Praise for
The Brethren and *Fortunes of France*

"Modern-day Dumas finally crosses the channel" *Observer*

"Swashbuckling historical fiction… For all its philosophical depth [*The Brethren*] is a hugely entertaining romp… The comparisons with Dumas seem both natural and deserved and the next 12 instalments [are] a thrilling prospect" *Guardian*

"Historical fiction at its very best… This fast paced and heady brew is colourfully leavened with love and sex and a great deal of humour and wit. The second instalment cannot be published too soon" *We Love This Book*

"A highly anticipated tome that's been described as *Game of Thrones* meets *The Three Musketeers*" Mariella Frostrup on BBC Radio 4's *Open Book*

"A vivid novel by France's modern Dumas… [there is] plenty of evidence in the rich characterisation and vivid historical detail that a reader's long-term commitment will be amply rewarded" *Sunday Times*

"A sprawling, earthy tale of peril, love, lust, death, dazzling philosophical debate and political intrigue… an engrossing saga" *Gransnet*

"A master of the historical novel" *Guardian*

"So rich in historical detail… the characters are engaging" *Sunday Express*

"Compelling… a French epic" *Kirkus Reviews*

Born in 1908, ROBERT MERLE was originally an English teacher before serving as an interpreter with the British army during the Second World War, which led to his capture by the German army at Dunkirk. He published his hugely popular *Fortunes of France* series over four decades, from 1977 to 2003, the final instalment appearing just a year before his death in 2004. *The Brethren* is the first book in the series, followed by *City of Wisdom and Blood* and *Heretic Dawn*.

Fortunes of France

CITY OF
WISDOM
AND BLOOD

ROBERT MERLE

Translated from the French by
T. Jefferson Kline

PUSHKIN PRESS
LONDON

Pushkin Press
71–75 Shelton Street
London WC2H 9JQ

Fortunes of France: City of Wisdom and Blood first published
in French as *En nos vertes années* in 1977

This translation first published by Pushkin Press in 2015

ISBN 978 1 782271 246

Set in Monotype Baskerville by Tetragon, London
Printed and bound by CPI Group (UK) Ltd, Croydon CRO 4YY

www.pushkinpress.com

CITY OF
WISDOM
AND BLOOD

1

CERTAINLY, I WAS THRILLED to be galloping along on this beautiful June day with my gentle brother Samson and our valet Miroul, traversing the highways and byways of France, and yet I kept feeling sudden waves of regret at leaving the barony of Mespech behind. As I rode along, tears filled my eyes every time I thought of the great crenellated nest where I'd hatched and got my first feathers, protected from the upheavals of our times by its ramparts, of course, but even more so by the bravery of my father, my Uncle de Sauveterre and our soldiers, in accordance with the Périgordian proverb: "The only sure walls are good men."

But it was no good crying. Now that we had reached the age of fifteen, with our heads full of Latin (vying for space in our brains with French and Provençal), our valour well tested in the la Lendrevie fighting, it was time to emerge from Barberine's sweet coverlet, and to quit, as I liked to say, our swaddling clothes. As younger brothers (and as my beloved Samson was a bastard to boot) we had to take up our studies in Montpellier, where my father had decided to send us.

It was in this good city that my father himself had studied in the flower of his youth. He loved this place and he claimed that his college of medicine, where Rabelais had defended his thesis, surpassed all others, even Paris, by the audacity, the variety and the novelties of its teaching, whose brilliance, he claimed, outshone even that of the school of Salerno in the previous century.

But we had a long and perilous journey to go from Sarlat to Montpellier, especially for three Huguenots who couldn't count fifty years among them yet had to travel in these times troubled by the recent wars, in which our people and the Catholics had so cruelly torn each other apart. To be sure, there reigned an uneasy peace between the two sides, but many grumblings and resentments could be heard. The uneasiness on our side had flared up again in 1565 during the Meeting of Bayonne, at which Catherine de' Medici had secretly met with the Duque de Alba, and during which the queen was rumoured to have proposed a marriage between her daughter Margot and Don Juan of Spain in return for a Spanish attack on the French Protestants. But Felipe II had ultimately disdained this renewed attempt to ally the French throne with the royal blood of Spain. Worse still, the following year, the Rex Catholicissimus became so irritated with the French for having settled so close to his own possessions in the Americas that he forgot his Catholic precepts in his wrath and ordered a surprise attack on our Breton colonists in Florida, massacring the lot. This, of course, had so greatly angered Catherine de' Medici that the Spaniard had lost much credit with the French court and no longer dared to exercise his papist zeal in the assassination of our Protestant leaders and the slaughter or exile of the masses of our brothers.

These bloody projects discarded, at least for the time being, Fortune seemed to smile once again on France. Peace seemed to be gaining some ground and the most rabid papists among the king's subjects seemed momentarily to lose heart at Spain's refusal to support them. The more moderate Catholics renewed their hope of reconciliation between the two faiths. Despite these more reassuring developments, we still had to contend, as we galloped across the French countryside, with the bands of rogues who, during the recent disorders of the civil war, had fled into the forests, setting up roadblocks at many crossroads and bridges to collect ransom from travellers and often, not content with mere robbery, inflicted the most horrible atrocities on their victims.

For our part, however, since we had learnt the arts of warfare from an early age—the last gulp of milk from Barberine's fulsome breasts having barely passed our gullets—and since we were armed to the teeth, well helmeted, breastplates firmly attached, swords at our sides, daggers hanging from our belts, pistols emerging from the holsters in our saddles and our arquebuses prominently displayed on the packhorses Miroul was leading behind him, Samson and I felt we had little to fear from these villains. But Miroul, young though he was, had already suffered from the assaults of the highwaymen and reminded us, as my father had done, that our safety lay not in combat where there was nothing to be gained by victory if one of us were wounded, but in flight, where the greater speed of our horses guaranteed our advantage. This was weighty counsel, for Miroul's prudence was hardly the result of cowardice. Slight of build, but agile to the point of being able to climb a wall like a fly, able to throw a pike with the speed and accuracy of a crossbow, he was worth three of the enemy all by himself. And don't accuse me of Gascon exaggeration! I'm telling the plain truth, as events would soon prove.

As for the timing of our departure, we had set out for Montpellier unusually early, given that courses wouldn't begin until mid October, but I well understood my father's intentions in sending us off a month beforehand. He knew I needed time to recover from the profound melancholy I'd fallen into after the death of little Hélix, my milk sibling. After terrible suffering, she had gone to her last sleep in the arms of the Lord the month before, in the flower of her nineteenth year. I had felt the deepest friendship for her despite the modesty of her birth and the evident disapproval of my older brother, François, who had stayed behind, in the safety of our walls, waiting for his turn to become Baron de Mespech when the Creator should call my father into his arms. And wait he would, and for many years to come, thank God, for my father, though well past his fiftieth year, was still lively and vigorous enough to have carried off Franchou, the chambermaid of his late wife, a year previously. Swords in hand, he, Samson and I had fended off a crowd of bloodthirsty vagabonds in Sarlat, and escorted her out of that plague-infested city.

To be sure, I was a Huguenot, but less fervently than my brother, Samson, who'd been raised from birth in the reformed religion. My own mother had insisted on raising me according to Catholic doctrine. On her deathbed—despite my having been converted to the new beliefs at the age of ten under heavy pressure from my father—my mother had given me a medallion of the Virgin Mary and conjured me to wear it as long as I lived. Thus it was that, while professing the reformed religion, I faithfully bore around my neck the symbol of the Catholic faith.

Might that have been the reason that the sweet intimacies little Hélix had shared with me during our sweet nights together seemed much less sinful than they would have to my half-brother Samson, whose great beauty was matched only by his ferocious virtue? Of course, the irony of his puritanical ways was that he was conceived outside of marriage—my father's Huguenot fervour not having deterred him from departing from the straight and narrow path, without, however, incurring the anger the Lord might have visited on the fruits of this sinful act, or, for that matter, on the sinner himself, since Mespech had continued to accumulate wealth and prosperity from the fruits of the Huguenot economy and agronomy practised there.

My father had advised us not to pass through the mountains to get to Montpellier since we would have been easily ambushed by the brigands there. He told us to take the road to Toulouse, after Cahors and Montauban, and then proceed through Carcassonne to Béziers, where the road cut through the plains and hence, though much longer, was also much safer because of the heavy traffic of horsemen and carts. However, at roughly the midpoint of our journey, as we arrived at the Two Angels inn on the outskirts of Toulouse, our hostess (a lively widow) informed us that just two weeks previously a merchants' convoy had been pillaged and massacred between Carcassonne and Narbonne by a large band of men who were hiding out in the Corbières hills.

This unpleasant news gave us a lot to think about, and in the room at the Two Angels, where Samson and I were lodged (with Miroul in a small anteroom next to us) we discussed our situation, sitting in a circle, with Miroul slightly farther away, holding his viol, from which he drew, from time to time, some lugubrious sounds to accompany our distress. We simply didn't know which saint, devil, incubus or succubus to invoke, not daring to continue our journey in the face of such imminent peril, and fearing to write of it to our father, whose answer would take at least two weeks to reach us.

"A fortnight at this inn!" cried Samson, shaking his handsome, copper-coloured locks. "'T'would be our financial ruin, a very blame-able recreation and an invitation to sin."

Whereupon Miroul, with a knowing look in my direction, plucked three notes on his viol to accentuate the triple danger that lurked in these quarters threatening our youthful innocence. Indeed, I was astonished that it hadn't escaped our pure Samson's notice that the buxom chambermaids who attended to our every need in this place were not the type to model their behaviour after the Two Angels who decorated the hotel's sign—who themselves suggested less than heavenly virtues, being cut out of iron.

I was about to respond to Samson's remark when, as Miroul plucked the third note on his viol, a huge tumult of horses' hooves, curses and cries could be heard below in the rue de la Mazelerie.

11

I rushed to the window (which we had to pull open in order to see since it was filled not with glass but with oil paper). Samson was at my heels, closely followed by Miroul, viol in hand, and, in the dusk outside, we glimpsed a group of about fifty men and women as they dismounted from their large, long-tailed bay horses. Their colourful and finely wrought clothes were covered with dust. Most of the women wore large-brimmed bonnets to protect them from the southern sun. Some of the men were armed with arquebuses, others with pistols or swords, and the ladies all carried daggers in their belts. They were of various ages and classes, most of them of considerable size and strength, golden-haired and blue-eyed, but a few others were of another type altogether: small of stature, dark-skinned and dark-haired, but all so happy to be dismounting and finding lodging in the inn that they shouted and babbled happily in an ear-splitting cacophony. In their relief to be setting foot to ground, they laughed uproariously, pushed each other, struck each other on the shoulders or on the arse and shouted boisterously at each other across the street while their huge mounts stood smoking with sweat, stamping their feet, shaking their blonde manes and whinnying so loudly for nourishment that they were like to break your eardrums. This crowd of horses and people made such an infernal row that you would have thought it was an army of rebellious peasants laying siege to the town hall.

All of the good Toulousain people were, like ourselves, at their windows, gaping, mute, eyes practically popping out of their heads, and ears wide open in astonishment, for the newcomers surprised us with a strange sort of jargon, in which French words (pronounced very differently from the sharp accent of Paris) were mixed with a dialect which no good mother's son could have understood.

The troop finally began to flood into the inn, pushing and shoving tumultuously, while a group of valets ran out to grab their horses' reins and lead them to the stables, buzzing with admiration for the size and power of these steeds. Beneath us, though we were lodged on the second floor of the Two Angels, the shouting continued with such brio that the walls shook with it. Someone knocked at our door, and, since Samson and I were busy watching the horses, I told Miroul to open it. Which he did, viol in hand, for it seemed he was never without it, even in bed.

There appeared—I noticed out of the corner of my eye, for I was still fixated on the herd of horses below us—the innkeeper herself, a lively brunette, all aflutter, beautifully dressed in a yellow petticoat with a bodice of the same colour, whose contents were so beautiful, so fulsome and so bouncy that it seemed a shame that she should expose them thus without some hope that they would be fondled.

"My pretty fellow," said the innkeeper to Miroul, in her Toulousain drawl, "are you not the valet to these two handsome gentlemen from Périgord whom I spy lounging at the window?"

"Indeed!" replied Miroul, plucking a welcoming chord on his viol. "I am at their service, and consequently at yours as well, my good hostess!" Another chord from his viol eloquently accompanied the smile he lavished on her.

"By my soul," cried the lady, laughing, "you're a very pretty fellow, I see, and your music too! What do they call you?"

"Miroul! At your service!" said he, plucking anew his instrument and singing:

> *Miroul—each eye a different hue!*
> *The right is brown, the left one blue.*

At this my heart was pinched with grief, for this was how little Hélix greeted Miroul, during the few remissions from her long agony, when

13

he arrived, viol in hand, to try to help her forget the flames of her suffering. But I quickly thrust this sad thought back into the satchel of my memories. From now on, I was determined to look forward and not back.

"Miroul!" laughed our hostess, batting an eyelash and sighing deeply. "I'm not sure I can trust these eyes! The blue eye may be a serious fellow, but that brown one is a rascal!" Their repartee was so lively that I wanted to put in my pennyworth, drawn as I was to this beautiful wench like a nail to a magnet.

"My good woman," I said, turning round and stepping briskly forward, hands on hips, "whatever aid or service your exquisiteness might require of us, you shall surely have it, for we are all quite undone by your beauty!"

"Your words, good Monsieur," she replied, "will be ever welcome—and the more so the more often you say them!"

"I shall repeat them as often as you wish, my hostess, at any hour of the day... or night!"

But our innkeeper, thinking no doubt that we had gone too quickly and too far from the very first word spoken, replied only by a quick curtsey that, to tell the truth, would have discountenanced the most austere of men, for she was obliged, upon rising, to rearrange her beautiful treasures in the sweet lodgings of her bodice.

"Monsieur," she said with feigned distress, "let's get down to business: fifty Norman pilgrims have just dismounted at our doorstep who are on their way to Rome under the holy guidance of a powerful baron and a dozen monks."

"Yes, I believe we may have heard them!" I laughed.

"Alas!" she replied. "That's not the worst of it! To lodge them I'll have to put four in a bed, and in this bed," she said, pointing to ours, "there are but two of you. Monsieur, would you be willing to accommodate two more companions for the night?"

"Men or women?" I smiled.

"Men," broke in Samson with a furrowed brow as he turned from the window.

The innkeeper thought about this for a long moment as she gazed on his manly figure standing before her in all the vigorous symmetry of his youth. She then sighed deeply, for though she believed herself in the presence of one of God's angels, she sensed how little she might profit from such a one and how much she preferred the hot-blooded version.

"Men, then," she sighed with a kind of whole-body shudder that convinced me that she would have gladly given up her own bed to the pilgrims to join us in ours.

"Men and *no* monkth," added Samson with his charming lisp, yet maintaining his serious demeanour.

At this, our hostess became very animated and reddened visibly: "By St Joseph and all the saints!" she cried. "Would you be the kind of pestiferous heretics and agents of the Devil who cannot abide the presence of men of God?"

"Heavens no, my good hostess!" I hastened to reply, knowing how thoroughly, since the victory of Montluc, the Huguenots were reviled and hounded by the people of Toulouse. "My brother meant nothing of the sort! He's only afraid that your monks will be too corpulent and take up too much space in our bed!"

"Sweet Jesus!" she sighed, and was once again all smiles. "Are you so hostile to the rotund?"

"Not in the least!" I rejoined, extending both hands in her direction. "There are some rotundities that are so pleasing to the eye that we'd like to help their owner bear their delicious weight!"

"Enough of that!" she countered, rapping my knuckles and feigning a frown. "These are for display only, not for common usage!" At this, Miroul plucked his viol two or three times in ironic echo, and our hostess laughed wholeheartedly, glancing conspiratorially at each of us in turn.

"If this cackling is quite finished," growled Samson impatiently, "I'd like to get to bed."

"Well, go right ahead!" our innkeeper replied. "You won't bother me in the least! And if the truth be known, I wouldn't mind seeing you all just as the Lord made you!"

"Shame on you, lady!" said Samson, blushing and turning his back.

"Easy there!" she exclaimed. "You gentlemen are a strange lot! One's too hot, the other's too cold and the valet's got brown and blue eyes! But now I have another request to make," she continued, calming considerably. "Monsieur, this morning I heard you talking with your brother in a jargon that little resembled the French of France."

"What? You don't understand it?" I replied.

"We speak only Provençal here," said the landlady, "just like you, Monsieur, only with a different accent and some different expressions. You should know that there isn't a single kid in the rue de la Mazelerie that understands French or who can read or write it. But," she said, drawing herself up, "I know my figures!"

"Well, you've never wanted for a figure, my good hostess!" I laughed. "But, good woman, tell me straight out if I can help you figure out this Norman baron's language."

"How did you guess?" she confessed.

"I'll follow you downstairs," said I, and, pushing our buxom hostess out the door, closed it behind us, happy to escape Samson's reproving stare.

Following our innkeeper, I found myself in a dark, winding staircase.

"This powerful baron," whispered my hostess, "is named Caudebec... By the Virgin, my noble guest, stop your kneading! Am I but a lump of bread dough that you press me so?"

"Am I to blame," I countered, "if your staircase is as dark as a black cow in a burnt-out forest? I've got to hold on to something!"

"Fie! By St Joseph, grab on somewhere else! Now I really *do* believe you're a good Christian and not one of those wicked heretics who want to forbid us to dance and play and celebrate saints' days as we ought! The plague take those cold cocks!"

"What did you say this Norman's name was?" I said, not wishing to reply and instead lavishing kisses on her neck and bodice.

"Caudebec. Remember this name well: Caudebec. This gentleman is so high and mighty he doesn't want anyone to know who he is."

"Caudebec," I repeated. "Like hotmouth," I added, to help myself remember the name.

"Hotmouth yourself!" she laughed, trying to twist out of my grasp. "By all the saints, your lips and your mouth are everywhere! Your kisses will be the death of me! You're making me crazier than a cat! Enough, I beg you! I've work to do in the kitchens for all of these pious pilgrims!"

But since I couldn't be bothered to obey her, she pushed me so hard that I lost my footing and dragged her down with me. We fell with a great clatter on the bottom wooden steps and, since at that very moment the priest had finished his benediction in the dining hall on the other side of the door, a great silence had fallen over the group of pilgrims gathered there for their dinner. All of the hungry travellers there assembled were thus pretending to be piously awaiting the priest's "Amen" to signal a happy end to his Latin formalities so that they could set to the meal they were so desirous of devouring. Into this pious silence there now resounded the fracas of our calamitous but happy fall as we rolled one on top of the other out of our stairwell, or, more precisely, I rolled on top of our hostess—a huge advantage from my perspective, since she was so wondrously well padded. Seeing which, the Norman pilgrims, being a very joyous and boisterous crowd, all burst out laughing like a swarm of flies.

"Silence!" shouted the Baron de Caudebec from the head of the table, his voice resounding like thunder, echoed by the violent clap of his hand on the oak surface. "Have you no shame? Your laughter at this wench's head-over-heels arrival has interrupted our holy father's prayers! 'Sblood! Is this the way devout pilgrims should behave on their way to Rome? Are you more crass than those mountebanks in Paris? Silence, I say! The first one who dares open his mouth before the prayer has ended will have his head smashed to pieces."

The silence that followed was deafening. Whereupon the baron said, "You may continue, Father."

"But... I've finished," said the monk.

"Amen!" cried the Baron de Caudebec, and all the assembled men and women echoed his "Amen!" in a shout that shook the entire house. After which the assembled guests fell upon their meal like wolves on their kill, hardily devouring the Bayonne ham, fresh trout, roast pheasant, truffle omelettes, Bigorre sausages, and the many other specialities for which the Two Angels inn was famous throughout the Toulousain region. And while they put their jaws to work on these delights, a dozen brunette chambermaids, whom I've already described as comely, curvaceous, amply endowed and hardly stand-offish, ran from one guest to the next, pouring streams of our excellent Guyenne wines into their avid goblets.

"Well then!" said the innkeeper as she rose to her feet and adjusted her bodice. "Well then!" she repeated happily as she surveyed the tables where a legion of sharp teeth and dry throats were having their way.

"Tomorrow we'll write very fat figures on your slate, my good woman," I laughed as I dusted myself off.

"Shush, Monsieur!" she cautioned, pressing her mouth to my ear—quite unnecessarily since none of our guests spoke Provençal.

"These Normans are very well appointed. Did you see the gold bracelets on these grand ladies? But, my friend, we can't linger here. I've got work to do in the kitchen. You must do as we agreed. For my part," she continued with a slight wink, her exquisite hand pressing my arm, "I'll find some way to catch up with you in some corner or other of my house today or tonight and will always be, my friend, humbly at your service." This said, she made a deep bow, but this time keeping her hand firmly on her bodice to prevent any repetition of the contents' escape in front of such a pious assembly.

"Monsieur!" cried the Baron de Caudebec, pointing a leg of guineafowl at me, his blue eyes blazing from a face already reddened by Guyenne wine. "Who do you think you are, disturbing our prayers? If you weren't so young, I'd take you in there and run my rapier through your liver!"

"Baron de Caudebec," I replied in my best Parisian French, as I bowed—but not very deeply, "please, I beg you, spare my liver, though I assure you I doubt it is the seat of reason as the ancient Babylonian doctors believed. My name is Pierre de Siorac. I'm the younger son of the Baron de Mespech, in Périgord, and I'm travelling to Montpellier to study medicine. I've come to offer my services as your interpreter since I speak Provençal."

"Well met!" cried Caudebec, raising his drumstick heavenward. "The saints in Paradise have sent you! Page, a stool for this gentleman! Next to me, here! You've saved me, my friend! I'm more lost in these provinces than a Christian in Arabia! These bumpkins don't understand my language!"

I stepped towards him and, as I drew near, the baron did me the honour of standing to greet me and gave me hardy pats on the shoulder and back which, in all honesty, I would happily have forgone, so powerful were his big hands. For big he was in all respects—bull-necked, broad-shouldered and barrel-chested. He was blonde-haired with a luxuriant drooping moustache that was carefully tapered. His blue eyes, as I've mentioned, leapt out at you from a ruddy complexion. He was elegantly clothed, though his doublet was somewhat soiled since he ate like a Turk, throwing his chewed bones over his shoulder. He wiped his hands on the serving girls' skirts when they came within range, and they daren't ever complain, given his wont of frowning and scolding at the least inconvenience, threatening to turn the poor wench's breasts into ribbons if she made the least objection. He spoke to them in French so that they understood not a word, but his angry look and grimaces told them all they needed to know. When he'd managed to remove all the grease from his fingers and moustache, the baron never tired of groping the backsides of these maidens, proving he was as lusty as he was devout—a trait I was able to observe at my leisure for the next two weeks, as you will hear.

"My friend!" he cried, after his welcoming blows. "Your doublet is covered with dust from your fall. Here, page! Take this gentleman's doublet and brush it!... Page! 'Sblood! The rascal is asleep again! By Christ, I'll disembowel him!"

In truth, he settled for a slap, which the miscreant dodged, but squealed nonetheless like a stuck pig. Then, throwing himself at me, he pulled off my doublet in a flash and disappeared with it, for far from asleep, the rogue was as lively as mercury, a liar, braggart, trickster and insolent lad with a saucy tongue—when he was out of his master's earshot. It was, moreover, a marvel to watch him as he stood behind his master's chair, catching half-eaten drumsticks on the fly as the baron threw them over his shoulder—not that this was his only provender. He regularly rifled the satchels of the pilgrims, extracting their prized possessions as soon as their heads were turned. This page was called Rouen, after the city where he was born, and although it was an odd cognomen for a Christian, I never heard him called by any other name. He had green eyes and a forest of red hair sticking straight up from the top of his head that no brush or comb could ever have tamed.

But I must go on with my story. My doublet removed, I sat down in shirtsleeves on the stool between the baron and a stocky monk whose massive dark eyebrows seemed to cut his face in two. This good apostle ate at some remove from the table out of respect for the enormous belly that protruded beneath his chest.

"Monsieur de Siorac," the baron began as he stuffed a huge Bigorre sausage into his maw, "this monk here is Brother Antoine"— the phrase, barely recognizable through the bits of sausage filling his mouth, having become, "This bonk is brover anwan." But then, the sausage having been sufficiently chewed, he emptied his goblet in a single swig to dilute it and continued, "Brother Antoine is entirely in charge of my finances. He's a very learned man. He has the authority to take confession and so I've assigned him the spiritual governance of our good pilgrims."

Brother Antoine gave me a friendly nod, but I couldn't help feeling penetrated by his little black eyes as he arched his thick eyebrows. "Aha," I thought, "I'd better be careful with *this* brother! I wonder if he's sniffed out my Huguenot leanings: I'll be on my guard."

"This wine is not so bad!" cried the baron as he seized another sausage in his great paw rather than picking it up delicately between thumb and index finger, as Barberine, ever attentive to good table manners, had taught me to do.

Having stuffed his entire prey into his mouth, the baron continued: "I must tell you, Monsieur de Siorac, that the reason I've undertaken this pilgrimage is that my wife is languishing, alas, with a slow but unrelenting fever that has sequestered her in Caudebec castle. And you must have guessed, my friend, that I'm on my way to Rome to ask our Holy Father the Pope to pray to the Virgin Mary to intercede with her Divine Son on her behalf."

"What idolatry!" I thought. "And so many intercessors: the Pope! Mary! Why not just pray directly to God—or through the mediation of His only Son, as it is written in the Gospels?" But as I suddenly felt the burning eyes of Brother Antoine on me, I remained silent, and put on my most contrite air.

"Monsieur de Siorac," Brother Antoine said in his most innocent tones, aren't you worried that in going to Montpellier to study medicine you will find yourself in a place where heretics are in control and swarm like a wasp's nest?"

"Ah, but a good Christian fears not the Devil!" I smiled.

"Ha! Nicely said!" broke in the baron. "Hey, wench! Bring us more wine!"

But the chambermaid he'd shouted to turned a deaf ear and I certainly understood why.

"Monsieur my interpreter," the baron said, turning to me, "this wench is definitely more to my taste than all the others, as I will prove to her tonight. So tell her to bring me wine and not to tarry or I'll cut her breasts to ribbons."

"I'll go and tell her," I said as I rose from the table, very content to escape from Brother Antoine's evil eye, but even more so to have to bring a message to such a comely strumpet. I headed for my trollop and to put her at ease I approached her and put my hands on her hips and gave her a big smile. "My friend," I said, "best that you don't put our noble friend on edge. He's calling for some of your wine."

"Problem is," she replied in her Toulousain dialect, "I don't want the pig to dirty my petticoats and skirts with his greasy paws the way he did to Madeleine."

"So what's your name, my girl?" I asked, smiling almost in spite of myself at the captivating twinkle that lit up her black eyes.

"Franchou, Monsieur," she replied, bowing politely yet managing to balance her pitcher without spilling a drop. More than the beauty of this tableau I was struck by her name: Franchou was the name of the chambermaid my father had liberated at sword-point from the plague-infested town of la Lendrevie!

"Franchou," I said, "if you don't obey the baron, he says he'll cut your breasts to ribbons."

"Sweet Jesus!" cried Franchou with a fearful expression that delighted me. "So that's what he's muttering in his bastard French! Holy Mother of God, would he really do it?"

"I don't know. He's a man of little patience. Go then, Franchou! I'll ask our hostess to compensate you for the damage to your skirts."

"Many thanks, my noble Monsieur!" she curtseyed with a winning smile.

Sadly the lass didn't manage to escape the baron's messy ways. Hardly had she served him when he ruined her skirt with his greasy fingers, and then, adding injury to insult, began pawing her.

"Ha ha!" shouted the baron as he burst into a belly laugh. "It seems, Monsieur Translator, that while pretending to represent me, you managed to do all right for yourself! This wench only has eyes for you, despite my caresses!"

"What's this big animal talking about now?" asked Franchou in Toulousain.

"He thinks you have a crush on me."

"Well, it's true," replied Franchou candidly.

"Monsieur de Siorac," Brother Antoine broke in, "you have a pretty chain around your neck! Might we see your pendant?" I pulled the medallion from beneath my shirts and showed it to him.

"Well!" he cooed, making the sign of the cross. "The Virgin Mary! Blessed be the Holy Mother of God! And who, if I may ask, gave you this beautiful relic?"

"My mother," said I quite simply.

"So your mother must be a person of great lineage, as the medallion is of pure gold, beautifully worked and, I would estimate, very old."

"No," I answered promptly, "our line is but recently begun. My father was knighted on the battlefield of Ceresole and named baron after our victory at Calais."

I was telling the truth but not the whole truth, just as my father had done with the monk after the fighting at la Lendrevie. For if my father, a commoner, had been ennobled, just as I reported it, my mother, as Brother Antoine suspected, could claim to be from a great and ancient family, a descendant of a Castelnau who had fought in the Crusades. I couldn't reveal her birthright to Brother Antoine, however, without also revealing that this family was well known to have supported the reformed religion in Périgord, Quercy and Agenais.

"I owe you a bit of an apology, my son," Brother Antoine crooned, leaning towards me with a compassionate glance. "I had my suspicions about you after seeing your black doublet—such unusual apparel for a young gentleman—believing you to be one of those pestiferous heretics who insinuate themselves into our company to corrupt our faith. But your worldly manner and this holy medallion have persuaded me I was wrong."

"My good interpreter a heretic?" cried Caudebec. "You're dreaming, monk!"

Thereupon, to dismiss her, the baron applied an altogether too forceful slap to Franchou's backside, seized a trout and crammed it, head, tail, bones and all, into his gullet. Franchou fled, her hand on her arse, whimpering and sobbing in pain and, truth be told, a few hours later, I could still see that her flesh was red and sore from the violence of his spanking and have never forgiven him for this revolting behaviour.

"My son," Brother Antoine resumed, his beady eyes fastened on the movements of the chambermaids who were serving us, "it benefits us not at all to attempt to hide from Our Lord, who is all-seeing and all-knowing, that we are but fashioned of fragile clay and that all flesh is piteously weak and that the demon beckons us from every petticoat that moves and breathes before us" (but saying this he turned not his eyes from the fetching demoiselles who moved among us—quite the contrary!) "and that this inn is all too inviting" (at this he sighed languorously), "that we eat too well, and drink too much and that these lively wenches—may God prove me wrong!—are accustomed to play the saddle to all comers."

He sighed again. "Tomorrow, my son"—and here he turned to face me, his eyebrows knitted in concern, and pierced me suddenly with his little black eyes—"I will hear your confession."

Oh, the treacherous scoundrel! He was trying to catch me out! His suspicions had not abated, as he had claimed, the hypocrite! He still doubted my word, and, knowing how much the Huguenots abhorred auricular confession, he had decided to set a trap for me.

"My dear Brother Antoine," I replied, displaying the most innocent expression I could manage, despite my animosity, "I cannot yet tell whether my night will be free of sin or not, but count on me to call on your good offices to wash me of my sins."

What a strange method, I thought to myself. They sin, they confess, they start all over again. But I had nary a chance to pursue this line of thought. The Baron de Caudebec suddenly gave a great shout, and, grasping at his throat, rose straight up from his chair, crying that he was dying from an enormous fish bone that was stuck in his windpipe, and that someone must straightaway go to find a barber. "Now, 'sblood! Right away! God's passion!" If not, he'd kill everyone in this house of the Devil: cook, kitchen boys, sauciers, serving girls and even the innkeeper herself!

Jumping to my feet, I urged him to remain calm. I managed to convince him that, since it was Sunday, the time it would take to get a barber here would mean hours of suffering, but that if he would take his seat, open his mouth, and show a bit of resolve, I would do what I could. Amazingly, he consented to my request. I had an oil lamp brought so that I could look into his mouth—a cavernous stink hole that I'll never forget—and could see that there was indeed a fish bone stuck in his throat just beyond his uvula. I quickly whittled two wooden sticks into long spatulas, and using them together as a pincer, succeeded in extracting the tiny cause of this great calamity.

Caudebec could hardly believe his senses when, after consuming an entire pitcher of wine, he realized he no longer felt the pain in his gullet.

"'Sblood!" he cried, leaping to his feet. "It's a miracle! Thanks be to the Holy Virgin Mary! And you," he continued, bestowing on me such a powerful embrace that I thought he would suffocate me, "you, my learned young friend, I will henceforth call you my true son, for my son by blood, compared with you, is nothing but a nincompoop who doesn't know his right hand from his left, who can hardly read, writes worse than I do, and thinks only of fox hunting and drinking and feasting, oppressing his labourers and bedding his serving girls. The plague take this ignoramus! *He* would have let his father die in agony. Monsieur de Siorac! The Virgin and all the saints brought you to me. God set you on this stool to save a poor sinner! My little interpreter, my gracious cousin, my eternal and immutable friend, what can I offer you in return for the immense gift you have bestowed on the barony of Caudebec? Ask and it shall be yours!"

And, just to prove that a Norman baron can bluster every bit as well as a man of the *langue d'oc*, he continued: "Speak up! What would you like? My purse? My horse? My daughter?"

"Hold, Monsieur! Your daughter for a fish bone?"

"My daughter? But I don't have a daughter!" he cried, laughing as much at himself as at me in his Norman way, which was less heavy-handed than simply boorish.

"Well, Monsieur," I replied, "since we're talking about girls…" and I leant forward and whispered a few words in his enormous ear.

"You scoundrel!" he laughed. "You lewd fellow! So that's what you want! But it's little enough. Though," he continued as if reconsidering, "I was thinking of having the hussy myself… But, so be it!" he went on with an air of immense generosity. "I'll leave her to you, my friend, since such is your pleasure." He seemed quite relieved, I thought, to have got off so cheaply—gifts not being his strong point, as I had already guessed.

At this point the page returned with my doublet, which I donned before taking my leave of the Baron de Caudebec, Brother Antoine and their pious assembly, who were but halfway done with their festivities, judging by the way they fell on the meats that were arriving periodically from the kitchens. As I started up the staircase, however, I paused to call the page.

"Hey, Rouen! Come over here!"

"At your service, Monsieur," he said, his green eyes averted in a way that suggested he was at bit uneasy.

"Rouen, you owe me four sols for cleaning my doublet."

"Four sols, Monsieur?"

"Exactly. They were in my pocket."

"Well then, they must have fallen out!" he retorted, lowering his eyes as if to search for them.

"Just what I was thinking. They must have fallen from my pocket into yours."

"Nay, Monsieur!" he countered—but without raising his voice. "As I am an honest lad!"

"For shame, Rouen, you swear so easily? What if I discussed my problem with your master?"

"He would whip me like green rye."

"So, to avoid this unpleasantness, Rouen, let's make a little deal. If by chance you find these four sols on the floor, they'll be yours by finder's rights. And if you hear Brother Antoine talking about me to the baron, you'll repeat every word."

"It's a deal! I'll shake on that, my master!" cried Rouen, smiling from ear to ear. I smiled back at him and, placing my hand on his head, gave his pointy red hair a rub that would have mussed it had it ever been combed.

After this I returned to my room, delighted with the way I'd fooled Brother Antoine, having behaved in every respect the way my father would have done, for my father always said that we owe the truth only to our friends and to our enemies ruses and guile, often comparing our Huguenots to the Israelites in the Bible as an oppressed people living among the Gentiles.

My beloved Samson had neither disrobed nor gone to bed, fearing the arrival of the two foreigners whom the innkeeper had assigned to our quarters. My own thought—which I was careful not to share with him since he was so innocent—was that he would have done better not to insist on male bedfellows since he was so handsome that he might have attracted the attentions of someone so inclined, should such a one be among our new neighbours.

I discovered Samson in deep reverie, sitting, spiteful and taciturn, on his stool, quite distressed by my long absence. Miroul was sitting opposite, not daring to open his mouth and content from time to time to play a few chords on his viol to console his master and, of course, for the pure pleasure of the music.

Samson became very upset when I had explained my plan that we should join company with these Norman pilgrims as far as Montpellier because they were so large and heavily armed a group that no bandits would dare cross swords with them.

"What?" he wailed. "Make common cause with these papists? Wear a mask? Hear Mass with them? Maybe even go to confession?"

I rose to my full height, hands on hips. "My dear brother," I answered coolly, "you've no right to scold me."

He was so shaken by my tone that tears came to his eyes. Such was the great love that, like a stream of red blood, flowed from one to the other. For my part, I couldn't bear that he should suffer the least bit on my account, and in a burst of feeling I ran to him, hugged him to me and kissed him on both cheeks. Seeing this, Miroul plucked on his viol.

"Samson," I explained, sitting him down beside me, "remember my father's wisdom in assigning you the management of our purse, and me the leadership of our little band—on condition I listen to Miroul, who, better than anyone, knows the ways of the vandals on the highways."

At this, Miroul, far from plucking his viol, lowered his head sadly, for he had watched his entire family have their throats cut by a band of these brigands on a highway south of Sarlat and would have suffered the same fate had he not had the presence of mind to bury himself in the hay in the barn.

"But still," argued Samson, "how can we break bread with these bloodthirsty papists who have sent so many of our people to the scaffold?"

"Bloodthirsty they were," I concurred, "and might become so again. But for the moment, peace has been declared between our two religions. Besides, these Normans are well-meaning folk despite their idolatry. Let me try to work this out, gentle brother."

"The problem is," said Samson, opening his big azure eyes and looking at me with such an honest demeanour that my heart swelled with affection for him, "I can't feign anything and you know it!"

"I do know it," I agreed, putting my arm around his shoulder, "so I'll have to pretend for both of us. As for you, Samson, all you have to do is remain mute as though you had been laid low with a terrible fever. Miroul will watch over you, and answer any questions they ask by plucking his viol. How say you, Miroul?"

"I find I think that you're right, my master," he replied. "There is certainly less danger for us among these papists than reduced to our own resources on the highways."

"But what will happen if we're found out?" Samson persisted.

"Nothing, I'd wager. The baron is a crude but not a cruel man."

A knock on the door interrupted our discussion and Miroul went to open it and found Franchou on our threshold, holding a heavy tray. "My mistress," said Franchou, her shining eyes locking on mine as she entered, "didn't know where to put you since our dining hall is entirely occupied by that crowd of pilgrims from the north."

"But this will do quite handsomely!" I answered. In helping Franchou bring in and lay the tray on a small table near the window, I managed to keep my back to Samson, although with the daylight waning and the oil paper letting in but little light this position was less an advantage for supping than for the exchange of looks we passed between us.

"Wench," I said, not wanting to name her in front of my brother, "I'm going to hurry my supper. As soon as you have finished your day's work, come and tell me whether the Baron de Caudebec needs my interpreting."

She understood my meaning, and her brilliant, lively black eyes told me quite clearly it was so. "At your service, my noble lord," she replied, bowing low—though her look was much less subservient than her curtsey.

The meats were succulent, but though I ate with a hearty appetite, my thoughts were elsewhere: I was listening to the sounds in the corridor outside, where I could hear the heavy and stumbling footfalls of the pilgrims heading for bed. Which my gentle brother did as well as soon as he'd downed his goblet of wine, perching, fully clothed, on the extreme edge of the bed in order to leave room for our guests.

"Miroul," I whispered, "when our bedfellows arrive—and let's pray they're neither too broad-shouldered or two pot-bellied—tell them to be quiet so as not to wake Samson."

"I'll take care of it, Monsieur," said Miroul, and I have no idea how he managed it, but at times when he was kidding, and didn't want to say or show it openly, his blue eye remained cold while his brown eye sparkled.

Someone scratched like a mouse at the door, and, without waiting for an answer, opened it. "Monsieur," said Franchou, her beautiful round cheeks aglow as she lied, "the baron is calling for you to interpret for him!"

I leapt to my feet and hissed to Miroul, "I'm off! Take good care of my brother!"

"I wish you a happy translation tonight, Monsieur," replied Miroul, as serious as a bishop on his cathedra, plucking two chords on his sweet viol.

It was a different tune altogether the next morning, when, at the break of day, I hauled up water from the well in the courtyard to begin my ablutions—a habit or a folly, I know not which, that I got from my father, who, in his early years as a student of medicine in Montpellier, and a zealous disciple of Hippocrates, claimed that water and our bodies have a natural affinity, the first helping the second to maintain its health. It would be a great thing, if you'll permit me to argue my father's case, if the use of this liquid element were more widespread in this century—and in this kingdom—than it in fact is, even among

31

the nobility. For I saw in my twenties, while at the court of Charles IX, many well-to-do and pretty women spend an infinite amount of time primping, but bathing? Not in the least. And isn't it a great pity that these feminine bodies, so suave and polished, remain, hidden beneath the silks and finery, as dirty as a day-labourer, who at least has the excuse of working the soil from dawn to dusk? Alas, how put off we are when we have sensitive noses and quickly detect the filth beneath the perfumes that these beauties spray on themselves!

At Mespech, my older brother François scorned my domestic dalliances, but I don't share his opinions on this matter. As for me, I prefer to say, "Long live Franchou, if Franchou bathes in pure water!" And the hell with the princess with her royal blood (whom I will not name) who dared to boast at court of never having washed her hands in a week! And it wasn't just her hands! I leave you to imagine the rest.

So I was spraying myself with cold water, however heretical such toiletries may have been—and may my sins be washed away by the Lord's grace as quickly on Judgement Day as the sweat and humours of the previous night—when who should appear in her yellow bodice, doing her best to negotiate the uneven paving stones of the courtyard, but our beautiful hostess. Her aspect was clearly not the least bit welcoming; quite the contrary, she looked very unhappy and spiteful, her eyebrows in a deep furrow, her eyes piercing me like daggers.

"Hallo!" she said with some bitterness, her hands on her hips. "Here's our handsome stallion all busy with grooming himself after his night's gallop!"

And, since I couldn't manage to say a word, so embarrassed was I, she added scornfully, "Your hocks seem to me to be sagging a bit."

"Not in the least!" I replied, stung and rising to my feet. "I'm always at your service, my good woman!"

32

"Ha! You scoundrel!" she cried. "Not a bit of it! You turned a cold shoulder last night to my feed and were whinnying after other oats!"

I decided to opt for bravado since repentance was out of the question. "My sweet hostess, to tell you the truth, I was intending to take my feed in two different mangers. Scarcely, however, was I set up comfortably at one than they slipped my halter on."

"If this halter, was, as I believe, two feeble arms, you could easily have broken free! You're a sweet talker but I no longer trust your palaver. You start out on one horse and end with another."

"But, my good woman," I protested, "the Two Angels inn is on the way to Montpellier and also on the way back to my home in the Sarlat region. We'll have many chances to see each other again."

"Enough of these empty promises! I don't eat reheated meat," she snarled, now wholly irritated with me. And, turning on her heels, she threw over her shoulder, "Can you imagine the conceited fop who'd believe I'd wait for him?"

The words "conceited fop" really stung, though I had to admit that my Gascon jokes about the two mangers deserved no less.

"Well then," I replied stiffly, "since there can be no more question of friendship between us, please prepare my bill of fare so I can be on my way."

"I've already added up your bill," she said, spinning around to face me with an air of vengeful triumph that set me to thinking. "Three meals at eight sols each, that's twenty-four sols. Six sols for the room since you had to share the bed. Twelve sols for your four horses. Plus eighteen sols for the wench you enjoyed last night."

I looked at her, speechless. Sweat suddenly started to trickle down my back at the idea I'd have to explain this last exorbitant expense to Samson, who had the entire responsibility for disbursements from our small treasury.

"What?" I gasped. "Pay for favours that were freely offered?"

"Depends on who offers them," she countered.

"'Sblood! as our baron would say! I'm supposed to cough up for a wench who's completely mad about me?"

"You misunderstand, Monsieur," replied my hostess, colder than a nun's feet on a chapel floor. "You're not paying for the wench, you're charged for having reserved her services for an entire night, to my great detriment, since she was unavailable for more general services."

"Where am I then?" I cried, standing to my full height. "In a brothel?"

"Absolutely not!" said my hostess, assuming her most authoritative posture. "You're a guest in a good, respectable, Christian establishment where all of our travellers' needs are fully attended to."

"Their Christian needs!" I laughed.

But I fell silent with the awful realization of just how bad this sounded, coming from me. Moreover, the innkeeper maintained such a stony glare that I had not the heart to continue in this vein. So I decided to adopt a completely different approach, and spoke in more honeyed tones, but this was no less in vain. She was not to be swayed in the least, and, ultimately, I realized that to soothe her I'd have to take an entirely different tack.

The how and what of this arrangement I will leave entirely to the reader's imagination, begging him not to judge me too severely for being a fledgling so recently cast out of his nest in Mespech that I couldn't help getting tied up in the skirts of both of these beauties. It's really not in my nature to be so irresponsible. And, in the end, it was the thought of offending my dear Samson, both in his morals and in the management of our purse, that led me to the course of action I chose.

Not that I mean to complain. It wasn't, after all, such a great sacrifice, despite my initial reluctance. To tell the truth, my hostess, even after the fatigue and stress of her evening, was well worth the bedding. My gods, what a furnace! And I can reminisce on our time together with some pride at being the bellows that set that fire burning. "Oh, what a pity," I mused as I crept back into our room (where Samson was still asleep, in the company of two fat monks), "that these delights, so healthy for our bodies and our spirits, should be, when enjoyed outside of marriage, such guilty pleasures in the eyes of God." But, alas, such is the way all of this is taught us. And it must be true since both of the religions of our country—both Catholic and reformed—are so fully in agreement on this matter.

2

I DIDN'T WANT TO RISK waking Samson with those two fat monks taking up so much space in the bed, so I slipped into the small adjoining chamber and, as Miroul was already out tending to our horses, I fell into his bed as the first light of dawn began to tinge the oil paper of his window.

When all our other voluptuous desires have been exhausted, there is always sleep, which is not the least among them. What a delight to find myself alone and able to stretch out full length on this little couch, my body so weary, arms and legs akimbo and eyes closing as soon as my head touched the blankets.

Samson was amazed to discover me so completely dead to the world when he decided to awaken me at noon—I who, at Mespech, was the first to rise and always the first downstairs in the great kitchens, arriving even before la Maligou had set the water on to boil. I explained as best I could, as I ran my fingers through my dishevelled hair, how exhausted I'd become doing all the interpreting the night before, but felt a bit ashamed at this lie since he immediately set about trying to comfort me. Oh, Samson you are such a guardian angel, but, thankfully, not so good a guardian, luckily for my sins!

For his part, Caudebec got softer by the minute in this inn whose two angels hid two devils, whose names were, respectively "good victuals" and "sweet wench". The night before he'd informed me he'd be leaving at dawn, but at noon he had no Samson to wake him and was still snoring at three in the afternoon. As he began to stir late in the day he immediately called for meat and wine. And, having lavishly eaten and copiously drunk his fill, he declared that the wise man always takes good care of his horses and, in the interest of the quadrupeds, he would put off his travels until the next day. But of course the next evening he fell asleep with the breasts of a wench for his pillow and didn't awaken until noon the following day. I do believe that, at this rate, he would have tasted every conceivable menu the Two Angels could prepare, and bedded each of their twelve serving maids, had not Brother Antoine, who still held some sway over him, reminded him that his wife was dying of the fever in their chateau and that if they continued to tarry thus they might well arrive in Rome after Our Lord had received her into His peace.

Thus it was that the two Siorac brothers and their page Miroul, having arrived on a Sunday at the Two Angels inn, did not take their leave of the place until the following Thursday at dawn—four days that seemed to Samson like lead weighing on his shoulders but to his brother seemed as light as cork, since I was not lacking for diversions; my "interpreting skills"—and I use the term without any ambiguity intended—were in such demand.

The innkeeper provided very good company for me during this period, though her friendship did not lead to any reduction in our bill—except for the supplement she'd threatened to add after our first night there. But when I asked her to reimburse Franchou for the damages to her petticoat inflicted by the baron she refused flat out. I sensed that if I insisted too much it would not help Franchou and that my hostess might well kick her out after we left, which would have left me feeling very guilty on her behalf, since, I confess, she'd garnered a bit of my heart in our short time together. She was a wonderfully good girl, with eyes more tender than my mare, Accla's, her lips softer than a baby's bottom, and so loving and trusting it brought tears to my eyes. In my arms, she melted like butter. Alas, poor Franchou! Although I'd taught her "the right herbs" and "where to put them"—one of la Maligou's secrets that I'd learnt from little Hélix—she ended up getting pregnant a year later from some guest or other, and died in childbirth. I find it so unfair that Nature can play evil stepmother to so many women who produce a life only at the expense of their own.

But, to come back to these petticoats, which the baron employed to wipe his greasy hands, I didn't want to betray either my promise or the hope of the poor girl, and had Samson advance me twenty sols (accompanied by a very severe sermon) on the pretext that I'd lost this amount playing at dice with Caudebec—a story that Samson believed willingly enough but that lit up Miroul's brown eye (while the blue one retained its perfect tranquillity).

Seeing herself so handsomely paid, Franchou jumped for joy, and, throwing her two wonderfully cool arms around my neck, pulled me towards her with such force I thought she was going to nest in my entrails. But then, suddenly remembering that I'd be leaving the next day, she went, in the blink of an eye, from happy to sad, mixing smiles with sighs, showering me with a thousand thanks, and as many kisses on the neck, watered by her tears. I was very moved, as you can well imagine, by these demonstrations of her affection.

Although my hostess was far from having the same effect on my feelings as Franchou, not being made of the same tender metal and her bright brown eyes too closely focused on her figures, I nevertheless wanted to help her as well, realizing that I would likely see her often on my travels between Mespech and Montpellier. I thus warned her that the payment that was due her from the pilgrims would not come easily since the baron was much quicker to undo his flies than his purse strings. She well understood my meaning, and was careful to fatten up her bill over these four days, a good bit more than she ought to have done.

Once alerted to the danger, and since she enjoyed the favours of the lieutenant of the Toulouse police force, favours she had more than one way to repay, the lady invited him (with four archers) to attend her settlement of accounts with the baron. He agreed to appear and his presence did wonders. When he caught sight of the lieutenant, the baron suddenly left off storming and thundering his threats to slash his hostess's breasts to ribbons and generally to reduce the entire household to a juicy stew.

When calm was restored, he argued nevertheless (through my translations) with such skill and at such length—the lieutenant being unable to validate the innkeeper's figures—that a goodly part of the bill's stuffing was removed and everyone parted company satisfied with the outcome.

But since all of this haggling took a good deal more time than we would have wanted, the troop didn't manage their departure until the sun was well up and they were unable to travel more than six leagues before nightfall.

We spent the night in a little village that was badly defended and in an inn that had meagre food at meagre prices. The chambermaids were a notoriously decrepit lot, and our host visibly on his guard against these Frenchmen from the north.

"Holy God!" Caudebec moaned, as he distastefully tested a spoonful of watery bean broth in which a few morsels of salted pork floated mournfully. "We've fallen directly into hell from our former Paradise. This wine tastes like piss! Monsieur my interpreter, ask this Lentenfaced innkeeper to provide me a good young wench to watch over my sleep tonight."

I translated his request, and, in response, our innkeeper frowned angrily. "Monsieur," said he, "I don't keep a shop, nor do I deal in women."

"What says this sad sack?" cried Caudebec.

"That there are none to be had."

"What? No women? In this whole town? 'Sblood! Are you making fun of Caudebec?"

"Not at all," I answered to appease him. "He claims they've all gone off to the hills to help with the harvest."

Whereupon Caudebec rose to his feet and, swearing he'd kill everyone in the house, unsheathed his dagger. But the innkeeper remained unmoved and, merely frowning harder, stood his ground.

"Monsieur," I urged, "put away your dagger. These people don't like us. Let's not start a fight. One night without a wench is quickly passed."

"Not so!" roared Caudebec, suddenly growing sad. "Without a pair of breasts to lay my head on, I'll end up thinking about my death, the fires of Purgatory and all my terrible sins!"

"Monsieur," said Brother Antoine, "if you could manage just one night without a wench, your sins would be less terrible…"

"Alas!" replied the baron. "I may well sin with a whore, but I certainly don't contemplate my sins while I'm at it! And sin is not really the question, it's how we think about it." This said, he began sobbing. Yes, this high and mighty baron was crying like a baby. Of course it *is* true that he'd been drinking heavily.

I turned to the innkeeper and assured him he could go in peace and that he'd not be molested by his guest. But our host answered in his dialect and with marvellous self-assurance of both voice and aspect, "I'm not afraid. No misery can touch the just."

From this quote from the Bible it was clear that he was one of ours. And indeed I'd guessed so from the outset, so hostile was his every look at the pilgrims' medallions and monks.

"Oh!" moaned the baron, the tears falling from his eyes like the autumn rain. "I'm already in Purgatory! To have to eat this slop and drink this vinegar! To be served by these toothless hags—and in such miserable and ugly surroundings! Oh, God help us! I'm already dead and damned!"

He was so despairing of his lot that he ended up drinking too much of this awful swill and rolling under the table. Nevertheless, when he finally awoke late the next morning, he hadn't forgotten his financial acumen, and spent the better part of an hour arguing with the innkeeper over the bill—which was entirely accurate. In short, it was high noon when we finally got under way again on the road to Toulouse and Montpellier.

That day we made barely five leagues, stopping this time at Castelnau d'Ary. Samson, Miroul and I were all very impatient with this pace, for our small horses could have easily covered ten leagues a day they were so fast and so strong. Samson, in particular, was unhappy at the expense of so many inns. Unfortunately for my dear brother, the inn at Castelnau was named the Golden Lion and this lion was no more angelical than the Two Angels in Toulouse, for it had a huge mouth to devour all it could and large claws to strip bare the tender prey that was foolish enough to enter its "lodgings"—as the innkeeper so humbly referred to them.

Our hostess, moreover, was an accomplished pastry chef and I couldn't possibly name all the astonishing array of tasty cakes that emerged from her ovens. Her pastries were displayed on the table throughout the day in the great hall of the inn and were available to the paying guests in such quantities that the most strident appetite could easily be appeased. What was even more surprising was the fact that these marvels were not considered additions to our bill of fare, but were offered as nibbles of little consequence. I didn't have to be urged to eat my fill of them. To this day I cannot pronounce the name of Castelnau d'Ary without drooling over the memory of these delicacies so freely displayed and offered at the Golden Lion.

Our good hostess, who had such nimble fingers to shape her pastry and such a giving soul to offer them, was a petite, dark-haired and quite rotund person, who was familiarly known as La Patota—the word for a doll in the *langue d'oc*—since her face was so round and rosy. She was, moreover, wholly enamoured of her husband's moustaches, as faithful as a diamond to him and, though thoroughly gracious, was to be looked at, not touched.

But many more palpable wenches were housed in these lodgings whom Caudebec ogled like a fox in a henhouse, and so we were trapped for five long days in order to "rest our horses", who were left to enjoy the ample supplies of oats provided in the inn's stables. We would still be there, combing the Lion's mane, to Samson's great dismay, given the deleterious impact on our purse, had not Brother Antoine, who confessed Caudebec each morning (the only time he wasn't in bed with a wench), finally knit those huge dark eyebrows into a serious frown over his baron's sinning ways. The next day we set out for Montpellier.

I found out from the little page, Rouen, that to get his master to leave, Brother Antoine had threatened to cut a hundred days from the indulgences the baron had just purchased. For if the good man was exceedingly parsimonious with his neighbours, he was quite the opposite regarding his salvation, and kept a very exact account of the number of days of indulgences he had bought with his offerings to the Church, which he counted on to diminish the number of days he'd have to spend in Purgatory. But on this subject, however scandalous these questions of Purgatory and indulgences may seem to me, I shall not expose my feelings here for fear of annoying those of my readers who may have different ideas on the matter.

Before leaving Castelnau d'Ary I went off alone—Samson claiming he was feeling poorly—to see the Norouse stones, which stood on a hill overlooking the town. It was said that an old dowager was passing on the road, took seven pebbles from her apron pocket and tossed them individually onto the infertile ground, swearing that these stones would grow larger and larger as long as the women in the village continued their shameful and dishonourable acts. I visited the site and walked around the rocks. And certainly, if this story is true, from pebbles these stones have grown into enormous boulders that together make a high wall. The townspeople seem to give credence to this wicked fable, though in my view the story was invented by some mad and spiteful husband.

As we were leaving the Golden Lion I went to say goodbye to La Patota, begging a kiss on her round cheeks, which I gave her quite chastely, my hands behind my back, without squeezing her or pinching her in any way. In truth I didn't know what to prize most in our hostess: her beauty—for she was a flower of a woman—her pastries or her virtue. I hope I shall be lucky enough, when it comes time for me to marry, to find a woman of my rank and condition who is her equal!

"My young Monsieur," La Patota said, "you have been so good to everyone during your stay here that I'm like to weep at seeing you set out to brave the dangers of the high roads with such an obliging valet and such a handsome and silent brother. May God keep you and care for your brother with his fever—though he looks much better already! Would you like another kiss in parting?"

With great enthusiasm and in wholehearted friendship, I kissed her again on both cheeks.

"By St Honorat, I'm weeping!" sobbed La Patota, overcome with tenderness. "I'm so silly to get so attached to my guests who pass by on the highway like boats on a river! My noble Monsieur, study well in Montpellier! Avoid quarrels and gambling and, by the Virgin, don't overdo it with the wenches there! They'll ruin your body and send your soul to perdition, as you know all too well!"

"But wait!" I countered. "Aren't you speaking ill of your fair and gentle sex? But, very well, I promise. I'll practise those arts in moderation... just as I did with your excellent pastries," I added with a smile.

At which my La Patota laughed heartily and I felt thus licensed to ask, "One more kiss, my dear hostess?" And I bowed reverentially.

"Just a minute, my friend!" cried her husband pulling nervously on his copious moustaches. "You're going to wear out my good wife's cheeks at this rate!"

My host was a solidly built fellow, bright-eyed, quick in repartee and certainly fully aware of how lucky he was to have such a valiant, virtuous and culinarily gifted wife. And though he was a bit jealous, his pride had taught him to hide his discomfort behind a ready laugh.

I was already in the saddle and off at a trot when a pretty chambermaid ran up behind Accla.

"Whoa, Accla, easy girl!" I called, reining her in. "What do you want, my pretty?"

"My mistress sends you this small provender of cakes to enjoy on your ride!" She handed up this delicious gift, wrapped in a clean cloth, the four corners tied together. I deposited the packet in my saddlebag with profuse expressions of thanks for the girl to pass on to La Patota, and spurred on my steed. I'm ashamed to admit that my throat got all knotted up and tears nearly clouded my eyes, so much did these feminine attentions remind me of the tasty little offerings Barberine prepared each time I left Mespech, even for an afternoon.

I caught up with the rear of our cavalcade, but as we were starting up a long hill I slowed Accla to a walk and fell into a long reverie about Mespech, which ended up being particularly painful since I was overcome with memories of little Hélix that I tried to push out of my mind in order not to feel again the sadness I had felt when she died. But even when I managed to chase her from my thoughts, Mespech remained all too vivid, with its large pond, green prairies and sunny hillsides. Ah, such a heartache gripped me when I thought of my warm nest and the sweetness of my little community.

What's strange is that I missed not only my father (my model and my hero), Uncle de Sauveterre, my little sister Catherine, my two cousins, as naive as they were sweet, but the very walls, the towers, the battlements, the drawbridge and the little fort at the entryway, as well as all of our people at the chateau, who were constantly coming and going, never idle, and seemingly never at a loss for stories, proverbs or practical jokes. I didn't doubt that they missed me as well, for almost all of them were already there when I was born and virtually all of them considered me (rather than my idiot of a brother, full of his haughty and superior airs) the prince of the castle, since I had the same open laugh, quick wit and amiable manners as my father. Forgive me, but I need to name each of them here in writing as I went over each of their names in my heart: Jonas the quarryman, Petremol and Escorgol, the most recently hired, Cabusse, my master-at-arms, Faujanet, Coulondre Iron-arm—these last three legionnaires who had served with my father—and lastly Marsal, who'd been killed by the shot of an arquebus in the fighting at la Lendrevie—all of them good and reliable people, along with their women: Cabusse's Cathau, Jonas's Sarrazine, Coulondre's Jacotte and, up at the castle, sweet Barberine, the gossip la Maligou, our severe Alazaïs (who had the strength of two men, not counting her moral strength) and finally Franchou, to whom Heaven, it seems, had given the mission of sustaining my father in the prime of his later years.

O Lord, how naked I felt at that moment without them—alone and dispossessed—yet still in command of our young troop on this perilous journey.

I was rescued from the depths of this melancholy—which, strange to say, had come over me as a result of La Patota's gift of pastries—by the little page, Rouen, who galloped up alongside me, hatless, his red hair sticking straight up into the rays of the midday June sun. With his green eyes—normally so merry, what with all of the tricks he played on people—gravely fixed on me, he asked me in a low voice if he could have a word with me. I nodded in acknowledgement, and slowed Accla to a walk so that we could let the rest of the party get some distance ahead of us.

"My master," whispered Rouen, "a dastardly plot is being hatched against you. Brother Antoine is trying to undermine you in the baron's eyes."

"What is he saying?"

"That he doesn't believe your story about your brother's slow fever, since Samson can clearly ride and looks the peak of health. And that he doesn't believe that you're of the true religion since you haven't been to confession since Toulouse, despite your conquests in the inns we've stayed in."

"And what does the baron say to all this?"

"He swears that he likes you well enough, but that if it's proved you're a heretic, he'll thrust his sword through your liver and thereby gain an indulgence from Our Lord Jesus Christ after his death."

"He hopes to reach salvation after his death through my liver!" I exclaimed. "Gentle Rouen, is that all?"

"Hardly! Brother Antoine believes that instead of killing you— which might have its risks—he'd rather have you remanded to the judges in Carcassonne to be examined as to your beliefs."

"Ah, what a good apostle he is!" I joked, feigning lighthearted-ness. "Rouen," I continued, smiling, "here is a delicious cake and two sols as my thanks for your fidelity. But I am no heretic, as I shall soon show you."

"Even if your were," replied Rouen, "I'd still like you better than Brother Antoine, who is always denouncing my foibles to the baron so that a day doesn't pass without my feeling the whip. The nine-tailed cat has so scratched and bloodied my buttocks that I can hardly sit in my saddle. Bloody hell, I say, death to this pig in skirts, and believe me, I'd happily set my dog on him to bite him where I'm in such pain."

"By the belly of St Anthony! I'll help you if I can," I promised, laughing.

And, offering him another of La Patota's cakes, I sent him back to the head of the cavalcade, happy and sworn to my service. As for me, I dawdled for a while at the back of the troop, musing as I watched Accla's ears. "Ah, Accla!" I thought. "You would never kick another pony in the stomach over a question of dogma! But, as I think about it, this is very unhappy news. What a terrible image I now have of my fellow men! This very unbrotherly brother whom I've never knowingly offended! This baron, whom I've faithfully served as interpreter! Did I pull a fish bone from his throat so that he could vomit blood and death on me? O Lord! I've hardly left my happy nest at Mespech and now must confront the awful truth about my fellow men, that they treat the least of the innocents as if he were the worst of the damned!"

For a while I was petrified and overwhelmed by the imminent danger that threatened me. And what course of action could the three of us take to avoid our impending fate? To remain with the pilgrims would be sure peril, but to leave them was equally perilous since the road beyond Carcassonne led right into the mountains of Corbières, where the brigands had their lairs. Words from the Old Testament came back to me and I recited a verse: "O Lord, I am counted with them that go down into the pit! O Lord, the wicked are as numerous as the blades of grass! Lord, how long will they triumph over your people and crush them?"

To this I added a short prayer and suddenly felt entirely relieved yet still uncertain as to the course of action we should take, since I was moving in a world of bodies and not souls. My first thought was to hide my worries from Samson, since I well knew that this beautiful angel would be of no help in this world. On the other hand, Miroul had his head securely fixed on his shoulders and his feet planted firmly on the ground. My father had urged that I take care to consult him in such danger and so, pulling him out of Samson's and the pilgrims' earshot I shared with him our situation.

He listened without batting an eyelash. "My master," he observed when I'd finished, "I've heard tell by your good nurse Barberine that your noble father and Monsieur de Sauveterre—at the time that they converted to the new religion but before they were ready to announce their faith, so great was the danger of being burnt—used a clever trick to appear to hear Mass at Mespech without really participating in it. They had a window pierced high up in the wall of the chapel that connected this sanctuary with their quarters on the upper floor. Thus could they hear the voice of the curate Pincers while sitting in Sauveterre's study. Without listening to it, of course. Their excuse for not attending Mass was the old injury to Monsieur de Sauveterre that made it painful for him to descend to the chapel. In reality, they were chanting the Psalms of David while the priest was intoning his paternosters and Ave Marias."

"Yes, I know all about their cleverness," I smiled. "My father showed me the breach in the wall of their study and told me all about it."

"So, my master," Miroul advised, "do as your father did. Use a ruse. Go to confession."

"To this diabolical priest? He'll see at my first words that I'm not a papist."

"So don't make your confession to him. Make it to Father Hyacinth, who's a bit hard of hearing and, to boot, a bit senile and forgetful. Plus he's no friend of Brother Antoine's, who used to lord it over him for not belonging to the same order."

"What a perfect idea! But how do you know all this, Miroul?"

"Oh, I talk to the valets. The servants always know more than the

masters. Sometimes more about them than they know themselves."
As he said this, his brown eye twinkled while the blue one remained
impassive, a sure sign that he knew all about the use to which I'd put
my nights in the arms of the Two Angels and between the paws of
the Golden Lion.

Brother Hyacinth, whom Miroul had just named, always trotted
along at the rear of the cavalcade, not because his horse was old and
weak, but because he didn't trouble to spur it on, preferring to leave
the reins limp on the steed's neck and, scarcely holding on to them,
make signs of the cross over his vast midsection, on which he seemed
forever to focus his meditations—or at least so it seemed, since one
could barely perceive his face hidden beneath his monk's cowl, which
kept the midday sun off a bald, greasy head that shone like marble.
Somnolent and dreamy, his fat loins leaning on the saddleback, he
plodded along the day through, as if in deep meditation. His nag
imitated him in every way and would only speed up to a trot if he lost
sight of the other members of his herd—without Brother Hyacinth
ever having to take up the reins or use his spurs. Never did he seem
to have a word to say to his fellow travellers or offer a response to
any who hailed him, but, feigning deafness, would always respond
to every question with "Eh? Eh? Eh?" muttering a paternoster so
that no one would dare bother him further. And so, since he always
seemed to be in deep spiritual prayer and meditation, he had acquired
a saintly reputation among the pilgrims, and even Caudebec held
him in high esteem.

Once we reached an inn, however, as long as the food was good,
our hermit awoke and lowered his cowl, revealing his polished dome,
bloated face and crimson nose. He suddenly regained his hearing well
enough to hear the hostess announce the various dishes and seemed to
find his voice sufficiently to call the serving maids to pour him more
wine, all of which he ate and drank quietly, his visage steeped in piety,

like certain religious people who offer themselves fully the pleasures of the belly, having renounced those of the lower organs. But, to tell the truth, I know some monks, including some among our Norman pilgrims, who cared as little for vows and rules as for an onion skin, and drank as deeply from the cup of lechery as they did from the cup of good cheer. And though these are, among the papists, terrible abuses that should be righted, they are far, in my opinion, from the worst of the true faith's shortcomings. What example should a shepherd give his flock, especially when among those lodging in the same inn with him are to be found chaste and virtuous women as were some of our Norman ladies? Is it not a shame, as Geoffrey Chaucer said, if the shepherd is dirty and the sheep are clean?

But to continue... I reined in Accla, which was not an easy task, since my little black mare, always so proud and spirited, wanted to break ahead of the heavy Norman workhorses, and was too highly bred to be content to hang back behind them. She had to obey, however, and follow my lead when I sidled up alongside the monk's mount.

"Brother Hyacinth," I greeted him loudly, leaning towards his cowled head. "May I ask you to confess me?"

"Eh? Eh? Eh?" he quavered without turning his head one notch in my direction, before beginning to mumble a paternoster. I waited until he had finished his prayer, but no sooner had he finished the pater than he was off on an Ave, so I had no recourse but to reach into my saddlebags and, pulling out one of La Patota's cakes, wave it in front of his nose.

"God bless you, my son," gurgled Brother Hyacinth as he stuffed the pastry into his vast maw. Finally, after having tasted it, chewed it, turned it over on his tongue, pressed it against his palate and swallowed it, he announced with a sigh, "I assuredly can. In 1256, our Holy Father the Pope granted my order the power to hear confession within the limits of our diocese."

"Do you mean, Brother Hyacinth," I asked with alarm, "that you cannot hear confession outside your diocese?"

"Assuredly I can. I received permission to hear the confession of these pilgrims wherever their calling may take them."

"Alas, I'm no pilgrim."

"No matter. You're one of our group, serving as the baron's interpreter."

This said, he fell silent for so long that I thought he must have fallen asleep, his cowl hiding his face. However, eventually he continued: "My son, I belong to the poorest of the mendicant orders and have in my purse not one single sol. I need not tell you that I am not one of those who goes about in leather boots or with golden clasps on my poor cowl like some Benedictines I could mention."

"Indeed," I concurred. "Brother Antoine looks very well appointed."

"Well appointed!" scoffed Brother Hyacinth with a bitterness whose intensity surprised me. "His abbey has locked away in its vaults behind huge iron doors a prodigious treasure: 17,443 relics, including several pieces of the true cross."

I confess that I did not immediately grasp, in my naivety, just how such relics "enriched" the abbey of Brother Antoine, but all I had to do was listen further.

"These relics," Brother Hyacinth continued, "are put on display once a year on All Saints' Day, and the faithful come out like flocks of sheep from all corners of the diocese to venerate them, for their eternal profit. You see, this veneration is worth, year in, year out, 130,000 days of indulgence! With such a great sum of days, my son, you can imagine the size of the offerings!"

I breathed not a word, so outraged was I by this shameful traffic.

"For my part," continued Brother Hyacinth, "I belong, as I believe I mentioned, to a mendicant order. Poverty is my lot. If you would like me to hear your sins, my son, you must make a donation to my order."

"Here is my donation," I replied, after digging around in my purse, not without some repugnance.

"Three sols!" growled Brother Hyacinth, holding them disdainfully in the palm of his large hand. "That's a very small sum for the son of a baron. Let's not haggle. To give freely and gladly to one's confessor is a sure sign that one is already repentant. Are you suggesting that your contrition is half-hearted?"

"Here! Two more sols," I conceded, furious that I'd let myself be fleeced.

"That should do it, I think," said Brother Hyacinth. "I'm listening."

Isn't it a marvellous thing, however, that, Huguenot though I am, rejecting the very idea of heard confession, and despising as I did the repugnant avarice of this particular priest—who barely listened to me—I nevertheless made a full confession of all of my sins from the most venial to the deadliest without mitigating any of them, but with heartfelt sincerity and in fear of having angered God, as though I had completely forgotten the secular design and useful ruse that had inspired my recitation? "Well," I thought, "maybe the papists are right about this, at least: that the confessor counts for a lot less than the confession."

"My son," said Brother Hyacinth when I'd done, "before I can absolve you, I must give you penitence, for you have committed sins of the flesh in the inn at Castelnau, and sins of irreverence and gluttony. For your sins of lust, you must recite ten paternosters and ten Ave Marias. And for your sins of gluttony, which is a cardinal sin as you know, you must remand into my care the pastries that remain hidden in your saddlebags—*all* of them!"

Alas, I doled out my delicious treasures one by one, but I cannot claim that I accomplished this penance in complete humility as I did so with feelings of bilious rage. Thereupon, Brother Hyacinth pronounced seriously and suavely my absolution—a shield I hoped would serve to parry the blows that Brother Antoine hoped to land on us.

Of course, the habit doesn't make the monk and, truth to tell, doesn't unmake him either. At the time the plague was so ravaging the townspeople of Sarlat I knew some Franciscans, so often decried by the Protestants, whose robes hid truly evangelical hearts. The bishop, priests, seneschal, judges, noblemen and rich bourgeois had all fled the town at the first signs of the outbreak. But these Franciscans remained and unstintingly brought aid and solace to the plague-ridden people in the poorer areas. All but two of them perished, the two my father liberated from the band of thugs in la Lendrevie in the battle in which Marsal was fatally wounded. One of the two, whom my father had praised for his marvellous devotion during the contagion, replied with a remark that is certainly the sweetest, most beautiful and most charitable statement spoken by the lips of a papist to a Huguenot: he thanked my father, saying that far from considering him a heretic he preferred to think of him as a Christian who had lost his way on the road to salvation, but whom he hoped to find waiting for him at the end of that road.

I caught up with my gentle brother, Samson, who was quite concerned by my extended absence and whispered (though I need not have taken this precaution, since none of the pilgrims spoke our dialect) that there were doubts about his "slow fever" and asked whether, to lend credence to my story, he couldn't suddenly pretend to be overcome by dizziness and fall from his horse, Albière, in the midst of the Normans. It took a great deal of work to convince him, since he so hated lies and pretence, but finally he gave in and, spurring his mare onto the grassy edge of the road, took a dramatic fall—so artfully that his breastplate was not dented but his helmet flew off and rolled noisily into the midst of the troop of horses. This produced a great stir, first much laughter, then jokes at his expense, but finally real commiseration, especially among the Norman ladies who, however prudish they might appear, had not failed to be struck by my brother's good looks.

"Good people," I shouted, dismounting and throwing my reins to Miroul, "please continue on your way. It's nothing. My brother has fainted—the effects of his slow fever."

However, a tall, beautiful blonde Norman woman, truly Christian and full of charitable sentiments, named, as I afterwards learnt, Dame Gertrude du Luc, insisted on dismounting as well, and knelt in the grass, with audible sighs of pity, seized Samson with all her strength and pulled him onto her lap, where my poor victim suddenly found himself nested in the protection of her very opulent bosom. Samson, eyes squeezed tight, turned bright red and I turned respectfully away, glancing at Miroul, whose brown eye was twinkling brightly, the blue one stone cold.

"Good lady," I said, "see how my poor brother is weakened by his fever. Might I ask you to let him drink from your gourd?"

"Assuredly!" answered Dame Gertrude du Luc, with great enthusiasm. And, holding his head tightly between her arm and her bosom, she gave him to drink as she would a baby, Samson daring neither to move a muscle nor to open his eyes.

"He's drinking, but I think he's still fainted away," Gertrude announced. "What a pity that such a handsome and well-built gentleman should be so feeble as to fall from his horse. By my Christian faith, he looks just like the beautiful Archangel Michael who's pictured in the stained-glass windows in our church. He has the same milky complexion, the same copper-coloured hair, the same strong shoulders, not to mention those beautiful blue eyes—when he opens them! I would be ashamed to speak thus of him if I thought he were not fainted away," she blushed, "but I don't believe he can hear me in his condition. Is he not unconscious?"

"Oh, there can be no doubt of that, Madame," I agreed, wrinkling my nose to keep from laughing, so thoroughly did the scene amuse me. "But with a couple of sharp slaps, he will wake up, and not remember a word that has passed between us."

"In any case, I mean no disrespect," said Gertrude with a sigh. "Certainly I'm not yet old enough to be his mother, but I love him as if he were my child. Monsieur de Siorac, before you awaken him, might I kiss his cheeks?"

"On the lips, Madame, on the lips! Such is our Périgord custom!"

Miroul's brown eye twinkled even more at this happy lie and the lady, leaning over him, gave Samson a devout kiss, just as I had bidden. To which, to my great surprise, Samson displayed neither resistance nor repugnance, no doubt seeing nothing blameworthy in this caress, which must have seemed purely maternal and which he received for the first time in his life.

I offered Dame Gertrude my hand to help her to stand, but she scarcely needed help as she leapt nimbly to her feet, so supple and vigorous was this noblewoman. She wore in her belt, besides her water gourd, a sizeable dagger, beautifully etched—which I guessed she knew how to wield—and a pair of pistols. Her mount was not just any nag but a beautiful bay mare that she easily and quickly mounted without my help. Then, nodding to me with some confusion of pride and shame, rode off to rejoin her party.

As soon as she was out of earshot, I burst out laughing uncontrollably, Miroul joining in unreservedly.

"Come on, my brother!" I said to Samson. "Open your eyes! Get up! Enough of this languor! Did you fall into a dream resting against this sweet bosom? And didn't you get a ravishing kiss!" And, turning to Miroul, I added, "The ruse worked perfectly! This good lady's virtue will have her relate how Samson fell, indeed, into a great faint. How else could she explain the liberties she took with him?"

"What liberties?" asked Samson, who, in his entire life, had never been approached or caressed by a woman. "Didn't she say she thought of me as her child? And wasn't she generous to share her wine with me? As for her honeyed way of talking, it reminded me of Barberine." Which said, and perhaps not said as innocently as was his custom, he remounted his mare and for the rest of the ride remained head down, lost in a dream.

As the three of us spurred our horses on to catch up to the cavalcade, we were met by a rider galloping at full speed towards us in a cloud of dust.

"The baron," cried Rouen, as soon as he emerged from the dust, "has sent me to ask if your brother has indeed died!"

"So this is how truth makes its way from one end of our column to the other, getting larger from head to tail. Gallop back and tell the baron, gentle page, that my brother is so little dead he can still ride a horse."

He was sitting up straight on his mare, to be sure, but didn't bat an eyelash, so profoundly was he lost in thought.

"So he's still living!" cried Rouen, running his hand through his thick carrot top of hair, his eyes practically popping out of their orbits from surprise.

"As you see!"

"But is it not a ghost I see?"

"Miroul," I said, "what a miracle! See what power a story has: before they doubted whether Samson had a fever; now they're going to doubt he's alive!"

We slept that night in Carcassonne, a splendid city, so well defended behind its magnificent, crenellated ramparts, with towers at regular intervals, that our Huguenots broke their teeth on it when they tried to take it. But our pilgrims decided not to spend more than one night there since neither our inn, the food nor even the chambermaids were to Caudebec's taste. The next morning, after they had sought a smithy and reshod several of their horses (for these Normans took great care of their mounts, which, when stabled at each inn, were thoroughly curried and properly dressed by their valets), we set off for Narbonne.

The baron would not allow a single rider to precede him on the road, so fearful was he of swallowing their dust or smelling the farts and dung of the horses before him, having a nose extremely sensitive to odours of all kinds except his own. What's more, he insisted on travelling at his own pace without hindquarters or rider's back to block his view of the horizon, or, worst of all, some rider to challenge him for the right of way. On his right, a few paces back, rode Brother Antoine; on his left, riding boot to boot, was his interpreter, and a bit farther back was his page, Rouen, who was constantly at work, riding back and forth, carrying messages, questions or orders from one end of the column to the other. Behind Rouen, astride their enormous warhorses, rode the baron's six massive soldiers, helmeted and corseted, skin leathered and scarred, each wearing a look that was hardly evangelical. If they hadn't signed on as the good baron's servants, they could easily have made fairly terrifying brigands.

With the exception of Brother Hyacinth, who inevitably brought up the rear, his reins loose and his hands crossed over his paunch, the rest of the company was free to take any place in the cavalcade according to what anyone had to say and to whom. Which created a perpetual coming and going in their ranks, as these Normans were great storytellers and practical jokers and, as I have said, loved a good laugh. They also loved to sing songs, some of which caused a frown to form on Brother Antoine's brow when he heard the refrains. But the impropriety didn't bother Caudebec one whit, who sent Rouen off to learn the couplets that had amused him. The dozen or so women who accompanied the baron veiled their faces under large headdresses that protected them from the sun but didn't prevent them from laughing on the sly at the scabrous songs. All but one were fairly young widows who had clearly enjoyed life's pleasures in their bourgeois, well-appointed homes in Normandy, and had joined the pilgrimage more for pleasure than for piety. All wore comfortable clothes, the finest boots and gold bracelets on their wrists, but none was more exquisitely adorned than Dame Gertrude du Luc, who seemed to be of higher rank than the others, her late husband having been a nobleman, as I was to learn later.

When we set out from Carcassonne, however, despite the good weather there was neither laughter nor song, everyone's mood having turned quite sombre, and all, the night before, had checked and readied their arms, for this was the stretch of road on which bands of brigands had attacked and murdered many Toulousain merchants.

The baron, who had shown remarkable moderation in his drinking the night before, was quite mute, his eye scanning the horizon to right and left, attentive to the least undulation in the terrain, as if he expected twenty highwaymen to emerge from behind every boulder. But, after a while in the saddle, he glanced over at me in a friendly way and said, "Monsieur de Siorac, if I am killed today, the company in which I find myself at the moment of my death will not be irrelevant, I believe, to the judgement God will pass on me."

These opening words really stung me, and I replied with some venom, "Monsieur, I hope that you find me of noble enough birth to merit dying at your side!"

"Oh, it's not a question of birth," replied the baron haughtily, "but of faith. Monsieur de Siorac, I must ask you outright, are you a good Catholic?"

"Aha," I thought, "it's come to this!"

"I am as good a Catholic as I can be," I equivocated. "But consider this. Would I be here with you, knowing your zeal, if I weren't?"

"But," the baron pursued, "do you make confession?"

"Once a year."

"Once a year!" exclaimed the baron. "'Sblood! That's very little! I, Baron de Caudebec, confess every day that God gives me."

"That's because you are so devout, Monsieur," I said with utmost courtesy, "but the Lateran Council demands only one annual confession." At this, as I well expected, the baron's mouth fell open and, turning to Brother Antoine, he threw him a questioning look.

"That is not strictly false," said this reverend fellow, his heavy black eyebrows bringing a dark cloud over his face. "But one can't be a good Christian if one remains from one end of the year to the other polluted in his sin, especially when one is in mortal danger."

"Ah, Brother Antoine," I replied, sighing sanctimoniously, "on that point, I couldn't agree more!"

"You couldn't agree more, Monsieur de Siorac," replied Brother Antoine, fixing his little dark eye on me, "and yet you have not confessed as I invited you to do in Toulouse."

"Oh, but I have!" I answered. "I obeyed you. Just yesterday, having fallen into a deep sense of regret over what I did at the Two Angels and at the Golden Lion, I suddenly felt so filthy from my terrible sins that I couldn't wait to have them washed away."

"But did you confess them?"

"Of course"

"And to whom?"

"Why, to Brother Hyacinth."

"To that idiot?" said Brother Antoine.

"Idiot?" boomed the baron, very surprised and angered. "Is that a Christian way to talk? 'Sblood, Brother Hyacinth is not an idiot, he's a saint! And the idiot is you, monk, if your suspicions have no better basis than this! Hey there, page! Page! God's belly, the rascal's asleep! I'm going to cut off his!—"

"At your service, Monsieur!" broke in Rouen, steering his horse clear of the baron's reach.

"Go fetch me Brother Hyacinth immediately, and be brisk about it! The skin of your backside will answer for your speed."

For the entire time it took Rouen to fetch the mendicant monk, Caudebec kept his peace, somewhat embarrassed, I thought, to be conducting this discourteous inquisition. For my part, I said not a word and sat straight up in my saddle, head held high, with the air of a man who does not brook insult. I'd often seen my father take on this air in his relations with his peers when some dispute arose, and I always loved that attitude, though regretted that my youth didn't give it more weight.

Brother Hyacinth appeared at last, his head bobbing and his paunch shaking at every step of his horse, who whinnied in displeasure at having to gallop up to the front of the cavalcade. Not that the monk had spurred him, but Rouen had ridden behind, whipping his croup, preferring to bloody the steed's backside than suffer the same fate to his own if he were too slow in returning.

"Brother Hyacinth," growled Caudebec, "is it true that you heard Monsieur de Siorac's confession?"

But I didn't want Caudebec to hold the reins or to whip this nag, so I broke in and said, "Monsieur, I beg you to desist from asking this question. It is an affront to my honour. The question supposes that I may have lied to you."

"Answer, Brother Hyacinth!" trumpeted Brother Antoine triumphantly.

"Hold your tongue, monk!" snarled Caudebec. "This is an affair between gentlemen. It does not concern you." And, turning to me, he said with utmost gravity, "Monsieur de Siorac, this is a question of my salvation. I've already told you that to die in the presence of a heretic today would be my damnation. If you don't wish me to pose this question I will not pose it. But if not, we will have to cross swords and the Lord God will judge between us."

I conjured myself to be silent, all the while inwardly enjoying this barbarous devotion, and especially the great distress exhibited by Brother Antoine, who, eyes throwing sparks beneath his great eyebrows, stood to his full height in his stirrups and, turning to Brother Hyacinth, cried with the utmost scorn, "Well, Brother Hyacinth, are you such a drunkard and an idiot that you cannot answer this simple question? Did Monsieur de Siorac confess to you, yes or no?"

Caudebec hereupon made an imperious movement with his right hand that silenced Brother Antoine, and I was able to catch, in the instant of this gesture, an exchange of looks between the mendicant and the moneyed monk, a look that was hardly tender. Brother Hyacinth, his cowl drawn low over his forehead, retained the most perfect silence and sweet immobility.

"Well then, Monsieur de Siorac, we must fight," said Caudebec, his face quite red, "and very much against our wishes, it seems."

This last remark touched me somewhat, but since I needed to push this scene to the conclusion I required, that is, to the greatest disadvantage and embarrassment of my accuser, I remained silent, stiff and upright on Accla, chin raised, eyes on the horizon.

"Monsieur," pleaded Brother Hyacinth, "may I have leave to speak?"

"I brought you here to do just that," Caudebec replied reproachfully.

"Indeed," answered Hyacinth, "yet I cannot in good faith answer a question that you do not wish to ask me."

"Why speak, then?"

"To tell you, Monsieur, that, as for myself, I would be marvellously sorry if two good Christians cut each other's throats in a quarrel of no consequence."

"A quarrel of no consequence! Did Monsieur de Siorac confess?"

"Did I not say so?" I cried as loudly and with as much offence as I could muster. "Say what you must, Brother Hyacinth, since you have now responded halfway."

"Oh, Monsieur, may I?" pleaded Brother Hyacinth.

"Speak, damn it!" shouted the baron.

"Monsieur de Siorac yesterday confessed to me in perfect contrition and entire humility."

Watching Brother Antoine out of the corner of his eye so as not to miss an iota of his discomfort, the good monk pronounced these words in the suavest possible tones, rolling them on his tongue with as much gluttony as if they were La Patota's pastries.

"Monsieur de Siorac," intoned Caudebec, his face scarlet and his eyes lowered, "I owe you my sincerest apologies for the evil suspicions I have cast on you."

Certainly he owed them to me, but hadn't quite offered them yet. Even in his words, Caudebec was not very forthcoming.

"Not at all," I replied, acting the generous one now. "You owe me nothing since the suspicions are not yours." This was intended not only to exonerate him, but to tell him in the same breath where to direct his wrath. Which he did without being begged to do so. It all fell where it was supposed to, with a directness, aim and devastation that were intensely satisfying.

"Monk," he said, turning to Brother Antoine, "although you are proud, learned and powerful within your abbey, you will henceforth ride at the rear of our column, alone, meditating on your errors. And Brother Hyacinth, whom you've so despised, will now ride on my right and will be my confessor."

The great advantage to being a monk is that one is not expected, as one is when one is a gentleman, to get one's dander up when humiliated. Quite the contrary: since humility is the very condition and the greatest of virtues of a monk, one can wear it like a cloak.

"Monsieur," said Brother Antoine, head and eyes lowered in a deep bow, "I will obey your orders, whatever they may be, in entire submission and respect."

Emitting as great a sigh as if he had been nailed to the cross, and looking heavenward to take God as witness to his martyrdom, he bowed a second time to the baron, reined in his horse and turned away. I'll wager that once he was alone and his face was hidden in his cowl, his black eyes spit flames and that these flames could have roasted me alive.

Upon reflection, I didn't want Caudebec to stew in his thoughts, and, changing the subject of his fears, I said to him, "Monsieur, my father always told me that when a company is travelling on a road in danger of being attacked, they should carry torches and send horsemen ahead and post soldiers on both flanks. If you would be willing to send two of your soldiers ahead to the crest of the hill, one on the right and the other on the left, my brother, Miroul and I will act as your vanguard."

"God's passion!" cried Caudebec. "Now, I like that kind of thinking! You've got a good head on your shoulders for such a young fellow! Of course, I'm not surprised. Noble blood does not lie! I should have been taking such precautions for a long time. Yo! Fromont, ride ahead to the top of the hill, and you, Honfleur, to the top of the next and keep your eyes open! Monsieur de Siorac, shall I send two soldiers as the vanguard instead of your little group?"

"No, Monsieur! Then you'd have no one here to protect your company."

"But that's a perilous mission to serve as the vanguard."

"Would I have asked for the mission if it weren't?" I said in my best Gascon boastfulness.

But the truth was, I was in a hurry to leave him to himself since I was fairly certain he would soon begin to resent me for humiliating his confessor. "But would you allow me," I rejoined, "to leave our packhorse behind and give his lead to your page? She'd be a bit of an embarrassment to us if we were attacked and had to ride hell for leather to get back here."

He agreed, and it was with no little relief that I found myself on the road to Narbonne with Samson and Miroul a quarter of a league ahead of the pilgrims. Miroul seemed as if he would love to hear my exploits, but I was loath to recite them in front of Samson, who didn't know I'd gone to confession the night before and who would have been passing troubled to learn of it. In any case, it wasn't a time for chatter but one for vigilance, for we were in great danger of being surprised and annihilated by a large band.

I told Miroul and Samson to load their pistols and unholster them, and to hold their swords at the ready. I did the same. Then, frowning, I remonstrated severely with Samson, for his slowness to unsheathe his sword and his repugnance to fire on his fellow men, even when they wanted to take his life, had nearly cost me my life during the fighting at la Lendrevie. I explained that, whereas my father had given him the responsibility for our purse, he had expressly given me the command of our little troop and that he, Samson, must now obey me in all things like a foot soldier his captain, without hesitation or objection, and that if he didn't he would surely endanger not only his life but mine and Miroul's as well. If he didn't, and even if nothing too terrible came of this peril, it would still be the end of our friendship.

At these words, my dear angel teared up. I felt some remorse for having so brutally shaken him up, and so, as we continued to ride along side by side, and still maintaining the severity of my look, I reached over and took his hand. He squeezed my hand tightly and said quietly but distinctly, "My Pierre, I will obey you."

Having thus cemented my authority over my little army, I felt more confident, though still very much on the lookout, my eyes darting in all directions. For the road at this point was not so straight and level as it had been. The hills had crept up close to the roadside and, at about every 200 toises, there was a curve, or a hill, or a descent that blocked our view of the rest of the way. I ordered my friends to ride on the grass at either side of the road so our hoof beats wouldn't be so easily heard by our attackers, but also so that we could better hear if anyone were coming. And it was good I'd had this idea, for a moment later I heard the sound of hoof beats and, glancing over my shoulder, spied half a dozen horsemen bearing down on us from 100 toises behind us.

"Miroul," I hissed, "don't turn around, nor you, Samson. We have a troop behind us who weren't on the road, since Caudebec would never have let them pass. They've come out of the hills. And who are these rogues who are cutting us off from Caudebec? We have to find out while there's still time. Miroul, I want you to hide in the thicket yonder, let them approach close enough to see them but not close enough to catch you. Then hurry back through the fields and tell me what they look like and how they're armed and mounted."

Miroul said not a word, but, as we reached the turn, hid himself so well that three toises away I couldn't have distinguished him or his mare from the leaves. As we distanced ourselves from him, leaving him alone, my heart was beating double time despite the fact that I was entirely sure of his skill and marvellous agility, and of the speed of his Arabian. Nevertheless, however much I tried to reassure Samson, I could not repress a profound sigh of relief when suddenly Miroul was there, smiling.

"There are five of them," he whispered, "ugly men and bloodthirsty, mounted on worthless nags, but well armed with pikes and lances, cutlasses and swords."

"Do they have firearms?"

65

"I didn't see either pistols or arquebuses, but from where I was, I couldn't really see their saddlebags."

"I'm thinking," I said after a moment's reflection, "these rogues have accomplices up ahead and when these men attack, the others will attack us from behind and on both sides using only swords so as not to alert Caudebec. If they crush the vanguard, they'll easily surprise the pilgrims and wipe them out."

To this, neither Samson nor Miroul replied, waiting for me to continue.

"Well then," I added, "let's not wait to be attacked and wiped out from two sides. At the next turn in the road, we'll hide and wait for them to come within ten paces of us, and as they reach the bend in the road, we'll gallop out, reins in our teeth and pistols in both hands."

"But what if they're peaceable workers?" said Samson.

"My brother, you're not serious?"

"No," said Samson, turning bright red. "I'll shut up and obey as I promised."

"My master," said Miroul, turning to Samson, "I've seen these rogues, and if they're peaceful workers and not the atrocious rascals I believe they are, I'll happily sell my part of eternity to the Devil."

"Miroul," replied Samson sadly, "please don't speak this way, especially in the teeth of death."

"Well, Death will sink his teeth into them and not us," I said categorically. "Enough talk, time is wasting. I will gallop into the middle of the road. Miroul, on my left, will fire on the two rogues in front of him. I'll take the two in the middle. And Samson, you must shoot dead the rascal who comes at you."

"I'll do as you command," said Samson, lowering his head.

He didn't. Either by chance or by secret will, despite the fact that of the three of us he was by far the best shot, his ball missed its target so that of our five assailants, his was the only one still on his horse when our horses ran down their nags, which were terrified by our detonations and the strange shouts we hurled at them. This survivor fled, but I ran him down and was lucky enough to wound him in the shoulder with my sword and cause him to drop his weapon. He surrendered himself to our mercy, Miroul strapped him to his horse, and we bore him back to Caudebec, our heads held high, right proud of our night's work.

3

BEFORE REJOINING CAUDEBEC, I slowed my little band to a walk, fearing that if we arrived at a gallop and in a cloud of dust the baron might mistake us for brigands and open fire. And indeed, I found the pilgrims, both men and women, in a state of alarm over the gunfire they'd heard so that some had drawn their pistols and others had readied their arquebuses and were lighting their fuses. As for Caudebec, his face was especially red and his hair was on end, unsure of what action to take as he was altogether better at bartering than fighting.

Nevertheless, as soon as he saw my prisoner and before I could open my mouth, he had two of his soldiers throw the man from his horse and set about torturing him in order to find out everything he knew about the brigands of the Corbières. This was done in the blink of an eye; they threw a hemp rope about his neck and brought him to his knees, all bloodied, on the stony road, and began tightening the rope by twisting it with a stick.

"Monsieur," I intervened, "this rogue is my prisoner, he's losing blood, he's terrified, and your soldiers don't speak his language and risk killing him before he's been able to speak. I request that you tell them to remove the garrotte and return him to me. I will interrogate him fully, but not right now when we are in immediate danger. I think what we must do is to abandon the road and move up the hill to our left, where, for lack of ramparts, we'll be able to see anyone who intends to attack, plus have the advantage of being above them."

As the pilgrims standing behind Caudebec were all overwrought, chattering and milling about in the most disorderly way, he agreed to everything I proposed since he had no plan of his own. Apparently he was also certain that I had inherited my father's knowledge of military science—an absurd idea, but nonetheless a common belief among gentlemen.

The summit of the hill that I had indicated was reached only with great difficulty since it sloped quite abruptly down on all sides (but that difficulty would also hinder our assailants). Everyone dismounted; we herded our horses into a copse nearby and posted several sentries to protect them. Of course the baron "gave" these orders, but he was simply following my advice. This hill would have been a sad place to end one's days, or even to live out one's days since it was rocky and treeless, as is often the case in this terrain, so different from the sunny and verdant one I'd known. Here the sun beat down and withered the frail and yellowing grasses that even the hungriest sheep would have disdained.

I pulled my prisoner off to one side, so that Miroul, Samson and I could guard him, and untied his bonds, washed his wounds with vinegar, bandaged them and gave him something to drink. He was astonished at this treatment, expecting only torture and death, which he accepted with the kind of brutal courage my father had observed in Sarlat among the gravediggers who were burying the victims of the plague.

This rogue was named Espoumel, spoke in a Catalan laced with Provençal, and although dirty and hairy, had a pleasant face and a look that was more naive than wicked.

"Espoumel," I began, "how many are in your band?"

"I can't say, Monsieur, I don't know my numbers."

69

"But you know their names."

"Surely."

"Then name them—all of them except the ones I killed."

The rogue named them all, one by one, and I counted nineteen on my fingers. Not so many. Rumours on the road from Narbonne to Toulouse had increased their number to at least double or triple the size of their present company.

"Espoumel, which of your fellows have firearms?"

"The captain and the lieutenant."

His answer relieved me enormously, and, leaving the prisoner under Samson's guard, I took Miroul with me to see Caudebec, who was ensconced under a meagre little oak tree, trying to get shade from the torrid heat of the noonday sun.

"Monsieur, you have among your provisions a small cask of Malvoisie wine that you take very good care of. I want you to give it to me in recognition of my good services."

I couldn't help laughing at his expression when he heard this. Certainly he didn't give this wine up gracefully—he simply didn't know how to refuse my request. With Miroul carrying the cask on his shoulder, we came back to our prisoner.

"Espoumel," I said, "how many firearms have you seen among our people since we brought you here?"

"I couldn't say how many, Monsieur, but lots, and even in the hands of your women."

"And how many of us are there?"

"Lots."

"More than your band?"

"'Tis certain."

"You're right. There are more than a hundred of us" (a figure that raised Samson's right eyebrow, since he hated to see me lie). "Well then, Espoumel, go tell your captain what you know about us and

70

take him this cask that my valet is tying to your horse. Tell him that the high and mighty Baron de Caudebec sends it to repay your loss of the four men we killed."

At this, Espoumel opened wide his little eyes and, standing there terrified, knew not what to do or say. Miroul brought him his nag and helped him mount, since the poor rascal was still weak from loss of blood.

"On your way, Espoumel!" I commanded, but he hesitated to spur his horse to leave.

"Monsieur," the rogue asked after some hesitation, "after I've said everything to my captain as you instructed me, must I return here to be hanged?"

"No, no, no!" I laughed. "Stay with your people and pray to God to forgive your sins."

At these words, Espoumel crossed himself, and with neither a word nor a look in my direction, fearing no doubt that I might change my mind, he gave spurs to his nag and rode down the embankment as fast as her legs would carry them.

"'Sblood, Siorac!" shouted Caudebec, rushing towards me and beating the air with his arms. "Your prisoner is escaping *and with my cask of wine!*"

"Not in the least, Monsieur, I released him. The man doesn't know how to count and he's going to tell his captain on my behalf that there are more than a hundred of us and that we're all armed with arquebuses. As for your delicious nectar, the bandit captain will suspect nothing, but in less than an hour he'll be sleeping like a babe."

To tell the truth, I would have been content to double the number of pilgrims without depriving the baron of his Malvoisie, but, in any event, Caudebec's inquisition had left a very bitter aftertaste, and I felt that since I had risked three lives in serving as his vanguard, it was certainly his turn to suffer some inconvenience.

I walked Caudebec back to the little bent oak tree that served as his shelter. He was stricken by the loss of his cask of wine but also pricked by the moral avarice that was so deeply rooted in his character, and he rather coolly—and very offhandedly—thanked me for what I'd done. I must say that, for my part, I would gladly have left his company altogether had it not been for the continuing danger that threatened us on the road. Ingratitude is a strange vice, despite the ironic truth that it is very widespread and none the less hideous for being such a common disease, for it despoils your soul like a bubo of the plague despoils the most beautiful body.

I consoled myself with these thoughts, yet I couldn't help feeling saddened by the baron's gracelessness in thanking me. My father often remarked that, for my age, and despite my temper, which I'd need to learn to control, I was very wise, despite my obvious need to subdue my passions, and even subtle in my observations of the world, with a certain instinct about others—wenches especially—which allowed me to deal effectively with all kinds of people. These were useful qualities in any man, of course, but especially in a Huguenot who was a member of the most persecuted group in the kingdom and who lived in constant apprehension of the potential wickedness of others. But I must qualify these observations by adding that I was but newly released from Mespech and from my native Périgord, and I knew but little of the outside world, so that my first exposure to it through these pilgrims, though it provided obvious pleasures, also left me feeling sad. Despite my success with ruses, I was still very green and very sensitive.

The baron had finally given the order to decamp, and when I came back to Samson and Miroul I found them standing by their horses; while Miroul was girthing them, Samson was leaning up against Albière with a very languorous expression and, at his side, Dame Gertrude du Luc was busily attending to him with great compassion, refreshing his temples with her perfumed silk hand-kerchief, these attentions necessitating her very close proximity to his person.

"Monsieur de Siorac," she said, giving me a pert nod, "isn't it amazing that your brother, weakened as he is by his slow fever, should have fought so valiantly against those rogues? Look at how he perspires with the return of his fever. I'm afraid lest he faint away again."

"And so he might," I replied gravely. "Given the condition he's in, he could collapse at any minute. Might I ask you, noble lady, to give him your arm while I regirth Accla?"

"Ah, gladly, Monsieur!" she answered. "I will indeed, for I love him like my child, despite being of an age to be his sister." And so saying, she put her arm around his waist and held him fast to prevent him from falling, although he was leaning comfortably against Albière, one hand behind him gripping the cantle of the saddle, the other holding the reins on the pommel, yet with eyes half closed and his body almost limp with his "fever".

"Samson, my beautiful angel," I mused, "you're doing exactly the right thing to close your eyes, if only on your virtue, for it is indeed on perilous footing, being so craftily circumvented."

Miroul's two Arabians and my mare, Accla, hid this scene from the rest of the pilgrims, clearly to Dame Gertrude's relief, since the most Christian of attentions are sometimes best accomplished without witnesses. I myself was scarcely present, so occupied was I with attending to my horse, and likewise Miroul to his, although his brown eye was all atwinkle when we glanced each other's way.

"Dear me," exclaimed Dame Gertrude, "he's fainting again!"

"Madame," I explained, "give him a couple of hard slaps and you'll revive him instantly!"

"God forbid!" she sighed. "I am a woman! It ill suits the modesty of my sex to strike a gentleman!"

"Well, in that case," I suggested, "do as our nurse Barberine has always done to revive him. Give him a couple of kisses in the Périgordian way."

"Ah," she sighed, "now that sits better with my natural sympathies!"

And whether she accorded him what I suggested I couldn't say, for her wide-brimmed sun bonnet, as broad as a shield, hid her face and Samson's as well from view for the entire time it took her to effect this resurrection. She hadn't quite finished when the whole hillside resounded to Caudebec's stentorian order: "Saddle up! Saddle up!"—cries that became all the more imperious the less he felt sure of his command in the present danger.

"Monsieur de Siorac," sighed Dame Gertrude, turning in my direction, "I must, alas, abandon my care here and find my horse. Will you permit me to visit from time to time during the day to learn of my patient's condition?"

"Madame," I replied, bowing, "I would with the greatest pleasure welcome such visits and any care you can provide my poor brother!" I spoke with entire sincerity, for if there were any imperfection in my beloved Samson, it was the distance he had always kept before this voyage from the gentler sex, without whom the green paradise God has provided would be but a mournful prison. The therapy to which he had just submitted was quite reassuring in this regard. To see how powerful Dame Gertrude's cure had been, and how quickly my brother had regained his usual colour and warmth, I understood that until now it wasn't so much lack of sensitivity but awkwardness—perhaps due to his being my father's bastard—that had inspired his secret resentment of women.

Without doing so too obviously, I watched him out of the corner of my eye as he mounted his horse in a kind of daze, his face flushed red enough to suggest he was still prey to the fever I had invented. For feverish he was, certainly, but this fever would never be cured except by the snows of future years. Throughout our ride to Narbonne, I could see he never lost the flame that turned his cheeks blood red. He kept to himself, eyes lowered, with a marvellously chaste expression—looking, broad-shouldered, his copper-coloured locks flowing over his collar, like the archangel in the stained-glass windows of the papist churches—and, indeed, hadn't Dame Gertrude compared him to St Michael? Looking at his candid face, I couldn't help thinking that, newly aware of the pleasures of the flesh, Samson preferred not to be too conscious of them, in order to keep his Huguenot conscience as clear as possible. And however much I was itching to trouble this hypocritical innocence, I invoked all the compassion I could muster to suppress the barbs I would have liked to prick him with.

And so it was that, with Samson all dreamy, my own attention focused on any possible surprises that might await us, and Dame Gertrude coming and going, her worries about her patient matched only by her concern for her reputation (which had already been the subject of much gossip) we quietly reached Lézignan well after nightfall, our horses, for once, put through their paces. At the Unicorn, where we put up, the Baron de Caudebec, as puffed up as a chickpea in brine, filled his hostess's ears with tales of his victory over the bandits. I had little role in his narration, as you may well imagine.

Our hostess at the Unicorn (I know not why so many of the women in this profession are widows, though perhaps it's because so many men require their attention that they have none left for their husbands) assured me the next morning, in response to my enquiries, that the Lézignan road was entirely safe, since so many merchants were headed for Lyons and Marseilles that they tended to travel in caravans as far as Montpellier. Of these, most appeared armed to the teeth and so resolute that no attacks had been reported for at least two years. She added, laughing, that she would have gladly kept me longer as her guest, so gracious were my manners, but that she well understood my impatience to be rid of these Norman pilgrims and their tendency to tarry too long at each inn where the food, drink and comfort were a welcome diversion from the apparent sanctity of their presumed goal. She also offered to introduce me to some merchants of her acquaintance who were heading out the next day—an introduction that would kill two birds with one stone since both parties would be the stronger for having joined forces. (She'd heard from Miroul what valiant service we had performed in killing the bandits in the hills.) I accepted her offer with effusive thanks and added a few cajoleries appropriate to my age. My hostess gently deflected my advances, bowing deeply and displaying with her pretty teeth such a gracious and knowing smile that I was overcome with passion. "Ah!" I mused as I watched her walk away. "Travel is such an education and the world so vast and full of infinite pleasures!"

Of course, I was delighted to part company with Caudebec and went happily to tell Samson the good news of our departure, thinking he, too, would be pleased to put a stop to these endless layovers, which were rapidly emptying our purse, and believing he'd be glad to leave these Norman pilgrims behind and to gallop off with people from our own region. But my beautiful angel, forgetting that he was the keeper of the purse, seemed less than enthusiastic about my news and, turning away, looked so bereft that I understood immediately why, and felt both remorse and the need to remedy the pain I'd caused him.

Taking Miroul with me, and advising him to go and have fun with the other valets and to take his time returning to our room, I sought out Dame Gertrude du Luc in her chambers, and took her aside, since there were two other ladies sharing her room, who pricked up their ears when I entered. I begged her most urgently, by the name of St Gertrude, not to reveal to a living soul what I had to tell her.

Breathlessly, she consented. I then informed her that we'd be leaving the next day without saying goodbye to the baron for fear that, bitterly angry to lose the services of his interpreter, he might use force to retain us, which would surely cause Samson and me to draw our swords in our defence. Hearing this, the good lady spun away from the eavesdroppers in the room and turned deathly pale. Then she whispered to me to leave her chambers at once but to meet her on the stairway that led down to the great hall. Which I did. The stairwell was quite dark and reminded me of the stairs at the Two Angels where my hostess and I had taken such a pleasant tumble.

A few minutes later—though it seemed much longer—I heard the sound of the lady's slippers in the hallway.

"Monsieur de Siorac?"

"I'm here!"

"Oh, Monsieur," she moaned, her bodice heaving—which I couldn't see but could certainly feel, for in her great emotion she had pulled me to her with as much force as if I had been my brother—and even though she intended not the slightest malice in this, and nor did I, I was prey to some extraordinary sensations at being thus embraced in complete innocence by a person of her sex.

"Oh, Monsieur," she continued, her voice choked with emotion, bathing my cheeks with her tears, "what terrible news! Oh, how unhappy I am! He's leaving! He's leaving tomorrow!"

"We must set out before dawn."

"But, Monsieur, why so sudden and brutal a departure? Is there no way to delay you?"

"Alas, no, good lady. Our poor students' purse will not tolerate so many inns!"

"But perhaps I could loan you what you need? There would be no shame in accepting, Monsieur. Thank God I'm not without resources."

"Fie, Madame! Borrow money! When we have no need!"

"A thousand pardons, Monsieur de Siorac!" she cried, hugging me ever more tightly, her hands clenching my back. "I must be losing my mind, I'll wager, so wretched am I at the thought of losing my little patient. But how is he taking all this?"

"Very badly indeed, but he won't say a word."

"Ah, he's so brave!" she said with such happy tones that I was very moved and almost envious of my Samson for having inspired such love.

"Good lady," I said, "when we get to Montpellier, we shall be lodging with Maître Pierre Sanche, apothecary, on the place des Cévenols, and we are counting on you to do us the kindness of paying us a visit there on your way to and from Rome."

"'Tis certain I will, Monsieur de Siorac! But will I be able to see your brother today in order to continue my care?"

"Dear lady, I was going to beg you to do him this very service! My valet, Miroul, and I have business to attend to in the town and my brother will doubtless be alone in our room while we're out, and doubtless too, in great need of your care."

Even though this was perhaps what she was most hoping for, she nevertheless pulled away and said, almost inaudibly, "But Monsieur, may I do such a thing? Alone with your brother? In his chambers?"

"Your sense of charity will answer for you better than I can," I replied, feeling a tinge of impatience with this display of modesty, which felt more ceremonious than real.

Groping in the dark for her hand, I seized it and kissed it fervently, then left without another word.

I realize as I reread this that some will raise an eyebrow at my behaviour since, as I have confessed, I am entirely devoted to Venus, yet now, rather than pursuing my own amorous desires, found myself pushing a beautiful—and oh! how ardent—woman into Samson's bed. It wasn't just my great affection for him that inspired this gesture, but also my, dare I say, fatherly concern that his life wasn't being lived in as full a way as his aspect merited: certainly there was nothing impotent or effeminate about him, for, aside from his great beauty, he was stronger, more muscular and more robust than any mother's son in France, and it was therefore a great pity, in my view, that this handsome stallion should live like a dried-up nun in a cell.

As for the sins that I committed then, and will commit, I'm afraid to say, until Death brings her chill upon me, and although I'm no Lutheran, I would like to share Luther's powerful and beautiful words on this subject: "I am a sinner and sin mightily, but mightier still is my belief in Christ and my joy in loving Him." A recommendation that is likely, I admit, to raise some objections, since it appears to allow for too much moral leeway. But that's not why I love these words; rather, it is because I cannot imagine loving God without loving his creatures. I deeply believe that, just as the body was not meant to be mortified, neither are faith and joy meant ever to be separated.

To cover the thirty leagues that separated Lézignan from Montpellier, we would need at most five days, not because our horses were faster than Caudebec's, but because they so much needed daily exercise that we could not spend more than one night in each inn.

Our three merchant fellow travellers were old greybeards, but still vigorous, full of animation, easy smiles and friendly words, though beneath their show of amiability, entirely battle-ready and hard as rocks. Their vigilance regarding the load of sheepskins they were carting to Montpellier was constant and unremitting, for they each repeatedly stopped to count their "harvest" to ensure that their valets hadn't made off with any of their store. They also seemed, as far as I could tell, just as mistrustful of each other, and kept up their surveillance on their fellows from dawn to dusk—and even throughout the night, I'd wager, sleeping with one eye open.

You may well imagine that for men like these a night's lodging was sufficient as long as they had victuals enough to fill their bellies and beds to restore their strength, their sheepskins stacked next to them at night despite the awful stench such a heap of skins produced. As for the rest, that is, all the things that make our French inns the envy of the entire continent—the fine cuisine, the bouquet of the wines, the sweet and pliable tempers of our chambermaids—none of that was of any interest to these three, who were so single-mindedly focused on their calculations, risks and profits that they went everywhere and saw nothing.

We were so impatient to discover Montpellier, which our father had told us so much about, that we took our leave of our convoy about two leagues before we reached the city. As we galloped away from them, I glanced over my shoulder at these merchants growing smaller and smaller in the distance and then disappearing at a bend in the road, along with their carts, valets and skins, whose putrid smell still permeated my nostrils no matter how deeply I breathed in the good dry air full of the perfume of this countryside. For although these lands seemed rocky and infertile compared to the verdant hillsides of Périgord, they nevertheless spawned a remarkable number of very aromatic plants that the sun cooked to such perfection that every breath of this air was an unmitigated pleasure.

One league from Montpellier, however, the terrain seemed to change dramatically, and suddenly we saw a field of harvested wheat at whose centre stood a hayrick surrounded by a group of labourers winnowing their crop. Their method was so surprising that we reined in our horses to watch, for in Périgord, which is so rainy even in June, we always flail our sheaves, to separate the grain from the straw, under a shed, whereas here, with the soil so hot and dry, they did this work right in out in the open.

As I walked up to them, I saw a man astride the hayrick, holding the reins of six horses, all blindfolded, and turning them endlessly in a circle by means of a long whip, while his companions, pitchforks in hand, threw the wheat stalks under the horses' shoes, so that the horses turned the stalks over each time they passed until they perfectly separated grain from stalks.

As they were just then stopping to breathe the horses and take a drink of wine, I went up to one of these labourers, who seemed quite clearly the leader of the group. He was a small, dark-skinned man with sparkling eyes and a ready tongue. He explained that they were waiting for the breeze that always came on towards the evening in these parts, in order to throw the straw and grain into the wind and onto a screen so that the lighter chaff would blow away and the grain settle on the screen. I asked him if they ever did their winnowing in the barn, but he assured me he'd never in his whole life seen that done since it never rained here in harvest season.

With his bright eyes fixed on me, he asked if he might question me in turn since it seemed only fair that if he'd satisfied my curiosity I should return the favour. I readily consented, and told him who we were, where we were headed and why.

He seemed infinitely flattered that we should have come so far and by such dangerous roads to study in Montpellier, which, he assured us, was the biggest and most beautiful city in all of Provence. He confessed that he'd heard that Toulouse was bigger but that being biggest was hardly of any consequence. Certainly, he claimed, there was no city in our provinces that could match Montpellier in beauty, commodities and climate. In Montpellier, he continued, there was hardly any cold season at all, whereas he'd heard tell that the king in his Louvre in Paris on certain winter days could see the Seine ice up before his very eyes. He added, jovially, that when he heard this story he got such a deathly cold in his back that he preferred to remain a field hand in Montpellier than to be king in the capital.

Of course the wisp of a smile that accompanied these words

suggested how uncertain the truth of his gasconades might be. As for me, I thoroughly enjoyed the give and take of this light and subtle jesting, and later, when I'd got to know the people of Provence better, I realized that this mirth was part and parcel of their customary finesse.

"A thousand thanks, my good peasant," I said, and to hear himself addressed in this way, the man smiled, though I couldn't fathom why. I spurred my horse away with Samson close behind, but Miroul, who had stayed to talk to the winnowers, didn't catch up with us for another half a league.

"Monsieur," he said, his cheeks swollen, or so it seemed, with the news he had to impart, "that man you took for a field hand is not one at all, however much he may be dressed for the part. His name is Pécoul, and he's a powerful bladesmith who sells daggers and swords and has a beautiful shop on the rue de l'Espazerie in Montpellier. He's the lord of this domain, and prefers to bag his own wheat since he doesn't trust anyone."

"By the belly of St Anthony, Miroul!" I cried. "Not much escapes your unmatched eyes! And even less your sharp ears!"

"At your service, Monsieur," said Miroul, feigning humility.

"And what else did you learn?"

"That if we continue on this road we'll cross through a field of olive trees where the city hangman exercises his trade; that we'll then see a high wooden palisade that protects the outlying houses round Montpellier and finally, after passing these houses, we'll reach the Common Wall."

"The Common Wall?"

"That's what the people of Montpellier call the wall that encloses the city."

"That's a very pretty name—sounds like commonweal! But this is marvellous, Miroul! You draw so many secrets out of so many people! Samson, did you hear Miroul's report?"

Alas, my beloved brother had ears neither for Samson's words nor for my question. He rode along, his eyes fixed on Albière's ears, the reins loose in his hands, colour leaving or flushing his face, sometimes deathly pale and sometimes scarlet, now biting his lip, now sighing mournfully. He scarcely even knew, I'll wager, that he was on a horse or in what direction he was heading. A couple of sidelong glances at his face told me that he was visited by such memories, such dreams, but also such remorse that the poor lad was being torn asunder in his mind, his eyes changing back and forth between tender and fearful looks as though hell might suddenly open up under his mare's hooves.

Although I'd seen more than one olive grove on our journey, I didn't have to wonder which one belonged to the hangman of Montpellier who had sent so many poor devils to their deaths, for at quite a distance we could distinguish the straight form of the gallows rising up out of the natural tangle of branches of the orchard that surrounded it. The young fruit that would be harvested in September from amid these light-green leaves gave an even more sinister aspect to the deathly form of the gibbet.

Besides the sword and the arquebus, killing a man doesn't require any stretch of the imagination. The simplest machine will suffice: three lengths of oak at right angles, the largest planted in the earth, the smallest bearing a rope at whose end our hanged man will dance as his judge goes on filling his belly, while awaiting his turn to go before the judge of us all, and then to rot in the earth instead of dancing around in the air as the man he'd condemned had done. A subtle difference, perhaps, which hardly justifies the high honour bestowed on the one and the deep disgrace heaped on the other.

This particular gallows bore no fruit, thank God, but I was too quickly reassured, for Accla bridled beneath me, and I quickly reined her in, my nose burning with a stale, sweet, unbearable odour that

I knew all too well. Raising my eyes, I found myself gaping at the strange spectacle before me, for, hanging from the branches of the largest of the olive trees, I spied various parts of a woman's body, her head tied to one branch by her own hair, and to others, attached by strands of hemp, the legs, arms and torso. Judging from this last that the executioner had stripped her bare to add to her shame, it was clear that the victim was a young wench, and although she'd been dead for at least a week, her body hadn't yet been too ravaged by crows so that the breasts and belly were still visible. The poor hussy, whose tender body was thus exposed to the curiosity of men and the beaks of the vultures, had been hanged, then, after her death, stripped of her chemise and cut up by the hangman like a pig by a butcher and the parts displayed on this beautiful tree, on which their sinister presence weighed no more than a dead bird.

Samson, suddenly awaking from his reverie, stared sadly at these rotting debris, and Miroul paled and went all sullen, perhaps remembering that he himself had barely escaped the gibbet at Mespech. Nearby, I spied a labourer hacking away with a dull scythe at the nettles along the road without ever raising his eyes towards these human fragments, so odious, I wagered, did he find their presence here.

"Friend," I asked, "is this your field?"

"Hardly!" replied this man, who was so tall and thin that he seemed scarcely thicker than his scythe, which he now lifted to lean on the back of the curved blade. "I own nothing in this beautiful Provençal land other than my mouth to eat with and my arms to nourish it. This field belongs to my master, and if you ask me, it's a great pity that he's rented it out to the consuls of Montpellier to use as a gibbet, though these olives are delicious—even the ones on the tree you're admiring"—this despite the fact that he himself refused to look at it. "But I don't like working in this stench, which the wind often carries right into my house."

"Friend, who was this poor wench, do you know? And what was the crime that earned her this torture?"

"I know not her name, but according to the archers who brought her here, she'd suffocated her child when she had no more milk to give it, the good-for-nothing who fathered it having left her penniless."

"He's the one they should have hanged," growled Miroul between his teeth.

"I don't know," answered the man, "I'm not learned enough to judge. But I do know enough to tell you that if the good-for-nothing had been a count or a baron, the littl'un would have been a glorious bastard and would not have wanted for victuals."

At the words "glorious bastard" Samson turned silently away, tears gushing from his eyes. He was three years old when his mother, Jéhanne Masure, died of the plague in Taniès, and I doubted he could still remember the face of the little shepherdess, but at least he knew she was his mother, since my mother never deigned to speak to him, never looked his way, never even spoke his name.

"But why in God's name did they quarter her?" I asked, saddened as I was by Samson's tears and the sight of her poor dismembered body. "Wouldn't it have been enough to hang her?"

"Ah!" choked the man. "It's all the same when you're dead to be cut up like beef on a butcher's table, or to remain in one piece. Here in Montpellier it's the custom to quarter the hanged."

"What an excessively cruel custom!" I gasped, turning towards Miroul and pretending not to notice Samson's tears. "When we end our time on this earth, don't our bodies belong to God, who will raise them from the dead on Judgement Day?"

"Well, that day is not coming tomorrow," sighed the peasant, "and while we wait for it we must labour on without a moment of joy. To little people, little comfort. And however beautiful the sun is in Provence, we can't eat it."

"Friend," I answered, "you are indeed very thin. Do you have enough to eat?"

"Enough?" he laughed bitterly. "I don't even know what that word means. There is great misery among the branches of this olive tree, and misery of another sort on the earth we walk on, and I don't know which is the worse."

"Miroul," I said, "give this man one of our loaves of bread."

"Monsieur," returned our peasant drawing himself up proudly, "I have never begged for anything, nor from any man in my life."

"Steady there, friend!" I replied. "Don't make your stomach angry! This is no curate's charity but the gift of a friend."

Miroul dug through our provisions and handed the man a wheat loaf, which the man seized with his meagre fingers, sniffed voluptuously, and devoured without a word or look of thanks, as though he were ashamed to accept food he hadn't earned.

"Let's be off!" I said, my throat in a knot, realizing that I had accomplished nothing in this gift but a small balm to my conscience without really remedying the man's condition.

We galloped along for a while, but soon slowed to a walk as the road became rough and hilly. As we proceeded, I tried to chase from my mind the terrible image of the girl's mutilated body left hanging as an example to all. But an example of what? Of the barbarous law that had made her its victim? And wasn't it a pity and a bitter coincidence, I realized as I thought more about it, that they had chosen for their executions this field of such beautiful trees and that it was precisely on the Mount of Olives that Christ had prayed in the last hours before his crucifixion?

The Common Wall (I don't know why my ear and heart found this expression so pleasing, but during the entire time I would spend in Montpellier I enjoyed repeating it) is a good thick rampart, though not as strong and well built as the one in Carcassonne. Arriving from Narbonne, you enter through the la Saulnerie gate, so named, I'll wager, because it was the route the salt carts took to enter the city.

We had to present ourselves unarmed at the guard house, show the safe-conduct passes prepared for us by the seneschal in Sarlat and explain the reason for our stay in Montpellier and the address of our lodgings there. Satisfied with my answers, the captain of the archers said with great seriousness: "Young scholars, you must always remember that carrying sword or firearm is expressly forbidden within the royal colleges and in the surrounding streets. Moreover, quarrels, insults, blows and, a fortiori, duels between students are rigorously outlawed by order of the police lieutenant. Any student violating these proscriptions, just as any other citizen of Montpellier, may be hanged for a capital crime, unless he is, like yourself, of noble birth, in which case he will be beheaded, but, in either case, he will be dismembered by the executioner."

"Monsieur," I replied, "we are studious people and not bloodthirsty rogues, although we bear the arms of war because of the dangers of the road."

"Nor should you be blamed for this in such troubled times. But here in Montpellier, things are, for the moment, quite peaceable, as Catholics and those of the reformed religion seem to be getting along." He frowned as he said this, as though this state of affairs were in no way to his taste, and, suddenly glaring at us, asked, "And you scholars, which side are you on?"

I was quite astonished by this abrupt question, and hesitated to answer. But another look at this captain of the archers, at the gravity of his expression and the stiffness of his bearing, convinced me that I was quite familiar with this type of soldier and so I opted for the truth: "Monsieur, my brother and I are both of the reformed religion, and my valet as well."

"I thought as much," said the head of the archers, softening his stance so much that he actually gave us a smile and welcomed us to his city, which he hadn't yet thought to do. "So, my young scholars, I heard you had a bone to pick with the brigands of the Corbières!"

"Indeed we did! We killed four of their number a few leagues from Lézignan."

"Say no more! Monsieur de Joyeuse, on my report, will send for you tomorrow for a report of this incident."

He bowed to us and with his usual gravity (but which now hid some warmth) closed the barrier behind us and ordered the city gates opened wide. And so it was that my little troop entered Montpellier on the twenty-second day of June in the year 1566.

Although assuredly less ancient than Sarlat, since it is but five centuries old, Montpellier is a much larger city, and though its streets are narrow and winding I found it quite beautiful, for its houses, or at least the mansions of the nobility and bourgeoisie, are built of cut stone without any wooden additions of any kind.

Our route took us through the magnificent place de la Canourgue, the most beautiful of all of Montpellier's open spaces, and, as I learnt later, the favourite meeting place of all the youth of both sexes, who enjoy walking round it of an evening, meeting each other and exchanging glances and gallantries. I was quite surprised as we entered this square to see a group of horsemen arrive in a procession preceded by some musicians playing lutes and viols. These young men, who displayed the easy grace of their noble birth, were wearing, over their vests and leggings, full-length robes of an immaculate white. And what so amused me and aroused my curiosity was that each one held in his left hand a silver shell and in his right a spoon of the same metal with which he struck the shells, keeping time with the musicians and making a most agreeable sound. This music was interrupted frequently, however, for every time they spied a pretty damsel—and there was a marvellous profusion of these—so many in fact that I have never seen their equal in any other city in France—they would head towards her and surround her, each one offering her a spoonful of the sugared almonds that filled their shells. It was a pretty spectacle to behold the happy confusion among the wenches prompted by the offerings and compliments that these cavaliers bestowed on them. When one of them actually accepted the proffered sweet, it appeared to be the result of much consideration, having less to do with what was offered than with the one who offered it. And yet, as soon as the damsel had poured the spoon's contents into her little hand, the rules seemed to require that her cavalier quit her side immediately (though not, perhaps, without some whispered rendezvous) and that the procession would immediate head for another maid, and when she'd been sugared in turn, to yet another, with the white cavaliers flying like a swarm of bees from flower to flower all around the place de la Canourgue, preceded or followed by their musicians.

This scene, which, at least momentarily, drove from my mind the awful spectacle of the olive grove, unfolded in the golden light of a June sunset. With my Accla standing still and warm between my legs, I happily watched my fill of this pretty commotion and especially the young maidens at its centre. Gripping Accla's reins, I stood straight up in my stirrups, craning my neck to the left and the right, the better to observe these goings-on, breathless, my heart palpitating. Frolicking about, laughing, batting their lashes at their cavaliers and so full of *joie de vivre*, these creatures of God inspired a greater love than I could hold. For, as transported as I felt, I was, at the same time, mindful that the infinity of choices in this beautiful city, by virtue of the very excesses of their beauty and rich diversity, made it difficult for me and might well end up impoverishing me. For immediately to take one of these damsels into my arms (supposing she were to accept) could only, I surmised, be cheating myself, for any kiss bestowed on one would necessarily exclude all of the others. The opposite of that cruel tyrant who wished that all men and women had but one neck, so that, by cutting it, he could make the heads of all mankind fall at one time, I would have wished that all the girls in Montpellier had but one single mouth that I might kiss them all at once.

I was in the midst of such delicious reveries when Samson suddenly said, "My brother, why are we watching this? All I can see here are silly frivolities and guilty dissipation. What are we doing here?"

To which, a bit put out, I responded half in jest, half serious, "We're here to forget our own enormous sins and criticize the peccadillos of others."

My poor Samson turned a deep shade of scarlet at this rebuff, and hardly were the words out of my mouth when I greatly regretted them, having no desire to add fuel to the fire that was consuming him. We rode on a bit farther and crossed the Jewish quarter, but never encountered so much as a cat there, so late was the hour, and finally reached the rue de la Canebasserie. Between this street and the rue de la Barrelerie stretched the place des Cévenols, where, every Sunday, the workers would come on their day off to show off their feats of strength.

On the far side of this square rose the imposing and handsome chemist's shop of Maître Sanche. To my great surprise, for I would not have imagined him to be so unassuming, I spied the great apothecary seated benevolently in front of his door, enjoying the coolness of the evening with his family. He looked exactly as my father had described him. I dismounted, threw my reins to Miroul and, removing my hat, made him a deep bow and said in Latin (for I knew that he liked to express himself in public in this learned tongue), *"Magister illustrissime, sum Petrus Sioracus, filius tui amici, et hic est frater meus, Samsonus Sioracus."**

No sooner had I spoken than he leapt to his feet with a degree of agility I would never have expected from a man of his age, and ran up to me, gave me an enormous hug, and another to Samson, and then gave me another, welcoming us warmly with a generous mixture of French, Latin, Provençal and Catalan.

Maître Sanche could hardly boast about his physical appearance: he had a bloated and ugly face, his globulous, crossed eyes placed unevenly in his dark-skinned visage on either side of an enormous, bony and twisted nose, which itself was perched over a mouthful of yellowing and badly arranged teeth. His body was hardly more attractive, with one shoulder set lower than the other, a caved chest, slightly humped back and bowed legs followed around by a prominent posterior. But despite his long grey beard and his more than fifty years, he was astonishingly lively, constantly in motion, jumping from one foot to the other, his eye as sharp as a dagger, his tongue not without its bite and his mind a source of deep wisdom. Twice a widower and with all but two of his grown children well placed in good professions, he had, he explained to me, remarried the previous spring and, turning towards her, he introduced me to his wife, Rachel, who was sitting next to him looking extremely pregnant, and told me in Latin that she was going to bear him a son this very evening as her contractions had already begun.

"Balsa," he cried in Provençal to one of his clerks, "help these gentlemen's valet unburden their horses and take them to the stable. My nephew," he said, taking my arm, "allow me to introduce you to my daughter Typhème, who is, as I'm sure you'll agree, quite beautiful, but whom you must be careful not to fall in love with since she's engaged to the venerable Dr Saporta, who will be your teacher."

---

* "Illustrious master, I am Pierre de Siorac, the son of your friend, and this is my brother Samson de Siorac."

I bowed to Typhème, whom I found, indeed, superb, with languid eyes, rich complexion and a luxurious head of Saracen hair.

"And this is my son, Luc," Sanche continued. "As he has reached majority and is consequently under his own guidance, he has decided to convert to the reformed religion. For my own part, I have sadly, as your father must have told you, remained a member of the very corrupt Roman religion, whose infinite abuses I must willy-nilly accept." This strange profession of his faith, mumbled rapidly in Latin, left me quite open-mouthed in surprise. However, I greeted Luc, as ugly as his sister was beautiful, but whose eyes were as expressive as his father's, and who, if left to his own devices, doubtless could have said as much, as rapidly and in as many languages as his progenitor.

"Luc," Maître Sanche added, "is fifteen. And may I present his teacher, whom I count a member of my household, for he is as rich in science as he is poor in silver. *Hic*," he added in Latin with a great sense of pomp, "*est Johannus Fogacerus, in medicina baccalaureus et procurator studiosorum.*"*

I bowed to this great personage, for great he was both in size and in titles. For it is no small honour to hold the title of bachelor of medicine and, on top of that, dean of students, and to represent them in assemblies of professors and doctors.

"Messieurs de Siorac, at your service!" replied Jean Fogacer with a large flourish, by which he seemed to mock both his own importance and ours.

He was clothed in black, somewhat threadbare robes, but his height and sinewy build gave him a kind of elegance that was seconded by his graceful gestures and remarkable physiognomy. I was struck by his very beautiful teeth, full red lips and aquiline beak; he had chestnut eyes and such black eyebrows that they appeared painted on his face, curling up towards his temples, all of which gave him the aspect

---

* "This is Jean Fogacer, bachelor in medicine and dean of students."

that we often attribute to Satan. But to tell the truth, if he were a demon, he was one jolly devil, for he smiled broadly and repeatedly laughed good-naturedly while Maître Sanche was introducing us to his family—and with especial gusto when the chemist told us that his wife was going to deliver a son that very evening. I have to admit that I also found it quite astonishing that Maître Sanche could pronounce on the sex of his child before the infant had emerged from his mother's womb.

"My nephews," said Maître Sanche, who was never to call us anything else, "you must be exhausted from your travels. Hey, Fontanette! Silly wench, instead of staring at these young gentlemen, show them to their rooms!"

My first unhappy thought was that our host had given Samson and me separate rooms, since we were so accustomed to sharing room and bed, but as I followed the pretty chambermaid up the stairs, observing that I couldn't take my eyes off her comely back, I realized that perhaps separate rooms wouldn't be such a bad arrangement after all!

"Here's your room, Monsieur," curtseyed Fontanette to Samson with a charming smile. "Would you like me to help you off with your boots?"

"My valet will do it," replied Samson curtly, averting his eyes. He was in such a hurry to be alone that he closed the door in our faces, and I could hear him throw himself down on his bed to continue his reveries.

I would have been quite vexed to see Samson behave so rudely with the poor girl had I not understood the reasons for it. Oh, what power a little wench can wield over man. When he falls into the snares of the flesh, he's stuck and wholly bewitched. Where his flesh has gone, heart and head will follow. At least I didn't have to worry that Dame Gertrude would abuse her considerable power over Samson, seeing as how she seemed to be in a condition so like his own.

"And here's your room, Monsieur," said Fontanette, visibly put off by Samson's rebuff and unwilling to risk renewing the offer of her services.

"Please come in!" I smiled as I sat down on the bed. "As for me, I'd happily accept your offer of help if it's still available."

"With all my heart, Monsieur!" said the wench, kneeling gracefully at my feet, her position in front of me affording a pleasant view of her bodice, which was so loosely laced as to give an ample glimpse of its contents. "I like you better than your brother, Monsieur! He may be prettier than you, but at least you're not so proud."

"It's not pride that makes Samson so cold," I explained, thoroughly enjoying watching the delicious effects of her efforts to remove my boots. "Samson is terribly lovesick over a lady and it has made him all dreamy and distant."

"And this lady has cast him off?" asked Fontanette, her light-brown eyes aglow with renewed interest.

"No, but she's far away, travelling the world."

"Ah," sighed Fontanette, "what a pity to love what you cannot hold and to embrace only the wind. And you, Monsieur, do you, too, mourn some faraway damsel?"

I looked at her half in mirth, half in tenderness, for I found her excessively pretty and pert, and melting under my gaze like butter.

"I'm not sure, Fontanette," I answered after some reflection, "I don't know you well enough yet."

"Ah, Monsieur, you're mocking me!" she blushed. "A future baron smitten by a chambermaid!"

"I'll never be a baron, Fontanette. I have an older brother. That's why I must study medicine!"

"But someday you'll be a famous physician, Monsieur," she sighed, rising to her feet, "like Maître Sanche or Monsieur Fogacer. And I'll still be as ignorant as a goat in the shed."

"That matters not a whit to me!" I replied, taking her about the waist and kissing her fresh cheeks.

"Hold, Monsieur," she protested, pulling away, "you're moving too fast for me! If you're giving me kisses today, what will you be doing tomorrow?"

I broke out laughing at her naivety, and, laughing with me, she said, "If it please you, Monsieur, I must go. I must go down and help with dinner."

This first supper in Maître Sanche's house, when we were all so famished from the long road, was a sad affair, for we were served but a salad and a thin slice of roasted meat—one only—and no dessert. Of butter there was not a trace either on the table or on the roast, since their cooking was done with olive oil, not butter. As for drink we had a rather bitter wine, ingeniously concocted to keep us from drinking too much: Fontanette passed around the table with two pitchers, one of water—from which she filled most of one's glass—the second of wine, with which she topped off the water. Happily the rye bread was good and copious and I devoured most of a loaf to fill the hole that still growled for its share in my stomach. "Ah, Fontanette," I thought as I watched her serve us, "I can certainly feast my eyes on you, but as our good people at Mespech always said, you can taste beauty but you can't eat it." As for Samson, he still didn't seem to know where he was, what was said to him or what he was swallowing. He was dining on his dreams. But I, alas, kept thinking about the Unicorn inn in Lézignan, the Two Angels in Toulouse, the Golden Lion in Castelnau d'Ary and La Patota's pastries, whose memory still made my mouth water as I sat before Maître Sanche's meagre board. Nor could I help wallowing in memories of Mespech and la Maligou's Périgordian cuisine, so savoury, velvety, appetizing and well cooked. For however silly, gossipy, idolatrous and superstitious she was—not to mention lecherous—she could make a roast melt in your mouth. Which was why my father had always

95

forgiven her transgressions, including having it away with the curate of Marcuays—under our very roof! Under our very Huguenot roof!

It didn't help my distress that, while we were trying to chew these unappetizing victuals, our host's wife was bedded down in the very same room, separated from our table only by a curtain, so that the moans and wails of a woman in labour punctuated our every bite, accompanied by the noisy encouragements of the two midwives attending her. Maître Sanche appeared in no wise troubled by these distractions, but simply raised his voice to allow us to hear his Latin dissertation on a new remedy he had devised, which he claimed to be a certain cure for inflammations of the stomach. Nevertheless, at one point, hearing a scream more urgent and higher pitched than the previous ones, he turned his head towards the curtain and said in Provençal: "My poor Rachel seems to be having a hard time making a son for me. Balsa, go fetch me the bottle of agrimony from my pharmacy—you'll recognize it as yellow poppy flowers."

Balsa, mouth still full of dinner, rushed off and returned with a phial, which he handed to his master, who, in his turn, called one of the midwives and said with the gravest authority: "Good lady, I beg you rub this ointment on the insides of the birthing mother's thighs and recite, as you rub, the paternoster. My wife's delivery will be greatly facilitated."

After having bowed deeply and made a sign of the cross three times, the lady took up the phial with the greatest respect and withdrew behind the curtain as she was ordered.

"Maître Sanche," I said, "I knew that agrimony was highly recommended for curing ulcers of the cornea, but I didn't know that it could be used so effectively for childbirth."

"Indeed it can!" he enthused. "I have it on great and worthy authority that the use of agrimony should be applied in such cases and is expressly recommended by Bernard de Gordon in his learned book, *Lilium medicinae*. I myself have tried it many times, not without success, in the parturitions of my late wives."

Fogacer, sitting to my right, broke out laughing hilariously. Whereupon Maître Sanche said, "*Medice, visne castigare ridendo medicinam meam?*"*

"*Non decet, magister illustrissime,*" replied Fogacer, his demonic eyebrows fleeing towards his temples. "*Felix est qui potuit rerum cognoscere causas.*"†

"Well then, why are you laughing?" continued Maître Sanche, though he was interrupted by a terrible cry. "My good woman," he shouted, turning his head towards the curtain, "continue to rub! Rub in the ointment! And don't spare your paternosters!"

The two remedies being applied, I imagine, with all the energy the two midwives could muster, a remission soon took effect, and in the ensuing silence, troubled only by a few moans, Fogacer said in Latin, "Illustrious master, first of all I do not contest the efficaciousness of agrimony. Secondly, I am too good a Christian to dispute the benefits of the paternoster. But I do question the alliance of the first with the second! It's one of two possibilities: either the agrimony is soothing the pains or else it's the pater. In the first case the pater is unnecessary, and in the second it's the agrimony."

"*Medice,*" Maître Sanche returned, "*navita de ventis, de tauris narrat arator.*‡ But winds and bulls are not the same thing. A woman experiences labour pains, but the pain is as much in her spirit as in her body. *Ergo*, it is beneficial to mix the two remedies: agrimony is the body's balm, the pater soothes the soul."

He was about to continue, when poor Rachel suddenly emitted a series of ear-splitting cries.

"My good women!" cried Maître Sanche in Provençal with great

* "Doctor, do you dare make fun of my medicine?"
† "That would be inconceivable, illustrious master. Happy is he to have been able to penetrate the deepest causes of things."
‡ "Good doctor, the sailor understands the winds, the farmer his bulls."

irritation. "We can't hear ourselves think in here with so much racket! Rub! Rub harder! And don't be stingy with the agrimony. For my good wife no expense shall be spared!"

"Master," I asked, when the cries had subsided a bit, "I heard you declare as something absolutely certain that your wife would bear you a son. May I ask on what you have based this certainty?"

Fogacer, taking advantage of another outburst from the other side of the curtain, which distracted Maître Sanche, leant over and whispered with a smile, "*Bene! Bene! Haec est vexata questio!*"*

But to tell the truth, it didn't appear to vex Maître Sanche in the least, for he replied, "There is not the slightest doubt, and even less discussion. She who delivers during a full moon will have a son and she who delivers in the new moon, a daughter."

However, despite the agrimony and the many paters, poor Rachel's wails grew more strident every minute. Maître Sanche finally decided that he'd better rise and go behind the curtain to offer his young wife the benefit of his great knowledge.

The dinner having long since finished, Luc, his sister Typhème, Balsa, Miroul and my beloved Samson had gone off to bed, and the only ones remaining at table were Fogacer and myself, when Fontanette brought us a pitcher of simple infusions she'd prepared.

"Ah, Fontanette," whispered Fogacer, "your master is going to scold you: an infusion! And sugar as well! And by your own decision?"

"I shall tell him I ordered it," I said.

"A thousand thanks, my noble friend," breathed Fontanette, with a grateful smile and a quick bow. Then, pivoting on her heels, she flew off to the kitchen. I followed her with my eyes.

Fogacer, raising one black eyebrow, leant over and touched my elbow, saying in a low voice, "*Nec nimium vobis formosa ancilla ministret.*"†

---

*   "Good! Good! This is a very debated question!"

†   "Never let yourself be served by a girl who's too pretty."

"Amen!" was my only response, since I didn't know what to say and my nose was in my goblet, but I smiled secretly at this feminine attention, and also at the delicious infusion that I was careful to drink slowly, while eating another crust of bread, for I had an appetite enough to start dinner all over again, so meagre were the servings here.

"The man," said Fogacer, pointing his bony index finger at the curtain, and lowering his voice (though this precaution was unnecessary given the diapason of lamentations that continued behind it), "has a few odd ideas, but he is a good person. Nevertheless," he cautioned, "empty your goblet so he doesn't scold the poor girl."

Just as I finished drinking, the curtain opened and Maître Sanche appeared, one shoulder lower than the other, his back bent over more than ever, but his two hands joyously combing his long grey beard. He stopped in front of us and crowed triumphantly: "It's almost over. I've seen the little rascal's hair!"

He'd scarcely finished his announcement when his wife let out a series of cries that would have awakened the deaf, and these were followed by a dramatic silence that astonished us all. Then, raising the curtain, one of the midwives entered, her head hanging low and her visage ineffably sad.

"Maître Sanche," she said in a mournful voice, "Madame your wife begs your humble pardon. It's a girl."

"What?" cried Fogacer, rising and feigning surprise at such a scandal. "A girl! Beneath a full moon!"

"Then necessarily," intervened Maître Sanche, without batting an eye, "another planet, sent by God, has mixed its rays with those of the full moon and undone her efforts." And, rising with great dignity, he added, "*Astra regunt homines, set regit astra Deus.*"*

---

* "The stars govern mankind, but God governs the stars."

4

A H, WHAT A SWEET awakening I had the next morning when Fontanette, entering my room, opened the oak shutters, which, from the inside, shaded the room. The windows, like those at the Two Angels in Toulouse, were made of oil paper, which blocked the view but not the warmth of the rising sun, which turned them a rich golden colour.

"By the belly of St Anthony, Fontanette," I said as I quickly combed my hair with my fingers, "how did you get in here? I bolted the door last night!"

"By this one, which opens onto my little room."

"Ah, Fontanette," I cried, "you're going to give me ideas…"

But Fontanette, who laughed and smiled so easily, became suddenly as serious as an abbess in Lent, and, putting on a grave face, made me a real sermon.

"Monsieur, if your ideas are what I suspect they are, you should not be having them. I am not one of those servant girls in inns who throws herself at men, but a chambermaid in a respectable Christian household. The door I used to enter your room can be bolted on my side. And as for me," she blushed, lowering her eyes, "I am a virgin."

"So, you're locked up twice over, my brave girl," I smiled. "But aren't you seriously inconvenienced by this state? Do you intend to persevere in this like a nun?"

"I just don't know," she lamented with a charming naivety. "I simply haven't made up my mind."

And for once, I, who normally have a ready tongue, found nothing at all to say in response, so divided was I between very conflicted feelings—my wicked desires and sweet pity haranguing each other inside me like two fishmongers. And to tell the truth, I thought then, and I still think today, that it's quite unfair that we ask these girls to clothe themselves in a virtue, just because they're girls, that one never seems to demand of men. But what would we do if they were always so strict? So I fell silent, and watched her coming and going in my room, so fresh and pert, arranging my affairs, which were in complete disarray, and, when she'd done with this, stopping to admire my various weapons.

"Monsieur, what do they call this short arquebus?"

"A pistol."

"And this short sword?"

"A pricker."

She giggled and blushed when she heard this name and so, observing her shame, I decided to change the subject: "So what do we eat to break our fast here?"

"Soup."

"What?" I exclaimed, grimacing. "Soup? No milk?"

"Ah, Monsieur, milk? You're not in Périgord any more! The flat countryside around Montpellier is all stone, sand and dust. Vines and olive trees do well here, but your cows wouldn't find much provender."

"So no milk. Does your soup at least contain some nice morsels of pork?"

"What, Monsieur, pork? You'll never find a shred of pork in this house! My master won't have it."

"What? No bacon, no ham, no sausages. What about pâté?"

"Not an ounce. But, now that I think about it," she confessed with some confusion, and I appreciated her transparency, for she was not one to play-act or pretend like some people, "the reason I came in was that Monsieur Fogacer desires to speak with you."

"Now you tell me, Fontanette! You must away before he comes looking for me!"

"Mayn't I stay, Monsieur, while you get dressed?"

"But, Fontanette, you'd see me naked!"

"I see Monsieur Luc stark naked every day and you're much better looking, better built and stronger than he!"

She went on like this while I was dressing. It was, I judged, her innocence that made her babble on, and though I was embarrassed to be dressing in her presence I didn't have the heart to send her away. So she remained, watching me the whole time, admiring my body in such a candid way; and clearly the poor girl in her naivety saw no wrong in telling me what she thought straight out, like a hen might do to a rooster if she could talk.

I found Fogacer slurping up his soup, which consisted, sadly, of vegetables without a scrap of meat, but I was still so hungry from the evening meal that I fell upon my breakfast with relish. Of Luc, the beautiful Typhème, Balsa or Maître Sanche there was not a trace, and when Fogacer had eaten his fill he said:

"Siorac, let's not stand on ceremony. Don't call me 'bachelor' and I won't call you 'Monsieur'. Finish your bowl and I'll take you up on the roof where we can speak our minds."

Little did I imagine that this roof, which we had reached by a narrow winding staircase, was in fact a wide and beautiful terrace from which one could enjoy various similar terraces spread across the city of Montpellier. In the distance I could discern a dark-blue line cutting across the sky blue of the horizon and shimmering with thousands of tiny fires from the rising sun—the Mediterranean. I, who in my young life had never seen such an expanse of water except on a map, stood transfixed before this spectacle.

"Ah, Fogacer," I cried, overcome with emotion, "should we not thank the good Lord for having created this miracle among all the wonders He has given the earth?"

"Certainly we should," he replied, raising his satanic eyebrows, "but we shouldn't stop there! We must also thank him for storms, hurricanes, flooding rains, droughts, lightning, volcanoes, earthquakes; give thanks as well for the vegetable kingdom: hemlock, belladonna, ranunculus, nightshade and the other innumerable plants from which we make our poisons; and for the animal kingdom: the bear, the wolf, the wild boar, the fox and the African cats of prey, not to mention the viper, the asp, the tarantula, the scorpion and the thousands of bugs, worms and fungi that attack the most useful plants. Is that all? Oh no! We also have to account for all the great benefits the Lord has visited upon us in the form of whooping cough, mumps, smallpox, dropsy, swamp fever, leprosy, consumption and those jewels of our human condition, syphilis and the plague."

I stared at Fogacer, surprised by this somewhat sacrilegious speech and by the mock seriousness with which he had pronounced it.

"Assuredly," I replied after a few stunned moments, "assuredly evil exists. But since God makes only good and right things, then evil itself must be some part of His plan."

"Plan?" mused Fogacer, raising his eyebrow even higher. "Plan? Of course there's a plan. But which one?"

"This is what we can't yet understand," I answered, "since God's ways are impenetrable."

"Ah," laughed Fogacer, "that's a very good and orthodox response, and quite proper, as Calvin would say, for convincing sober and docile people. But observe, however, not your reply but the very spare way in which you proposed it: without the bother of deductive reasoning, absent of any sustained argumentation, unadorned with any art whatsoever, and concluded *ex abrupto*, drawn to a close with this opaque curtain of human ignorance. By my bachelor's robe, we need more words to say that we know nothing! According to the rules of rhetoric, you should have pushed your position further, articulated your principles in syllogisms, used rigorous logic to reach your conclusion—the whole bolstered by an abundance of quotes from the ancient philosophers. 'Sblood, you can't pretend to speak wisely when you go about it so tersely!"

I blushed to see myself treated with such pleasant irony, and, seeing my scarlet face, Fogacer laughed even harder, and turning away sat—or rather threw—his large body on the stone bench situated next to the little overhang that sheltered the stairway we'd just taken from the rain.

"Siorac," he said, seeing me so silenced and flabbergasted, "come sit next to me here in the shade, out of the heat of the sun. It was not my intent to humiliate you or overwhelm you to test your knowledge. I cannot, however, in my capacity as dean, register you in the Royal College of Medicine until you have satisfied me that you have sufficient command of logic and philosophy."

"Very well," I replied as I took my place beside him, quite crestfallen. "What is your opinion of my capabilities in these matters?"

"Quite weak, despite your already remarkable knowledge of medicine, thanks to your father. But logic and philosophy being the two breasts by which the milk of knowledge is believed to flow into us, you will never be accepted to the rank of doctor if you haven't learnt how to suck from these inept teats."

"What?" I gasped. "Inept? So you despise them?"

"*Medicus sum et in medicinam solam credo.** As for the mammary glands to which I referred, I hold them to be empty, vain, insipid and scholastic. But this does not mean that I don't know how to manipulate

---

* "I am a physician and I believe only in medicine."

them. There is no better debater in the Royal College, in the opinion of all, than your devoted—but not humble—servant. However," he added, "for reasons of courtesy as well as prudence, I concede this point to my royal professors."

I was dumbstruck to hear Fogacer bite so fiercely the venerable breast that fed him. So is this how it is? Philosophy is secretly despised by the very people that make such a public display of it? Here I am waiting in the wings to go on stage, wearing such wigs and make-up!

"Meanwhile," Fogacer added, "there's no danger as long as you follow my advice. Today is the twenty-seventh of June and the courses in medicine begin on St Luke's Day, the eighteenth of October: so I have all the time I need, if you're willing, to whip you and your brother into shape."

It was not for nothing that I'd been raised according to a strict sense of Huguenot economy, and my hair stood on end as I calculated all of the gold and silver coins that I could hear jingling in the background of Fogacer's apparently disinterested proposition. "I'll tell you what, Fogacer," I replied coldly, "Samson and I are younger sons and our resources are thus quite limited. So, as you invited me to do, let's speak frankly. How much will it cost us to benefit from your lessons in logic and philosophy for the next three months?"

"Ah, you son of a Huguenot!" laughed Fogacer, raising his diabolical eyebrow, if possible, even higher. "Are you a cheapskate pinchpenny? Do you suspect me of trying to fleece you? You're wrong, Siorac. My fees are remarkably moderate. I'll offer the two of you two hours every day of my time and it will cost you a mere two sols a day plus, twice weekly, a meal at the Three Kings inn at which the three of us can enjoy a delicious roast pork for only eight sols. So then, what say you? Dr Saporta will charge you much more than that to take his summer course for new candidates."

"But do I have to take his course if it's so dear? Will it be worth it?"

"Silly boy!" replied the wily Fogacer. "You are required to take his course even if it profiteth you nothing. Saporta is, with Rondelet, Feynes and Salomon d'Assas, one of the four royal professors, and when Rondelet, who is old and feeble, passes out of this world, Saporta will be elected chancellor. Would you disdain the private lessons of your chancellor?"

"Or those of my procurator? Let's shake on it," I laughed. "Let's shake on it, Fogacer! I shall be your pupil in logic and philosophy. And 'sblood! However meagre this provender, I shall gulp it down with gusto!"

"Now you're talking!" agreed Fogacer, happy with himself and with me. "I like a man with a big appetite. We'll start tomorrow."

Thereupon, he looked me up and down without a word, and I calmly returned his gaze. His lifeless black hair was thinning at the crown of his head so that he appeared to be older than he was (roughly twenty years old, as I learnt later). Under those impressive eyebrows gleamed two piercing chestnut-brown eyes, and his nose, as I've said, had the curve of an eagle's beak. He would have appeared altogether severe had he not on occasion broken into a sinewy smile, particularly when he was spouting paradoxes, irreverent comments, jokes and veiled impieties, which he restricted to his private conversations, for in public he was as guarded with his tongue as a shepherd with his lambs, carefully separating out the black ones and displaying only the lily-white members of the flock.

"So, my young friend," he said at length, feigning an air of gravity, "you're a skirt-chaser."

"Monsieur," I replied in the same vein, "I do chase them, yes."

"And, as fast as these skirts run, I doubt not that you catch up with them. You're blonde, blue-eyed, fair-skinned and pretty vigorous."

"Well, I'm not at all as handsome as my brother."

"True enough, but he's a mute, and you have a ready enough tongue. There's also something lively, strapping and quick about you which must please the fairer sex."

"Monsieur, I cannot complain."

Here, Fogacer paused and, suddenly quitting his jocular manner, said with utter seriousness, "Siorac, this is just my opinion, but I urge you to take heed. There are in this house two damsels of very different status whom you must, for different reasons, give a very wide berth. The first is Typhème, who's promised, as I'm sure you've been told, to Dr Saporta, a very good man twice her age. But he's Sephardic, like Maître Sanche."

"Sephardic?" I echoed.

"What? Didn't your father explain this to you when he arranged for you to lodge with Maître Sanche?"

"He did not."

"You must know that Sephardics are Spanish Jews—though some are Portuguese—who were forcefully converted and then chased out of their country by the stinking intolerance of the priests, but who were welcomed to Provence by Louis XI. Which was a very wise thing to do, for these Sephardics brought with them their knowledge of Jewish and Arabic medicine, without which the Royal College of Medicine in Montpellier would not be what it is today."

"But Maître Sanche described himself as a Catholic."

"He's forced to. He is Catholic in the same wise as myself: a prudent and purely exterior and nominal adherent."

Fogacer had given me much food for thought, but I decided against this discussion on such dangerous terrain, and said, "Is it because Saporta is Sephardic that Typhème is betrothed to him?"

"That's one of the reasons," replied Fogacer with a smile. "The other is that Maître Sanche is very well-to-do and Saporta even more so, possessing vineyards and farmland throughout the region, many fine houses in Montpellier and, what's more, in the rue du Bras-de-fer—so steep and narrow that it's called 'the slide' in Provençal—he owns a tennis court from which he makes a handsome profit and which you would do well to frequent."

"But I've never in my life touched ball or racquet!"

"That's nothing. I'll teach you."

Mercy! I thought. That's city folk for you! They have both hands in your pockets. "But, Fogacer," I said, "help me understand. The father of this house is Catholic. His son is of the reformed religion. Maître Sanche and Luc are thus mutual heretics each to the other. How is this possible?"

"It's a purely sartorial question," replied my teacher with his sinewy smile. "The father wears the coat of a papist; the son dresses in Calvin's coat. That way each covers for the other. Which is very well advised in the uncertain times we live in. Siorac, take a good dose of this infinite prudence. Don't go about Montpellier trumpeting your reformism. It's true that there are many of your people here, but always remember that the king and his mother are papists and ultimately you will have to match our own beliefs to theirs, if only by force."

This said, he laughed, as if all this—anything that wasn't medicine—was a comedy of little consequence, and rising to the full height of his long, elegant legs with the agility of a greyhound, he went on, "I must go, Siorac. The sun is already up, and Rondelet, who's leaving soon for Toulouse, has left me his patients to attend to."

"But you haven't talked about Fontanette."

"Aha, I see the subject interests you! But we'll speak of this another time," he laughed over his shoulder as he descended the spiral staircase.

At the bottom of the stairwell, Fogacer having already disappeared from view, stood Fontanette, who was, I wagered, waiting to meet me to exchange a few meaningful glances.

"Fontanette," I said, "is my brother up yet?"

"No, Monsieur, he's sleeping like a marmot. I knocked several times but there was no answer."

"I don't like this," I answered, feeling apprehensive, and went directly into Samson's room without knocking. He was stretched out on his side and, given the heat of the morning sun, had thrown off his sheet, and was lying buck naked, so strong and muscular, his snow-white skin contrasting sweetly with the pink of his cheek resting on his hand; his eyes were closed, almost hidden by the tangle of his copper-coloured locks. At this sight, my anger and bitterness disappeared and, putting both hands on his shoulder, I shouted his name, shaking him so roughly that he finally came to his senses.

"My brother," I said trying to appear angry but already overwhelmed by the tenderness I had always felt for him, "did you come to Montpellier to lounge about all day in your bed and wallow in your room? The sun is up, it's almost noon and here you are lazing about!"

"Dear Pierre," he replied in a piteous voice, as he got up and hugged me. "Please don't scold me! I haven't closed my eyes once this whole night! I feel like hell has loosed a thousand flames on me, so great is my distress at the resolution I've taken!"

"Resolution? What resolution? About what?"

"Not to see Dame Gertrude du Luc when she passes through Montpellier, or on her return from Rome."

"And why ever not?"

"Because lust outside of marriage is a cardinal and mortal sin!"

"'Sblood!" I cried, raising my hands heavenward. "Who gave me this lovesick idiot for a brother? Have you taken vows? Are you a nun? A monk? A hermit? Are you a eunuch escaped from a harem? Are you going to remain stuck in the bile and vinegar of chastity until you marry? By the belly of St Anthony," I exclaimed, raising my voice, "are you so presumptuous as to believe you're more virtuous than your father?"

"Me?" he blushed, putting his hand on his heart. "More virtuous than my father? I wouldn't think of it!"

"You must have! You can't be ignorant of the fact that he fathered you outside of marriage, a sin that I *bless* since he gave me a brother whom I hold dearer than my legitimate brother."

"Ah, Pierre," he cried, throwing himself in my arms, "I love you too, with all my heart!"

"Perhaps," I growled, pushing him away, "but I'm not sure I mustn't stop loving you since you're beginning to smell of heresy."

"Me?" he cried, open-mouthed and so visibly horrified that I almost felt guilty for taking such advantage of his pure heart, even if it was in his own interest.

"Don't go imagining, Samson," I said, frowning and getting very serious, "that in sacrificing Dame Gertrude to your monkish ideas you are going to achieve salvation by works, which, as you know very well, is contrary to Calvin's doctrine."

Poor Samson was brought up short by my empty sophistry, and, completely at a loss for words, just stood looking at me, unable to say a word in reply.

"But go right ahead!" I said, sensing that he was weakening. "You're on such a high road. To heresy you can add cruelty! Refuse to see Dame Gertrude? You're inflicting on this sweet and noble lady a barbarous punishment and on yourself a deep wound without either punishment or wound serving a living soul! Think about it! Whom are you hurting in loving her? She's a widow, and mistress of her own person!"

"But, Pierre, God in heaven sees my abomination!"

"Which is a good deal less abominable than many sins I could name. And believe me, the Lord would have his hands full if He had to keep track of every grain of dust dancing on the earth's surface. In these times of trials, executions, stinking betrayals, innumerable murders of brother against brother, do you really think He is interested in your peccadillos? And if He sees them, what do you think they weigh in the great balance of things?"

"It's not a peccadillo," Samson assured me, regaining his stiff manner. "The law is the law."

"Then didn't Christ break the law when He prevented the crowd from stoning the adulterous woman? Oh, Samson! You no longer want to see Dame Gertrude du Luc, this beautiful angel of heaven, this sweet and gentle creature! Will you ever have a sweeter sister? A more loving companion?" (At this he weakened all of a sudden and tears leapt from his eyes.) "You owe her a debt of gratitude for having taken care of you!"

"But," he said from the depths of his naivety, "I wasn't sick! I was only following your orders to pretend to be so."

"You were so, Samson! Not from fever perhaps, but from a terrible lack. If it weren't so, you would never have welcomed the attentions of Dame Gertrude with such appetite."

This at least gave him pause, for he fell silent and began to get dressed, still weeping hot tears. I remained quietly at his side, for I wanted to let my words sink in, doubting not that they would find powerful allies in him to prolong their echo.

And isn't it marvellous, when I think on it, that I had to battle tooth and nail with him, arguing from all possible angles to prevent him from undoing with his own hands his very happiness? "Ah," I thought, "I wish I were in his shoes! If I had a Dame Gertrude du Luc, I would faithfully and worshipfully bend the knee before her instead of chasing from one skirt to another—which I do not without some pleasure, of course, but without ever finding anything spiritual or nourishing in these encounters."

*

I left Samson's room with my brother right behind me—his eyes dried and, it seemed to me, a good deal less upset and sullen than when he woke up—and, as you would expect, we passed Fontanette wiping the banisters, though I suspected that she'd been listening at our door, for she seemed to be turning something important over in her mind that brought a bright blush to her cheeks and heavy breathing in her bosom. To Samson she threw a most compassionate look and to me an even more tender one as she announced that her most illustrious master (for this is how his servants referred to Maître Sanche) wanted to see me in his office, adding, as if she feared I'd lose my way, that she'd be happy to take me there. I was careful not to reject this offer and so, leaving her dusting cloth on the railing, the lass preceded me down the stair, moving with such a lively step and so gracious a movement of her hips that my eyes must have warmed her for the entire descent.

The office was a large and beautifully appointed room, lit by two leaded windows filled with small diamond panes of real glass of different colours. Across the entire width of the middle of the room stood a counter of polished oak on which a large number scales of the reddest copper were displayed, all shining like a heaven of suns, so carefully were they polished. Behind this counter stood two assistant clerks and the chief clerk, Balsa, who bore some resemblance to the Cyclops, since he was one-eyed, with the chin, shoulders and hands of a giant, though in fact he wasn't very tall since he had such short legs. He made a deep bow to me as I entered, which I answered politely, calling him by name with the cheerful familiarity my father always used with his soldiers. I couldn't tell whether my behaviour pleased or displeased him, for his face remained as impassive as marble as he tapped with his pointer on the counter and the two clerks greeted me—to which I responded with a nod, not knowing what to think of these ritual civilities. Then with a very sweet voice, which I was aston-ished to hear emanating from such a hideous face, Balsa invited me to have a seat and my brother as well, adding that the very illustrious master would soon be here.

I sat down. Behind the counter, running the full length of the wall and from floor to ceiling, stood a set of dark-brown shelves on which were arranged an infinity of jars, some made of clay, others of clear glass, all of which bore labels with the Latin names of the drugs, condiments, medicines or spices they contained. This display somehow, I knew not why, awakened an intense interest in Samson, who, for the first time since his encounter with Dame Gertrude had cast its spell on him, suddenly opened his eyes and began inspecting each one of these jars with as much ardent interest as if they'd contained a treasure. And, although no apothecary in Sarlat could have rivalled the rich profusion that was displayed here, nevertheless Samson's delight and the way his eyes lit up as he examined these curiosities wholly surprised me.

For my part, I confess that, rather than continue to survey the entire array on these shelves, my eye was arrested by a series of glass jars set way up on the top shelf and filled to the top with sweets of all colours, nougats, dried fruits and other delicacies, which seemed to me so beautiful and tasty that, both because of their arrangement behind this shiny glass and because of the hunger which never seemed to get entirely sated here, my mouth began watering almost uncontrollably. But that was the only way that I ever enjoyed them, for during my entire stay at Maître Sanche's lodgings, none of the contents ever appeared on our table.

"Here is my illustrious master," announced Balsa, tapping with his pointer on the counter. And Maître Sanche appeared on the threshold. He had quit his simple doublet of the previous evening and was now clothed, as I was to see him every day in his shop, in a resplendent black silk robe, decorated by a silver belt, and his head was covered by a cloth hat, topped by a tuft of amaranth.

He was holding, as Balsa did, a fine reed pointer, but, as was fitting for his status, much longer, more beautiful and finely worked than his clerk's, being varnished and encircled at the centre and both ends by silver rings. Maître Sanche used this symbol of his power to emphasize each of his pronouncements, or to punctuate a command by tapping it on the counter, or else—and this was probably its original and primordial function—to indicate a particular jar on one of the higher shelves that his assistants were to climb up and fetch for him. But, though he waved this reed frequently in his wrath to reprimand one or another of his clerks, I never saw him use it, as the lictor of Rome did, to strike anyone, not even the drunken and disorderly rascal who ran errands for him. For however puffed-up and self-important he was, Maître Sanche was not of a hard-hearted or cruel nature.

The master crossed the room to greet us, and I must confess that the light of day did not favour him as much as candlelight, given his crossed eyes, long bony nose and… well, no need to revisit the rest of his body, which no sculptor, however drunk, would ever have taken as his model. But then, Socrates was also said to be ugly, and I could not help being impressed by the majesty of his apparel as he paraded towards us in his long black robe and tufted bonnet, holding his silver-ringed pointer as a king might wield his sceptre. I rose quickly to my feet.

"*Te saluto, illustrissime magister,*"* I said, bowing low. At the sound of my voice, Samson tore himself away from his awestruck contemplation of the pharmacist's jars, and stood up as well, bowing silently in his turn.

"My good nephews!" trumpeted Maître Sanche, and, opening his arms, he enfolded us into them, rubbing his long grey beard against our cheeks.

---

*   "Greetings, very illustrious master."

He put so much warmth and good Provençal humour into his greeting that I couldn't help feeling great tenderness towards him despite my unhappiness over his miserliness when it came to his kitchens. It's true that he himself did not eat much and it was surprising, given how daintily he took his food, what a round and prominent stomach preceded him through the room.

After many compliments in Latin, French and Provençal, and a flurry of words of welcome, Maître Sanche declared: "My nephews, I've invited you in here to show you the secret laboratory in which we store, concoct and mix the medicines of my pharmacy. You should know that *adeo in teneris consuecere multum est.*"*

At this offer, Samson's eyes lit up prodigiously and I too felt enflamed by the thought of seeing so close up the rarities and infinite curiosities of which the drugs my father had spoken so much about were composed. I immediately expressed my gratitude to the master apothecary for his generosity, assuring him that for my brother and me it was an immense privilege to be initiated into his arcane science.

"You will learn, of course," Maître Sanche continued with a mysterious smile, "only the most superficial aspects of this science, but that is already a lot. Except for the royal professor of the college who, once a year, is authorized a visit to this place, *pauci sunt quos dignos intrare puto.*"†

Having said this, changing his pointer from his right to his left hand, he took from beneath his robe an enormous, shiny key and after giving each of us a very significant look, he inserted it with great pomp and ceremony into the lock of a great oaken door that seemed so ancient that I reckoned it would be extremely difficult to drive a nail into it and harder still to break it down with an axe, given that it was reinforced by three metal bars. Maître Sanche had, moreover,

---

* "Training the mind is of especially great importance in our youthful years."

† "Few are those judged worthy to enter here."

no easy task to turn this powerful key. That done, however, the heavy door pivoted noiselessly on its enormous, carefully adjusted and generously oiled hinges.

We then had to go down a few stairs into a room with a vaulted ceiling, which seemed very dark after the well-lit office above, but which I gradually realized was sufficiently lit from a large vent at one end that was well fortified by strong bars.

"In here I keep my treasures," said our host with a sudden gleam in his eye. "Ali Baba's cave never held greater riches that this. So I must defend them against the thieves and treasure seekers by means of the unbreakable door you've just passed through and by the iron bars that darken yonder vent, which looks over a walled-in courtyard, itself guarded day and night by two bulldogs, so ferocious and hungry that Balsa and I can scarcely approach them to feed them."

And indeed, as he spoke, the two mastiffs began snuffling and growling, their hair bristling, and pushed their snouts through the bars and bared teeth worthy of guarding the entrance to hell, as if access to that place needed defending...

"This room," Maître Sanche continued, "contains all the bodies and substances needed for the composition of my medicines, all of which, you should realize, my nephews, can be found in nature, since it is sure that Our Lord, in His infinite wisdom, took care to include in His world a cure for every evil therein."

I was very happy to hear this remark, and packed it safely away in my memory pouch so that I could take it out again to counter Fogacer, whose nearly sacrilegious thoughts about the world's evils had so silenced and troubled me up on the terrace.

"The substances from which I make my drugs are of three orders," Maître Sanche announced, holding up three fingers of his left hand, "animal, vegetable and mineral."

Here he paused.

"Those we get from the animal world are few," he went on, after pulling a key from beneath his robe and opening a small cabinet, "though sometimes extremely dear, because they must be obtained from the East, and travel here by perilous roads. Of course, we don't have to search so far away to find among the fields round Montpellier the honey that the bees suck from the sweet flowers and deposit in their combs, which furnish us with wax. Honey and wax, though they have medicinal applications, are also well known for their domestic uses. But here's something you'll find a bit more surprising: these are scarlet grains used in dyeing."

"Are these grains," I queried, "of vegetable origin?"

"Not at all, my nephew! They come to us from a cochineal, an insect that prospers at the expense of the trees you'll see as you ride through the oak forests throughout Provence. You just pull them off the trees as if you were a bird."

Here Maître Sanche made a quick pause, to ensure that we were duly impressed, before continuing. "My nephews, this jar I'm opening now, but only a tiny bit in order not to intoxicate you, contains a very expensive substance, for it comes to us from an Asian stag, which carries it between its legs next to its pudendum. It's called musk, and its odour is marvellously violent and powerful, but, in minute doses, can be used in the composition of perfumes and some drugs that I won't mention."

"Do these medicines," I asked, "stimulate our venal pleasures?"

"Nay, nay," replied Maître Sanche, his eyes gleaming, "but remember, my strapping young man, that at your age, blood is its own drug. Over here we have a very small amount of a very precious substance that is worth its weight in gold: ambergris. It can be found in the intestines of a sperm whale, a ferocious mammal that can swallow a man in one gulp."

"Is that the one in the Bible that swallowed Jonah?" Samson asked.

"The same, and not his cousins the other whales, who would have had a lot of trouble swallowing our ancestor since their throats are so narrow."

Having closed the bottle of ambergris and locked the cabinet that contained all of these animal substances, Maître Sanche took us to another, much larger and wider cupboard, which he opened with a second key. "In here," he explained, "we have beneficent vegetables which are used in my remedies; they grow in great profusion, thank God, and the simplest of them are so widespread in our region that it's hardly worth bending over to pick them. Then there are the plants, grains, saps, juices, extracts and crystals that we have brought here from faraway places at great expense: sugar from Candia; pepper from Malabar; rose water from Damascus; indigo from Baghdad; saffron from Spain; henna from the Levant; henbane from Persia; opium from Thebes; ginger from India; cinnamon from Ceylon. As for senna, my nephew," he continued, putting his hand on my shoulder, "whose purgative properties you are familiar with, you should know that in Paris and even in Montpellier there are certain penny-pinching and underhanded pharmacists who import it cheaply from Algeria, but I," he announced, raising his voice, "consider this kind of senna vile, rough, full of mud and gravel and unworthy of being administered to an ass, and I prefer a thousand times over the senna from Alexandria, more costly to be sure, but clean, pure and healthy."

Maître Sanche seemed to get very aroused as he spoke these words and brandished his pointer—his large features even more scarlet than usual, his fingers vigorously raking his beard—and I was struck once again by the contrast between his abstinence at table at the cruel expense of his stomach (and ours) and the remarkable generosity of spirit and deed when it came to the composition of his drugs. I felt my admiration grow even greater for the high priority the master placed on his art and on his duties to the sick.

"And finally," said Maître Sanche, leading us over to a little walnut cabinet, attached firmly to the wall by four thick iron bands, "here are my most precious possessions, surpassing in value all the treasures of Araby: the *minerals*—few in number, to be sure, but some quite beautiful and others extremely effective in curing disease."

This said, he took from his robe two keys with very complicated patterns and, having inserted them in two keyholes, one at the top of the cabinet door, the other at the bottom, he handed me his pointer for the moment, and with his two hands turned them simultaneously. The door opened but revealed nothing more than a series of small drawers. Each of these bore a small opening in its centre, into which Maître Sanche, as he spoke, introduced a piece of metal that was squared at the end and, it seemed, had the effect of "open sesame", for scarcely had he inserted it when the drawer immediately unlocked with a little click and slid open towards him.

"Here we are!" exclaimed the very illustrious master. "Verdigris that the women of Montpellier prepare by using copper plates that they bathe in alcohol. Alum, bitumen, borax, cinnabar, arsenic, quicksilver, coral and, in this drawer," he said, pulling the drawer all the way out and holding it close to his chest, "pearls, gems, gold and silver."

What fires, what dazzling brilliance, what scintillating colours this pile of beauties projected onto the velvet around them! This jumbled mass contained gems that any queen or king's favourite would have proudly displayed on her breast, but instead these stones were destined for a darker and more interior use and would lose their splendid lustre when ground into a powder that would end up bran in some intestine. Scarcely had our eyes had time to take in these marvels before Maître Sanche, with the demeanour of a magician, had whisked them back into their drawer, slid it closed, locked the cabinet with his specially made keys and concealed these under his robe.

"Can it really be," asked Samson, "that such precious stones are used in the composition of medicines?"

"Most assuredly so!" said the master pharmacist as he reclaimed his pointer from my grasp. "You should know that at the very foundations of the innumerable drugs that the apothecary sciences create are four major and sovereign preparations—remember these names: theriac, mithridate, alkermes and hyacinth. Now hyacinth, which is itself a gem, is composed of twenty-nine ingredients which include gold, silver, sapphire, topaz, pearl and emerald."

"But only a king could afford such costly medicines!" cried Samson.

"A king, a prince, a bishop, His Holiness the Pope or a rich financier," said Maître Sanche with a subtle smile. "Jacques Coeur was said to be quite addicted to this drug."

"Very illustrious master," I said, "you mentioned alum. My father used this same drug to stop stomach ulcers."

"*Bene! Bene!* Alum is an astringent. But," he added, stroking his beard with a suggestive air, "there are other, more esoteric uses." At this he gave me a half-serious, half-amused look. "And perhaps when you've become a doctor of medicine, you will prescribe this drug to some of your beautiful patients, my nephew. For it is claimed that alum does miracles in the secret parts of a woman, and that Cleopatra used it to strengthen and restrict the interior walls of her vagina, which gave Caesar each time the illusion of her renascent virginity."

I laughed out loud at this and looked at my host with a renewed appreciation, for beneath his haughty expression lay a very human and lewd humour, which pleased me no end. But to tell the truth, I should have noticed this earlier, having observed the fresh beauty of his wife. Meanwhile, Samson was nearly overcome with embarrassment and, blushing, quickly changed the subject:

"Illustrious master, if we can return to the subject of hyacinth, how can one get a patient to swallow so many stones at once, no matter how precious they are?"

"*Haec est bona questio!*"* cried the master, who clearly appreciated Samson's genuine interest in his profession. Moreover, given his own ugliness, he may have felt a natural tenderness for someone so beautiful as Samson—whom he never encountered at the dinner table without murmuring to himself: "Ah! *Que matador! Que matador!*"—which Fogacer translated for me as: "Ah, how beautiful he is!"

"You should know, my nephew," said Maître Sanche, seizing Samson by the arm, "that we put these precious stones in a mortar according to the requirements of each drug. Then having ground them into a fine powder, they are mixed with an equal quantity of honey, working this mix into a sort of paste, which we call an *electuary* and which, given the worth of its contents, we present to the patient in a little ebony box."

"What riches are swallowed up!" cried my naive Samson.

"Yes, of course," replied Maître Sanche, dropping Samson's arm and raising his pointer. "But the health of great men costs great sums!"

"But," I asked, "what ills does hyacinth cure?"

"This is what your professors at the Royal College of Medicine are going to teach you," said our host. "*Non medicus sum,*† and, according to the rules of my profession, I cannot make any drug without a prescription signed by a doctor. To tell the truth," he added with a smile in which mirth wrestled with feigned humility, "I have a few ideas about the ills that can be treated with hyacinth, but I must be careful not to voice them, my good nephew, out of respect for the territory of the royal professors."

And yet trespassing on these territories was exactly what he would do in our subsequent discussions, as I was to have ample opportunity to observe.

---

* "What a good question!"
† "I am not a doctor."

"I will now introduce you into the secret laboratory where we make our drugs," continued Maître Sanche as he headed towards another very low door, as well fortified by iron bars as the one that had afforded us entry into his office. He unlocked it and we followed him into a second vaulted room, much larger than the first and brighter, lit as it was by two vents at floor level, between the bars of which the two mastiffs immediately thrust their toothy snouts and recommenced their snarling. But, unlike the others, this room was not empty of any human presence, for two assistants were diligently at work, both wearing shirts without doublet or collar, for the heat emanating from several different hearths was intolerable.

These two assistants were about twenty years old and dangerously thin, which was not astonishing given that they were doing work from dawn to dusk that robbed them of their substance and weight—not to mention that there was no way to regain what was lost once they sat down to Maître Sanche's meagre suppers. Moreover, they were extremely pale, skin hanging loose and colourless on their bones, their moist hair flattened to their skulls, their eyes empty and lustre-less, no doubt because they lived under lock and key in this cave, like prisoners in their jail; perhaps also because they breathed, day in, day out, the horrible fumes, vapours and odours that emanated from their preparations.

"In here," explained Maître Sanche, after a nod to his assistants to which they responded with deep bows, "we keep various very costly machines, all of which were invented by the Moors, who were our teachers, as you know, my nephews, in everything connected to alchemy—a word which comes to us from the Saracen, as do all the names of the machines you see here. This slow-combustion oven is called the 'athanor', deriving from *al-tannur* in the Arabic language. And this series of clay tubes, each connected to the next, which we use to sublimate solid bodies, is called the 'aludel'—in Arabic, *al-utal*.

Here is the alembic—in Arabic, *al-anbiq*—which is used, as you know, for distillation. In truth, everything in here is Saracen, from the pot and the casserole to the long funnel over there."

"But, illustrious master," Samson said, his eyes shining with a degree of enthusiasm I'd never seen before, "what is sublimation? What's it used for?"

"Through sublimation," replied the master, "we transform a solid body into vapour, a vapour that we then freeze so that it turns into crystals which are purer and lighter than the original solid. Thus, from mercury we can derive a corrosive sublimation which is used in the cure for syphilis."

This said, Maître Sanche turned towards me and, stroking his beard, gave me a very severe look. "My nephew," he advised, "you must be very careful. Syphilis is all but unknown in the regions where you were born, but not so, alas! in a large city like Montpellier. Fogacer will confirm this. In the rue des Étuves, where the students usually go for their baths, there is a group of ladies of the night who swarm around the young men like flies to carrion and who keep rooms nearby to turn their tricks. Some of these wenches are young, pretty, firm of flesh and well endowed. But the young rogues like you, my handsome nephew, dreaming of amorous conquest, taste these fruits which are so luscious on the outside but so rotten within and wake up one morning with their *nephliseth* all withered and gangrened, and no matter how much this drug helps with their infection, their hair falls out and their teeth as well."

"Goodness!" I thought, shaking my head with compunction. "How many taboos I'm having to confront in this house! Typhème, since she's betrothed to Dr Saporta; Fontanette, for reasons I don't yet know! And now the pretty harlots in the rue des Étuves! Is there no wench in this town to whom a young man may entrust his poor neglected *nephliseth* without losing his hair and teeth? Am I going to be famished at table, unmanned in bed like a hermit, and obliged to sublimate my body by the bitter vapours of chastity? How will I last the year? If you close up the kettle on the aludel it will be so oppressed with the heat that in the end it will explode!"

All the while, Maître Sanche continued to gaze at me with the same severe countenance, and, for his part, Samson appeared dumbstruck to see me thus counselled by our host. I tried to hide my embarrassment and, turning away, approached one of the assistants, who was dripping with sweat as he worked. "Friend," I said, "what are you crushing with such energy in this mortar?"

"He is not able to answer you," Maître Sanche explained as he approached in turn. "He is, like his twin brother, quite backward in his speech. They emit sounds, of course, but I'm the only one who can understand them, which is fine by me, since, in this way, they're unable to reveal to a living soul the secrets of my formulas."

This was spoken in a half whisper, with a knowing smile. But having said this, Maître Sanche looked both of us in the eye (as much as his crossed eyes permitted) and said gravely, "My good nephews, what varies from pharmacist to pharmacist is not so much the composition of these drugs, which is *grosso modo* common knowledge in our profession, but the exact proportions of the various ingredients and the art of mixing them, whether it's to be by decoction, sublimation or reduction. There are in these operations, *crede mihi experto Roberto*,* an infinity of occult recipes that many of my colleagues envy me and would gladly steal. And so I must be on my guard to prevent any such thievery of these secrets, which are worth more to me than the king's treasure, since I learnt them from my father and he from my grandfather—to whose knowledge I have added considerably through the incomparable diligence and unceasing labour of my entire life. For this I am respected and held, *omnium consensu*, as the first among

---

* "Trust me, for I have the requisite experience."

my peers by the pharmacists of this city, of the whole of Provence and of the entire kingdom."

All of the preceding was spoken with such bombast, our host waving his pointer with haughty pride and self-satisfaction, that Samson gazed in dove-like awe, whereas I felt secretly impatient and quite put off by such parading, though I was very careful to display a respectful and impressionable face.

I was wrong to be impatient, however, for, despite his puffed-up and vainglorious airs, it's true that Maître Sanche's reputation extended as far as the king in his Louvre, as Fogacer explained later that same day. In 1564, two years before, Catherine de' Medici and Charles IX had visited Montpellier during their tour of the kingdom and had insisted on visiting the famous apothecary and its curiosities, so great is men's trust in and veneration of the medicines thanks to which they believe their ills are cured and they themselves are spared from death.

"Of course," our host continued, "the pharmacist's science had not yet achieved the seriousness and effectiveness in my grandfather's day that it has today. Back then there were many so-called remedies that had more to do with superstition and ceremony than with medical knowledge. For example, to stop a wound from bleeding, it was recommended to tie a red thread from the codpiece of a newly wedded man around the little finger of the patient. Or it was believed that a woman who had just weaned her baby and desired to stop her flow of milk should, on three successive mornings, jump over a sage bush in the priest's garden. To cure jaundice, all one had to do was to find ribgrass growing from the side of a house and to piss on this ribgrass every morning and night until it died—so the jaundice would die as well."

With both hands clasped on his paunch, Maître Sanche laughed uproariously at these silly and ritualistic remedies that credulity, the daughter of ignorance, had planted in people's minds. We all laughed so much that even the two assistants, as thin and sweaty as they were, permitted themselves a quick smile, for they understood everything we were saying despite their own mute aspect.

Then, turning to me, Maître Sanche said with great pride, "As for the question you asked my assistants, young man, I am going to answer you. What they are preparing in this mortar is *arthanita*. It is derived from sap from the scrub pine and contains twenty-one vegetable substances, including saps, juices, resins, bark and seeds. It is an ointment that is effective for many different complaints." And, forgetting that, not being a doctor, he had resolved not to reveal the uses of any of his drugs, he added, "*Arthanita* is rubbed on the patient and the results depend on the site where it's applied: if on the bowels it's a purge; on the stomach it's an emetic; on the bladder it releases a great quantity of urine."

To hear the miracles spawned by this universal remedy, I confess that I began to have my doubts about *arthanita* and wondered how much more effective it really was than the red thread of a newly married man's codpiece. Overwhelmed, however, by the man's bombast and careful to avoid arguing with such an amiable host, I said, feigning naivety, "But isn't it a marvel, most illustrious master, that a single ointment can have so many different effects?"

"Such are the virtues," Maître Sanche replied gravely, "of these ointments when mixed together. Used separately, they would produce none of these so happily diverse consequences."

We were interrupted at this precise moment by the ringing of the dinner bell and Maître Sanche said: "Let's go to dinner, my worthies! We must, if only to replenish our veins and arteries and to defend them by pumping them up against the air's contagion. Of course, we must not overeat to the point of blocking them up entirely. In that case, the encumbered brain becomes lethargic and weak. *Impletus venter non vult studere libenter.**

---

*   "An overfilled stomach won't readily turn to study."

Seizing gentle Samson by the arm, evidencing the sudden affection he'd gained for him, he drew him towards the door, with me at their heels, as my brother was saying, "And when do your assistants get to eat, illustrious master?"

"When I've eaten my fill, I take their place here, *ego ipse magister Gabrielus Sanchus Dominus Montoliveti,** in order to keep an eye on all the decoctions and sublimations in progress. And while I'm down here, they can wipe themselves clean of the sweat they accumulate in this terrible heat, change their shirts and don a doublet, and eat their soup in the little courtyard where Balsa has tied the dogs. And there for a full hour they can sun themselves and purify their lungs of the infection of the medicinal vapours they've inhaled. Thus have I arranged, in my paternal and humane concern, to keep them healthy and happy in my service."

Assuredly, if one compared Maître Sanche's behaviour towards his assistants with the way the burghers of Sarlat treat their workers and other servants, he was entitled to call himself "paternal and humane". But as for the midday broth, God help us and them! There was absolutely no danger in devouring it that one would stop up any arteries or veins! This broth was no more soup than the watery concoction that greeted us in the morning. With nothing to eat before or after! A naked broth in which garlic and onion replaced pork and fat! Sometimes one could see tiny bits of boiled meat floating here or there in this gruel that had to be supplemented by the few crusts of bread we were allowed, but they'd go down our gullets before we could taste them. (A pretty weak defence against the air's corruptions!) And to drink, a vinegary liquid, diluted with lots of water and served sparingly. "Ah, Fontanette! Fontanette!" I thought. "Why can't I be a cannibal from the Barbary Coast and feast on your pretty flesh? That's the only way I could ever be fully satisfied at table in *this* house, since

---

*   "I myself, Maître Gabriel Sanche, lord of Montolivet."

civil and common usages are so completely lacking here. Ah, to be sure, there is much to be learnt here, for Maître Sanche's lessons are full of choice morsels and gravied with knowledgeable sauces, but as for victuals, the sustenance and pleasure of our bodies, the meats are scanty and far between."

But I'm getting ahead of myself. The bell sounded a third time. Typhème and Luc, the latter followed by Fogacer, appeared in the common room just as we did. We all greeted each other, and Typhème, her Moorish beauty more resplendent than ever, told us in a hushed voice that only made my heart beat faster, that Dame Rachel begged to be excused from dining with us, and would remain in her room. Of course, we understood why. So Dame Rachel had a room after all (and one of the most beautiful rooms of the house, according to Fontanette), which made it all the more surprising that she should have had to give birth to her son in the common room, virtually in public.

With that certain pompous air that never left him, Maître Sanche, removing his silver belt, took off his silk robe and hung it on one of the antlers of the stag's head that decorated the wall behind him. On the highest antler of all, he hung his tufted hat and, seizing a little black cap embroidered with silk that was perched on another prong, he pulled it over his thick, curly grey mane. All the while, we remained at quiet attention, watching his divestiture.

However meagre the fare was in this house, it was not lacking in ceremony, whose first act we had just observed in this royal and public undressing.

Secondly, whereas on the previous evening we had been seated in no particular order, now Maître Sanche, as soon as he'd seen to his sartorial needs, indicated to each of us our stool by tapping it with his pointer, requiring that we remember our place and always occupy the same one. Taking the seat at the centre of the long table, he placed Luc on his right and—what an honour he now bestowed!—my beloved

Samson on his left. Opposite him, as though power was paired with power, I was seated, with Fogacer on my right and Typhème on my left, who after all was only a maiden and unmarried. At the high end of the table, Dame Rachel's seat remained vacant, though her place was set for reasons of decorum, and at the low end were Balsa and Miroul. For the latter to be granted a place at table with us, I'd had to make a special request, but it was an arrangement that was displeasing and, indeed, heart-breaking for the cyclopean Balsa, whose pride suffered no end for having to share his end of the table with a simple valet. It's true that Miroul sat on the side of his blind eye, so that if he didn't actually turn to face his neighbour—which he never once did—his view wasn't afflicted by him.

Thirdly, after our places were assigned, we had to remain standing for the entire time it took Fontanette to pass around the table with a basin and her sweet smile, and offer us water to wash our hands. This each of us did silently and with great seriousness, for Maître Sanche would look askance at anyone who breathed a word during these ablutions.

Fourthly, once our hands were washed, Maître Sanche, leaning his wand against the wall, intoned, without joining his hands, a sort of benedìcite, which I didn't understand a single word of, since it was spoken neither in French, nor Latin, nor Provençal, nor Spanish, nor even Greek (which I knew a smattering of). And what was even more mysterious was that, while he spoke this prayer, our very illustrious master turned towards the wall (in this he was imitated by Typhème and Balsa but not by Luc) and began to rock back and forth, chanting his prayer more than speaking it.

Which done, he turned back to the table and said in French: "In the name of Lord Adonai, Amen!"

To which Luc added quietly, "And of the Son and the Holy Spirit, Amen!"—words that his father appeared not to have heard, any more than he seemed to have seen the somewhat furtive sign of the cross that followed them. With a bit of a delay, I imitated Luc, and was imitated in turn by Samson and Miroul, but not by Fogacer, who, throughout this exercise, remained silent, eyes closed, lips curled in a sardonic smile.

"You may be seated," said Maître Sanche, clapping his hands. And so we did as we were bid, I, for my part, still wondering about the strange benedicite in this unknown tongue, and pronounced in such a bizarre manner, facing the wall and calling the Lord Adonai, one of His biblical names. But no invocation of the Son and Holy Spirit or any sign of the cross.

In the midst of these marvels, Fontanette served each of us a ladle of soup, into which I dipped my spoon, hoping that this was the appetizer for the main meal.

"Illustrious master," said Samson, who was looking at the apothecary with such awe that I would have been jealous if I were of so small-minded a nature to permit such a feeling. "What is the Montolivet that you are lord over?"

"Some lands that I acquired," replied the master, with an air of immense modesty. "It's large enough and beautiful enough to allow me to bear the title Monsieur de Montolivet—just as my friend, Dr Salomon, holds the title of Monsieur d'Assas, the name of his little fiefdom. I don't blame him, but I myself am too proud of my name and my nation to want to disguise them more than is necessary to live in peace in this kingdom. It's already enough to be among the converted, what they call *anusim*," he whispered, a word which took me quite by surprise. "My lands, my house and my fields, my nephew," he continued, turning towards Samson, "are situated to the west of the sad hanging ground that you saw on your way into Montpellier, and adjoin the lands of Monsieur Pécoul, the prosperous merchant on the rue de l'Espazerie, who sells the swords, daggers and knives

130

with which our good countrymen slit each other's throats during our civil wars."

"I saw this man Pécoul," I replied, "on our way here. He was out threshing his wheat, and I spoke to him."

"I know," replied our host, with the air of one who knew about this encounter even before it took place. "My land at Montolivet," he continued, "produces enough wheat to bake my own bread, and olives aplenty to make my own oil and the brew that we drink. There's also a small vineyard from which I get our grapes for the table and, when the time comes, I'll take you and your brother to pick olives and the grapes for our wine."

I was delighted with this promise since I so missed our own farmlands, little accustomed as I was to being shut up between four walls, forced to breathe the stale smells of the city and deprived of the view of the green hills and valleys where I'd spent my childhood. But Fogacer nudged my elbow while our host was speaking to his son and whispered, "Be sure to eat lots of bread. This soup is the only course in this meal."

"What?" I answered, sotto voce. "No meat?"

"Other than the bits floating in this gruel, not a whit."

'Sblood! I was going to dry up here, having nothing to consume but knowledge.

"Monsieur Fogacer," broke in Maître Sanche, "tell us about Dr Rondelet's patients you visited this morning in his stead."

The reader should not imagine that the conversation at the dinner table was spontaneous and flowed freely between the various members of the party, involving quiet, tête-à-tête exchanges, asides or off-colour explosions of mirth or silliness apropos of nothing. Oh no! Maître Sanche was possessed of as great an appetite for learning as he was for teaching and thus could not imagine that we could employ our precious time together at table for any purpose other than sharing some new discovery with one another. So in his greedy and insatiable thirst for knowledge, casting his squinting but piercing eyes around him, and opening wide his enormous ears to receive any new fact, however seemingly insignificant, he would toss it, while still hot, into his bag of memories, from which he could withdraw it later to lend sauce to his teaching. And while thus passionately occupied, he was so oblivious to the meat or sauce that his spoon threw into his maw that, doubtless, he could not have told you what he'd just eaten.

He asked innumerable questions of Fogacer about each one of his patients and their specific complaints, descending happily into such truly disgusting details that, had I not myself been destined for medical practice, I would certainly have thrown my dinner back up into my soup.

"And his stool, Fogacer? His stool? What was the stool like?"

"Greenish in colour. Very liquid in consistency and, in odour, nauseating."

"Aha! I would have sworn it!" cried Maître Sanche with great satisfaction, gleefully rubbing his hands together. "And what did you prescribe?"

"Fasting."

"*Bene! Bene!*"

While lending an obedient ear to these discussions, as was appropriate for my future profession, I couldn't help sneaking a look from time to time at Typhème, whose profile was half hidden by her luxuriantly abundant hair, which was as blue-black as a raven's feathers. But what I could detect in her features was surpassing beauty, sweetness and natural distinction. Her eyes were large and liquid; her lips were so full and beautifully proportioned that I wanted to take their measure with my own. Her small, pointed teeth were as white as sea foam; her complexion was warm and ardent, with something suggestively sombre in which any mother's son would have wanted to lose himself.

I observed that she ate very properly, taking a small amount of soup in her wooden spoon with its copper handle, and carrying it carefully to her mouth so that not a drop spilt on the table or on her bodice. Each time she drank, she wiped her lips gracefully with a small, embroidered napkin, never leaving a trace of grease on her glass, which was decorated with different coloured designs (she did not use a goblet as the rest of us did). Her plate was also very beautiful, fashioned of pewter and engraved with her initials. When she'd finished her soup, she wiped her plate carefully with a piece of bread, doubtless not because she didn't want to miss any of the gruel, but more likely in order to return the pewter to its pristine brilliance. She wore no frills, just a simple morning dress of a beautiful pale blue, and sat very straight on her stool, cutting, as best I could observe, a trim figure deliciously endowed in just the right places.

And so I watched her out of the corner of my eye while seeming to pay close attention to the discussion between her father and Fogacer, proof that our eyes can carry out one task while our ears are occupied with another, my brain divided into two very divergent thoughts—one the unmatched beauty of the Sephardic demoiselle on my left and the other the talk of abscesses, swollen stomachs, high fevers, urinary blockage and unremitting vomiting.

Having pressed Fogacer on the patients he had visited that morning the way an oil press extracts juice from the olive, the very illustrious master turned to his nephews and began to test the knowledge we had—or were supposed to have, since we were of the reformed religion—of the Holy Bible. He asked various difficult and curious questions of each of us in turn, which we were hard-pressed to answer.

Thus, turning to Samson, he said, "Samson, what colour is David's hair?"

To which Samson could answer nothing; he blushed as he replied, "I know not, very illustrious master."

"And you, young master, student of medicine, do you know?"

"In truth, I have no idea."

Maître Sanche looked us up and down, and, after a dramatic pause, which afforded us the time to reflect on our ignorance, he said, "His hair was red. We read in the first book of Samuel, chapter 16, verse 12: 'His hair was red. He was a handsome man with beautiful eyes.'" And, looking at Samson, he said with grave authority: "A description that applies to you, my good nephew. For you are handsome, with beautiful features, eyes of blue and hair as copper-coloured as my scales. That's why you should have been named David and not Samson, for Samson allowed himself to be undone by a wicked and perfidious woman."

To this, whether he was upset that anyone could doubt his father's good judgement, or because he suddenly thought that Dame Gertrude du Luc might one day be his Delilah (a role that this good and sweet lady seemed poorly suited to), Samson blushed to the roots of his copper-coloured hair, and with tears in his eyes he looked at Maître Sanche with filial adoration, full of respect, admiration, love and, simultaneously, a sort of questioning, as though he were about to ask the master if it would be possible for him to be rebaptized to keep him from the clutches of evil women. As for me, while glancing at Samson, melting with tenderness for his dove-like innocence, I also managed to keep my left eye on Typhème, and noticed that under her half-closed lids—but how many things a young woman can see with her eyes shut!—she shot Samson a look—one single glance—but so rapid yet so penetrating that I wondered whether my eyes deceived me. Oh, Dr Saporta! Dr Saporta! Think about it while there's still time: *cave tibi a cane muto et aqua silenti.*"*

All the while, the master was pursuing his interrogation, and when he posed us a question that neither Samson nor I could answer, it was Miroul who spoke up.

* "Beware of silent dogs and still waters."

"My my, Miroul," cried Maître Sanche, prodigiously astonished, "you know that?"

"Oh, very illustrious master," Miroul murmured, "I read the Holy Bible every day God has made."

"You mean you know how to read?"

"When he took me in, the Baron de Mespech had me taught."

"I did as much for Balsa when he was younger," said Maître Sanche, shaking his head, "so that he could read the Holy Scriptures, and although he has only one eye, he reads very well."

At this, the eye in question glowed with gratitude, which touched me deeply since this is a rare feeling in men.

Meanwhile, remembering that our host had begrudgingly agreed to have Miroul take his place at the table next to his cyclopean servant, I ventured to try to raise Miroul further in his esteem, adding, "But Miroul has many other talents. He is a good and brave soldier, sings the Psalms of David beautifully, and accompanies himself on his viol."

"But this is marvellous! It is the God of David who has sent him," cried Maître Sanche, whose eyes sparkled with happiness as he rocked back and forth on his stool, furiously stroking his greying beard. "If it please you, my nephew, would you ask your valet to fetch his viol?"

But Miroul was already on his feet, questioning me with his eyes of blue and brown.

"Go ahead, Miroul," I said.

Slender, rapid, he took off like an arrow from a crossbow, and in the silence that followed, Luc, who hadn't breathed a word during the entire meal, except to amend his father's benedicite, now raised his head and looked at the apothecary as if to warn him of some danger that he couldn't name out loud. Seeing this mute prayer, his father nodded and said, "Balsa, when Miroul begins to sing, go stand outside the door to see if there are any passers-by in the street who might hear the words of his Psalm, and if so, come back in and tell me."

Scarcely had Balsa gone out with his rolling giant's gait when Miroul, flying across the room, came up to the table and placed his winged foot on his stool with the viol on his knee.

"Very illustrious master," I asked, "which Psalm should Miroul sing?"

"The one that God inspires him to choose," said Maître Sanche, quietly.

Miroul bowed his head over his instrument, his face suddenly marvellously focused, and lightly plucked a few sweet chords that seemed to make all the angels in heaven descend from the skies into the common room. But, at this moment, Maître Sanche raised his hand to interrupt him: "Fontanette," he commanded, "go into the kitchen. Close the door tight behind you and stay there until I call for you."

"Yes, master," replied the poor chambermaid, making, with evident reluctance and reticence, a small bow that perfectly expressed her displeasure at being asked to leave just as the music was beginning to enchant her.

With more spite than a one-eyed cat with its back up, she left, slamming the door behind her. It was only later that I understood that the reason for her exile was the master's fear that, as a good Catholic, she might talk about it outside the house. Maître Sanche, with evident emotion, made a sign to Miroul, who recommenced his playing, and then, suddenly raising his eyes to heaven with a serious look I had never seen before, since he was always so full of laughter, he began to sing with a voice so clear and limpid that one would have thought a mountain stream were flowing over smooth white stones.

> *Hear my prayer, O Shepherd of Israel,*
> *Your people walk along the road*
> *Like a flock that You are leading.*
> *Bring them out of their troubles!*

I'm not going to quote the entire Psalm. But those of my readers for whom it is not a sin to read the Bible (as, alas, the papist priests attempt to make us believe, making it a crime to have translated it into a vulgar tongue) know that in this Psalm, David compares the people of Israel to a vine that He has planted, but which the wicked seek to destroy:

> *What has broken down your fences?*
> *Why are you exposed*
> *Like prey to every passer-by?*
> *And how does it come to pass*
> *That wild boar have destroyed*
> *What God Himself had planted?*

Hearing this lament, which recalled the terrible persecutions that Israel had suffered, first Typhème, then Luc and finally Maître Sanche began shedding silent tears, since each of them knew the tortures, the autos-da-fé in Spain and Portugal, where so many had perished before being exiled. The terrible accounts and bloody stories of their ancestors—the very people whom Louis XI had welcomed to Provence—were so many open wounds lodged in their memories through their secret adherence to the Jewish rites, which even today risked exposing them to denunciations by their neighbours, inquisitions by the priests and trials by hostile judges, not to mention the blind fury of the populace. Certainly, I was not ignorant of the fact that the reformed religion's belief in the divinity of Christ separated us from these Sephardic people, and yet Rome had inflicted on our people, ever since François I, so many jailings and executions, that our common persecution and our daily practice of the Bible tended to connect us, if not in our beliefs, at least in our feelings. For "the people of Israel", for whom this inspired Psalm was written, designated, in our heart of hearts, our own people every bit as much as theirs. I had only to recall how much my father and my uncle were troubled as they listened to Miroul sing these verses, remembering that, in 1562, the Huguenots had been outlawed by parliament, so that in Sarlat the Catholics, who considered that the law authorized it, began to pillage and murder our fellow religionaries. This was the prelude to the first of our civil wars. Meanwhile the Psalm finished on a note that, after so many tears and lamentations, restored our pride and called us to hold our heads high and inflate our chests:

> *Oh Lord, have pity on Your vine!*
> *If the people You have chosen*
> *Are now deemed unworthy of You,*
> *Deign now to pardon them.*
> *Let Your arm uphold this day*
> *The children whom You once supported.*
> *Raise us up and give us Your grace:*
> *And we will walk before Your face.*

On the last word and the last chord, Miroul, who had been standing with one foot on his stool, his viol on his knee, sat down, and for several minutes no one could speak, and we all looked at each other, our eyes red with tears, our lips trembling, communing together, Huguenots and Sephardic Jews together in remembrance of a cruel past and in the hope of a triumphant future.

5

WE'D BEEN IN Montpellier scarcely five days when, one morning as I was getting dressed, Fontanette burst in, visibly alarmed and out of breath, to tell me that an officer of the watch was asking for me downstairs. I immediately rushed down to see what could be the matter and discovered in the entryway the same captain of the archers who, on the day we arrived, had opened the la Saulnerie gates for us after enquiring about our religious beliefs. He was a heavy-set fellow, but very trim, without an ounce of fat on him, straight-backed and with head held high, very dark-haired, dark-eyed and dark-skinned. He was armed with both sword and dagger, but wore no coat of mail, only a red doublet and breeches of the same colour, with black hat and sleeves. He looked very serious indeed, though neither rude nor as aggressive as his dress at first seemed to indicate. Indeed, as he looked me over, I noticed a very friendly light in his eyes. He greeted me right civilly, told me he was called Cossolat and that he was ordered to bring me to Monsieur de Joyeuse, who desired to speak with me.

"What is it?" I asked, half alarmed, half pretending to be. "Are they going to arrest me, lock me in prison and try me for the crime of being a Huguenot?"

"Nothing of the sort," Cossolat replied with a smile. "I told you before that I'm of the reformed religion. Joyeuse is a Catholic, but, in truth, not a very zealous one and I faithfully serve a papist governor. I wish to God that all the papists and Huguenots in this city got along as well as he and I do. But it's not always the case. Ever since the Edict of Amboise re-established the papists and their former domination, we've had nothing but troubles, plots and back-stabbing. The papists are intending to get their revenge on us. They're growing uneasy at our numbers. They've been organizing labourers' parades in town and getting these ignorant peasants to throw stones at our houses. In response, some of the most hotheaded of our people have been sending their children to sing the Psalms of David as loud as they can in front of the cathedral of St Peter while the papists are celebrating Mass."

"But what's all this got to do with me?" I replied in astonishment. "I've scarcely arrived. I'm here to study medicine, not to become embroiled in local passions."

"This is precisely what Monsieur de Joyeuse would like to know. It seems that some Catholics in Montpellier, having heard of your bravery in the Corbières hills, suspect that you've been sent here by the Prince de Condé to lead an uprising of the reformers and take over the city."

"Me?" I gasped. "What kind of story is this? Me, captain of the reformers? At fifteen? Who would believe such a thing?"

"Ah, Monsieur scholar!" replied Cossolat with a gleam in his dark eyes. "You'll be all right with Monsieur de Joyeuse. You have a ready tongue. Is your brother your equal at this?"

"Sadly, no, he's practically a mute, and when he does speak, he has a most regrettable degree of honesty and strictness of faith that expose him to the greatest peril."

"Well then, we'll report that we had to leave him behind to recover from this fever that you reported he'd been fighting during your trip here."

Hearing this, I beamed at Cossolat and found myself suddenly quite unable to say a word.

"As you see, I know a lot of things," smiled the captain of the archers. "My work requires me to be exceptionally well-informed. Come, Monsieur scholar!" he said, taking my arm. "Let's not dawdle here. My lieutenant will lend you his horse. Like all great men, Monsieur de Joyeuse doesn't like to be kept waiting."

We didn't ride as fast as Cossolat would have liked, since the narrow, winding streets of Montpellier were crowded with people, especially girls and housewives heading out to do their shopping. We had to slow our horses to a walk, which I was happy to do since there was so much to see in these streets.

"Monsieur scholar," said Cossolat with a smile, "you seem to enjoy looking at skirts."

"Not at all, my friend," I replied, "I don't aim so low. But I notice that my position on horseback offers very nice views of the local topology."

"Especially when it is so hot as it gets here in Provence. And anyway, why hide the gifts nature has given you? The maids of Montpellier are reputed to be the prettiest in the kingdom, and some claim they've inspired the name of the city itself: *Mons puellarum*—the hill of maidens. In any case, I think it's the most beautiful city in France. I wouldn't leave it for all the treasures of the earth, even if the king gave me Paris and his Louvre."

This made me remember the knife-maker Pécoul's boasting about Montpellier. "And yet," I replied to prick my guide's pride a bit, "some say Toulouse and Marseilles are bigger than Montpellier."

To which Cossolat, as Pécoul had done, furrowed his brow. "Size is not important. How do you judge a wench, by her size or by her beauty?"

"Beauty, of course. And I'm willing to grant you that Montpellier is the most magnificent city I've yet seen. Though I don't know Paris."

"You won't fail to be disappointed when you see the capital," replied Cossolat. "Here we have little subterranean canals that drain off our sewage. But Paris has nothing like these conveniences. It's an ugly town, Monsieur scholar, a disgusting town! Kitchen water, piss and faeces all end up in the street. What's more, you can't get anywhere there are so many carts and carriages in the streets. Everywhere you go the noise is deafening! And the insolence of the Parisians is legendary—pages, lackeys and other rascals included— and you'd be drawing your sword every three steps if you weren't a good Christian."

Such comments deprecating Paris and the other cities of the kingdom and putting Montpellier on a pinnacle were common on the lips of the Montpellier citizenry, who were besotted, nay entranced, by the beauty of their city. And however agreeable I'd found Cahors, Toulouse, Narbonne or Carcassonne on my travels, the inexplicable charm and contentment one finds in Montpellier are so great that, after only a few months of living there, I began repeating these out-landish praises and considering Paris to be the lowest of the low—I who had never set foot farther north than Périgueux.

"Here we are in the rue de l'Aiguillerie," announced my guide, "so we'll take this next right on the rue Bocador. Monsieur de Joyeuse lives in the beautiful house that the financier Jacques Coeur built—worthy of a king, and indeed, in 1564, our own sovereign Charles IX stayed here, God protect him! You'll find another dozen houses like this in Montpellier where the rich nobles and well-to-do merchants live."

I was indeed astonished by the monumental stone staircase that led up to the apartments of Monsieur de Joyeuse, and by the very rich rugs, paintings and furniture that adorned them. I'd never seen the like nor in such profusion. I followed Cossolat through two reception rooms and we stopped on the threshold of a third, even more mag-nificent than the first two, illuminated by three large, sunny windows.

The Vicomte de Joyeuse was in the middle of his breakfast, and since he was sitting facing away from the doorway he didn't see us—or perhaps pretended not to see us—standing there, so absorbed was he by the choice of delicacies laid out before him. Cossolat signalled to me to remain still and silent, so I had the leisure to observe the king's representative.

He was, in truth, a very tall and handsome gentleman, dressed in a brocaded doublet with a large ornate ruff around his neck. He was seated on a high-backed chair at the head of a long table of polished walnut, with a young lad standing at his right—also very good-looking and, judging by the great likeness between the two, his son. Both father and son had the same azure eyes, curly blonde hair and long curving nose that, despite its size, detracted not a whit from their beauty.

There emanated from this table such delectable odours of the many sweetmeats laid out there, that I was like to faint—especially given the hunger that gnawed at me due to the fact that I'd left the pharmacist's house before consuming even the weak gruel that was our normal morning fare. On this walnut, polished like a mirror, I counted no fewer than eleven silver platters, each with an elaborately worked cover, which Monsieur de Joyeuse lifted at his pleasure, tasting one or another and, after each mouthful, rinsing his throat with a sip of wine from his goblet.

He exhibited a rare grace in all of this that pleased me no end, however much my own mouth was salivating at the sight and smell of his choices. I also noted that included in his table setting was a small fork of gold-plated sterling, a new refinement that the brother of Charles IX had reportedly introduced to the court. However, Monsieur de Joyeuse did not use this implement the way the Duc d'Orléans did to pick up morsels from the plates. My host preferred the old way of picking up each piece very daintily between his thumb and index finger, as Barberine had shown me how to do when civility required, and placing it on his plate, and if these morsels were too big he would then use the fork to hold them in place while he cut them with his knife into bite-sized fragments. After which he picked them up with his fingers (very daintily, as before) remembering to wipe his hands and mouth each time with a richly brocaded napkin that an overdressed valet handed to him from his left.

As for the young rascal standing on his right, who seemed to be about five and of a mischievous, playful and sunny disposition, he was dressed from head to toe in pale-blue silk, but instead of a ruff wore a wide, open collar which displayed his tender, soft neck. He divided his attention between his father, on whom he bestowed a very touching degree of affection, and his father's plate, on which the latter placed his meats. When he saw a morsel that he wanted, he pointed at it with his little pink finger and said in a charming voice, as clear and musical as birdsong, "May I, my dear father?"

To which his father, after smiling sweetly, replied very civilly, "You may!"

Anne de Joyeuse, for that was the lad's name, with the same daintiness as his father, seized the coveted morsel and put it in his mouth. Oh, how far I had come from the rude and coarse manners of Caudebec who, however baronial he claimed to be, behaved at table like a pig in its sty.

"What's keeping Cossolat?" asked Monsieur de Joyeuse, raising his head and addressing his lackey with a lively impatience. "Isn't he back yet?"

"I'm here, Monsieur," said Cossolat without quitting the threshold. "Monsieur de Siorac is with me and we're awaiting your good pleasure."

"Well, come in! Come in, my good man! Don't stand on ceremony!" answered Joyeuse, who certainly did not appear to be a man who would waive or curtail ceremony of any kind. "Monsieur de Siorac, please excuse me, I beg you, for having failed to rise to greet you!" he said, giving me a nod that denoted very precisely the difference in rank between us.

To which, advancing towards him, I responded with a very low bow, as befitted the king's representative. Then, straightening, I greeted little Anne de Joyeuse with feelings of real tenderness, for I felt I already liked him. In return, the boy greeted me with great seriousness, but suddenly broke into a huge smile, revealing a pair of dimples in his cheeks.

"Well, Monsieur de Siorac," said Monsieur de Joyeuse, "if my son likes you, then I'm sure I will like you too, for, though he's only five, he has a very sure sense of things, even if he can't express it so well in words just yet. But, please, Monsieur, be seated!"

"Monsieur," I replied in French (since Joyeuse had spoken in the language of the north without a trace of our Provençal accent, though he'd spoken this language to his lackey), "I'm happy to remain standing."

I bowed a second time.

"No, no, Monsieur de Siorac! Take a seat, please! Couiza," he said to his lackey, "bring a chair for my guest."

And, since he hadn't begun by requesting a chair for me, I understood how right my instinct was to refuse the first offer, and that such a refusal was expected of me, and had to do with certain protocols that Joyeuse expected of his guests.

And so I sat down, whereupon the captain of the archers, bowing deeply in his turn, said in his very poor French, "Monsieur, shall I withdraw?"

"No, no, my dear Cossolat, stay! I may need your advice. Sit down."

"Monsieur," said Cossolat, with a second bow, which felt more like a military salute, "I am too conscious of my soldier's duties to sit in your presence."

"Enough ceremony, my dear Cossolat!" replied Joyeuse as he uncovered one of the dishes on the table, releasing a mouth-watering odour that made me nearly dizzy with hunger. But he did not ask Couiza to bring up a chair, and Cossolat remained at attention beside the table.

"Aha!" I thought. "Here's a pretty kind of etiquette that's full of pitfalls. They tell you to sit and would be offended if you obeyed!"

"Siorac," Joyeuse continued, "I beg that you excuse me for having taken the liberty of disturbing you this morning. My duties require me to know everything that's going on in this city, and if it's agreeable to you, I'd like to hear from your own mouth the story of your engagement with the brigands in the Corbières. But pray, Monsieur, will you do me the honour of sharing my humble breakfast?"

By the seventy-seven devils of hell, I was sorely tempted! Such meats, such wines, such delicious odours! And under my very nose! So close I could touch them! But just as I was about to give in, I realized that my cruel tempter had not ordered Couiza to set a place at table for me, and so, lowering my eyes, with a thousand thanks I declined.

"Well then, I'm listening," said Joyeuse as he delicately took a mouthful of crispy roast pigeon wing, whose last flight I was unable to prevent my eyes from following until the baron's beautiful white teeth closed over it.

Remembering how, after his return from the war, my father recounted to our assembled household the siege of Calais, improvising his tale with amusing embellishments, I decided to imitate his manner. I believe audiences are often annoyed when the author of the story too obviously vaunts his own prowess and courage, but, on the contrary, are grateful when he makes light of his achievements, giving you the impression you would have done the same thing if you'd been in his shoes.

Joyeuse seemed prodigiously tickled by my story and, when I described the way I unburdened Caudebec of his cask of Malvoisie sherry to give it to Espoumel, and how the latter, after I'd freed him, asked if he must come back to have himself hanged, Joyeuse, rocking back against his chair, laughed uproariously until his eyes watered—but did not have the decency to cover his mouth with his brocaded napkin.

Anne de Joyeuse, listening wide-eyed and open-mouthed to my tale, asked his father permission to speak and, once it was granted, asked, in his sweet little sing-song voice, a thousand questions about various details of my story, either because he hadn't heard them or because he wanted to hear more about the event. To each of his queries I responded patiently, choosing very simple language and accompanying my words with mimes and dramatic gestures.

"Ah, Siorac," cried Joyeuse when I'd finished, "if you weren't a student of medicine, what an excellent teacher you would make instead of this old pedant who's teaching my son the history of our kings. But I wanted to ask you, Monsieur, if your father, Baron de Siorac, took part in the fratricidal war that so devastated the king's subjects?"

This question brought me up short, for, from the tone in which it was posed, it seemed to me that Joyeuse already knew the answer.

"No, Monsieur," I replied promptly. "Although my father was devastated by the outlawing of the reformers, he never wanted to take up arms against our sovereign, having so well served the king's father, Henri, in Calais, and his grandfather, François, at Ceresole, and owed to each his entire allegiance for having ennobled him."

"Your father did well," admitted Joyeuse. "Monsieur de Siorac," he continued, I am Baron d'Arques, and my barony includes hills and valleys in the Corbières between Mouthoumet and Couiza, where my valet, here, was born. I am infinitely indebted to you for having killed some of the brigands who have terrorized this countryside. It's a great pity that I, myself, am unable to punish these rascals. But, alas, I cannot; there is so much to do in Montpellier, trying to make peace between Catholics and Huguenots, who zealously provoke each other to some trouble or other, scratching each other like tomcats, and who would massacre each other if I let them. Siorac, believe me, you must not get drawn into these troubles."

"Aha!" I thought. "Now it's clear. Cossolat advised me well: they're sounding me out and warning me."

"Monsieur," I answered with all the gravity I could muster, looking him straight in the eye, "I came here to study medicine and not to shake things up. It is neither my nature nor my inclination to do so. I'm a younger brother, and although some might consider medicine an unworthy occupation for a gentleman, I have to make my fortune, so my firm and abiding aim is to make my way by my studies and not by rebellion."

"I understand," replied Joyeuse, who fixed on me his most penetrating stare as we spoke. "And yet I must ask you to explain a circumstance which I find most intriguing. This man Caudebec, whom you mentioned, arrived in Montpellier yesterday. He's lodging at the inn of the Three Kings. He has lodged a serious and public complaint against you for having villainously fooled him. He claims that you tried to pass yourself off as a Catholic and even went so far, to dupe him, as to make confession to a priest."

I scowled at this accusation, and said with some heat: "I have not deceived this gentleman. I served as his interpreter without any remuneration of any kind for a fortnight. At my risk and personal peril I spared him a battle with the Corbières brigands in which more than one of his troop would have no doubt perished or been wounded. If I confessed to one of his monks, it was a ruse of war, to protect my life, for Caudebec, in his fanatical zeal, had threatened to pass his sword through my liver if he learnt that I was a heretic."

"May I speak, Monsieur?" asked Cossolat.

"You may, my dear Cossolat," replied Joyeuse, who was good enough to call him "my dear" but not good enough to offer him a seat.

"Monsieur, according to what I have discovered, when Caudebec arrived at the Three Kings, where he learnt of Siorac's religious beliefs, he began shouting violent threats and horrible, nasty slurs against this man. I went to the Three Kings and met individually with different members of the Norman pilgrims. They confirmed the report that Siorac has given here."

"And you questioned everybody?"

"Everyone except the women and monks."

"And why not these?" said Joyeuse, raising an eyebrow.

"The former because they love our hero too much. The latter because they love him too little."

"Ha, my dear Cossolat," laughed Joyeuse, "you're not just a good captain! You have a ready wit as well. And you're going to need it," he continued, "to smother this chick while it's still in the nest. I don't want the hens to go about cackling and pecking at each other and making blood and feathers fly. For if this Caudebec, who strikes me as too excitable, ends up killing or wounding Siorac here, the Huguenots are going to seek revenge on these pilgrims, the Catholics will come to the aid of the pilgrims and, from this quarrel, we'll see a tumult arise that could lead who knows where. Siorac," he added, turning to me with great civility, "if it suits you to follow my counsel, I would dare advise you to go immediately to the Three Kings and lower the horns of this Norman bull."

"But I'm not armed!"

"Nor should you be, since you're such a high-handed, proud fellow as suits your courage and the bloom of your youth. But Cossolat will accompany you and won't let you out of his sight. I very much hope that he'll know how to make peace between you and the baron. This is what I want: a reconciliation that is public and complete."

The Vicomte de Joyeuse pronounced this request in a stentorian voice, his head held high, his brow furled and looking me straight in the eye, as if he wished me to understand that he was speaking in the name of the king. At this, I made him a profound bow and assured him that to keep the peace in Montpellier I would be as easy and flexible as he desired.

Joyeuse took his leave of me politely but without getting up from the table, and if a nod can be interpreted by the degree of inclination, then the one he gave me seemed to signify several degrees more of respect than the one he gave my companion.

"Well," said Cossolat on our ride over to the Three Kings, "what do you plan to do?"

"To stand entirely on ceremony."

"Which is not always a question of vanity, but sometimes a way of governing. Remember that not all Catholics use cruelty as their opening gambit the way Montluc did. Some do the opposite."

Cossolat was not wrong in this opinion of Joyeuse, as we discovered six years later when, on the morning after the dreadful night of the St Bartholomew massacre, in which so many thousands of reformers perished, the governor of Montpellier received an order from Charles IX to put to death all the reformers in his city. Great courtier that he was and as worried as he was about his own career, Joyeuse considered this infamous commandment dishonourable and refused to comply, saying publicly that he was "a soldier, not an executioner".

And indeed, when, both before and after this incident, he was ordered by the king to fight the Huguenots—along with his son Anne, who was to die in the flower of his youth—he acted as a loyal soldier, without bitterness or hatred, conducting himself throughout these battles with the moderation and elegance that were integral to his character.

The inn of the Three Kings was a large and handsome lodging, where Samson and I had, two nights previously, invited Fogacer to enjoy a succulent roast pork as payment for his lessons. I thus knew how good the food was and realized that such fare would keep Caudebec there indefinitely. On the other hand, despite knowing that my reconciliation with the baron would be a fractious and arduous affair, I was delighted that this extended stay of the Norman pilgrims in our city would afford Samson the occasion to court Dame Gertrude at his leisure, rather than sit around "kissing the wind", as Fontanette put it.

As soon as we dismounted, the hostess of the Three Kings appeared in the doorway and greeted Cossolat with a huge smile and told him that the *roumieux* (which is what the people of Montpellier call the pilgrims heading for Rome) were already sitting at breakfast inside, gorging themselves on large quantities of meat and wine. I entered the inn first with the hostess and Cossolat behind me, and, believing that the captain was still right behind me, went into the common room and headed straight for the baron to make peace with him. But scarcely had he caught sight of me before Caudebec leapt to his feet, throwing the drumstick he was eating behind him and, trembling with anger, eyes bulging and face bright scarlet, screamed, "Ah, heretic! You villain! You monster! You dare show your traitorous face in here? 'Sblood, I'm going to make you pay for your audacity!"

Drawing his dagger, he rushed at me. I turned, but Cossolat was no longer behind me, and terrified by his absence and at finding myself unarmed before this ball of fury, I began to back up, and, being naturally quicker than the baron, would have escaped had not one of the monks stuck out his foot behind me and caused me to fall. Caudebec, brandishing his dagger and shouting "Kill! Kill!" would certainly have caught me and killed me if the page, Rouen, feigning confusion, hadn't thrown himself at his legs, for which he was rewarded with a powerful kick that sent him rolling halfway across the room. But that provided only a brief respite, and, jumping to my feet, I grabbed the stool the monk had been sitting on by one of its legs and ripped it out from under him with such force that he fell in his turn, and Caudebec, still in hot pursuit, fell on top of him. Would that God had made Caudebec run the monk through as he fell on him, but alas! that didn't happen—Providence must have been looking the other way.

Caudebec, jumping to his feet and growling like a wild boar, immediately recommenced, dagger in hand, chasing me round the table, while some of the pilgrims cried "Kill! Kill!"—though they did not venture to lend a hand—and others shouted, "For shame! An unarmed man!" Some of the good Norman wenches even went so far as to begin bombarding the baron with their goblets and spoons to slow his progress. But realizing that, though I had no sword, I did possess a shield, I turned to meet my assailant, grabbing the stool by its legs and holding it firmly in front of me, bracing my feet and head held high. My stance clearly unnerved Caudebec, and served to cool his anger a little, especially since among his superstitions was the belief that I had inherited from my father the gift of invincibility in battle. He nevertheless made two or three dagger thrusts that I easily parried. However, not content with being on the defensive, which didn't suit my disposition, I was considering suddenly throwing the stool at his head when Cossolat's stentorian voice was heard above the confusion in the room. "Baron de Caudebec, I arrest you in the name of the king!"

This had the effect of a thunderbolt, and the terrified pilgrims immediately fell silent.

"Monsieur!" said Caudebec, turning as if a viper had bitten his heel, and his crimson face now as white as a candle. "Monsieur, what are you saying?"

"Monsieur," Cossolat continued when silence was restored, "I'm arresting you for the attempted murder of the nobleman Pierre de Siorac, here present."

"But he's only a Huguenot!" cried Caudebec, whereupon several of the most zealously papist monks among the pilgrims shouted "Have at him!" in support of their master.

To these, Cossolat replied by leaping on Caudebec's empty stool, suddenly drawing his sword with a clash of steel, and shouting loudly: "Good people, who among you dares to challenge the captain of the archers in Montpellier? Shall I send for my men and have you all arrested? Or would you rather I have the lot of you—you and your horses—thrown in the garbage pits of the city?"

Cossolat's sword, and his vigorous frame, the light in his dark eyes and even his terrible Provençal accent in French worked wonders on the pilgrims, who lowered their heads, quite undone by the idea of suddenly losing the delicious fare and amenities of the Three Kings inn, which they'd so looked forward to.

"Captain," said Caudebec at last, quite annoyed to see his people abandon him, yet attempting to regain his credibility, "you cannot arrest me, I am a baron."

"Perhaps in Normandy I wouldn't be able to," said Cossolat, his voice as chilling as a November breeze, "but here I can. And I will, unless Monsieur de Siorac agrees to reconcile with you and you with him."

"Me? Reconcile with this baron?" I cried, wanting to add a few strands to this knot so that the baron would have to work harder to untie it. "I, who saved his life, saved his entire company by standing up to the brigands in the Corbières and chasing them away? I, whom, as my reward for saving him, he tried to kill, naked and unarmed, adding insults to my honour in front of these assembled pilgrims? No, no! Either you arrest this baron forthwith, Captain, or else I shall ram his damnable insults down his throat!"

At this, the baron turned even paler, seeing himself dead and buried, having to pay for his mortal sins, or already roasting in

Purgatory longer than the days of indulgence he'd purchased by the thousands from his monks, his fat carcass turning on the Devil's spit until it had browned sufficiently to pay the Lord for his sins of gluttony and adultery. Thinking these terrible thoughts, white as a sheet and head lowered in shame, the baron remained silent. But Dame Gertrude du Luc, with her feminine intuition, having understood the element of comedy in my speech, and very desirous, for her own special reasons, of seeing a reconciliation between the Siorac family and Caudebec, and wanting her own reconciliation with him since she'd been among the first to hurl goblet, spoon and table knives at him as he was chasing me through the room, rushed to my side and with her sweet white hands seizing my right hand (into which she slipped a little note that I quickly hid in my doublet), fell graciously to her knees and said in a piteous voice:

"Oh, Monsieur de Siorac! Are you a Turk or a Christian? If you are a Christian, as I believe, reformist though you may be, I beg you on my knees, in the name of Christ, spare the Baron de Caudebec, who is like a beloved father to all of us, and without whom not one among us could go on living!"

At these words, the Norman wenches, who are all quite tall, as I've said, and quite beautiful, blue-eyed, with hair like ripened wheat, and who, however manly their height and vigour, were nonetheless possessed of all the feminine wiles, added their prayers to Dame Gertrude's, and pressed up against me from all sides, moaning, sighing and crying hot tears (real or feigned) and begging me not to kill the baron, their beloved father. To which the baron testily replied, "The plague take these silly wenches! Am I so weak? You'd think I were already dead!"

Scarcely had he spoken when there appeared in the hall a very handsome and majestic gentleman, followed by a lackey carrying, with the respect ordinarily given the reliquary, a barrel I hoped would be full of precious wine. Cossolat immediately leapt down from the stool, resheathed his sword and bowed deeply to the new arrival.

"What's all this?" said the gentleman, frowning. "My dear Cossolat, I see that you had unsheathed your sword. Was there some trouble here?"

"Things are calming down, Monsieur de Lattes," replied Cossolat.

And, indeed, already Caudebec had furtively replaced his dagger in its sheath and was looking at Monsieur de Lattes without saying a word or moving a muscle, so astonished was he by the man's presence and appearance.

"Are you the Baron de Caudebec?" enquired Lattes.

"I am," replied Caudebec.

"Monsieur, I want to thank you for the good grace you have shown in making a reconciliation with Siorac," said Lattes, "and Monsieur de Joyeuse wishes to make you a gift of a barrel of muscat to replace the one that you so artfully used to fool the brigands of the Corbières. Are you two indeed reconciled?"

"We are working on it," I said, bowing deeply to Monsieur de Lattes. "All that remains is the apology that the Baron de Caudebec intends to offer me for a few unfortunate words that escaped him in a moment of anger."

Caudebec looked from Monsieur de Lattes to Cossolat, to the barrel of wine, to me, and, with ashen face, he mumbled, "Monsieur de Siorac, I offer you my apologies."

"Monsieur," I replied, "I am at your service." And stepping up to him, I smiled, embraced him warmly and kissed him on both cheeks. He responded with much more good grace than I would have expected, for he was doubtless secretly relieved to have got off so easily.

"Monsieur," I whispered as we hugged each other, "you must promise me that you won't whip your page tonight. Without him,

I'd be dead and you would be languishing in a fetid jail waiting to be beheaded."

He promised. I won't repeat all the compliments that were exchanged and all the beautiful (and lengthy) phrases that were passed back and forth, Lattes displaying an easy mastery of French and loving to hear himself speak. As soon as this handsome gentleman had left the common room, and while Cossolat was accepting a glass of muscat from the baron, I bid everyone good day and took my leave. As I left the Three Kings, however, I ducked into a doorway and pulled Dame Gertrude's note from my doublet and read:

> My gentul brother. Pleez fine me a diskreet place which I will pey for, to meet my little sikke frend, since we can't meet heer four I've been under hevey wach since Lézignan. I will wate for you pressenly at the chursh of Saint-Firmin. Pleez, my sweat brother, due what I sae or I shall dye.
>
> G.

"Ah," I smiled, "wouldn't it be better for these two to live side by side instead of dying far from each other?" But rereading the letter, laughing at her spelling, I suddenly remembered the note little Hélix had sent me when Samson and I were locked up in the north-east tower at Mespech when we returned from our expedition to the plague-infected Sarlat. I fell into a brown study thinking about the poor girl, dead in the bloom of her youth, and how I was like a widower, deprived of the company of one whom I'd know so well and so closely since my earliest memories. These thoughts pained me deeply but fortunately were interrupted by the appearance of Cossolat on the threshold of the Three Kings. I rushed up to him and pulled him aside to whisper to him that I was looking for a "diskreet place" for a few days.

"Oh, Monsieur scholar!" laughed Cossolat. "What a man you are! You're scarcely free of the clutches of this *roumieu*, and there you go again throwing yourself at the feet of some she-wolf."

"Not at all! This she-wolf is for my brother and not for me."

"What are you telling me? That he can't find the den for himself?"

"Ah, that he can't, he's one of God's angels, wandering dreamily around this earth, and full of remorse for having feelings about this woman."

"Well, you're a good brother!" said Cossolat with a laugh. "Given how much you're doing to help him exercise his member, which, without your aid, would fall into total disrepair. Come with me!"

Taking me by the arm, laughing and joking, this man, who had seemed so serious and humourless, led me through the city to the rue du Bayle, a little street that bordered on the Saint-Firmin church, and there he showed me a little shop with a first-floor garret. "Thomassine lives here," he explained. "She owns this needle shop, but rents out the room above to certain rich merchants who, like the camel in the Bible, don't dream of passing through the eye of the needle." (He laughed heartily at his own joke, which I suspected he'd told more than once.) "Thomassine arrived here ten years ago, chased from her home in the Cévennes hills by a terrible famine that wiped out her entire family. The poor wench was so defeated when she arrived in Montpellier that she had to sell her blouse to buy a skirt. But ever since, choosing her clients from among Montpellier's finest families (including some canons of the cathedral of Notre-Dame des Tables), Thomassine has so prospered that she now owns this shop and a very handy lodging only forty toises from the door of Saint-Firmin. It's a very nice trick. The client enters the shop to buy needles and thread, finds himself upstairs where the bawd is waiting for him and then leaves by the back door which gives onto a little alley which no one ever uses."

"But isn't this a brothel? The lady is very refined."

"Not at all! It's just a shop with articles for women. It's like in Spanish inns. Everyone eats the food they bring in. Monsieur scholar, I'll take my leave. I just noticed the red curtain upstairs is moving, so Thomassine is watching us. Adieu. She'll like you. She's a beautiful and strong woman. Having known many men has not soured her view of our species."

Turning on his heels, Cossolat marched off in his abrupt and military way. I couldn't help feeling surprised all over again by this rather schoolboy-like side of him. I watched his broad shoulders disappear from sight. "Well now," I thought, "Huguenot he may be, but a captain of the archers is no toddler who has to have his bread buttered for him. No doubt he knows each paving stone in this city by day and by night and all that goes on behind every facade."

Scarcely had I set foot in Thomassine's needle shop before a very trim chambermaid appeared and said with an inviting smile, "My mistress is awaiting you." She preceded me with a lively step up the staircase, her ample hips rolling in a way that left me feeling cradled in her beauty. "Ah," I thought to myself, "hasn't this poor beast been bridled enough? Since the inn at Lézignan, I've been languishing in a nun's chastity, and in Maître Sanche's house growing thin on his meagre fare. Did I come to Montpellier to dry up, studying logic and philosophy, labouring all day with my head, my stomach empty and my arms unencumbered?"

Aha! I was sure of it! Thomassine was at breakfast and her table laden with sumptuous meats and delicacies. Joyeuse in his mansion, the *roumieux* at the Three Kings and now Thomassine in her rooms! "By the belly of St Anthony!" I thought. "Everyone in this town is gorging themselves, everyone except me! I haven't eaten a morsel since last night." Let me just say, without wishing to offend anyone: let the

Lord protect Thomassine to the end of her earthly days for having guessed from her first glance at me that I was weak from hunger and, in her sweetness and hospitality, for having said as soon as I crossed her threshold, "Monsieur, no ceremony! Sit, I beg you, and enjoy my table. You're my guest, it won't cost you a sol. No! I won't take no for an answer. Azaïs, set a place for the gentleman, and quickly! Here, next to me. Eat, my noble friend, eat! Without meat to fill our bellies, there's no life! Without life, there's no love. Without love there's no life! Azaïs! Where's the man's goblet? Fill it to the top! Don't hold back! Serve him some more of this Bigorre sausage! Oh, my! What a pleasure to watch him eat with those beautiful white teeth! Azaïs, give him more ham! He's eating a whole slice in one bite! It's wonderful! Monsieur, have some more of this Corbières wine! Something to wash down your breakfast with! Azaïs, remove this man's ruff! Take off his doublet! It's too hot in here! Help him off with his boots so he can make himself at home! Good Monsieur, have another slice of this cherry pie! Finish your wine so that Azaïs can pour you some of this muscat. It's from Frontignan, smooth and sweet, and flows down your throat like Lyons velvet."

To be sure, there were no silver platters, or gold-plated tableware, or golden-handled little forks, or tall valets in superb livery, but by the belly of St Anthony, it was very pleasant here! I devoured healthy but simple food and drank these excellent regional wines in the cool darkness of the room, whose shutters were half closed against the sun and flies. And there was beautiful Thomassine, watching me with generous eyes, she of the easy saddle but heavenly soul, may God watch over her! And, to top it off, here was a trim chambermaid, taking off my ruff, my doublet and my boots with light and caressing fingers and a cheerful smile.

While I was wolfing down this repast, and already three-quarters full (but this chasm was woefully deep), I glanced around the room and what struck me, other than the tapestries and many Persian rugs, was a bed so large that five people my size could easily have slept in it. The coverlet was of red velvet, matching the curtains that enclosed its alcove. Of other furniture there was none, excepting a trunk where, doubtless, Thomassine kept her clothes, and the table at which I was seated. As for Thomassine, she was not yet thirty and very beautiful, with black, luxurious hair, a round face and large red mouth. She had a robust neck and certainly, exposed as it was by a largely unlaced bodice, the largest, firmest, most milky and round bosom that I ever saw on a wench—except my beloved Barberine, whom she strongly resembled, though my nurse lacked Thomassine's saucy effrontery.

"Monsieur de Siorac, are you well filled?"

"Oh, Madame, marvellously so! What gratitude and thanks I owe you! But, pray tell, how do you know my name?"

"My bed is more talkative and warmer than ten confessionals, and though my little ear hears secrets a plenty therein, my tongue never repeats a one. What do you need?"

"A room, Madame, for five or six days."

"As you've an older brother in Périgord, young man, and you're a medical student without much money, I'll let you have it for six sols a day."

"A thousand thanks, Madame," I replied, "but I do not want to take advantage of your goodness. It is not I who will pay for the room but the lady, who herself is quite well-to-do."

At this naive remark, Thomassine threw her head back and laughed until tears came to her eyes.

"My noble Monsieur! I like you! You're as frank as a freshly minted coin. And so good-looking! You're pawing the ground like a stallion in a pasture! So, it will be ten sols a day! Go find your lady right away! Where did you leave her?"

"At the Saint-Firmin church, saying her prayers. But alas, she is not mine but my brother's. I wish to God she were mine, for in these last ten days I've kissed only the wind."

"If I understand you," laughed Thomassine, "you're pretty hungry in that way too! But tell me, is your brother's lady so beautiful that you covet her yourself?"

"Oh, Madame, she is not half so pretty as you, her blonde hair seems so pale compared to your jet-black curls."

At this, Thomassine laughed again, and what gay and inebriating music that laugh was to my ears!

"Azaïs, did you hear this gallantry? What a clever boy he is with his compliments. And the look in his eyes! They're flashing fire! Azaïs, what are we going to do with this poor lad and his strident hunger?"

"Satisfy it, Madame. Charity demands no less. After the belly comes the ballet."

"Well said!" replied Thomassine. "Monsieur, I've heard you're a valiant fellow. Here's your citadel," she continued, rising, her cheeks on fire and her legs spread invitingly. "Arise and have at 'em! Give no quarter!"

"What, Madame! Laying siege at this hour of the morning? And with that lady waiting?"

"Let her pray! Let her pray to her God since she's going to offend him! The more she prays, the lighter will be her soul when the pleasure comes. Come, Monsieur, I'll brook no refusal. Azaïs, close the door behind you. And don't go listening at the keyhole or I'll whip you tonight like green barley."

I don't know which of us carried the other to bed but we were there in the blink of an eye, our clothes discarded and thrown to the Devil, the velvet curtains closed around us like the future baby in it's mother's womb. My head buried in Thomassine's ample bosom, I felt myself flying so high, so high that I could scarcely believe my senses.

"Oh!" I thought in absolute wonder. "Is this really me in here, so well lodged and received?"

These pleasures finished, which always finish too soon, I had a lot of running to do. First to the church of Saint-Firmin where I saw Dame Gertrude du Luc on her knees, deep in prayer in front of a statue of the Virgin, a thick black veil over her beautiful straw-coloured hair, which I'd dared to malign just minutes earlier. She had chosen Jesus's mother for intercession, hoping no doubt that since Mary was a woman she would better understand the mix of scruples and desires she was feeling. I came up to her from behind, touched her gently on the shoulder and, when she turned, I saw her face bathed in tears, either because of her conscience or because she feared I might not come, for she whispered to me that she had despaired of seeing me. I didn't want to lose any more time in excuses or civilities and told her to follow me at a distance of ten paces to the home of a woman who was a friend of mine—which she did immediately, hiding her identity behind a mask she'd brought for the occasion. Her face thus disguised, she crossed the street separating the Catholic church from the needle shop, where another idolatrous rite was celebrated daily, by which I mean that of our mortal flesh. Alas, I agree wholeheartedly that men should love God. But are we able to, constructed as we are and as He created us? It is not I who sin, says St Paul, but the sin that is in me.

As soon as Thomassine saw Dame Gertrude du Luc before her, all blushing and ashamed, she understood what a novice she was dealing with, and took compassion on her from the depths of her generous heart. She caressed her new acquaintance a lot and gave her a goblet of Frontignan wine, told Azaïs to brush her blonde hair, perfumed it with essence of musk, which, as everyone knows, is an aphrodisiac, and, in an attempt to distract her thoughts from images of hellfire, asked her straight out what kind of man her lover was. To which, Dame Gertrude, who, up until that moment, had been sitting still and quiet on her stool as though paralysed by fear and shame, suddenly grew quite animated and, blue eyes shining now, cried, "Oh, good hostess! He is so handsome and so radiant, and so suave that there is no angel in God's heaven his equal."

Happy to see her so restored, she who had appeared so enfeebled, I immediately left and ran all the way to the apothecary to seek this beautiful angel, from whom very unangelic things were expected. I was careful not to tell him where I was taking him or what he would see, wishing to avoid any argument such as we had already had, and counting on the sight of the lady to dissipate all his heroic resolutions. To tell the truth, the effect exceeded all of my expectations, for scarcely had he caught sight of Dame Gertrude standing in the upper room of the needle shop before he paled terribly and fainted dead away. I gave a few slaps on his cheeks to bring him round, and Gertrude du Luc, when I had done, applied a few kisses, both remedies having remarkable success: his pale face regained its colour immediately, and his eyes, upon opening, fixed on his lady with such an air of adoration that I was seized with respect for such a noble and powerful feeling. I withdrew. And leaving them to celebrate the rites of their great love, I went away all pensive, pricked a bit by envy—not of the lady, but of this unique happiness into which I had watched them melt.

I returned on the run to the apothecary, for it was close on noon, and I didn't want to offend Maître Sanche by my tardiness. It was excessively hot for early June and the citizens of Montpellier had, from house to house, strung cords at the level of the first floor, on which they threw branches and reeds, so that passers-by would be shaded from the terrible midday heat. They had also thrown water they'd drawn from wells or cisterns on the paving stones, since there is only one fountain in Montpellier, in the place Saint-Gély. The sun, even through these branches, fell heavily on the heads and shoulders of the crowd of pedestrians, who seemed unaffected by it, but strolled through the streets laughing and chattering gaily, young men and women eyeing each other carefully. Running as I had to do, I arrived at Maître Sanche's house all moist with sweat. The dinner bell was ringing and, in the great hall, all were standing at their places round the table, waiting for the illustrious master, whom some business must have detained in his office.

"Where is your pretty brother?" asked Fogacer.

"I left him at the Three Kings with a *roumieu* who invited him to dine there."

"And this *roumieu* didn't invite you?" asked Fogacer, raising one diabolical eyebrow.

"No," I answered curtly, hoping to put an end to this line of enquiry, to which Typhème on my left lent an avid ear.

Then, parading in majestically in his black satin robes, the very illustrious master immediately noticed Samson's absence, and he, too, enquired after his nephew, but seemed to accept my lame answer without any reaction, focusing instead on removing his robe and replacing his tufted hat with a his little cap. After which he intoned his strange benedicite.

"Good nephew," said Maître Sanche as soon as Fontanette had served the midday soup, "is it because you had such an exciting morning that, as hungry as you must be, you're picking at your food without appetite?" However cockeyed he was, his look was now very penetrating.

"No, no, illustrious master," I pleaded, reddening so much that Typhème, on my left, looked at me very curiously without turn-ing her head. I blushed even more when, to my infinite astonish-ment, Maître Sanche began recounting, as if he'd been present, my interview with Monsieur de Joyeuse and my fight with Caudebec at the Three Kings. He stopped there, but I had no doubt he also knew the rest of my activities of the morning, so I sat quite still on my stool, suddenly aware of what would later be confirmed by Fogacer: that among the Sephardic families of Montpellier, news travelled like lightning, since these people lived in constant fear that some popular uprising or machination of the priests might put their lives in danger, as had been the case in Spain with their security and well-being.

"Wherever Samson is," said Maître Sanche after a short pause, "I hope he's happy, since he has such great merit. Besides having much to his advantage physically—a blessing not only for him but for those who are close to him—Samson has a great appetite for goodness; his heart is as pure as the most azure sky, and he feels a great tenderness for his fellow man. As for me, I am excessively touched by his ravishing beauty and his rare virtue. *Gratior et pulchro veniens in corpore virtus.*"*

I must confess that this adulation of my beloved Samson, which I hadn't expected, moved me to tears.

"And yet," continued the master, eyeing me with a look that was half serious, half jocular, "Samson doesn't have a brain or a tongue as agile as some people I could mention. Being more at home in heaven, he sometimes has trouble living in the mire in which we live, and he badly needs a more worldly brother to help him find his way—*frater qui arranti comiter monstrat viam.*"†

I lowered my eyes and silently ate my soup, not sure whether this praise of the more worldly brother was pure gold or gold-painted lead, or intended to let me know that our illustrious master knew all. But perhaps there was some of each in these words of Maître Sanche, who, despite his posturing and Latin pompousness, was

---

* "Virtue is only more agreeable when present in a beautiful body."

† "A brother who graciously shows the way to him who has lost his way."

more subtle than I would have thought. What added to my confusion was that the sibylline words of the chemist had made me the focus of everyone's attention, and I felt quite uneasy being put on the spot, feeling Fogacer's stare from under his satanic eyebrows on my right and Typhème's more furtive glance between two blinks of her eyelashes on my left.

"My nephew," Maître Sanche continued, lapping and slurping his soup, with sucking noises that the Vicomte de Joyeuse would have found most unappealing, "Fogacer will tell you, as he told me himself, that your gentle brother Samson is not getting the hang of logic and philosophy (in which, our Fogacer believes, you will someday shine, since in you the vital spirits pass more subtly from the blood to the nerves and from the nerves to ideas and from ideas to words). Alas, Samson is slow, having a mind little given to conceptual thought, a tongue little given to the ready word and not much facility for argumentation. He prefers to these abstract ideas things he can see, touch and smell. But if Samson has little appetite for the subtleties of the logicians, how will he ever defend himself against the chicanery of the lawyers or, given his purity, against the corruption of the judges? Maître François Rabelais said, justly, that 'the law is only a beautiful robe embroidered with shit'.

"This is all the more a problem since the Saint-Benoît college of law in Montpellier has no reputation for brilliance. All they've got there are three lice and a bunch of mean-spirited, senile lawyers, papist zealots all, who have no love of Huguenot students and will prove it to Samson in refusing his admission. Which is why, considering the extraordinary fascination your brother has displayed for the apothecary sciences, my advice and counsel is that he be urged to follow this path, which, if my memory serves me correctly, was also that of your grandfather, Charles, in Rouen. And, God willing, may your father give his blessing to this plan, so that someday we can say to Samson what will be said of me: *scire potestates herbarum usumque medendi maluit, et mutas agitare inglorius artes.*"*

Whether our most illustrious master had dedicated himself humbly (*inglorius*) to this peaceable art (*mutas artes*) is not a matter I would venture a firm opinion on, but I felt a rush of gratitude for his fatherly interest and all the more so since the students of the apothecary sciences, while not authorized to be called scholars, were nevertheless able to take courses at the Royal College of Medecine, but did not have the same rigorous requirements as the future doctors. So if this arrangement were approved, I'd have Samson near me, and would enjoy his radiant presence and the opportunity to "to help him find his way", as Maître Sanche put it.

And so I happily agreed to the proposal, and, with many thanks for his solicitude, I told the apothecary that I would go straightaway and write to my father. But the master, stroking his long grey beard, in which, to be honest, you could see bits and relics of his soup, turned to Fogacer and began questioning him about Rondelet's patients, asking for details that, had medicine not been my future art, I would have found disgusting. "And the pus, Fogacer? How was the pus? Liquid? Unctuous? Yellowish? Bloody?" But before Fogacer could answer, he turned to me and said, "My pretty nephew, I'm going to put you to the test about these matters. Take heart. Urine, faeces, pus and the humours are the focus of our profession. And when the lawyers of Montpellier affect superior airs with us and have the gall to say: '*Stercus et urina medici sunt prandia prima,*'† we never fail to reply, as Maître François Rabelais once did, '*Nobis sunt signa. Vobis sunt prandia digna.*'"‡

We all laughed uproariously at this excellent repartee. And, at that, Fogacer began his daily report on his patients, using the crudest

---

* "He preferred to know the virtues of plants and their medicinal uses, and dedicated himself humbly to this peaceable art" (Virgil).

† "Excrement and urine are the appetizers of medicine."

‡ "For us these are symptoms, for you they're your dinner."

terms to answer his master's questions. I noticed that Typhème herself, taking dainty spoonfuls of soup, didn't bat an eyelid at these disgusting terms, being, I imagined, quite used to such language, but remained calmly seated on her stool in her Moorish beauty, her head held high, looking at her father with infinite respect as if he were Moses coming down from Mount Sinai. As for Luc, like everyone else at this table, more accustomed to listening than to being heard, he also sat silently, but was listening avidly to their discussion, gleaning whatever he could from it. As ugly as his sister was beautiful, he looked uncannily like his father, but without the latter's squint or hunched back. Meanwhile, inside this carnal envelope there burned the same inextinguishable fire, having no other ambition than to become a learned man like his father.

That was a Friday, so I spent the afternoon in my room, reading Aristotle's *Organon*, a treatise on logic, and since my reading was so dry, I snuck down to the kitchen several times to beg a glass of cool water from the Sephardic cook, Concepcion, a big, fat, resentful woman, who grudgingly provided me water as though it were costing her personally to do so. I was surprised, each time I went downstairs, by the busy goings-on in the house that day: the laboratory assistants were going back and forth with a great clatter of pails, throwing water on the kitchen tiles and scrubbing them with large brooms. As for Fontanette, I saw her in passing through the common room, her cheeks red, working feverishly to iron all the shirts and blouses for the men and women of the house and then taking them up to each of their rooms.

Taking up the *Organon* again, I thought ruefully that my beloved Samson was better occupied than I, as I wandered through the arid parched deserts of syllogisms, the first and second premises, the great and medium terms, when there was a tap at my door and in came Fontanette, still red from pressing clothes, and whose arrival was like an oasis in my desert.

"Oh, Fontanette," I greeted her, "I'm so happy to see you looking so fresh and trim, your cheeks like cherries and a gleam in your eye."

"Ha, Monsieur! The gleam in my eyes is not as saucy as yours, however blue they may be. I feel all naked when you look at me like that."

"'Sblood! If my gaze had that power, I'd look at you all day long! But come over here, Fontanette, that I may greet you properly."

"No, no, my noble friend, I'm not coming anywhere near you!" (But as she said this she took two steps towards me.) "You're the only one in the house who gives me kisses, and, however much I may like that, I don't think it's right. Monsieur," she continued, "might I ask you to carry your table into your brother's room so you can work undisturbed tomorrow?"

I looked at her wide-eyed with surprise.

"But, Fontanette, can't I work in here tomorrow?"

"Ah, no, Monsieur, you can't! You'd be cooked like a crayfish in a kettle! Every Saturday I have to keep a fire going in your room."

"By the belly of St Anthony! A fire in my room? In June? In this suffocating heat? Fontanette, what's all this about? Have they lost their minds?"

"I know not, Monsieur," she replied naively, "but the illustrious master has ordered that there be a fire every Saturday in your room, in summer as in winter. And it's my duty to light it and keep it going, and no one else."

"What? All day long?"

"Morning, noon and evening."

"This is most strange, my brave girl," I replied. "But tell me why is there such a bustle about the house this morning?"

"That's the way it is on Fridays," she explained as she took two or three steps towards me. Seeing that she was now quite close to me—whatever she might have said about this—her hip pressed against the table where I was seated, a bloom in her cheeks that was *not* due to the effort of pressing clothes, her breath coming in short gasps and her bodice unlaced, as she should have noticed before knocking on my door, I put my arms around her waist, pulled her towards me and, with my face now pressed against her breasts, feeling again the terrible thirst I'd felt the first time I saw her, kissed them avidly. As dry and meagre as Aristotle's logic seemed, so now did the wench seem to be full and refreshing as she sank into my arms, melting like butter in the sun. But alas, this pleasure was short-lived, for, suddenly stiffening and pushing me away, Fontanette pulled free of my embrace.

"Oh, Monsieur!" she cried, terrified by a tardy scruple that had her retying her bodice in haste. "Sweet Jesus, if Dame Rachel caught me at this she'd dismiss me forthwith!"

"And that's why you're not allowed to touch me? You'd lose your place here? For a couple of kisses? Fontanette, do you really expect me to believe that?"

"Indeed I do, Monsieur! You must believe it, it's the truth. Dame Rachel doesn't like me. She tells me I'm rebellious and stubborn and, what's more, I'm not a Sephardic like the rest of the servants, save one."

"So why does she keep you on?"

"The most illustrious master has a weakness for me."

I laughed at this and asked, "A weakness that goes how far?"

"Not as far as you'd like to go, my noble friend," she said with a little bow, before rushing away with a teasing laugh, leaving my room full of the sadness of her absence. And so, reluctantly, I returned to Aristotle, who seemed quite vapid after such passion. "By the belly of St Anthony," I mused as I progressed from the "major premiss" to the minor one and on to a conclusion, "why do we need a syllogism to discover that 'Socrates is mortal'? Didn't we know this before beginning to reason it out?"

The dinner bell freed me from the *Organon*, and, little nourished by this empty meat, I hurried downstairs, little concerned about

Samson, who hadn't yet returned, knowing how easy it is to forget the passing of time when you're enjoying the pleasures he was. Imagine my surprise when, reaching the bottom of the staircase, I discovered the house brightly lit by new candles, which had replaced the old ones, which, as I'd observed the night before, were far from burnt down. But I didn't want to ask my host the reasons for this prodigal illumination, any more than I dared enquire about the other strange customs I'd noticed here since my arrival—not to mention Fontanette's disclosure about the fire that, despite the June heat, she would light in my room the next day. Nevertheless, after the meagre repast, having climbed up to the terrace with Fogacer to enjoy the evening breeze, I shared my astonishment with my tutor.

"Ah, Siorac!" he explained. "It's time you knew, living as we do in this house, that these Sephardics are turtles."

"Turtles? What do you mean?"

"Turtles whose shell is the Holy Roman Apostolic Catholic Church, which was previously in Portugal and Spain their great and cruel persecutor. Having been forced to adopt the religion of the tyrants who were oppressing them, they've made of it a shield to protect them from further persecution. But beneath this carapace that weighs on their backs, but protects them, beat their turtles' hearts. And those hearts have remained Hebrew and piously faithful to their former religion. And that's the explanation for all the strange goings-on that have confused you since your arrival. Tomorrow, Saturday, is, for Maître Sanche, the true Sabbath, and the reason for all this bustle you've witnessed today: the house cleaning, the change of linen, the lighting of the candles."

"But why the fire in my room tomorrow?"

"Ah well, that's more subtle and Ulysses couldn't have imagined a better scheme. As you know, no Hebrew is allowed to touch fire on the Sabbath and the fireplace in Concepcion's kitchen must remain unused for the entire day, so that we'll be eating cold meats. But there's a great peril in this for our Sephardics. For some of the neighbours who are jealous of Maître Sanche's fortune might get suspicious that there is never smoke coming from his chimney on Saturdays and share their suspicions with their priests—who would immediately stir up trouble. So, here's the trick: the flue of the fireplace in your room joins the one from the kitchen, and Fontanette, who is not of their religion, can tend the fire and thus produce enough smoke at the right times to allay the suspicions of our evangelical neighbours."

"Ah, I like this trick! And all the more since I hate the papist repressions."

"Would to God," replied Fogacer arching his black eyebrow, "that you hated the Huguenot version of repression in those areas where you are stronger."

"I hate that every bit as much. I am not a zealot."

"As I have observed," conceded Fogacer.

"But," I added after a moment's thought, "this pork that is so abhorred by the Hebrews, despite its succulence, is there not some danger in never buying it? What will the neighbours say to that?"

"Which is why the houseboy, Jean, who is no more a Sephardic than Fontanette, goes to buy pork at the butcher's every Thursday."

"What? They allow pork in this house? Is it possible?"

"It's never served at our table, since Concepcion won't touch it. Jean cooks it up with the dogs' food and serves it to them."

"What a pity!"

"Truly a great and horrible pity. You know how much I love pork!"

"But," I said, "how does Maître Sanche manage to spend all of Saturday not working, since the laboratory is open to his customers?"

"Every Saturday at dawn, Maître Sanche, his assistants and Balsa head to Montolivet on horseback under the pretext of working in the vineyards there. He doesn't return until evening."

"And what about the laboratory? Who does the work there?"

"Jean, the houseboy, and I. That makes two and," he added laughing, "there will be three of us when Samson becomes my apprentice!"

I laughed with him, but perhaps not as heartily, and not bitterly either, for I realized that Maître Sanche's interest in Samson happened to coincide with his own needs, a detail which escaped me when the master made his "beneficent" offer.

"And what about Sundays?"

"Ah!" replied Fogacer. "It's a sad and painful day for these Sephardics who must sacrifice their shell! With the exception of Luc, who goes off to the reformed temple where you will meet him, Maître Sanche and his entire household go with great pomp to Notre-Dame des Tables, where an entire pew is reserved for him. And there, holding the Roman missal, whose abominations must burn his fingers, his eyes lowered so as to avoid looking at the idols, the crucifix, the paintings, the stained-glass windows and other damnable idols, he prays secretly to the God of Moses to pardon him for being there."

As I remained silent, stuck by this sad tableau, Fogacer added, "So what do you think? Do you blame the Sephardics for these dissimulations?"

"Not at all!" I replied. "They are daughters of constraint and tyranny."

For I well remembered the clandestine cult to Mary that Barberine and la Maligou practised in the loft of our Huguenot enclave at Mespech: proof that conversion through fear and threats is merely an affront to conscience and of no profit to anyone. I added, "If I were threatened with the scaffold, I'd do the same."

Fogacer smiled.

"As for me," he said, raising that diabolical left eyebrow, "the conditional is unnecessary. I do the same. And it costs me very little. Listen, Siorac, here's how I've limited my practice: I confess and take Communion once a year. I go to Mass on Sundays. I cross myself at

173

crossroads in front of the crucifix. I take my hat off when processions are passing. And if required, I'll kneel. In short, I have my carapace too. Where I differ from the Sephardics…"

And since, smiling his sinuous smile, he left his sentence in suspense, I said:

"Well?"

"Is that under my shell, there is nothing."

'Twas thus that I discovered that Fogacer was a sceptic in theology as in philosophy, and believed only in medicine, and even there, only, as I had observed, with a very limited degree of faith and only in certain of its practices.

Remembering suddenly that I was supposed to go and fetch Samson, I took my leave of him and he said, "Take Miroul, arm yourselves, and walk with your swords unsheathed in the middle of the street, a pistol in your belt."

Then, taking my arm and squeezing it, he whispered:

"*Thomassina bona mulier est, et formosa et sana. Bene, bene.*"*

"Well, well," I thought, "the whole city knows about it! But 'sblood! What do I care?" And dragging Miroul along, I ran through the streets and alleys like a stallion in his pasture, so anxious was I to see my beautiful hostess. And although, as I write this in Paris many years later, I am still as healthy and vigorous as my father was at my age, I doubt I could now run through the town for as long or as fast as I did that night in the bloom of my fifteen years, sword in hand, in the cool of the evening, feeling invincible. Oh, my beloved Provence, which I miss so much in my golden exile! Oh, the sweetness of life in Montpellier. Oh, Thomassine!

---

* "Thomassine is a good woman, both beautiful and healthy. Good, good!"

6

FONTANETTE WAS RIGHT: I couldn't work on Aristotle's *Organon* all day Saturday, because the heat was so intense, even with the window wide open, that I simply couldn't think. Luckily, Samson was harnessed all day by the tender arms of you-know-who, and I was able to use the little room next to mine, visited at least once an hour by Fontanette, who flitted around me like a butterfly to a candle flame. With a gleam in her black eyes, she kept asking whether I was all right or whether I needed anything. "But it's you I need, Fontanette!" I'd reply. "For shame, Monsieur! Watch your evil tongue!" she would retort, but she would have been disappointed if I'd said anything else. Sometimes as she passed she'd permit me a few kisses, but then, pulling away, she would refuse them according to whether her inclination or her will was stronger, but the latter certainly seemed to me to be weakening.

Samson didn't return until evening, dreamy and dazzled and with an uncertain step, as if, on leaving his paradise, he was scarcely able to get a proper foothold on our sad earth. He hardly touched his meal, which consisted of cold meats since it was the Hebrew Sabbath. But Thomassine, I'll warrant, in the generosity of her heart, had seen to his appetite every time the two lovers caught their breath.

My honest Samson was very closely—if surreptitiously—watched by Typhème, who batted her eyelids at him quite liberally in the absence of her father, who was retained at Montolivet by the enforced idleness that the law of Moses imposed on him. Watching my beautiful brother, and, in turn, watched by me, our beautiful table mate's cheeks were deeply flushed and her breath was so short it was almost a sigh. But however obvious her emotion was to me, Samson remained entirely oblivious to his effect on her, ensconced as he was in his delirium like a snail in its shell. Scarcely had he downed his dinner (without the slightest idea of what he'd eaten) before he was off to his room, staggering from fatigue and so tired he could barely undress before he fell into his bed.

I could only extract him from his slumbers by force the next morning and drag him to the former Bailiff's residence where our fellow religionaries in Montpellier worshipped. Luc and Miroul joined us, and despite the branches shading the freshly watered paving stones of the streets, the sun shone so ardently that you could have fried an egg on them. While the four of us walked along, my brother's face, ordinarily so serene, was darkened by worry. Psalter in hand, he was heading to the temple as though to hear himself condemned to eternal damnation for his fornication, for he followed the Ten Commandments very literally. Since I could find no remedy for the rigour of his beliefs, I turned to Luc, as we walked along, and begged him to explain to me how, from his original papist faith, he'd come to embrace the Reformation. But, heavens! What had I said? Paling visibly, he cast a terrified look around him and begged me in Latin, in a trembling voice, not to ask such questions of this kind *coram populo*.* Clearly, Maître Sanche's heir was extremely prudent despite being in the bloom of his youth.

I was very happy to discover that there were so many people in our cult, and of such different social backgrounds and professions: weavers, shoemakers, shopkeepers, but also doctors, schoolmasters,

---

*   "In the presence of the people."

rich merchants and noblemen—whom I recognized by the swords they wore at their sides—as Samson and I did. What a difference from Sarlat, where, after the failure of the siege by Duras, which I have recounted elsewhere, the Huguenots didn't dare show their faces, let alone gather to celebrate their cult, even secretly. Here, our people seemed to have the advantage, and were very vocal about it, showering the papists with insults. My brother and I, well before we arrived in Montpellier, were already well known for our exploits at the Corbières, so that, after the service, when we were greeting the deans, elders and minister of the temple, the latter, Abraham de Gasc, a candle merchant from Lyons, introduced us to each of the members of his congregation. We were very warmly greeted, and in response to each of the compliments we received, I responded in Provençal, with my habitual Périgordian openness, as much for myself as for my brother. Samson, of course, stood silently by in his remarkable and luminous beauty and couldn't have failed to trouble more than one young woman's heart. Indeed, there were several of these present, and, being from Montpellier, they couldn't help but be beautiful, though because of the gravity of the place and the circumstances I kept myself from eyeing them too obviously, but managed a quick, hypocritical glance at a couple of the comeliest.

Throughout these introductions, Luc watched us benevolently and evidently not without some sense of pride and possessiveness, as if he were happy to have such heroes as his guests. He took me by the arm as we left the temple and asked whether, after our midday meal, we could repair to the rooftop terrace to be able to talk at our leisure without being overheard. Once there, we sat on the stone bench protected from the noonday sun by the shadow of the stairwell entry. We sat in silence for a moment and I had the opportunity of looking closely at him for the first time—since so much of my attention had been directed to his sister, whose Sephardic beauty had completely

177

captivated me, even though I knew I had no chance of ever marrying her, since I was neither rich nor Sephardic myself. I was now surprised to discover that Luc, despite his long angular nose, had beautiful, luminous eyes, whose long dark lashes reminded me of Typhème's, a resemblance I found quite moving.

He himself seemed quite distraught. He was of a sickly and fragile constitution, since he'd never been trained to bear arms, and so, his whole frame trembling with emotion, and in a very low and uncertain voice—though in beautiful and rich language, mixing French and Latin—he began speaking. "Monsieur de Siorac," he said, but I immediately broke in, saying warmly,

"No, no! If your very illustrious father calls me his nephew, then you are my cousin. And to you I am Pierre, pure and simple."

He reddened at this as if he were a girl, with his sensitive and timid complexion. "Pierre," he said, "I offer you a thousand thanks for your gracious generosity. There is no one my age I admire more than you, and, to be honest with you, I'd like to be the way you are."

"Oh, Luc! Your humility has blinded you! You speak Spanish and Portuguese. You know Greek, which I only have a smattering of, and Hebrew, which I don't speak a word of."

"But that's not the way I see things," returned Luc. "You not only have all the gifts of intelligence, but you have so much to be proud of in the flesh. You are agile, strong, an excellent soldier and horseman, and, according to Fogacer, a superb tennis player. What's more, he added, lowering his long dark lashes, they say women find you irresistible."

I was deeply touched by his words, but also embarrassed by them, fearing that Luc, who was very perceptive, had discovered my little games with Fontanette.

"Oh, Luc!" I said, affecting an offhand and jocular manner. "Enough of this. A man's virtue is in his mind, not in his body, which he has in common with other mammals. Tell me what's on your mind."

"Well, I'll tell you then," said Luc with a sigh, as if it were difficult to put an end to singing my praises. "I know, from Fogacer, that, the day before yesterday, you were astonished by the strange goings-on in our house."

"I was astonished, yes, but not offended. We Huguenots also have to dissimulate at times."

"If you know that, then you know that the secret of the mysteries you've observed here can be summed up in one sentence: *Marrani novi Christiani appelantur, sed in facto judii occulti sunt.*"*

"That's exactly how I understand it."

"But, Pierre," moaned Luc, looking at me with an air of extreme anxiety, "do you think such duplicity can be justified before God?"

"Speaking frankly, I don't know. But if it is, why do we then venerate the martyrs?"

"Pierre! Pierre!" cried Luc with great vehemence. "It is written in the Scriptures that it is lawful, in the greatest extremity, to give in to tyranny and to save one's life *by any means possible*, with the exception of murder, incest or idolatry."

Hearing this, I realized that to embrace Catholicism, even for appearances' sake, meant accepting some sort of idolatry, but I restrained myself and said not a word, not wishing to add to the infinite distress I observed in my companion. Moreover, since Luc was of the reformed religion and, from all appearances, with great sincerity, he didn't have to dissimulate so much, so that I guessed that it was his father and Sephardic brothers that he was trying to exculpate.

"Pierre," he continued, his voice full of emotion, "we received yesterday from one of our friends who stayed behind in Spain a letter

---

* "Sephardics are called the new Christians but are, in fact, secretly Jews."

179

in which he tells us what happened to a Sephardic woman from Toledo, Doña Elvira del Campo. This lady, a very rich and beautiful person, was arrested last month by the Inquisition as her neighbours and the butchers of her city accused her of never purchasing or eating pork. For this crime, she was hauled before the Grand Inquisitor. There she was stripped naked, and while her judges, hiding their hypocrisy beneath their robes, enjoyed her nudity, two executioners tied her hands behind her and passed a rope around her arms. At a sign from the judge, they give the rope a twist, then another, and another until the rope broke… I have the letter here, Pierre," he said pulling it from his doublet, "it's in Spanish, but I can translate it for you. This is the interrogation to which Doña Elvira submitted:

"'Why don't you eat pork?'

"'Señor, pork makes me ill. Please, señor, have pity! Ah, these men are killing me!'

"'Why don't you eat pork?'

"'Because I don't like it… Oh, señor, stop these men! I'll tell you anything you want to hear!'

"'Why don't you eat pork?'

"'I don't know… Oh, you're killing me! You're killing me!'

"'Why don't you eat pork?'

"'Because I don't want to eat it… Oh, señor! Oh! I'm dying! Tell them to loosen the rope! Señor, I've already said that I don't eat pork!'

"'Why don't you want to eat it?'

"'For the reason I told you! Ah, señor! What do I have to say? Tell me what to say and I'll say it! Oh, I'm dying, I'm dying! Have you no pity on me?'"

Here Luc stopped reading, tears streaming from his eyes, and I put my arm around his neck and hugged him to me, kissing his cheek, which was as soft and smooth as a girl's since he had no beard. He collapsed into my arms and remained there, pressed against me, crying for a long time, but happy in the embrace of my arms, his sobs preventing him from saying anything more.

"Oh, Pierre," he said, finally, as he pulled himself away, and with those eyes that looked so much like Typhème's he threw me a look of immense gratitude, "even at times when the Inquisition sleeps, you can never believe the injuries our people suffer in Spain. Did you know that the word '*marrane*', which we use in Provençal as a sign of nobility, was originally an insult that derives from the Spanish word for pork? And did you know that sometimes our torturers make fun of us by calling us 'Los Alboraycos', from the name of Muhammad's famous steed that was neither male nor female, insinuating that we are neither fish nor fowl, neither Christians nor Jews? Pierre, our Hebrew brothers who have succeeded in maintaining their religion in the ghettos of France call us in our language *anusim*: the forced ones. And indeed we *were* forced, and by what atrocious means! Pierre! Pierre! Is it not the worst of atrocities to be obliged to live a lie and see yourselves reproached for it by the very people who constrained you to it?"

"Certainly it is an abomination that cries out for vengeance and I firmly believe that the monsters who treated you this way will be punished, if not in this world, alas! then in the next. But Luc, you haven't told me the hows and whys of your own conversion."

At this, throwing me a searching look, he fell silent. And as if I were continuing to press him, suddenly he blurted out:

"If I hesitate to confide in you it's because I'm terribly afraid of offending you."

"Luc, there is no way you could offend me. There is no offence without evil intent. And of that intent you are innocent. Please, continue."

"Well then," said Luc with a sigh and a very sad face, "I will beg your pardon in advance in case I offend you. But here goes: certain of our Sephardic women, secretly despising the religion they profess publicly, not only do not admit the divinity of Christ, but go so far as to make fun of Him in the privacy of their homes, calling Him derisively 'the little hanged man', or else they draw a cross on their stools so they can say they've sat on it: nasty and offensive practices that my father condemns. But he doesn't make the sign of the cross and, at the end of the benedicite, omits the name of the Son."

"Yes, I've noticed he forgets to say 'the Son'."

"He doesn't forget. Pierre, if I tell you this it's so you'll understand that I've been raised in this stubbornly tacit refusal, which is sometimes injurious to Christ. In this house, you'll never see a crucifix in the common room except when we have papist guests. Ordinarily, it sleeps at the bottom of a chest, on the pretext (which only Fontanette is silly enough to believe) that, being made of precious ivory, it would yellow in the air we breathe. So, Pierre, here's what happened. When I outgrew my little boy's dresses, I heard the Gospels, but I really listened to them, and in their core and substance, I couldn't help being struck by their beautiful nobility of spirit, whose morality seemed to me something new and beautiful, more attuned to human tenderness than anything I'd see described in the Old Testament, in such rough and primitive colours. I couldn't doubt, then, that the Old Testament had been corrected by the New according to God's specific will and decree. Consequently, not only the teachings of Christ, but Christ Himself must be considered divine."

"But how did it happen that, believing in Christ, you didn't become a Catholic in your heart, since you were already one in appearance?"

"I simply couldn't!" Luc said, his teeth clenched and his eyes suddenly very bright. "For I couldn't accept the ignorance of the Bible in which the faithful were kept by the priests, nor the idolatries that they imposed on the word of Christ. And even less could I pardon the atrocious persecutions that they wreaked on my ancestors. But, once I'd studied the reformed religion, and finding none of these grievous faults in it, I decided to embrace it."

Having said this, he fell silent, wiping the tears from his cheeks and a bit ashamed, I think, for having shed them. And, silent at his side, I held his right hand between mine to comfort him as best I could, remembering that having been raised by my mother in the Catholic religion, I had been converted by the imperious order of my father. And I recalled that he'd been so spiteful and angry when he discovered the medallion of Mary that his late wife had hung around my neck that he had nearly cast me out of Mespech. And as I recalled these memories that were so painful (precisely because I loved my father with all my heart and because he was my guide and example in all things), Luc and I looked at each other, and I was impressed that he'd had the liberty to choose that which had been refused to me.

"But, Luc," I asked, "what did the most illustrious master say about your conversion?"

"Ah!" cried Luc. "My father is the best father in the world. How could I ever praise his goodness, and benign tolerance sufficiently? He didn't consider his own feelings or advantages in the matter, but bent his authority generously to my own free will. 'My son,' he told me, 'I respect Christ, but I do not consider him divine. But if you do, and believe in the Reformation, go your own way. Your way will have the advantage over mine of matching your beliefs to your outward practice. For I tell you, it's a strange faith that believes what it believes only because it doesn't have the courage not to believe it. But I beg you, always be extremely prudent in your conduct. When the papists get zealous, they are a terrifying bunch. Think about this: whether you're burnt as a Jew or burnt as a heretic, it's the same fire and the same death.'"

Then, remembering that I wanted to see my beloved Samson before he left to visit Dame Gertrude in the early afternoon, I took

183

my leave of Luc sooner than I would have liked, but not without embracing him and kissing him on both cheeks, moved as I was by his combination of moral rectitude and bodily weakness. As I left, I pledged him my friendship. From the confession he'd made to me, I couldn't doubt that, in his weakness, he sought my protection at the moment he was to enter the Royal College of Medicine, whose older, rougher students could be very hard on the new arrivals.

As for his conversion to the reformed religion, I was now wholly convinced of the solidity of Luc's faith, contrary to Fogacer, who joked about his "Calvinist coat", which was as hypocritical as Maître Sanche's "papist coat". And the more time I spent in Montpellier, the more I became convinced that age had a great deal to do with this question—fathers were anchored through fear and habit in the papist traditions, whereas sons, attracted by the audacity of the Reformation, found that it matched the spirit of the wonderful renewal in the arts that the sixteenth century had ushered in.

I found Samson clad only in his shirt, his copper-coloured curly locks all a-tangle, sitting dreamily on his stool, his azure eyes clouded by tears. His normal vigour and virile symmetry were now sapped by sadness and despair, his face more lined with worry than an apple in winter.

"So, my brother, what are you doing here undressed? Have you forgotten your rendezvous with Dame Gertrude?"

"No. I'm not going. Women are false beings who lead our souls to hell! I would be a terrible merchant if I traded my eternal salvation for such short-lived joys."

I was, as you can imagine, very impatient and angry with such silly words, but surmised that, during the service at our temple, Samson had become fortified in his resolution, and so I stifled my first angry reaction and, looking at him calmly, simply agreed, "Very well. Don't go to see her since this is what you've decided."

I withdrew into my room, and, as expected, he immediately rushed in after me. I pretended to be combing my hair with my fingers in front of my mirror and did not turn round.

"So?" he said after a fairly prolonged silence. "You're not going to argue with me?"

I could have kissed him, I was so touched by his dove-like simplicity.

"Argue with you?" I threw over my shoulder. "Why should I do that?"

"So you agree with me?"

"Absolutely! And with all my heart! Dame Gertrude has such an angelic face that Satan himself wouldn't dare harm her. Her voice, her eyes, her hair, her body—everything about her is entirely alluring. And she has more goodness in her little finger than in the longest of papist sermons. In short, she's a flower, she is. So of course I approve of the fact that, straightaway, you begin tearing off her petals one by one, throwing them on the ground and stamping on them."

"You're joking!" he blurted out in a strangled voice. "You're making a jest of my feelings! And while you make light of it, my soul hangs in the balance!"

"Ha!" I said as I looked at his pale and defeated features in the mirror. "Your salvation, is it? Your great concern for your own interests is more important than your lady's pain?"

At that he seemed completely undone, and started pacing aimlessly around the room, sighing inconsolably.

"Ah," he groaned, "I see that you don't approve of me."

"'Sblood! You're mistaken! I entirely approve of your murderous ways. You used her for your pleasure, and now you're strangling her. Kill, by God, kill!"

"What would you do if you were me?"

"Am I such a monster that I would accept to be in your shoes?"

"Be reasonable! Tell me what to do!"

"Would I reason with a mule?"

"Oh, my brother," he said, impatiently pushing me away—something I'd never seen him do before, "don't make light of this! I'm neither a monster nor a mule, but a Christian who must think about his salvation."

"I'm also thinking about your salvation. But as for me, I'd never have such outrageous arrogance as to second-guess my sovereign judge."

This brought him up short and seemed to leave him wracked by doubt and perplexity.

"But," he said weakly, "the law says hell is promised to all who fornicate."

"The Lord is above the law, since He made it."

"But, my Pierre, are we to sidestep all thought of sin?"

"As for me, if the Lord wants to throw me into the flames because I love my mistress, let Him do it. You only burn once!"

"Oh no!" he cried, his beautiful face twisted in distress. "The tortures of the damned last for all eternity."

"In that case I will be reborn from my ashes and get roasted all over again. I am no coward."

At the word "coward" he looked quite surprised and then his face darkened dramatically, but he didn't make a sound and stood looking at me, his gaze so pure and tender that I felt terribly sorry for him as I buttoned my doublet.

"Wait! Where are you going?" he gasped.

"To throw myself at Dame Gertrude's feet and ask her forgiveness for your hateful cruelty"—he shuddered to hear this—"and tell her that I love her like a brother, but would be disposed to love her otherwise if she were so disposed."

"*What?*" he cried, entirely beside himself. "You would do such a thing?"

"Certainly. If an ignorant savage from the East Indies found a pearl in an oyster and, having no idea of its value, threw it into the dust of the road, what would keep me from going to pick it up?"

"My brother," he yelled, "you would break my heart!"

"You don't have a heart!" I threw back at him, yelling even louder. "Oh, Samson, how can you bear the thought that, at this very moment, this noble and sweet lady, her beautiful hair strewn carelessly over her shoulders, is crying hot tears at the thought of having lost you?"

Her "beautiful strewn hair" carried the day, for I watched him rush about his room like a madman, return with his doublet, which he was drawing on any which way, and bolt down the stairs, his ruff in his hand.

"'Sblood, where are you rushing off to? Wait for me, I'll follow you!"

"Oh no, you won't!" said Fogacer, ripping open the door of his room and emerging into the hallway in his rumpled black robes, his long spider-like arms extended to block my passage. "No, no, my dear Siorac! You're not going to follow your pretty Samson along the path you used so much fraternal cleverness to set him onto." (So he'd heard everything from his room...) "You've got many more fish to fry than the ones you're chasing after. No thread through the eye of the needle this afternoon, my son! And as for the needle itself, which you seem to have such a strident appetite for, your religion would prefer that she be *aut formosa minus aut improba minus*."*

"*Improba!*" I returned, stung by this insult.

"That's what your minister would say, not I, who, being less austere"—and at these words he laughed heartily, raising his diabolical eyebrow—"absolve you of all sin in this matter. Allow me, however, Siorac, to tear you away from these beautiful needlepoints where you risk pricking your finger"—he laughed again—"in order to lead you to a person of the male sex who's got a beard, snubbed nose, bony

* "Either less beautiful or less impure" (Ovid).

187

forehead, short legs, fat belly and stumpy arms—not a handsome man to be sure, but one who could nevertheless say of himself, *ingenio formae damna rependo meae.** In short, one of the most illustrious doctors of the kingdom and, what's more, one of the best."

"Rondelet!" I cried, overcome with joy, and hardly able to believe my ears, so great was the honour he was doing me. "Rondelet has asked to see me!"

"*Ipse,*"† replied Fogacer, with his left hand placed elegantly on his hip, his interminable right arm sketching an ample gesture. "*Gulielmus Rondeletius, venerandus doctor medicus et medecinae, professor regis et cancellarius in schola Monspeliensi.*"‡

"But isn't he a Huguenot? How is it that I didn't see him at the temple this morning?"

"He has been very ill for three days with a stomach ulcer and terrible headaches. Nevertheless, having felt somewhat better towards noon today, he asked to meet you before he leaves for Bordeaux."

"What? He's leaving? Before he's fully recovered? On such a long, uncomfortable and perilous journey?"

"I agree, it's pure folly! But Rondelet is a man of infinite goodness and his two brothers-in-law have been asking him for the last three months to come to straighten out their affairs, so he's decided to go."

Saying this, Fogacer took me by the arm and led me towards the street, whose paving stones were already burning hot, though the sun wasn't yet at its zenith.

"Siorac," he said, "you're walking like a country bumpkin, too fast. In the city, you have to stroll, looking here and there, studying and enjoying the spectacle of street life, not losing a single detail of the shops, the carriages or the passers-by. Isn't this a pleasant spectacle

---

*　　"I make up for my lack of beauty by the gifts of my mind."

†　　"The very man."

‡　　"Guillaume Rondelet, venerable doctor of medicine, chancellor and professor at the Royal College of Medicine of Montpellier."

with all these people coming and going, of different ages and conditions, each one thinking about his own business? Ah, humanity is so beautiful and diverse, and since we are humans we should treasure it and study it diligently, beginning with our mortal bodies, each of which is, in itself, a world that we're only now beginning to explore. And if we hope to assuage some of the innumerable ills that assail it, shouldn't we begin with the study of it? Have you read Rondelet's memorable *Methodus ad curandorum omnium morborum corporis humani,** which I gave you the notes for?"

"I've read and memorized the book *De morbo italico.*"†

Fogacer burst out laughing so loudly that all the passers-by turned to look at us, so he went on, but in Latin: "Young and brilliant Siorac! My young friend, you're brilliant, but your brilliance is deflected towards Venus even in your studies! And you're starting to look right where the shoe risks pinching you the most. That's good! Rondelet will want me to test you in front of him."

"Test me?"

He laughed and continued in French: "Don't worry! A few little questions. It won't be an exam or a debate."

I fell silent and, for the rest of the walk, thought excitedly about meeting such a great man, whom I placed far above the Vicomte de Joyeuse, because the doctor possessed the knowledge and skill to heal his fellow men, not to kill them. I was so nervous about the idea that Fogacer would be grilling me in front of such a great doctor that I didn't even notice the profusion of skirts in the streets, but walked with my eyes on the pavement trying to recall what I'd learnt about syphilis—or, as Rondelet called it, "the Italian disease"—not a very gracious label for our friends on the other side of the Alps. And, despite the painstaking work, I was glad I had copied *On Syphilis* line by line,

---

*   *The Method for Curing All the Sicknesses of the Human Body.*

†   *On Syphillis.*

according to Fogacer's notes, since this learned treatise, despite being well regarded among the wisest doctors in the kingdom, hadn't yet found a publisher, printing costs being so high and the audience for such a book being so uncertain.

Rondelet's house was situated in the rue du Bout-du-monde—"end of the world" being a strange name for a street in the very centre of Montpellier. It was also situated conveniently close to the Royal College of Medicine where the chancellor taught. It was a beautiful dwelling, with mullioned windows and a little tower, in which a spiral staircase gave access to the upper floors.

As Fogacer stepped up to knock at the door, I ventured to observe, "Judging by his mansion, our chancellor must be very well-to-do."

"Indeed," replied Fogacer with a smile. "And would be even more so, if he weren't obsessed by demolishing and rebuilding, changing square shapes into round ones, *quadrata rotundis*—squaring the circle—or vice versa. So this little round tower you see used to be square, but our chancellor had it knocked down at great expense and rebuilt it round for his particular pleasure. He affects a great love of everything round, including women and their finer parts."

At this description, I knew I would like this man, and, indeed, when I saw him, although he was still recovering from a serious illness, I wasn't disappointed. Fogacer had already provided an excellent portrait, saying that he had "short legs, fat belly and stumpy arms". I immediately understood that Maître François Rabelais had used his appearance to describe the doctor Rondibilis in his *Third Book of Pantagruel*. Indeed, it wasn't just his body that was round, but his very features, or as much as one could see of them, for a long grey beard hid the lower third of his face. And yet his ample forehead, twinkling dark eyes, full lips, robust neck and warm bass voice all appealed to me.

"Fogacer," he said, "no compliments, please! Have a seat, and you too, Siorac, and let's talk. Siorac, I did not have the honour of meeting your father since I was not in Montpellier when he was a student here and didn't return until after he'd left under the unhappy circumstances I'm sure you're familiar with. Doubtless you know that he was accused of murder, although everyone knew that he'd only acted in self-defence after a minor nobleman had provoked him to a duel. But everything I've heard from Maître Sanche about your father indicates he was an ardent student and an ardent lover—exactly what I've heard about you! Which is why I was so anxious to make your acquaintance and discover what you know about medicine."

I began to thank him profusely but the chancellor stopped me with a wave of his hand and, settling into a capacious armchair, he eyed me with a most encouraging—yet also very penetrating—look.

"Siorac," he said, "I see you have the inquisitive and restless eyes of a squirrel, who, snatching up here and there a thousand different things, lays them up as provender in his nest. So I don't doubt that someday you shall become what François Rabelais recommended us all to be: 'an abyss of science'." (Here he laughed.) "However, I see that your mouth is presently more full of questions than provender that your good manners prevent you from asking. Go ahead, Siorac, be my guest! Satisfy the squirrel in you. However, I'm going to ask you to make a choice, which I consider most illuminating: of all the questions pressing on the back of your teeth, you must choose but one, and to that one and *only* to that one I shall respond."

"Monsieur Rondelet, here is my question. Were you, in fact, the model on which François Rabelais based the character of Rondibilis?"

"Siorac," parried the chancellor, "are you a good swordsman?"

"Not bad, and I'd be better if my defence were as good as my attack."

"That's exactly what I would have guessed from listening to you," smiled Rondelet. "In order to discover my position, you've uncovered too much of your own."

At this, Fogacer let out a quick laugh and arched his black eyebrows.

"Here is my analysis of your character," announced Rondelet. "*Primo*, you're a man of instinct and possessed of a generous disposition. *Secundo*, you walk through life with your head held high, giving and taking the blows that come your way. *Tertio*, you have great confidence in yourself, which is good, though you have an equal amount of confidence in others, which is not very prudent. *Quarto*, your curiosity about people overrides your curiosity about things."

"Ha ha!" laughed Fogacer. "You've said a mouthful, my friend."

"Monsieur Rondelet," I replied, "I'm not sure I understand your fourth point."

"Well, then, here it is: since you, by my orders, had but one question you could ask, you might have asked me some very ticklish question about medicine. Instead you preferred to get to know me better."

At this I blushed and remained silent, having no idea whether this was intended as criticism or praise.

"Fogacer," the chancellor continued, "take this stool and fetch me from the top shelf on the right my copy of *The Third Book* by François Rabelais, whom I knew quite well, for I was, in the bloom of my youth, in the same position in relation to him that Fogacer is today in relation to you. I was an advanced student and the procurator of the students when Rabelais, then in his forty-second year, came to enrol in our Royal College. And although I was his junior by four years, we became best friends and companions in feasting and drinking, and had many learned discussions and other entertainments at the Golden Cross tavern in Montpellier. A greater *joie de vivre* I never saw and I would call him very nearly divine for the love he bore humanity."

"Master, here is your Rabelais," said Fogacer, handing the volume to Rondelet, who, taking it on his lap, saw the book fall open to the same passage that, these last twenty years, its owner had so often reread.

"Siorac," the chancellor continued, "you will remember that Panurge was going around asking everyone if, when he married, he'd be a cuckold. In response, the doctor, whom Rabelais named Rondibilis—ah, here it is—says yes, and opines that it is the common fate of any man who takes a wife. Here's the end of the chapter, which I'll read to you:

> "Panurge approached Rondibilis and silently placed four gold pieces in his hand. The doctor took them easily enough but then said with great surprise, 'Oh no, no, no, Monsieur! You didn't need to pay me a thing. But, great thanks anyway. From the wicked I never accept anything. But I never refuse anything offered by good people. I am at your service.'
>
> "'But only if I pay,' said Panurge.
>
> "'Of course!' said Rondibilis."

Rondelet closed *The Third Book* and, with his two hands resting on his stomach, asked, "Well, what do you think, Siorac? Is this Rondibilis me?"

I was brought up short by this question, as you could well imagine, and was plunged into complete confusion, unable to pronounce either way, and wishing I were a thousand leagues away. But, as Rondelet had observed, I have a lively temperament, and before you could count to five, and without thinking what I was doing, I'd leapt to my feet, drawn my sword and cried, "Ah, what treachery is this? You're playing with fixed dice! You answer my question with a question!"

"Touché!" answered Rondelet, laughing.

Fogacer, too, was laughing.

"God in heaven, Fogacer, this young recruit fences well! Did you notice how well he parried my thrust and counter-attacked?"

Laughing uproariously, he continued, "But since you won this round, my lively young friend, I'm going to provide an honest response to your question: this Rondibilis with his four gold pieces is not me, but some cagey, hypocritical and dishonest doctor, like so many of our profession, interested only in gold while pretending not to be. But if you were to portray me, it would have to be in a very different way. Rabelais would have had to change the doctor's words to: 'I'll never take a sol from the poor, / It's the rich who will pay more and more!' Is this true, Fogacer?"

"'Tis God's truth, Monsieur," Fogacer replied with some emotion. "You've always cared for the poor for no fee and are, in this, a model for our entire art."

Hearing this, I blushed to have had such an unflattering opinion of Monsieur Rondelet and was upset with Rabelais for having compromised the reputation of his friend from college days.

"But here's another passage from the divine Rabelais," said Rondelet, opening the book at another place.

"Aha!" I thought. "Divine! He called him divine! In his heart he must have forgiven him."

"In this passage, Rabelais has Rondibilis say the following about women and their physical nature:

"Nature placed in a secret place inside their bodies an animal that is not found inside men, and which engenders salty, nitrous, pungent, biting, piercing, bitterly ticklish humours whose pricking and vibration (for this member is very nervous and quite sensitive) upsets their entire body, ravishes their senses and confuses their minds. If nature hadn't also endowed them with a sense of shame, you'd see them running amok like criminals."

"Oh, Monsieur Rondelet!" I laughed. "I understand! Rondelet and Rondibilis are the same after all and Rabelais has Rondibilis expressing your thoughts!"

"Very good! You understood perfectly," said the chancellor. "But, when you think about it, what do you think this character is saying?"

"That the two sexes are, in this respect, equals: man also harbours an animal inside his body and this animal is also pungent, biting and ticklish, and seeks exactly what you were just saying."

Hearing this, the chancellor, raising his arms heavenward, cried, "*Crede illi experto Roberto!*"*

And looking at each other, the chancellor and I burst out laughing again.

"Ah, Siorac, I like you! You're just the sort of funny and hardworking son I would have wanted to comfort me and lighten my old age. Alas, my first wife died. And so did the daughter she bore me and whom I'd been able to marry off to Dr Salomon d'Assas. And as for the four sons I had from my two marriages, the Lord has called them back to Him one after the other."

Rondelet's head fell to his chest after he said this, and he was overcome with sadness. Astonished to see him pass so quickly from hilarity to sorrow, I maintained a respectful silence, and Fogacer gave me a quick look to let me know that this would soon pass. And, indeed, Rondelet suddenly sat up in his chair with an "Umph!", squared his shoulders as if ready to take on the world and opened his eyes, which flashed with energy and combativeness.

"Siorac," since you're taking a little informal exam for me, here, before enrolling in our illustrious college, I'm going to ask you a difficult question: twenty years ago, my second son having died of the same strange and unknown sickness that had carried off his elder brother, I sent my wife, my daughters and my servants off to our

---

* "Trust him, for he has the requisite experience!"

country home and remained here alone with the body of my poor little son, and dissected him."

"Oh, Monsieur," I cried, overcome with the memory of how, after little Hélix had died, my father had sawed off the top of her skull to determine the cause of her death. "What great courage it took to do such a thing!"

"The greatest," sighed Rondelet, his eyes full of tears. "And all the more since, to educate my more timid fellow physicians, I published what I had done. A great clamour arose against me, *urbi et orbi*,* and I was assailed by a hailstorm from those you would expect, a host of libels and hateful pamphlets, which continue to this day, in which I was called a pagan, a Turk, a blasphemer... Well, Siorac, what do you think? Did I do the right thing or the wrong thing? Speak without fear of offending me and in the sincerity of your heart. But don't just say yes or no: make your arguments and present them in order."

"Ah, Monsieur," I cried. "I've already thought it all out. You did the right thing and there are two reasons why. *Primo*, since your second son died of the same symptoms as the first, you had to discover the causes of this death to protect your third son."

"But, alas," sighed Rondelet, "I didn't succeed. He died too."

"But at least you tried to save him by attempting to find the cause of his illness. *Secundo*, by publishing the dissection of your son that you'd performed in the secrecy of your lodgings, you wanted to demonstrate that, as painful as this was for you, it was necessary. And so you struggled, in the teeth of considerable risk to your person and your reputation, against the unreasonable interdicts of the papists."

"Excellent!" cried Rondelet. "Well thought-out, well supported and well argued. Fogacer, we're going to make a handsome doctor out of this young man from Périgord."

"So I believe," agreed Fogacer.

---

*   "In the city and in the world."

"But let us continue," said Rondelet, rubbing his hands in excitement. "Siorac, a few more questions. In what year and by whom was the medical amphitheatre in Montpellier founded?"

"In 1556, Monsieur, by yourself and the doctors Schyron, Saporta and Bocaud."

"Which of these doctors belong to the reformed religion?"

"All of them, yourself included."

"And is there a connection between the foundation of this *theatrum anatomicum* and our religious affiliation?"

"Certainly!" I said with some heat. "In their practice of free examination, the doctors in question placed themselves above the prejudices of the priests of secular superstition."

"*Bene, bene.*" So saying, he rubbed his hands together more vigorously, as happy with my answers as if I'd been his son, so much did he already like me. And this feeling was certainly mutual since he was a man of such good-naturedness, wisdom and love of humanity.

"Fogacer," he continued, "I cannot myself imbibe, given my recent illness, but please offer a glass of muscat to this young scholar and help yourself as well."

"Great thanks!" replied Fogacer. "It's very hot and I'm exceedingly thirsty."

Like a long black insect, he leapt up on his long legs, filled two goblets from a bottle on the table, handed me mine and then drank his slowly but in one continuous draught. "Not a bad wine," he said, smacking his lips.

Rondelet smiled, visibly happy at the pleasure that we were taking and that he was denied: "My son-in-law, Dr d'Assas, has a very pretty vineyard near Frontignan, and gives me two barrels each year. But serve yourself another, drink up! Don't sit there thirsting for this excellent muscat!"

"A thousand thanks," said Fogacer, who didn't need to be prodded. He offered me a second glass as well, but I refused, wanting to keep a clear head for the rest of my exam. Fogacer raised his goblet high in the air and said with great pomp, "*Ad maximam gloriam domini d'Assasii et venerandi cancellarii nostrae collegiae regis.*"*

"Amen!" added Rondelet.

And standing there on his interminable legs, Fogacer poured this precious velvet down his throat. "Monsieur," he said, his eyes sparkling, perhaps aided by the wine, "as I stand before you as the only representative in this house—though unworthy and of little faith—of the Holy Roman Catholic Church, I would like to remind the two Huguenots here present that Pope Boniface VIII allowed, as early as 1300, the practice of dissection by some doctors in Rome and Boulogne."

"*Ab uno non disce omnes,*"† replied Rondelet, making a gesture as if to swat away a swarm of flies. "What does one Pope's generosity mean if two and a half centuries later a swarm of priests continue to pester us? Siorac, have you drunk your thirst? Shall we continue?"

"I am at your command, Monsieur."

"Fogacer," said Rondelet, "did you give him your notes on my *Methodus ad curandorum omnium morborum?*"

"Indeed I did, and though he's only arrived very recently, he has diligently studied your treatise on syphilis."

"Holy of holies!" exclaimed Rondelet, laughing. "This rascal is prudent and is well advised to consider the dangers he risks in sowing his seed to all winds! So, Siorac, please, no frowns! I'm not preaching at you. Just a little fatherly joke."

"Which is how I understand it, Monsieur."

---

* "To the greater glory of Monsieur d'Assas and of the venerable chancellor of the Royal College!"

† "From one example we don't know all of them."

"So, let's move on and see to what profit you've put my study of syphilis. Siorac, is syphilis a dry, cold inclemency?"

"On the contrary, Monsieur, that is the grave mistake made by the learned Montan. Syphilis is, rather, a hot and humid inclemency."

"*Bene, bene.* And is its origin, as many doctors claim, in the conjunction between Mars and Venus?"

"Excuse me, Monsieur, but that's pure astrological fantasy. It's absurd and without any foundation whatsoever."

"Does one contract this disease by breathing it in?"

"No, by venereal contact. The infected person only infects another by a *liqueur* that flows from one part of the body to another body. Though the infection can also be spread by infected linen."

"How do we recognize this disease?"

"After intercourse, the phallus is covered with pustules, pimples and ulcers."

"And how does one guard against syphilis if one suspects he has had intercourse with an infected person?"

"By purgation and bleeding."

"What is the principle of this cure?"

"Since the disease comes from repletion, it will be cured *primo* by depletion: enema, purgation and bleeding." At this point, out of the corner of my eye I noticed that Fogacer was frowning and looking unhappy, as though he doubted these remedies.

"And *secundo?*"

"One must apply to these ulcers sublimated quicksilver, and have the patient take aloe pills so that the aloe can cure the disease from inside by drying it out."

"Should ointments be used?"

"Yes, derived from pig grease and quicksilver."

"Though," corrected Fogacer, "Maître Sanche has replaced the pig grease with chicken grease."

"It works just as well," smiled Rondelet, "and is surely more acceptable to our worthy chemist. But let's move on. If the syphilis patient complains of terrible headaches, what should be done?"

"He should be given theriacal water to drink."

"What should be done if the ulcers are large and putrid?"

"Sublimated mercury should be applied, since it is an active agent against that which is rotten."

"What relief can be given to patients who cannot remain at home but must go about their business on horseback?"

"Give them mercurial pills."

"Wonderful!" exclaimed Rondelet throwing open his arms from his wide body. "You've got it all, learnt it so quickly! Fogacer, if by St Luke's Day in October your pupil has satisfied your expectations in philosophy and logic, then you may enrol him in the Royal College. *Dignus est intrare.*"*

"Oh, Monsieur," I cried, blushing to the roots of my hair from happiness, "how can I thank you?"

"You don't owe me any thanks. Your merit alone is responsible for this decision. Monsieur scholar," he said, pronouncing for the first time my new title, which made my heart beat even faster, "have you thought of a choice for your doctor-father among the four professors of the college?"

"But, Monsieur," I blurted out, forgetting in the heat of the moment Fogacer's advice, "may I not ask you to serve in that role for the duration of my studies?"

"You should not make this request," said Rondelet, suddenly growing sad and looking at me gravely. "I am old and infirm, my stomach is wrecked by some disease and, stricken with fever, I am growing weaker every day and, alas, near the end of the skein the fates have woven for me."

---

* "He has earned his entry."

"And yet," cried Fogacer with some heat, "you're leaving tomorrow for Bordeaux! Monsieur, this is madness! I've told you a hundred times!"

"Easy now, don't scold me, Fogacer," said Rondelet, "my brothers-in-law badly need my help."

"What about you? Don't you need it?"

"Ah, my friend, to die there or somewhere else… If I were master of my destiny I wouldn't raise my little finger to prolong my life by a year. I've suffered abominably in my personal life, devastated by more losses than the face of a hanged man is by pecks of the crow. Death has ravished too many of my family, dismembering me alive, taking such beautiful children. And all I dream of today is to be reunited with them in heaven, if the Lord in His pity allows me in. I've lived long enough on this earth."

At this Fogacer fell silent, feeling, I guessed, as I did, his throat knot up to hear such melancholy. But Rondelet, seeing our discomfort, managed a smile and, recovering the glint in his eye, he said to me, "Siorac, take Dr Saporta for your doctor-father. He's not an easy man to get along with," he laughed, "but he's an excellent physician, exact and diligent in discharging his duties."

"Monsieur," I replied, "I shall do as you bid me."

Having arranged this, and being no doubt fatigued by the interview and the many preparations for his voyage to Bordeaux, Rondelet rose from his chair with some difficulty, and gave us our leave, after embracing each of us tenderly.

"Siorac," he said, placing his hands on my shoulders, "listen carefully: the practice of medicine should never forget study. All your life you should study. Engrave this word 'study' in your brain with a golden pen. It will only be through unceasing and indefatigable effort that we will vanquish one after another the diseases that kill us and ravish our loved ones. But remember, too, not to overdo it. Don't work to the point of wearing out your brain. You are a man and will retain your vitality if you exercise all of your faculties, and I mean *all* of them: mental, corporal and erotic. But for these last," he added with a delightful smile, "I'm sure you don't need urging. *Vale, mi fili.*"* And embracing me one last time, he sent me on my way.

"Siorac," said Fogacer, with a long face as we walked along through the crushing heat of the Provençal sun, "think about Rondelet's example: if you cherish a wench, don't marry her! She'll die in childbirth and your children in their youth. Maître Sanche, as great a pharmacist as he is, has lost, despite his great knowledge of cures, two wives, and of the ten children they've given him, only four have survived. As for Rondelet, of his seven children, five are no longer with us. This is our miserable lot on this earth: whoever marries gives hostages to death. Adieu, Siorac, I see there's no use in sermonizing you—you love women too much, and with too much tenderness. You will suffer greatly."

This said, he abruptly turned on his heels and walked away, leaving me quite astonished at his mood. But what should we do? Should we live like monks because of the frailty of women, and have no children because they might die in the bloom of their youth? We are all going to die and are headed to death from our swaddling clothes on, though no one thinks about mourning when he's young. Long after my student days, I heard Michel de Montaigne tell me in his library, "I lost two or three children when they were still nursing—not without regret, but without anger." That Michel de Montaigne didn't even know the exact number of children he'd lost really surprised me. And that he learnt "without anger" of their passing recalled by contrast the bitter tears that Rondelet wept at the loss of his three sons, so quickly and so early gone to their maker. I'm not trying to make a parallel between them. Montaigne was a philosopher, and as such, for better or for worse, managed to detach himself from human events. If he'd been a philosopher, Rondelet wouldn't have chosen to

* "Be well, my son!"

spend his life struggling against death, which is the lot of the doctor, and, I believe, his honour.

Coming back to Fogacer's bitter advice, I still found it very strange, and would have thought more about it, had not Miroul suddenly appeared at my side as if out of the ground.

"Well, Miroul," I said, "is it really you? What are you doing strolling around the rue de l'Espazerie?"

"Monsieur," he replied without turning his head, "step into the next shop; I need to speak with you without anyone seeing or hearing us."

I did as he requested, and found myself in an enormous shop in which knives, swords and daggers were for sale. Behind a counter, two assistants were busy with customers, and other customers were waiting to be served—there was so much demand for weaponry in these troubled times. I got in line, and Miroul stood just behind me.

"Monsieur," he whispered, "you were followed from the pharmacy to the rue Bout-du-monde by a beggar who looked very desperate and bloodthirsty. He waited for you the entire time you were visiting there, hidden in an entryway. When you came out, he followed you all the way here. Here's your short sword, which I've wrapped in your coat. Take it without revealing what it is."

"You're a marvel!" I said, taking the coat and its contents. "Now I feel less naked. Tell me, Miroul," I said over my shoulder, "should I confront this man here and now?"

"No!" he urged. "There are too many people in this street. He might take advantage of the crowd to flee." And then, looking me in the eye with his brown eye twinkling and his blue eye cold as ice, he said, "Monsieur, are you heading to the needle shop?"

"I might be…"

"Confront this beggar in the alley. It's deserted. I'll be behind him, dagger in hand. This way, when you confront him, he won't be able to get away and we'll take him dead or alive."

"Alive, Miroul, alive! I want to know who's put him up to this!"

After Miroul departed, I left in my turn, gripping the sword under my left arm, and pretended to be deep in thought, my nose in the air as if lost or just gaping at the scenery. But I managed to look around a bit, and caught sight of my shadow; strange to say, I recognized him, though I couldn't for the life of me remember where I'd seen him.

I headed towards the needle shop, which I intended to reach not by the rue du Bayle or from the side of the Saint-Firmin church, but, as Miroul had suggested, through the narrow, winding alley that led to the back entrance.

The closer I got to my destination, the fewer passers-by there were, until, as I neared the shop, I found myself alone in the street, gripped the sword with my right hand and pricked up my ears for any sound behind me, guessing that my man was wearing some sort of matted sandals.

I was so tense that, with the midday sun, I was sweating profusely when I reached the little alley, and, following its curve, I turned my head just enough to see my assailant at the corner, only a dozen or so paces from me. I don't know whether it was my imagination that misled me, but I felt, or thought I sensed, that he was going to attack me, and so, suddenly turning, I shouted as menacingly as I could, "Halt, you rascal! What are you doing following me around?"

The beggar was completely taken by surprise; he stopped dead about ten paces from me and stared at me with his little black eyes, which seemed more taunting than menacing. This done, he very civilly removed the dirty cap covering his dusty hair and said: "Monsieur, begging your pardon, but I have orders to kill you."

"'Sblood!" I said, amazed to be confronted by such a polite assassin. "And with what?"

"With this, Monsieur," said the beggar, taking from beneath his rags a heavy cutlass.

"And what do you think of this?" I countered, pulling my sword from its sheath. "I think I've got more reach than you."

"Sorry! But no," said the man, "again begging your pardon, but your sword will be no use. I don't use my knife in a mano-a-mano. I throw it. Before you can take a step, you'll have it sticking from your gut."

This said, he took his knife by the point, as if to throw it. I won't deny that I was now sweating from head to foot, but my distress didn't paralyse my tongue.

"You knave," I said, "if you throw your knife, you won't have it to defend you, and my valet, Miroul, who's right behind you, will plant his dagger in your back."

Unfortunately, I was lying, for as desperately as I sought to catch sight of him, I couldn't see a trace of the rascal. However, at the name of my valet, my assassin pricked up his ears, raised an eyebrow and without even turning round to check whether I was telling the truth, said, "Miroul, isn't he the rogue with one blue eye and one brown eye?"

"That's the one!"

"Aha, Monsieur! I thought so! I know him! And you too! You're the gentleman who wounded me in the Corbières, captured me, and then saved me from the rope."

"Espoumel!" I cried, infinitely relieved. "It's really you? What are you doing here?"

"Monsieur," explained Espoumel, resheathing his knife under his rags and speaking with a certain swagger, "I'm not going to kill you: my honour forbids it."

Just at that moment, running up behind him, Miroul arrived, dagger in hand, sweaty and out of breath. "Oh, Monsieur Pierre, thank God you're all right! I had to put a lackey in his place back there, who wanted to fight me since I bumped him as I ran by."

"Put away your dagger, Miroul," I laughed, resheathing my own weapon. "This assassin is a friend. He calls himself Espoumel."

Miroul opened his unmatched eyes very wide, but I didn't give him much time to enjoy his surprise, for I took my Corbières bandit by the arm and invited him to take refreshment in the needle shop, where Azaïs served each of us a large goblet of wine, before going to fetch Thomassine, for I wanted her to witness our conversation. And it was lucky I did, for without her, I wouldn't have been able to clear things up.

Espoumel, who now sported a thick beard, and was tall and as thin as Good Friday, had eyes and mouth only for his wine, which he drank in little sips, appearing to think it quite normal that his victim should be offering him a drink. As for me, as concerned as I was by the present adventure, I couldn't help following Azaïs's every step as she left the kitchen, her body undulating like a snake and displaying her modest but very appetizing charms. But I also remembered my mistakes at the Two Angels inn in Toulouse, when Franchou was very put out by my dalliance with the innkeeper, and I didn't doubt that the same difficulties would ensue with Thomassine if my hands followed my eyes with her maid. But I suddenly became aware that Miroul's blue-brown gaze had followed the same path as mine, and that he continued to watch with a mix of pleasure and intensity the door through which Azaïs would re-enter the kitchen. I decided it would not sit well with my valet if I robbed him of his portion, and that today's chicken was worth much more than tomorrow's egg, and that wanting both risked losing both.

Azaïs returned, now eclipsed by her beautiful mistress, her luxuriant hair falling loose on her shoulders, looking all pink and blooming from her siesta. I told her what had happened, a tale that cast a dark shadow over her sunny disposition. Turning to my would-be assassin, I said, "Espoumel, now that you've enjoyed your wine, tell me who commanded you to kill me and why."

"The why part," said Espoumel, wiping his mouth on his sleeve, "I couldn't tell you. But the churl who ordered me to do it I know very well. The day after you captured me, I fled with him from the Corbières hills, fearing the wrath of our captain if he suspected us of having cheated him."

"Well now, what a pack of wolves! But what are two good fellows like you doing in Montpellier?"

"My friend knows some sweetmeat from whom he was going to get a few 'subsidies'. But she threw him out penniless last Friday, so he went and killed a peddler who was connected to her and took his purse."

"Nasty business."

"I'll say! Worse than nasty!" replied Espoumel, shaking his head over his wine. "And all the more so since the take was small and quickly drunk up. 'Tis a pity to kill for so little."

"Well, there wasn't much in my student's purse either, Espoumel. Why me? Why was I next?"

"Monsieur, I know not, except that my companion swore that there'd be a huge reward if you disappeared."

"How much?"

"Upon my life, I don't know," said Espoumel, putting both hands on the table and looking intently at the bottle of wine.

I wouldn't have got anything more out of him if Thomassine hadn't entered the lists at this point, her helmet lowered and her lance levelled at her opponent. "Espoumel, what's the name of your partner?"

"Doña, I dare not tell."

"Are you hungry, Espoumel?"

"Hungry, Doña? You'd better believe it! I could eat this goblet after drinking the wine, if you gave it to me."

"I'll give it to you, believe me, and a capon with it that I roasted yesterday that's waiting in my larder. Would you like a taste?"

"Would I like a taste, Doña?" said Espoumel, saliva flowing from his lips, his eyes fastened on the bottle.

"His name, Espoumel?"

"Le Dentu."

"Aha!" cried Thomassine. "Le Dentu! That's exactly what I would have thought! Azaïs, go and get that capon and serve it up to our friend here. So, it's Le Dentu…"

"Le Dentu," I said. "Is that his real name?"

"No one knows his real name, not even he does. But the beggar's got teeth, and beautiful teeth at that. Teeth that will chew up anything you give him. I know this man, my Pierre. When I arrived here from the Cévennes mountains, almost dying from hunger, as thin as a needle, Le Dentu was my pimp and introduced me to sin. He was with me for two years and certainly I loved him. But he was a drunk and a brutal rowdy and was interested only in my take. So I kicked him out as soon as I met Cossolat, whom he was very afraid of, since he'd robed and killed many people. So Le Dentu headed for the Corbières hills, where he's spent the last eight years or so, and last Thursday he suddenly reappeared. Espoumel, I'm the 'sweetmeat' from whom he was going to get some 'subsidies' and who'd kicked him out."

"Doña," corrected Espoumel, his mouth full of capon, "I'm a polite man, I am. Never called you a 'sweetmeat'—that's not me!"

"What do I care?" laughed Thomassine, her shoulders rocking with mirth. "I am what I am and not ashamed of it. What's more, now that I have enough money, I no longer sell my wares. I offer them to whom I please. And my love along with them," she said, throwing me a tender glance.

"Thank you, my good Thomassine," I said, rising from my stool and giving her a kiss on her crimson lips. "I'm grateful for your love and I return it."

"Ah, gentle liar!" she breathed as she returned ten kisses for my one, and ran her plump fingers through my hair. "You're sweet and courteous, like a good Périgordian lad. But I don't believe you! At least you're not like these bastards who piss in the well after drinking from it."

At which Miroul's brown eye twinkled while his blue eye remained cold as ice.

"But, Madame," said Azaïs, who enjoyed a degree of familiarity with her mistress I'd never seen before in a chambermaid, "that's all well and good, but doesn't explain why Le Dentu wanted to murder our gentleman."

"Oh yes it does!" rejoined Thomassine. "I know the cad! He viewed Siorac as a rival and reasoned that once he got rid of him he could get his hands on me and my money."

So finally everything was clear, and, as everyone fell silent, Azaïs sat up on the table and dangled her legs invitingly, something that, naturally, caught my eye, but, since I had killed that chick as soon as it had hatched, I kept on the straight and narrow. But Miroul was clearly heading right for the trap and the sight of it made me happy, since it would be convenient if the valet were to find pasturage in the same field where his masters sowed their oats. If, that is, I could refer to Dame Gertrude du Luc as "oats", since at that very moment she was in a room above offering her ambrosia to my beloved Samson. "Oh, my brother!" I mused. "Give in to your pleasure without a thought or worry in the world! How can you possibly believe that our divine master, who has so prodigally bestowed on us the grains and flowers of the fields, could have been so niggardly as to deprive us of such brief pleasures in our short lives?"

But a knowing look from Thomassine tore me from my reverie and abruptly brought my attention back to our Corbières bandit. "Espoumel," I said, as I watched him devour his capon, grease dripping from the corners of his mouth, "you tried to kill me once in the mountains, and again here in town. Twice is too much! What are we going to do with you?"

"Hang me," said our brigand, as he lapped up his wine with little pensive sips. "It had to come to that. He who one day mocks the hangman's noose will wear it the next and it won't be loose. And may God have pity on him! It's poverty that led me to robbing and killing in the Corbières hills. If I'd been a girl I would have had to live by my skirt. As a boy I learnt to live by the sword. May the Lord Jesus Christ pardon me and I'll die happy."

"Espoumel, you'd be happier still if you lived. If you tell me how and where to find Le Dentu, I'll ask the king to pardon you."

"You'd do that for me, Monsieur?" he gasped, half rising from his stool, his little black eyes wide with disbelief.

"Assuredly I would."

"I'll have to think about it," he said, sitting back down.

7

S ITTING IN HIS JAIL a week later, Espoumel confessed: "Ah,
Monsieur de Siorac, my honour would never have given me a
minute's peace for having told Captain Cossolat where Le Dentu was
hiding if the rascal hadn't tried to kill me three days before."

"Kill you? But why?"

"To steal from me."

So Espoumel explained that he'd kept hidden in his belt forty
sols that he'd acquired illegally, but not without some difficulty, by
stealing and reselling a *flassada*—the name given in Montpellier to a
wool blanket.

"Le Dentu," he continued, "doesn't throw a knife like I do. He
just stabs you at arm's length. So very early one morning, as I was
sleeping under one of the flying buttresses of the Saint-Firmin church,
I saw him in the shadows, creeping towards me on all fours with his
blade in his hand.

"'Friend,' I shouted, 'where are you going?'

"'I just have to piss,' he said, standing up.

"'A man who gets up this early can piss wherever he likes. Go
ahead, my friend, go right ahead. There's lots of room and I want
to go back to sleep.'"

After telling me this story, Espoumel looked at me with his beady
black eyes, and said, shaking his head, giving great weight to his words,

"My noble Monsieur, listen carefully to what I'm going to tell you. Le Dentu is a man of little conscience."

"This I believe!" said I.

But to continue my own story. Le Dentu was waiting at the Golden Cross tavern for good news from my assassin and smiling into his beer with his big teeth, thinking of the fun he'd promised himself, when, instead of Espoumel, it was Cossolat who appeared.

The beast, surprised in his lair, tried to defend himself with teeth and claws, but he'd picked the wrong adversary, for Cossolat, angry to be confronted by such a ruffian, drew his sword and split his head right down to his jaw.

This exploit grew in magnitude as the news of it spread through Montpellier, and some heard that he'd split his man from the guzzle to the zatch. It's a pretty tale, but I can attest that it's false. Fogacer collected the body for the anatomical theatre before it could be dismembered by the executioner, so I was able to examine it at my leisure and can affirm that it was only the cranium that was cut in two.

I was not sorry to hear the news, though, having no desire at all to go to court to testify against this brigand. Cossolat had even stronger reasons for not wanting Espoumel to appear in court, because he had him locked away in secret in the city prisons for as long as it would take to get him to provide information on the secret camps and caches of the Corbières brigands.

These he obtained, not by torture but by persuasion. Cossolat promised him, in the name of the Vicomte de Joyeuse, that the king would pardon him if he ratted on his former allies. Having myself developed a kind of affection for this honest scoundrel, to whom I owed my life, just as he owed me his, I visited him twice a week in his jail, bringing him provisions of meat and wine, all of which turned out to my advantage, as I shall relate.

The Vicomte de Joyeuse had every reason to be satisfied with my services, for piecing together what Espoumel had told the captain of the archers with what he had confided in me, he knew enough about the camps and caches of the Corbières brigands to mount an expedition against them that wiped them out, ensuring, at least for a time, the security of the road from Carcassonne to Narbonne, and returning peace and prosperity to his barony of Arques.

This handsome result hadn't yet been achieved when Caudebec and his *roumieux*, well rested and refreshed from six days of orgiastic feasting, had resigned themselves to leaving the Three Kings for the city of the Pope, though not before Cossolat had to intervene in a quarrel between the innkeeper and the "pilgrim", who, as I'd already had occasion to observe, didn't willingly open his purse, and was more miserly and cheap than any Norman in Normandy.

I agreed to serve as interpreter in this ugly dispute, which was long and difficult, the scales of justice having been weighted a bit unfairly, since Cossolat didn't like the baron, who had dared insult him in his own city, but did like the inn's hostess, who daily bent so willingly to his authority.

When at last everything was settled, I went looking for Samson and Dame Gertrude, who, hidden away in their little room at the needle shop, were stricken with grief at the idea of leaving the few square feet that had so happily enclosed them for six days and nights in such incredible happiness.

I found them beyond tears, pale and dazed, plunged into a deep silence, no longer knowing what else to do but hold hands in desperation and gaze at each other with love and astonishment, waiting for the knife that would soon inflict such wounds on their bodies and souls. Alas, I was to be the one to inflict that wound, since the time of the pilgrims' departure had come, and had to witness their great pain, their last desperate embrace, and then, after kissing his beloved from head to foot, Samson's flight from the shop, during which (according to Miroul) he bumped into Thomassine and Azaïs without even seeing them, and ran straight to Maître Sanche's house.

At my request, Miroul followed him, but couldn't enter his room since Samson locked himself in and threw himself on his bed, overcome with heart-rending sobs. Seeing which, Miroul went into my room, which was separated from Samson's by wooden planks and, sitting next to this wall, sang one of Barberine's lullabies to comfort his master.

For my part, I would love to have been able to flee from poor Gertrude's despair, but once Samson had left she threw herself into my arms, and cried in such a piteous voice that I could hardly restrain my own tears, "Oh, my brother! Don't leave me now, for I couldn't bear losing all of him at once! Let me keep you a minute longer, you who belong to him as I do, since I know with what great love you watch over my beautiful angel to ease his way on this earth! For my Samson tells me everything in his heavenly simplicity, so I know what torments he suffered at the idea of his terrible sin and how you dissipated his suffering. May Heaven—if I dare invoke Heaven!—thank you for your care. If Heaven won't, I will, poor sinner that I am, but is it a sin when we love another so much and would dedicate our heart, body and everything we have to our love?"

"Oh, Madame!" I pleaded. "Enough! We don't need to argue this point! Let's put ourselves in God's hands. He is good. And how could his goodness sanction the cruel punishments that threaten us in our brief instants of happiness here on earth?"

"Pierre," she said, calming considerably, "how I would love it if you could persuade me, as you've persuaded Samson! But, my brother, after my departure from Montpellier, when you'll have such great influence over your brother, are you not going to convince him in the interests of his health to lay his cares at the feet of some commonplace wench, who, despite being younger than I (though I'm hardly old enough to be his mother) would certainly not bear him the love that I do? Don't think I haven't noticed the tender looks that the little viper Azaïs gives him every time she sees him."

"Azaïs, Madame! It's not just Azaïs! All the women in God's creation would be at Samson's feet if he wished! But he loves, and will never love anybody but you, I solemnly swear to you. And as for me, I'll watch over his fidelity as carefully as I'd watch over mine if I were so lucky as to deserve your love."

"Oh, my brother," she cried, giving me a fierce hug, and covering my face with kisses, which, in the extreme emotions she was feeling, weren't perhaps entirely innocent. "You're lifting a huge weight from my heart! You know," she added with a look that pierced my heart, "I love you like a brother and much more than that. Watch over my beloved Samson and, if he doesn't do it himself since he tells me he's not good at composing letters, write to me in Rome, telling me how he's getting on, and I'll be eternally grateful!"

Thereupon, after the promise I'd made, she gave me another kiss, with such gratitude and so much tenderness that, after she'd gone, I had to sit down on a stool and cry copious tears.

"What's this?" demanded Thomassine as she entered the kitchen. "*You* in tears? This Norman lady has turned both my Périgordian boys into fountains. Pierre, are you caught up in her charms?"

"I'm not sure…"

"Or is she caught up in yours? The wave that covers one rock can, in the next breeze, cover another one. Beware, Pierre, women are like winds and tempests, no one can predict them."

But since I sat there silently, sadly looking at the ground, Thomassine said with a smile, "I see you are badly wounded. But as you are a doctor, Pierre de Siorac, you know very well that the soul can be healed by working on the body. Come along, my Pierre, let me take care of you. I have the sovereign cure for what ails you!"

Certainly of all the remedies that Monsieur Rondelet forgot to include in his *Methodus ad curandorum omnium morborum*, hers is the least costly, the surest and the most delicious, for from Thomassine's arms I emerged as healthy as the giant Antaeus after he'd re-established contact with the goddess Earth, his mother. So I too believe that I'm a son of Earth and of earthly women like Barberine and Thomassine, whose milk of divine kindness has never failed to nourish me throughout my life.

But an entire month went by before I could console Samson, ever so little, for whom the particular remedy I'd just enjoyed was, as you would imagine, of no help whatsoever. Every week I wrote, not without a secret pleasure, a long letter to Dame Gertrude du Luc, to which Samson would add a few words whose simplicity was heart-rending.

Since not a week passed without some *roumieux* appearing in Montpellier, either on their way to Rome or returning therefrom, the letters in both directions arrived with marvellous speed. Our letters even crossed at times, for although Dame Gertrude was presumably in Rome for her devotions, she managed to cover numerous pages (using spelling that recalled little Hélix's), addressed to Samson and me, filled with feelings so tender and caressingly sweet that if you closed your eyes you could almost see her generous heart beating between the lines. At least, that's how I imagined it, since I felt I was included in her effusions.

On the other hand, towards the end of August, the apothecary's shop received two other letters that had taken an infinitely long time to reach us, having been passed from merchant to merchant and from town to town: a very auspicious one from my father and a very inauspicious one from a lawyer named Coras living in Réalmont in Albi, addressed to the very illustrious Maître Sanche, which plunged us all into despair, as I shall explain.

You can easily imagine the mixture of feelings evoked by my father's letter, since, in reading his vivid description of life at our beloved Mespech, now so far away, we could not help being overwhelmed with a sense of pride, accompanied by a wave of homesickness. Everyone seemed happy and healthy within its walls; the harvest was plentiful, with the hay already safely in the barns and the vineyards and the orchards heavy with ripe fruit; the cut stones from Jonas's quarry, Faujanet's barrels and Sarrazine's baskets were fetching good prices in Sarlat; Cabusse's sheep were bearing wool; the mill's pigs were fat and ready for slaughter; and Coulondre's mill was prospering under his adroit management, since townspeople brought him their grain not by fiat, as the rule used to be, but by choice, trusting in the integrity of this honest Huguenot—something that did not prevent him from making a fair profit. And it wasn't just grain that was milled, but walnuts were pressed on another millstone in late autumn to produce oil for our lamps. Even Petremol got into the act, since, after making harnesses for Mespech's horses and mules, he'd turned to making saddles so beautiful that the Brethren had no trouble selling them at very good prices to the Catholic nobility in Sarlat, who were always interested in fine saddlery, for show.

All of this was recounted in my father's lively and communicative style, which made him seem so present: his light-blue eyes, his way of standing straight, his sonorous laugh, his off-colour jokes and the warm love he bore all of his people, whose names he cited in the letter without omitting a single one.

"As for Samson," he wrote,

far from discouraging the extraordinary appetite he has shown for the apothecary's trade, I'm wholly satisfied and give my enthusiastic blessing to his learning this science. All the more so since it reminds me that my father Charles de Siorac wanted to make his eldest son a chemist and his second son (myself) a doctor so that we could both work in Rouen treating our patients from first symptoms to final cure, and God willing, greatly prosper from their collaboration. And who knows whether what my father failed to accomplish with his sons might be accomplished with mine.

My sons, you will be no doubt happy to learn that your older brother, François, and your gracious sister Catherine are well and my young bastard son David is turning into an exceptionally beautiful young man—seemingly profiting from some mysterious grace that attends children born out of wedlock. [This was written, I thought, as much to comfort himself as to comfort Samson.] Such is the case with Little Sissy, as brave and pretty a lass as any wench in the Sarlat region, though she's not the daughter of a Gypsy as la Maligou claims.

My dear Pierre, I'm as proud of you for attempting to master logic and philosophy as for your exploits in the Corbières hills. Art lasts so long, life is so short. And as you know: *absque sudore et labore nullum opus perfectum est.** As for skirts, if you find a good one, stick with her and only her. But I trust your wisdom, which far surpasses that of most young men your age.

So much for the flowery part of the communication, which my father always reserved for himself, never liking to scold, the role of disciplinarian having fallen to Sauveterre—but no one should imagine that censure didn't come from both of them. After the roses, then, the thorns. For there was, alas, a *postscriptum* to this lovely letter, and this addition, like the rattles on a poisonous snake, excessively bitter and stinging, was signed by our Uncle de Sauveterre. In his inimitably acerbic style he chastised us for spending far too much on food and drink at the Three Kings, and rejected as "futile and frivolous"

---

* "Nothing can be brought to perfection without sweat and labour."

my suggestion that Samson and I order suits of blue satin with red slashes, matching shoes and plumed velvet hats. "My nephews," wrote Sauveterre, "dress in black, as befitting your learned pursuits, and not like vile ladies of the night who parade the back alleys of Montpellier."

That's our Huguenot style, I thought, despising proper dress and appearances, and skimping on everything, even necessities, in order to fill the coffers. "Samson," I said, after having read the letter, "remember the time Sauveterre found a needle in the courtyard of Mespech, and limped all the way up to my mother's chambers to tell her, 'This is yours, I believe. My cousin, don't go losing your needles, they're too dear.'"

"But he was right!" countered Samson stiffly. "Waste is godless, and as for ostentation, she is the mother of lust!" I made him no reply, but there were many things I might have said. I could, for instance, have cited to my naive brother instances of lust that, far from being daughters of excess and ostentation, hadn't cost a single sol to those who had wallowed in them. But I preferred to remain silent for fear of troubling my dear brother, for in his dove-like innocence Samson had never asked who had paid for his love nest at the needle shop, or where the delicious meals had come from on which the two lovebirds had feasted for six days.

Dame Rachel, whom we'd caught sight of sitting very pregnant in front of the house when we arrived in Montpellier—and who, as you remember, while hidden behind a curtain in the common room, had given birth to a daughter, in violation of our medical rule that dictates that babies born under a full moon will be male—had returned to our midst after her churching, brilliantly regal in her oriental beauty. As Fogacer had said, Maître Sanche had displayed excessively good taste in his choice of wives, and the most recent version, younger still than the previous one, being some forty years her husband's junior, was of a beauty that overshadowed even Typhème, who was not her daughter any more than Luc was her son, both being children of Sanche's first wife. This lady was as cold as a diamond, whose brilliance she shared, and had no love for these, his other children, nor, for that matter, for me, Samson or Fogacer. She was feared, moreover, by the entire household like the plague in Lent, and especially by the cook, Concepcion, by Fontanette and even by the cyclopean Balsa. To her very illustrious master, she gave the respect he was due, but nothing more, and gazed at him with cold eyes, which were never tarnished by tears—at least as long as I was a guest in this house.

The letter from the lawyer named Coras, which arrived two days after my father's, was, alas, of an entirely different ink from my father's, which breathed his habitual gaiety and joy of life.

At dinner that day in Maître Sanche's common room, we all stood at our stools, waiting for our illustrious host—Dame Rachel, given her condition, or perhaps because of some permanent decree that exempted her from this form of respect, was seated, leaning easily against the back of her chair, hands on her knees, seeming to look at no one with her cold eyes, but perhaps at the spectacle of her own beauty inside her head.

But our wait for the master being prolonged more than usual, imagine our surprise when he appeared, finally, his head lowered and looking very dejected, holding in his right hand a piece of paper folded in four, sadly stroking his long grey beard with his left. Placing this paper next to his plate with a deep sigh, he undid his silver belt and removed his silk robe, but he was so lost in thought that he accomplished these rituals with a great deal less pomp than was usual. Then, hanging his robe on one of the antlers of the stag's head behind his chair, he sat down looking wholly devastated.

"But, my dear husband," said Rachel, "you've forgotten to remove your plumed hat."

"By my faith, 'tis true," said the master, who, rising without the least trace of a smile, his face still contorted in sadness, took off his bonnet and hung it next to his robe. This done, he put his little black silk brocaded hat on his head of curly grey hair and, with another deep sigh, sat back down, posing his trembling hand on the paper he'd brought.

"But, my dear husband," said Rachel, "you're sitting down!"

"Yes," he returned with some impatience at being distracted from his reverie, "why shouldn't I?"

"My dear husband," repeated Rachel, stung by his tone, and raising her nose even higher than usual, "you've forgotten the benedicite… Are we going to dine like Turkish pagans?"

"Ah, to be sure," admitted Maître Sanche, and, rising, he waited for Fontanette to bring him water to wash his hands. He remained standing, eyes cast down, while the good wench passed round the table, giving each of us water to rinse our hands, which she did without her usual smiles, Dame Rachel's cold eye watching her throughout like a hawk its prey.

Fontanette having retired to the pantry, Maître Sanche pronounced his particular benedicite in Hebrew, facing the wall and bobbing his head back and forth, as was his custom, and then turned to us to say: "In the name of the Lord Adonai, Amen." To which Luc added with his throat in knots and in a hushed voice, "And of the Son and Holy Spirit, Amen."

However, instead of inviting us to be seated, and sitting down himself, Maître Sanche remained standing, and, reaching with reluctance towards the paper on the table, he unfolded it with trembling fingers and said in a mournful voice: "Oh, Fogacer! My good nephews, my beautiful children and you, Madame, my spouse! I am so sad to have to read you this unhappy letter and sad you will be to hear it! But in truth I will not read it to you. My heart fails me. I can only tell you its substance and that will suffice."

With the paper still trembling in his hands, and tears gushing from his eyes, Maître Sanche went on, although in a somewhat stronger voice, as though he were ashamed of the weakness he was displaying: "This letter is from my great and learned friend, the lawyer Coras, who is from Réalmont in Albi, who studied law in Montpellier at the time I was studying pharmacy here, and Rondelet was studying medicine."

"Rondelet!" cried Fogacer as though seized with terror. "It's about Rondelet?"

"Read it, Fogacer, read it and weep!" said the master. "I cannot go on." And handing him the letter across the table, he fell onto his stool, savagely stroking his beard with both trembling hands.

Fogacer, his eagle's beak of a nose pale and pinched, his eyebrows raised, first read the letter, which was full of Latin phrases, as I could see by sneaking a look over his shoulder, in silence. While this was happening, seeing the great torment that had overcome his master, my beloved Samson, angel of God that he is, approached the apothecary and placed his hand on his shoulder, a bold gesture that was appreciated, since Maître Sanche left off stroking his beard and placed his hand on his nephew's. Luc, too, came over to his father, but so great was his respect for him that he dared not touch him. Typhème was crying in her corner, not so much in apprehension of what she feared to hear, but out of sympathy for the terrible emotion she saw in her father. For her part, Dame Rachel, ever sufficient unto herself, made up like a china doll, not a hair out of place, sat in serene silence, her eyes as dry as the agates they were made of.

"Here is what Maître Coras writes," said Fogacer at last, his voice and countenance laden with grief. "I will not read it but give you a summary. As was expected, and as I myself had foreseen at his departure, Monsieur Rondelet was afflicted greatly by his illness both during the ride through hill and vale to Toulouse, but also during his stay there, where he suffered from the terrible heatwave and from the great fatigue that ensued from his extensive consultations with the lawyers who were trying to sort out the affairs of his brothers-in-law. Hardly had he finished his work with these lawyers and started to look forward to some rest from his labours when he received a letter from Coras (who knew nothing of his friend's illness) begging him to hurry to Réalmont to care for his wife, who was suddenly stricken with a serious and mysterious illness. Although his stomach ulcers had only got worse since his arrival in Toulouse, Rondelet nevertheless decided to leave immediately for Albi, despite a dangerously high fever and the pleas of his brothers-in-laws to take to his bed. Thoroughly exhausted and shaking with fever, Rondelet set out from Toulouse the very morning he received Coras's letter. Réalmont is a day's ride from Toulouse, but it took the doctor two days to make the journey, as he was forced to stop at every inn, tortured by the pain from the inflammation in his stomach. Once in Réalmont, he went immediately to Coras's wife's bedside to try to determine the cause of her illness and to prescribe a remedy—which, in fact, cured her. But scarcely was she back on her feet before the doctor took to his bed, never more to rise from it. Deciding that his case was beyond help, he refused any remedies, dictated to the notary his last will and testament and spent his final hours making his peace with God. He died on the twentieth day of July."

As soon as Fogacer had finished his account, Maître Sanche, who'd had time to regain his composure, bid us be seated and then spoke with the same quiet despair in his voice as before. "And so it's because of his astonishing devotion to the sick that this great doctor rendered up his beautiful soul to God. He was as exemplary in death as he had been in life. His brief life has not completely ended, however, since the work of this humanitarian will live on in us and in those

223

who will come after us. *Brevis a natura nobis vita data est, at memoria bene redditae vitae est sempiterna.*"*

As he quoted this adage, Maître Sanche's voice gained its former assurance and his face recovered some of its colour, as if the Latin words had had a restorative effect on him and, simply by the magic of their sonorities, given him back his courage and faith in the conduct and purpose of his life. Thus fortified, the master seized his spoon, less from force of will than from force of habit, and plunged it into the humble broth that Fontanette was serving us, her manner very sombre to see us all so desolate. She nevertheless found a way to touch my hand as she served me, but I withdrew it immediately, since I could see that Dame Rachel's agate eyes hadn't missed a single gesture made by this poor wench. But I must admit, without too much shame, and hoping not to annoy my reader, that, despite the afflictions of the moment, and my sincere participation in the general grief, this touch gave me extreme pleasure, given how difficult it was, in the bloom of my youth, to linger too long on thoughts of death, or to believe, swollen as I was with sap, that one day it might catch up with me.

Meanwhile, this tragic news, coming as it did after the letter from my father, caused me to long even more for my nest at Mespech, Barberine's enclosing arms and the friendship of all our people. I wish to God I'd been as wise beyond my years as my father claimed in his letter. But, alas, as the following will demonstrate all too well, my blood boiled too hot in my veins and neither solitude nor sadness could hold me back for long.

That same evening, still feeling stirred up by the death of this good man, and by the effect it had produced on Maître Sanche and Fogacer—for whom Rondelet had served as "doctor-father" during his studies—I was unable to fall asleep in my room and went to

---

* "The life Nature has given us is brief, but the memory of a life dedicated to good works is eternal."

tap on Samson's door, but got no answer. No doubt he was already asleep, naked on his mat in this suffocating heat, and dreaming of the sweet embrace of his lady. Without my beloved brother's company, my solitude weighed all the more heavily upon me, so I headed for Fogacer's room, and entered without knocking, since he never bolted his door. But my tutor was not in his lair, having, no doubt, gone off to seek comfort I knew not where, nor from whom, since Fogacer was always so secretive about his love life. As for me, no matter how much I needed tender arms to comfort me on this particular evening, there was no recourse since it was Friday, and on Fridays Thomassine entertained her canon, who, being a very sensible man, put to the best possible use the generous sums he received from his parishioners for the indulgences he granted them. And so these pennies for salvation passed from the purse of the sinner under the pillow of the temptress, without anyone in this world or the next being hurt, the sinner gaining access to Purgatory, the bishop achieving his personal serenity and the temptress getting paid for her services and then being absolved of her sins. For although Thomassine had told Espoumel that she no longer sold her bodily wares, in truth she loaned them out at very advantageous interest rates to two or three very well-to-do members of the community. These activities did not make me jealous, but I did find them inconvenient since I didn't have access to my consoler as often as I might have liked.

Thus deprived of my brother, my tutor and of Thomassine, I returned to my room quite downcast, where I found the heat—even at night—almost unbearably oppressive. I gazed out of my window at the rising moon and thought that at least *she* could keep me company—as she had once done for Endymion in his cave—and, naked as I was, hoisted my straw mat on my shoulders and made my way up the staircase to the terrace at the top of the house where the stone floor was still warm from the afternoon sun, but there was at least a cooling breeze. However, my efforts had covered me with sweat, so I returned to my room to splash some water on my body and, may Uncle de Sauveterre forgive me, spray myself with some perfume that Thomassine had given me. Thus refreshed, I returned to the terrace, making more noise in my comings and goings than I would have liked.

Oh, how beautiful and white Montpellier appeared in the moonlight, with its superb terraces, and how friendly was this silence, for all the noise of the day's bustle had quieted. No street vendors' cries, no sounds of boots on the uneven paving stones, no shouts between friends, grinding cartwheels or hoof beats. All were happily and snugly ensconced in their beds behind tightly closed doors. But as moved as I was by the nocturnal beauty of this unique city, my pleasure was incomplete, for I had no one to share it with. My unhappy thoughts were redoubled when I caught sight of the clock tower of Saint-Firmin, which made me think of a needle, which, of course, brought to mind the needle shop and Thomassine, busily occupied, as you may imagine, behind her red velvet bed curtains. And the more I thought about it, the less I liked it, especially since it was with a papist.

I lay down on my straw mat, clasping my hands behind my neck, and abandoned myself to thoughts of Rondelet's death and that, in turn, brought back memories of little Hélix, whom I'd loved so tenderly. But I realized that, in the long run, the generous and naive love that she bore me while alive had gradually turned into bitterness, stricken as I was by the belief that her death meant that I would never find such complete satisfaction again.

"But, by the belly of St Anthony!" I cried out loud, sitting up on my mat. "I refuse to dwell on such melancholy! It's the mother of all the inclemencies of the body and any good doctor must begin by healing himself!"

Having said this, I arose, and, naked though I was, walked back and forth on the terrace, and, though my throat was in a knot, I held my head high and, fists on my hips, took up the pose I'd so often seen my father adopt. Which made me feel better, no doubt, but I felt better still when I caught sight of Fontanette, barefoot and in her nightgown, her hair falling about her bare shoulders, standing at the top of the staircase. "Oh, my noble friend," she gasped, seemingly terrified, but surely not by my nakedness, which she'd seen before. "What strange behaviour! What goings-on in your room and over my head! Are you a madman, that you prance about naked as a babe, sleeping up here like a wild man in Arabia under the moon, with no roof to protect you from the contagions of the air and the pestilence of the night? You'll catch your death!"

"Ah, Fontanette!" I breathed, happy to see her in such charming disarray. "The contagions of the night are nothing but vulgar superstition; the night air is as good for you as the air of the day, and much cooler and fortifying if the day has been too hot."

"Well, of course I'm just a silly, unreasonable girl, unable to read or write, while you, Monsieur, are already a learned doctor, speaking Latin and reading your enormous books. Nevertheless my mother and grandmother taught me that that the moon is the hares' sun, and hares are mad as everyone knows who's watched them hopping around the fields. And where I come from, they say the March moon is mad, and if she's that crazy can't she make you so loony as to run around naked on a rooftop instead of sleeping in your room like a good Christian?"

"Fontanette," I said jokingly, but with a serious face, "it's August! And in August the moon isn't nearly as mad as she is in March; she's madly in love and dreams only of running amok and seducing all the rascals she pleases. That's why I'm up here on this roof tonight in my sadness, hoping to accommodate her."

And saying this, I went and sat down on the right side of my mat, leaving room on the left side, as if I were expecting a night-time companion.

"Sweet Jesus!" cried Fontanette. "Is it true you're plunged in melancholy? Oh God, is it possible that the moon will come down here to caress and be caressed by you?" And so saying, she dropped down on the left side of the mat and placed her plump hand on the covering of the mat to feel it, saying, "But I don't feel anything!"

"That's because the moon has only sent her beams to caress me, but soon she will be here in person, cool and golden, having taken the form of the prettiest girl who was ever seen in Montpellier."

At this, Fontanette's eyes grew wider. "But that's villainous blasphemy!" she cried, making the sign of the cross. "And satanic magic! With all due respect and friendship," she cried, "I must flee!"

I grabbed her arm to restrain her. "Stuff and nonsense," I said. "You should be ashamed of such silly terrors! The moon is every bit as Christian as you or I! If it were otherwise, would God have hung it up there in His firmament when He created the world? Would He have tolerated all this time a pagan or impious moon, He who can do anything?"

"Even so," she said, somewhat reassured, "I don't think it's good when the moon comes down and takes over the functions and pleasure of the poor wenches of this world. So if you're plunged in your melancholy, my noble Monsieur, isn't there some earthly woman who can comfort you? I've heard you're very much in Thomassine's good graces…"

I did not expect this, and was so taken aback by her words that I couldn't think of a thing to say and just sighed deeply.

"You're sighing," she said, her voice full of emotion. "Did I say something bad? Did I make you angry?"

"Not at all, Fontanette," I replied. "I'm looking at the moon," I added, raising my eyes, "and now I know she won't come, having found provender elsewhere. So I'll just sit here alone and naked, rejected by all."

"Oh, Monsieur! Don't say that! You're loved here. Of course, you're not as handsome as your brother, Samson, but he's so dreamy he doesn't even know he's here. But here you are, and very much here, lively, funny, saying such clever things, seducing young girls with stories of the moon."

"Oh, Fontanette!" I sighed, speaking from the heart, all joking and tricks aside. "I'm not trying to fool you. I love you with great friendship and I have such a great appetite for you, you can't imagine."

"Oh, yes I can!" she cried, her eyes shining in the soft light of the moon. "Of course I can imagine, since I feel the same way! And so violently! Ever since you arrived, I've thought of you every night the Devil has made. I toss and turn a thousand times in my sleep, twisting my sheets into knots and making a complete mess of my bed. Holy mother of Heaven, what fevers, what sighs, what disorder!"

She spoke with such simplicity that I was altogether moved by the naive way she dismantled all her bulwarks and defences. And as tempted as I was to take her in my arms and bed her in the place I'd reserved for the moon, I did not do it—at least not yet—my heart was so rueful at seeing her so defenceless, and regretting having told her such tales that she'd believed without *really* believing them, good girl that she was, so pretty and prim, her hair falling about her shoulders and her nightgown all askew.

"Monsieur," she said in her Montpellier accent, so much more sing-song than our Périgordian dialect, "have you nothing to say?"

"Fontanette," I replied softly, taking her hands, "what can I tell you except that there's a very simple remedy for the sickness from which we both suffer."

"Oh," she sighed, "it's so easy for you to say, being a man and a nobleman. But I'm a chambermaid, as closely watched by Dame Rachel as a field mouse by a falcon, and risk being sent away and, worse, sent away pregnant."

229

"Oh, as for that," I whispered, "I know all about certain special herbs and where to put them. A very safe precaution that my father taught me."

As I whispered this, my lips were so close to her ear that I gave her lobe a little kiss, and then a second, and then a little nibble that made her laugh. And, laughing, she melted into my arms and offered her neck to my kisses.

"Oh, Monsieur," she said, as I laid her down beside me, "what is this? I'm sharing your bed! This is a great sin!"

"Which you can confess to your priest."

"Heavens no! He'll go straightaway to Dame Rachel to repeat it."

"Then tell it to another priest."

"But I know no other. Oh, Monsieur, if it weren't a cardinal sin, I'd love this. But since it *is*, I don't want to. I don't want to!"

Her hair falling loosely around her pretty face, she kept repeating "don't want to" more softly with each kiss, until finally, with the help of the moon, her silence and the softness of the night air, she was mine and I was hers.

Cicero must be wrong when he states "*ignoratio rerum futurorum malorum utilior est quam scientia.*"* For if I'd been able to foresee the terrible consequences that were to devolve onto my poor Fontanette as a result of our embraces, I would have forcefully pushed her from my arms, to which she was attracted—I wouldn't say like iron filings to a magnet, for the magnetism belonged both to her and to me, and was, for each of us, irresistible, given the bloom of our youth.

But how could I not have marvelled to have enjoyed this flower in its first burgeoning, and to have had her all to myself at a time when I had to share Thomassine with three or four fat merchants and a canon who was flogging indulgences? Alas, of all the pleasures I've enjoyed on this earth, this was to be the briefest, and ended in a way

---

* "It is better to be ignorant of our future ills than to know them in advance."

that broke my heart. We were to enjoy this delicious secret relationship for only three months—but I must ask my reader's forgiveness for not saying any more about it, for even today I cannot even think about what happened without my throat tightening and tears coming to my eyes, given the awful sequel that fate reserved for our lunar love.

As Fogacer had foreseen, after Rondelet died, Dr Saporta was elected to serve as chancellor of the Royal College of Medicine. Accompanied by Fogacer, I went to see him at the end of September.

Although he was very well-to-do, Saporta, a Sephardic and a Huguenot, lived more simply than any other physician in the city, lodging in an unremarkable house in the rue du Bras-de-fer, which was so steep that it was known in Montpellier as "the slide"; neither horse nor wagon would have dared attempt it, and so the street would have been very quiet had it not been for a bunch of noisy kids who frolicked there day in, day out on little wooden discs on which they slid from the top of the street to the bottom at considerable risk, for they would frequently crash into a wall, collecting bruises and wounds and leaving their discs in splinters.

All of this activity made a deafening din in the rue du Bras-de-fer. And this noise, which died down as the urchins went off to their beds, was replaced by another that was even worse, produced by the oaths, quarrels, fights and filthy songs that emanated from a tavern known as—may Christ pardon it!—the Golden Cross, where Montpellier's worst rabble gathered to drink, gamble, fornicate and brawl the whole night through.

And so the chancellor of our school lived night and day in the noisy hell of this disreputable place—more ignominious even than the rue des Étuves, where an assembly of harlots held sway—but patiently tolerated all of these incredible goings-on since he was sole owner of No. 32 on the same street, a beautiful tennis court, and wanted to keep a close eye on this establishment, from which he drew a handsome profit.

Having followed a summer course with Dr Saporta, I'd seen this terrifying regent, though from a distance since his lectures were so well attended, and I'd also caught sight of him from time to time while Fogacer and I were enjoying a game of tennis at his club, which we did partly because my tutor was convinced that one could never enter the good graces of the master unless one brought him his business. At each one of these visits, after a rapid glare from his dark and suspicious eyes at the players, without a single smile or sign of recognition to Fogacer, who bowed obsequiously to him, Dr Saporta, looking impossibly grim, spent his time in discussions with his manager, who, bent double in what appeared to be a permanent bow, accounted in a low and trembling voice for all the monies he'd received.

When Fogacer had knocked at his door, a long moment elapsed before the sound of footsteps could be heard, then a peephole opened revealing a wrinkled and suspicious eye. "State your business," growled a rough voice, though whether a man's or a woman's I couldn't tell.

"My name is Fogacer, and this is my tutee, Pierre de Siorac. The chancellor is expecting us."

The peephole closed abruptly and we heard the footsteps heading away again, and again there was a long wait.

"Fogacer," I said with a scowl, "can this be the house of a man who is said to be so well-to-do?"

"Ah, but it is! He is wealthier than the other three professors of the Royal College, Bazin, Feynes and d'Assas, put together. Our Dr Saporta has vineyards, wheat fields, pasturage and mills, not to mention his very profitable tennis court, as well as shares of a merchant marine company, and, to top it off, some very beautiful houses in

Montpellier that he rents to noblemen, contenting himself with this humble abode."

"Isn't it a pity that a man of such wealth should live so badly?"

"Badly? You're not taking the pleasures of avarice into proper account! Avarice surpasses all the others in pure voluptuousness—including the pleasures you seem to prize so highly!"

"Well, Saporta certainly can't be insensitive to those since he's marrying Typhème."

"Capable of love, you mean? I doubt it. All he wants from Typhème is children to whom he can leave his fortune, and nothing else."

"How's that possible! Typhème is so beautiful!"

"That's how you see her, Siorac," said Fogacer, raising his eyebrows and looking at me out of the corner of his eye, "because you've made skirts your pantheon, good Huguenot that you are. But for Saporta, who worships lucre, Typhème is nothing more than a girl from a good family who will bring him a handsome dowry and guarantee the perpetuation of his line. So goes the world: everyone has his own idol; for you it's wenches, for him, gold."

"Oh," I said quietly, "if that's the way things are, then I pity the poor girl for having to come and live in this hovel with that miser."

"Pity her," cautioned Fogacer, "but don't go consoling her. He'd roast you alive. But why do I bother? You pay no attention to my advice."

And whether he was alluding to my secret commerce with Fontanette—whom he'd warned me about—I couldn't tell, either from his expression or his tone, and had no time to consider the question, for we heard the footsteps returning and there was a loud noise behind the door of locks being unlocked, bolts unbolted and bars raised, as if we were entering a citadel.

But if, as my father warned, the only good walls are good men, then the defence of this place was weak and precarious, for once inside, aside from the master of the house, we found only the old woman who had ushered us in, and she was a tiny, dried-up and fabulously wrinkled old prune. No Fontanette here to welcome you in with shining eyes, pretty face and gracious figure… Nothing but this poor old skeleton, flat as my hand, nearly bald, her beady eyes full of mistrust, her upper lip well moustached and her voice as rasping and hoarse as a man's.

This personification of Fate showed us into a small room adorned with neither tapestries nor rug to cover a cold floor of old cracked and broken clay tiles, devoid of any furniture other than a table and a few stools, and feebly lit by one small window, covered by a curtain, the houses on the other side of the rue du Bras-de-fer leaning so close over the street that you could have grasped the hand of your neighbour from one window to the other.

She did not invite, but rather commanded us in her bass voice to be seated, and disappeared, but not before throwing us a nasty, suspicious look as if in her absence we would run off with the table, which, frankly, wasn't worth stealing.

The awful hag gone, the very walls of the room seemed so hostile that we sat in silence until the chancellor appeared. Which he did without the pomp or parading that we were accustomed to from Maître Sanche. By contrast, Saporta appeared almost by stealth, quietly slipping sideways into the room as though he were afraid to waste any air by moving too suddenly. Then, keeping the width of the table between us, he stood silently, arms folded, occupied not in looking at me but rather in inspecting me as though he would have liked to use his scalpel to cut up my face and study its fragments under a magnifying glass. I returned his gaze, having never seen him so close up, either during his lectures or at his tennis courts, and found him pretty terrifying.

Chancellor Saporta wore a doctor's four-cornered bonnet—which, I imagined, he removed only when he went to bed—and he had a thin, bony and hard face, with hair as black as a crow's wing, black eyes that sat far back in their sockets but bored into you with unbearable intensity. Two bitter and disdainful wrinkles framed his mouth and disappeared into his thick black beard. Standing there, prey to these piercing eyes, I was all the more troubled to find his countenance so bilious and tyrannical since I had agreed with Rondelet, before his departure, that I would ask this ogre to serve as my sponsor for the duration of my studies. What a haven of grace *he* would be! What sort of father would he be to me, as a replacement for my natural father, who, except when he was angry, treated me so sweetly and tenderly?

We had risen when the chancellor had slipped into the room and Fogacer and I had, each in our turn, greeted him in Latin, to which he replied not a single word, but kept us standing during his long and minute inspection of my visage, before seating himself, without inviting us to do the same. Then, continuing to hold me in the pincers of his gaze, he said in Latin, in clipped tones: "Tell me who you are and what you want. Be brief. I don't have much time."

"Monsieur," I replied, "my name is Pierre de Siorac," knowing that in naming myself I wasn't really telling him anything, but very surprised that he would adopt such a rude manner for our interview. "I would like you to consent to serve as my doctor-father for the duration of my studies."

"Have you enrolled in the college?"

"Not yet, Monsieur."

"Then I can't be your doctor-father," he said in a way that brooked no response.

An unbearable silence followed, and, seeing my predicament, Fogacer intervened. "May I speak, Monsieur?" he said with abject humility—a tone that astonished me, coming from him.

"You may."

235

"I have tutored Pierre de Siorac in logic and philosophy, and can attest that he is worthy of admission to the college."

"I cannot so declare this until I have a signed document from you to this effect."

"I shall provide you with such a document."

"Nor can I accept him into our college without his having been examined as to his medical knowledge by one of the four royal professors."

"Dr Rondelet carried out just such an examination before his departure for Toulouse, and found him well qualified."

"But Dr Rondelet is dead," said Saporta without moving a muscle in his face. "Therefore the good doctor cannot provide a written report."

Although there was no disputing the logic of this assertion, its insensitivity, under the circumstances, left us flabbergasted—all the more so since Dr Saporta's ensuing silence seemed to be burying my application to the college along with Rondelet.

"So what should we do?" said Fogacer finally in the same obsequious tone, which I already guessed was the only tone to take with the chancellor.

"Let me tell you," said Saporta. "You will take Siorac to Dr d'Assas, who, after examining him will send me *in writing*" (raising his voice with these words) "his opinion. If Siorac is worthy to be admitted, he will receive from my hand *a document*" (again raising his voice for emphasis) "ordering him to pay 300 livres for tuition. This done, Siorac will receive from Dr d'Assas a *document* apprising him that he is now a student in our school. When he is in possession of this document, Siorac will send me a *document* requesting that I serve as his doctor-father. And whether my reply is positive or negative, you may be sure that it will be *in writing*."

Having practically roared this last word, Dr Saporta sat down, not deigning to cast his eyes on my poor being—I did not yet exist since

I hadn't yet enrolled *in writing* in his college—but instead scrutinized Fogacer with his beady, penetrating black eyes.

"If I understand correctly," said Fogacer in the same submissive tone, "you have decided to remedy things, and from now on everything will be in writing that, under Rondelet's administration, was done by word of mouth."

"Exactly. *Vox audita perit, litera scripta manet.*"* Then, passing from Latin to French, Saporta continued, "Fogacer, the good management of a school requires that the chancellor keep a written record of everything. But," he said quickly and with an evil gleam in his eye, "that is but one of the innumerable abuses that I need to rehabilitate here. When I have restored order to the anarchy of our enrolments, I will rain down fire and brimstone on the counterfeiting of diplomas. Every year I will change the chancellor's seal so that it can't be copied by miscreants and fakers. I will make sure that no doctor may practise medicine in Montpellier who does not have a diploma from the Royal College and who has not demonstrated his knowledge and competence to me personally, Fogacer—even if he holds a doctorate from Paris, whose school of medicine is, as everybody knows, empty, scholastic, full of superstition and infinitely mediocre."

What astonished me was Saporta's passionate and unreasonable disdain, which those in Montpellier heap on the capital—a scorn enthusiastically endorsed by Fogacer. Of course, I kept this opinion to myself, knowing full well that a straw can't hold back a torrent. And anyway, what would be the point of saying anything at all since, not yet being enrolled in his college, I didn't even exist in Saporta's eyes?

"I shall severely punish," continued the chancellor-elect, "all those who dare to practise our art without a diploma, and I shall revive the healthy custom that fell into disuse under Rondelet, whereby, every time we catch one of these charlatans, our students parade

* "What is spoken perishes, but the written word remains."

him though the streets of the city tied backwards on an ass, and then forcibly throw him outside our walls."

"*Bene! Optime!*" applauded Fogacer with total sincerity, as far as I could judge.

"But above all else," Saporta went on, "I'm going to put firmly in their place (which is secondary) all of these apothecaries who have taken advantage of Rondelet's notorious weakness to commit secretly innumerable abuses." Catching his breath, and raising his meagre torso to its full height, he continued, now directly addressing Fogacer with his black eyes gleaming, "I respect Maître Sanche for his wisdom and science. I'm honoured that I shall soon be his son-in-law. But I will no longer tolerate the way that, in the secrecy of his laboratory, he performs examinations of urine. It is a heretical and damnable encroachment of the prerogatives of the doctors! Maître Sanche conducts urine tests!"

"But every chemist does the same, Monsieur!"

"It will no longer be tolerated!" yelled Saporta in anger with a cutting gesture. "Urine belongs to the doctor! Fogacer, remember this inviolable principle! Everything that comes from the patient belongs to us as doctors, and only to us: urine, excrement, blood, pus, humours—all of these substances, given their natural origins, fall infallibly under the jurisdiction of the doctor. And let no apothecary dare touch them! Of course, I take nothing away from those who manufacture remedies, though they hold master's degrees and not doctorates, and thus belong more to a mechanical trade than to a real art. But if the chemist, is, as has always been acknowledged, the servant of medicine, the servant should never attempt to arrogate to himself the rights of his master. I'll make this quite clear to all these asses in aprons!"

"Monsieur, may I speak?" said Fogacer in his most submissive voice.

"You may."

"Monsieur, would you grant me permission to plead Maître Sanche's case?"

"You may."

"Monsieur, what doctor would ever disagree with you? There is no doubt that it is a damnable abuse on the apothecary's part to study urine. But Maître Sanche is, in fact, more than any other chemist in Montpellier respectful of our rights. He never, even when his practice would seem to require it, applies leeches or does bloodlettings, as certain of his colleagues do, and do in secret."

"Oh, I'm fully aware of these diabolical abominations, and I'll raise my sword against them!"

"Maître Sanche," continued Fogacer, "never does diagnoses or prognoses, is always saying '*Non sum medicus*'* and never fills an order without a signed prescription from a doctor."

"This is true," said Dr Saporta. "Maître Sanche is not one of the worst offenders. And yet, he studies urine! This is a capital crime and such a horrible infringement on our rights that I could not tolerate it even from Maître Sanche and even if he had ten thousand daughters to give me in marriage."

I would have laughed at this if I'd been of a mind to laugh, seeing the horrible face of our angry chancellor. Frowning fiercely, his black eyes throwing sparks, all his features contracted into an awful grimace, his pale nose pinched, his breath coming in gasps, he seemed to be condemning not only the abuses that so angered him, but the people who committed them as well. "What a sad and choleric personage!" I thought. "My heaven preserve me if he accepts me as his student and I do anything to anger him!"

Fogacer, who had the most marvellous ability to keep his mouth shut when it mattered, didn't pursue his defence of Maître Sanche any further, and, bridling his feelings, fell silent. As for me, I'd neither

---

*   "I am not a doctor."

spoken nor moved a muscle during this conversation, since I was in limbo, as behoved my status as a nonexistent being. The sum of our two silences finally weighed enough for Saporta to notice them despite the fire and brimstone he was emitting. But as his flashing eyes suddenly noticed us, he seemed surprised to see us still there, and said very abruptly and rudely in Latin: "Our conversation is over." And, without responding either by look or by gesture to our words of adieu, he summarily took his leave.

It was no mean accomplishment to find our way out of Saporta's stingy quarters and to negotiate "the slide", so large and boisterous were the crowds of snot-nosed good-for-nothings who were out in force, playing at marbles and tops with shouts that would make a deaf man cringe, banging on pots and pans of all sorts, defiling the pavements with their offal, pissing on passers-by or shaking their members at them, singing filthy songs or throwing their hoops or sticks under their legs to trip them up—not to mention that we had constantly to be jumping out of the way of their sleds as they hurtled down the hill fast enough to break our arms and legs if they'd bumped into us.

"Oh," I cried, "now I know what hell must be like!"

"'Tis worse at night," said Fogacer. "During the day all you see here is shit and piss, but come night-time it'll be blood. No wench can pass through here without getting raped, nor man escape without being traitorously stabbed in the back and left as naked on his last day as he was on his first."

"What about the nightwatchman?"

"These ruffians would beat him bloody if he ever showed up here. They fear no one but Cossolat and his archers, and perhaps a few rich merchants in town, who, if their serving girl has been molested or a valet has been dispatched, swear vengeance, arm a small platoon, swoop in on the area, grab a few of these rascals and send them, boots and all, to their maker. But that's merely a nobleman's pastime; the anthill is still there, active as ever."

"It's a living hell! How can Saporta manage to live here, unless he's a veritable Pluto? Oh, Fogacer, he's a terrifying specimen! Why does he have to be my doctor-father? Wouldn't I have done better to choose Dr d'Assas, who's reputed to be so nice?"

"Hah! Not on your life!" returned Fogacer. "You know that his late wife Catherine was Rondelet's daughter (all of these physicians and apothecaries intermarry, as you've noticed). D'Assas would have invited you to his beautiful estate in Frontignan, amiably served you some of his wine and meat pastries, and talked your ears off about his vineyard. But that would be it. Saporta is a man of iron, Siorac, but you can use this iron to stand on and move forward. What's more, he'll be a much more effective director of the Royal College than Rondelet, who was a great doctor, but allowed incredible abuses to spread within his walls without any retribution. Don't judge Saporta by his looks, or by his avarice, or by his moods, but by the advantages he can bring both to the school and to you."

Having offered this explanation, which comforted me somewhat, Fogacer stopped in front of No. 32, rue du Bras-de-fer. "Shall we play a game of tennis? Would you enjoy that?"

"I must decline. I have another appointment."

"Aha!" smiled Fogacer, raising his satanic eyebrows. "Doubtless you're going to offer your devotions at Saint-Firmin?"

"No, no!" I laughed. "For once you're wrong! I'm going to visit Espoumel in his jail cell."

"'Tis strange that you should have developed such affection for this rascal, and go visit him so faithfully."

"I owe him my life."

"He owes you his. You're even."

"Oh no! My life is so much more beautiful than his: I'm still in his debt."

"Ah, Siorac! Siorac!" sighed Fogacer. "Despite your unbridled habits, one just can't help liking you!"

Thereupon, with a sly smile, he skipped away, leaving me quite perplexed, for he clearly knew everything about my habits though I knew nothing at all about his. I had no idea that his more basic desires might be as well tended as my own.

I was given free access to the Montpellier jail thanks to Cossolat, who had said a good word for me to the superintendent, who, in turn, had spoken to the jailer, who continued to open the door to me because I generously greased his palm. And so I'd managed to get Espoumel moved from the dark and fetid dungeon into which he'd first been thrown, to the cell where those condemned to the noose would spend their remaining days. This room had a large window, well defended by strong iron bars, of course, but which nevertheless admitted the sun, since these miserable creatures were given the privilege of seeing the beauty of the sunrise on the very day when they'd be deprived of it forevermore.

After the jailer had admitted me to this cell and relocked the door behind me, Espoumel stood, dominating me by a full head, being tall and thin, though his meagre frame disguised his great strength since he was made all of muscle and sinews. He would have been handsome enough if one had hacked away his voluminous beard and cut his long tangle of thick dirty hair. He greeted me warmly, his little black eyes full of a canine gratitude, while I set out on the table a store of meats and provisions which I'd purchased on my way here.

"Ah, Monsieur!" he gushed. "What would I do without your help? I've been here a month already, eating the bread of grief and drinking the water of anguish, plunged in remorse for my terrible sins! I had a pleasant companion to keep me company, but the archers took him off this morning, and hanged him in the olive grove for having stolen ten écus from his master. I can't help thinking that there's no justice when you take an honest lad's life for such a paltry crime… while here I sit, who've committed so many robberies and murders, awaiting the king's pardon."

"Espoumel," I said, "man's justice is flawed by the infirmity of his nature, but in heaven all will be righted by the grace of God."

"And who's come back to tell of it?" sighed Espoumel, freezing the words in my mouth with this naive but heretical question. "Oh, Monsieur, if you could only have seen this nice fellow as he readied himself for death, tender-hearted as you are, you would have given the hangman an écu to strangle him before he was hanged."

"But isn't it the same death?"

"Not at all! When the hangman is putting the rope around your neck he can crush your throat bone with his thumb without anybody seeing, and you die instantly. But when you're hanged alive, it's your own weight that suffocates you little by little. It takes a long time to die and so 'tis a horrible death."

"And how do you know all of this?" I asked, quite amazed that Espoumel knew more about it than a medical student.

"Because I was born a villain," replied Espoumel, "and that's the fate of men who are hanged."

I had nothing to answer to this, and sat down on his little stool, but at some distance from him, as my father had advised in such cases, so as not to catch his lice, and, to tell the truth, because he smelt like a skunk in a cage, having no water in this cell except an occasional cupful to drink.

"Espoumel," I asked, "what's that you're holding?"

"Oh, it's nothing," he said, "just an image of my jailer that I carved in a piece of wood to keep from pining, since the days are so long."

"Let's see it," I said. He handed me a little statue about four inches high, beautifully worked and proportioned and looking a lot like its model. "Espoumel, this is beautiful work!"

"It's not too bad, is it?" he confessed, smiling with pleasure at the praise I'd given him. "But I could do better if I had a better knife, a chisel, a rasp and some wood that was easier to work."

"You'll get them."

"Oh, Monsieur Siorac, if you like my little *peteta* so much I'd give it to you, but I promised it to my jailer. But I can carve another for you if you'd like."

"Could you carve it from a model if I drew it for you?"

"Yes I could, if the drawing has the right dimensions."

"And how much time would it take you to carve your *peteta*?"

"About a day, if you give me the right wood and the right tools."

I thought about this for a moment, for I'd conceived a plan that held out great promise. "Espoumel," I said, "I tell you what. You will give me the first *peteta* you carve, but I'll pay you for the others, and I want you to make one every day that God has made and that you spend in here waiting for the king's pardon. That way, you won't while away your time with nothing to do, and when you get out, you'll have some money for your food and drink."

"Oh, Monsieur," cried Espoumel, "your kindness is infinite, but if I have to be here a month, or more than a month, to what conceivable use will you put all these *petetas*?"

"Soldiers, Espoumel!" I laughed. "Some French and the others English. And with the two armies, set up one against the other, I can stage the siege of Calais where my father fought with such distinction."

And so, promising to visit him the next day, and to bring him the tools he needed and three pieces of soft wood, I took my leave, very happy with him and with myself, believing I could make a handsome profit with these carvings. Now, I realize I may be raising some eyebrows among my readers, who, having perhaps already found it unacceptable for a nobleman to study medicine, are now turning up their noses at the idea that he should try to make a profit from such an enterprise. For them, no doubt, the only noble way to live is, for the eldest son, to exploit the labourers on his lands, and, for a younger brother, to embrace the Church or the army. However, for me, my faith has closed the door of the Church, and, as for the army, must I enter the service of a king who, tomorrow, could declare that all Huguenots are outlaws?

My father and Sauveterre have adopted Calvin's belief that all money is good that is honestly earned, and that it's a sure sign of God's favour that He puts in our minds that which is most profitable to us. It is to this maxim, so faithful to the spirit of the Bible, that they owe the incredible prosperity of Mespech.

As for me, inspired by these same ideas, I disliked costing the Brethren so many écus, just as I disliked having to depend on them at all, for in my view, any man who owes his livelihood to another—be it his own father—is nothing more than a child. Being a younger son, and thus able to count on no one but myself for the advancement of my fortunes, I found it lamentable to dress all in black since I was already in Joyeuse's good graces—and would have been even more so if I could appear before him dressed in clothes that would enhance rather than demean my situation. May I say that I saw nothing in the blue satin suit that I hoped to acquire that could be described as "futile" or "frivolous", as Sauveterre wrote, but regarded it rather as a means to an end, as these *petetas* would be, for certainly I would not open a shop on the public street to sell them, but would turn them to my advantage in a more subtle and honourable way, as I shall recount.

While thus meditating on my fortunes, I realized my steps had taken me to Saint-Firmin, but it was not to the papist church, but to what stood opposite it, that I directed my particular idolatry. The workings of man's brain are strange indeed! And how easy it is, no matter what some might say, to have two ideas at once! For, however absorbed I was in my schemes for the future, I had, nevertheless, the minute Espoumel had said the word *peteta*, begun to remember that the innkeeper in Castelnau d'Ary was called La Patota, which is the same word in a different dialect and means "doll" in our Provençal tongue. And remembering the delicious cakes that our good hostess had offered me as I left her inn, I arrived at the more recent memory of the pastries I'd swallowed at the needle-maker's shop the night before, and slipped insensibly from the pastry to the pastry chef, the second no less succulent than the first, and was so overcome with desire and appetite for Thomassine that I had to satisfy them without delay.

But I couldn't. Thomassine was not there, wouldn't be back all day, as Azaïs informed me, writhing like a little snake, attempting to provoke me, ticklish as she was. But I would have none of it—as ticklish as I might be myself—for I did not wish to be the cause of her dismissal: a scruple, however, that had not stopped me in my dealings with Fontanette.

And so I left, quite dissatisfied by my own good behaviour, which for once was prudent. I make no attempt to hide, though, that prudence is hardly my cardinal virtue. For a month later, and in an arena that had not to do with wenches but with study, I committed, along with some other students from my college, an action that my father deemed, after reading my letter of confession, sacrilegious, stupid, and, to quote him directly (for his conclusion was written in Latin, to give it more weight) *atrocissimo*.*

---

* "Most cruel."

8

ON THE TENTH DAY of October, I set out on my mare, Accla, to visit Dr d'Assas in Frontignan, accompanied by Fogacer, riding Samson's Albière, who would serve as my guide on these unfamiliar routes, but whose real interest in the journey was the schoolmaster's muscat wine.

This doctor, Fogacer explained as we trotted along the stony roads, was a Sephardic and was called, in reality, Salomon, but, finding that his name was too obviously Hebraic, he adopted the name of his property, d'Assas. At first this had raised some eyebrows among his Sephardic friends, especially since, after becoming a Huguenot, the good doctor had abandoned the secret rites to which many of them had remained faithful. D'Assas's adoption of the noble "de" had elicited much ridicule among the papists of the town (but then hadn't my grandfather ultimately done the same thing?), but everyone eventually got used to it. As for the reformists, who were too austere to laugh at his change of name, they were very disappointed that d'Assas was such a tepid convert, for he seldom went to their temple, claiming that the long ride made his backside too sore.

When we dismounted and I saw him emerge from his lush garden under the sunny blue skies of a Provençal autumn, approach with arms outstretched and give me a warm hug, so full of goodwill and tolerance, my heart swelled with affection for the good doctor!

Everything about him was round: his head, his face, his shoulders, his paunch—his heart and soul as well. And around these rotundities, so different from those of the late Chancellor Rondelet, the thorns of life seemed to have slipped by without scratching him, for d'Assas had endured a like number of funerals as his father-in-law, successively mourning two wives and four of his six children, but unlike Rondelet, at each loss, after many tears shed, his former serenity seemed to be reborn from those ashes. D'Assas appeared perpetually able to draw forth from himself a *joie de vivre* as sweet as the muscat he drew from his wine barrels.

Indeed, the better you got to know him, the more you realized that the drinker shared a deep affinity with his drink. For d'Assas was personally sweet, suave and fruity, a true nectar of a man, self-indulgent, indulgent of others, tender with everyone, pardoning each one, wishing for no enemies, seeking accommodation with all. But of course, since every medal has its reverse side, he was also very little inclined to take pains, even in his art, since he had little trust in medicine, as became obvious very quickly, and instead was entirely devoted to the management of his Frontignan vineyards, which, if truth be told, he valued more than the king his kingdom.

Having invited us to sit down in the shade of his lovely garden, Dr d'Assas showered us with compliments and ordered his valet to see to our horses, and his chambermaid to bring us wine and cakes. Which she did, all smiles and alluring glances. She was a pretty brunette, as long and supple as a creeper vine, her large green eyes speckled with gold. She was imbued with a languid Italian grace—as appetizing to look at as her cakes, which were spread out on a small table placed between our legs, and which I attacked with gusto, as did Fogacer. Dr d'Assas smiled benignly to see us so hungry and thirsty after our long ride. He sat at his ease in an armchair, his head bobbing gaily and—I hope my reader won't take this amiss or be angry at my telling it—time

248

and again baritoning from his arse. For, to tell the truth, and despite his otherwise perfect manners, he farted often and loudly, though not odoriferously, and expelled from his anus the air he breathed in excessively through his mouth, being accustomed, God knows why, to yawn mightily between each sentence like a fish out of water.

When I was half full (for in the bloom of my youth I never discovered a bottom to my abyssal stomach), Dr d'Assas said, in between mouthfuls of cakes and wine: "Monsieur de Siorac—but let's drop the formalities! I'll just call you Pierre, since I already like you so much with your frank appearance and good manners—I hope you'll forgive me." (And here he gave a strange intake of air with a curious sound as if he were saying, "Haaamm".) "Please, eat while we talk. Eating and drinking belong to the living, for the dead no longer have any appetite but for God, and since God is eternal, why should we be in a hurry to join him? Pierre, forgive me if I must ask you a few little questions about medicine, but I must since I must give my evaluation in writing to the chancellor (Haaamm!), so I'm going to ask you right off to tell me what you know about syphilis, since this disease is, it seems, your strong point." (He laughed.) "Pierre, is syphilis a dry and cold inclemency?" (Here he abruptly... but if it please you, reader, I shall leave to your imagination the number of times he yawned or broke wind as we conversed, since it would be bad breeding to insist on these, the good doctor being a man of otherwise impeccable manners.)

"No, Monsieur, it's a hot and humid inclemency."

"Fogacer," said d'Assas with a sly look at the tutor, "do you believe that? 'A hot and humid inclemency?' What the devil is this kind of talk?"

"I'm really not sure," said Fogacer, who was amused by the doctor's scepticism. "But the distinction is classic."

"Very good then. Let's distinguish. Zara," he said to the pretty chambermaid, "come over here, my sweet, and stand on my right, next to me. *Bene, bene.* Pierre, how does the sickness spread?"

To which I parroted back to him, "An infected person can only infect another by the passage of *liqueur* from one body into a part of the other body."

"Well that makes sense, though I'm not partial to the word '*liqueur*'," said d'Assas, and with his left hand he brought his goblet to his mouth, with his right caressing his chambermaid's back, at least that part of her he could reach since he had such short arms and she was so tall.

"Pierre," he said with a delectable smile, "we've worked hard enough for one afternoon, under such a bright sun and blue skies. One question more and we shall be done. How can we protect ourselves against syphilis when we suspect we've had relations with an infected person?"

"By purging and having blood drawn."

"Fogacer," said d'Assas with an even more ironic expression than before, "do you believe that?"

"I don't know, but that's what they teach."

"Very good then. Let's teach it that way. Pierre," he continued, "you've said enough to convince me that you know the *De morbo italico* of Rondelet by heart. *Dignus es intrare, mi fili.** I will write to Saporta soon."

"Venerable Doctor," said Fogacer, who did not trust d'Assas's lazy habits or his well-known tendency for procrastination, "why not write this note immediately? I'll deliver it to the chancellor myself since I have a meeting with him this evening."

"As you wish," sighed d'Assas. "Zara, fetch my writing desk!" And this said, as she rose to do his bidding, he accompanied her departure with his hand on her backside for as long as his stubby right arm would permit.

Having wrapped up my examination in two easy questions, and disposed of his recommendation to Saporta in two short lines, d'Assas finished his wine, and rising with unexpected sprightliness, invited us

---

* "You're worthy of admission, my son."

to visit his vineyard, which he described in excruciating detail for an entire hour, punctuating his diatribe with you-know-whats, while Zara, as ordered, walked along on his right for his tactual enjoyment. She seemed so constantly necessary that I was surprised that, when he offered his lectures at the Royal College of Medicine, he didn't bring her with him for his continued pleasure. As for the punctuation I've mentioned, he did not fail to display that particular habit during his lectures, which offered a subject of great merriment to his students, who enjoyed imitating his airy offerings. However, despite the jokes he inspired, his courses were well attended and were fairly good, and would have been better if he'd put more thought into them.

"Make no mistake about it," Fogacer told me as we rode slowly back to Montpellier, our pace determined by the amount of muscat wine we'd absorbed, "Dr d'Assas is extremely intelligent. In fact, he would have been the greatest doctor of his time if he'd only taken the trouble. But he is a true hedonist. His only care in life is to make the most of every passing moment since we don't get another chance at it."

"And don't we all do the same?" I asked. "Each in his own way, some through avarice, others though love, still others through austerity."

"I have an answer for that," said Fogacer, "but my head is spinning, and I can't seem to find it." Having said this, he reined in Albière, grabbed the pommel of his saddle and, bent over double, burst out laughing uncontrollably. Seeing this, I broke out laughing myself, so happy to see this side of my wise mentor, and we remained lost in our mirth for quite some time.

On 11th October, Chancellor Saporta sent his beadle to me to request payment of three livres for my inscription in the college register, and to remind me that I must not consider myself officially enrolled until I received *written* confirmation from Dr d'Assas; hence I should make no attempt to request *in writing* that Saporta serve as my doctor-father until I had in my possession d'Assas's letter.

But on the 16th—two days before St Luke's Day, the first day of the semester—having heard nothing from Dr d'Assas, and attributing his silence to his proclivity for procrastination, I saddled Accla and went straight to Frontignan, partly since I enjoyed his benign presence, not to mention his cakes and wine and, I confess, Zara's green eyes, with which she bewitched all the young men around her. And even if this *non licet toccare** had been written in golden letters across her pretty forehead, and enjoying her favours was only a dream, who wouldn't love to get lost in such a beautiful dream? As our stonecutter at Mespech, Jonas, would say, chastely ensconced in his cave and hence deprived of the sight of Sarrazine, "A fox likes to watch the chickens go by even if he can't catch them."

In short, I had all the pleasures of *sight*, in seeing the pert chambermaid again; of *hearing*, since Dr d'Assas held forth on his various disquisitions; of *taste*, as I partook of his exquisite wine and cakes—and, to top it all off, I finally got my letter of enrolment, which was as prompt as it was bizarrely conceived:

> *Descriptus fuit in albo studiosorum medicinae Petrus Sioracus, per manus, anno Domini 1566 die vero 16 octobris; cujus pater est Venerandus Doctor Saporta, nostrae scholae Cancellarius, qui ejusdem jura persolvit. Datum Monspessuli ut supra. Doctor Dassassius.*†

I found these terms curious because they stated that Dr Saporta would serve as my doctor-father whereas it was precisely *this* document that

---

*   "No touching permitted."

†   "Pierre de Siorac has been inscribed by my hand in the book of scholars in medicine on 16th October in the year 1566. His doctor-father is the venerable Dr Saporta, chancellor of our school, who has authorized this action. Montpellier, on this day (as inscribed above). Dr d'Assas."

was required before I could ask him to serve in this capacity. I dared to point out this anomaly to Dr d'Assas, but he, with a twinkle in his sly eyes, assured me that such a contradiction or absurdity would in no wise bother Dr Saporta, as long as it was stated *in writing*. As he said this last, he pronounced "*in writing*" in a perfect imitation of the tone and voice of Dr Saporta, which provoked a huge laugh from both of us.

The school of medicine in Montpellier was situated on the rue du Bout-du-monde (the idea that we should be located at "world's end" always amazed me) and, aside from the anatomical theatre that Rondelet had founded, consisted of but two large halls, one for lectures and the other, called the graduation hall, for examinations and assemblies, but where, for lack of space, some lectures were also given. Attached to these two halls was a large tower, whose solemn bells were rung by the beadle Figairasse to announce the beginning and end of each reading. I use this word advisedly, for our teachers, whether they were royal professors or ordinary doctors, invariably *read* selections from ancient texts, accompanied by commentaries that varied enormously from reader to reader in both quantity and quality.

Also attached to these two halls was a small but very precious garden, for, since the arrival of Rondelet, who was a great lover and observer of natural phenomena—and to whom we owe a book entitled *Fish*, which is an extraordinary study—a great variety of medicinal plants were cultivated there. We all took turns weeding this garden, but the most assiduous of us all was my beloved Samson, even though he was not a regularly enrolled student in the college, but was admitted to certain courses deemed relevant to his interest in the apothecary arts.

But I'm getting ahead of myself. What a grand occasion it was for Luc, Samson and me to hear the solemn bell ringing, announcing a plenary session of all of the teachers and students of the school in the graduation hall.

Enthroned on a platform at one end of this great hall were the college's four professors, sitting behind a long oak table, all equal in rank, but not in power or function. Neither Dr Feynes nor Dr d'Assas could claim to enjoy the same power or privileges as Chancellor Saporta and Dean Bazin—the first responsible for the school's management, the second for its curriculum, the latter little disposed to give way to the former, or so it appeared. But since he was a thinly built, white-haired little man, bent over with age, Bazin looked like he had little chance of carrying the day against my terrifying doctor-father—for my "father" he now was, as the very laconic *written* attestation I'd received on the eve of this plenary reunion, and signed by Saporta's abrupt hand, was, henceforth, ample warrant.

As for Dr Feynes, a good man and a good doctor as I was to learn later, and the only one of the royal professors who was a papist (the only one that Bishop Pellicier had managed to impose on the school), he had thinning hair and watery eyes, and such wan, pale and indecisive features that he had no need of effacing himself any further as was his wont, since he lived in a state of perpetual terror in this Huguenot lair.

Chancellor Saporta and Dean Bazin occupied the centre of the table, with Dr Feynes at one end and, at the other, my gentle Dr d'Assas, well rounded in body and lively in spirit, playing the toady but not missing an iota of what was going on, and, I would guess, inwardly laughing at the entire spectacle, yet able to respond with appropriate civility and modesty when addressed by his chancellor or his dean.

Opposite this august platform were seated, in order of their rank and importance, ordinary doctors in the first row, the masters of science in the second and the bachelors of science in the third, all in robes, with the doctors wearing a four-cornered cap of black cloth adorned with a tassel of red silk, each bearing a large golden ring on his right hand and girded with a gold belt. The reader will perhaps remember that Maître Sanche wore only a dark purple tassel and a silver belt... So the difference between a doctor and an apothecary was immediately obvious, even when the latter was as illustrious as Maître Sanche.

Behind the bachelors of science, the second-year medical students were seated, and these were a raucous and rowdy lot when compared to the more reticent novices, who sat humbly behind their elders, subjected to the dismissive and haughty stares emanating from the older students. Luc was terrified by their very presence, and pressed himself against me, seeking my protection. And behind all of these stood—and I emphasize the word "stood" even though there were vacant seats aplenty directly in front of them—the apothecary companions and the surgical apprentices who had no right to be there since they were not, properly speaking, medical students, but who had been specially granted admission to this ceremony by the chancellor, who deemed that it would be good for them to hear the statutes of the school since they'd been given permission to sit in on the lectures.

But in all this assemblage I don't want to forget to mention the guarantor of the security of our institution, the beadle, Figairasse, and I have excellent reasons for remembering him. Between the platform where the four professors were aligned, and the general seating of the rest of us, Figairasse stood in all his power and glory, decorated with all his trophies from other St Luke's Day ceremonies and plenary meetings, his head adorned with a helmet (a souvenir of his soldiering days) and clothed in a black vestment decorated with gold buttons, padded red stockings with black slashes and short, high-heeled fur boots, which contributed to his imposing, broad-shouldered and barrel-chested stature. He had a large face, bright and merry chestnut eyes, a round puffy nose, reddened, no doubt, by his love of drink, his left hand replaced by an iron hook, just like our own Coulondre at Mespech, his right hand proudly holding a long flexible staff that was both the sign and the instrument of his work at the college. I had no idea that I would feel its bite so soon and so painfully.

Although the royal professors had already taken their places on the platform and were deep in conversation with each other, the assembled students were making a great deal of noise. They loudly and shamelessly jeered at each other and their teachers, made merry, ate their bread and onions, drank noisily from their gourds, played hand games, dice or cards, or heads-or-tails with an old coin; some were even off in a corner singing dirty songs or exchanging anti-papist jokes, one of which (that I judged to be inspired by Rabelais) went thus: "Is it better to say 'This fat woman who goes to Mass?' or 'This mad woman's got a fat arse?'"

Still others of these turbulent rascals (among them a ruffian named Merdanson, who seemed to be their ringleader, a big red-headed devil, and who was seated directly in front of me) turned round and stared pointedly at the new students in a nasty way that I thoroughly disliked. Merdanson then shouted as if surprised, "Hey! Who are these rogues? What are they doing in here? They look scarcely human! Are they asses? Monkeys? Apprentice mechanicals? They've got ugly faces and their feet smell so bad I could vomit!" Then, holding their noses, Merdanson and his acolytes arrogantly turned their backs on us.

The chancellor, who had been in deep discussion with Dean Bazin, seemed suddenly to notice the racket that was going on, and, glaring at the assembly with his black eyes, his face twisted in a terrible grimace, struck three blows on the oak table with a wooden gavel, and, the hullabaloo subsiding only slightly, he said in a stentorian voice: "The first student who dares open his mouth without my express consent will be thrown out by the beadle, Figairasse, and will *never* be allowed to return. I am the chancellor of this college and it is my duty to assure that order reigns here *and I will make it reign!*"

This last was not so much shouted as bellowed, with such violence, accompanied by such a sharp rap of his gavel on the table and punctuated by the menacing whistle of the beadle's supple staff, that the students fell silent immediately. Cards, onions and gourds disappeared. Songs and jokes were sucked back into throats and devils were transformed as if by magic into toadies.

"Aha!" whispered Merdanson to his henchmen. "What a difference from Rondelet! By St Vitus's belly, my lads, the party's over!"

Meanwhile, Saporta stood staring angrily at the assembly, looking everyone one by one in the eye, convincing each of us that his look had pierced us to the bone, and the silence became so profound that you could have heard a silkworm turning over in its cocoon.

"My scholars," Saporta continued with an unbearable gleam in his eye, "I'll have you know that every abominable abuse that has been tolerated in this school under Dr Rondelet is going to be quickly redressed. And to begin with, I'm going to remind you of the statutes that you swore to uphold a year ago, but which have been treated as dead letters. I *tell* you, I *remind* you and I shall herewith *repeat* these statutes: first, you are to attend every lecture, assembly and professional graduation and the cavalcades that follow them. Second, under penalty of immediate expulsion, you must not bear arms of any kind—daggers, swords, firearms or others—in the school, in the rue du Bout-du-monde or in the neighbouring streets."

"Oh!" hissed Merdanson to his bullies. "This is going too far, and encroaches on our rights." But, at this outburst, no one around him dared crack a smile.

"Third, any scholar who dines or drinks in the taverns of our city but is unable to pay his bill will be expelled. Fourth, expulsion will result if any student is discovered to be living in sin with a harlot in a brothel, supporting her in her sin or receiving money from her; the same applies a fortiori to any student guilty of stealing, even if it's only a sausage or an onion. The whip will be administered to any student walking around the hall during lectures, talking loudly, eating, drinking, tapping his feet, rolling dice or urinating in the window recesses. The whip will also be administered to any who come to blows on the school premises, or injure others by blows, slaps, punches or kicks in the arse. The same whip will be exercised on any student who dares affront with dirty, ugly or outrageous language any of our royal professors, our tutors or the beadle, who shall henceforth be addressed as Monsieur in a respectful manner.

At this, Figairasse, delighted that he should be called "Monsieur" by the students, who, under Rondelet's administration, had called him—at a prudent distance—"Fig arse" puffed out his chest with pride and made his switch whistle menacingly.

"Monsieur Figairasse," said Saporta, "from now on, you will make your switch whistle only when I've rapped my gavel on the table."

"At your orders, Monsieur," said Figairasse bowing low, his entire face (and not just his nose) crimson with shame, and, though he looked chastened, not a single student dared smile, so much did their backsides begin to warm uncomfortably in anticipation of this terrible switch which, under Rondelet, had been left to droop ineffectually.

"And finally, I will remind you that in honour of our master Hippocrates, there will be no lectures on Wednesdays, except in a week in which we celebrate a…" And here I imagined he would say "a papist saint" but, catching Dr Feynes's eye, who was sitting beside him, he said: "Catholic saint. In which case," he continued, "it goes without saying that we'll work on Wednesday to avoid having two idle days in the same week."

At this, Dr Feynes, who caught the polite nuance intended for him, made an amicable nod towards his chancellor, which made me realize that Dr Saporta was not such a madman as I'd supposed, but that he also knew how to govern with finesse.

"The returning students have already sworn to obey our rules," continued Saporta, "but the new arrivals must now take their oath which they will each pronounce in turn. Master Fogacer, please take the roll call and write the results on the register."

Fogacer rose from his bench to his full height, a long black shadow, and proceeded to the platform where Chancellor Saporta handed him the school register.

"Luc Sanche!" called Fogacer, who began by the last ones enrolled.

"What must I do?" asked Luc as he rose, his face deadly pale.

"*Juro.*"*

"*Juro!*" said Luc.

At this, Merdanson turned around to look at Luc and, glaring at him, said, "He's got balls…"

"But they're soft balls!" the chorus of his acolytes intoned quietly.

I would have bet that our chancellor was going to throw a thunderbolt and reduce these idiots to ashes, but, amazingly, he remained as quiet as a log in a forest, his eyes quite calm and his brow serene. I only learnt later that it was a tradition of the school (which even this chancellor was loath to correct) that the older boys would greet the new arrivals with this taunt, which was borrowed from the author of *Gargantua and Pantagruel*.

"Pierre de Siorac!" called Fogacer.

"*Juro!*" I said, raising my hand.

"He's got balls," said Merdanson.

"But they're soft," chanted the chorus.

There were thirteen of us novices and each was called in turn, responded "*Juro*" and was greeted in the same manner. After the thirteenth, the veterans, emboldened by the success of their chant, tried to humiliate us with other jokes, barbs and jeers, but Saporta

* "I swear."

259

suddenly banged his gavel down on the oak table and Figairasse made his switch whistle through the air, and a palpable silence reigned.

"Good students!" Saporta announced. "Dean Bazin will now speak to you about your studies."

Dean Bazin, as I have said, was a small, thin gentleman, bent with age, who spoke in a weak voice, but his eyes were so sharp and viperous that he compensated for his lack of physical vigour with the venomous fire in his pupils. He spoke in few words as a man who is economizing his breath.

"I will speak first of all," he said, "of the school library. In 1534 it could boast but fifty-two volumes. Today these number eighty-six. It has thus acquired thirty-four volumes in thirty-six years. This growth is of particular consequence given how dear these books are, but I would like henceforth to be able to purchase two volumes a year. We have therefore decided to exempt each student from the banquet he's expected to provide the school on his graduation if he donates one écu to the library."

Although for the most part contained, and nearly stifled, the indignation that followed this proposal was so lively and so unanimous throughout the students' benches that Saporta was obliged to give a blow of the gavel to the table, and before Figairasse could whip his switch into a whistle, he growled, "Who would like to speak?"

"I would, begging your permission, Monsieur!" ventured Merdanson, not without some courage, as he rose from his seat.

"Merdanson," snarled Saporta, "are you speaking on your own behalf, or are you mandated by your peers?"

It didn't take me long to realize that Saporta had set an insidious trap for him, and Merdanson had stuck his nose in it like a simpleton.

"I am mandated by my peers," he asserted. "They elected me to be the students' abbot."

"You are nothing of the sort!" screamed the chancellor with a voice so thunderous that the windows rattled in their lead frames. "The title and functions of the students' abbot were eliminated by the Royal Council of Béziers, because some of these so-called abbots were abusing their power by leading the novices to the baths and introducing them to the sluts who frequent these places and having them robbed blind. Very abbot-like, don't you think?"

"But I'm not guilty of any such abominations," countered Merdanson, his face turning as red as his hair from shame and humiliation.

"Perhaps, but you were elected illegally, and now you challenge your professors by virtue of a title you cannot lay claim to."

"But," objected Merdanson, "the title of students' abbot was reinstated here under Chancellor Rondelet."

"I am the chancellor of this college," thundered Saporta, drawing himself up to his full height, his eyes glowing like embers, "and under my governance no local custom will ever prevail against the law! Merdanson, you represent no one but yourself, so if you wish to speak, speak in your own name."

"Monsieur," said Merdanson, making a visible effort to get a grip on himself, since he'd been so thoroughly bloodied in the first skirmish.

"I'm listening," sneered Saporta in a tone that made it abundantly clear he was listening with only half an ear.

"Monsieur," continued Merdanson, "this is what we believe—"

"Merdanson!" Saporta interrupted. "Are you the king of France that you speak in the plural?"

"Monsieur," Merdanson replied, once again brought up short, "it is my belief that it is against all traditions of this college to annul the banquet the graduating student has always offered to the school."

"Unstop those big ears of yours, Merdanson," scoffed the chancellor. "You misunderstood Dean Bazin. The banquet hasn't been annulled. Each student has the choice of offering a banquet *or*, in lieu of a banquet, offering an écu to the library."

By this cunning reply—since no student would choose to spend five livres on a banquet when he could get away with a donation of one écu to the library—Merdanson had his trap shut tight, and, defeated, sat back down. And although Saporta's victory was not carried out by entirely irreproachable tactics, I had to admire his cleverness as well as the good sense of the royal professors. Indeed, as my father had often remarked, medical schools throughout the kingdom, like their sister law colleges, abused their students' purses by requiring these ruinous celebrations that left no legacy other than latrines full of excrement the next morning, whereas the money that was thrown away on such excess would be much better spent on furnishing their scholars with books.

"Dean Bazin," crowed Saporta, with a royal gesture that seemed to me to irritate his colleague, "please continue."

"*Secundo*," said the dean, "dissections are very dear both for the school and for the students. Under Chancellor Rondelet, we were abusing our quota by performing up to six a year, whereas the Royal Council of Béziers established a limit of four. As a cost-saving measure, we will return to this number."

Again there was a great stir among the students, and, even though it was certainly more justified than the previous one, no one dared any insurgency against this baneful economy, not even Merdanson, still stinging from his defeat. I know not what demon possessed me, but I madly undertook to incite him to battle. "Friend," I whispered, lightly tapping his shoulder, "now's the time to fight back!"

Merdanson turned as suddenly as if he'd been stung by a wasp and frowned, his green eyes dismissing me with infinite scorn. "You little turd," he spat, "you dare tap the shoulder of your elder?"

"Ah, Monsieur! If I'm a little turd then you're a turd and a half since you're bigger than I am!"

Merdanson couldn't believe his ears. "Lads!" he hissed to his acolytes. "Did you hear this novice? This idiot? This conceited ass? When this assembly's over, we'll whip him like green barley to cure him of this madness."

"My friend," I replied, voice trembling with rage but still managing a whisper, "I crushed the Corbières bandits and I'll crush you too!"

"Listen to this gentlemoron!" hissed Merdanson. "If he's interested in crushing, it's his arse that will get crushed and his shit with it!"

"Silence!" cried Saporta, banging his gavel down on the table, which, of course set Figairasse's switch to whistling, and the tumult died down.

"Who wishes to speak?" asked the chancellor, and, since no one dared confront him, he continued with the same princely condescension, "You may continue, Dean Bazin."

"Let me continue then," said Bazin, gnashing his teeth at being subjected to Saporta's high-handed tones. "To conclude, my young scholars, I shall read you the *ordo lecturarum** for this year—"

"But, before continuing," Saporta said, shamelessly interrupting the dean with an incredibly superior attitude, "I will ask my 'son', Siorac, who has such beautiful handwriting, to come up here on the platform to write, from your dictation, the *ordo lecturarum* in the school register."

I stood up.

"His son! By the belly of St Vitus, my brothers!" hissed Merdanson. "Our revenge promises to be all the sweeter since we can think about the father as we administer a good spanking to the son."

"Monsieur," I said, as I rose to leave, "however much your ears flop about, they're nothing compared to the way your tongue wags, which would put every dog's tail in France to shame." Whereupon I walked up to the platform and took the stool the chancellor indicated at the end of the table. Dr d'Assas greeted me with a

* "The list of lectures."

263

delectable smile, handed me the school register and provided me with a writing desk. You can imagine how, despite my quarrel with Merdanson and the apprehension it produced (for he was very solidly built and could undoubtedly land a strong blow), I strutted a bit as I ascended the platform and took my place in such illustrious company.

"Here's the *ordo lecturarum*," said Dean Bazin, and judging by the venomous look he gave me, despite the fact that we were meeting for the first time, I realized I should not look for any excessive tenderness on his part when I sat for my exams at the end of the year.

"To great men, great honour," intoned Dean Bazin, and removing his cap he continued with great pomp. "First, Hippocrates, *The Aphorisms…*"

At the name of the venerated master of Greek medicine, the royal professors and ordinary doctors removed their bonnets and did not put them back on until he had finished his reading of Hippocrates.

"Second: Galen, *Libri morborum et symptomatum*."*

How strange, I thought as I wrote this name ("Galien, with only one 'l'," whispered d'Assas, reminding me of the correct French spelling. "Gallien with two is a Roman emperor"), how strange that they remove their hats for Hippocrates but not for Galen. Could it be that, although both were Greeks, the first of whom lived 400 years before Christ, and the second of whom lived two centuries after, Galen is too recent to merit the same respect?

"Third and fourth," Bazin continued, "we will study Arab medicine, as our school has always done: Avicenna's *The Canon of Medicine* and al-Razi's *Treatise on Smallpox and Measles*."

Here Dean Bazin paused, as if conscious of the scandal that he was going to provoke. "Fifth: Vesalius's *De humani corporis fabrica*.† Sixth:

---

* *The Book of Maladies and Symptoms.*
† *On the Composition of the Human Body.*

Ambroise Paré's *The Method of Treating Wounds Made by Arquebuses and Other Firearms.*"

At this point there was such a commotion on the ordinary doctors' bench that I couldn't help noticing it, since I was up on the platform. Not that there was a struggle or uproar, but, in a more muffled way, there was a series of consultations and angry whisperings and along the entire bench, a wave of resentment, with, here and there, expressions of great dismay among the doctors—some turning their backs, some turning crimson with anger, others jumping to their feet and actually spitting like tomcats.

"What's all this?" said Saporta, frowning deeply.

"Dean Bazin," cried one of the ordinary doctors, "I cannot stifle my indignation any longer: Vesalius and Paré are modern doctors and it's an abomination to put them in our *ordo lecturarum* beside such venerable masters of the ancient practice of medicine."

This doctor had very black, fanatical eyes set in a long, narrow, wrinkled and jaundiced visage, and his bilious vehemence so surprised Dean Bazin that he stood there unable to say a word. But of course, as you may surmise, Chancellor Saporta was not to be undone by such a one.

"Dr Pennedepié," he said, with his regal air of disdain, "if you wish to express yourself in this assembly, be so good as to ask my permission so to do."

"I so request it," said Pennedepié, raising his cap of bright-red silk.

"I so grant it," replied Saporta, "and in granting it, I request that you use it moderately and wisely."

"Very well then," cried Pennedepié, raising his red bonnet, "I shall repeat here my thoughts on the choices of texts for the fifth and sixth books of our *ordo lecturarum*. I think these books are a great scandal, and I am not the only one here who thinks so. Vesalius and Paré are modern writers, and what's worse, they're our contemporaries! Vesalius died in 1564 and Ambroise Paré is still alive!"

"And may God grant him long life," answered d'Assas, with his benign look, suave voice and gestures so caressing you would have thought his chambermaid were standing at his right hand.

Dean Bazin, having regained his composure, now adopted an entirely different tone as he replied, "Dr Pennedepié, I would like you, from the depths of your ignorance, to *try* to understand that nothing, absolutely nothing in the Béziers decrees forbids including moderns in our *ordo lecturarum.*"

"But we never did this under Rondelet!" said Pennedepié.

"Dr Rondelet is dead!" cried Saporta in a thunderous voice. "And I find it passing strange that seeing me standing where I'm standing you haven't yet noticed his demise."

Dr Pennedepié, accused of rank ignorance by the dean and so brutally snubbed by the chancellor, was so humiliated that his eyes were popping out of their sockets and his lips were trembling, and he rose as if to leave. Dr Saporta, seeing him stand, and fearing no doubt that Pennedepié's departure might start an exodus of the other ordinary doctors and gain enough momentum to create a cabal against him, immediately resolved to mix some oil with his vinegar.

"Being uninformed about the Béziers decrees does not necessarily imply ignorance," he said in his most soothing voice. "Dr Pennedepié's disdain for the moderns in no way diminishes the fact that he himself is one of the most learned doctors in Montpellier, and that someday he will take his place among the royal professors."

Despite the fact that this empty promise was clearly intended as nothing more than a temporary balm, it had a marvellous effect on Dr Pennedepié, who, seeing the chancellor in an entirely new light, sat back down and dreamily fell silent.

Immediately, however, another David emerged from the ranks, "Monsieur, may I speak?"

"You may, Dr Pinarelle," said Saporta.

This Pinarelle was a small, bony fellow with a pointed nose, thin lips and ears that stuck straight out from his head and looked, if I may speak of an ordinary doctor with such candour, entirely senile.

"Monsieur," he croaked, "it doesn't seem fitting to include Vesalius in our *ordo lecturarum* since he dared to insult Galen."

"He did not insult him," corrected d'Assas in a soft voice and with a caressing gesture, "he respectfully criticized him."

"But it's all the same!" cried Pinarelle. "Criticize Galen? One of the masters of Greek medicine! Who is Vesalius to dare such a thing?"

"If Galen were infallible, he would be God Himself," replied d'Assas with his most disarming smile. "You must admit that Galen's methods were very strange: he dissected animals and applied to men, without even checking them, the observations he'd made. So it was that he declared that a woman's uterus is split in two because that of the rabbit was. Vesalius corrected this error."

"I don't care!" cried Pinarelle furiously. "I'd rather be mistaken with Galen than right with Vesalius!"

At this the entire assembly, which, up until Pinarelle's statement, had been noisily commenting on the proceedings, was struck dumb with disbelief and then burst into waves of laughter, which moved from bench to bench uproariously. An angry frown from Saporta put an end to this brouhaha, and, in the silence that followed, Dean Bazin said in his most venomous tone: "Dr Pinarelle, if you were treating the uterus of a sick woman, it would not be of little consequence that you were, as you put it, mistaken with Galen."

At this witticism, another huge burst of laughter shook the assembly. Even the apothecary students and the surgical apprentices sniggered at this, despite the fact that, unworthy of seats, they listened to this squabbling while standing at the back of the hall. Pinarelle felt both the viper's sharp bite penetrating his skin and its hot poison burning in his veins. He fully realized that it would take a long time to recover from this cut Bazin had inflicted, and that, for months to come, it would offer to the entire city of Montpellier an immense source of humorous jibes. He turned ashen to have been so pricked by his dean, and, in his silent resentment, threw Bazin such a hateful look that Chancellor Saporta understood that Pinarelle, like Pennedepié (and even more easily than the latter) could be won over to his devotion. It was clear to me, as I watched open-mouthed and excited, that if Saporta was defending Bazin's *ordo lecturarum*, he was in no way defending Bazin's person. Quite the contrary.

The unhinged laughter of the assembly would have continued unabated if Saporta, who'd been careful not to take part in it, had not suddenly frowned, rapped his gavel on the table, signalling the beadle to make his switch whistle in accompaniment.

"No one," said the chancellor in a grave voice and with a feigned appearance of equity, "no one here may question Dr Pinarelle's science or his conscience. Monsieur de Joyeuse owes to our colleague here his recovery from a nasty catarrh and would agree with what I've just said since he has only praise for Pinarelle. I wanted to make that clear. However, to satisfy Dr Pinarelle's scruples regarding the late and illustrious Vesalius, I must inform him of something few in this city know, that Vesalius was a student at our school of medicine in Montpellier."

"I didn't know that!" cried Pinarelle. "That changes everything!"

And even though this joke proved Pinarelle to be even sillier and more naive than the one that had just caused him so much embarrassment, the love that all of us, novices and veterans alike, bore our college, caused this announcement to be met with general applause. And Pinarelle, smiling gratefully at the chancellor, tipped his crimson hat to the assembly and sat down.

I imagined that after such tempest and tumult that the assembly would finally be becalmed, but scarcely had Pinarelle returned to order than a third champion threw his glove into the arena.

"May I speak, Monsieur?" said a stentorian voice.

"You may, Dr de La Vérune," answered Saporta.

This fellow, as I learnt later from Fogacer, was named La Verrue, too similar to the word for smallpox to avoid ridicule in the medical community, and so he changed it to La Vérune. But this transformation did not bring him the satisfaction he'd hoped for, so he'd added a noble "de" to it, which raised many an eyebrow before people grew accustomed to it. I was surprised by how voluminous Dr de La Vérune was in every part of his body: cheeks, neck, chest and belly, but unlike Figairasse, who looked so strong, this fellow just looked swollen.

"All right, we can accept Vesalius," he cried in the most scornful tone. "He's a doctor and studied at our school. But Ambroise Paré! Words fail me to tell you how scandalized I am that a book by this *surgeon* (he pronounced the word with infinite disparagement) should find its way into our *ordo lecturarum*! How can we tolerate it, Monsieur, that doctors of medicine—I said doctors!—should open Ambroise Paré's book, which, by the way, is written in French, read it and write commentaries on it? I blush with shame and confusion at the very thought! Is this, I ask you, a reading worthy of our school? Should a doctor, I say a *doctor*, read a book in French by a surgeon who is merely the holder of a master's degree and not a doctor? Are we going to allow ourselves to sink down into such mud?"

In the silence that followed this remonstration, which greatly embarrassed both dean and chancellor since it touched on their rank and the privileges that accompanied it, which are considered by all to be perhaps more sacred even than their science, Dr d'Assas, smiling genteelly and, speaking softly, replied, "If 'mud' there be, than I would be happy to be relegated to the rank of master of science if I had the genius of Ambroise Paré. For I hold him to be a very great doctor and a surgeon without peer. On the battlefields, he saved countless amputees by tying the ligature of their arteries, rather than cruelly cauterizing them by fire. And as for his treatise on the wounds made by firearms, he has no equal to this day in the accuracy of his descriptions and in the efficacy of the remedies he has proposed."

"Nevertheless," cried Dr de La Vérune with a sweep of his hand as though he were brushing away d'Assas's arguments like straw, "Ambroise Paré is not a doctor! He has only a master's degree! We might admit to have read him in the secrecy of our rooms, though he doesn't write in Latin. But to read him *ex cathedra** and in French would be unacceptable and beneath us."

"Dr de La Vérune," said Chancellor Saporta, who, as I observed once again, had the ability to change from devouring wolf into lamb, "I want to praise you for the zeal you have displayed in defending the glory of our title against the encroachments of our subalterns: it is true that Ambroise Paré is only a master. He is not a doctor. Worse yet, he's a surgeon. And for all of these reasons, I share your views and stand wholeheartedly with you. However, the authority of the surgeon in matters of wounds inflicted by firearms is, as Dr d'Assas said, unequalled, and as these wounds are so frequent in these troubled times that we live in, we have thought it wise to instruct our scholars in these arts. Are we mistaken in doing so? Should we strike Ambroise Paré's book from our *ordo lecturarum*?"

"If I were you, yes! I would do it!" cried Dr de La Vérune, who, complete idiot that he was, thought he'd won the day.

"And yet!" countered the chancellor with a sudden gleam in his eye. "And yet! The case merits reflection. Ambroise Paré cared for Henri II during his long agony. Charles IX has chosen him as his personal physician. So I ask each and every one of you," he added, raising his voice, "should we take lightly the serious risk of offending our king and sovereign by striking his personal physician's work from our *ordo lecturarum*? Let all who so believe raise their right hands."

* "As if he were infallible."

270

This question, by its tone and by its captious form, was posed in such a menacing way, the entire assembly was so cowed, and their rebellious spirit so completely crushed, that not a soul moved so much as a finger. And profiting from this cowardly and tacit acquiescence, the chancellor, his brow still furrowed in an angry frown, raised his gavel and, as the entire assembly continued to keep as still as a mouse in its hole, he struck the table with brute force, saying in a thunderous voice: "The *ordo lecturarum* for the year of Our Lord 1566 has been unanimously adopted."

One might have thought that we had done with the twists and turns that had marked the beginning of the school year. But this was not to be, either for Chancellor Saporta or for me, however paltry my involvement had been in the larger questions that had just been debated here. I was more troubled than astonished by the spectacle provided by the angry doctors. (For example, if examined by Dr Pinarelle at the end of the year, was I to argue with Galen that the uterus was a double-structured organ, or agree with Vesalius on its unity?) And, as I was lost in these thoughts, I realized that I hadn't yet written the name of the book by Ambroise Paré in the school register (though I knew the title well enough, having seen it in my father's library at Mespech) when Saporta, leaning over my shoulder like a great crow, suddenly said in his inevitably brusque and imperious voice, "Well, Siorac, where are we?"

"Monsieur, I'm just finishing." And scarcely had I written the last word when the chancellor took—or rather snatched—the pen from my fingers and, in his large handwriting, all of whose letters bristled with pikes and shields, wrote on the bottom right of the document:

Dr Saporta
Chancellor

Then, with an air of superiority and swagger, handing the pen to Dean Bazin (who was gnashing his teeth at being treated so cavalierly), Saporta walked away, his nose in the air, to discuss some matter with Dr d'Assas, who, despite his many human failings (his vineyard and his chambermaid), was still held in great esteem. I remained sitting on my stool in front of the register and saw Dr Bazin, his meagre body trembling with fury, approach the register, pen in hand, like a viper its prey, reflecting for a moment on what he intended to do. Then, his jaundiced face illuminated by the ruse he had settled on, he signed his name (despite his trembling hand) in the space between Saporta's name and the text of the *ordo lecturarum*, inserting it thus:

Dr Bazin
Dean
Dr Saporta
Chancellor

In this way, despite being constrained to sign second, he demonstrated in the most dazzling fashion that he came first in the hierarchy of administrative functions, the responsibility for the curriculum having, in his eyes, priority over the management of the school.

"By the belly of St Anthony!" I thought. "Here's a nasty trick! What cleverness! What a hypocritical tactic! And what frightful carnage we're going to see in this swamp between these two crocodiles!"

For my part, however much I was inclined to side with Dean Bazin (since, after all, it was a question of the *ordo lecturarum* that he'd read and, for the most part, composed), Saporta's (admittedly minuscule) support and the loyalty I owed my doctor-father had me sneak away like a cat who'd just stolen his dinner, slipping in among the black robes to tug on the chancellor's long sleeve and alert him, sotto voce to the sacrilege that had just been committed.

"I'm going to find a remedy for that!" mused Saporta, his feathers up and his nostrils whitening in the heat of his anger.

Saporta returned with great strides to the table of the royal professors, where Dean Bazin was licking his chops, eyes modestly lowered as he tendered the pen to Dr Feynes for him to sign in his turn. Saporta, however, grabbed the book out of his hands and, holding it up to the light, carefully reread what I'd written.

"Siorac, my son," he said finally, "you've got beautiful handwriting. But unfortunately, you've misspelt al-Razi. Since we can't have the name of the great master of Arab medicine disfigured in this manner, you must"—and here he ripped the page from the book and tore it to shreds—"do it over."

At this, Merdanson and his acolytes burst out laughing and began shouting and razzing, "Pierre al-Razi de Siorac!"—so much that Saporta again had to rap his gavel three times on the desk and Figairasse had to whistle his switch through the air with particular vigour before the rascals would calm down.

Quite understandably ashamed for having publicly to take the fall for this dark disputation between our regents, I recopied the *ordo lecturarum* from one end to the other on a new page of the school register. This done, Saporta, seizing the pen, signed his name on the lower right-hand side of the text, but close up against my own script so there was absolutely no space in which Bazin might insert his own name. Next, fearing that the dean might try to sign the document on the left side level with his own name, Saporta made a series of hash marks on that entire side which barred any access to the area. Thus Bazin was forced to sign not only after his chancellor, but directly below the signature of Saporta, who, on this first day of the new school year, carried the day against his dean and established his complete domination of the college.

I still believe this was a good thing, years later, although at the time it caused a lot of problems both for me and for others, as we shall see.

After formally closing this session of the assembly, the chancellor was the first to leave, which he did with great majesty, followed by Dean Bazin and the two other royal professors; next came the ordinary doctors in order of seniority, then the masters and then the tutors. Against this exodus, the second-year students, the novices, the apothecary students and the surgical apprentices all stayed in the hall to meet up with their various groups and clans. Fogacer returned, however, to announce that Saporta had ordered everyone to vacate the hall immediately and to return quietly to their various dormitories. The chancellor had expressly forbidden any of the initiation rites, to which, in previous years, the second-year students had submitted the novices. Of course, Merdanson and his henchmen loudly protested this order and became very noisy in their opposition to it.

"Listen carefully, all of you!" said Fogacer, raising his long spidery arms to quiet the tumult. "You've heard the orders of the chancellor. As for me, I've got little to say to you, since I'm not your abbot, nor your prefect—but at best your advisor. And yet, if I had any advice to give it would be this: if I were you I'd be very careful about obeying the chancellor's orders. He's looking for an excuse to make a strong statement on his first day and is itching to have a reason to use one among you to serve as an example for all the rest."

"But, by the belly of St Vitus! Our traditions have been indisputably violated!" complained Merdanson, his face as crimson as his flamboyant hair.

"Ah!" said Fogacer, raising an eyebrow. "Traditions are like forced women. They cry but submit." Which said, he turned on his heels and left, as the shouting echoed behind him.

In the midst of all this shouting and shoving, Luc slipped in next to me and, taking my arm, said in a soft and trembling voice, "Pierre, let's obey the chancellor! We've got to get out of here as quickly as we can! Let's go home!"

"What? Leave the field of battle? Flee from Merdanson? Oh no! I must stand up to him now whatever it costs and lance this abscess."

To be sure, I wasn't looking forward to this, since the churl was tall, broad-shouldered and strong, and we were going to have to fight bare-handed and without swords. Frankly, fear gripped my stomach at the very moment I was pretending to be so brave, but I was careful to pay it no mind, since it's not our guts that should rule our conduct, but our brains.

Meanwhile, despite the order that Fogacer had announced (and, as I realized later, was arranged as a Machiavellian ruse by which the chancellor seemed to weaken his own command by having it carried out by another), the students refused to leave the hall: Merdanson and his henchmen because, though they didn't yet dare set to it, wanted to "initiate" the novices and wreak their vengeance on me; the novices because they now regarded me as their champion and were grouped behind me, terrified by the tyranny of the older boys. In both groups, hurried discussions were being held in hushed voices and, considering the one and the other, you could have more easily got a fart out of a dead donkey than a resolution from either, since both were reluctant to countermand the orders of the chancellor.

While we were thus temporizing, two acolytes, Gast and Rancurel, the one round as a barrel, the other thin as a plank, whom Merdanson had sent off to reconnoitre the activities of the adults, came running back to announce that they'd seen Saporta get in a carriage with Dr d'Assas and that they were heading off to Frontignan to celebrate the new school year and drink *sicut terra sine aqua.**

"By the belly of St Vitus!" cried Merdanson, leaping onto the platform. "My boys, the school is ours! When the cat's away, the rats will fornicate in the hayloft. Belly of St Anthony! You novices,

---

* "As if the earth were without water."

apothecaries and surgeons, we're going to make you the most harassed asses in creation."

"What?" shouted an apprentice surgeon, whose name was Carajac—and he was well named, for he was built like a wagon with a pair of shoulders that didn't fear God or the Devil. "So you plan to 'initiate' surgeons and apothecaries who aren't even students in your school?"

"Lads!" cried Merdanson. "Did you hear this turd? Ever since that foetus Bazin decided to add that beggar Ambroise Paré to the *ordo lecturarum*, these filthy barbers don't even know when they're pissing. Confirmed turds that they are, they dare open their shitty little mouths and dare question the ancients!"

A loud murmur arose among the surgeons, outraged to be called barbers, and to hear their venerable master insulted. Carajac, raising his head, cried, "Monsieur, you haven't answered me!"

"And here's your answer!" shouted Merdanson, behind whom, on the platform, the second-year boys had eagerly massed, ready for a fight. "And the answer is *yes*! As the students' abbot, legitimately elected by my peers according to the traditions of the school, and having the power to decide such matters, I will spare neither barbers nor remedy grocers. And you, you miserable little cowpat, I answer: eat my shit!"

I decided that it was time I entered the fray, so I stepped forward and said loudly and clearly, "Merdanson, though you pretend to be a second-year student, your knowledge of anatomical science is laughable and completely arse-backwards. For hearing so many 'turds', 'cowpats' and 'shit' fall from your mouth, I'm convinced you've got your anus where your mouth should be."

This witticism left our novices, surgeons and apothecaries doubled-up with laughter, while the veterans on the platform howled with rage to see their abbot so rudely treated. Meanwhile, Merdanson was so stunned he couldn't utter a word, so it was Gast (the lieutenant who was round as a barrel) who cried, "Lads! Are we going to let this earthworm insult our abbot? By God, we're going to give them a historic hiding! Let's rip the pants off this al-Razi de Siorac and paint his prick red!"

"And as for his balls," shouted Rancurel, "which are so soft"— laughter from the older boys—"I'm going to rip 'em off with my teeth and either fry 'em with onions or eat 'em raw with vinaigrette!"

"Well said!" cried Gast. "I'll eat some too!"

This disgusting joke bucked up the courage of the older boys, and they gathered to plan how to rush at me, when all of a sudden my beloved Samson stepped up in all his incomparable beauty and strength, God's chosen angel that he was, and said, softly and with his usual lisp, "Whath's thith, Monthieur? Are you talking about cathtrating my good brother here? If it'th jutht wordth, they're ugly and dirty. But if you mean it, I'll fight you."

"Where did this idiotic sweetie pie come from?" cried Merdanson. "Who is he?"

"Friend," said Samson in his dove-like simplicity, "I'm Thamson de Thiorac, I'm an apothecary's apprentith and not so thtupid ath to countermand the chancellor'th orderth forbidding initiationth."

This naive statement was not without some effect.

"Well said!" I cried, wanting to seize the ball and run with it. "Apothecaries, Merdanson has had the temerity to reduce your art to the sale of spices. Surgeons, he's called you barbers. And you, novices, he's telling you you're going to be harassed like donkeys in a barnyard. Are you going to be cowards and accept the arrogance of these bullies, just because they started school a year before you did? Or are we going to unite and resist their insults and humiliations?"

Sadly, the idea that novices, who were, after all, medical students, should join with the apothecaries and surgeons was so new, and the respect in which the novices held their "elders" so strong, that my speech did not have the success I'd hoped among those it was intended to protect. From the silence of some of the novices and the catcalls of others, I could measure just how isolated I'd made myself.

"Courage, Monsieur," said a voice from directly behind me, "we've been up against worse than this when we were fighting in la Lendrevie"

"What are you doing here, Miroul?" I hissed, turning round. "Get out of here!"

"Oh no, Monsieur! Your father ordered me to stand by you through any and all dangers, and knowing your temperament, I figured your first day of school would be one of those dangers."

"You were right, Miroul," I conceded. "Stay here. Against these fifteen hardy rascals, three of us certainly aren't in danger of out-numbering them!"

"Four!" said Carajac, the surgeon's apprentice who had dared stand up to Merdanson. "I won't tolerate this kind of tyranny in the name of school traditions."

"Thanks, Carajac," I said, admiring his strong frame, and much relieved to see one of his size and strength join our ranks. "Looks like we have a fight on our hands."

At these words, as if I'd given the signal to attack, Merdanson and his acolytes rushed from the platform, down the centre aisle between the benches, shouting, "Kill! Kill! Kill!" and these madmen would definitely have killed us, I'll wager, had they had swords or pikes, so extreme was their fury.

Our assailants had the advantage of numbers, but we had the better situation, for they were forced to climb towards us in the narrow passage between the benches, which restricted their numbers.

"Your feet, Monsieur! Use your feet the way you did with me the day I was caught stealing at Mespech!"

Excellent advice! As soon as Merdanson was within reach, his red hair and face glowing, his mouth spitting ugly insults, I unleashed a booted kick that knocked him screaming back into the arms of his henchmen. And although in the next few minutes I had plenty to do to defend myself, which I did like a stallion in heat (feeling sorry that I had only two boots instead of four hooves), I couldn't help noticing that Carajac was doing some excellent work with the windmills of his arms, and Miroul better still, tripping some of his adversaries and using other sly tricks he had learnt on others. As for Samson, who was always slow to figure things out and to act, and of course very little inclined, given his angelic nature, to hurt his fellow men, it took an attempt by Gast and Rancurel, in their fury, to attempt to take him prisoner, to wake him up.

"Friendth, whatth thith?" he lisped politely. Lifting Gast with his left hand and Rancurel with his right, he knocked them one against the other and threw them bodily into the group of assailants. And what a pretty fall that was! In truth, I didn't see it, but a year later there were still stories circulating in the rue du Bout-du-monde about it.

Meanwhile, Luc, who, given the weakness of his constitution, dared not enter the fray, but who did not lack the best kind of courage or eloquence, was exhorting his fellow apothecaries and surgeons to come to our aid, calling them cowards, cads, spineless milksops, sheep for the slaughter. "Look at you," he jeered, "standing there in the corner trembling like jelly with not a thought for your champions! Isn't Siorac a novice like you? What are you novices doing? Samson's an apothecary, what about you? Carajac's a surgeon. What are his brothers doing? Nothing! All three are fighting to save you from the humiliations of an initiation that Saporta has outlawed. And you miserable impotents, you're letting them get crushed!"

Finally his eloquence began to have some effect, and Samson's epic exploit so astonished them that it pushed them to action. And, as the older boys were attempting to surround us by leaping over the benches, the novices marched to meet them by the same means, and even though they fought a bit half-heartedly (perhaps still fearing the veterans) there were enough of them to keep the others from surrounding us. And these latter lost some of their ardour when they saw our flock of sheep heading their way.

We were in the thick of battle and it was slowly but surely turning to our advantage when we heard above the general din three thundering gavel strokes struck on the oak table. And turning towards the platform we beheld, standing behind the table, terrible in his wrath, Chancellor Saporta. He was flanked on either side by Dr d'Assas and Fogacer, while Figairasse, standing in front of the platform, was whipping the air with his switch with such fierce pleasure it was enough to send your heart into your bowels.

"Ah, you miserable scoundrel!" Merdanson hissed at Rancurel. "You said you saw them with your shitty eyes leaving for Frontignan!"

"By God, we did see them leave!" said Gast, as downcast as Rancurel. "They left and came back! It was a ruse to catch us!"

"Silence!" roared Saporta.

And a silence fell so deafeningly on the hall that I don't have words for it since I've already used the metaphor (which I made up) of the silkworm turning over in its cocoon. And yet, how suddenly mute we'd all become! And aching all over! And bruised! And bloody! And to top it all off, more sheepish and abashed than thieves caught at a fair.

After having held us spellbound for a long moment under the fascination of his dark eyes, Dr Saporta cried angrily (though without sacrificing his usual rhetorical finesse), "Oh, you miscreants! Scarcely have you sworn to uphold our statutes and not to come to blows here before you've violated your oath! Where am I?" he continued with a majestic gesture that set his large sleeves flying. "In the medical college of which I am the chancellor? Or among Joyeuse's stable hands? Or perhaps among the crooks of the rue des Étuves? Did I, or did I not, read you *coram populo** the article of our statutes that states that anyone caught fighting or inflicting harm on another by blows or kicks will be subject to public whipping? From what I saw when I came in, you shall *all* be whipped!"

He shouted this "all" the same way he'd emphasized "*in writing*" during my interview, these sudden inflections being part of his customary method of terrifying his audience. And it worked very well, to judge by the anguished faces of our combatants, who were already turning the scarlet hue that our backsides would soon match.

"However," Saporta continued, "not wishing to overtax the good offices of our beadle Figairasse—"

"One must never flinch before one's duty!" interrupted Figairasse as his switch whistled through the air in anticipation of the pleasure to come.

"Figairasse," said Saporta sharply, "remember, I beg you, that you are not to open your mouth unless I speak to you!"

"I beg your pardon, Monsieur," said the beadle, "I'm at your service!" And though he spoke humbly, he looked at us proudly to let us know on whom and on which body part he would take his revenge for this rebuke.

"However, on this first day of my chancellery," Saporta added, "it is my pleasure to show you all mercy"—at this Dr d'Assas smiled faintly, as though he knew quite well how to interpret this "mercy"— "and instead of punishing all of the soldiers, I shall punish only the leaders. Let them come forward and identify themselves, though I already know who they are."

I had no choice.

"Monsieur," I said immediately, "I commanded one of the sides."

"Monsieur," said Merdanson, "I commanded the other."

---

* "In public assembly."

"What distinguished captains!" sneered Saporta. "And which one started this tumult?"

"I did!" I said. "I antagonized the second-year boys."

"I did!" said Merdanson. "I humiliated the novices."

"*You did worse than that*, Merdanson!" thundered the chancellor in a terrible voice. "You attempted to reinstate the initiations that I had expressly forbidden!"

Here Merdanson, paling suddenly, nodded "yes", without being able to articulate a single word, so much did he fear, as he told me later, to be expelled from the college, as he loved medicine with a great and passionate love, however loutish he may have been or appeared.

"Monsieur, may I speak?" I enquired, feeling that things were going very badly for Merdanson, and hoping to patch things up with him and make my peace.

"You may, Siorac."

"I have to confess to you that I was responsible for greatly inflaming the dispute by my angry and biting words: I accused Merdanson of confusing his mouth with his anus."

At this point something very strange happened: Chancellor Saporta smiled. Whether this smile was sincere or calculated I'll never know. In any case, as if to encourage this lightening of the mood of the chancellor, d'Assas and Fogacer hastened to smile in turn, though we students, however comforted we might have felt, didn't dare to imitate them.

"Siorac," said the chancellor with a sort of good-natured scolding I'd never imagined he could feel or express, "that was a very unfortunate and regrettable joke and I will consider that it attenuates the charges against Merdanson. I will also consider as attenuating these charges the fact that, though Merdanson intended to reinstate the initiation, he did not in fact do so."

Hearing these words, as captious and scholastic in form as they were clever and merciful in their effect, Merdanson heaved a great sigh of relief to have avoided the ultimate punishment.

"However," said Saporta, with a brusque and apparent return to his implacable severity, "Merdanson can't deny having provoked this tumult."

"Monsieur," said Merdanson with what very much resembled a rush of gratitude, "I do not deny it."

"Hear my verdict, then," said the chancellor, removing his doctor's cap (which gesture d'Assas and Fogacer immediately imitated). "I condemn Merdanson to receive ten lashes from Monsieur Figairasse's whip. To which, because he started this tumult, I add ten more. I condemn Siorac to receive an equal number of lashes, to which I add an equal number in addition because he is my son."

"Ah," I thought, "those ten additional strokes, however paternal they may be, won't hurt any less!"

"Merdanson," continued the chancellor, "do you accept my verdict?"

"Yes, Monsieur," replied Merdanson.

"Siorac, do you accept my verdict?"

"Yes, Monsieur my doctor-father," I said, but to myself I thought that the son was paying too dearly to help maintain the equilibrium the father wanted to establish in the punishments meted to the older students and the novices.

"The punishment will take place here within the hour," announced Saporta, "before the assembled students and in the presence of Dr d'Assas and Fogacer."

A silence followed this sentence, which, I'll wager, the chancellor savoured greatly, and which I enjoyed a good deal less than he did, but it was suddenly broken, to the prodigious astonishment of all, by my brother Samson.

"Monthieur, may I thpeak?" said he in his soft voice, his beautiful visage reddened as though he were surprised at his own marvellous audacity.

"Who are you?" demanded Saporta, who knew very well who he was, but who seemed to be astonished by the radiant appearance of my beloved brother.

"Monthieur, my name ith Thamson de Thiorac, and I'm an apothecary apprentith."

"What?" said Saporta. "You're an apothecary apprentice and you ask to speak to this assembly?"

"In all due humility," replied Samson, and so powerful was the effect of his beauty that Saporta didn't manage to remain angry, even though he was itching to. "Well, say your piece," he conceded.

"Monthieur," said Samson, "I led the group of apothecarieth in the tumult. I demand to be treated like my brother."

"Young man," said Saporta, barely repressing a smile, "cognisant as I am that you are not a student in our college, I cannot, to my great regret, apply statutes to you that you have no reason to obey. You shall therefore not be whipped, however much you desire it."

He then put on his doctor's cap and smiled, which had the effect of eliciting from the assembled students laughter and applause, which continued and increased, making Chancellor Saporta's intervention a huge triumph, especially since the older boys and the novices in their heart of hearts were infinitely relieved that everything had worked out so well, and that the punishment would be meted out on other backsides than their own.

After his verdict, Chancellor Saporta was able to leave the college for the second time, and this time with no plan to return, his spirit hovering over the college that he now dominated and inhabited in all its parts.

"Merdanson, and you too, Siorac," said Figairasse, his big face red with anticipation as he paraded back and forth on the platform, tapping the handle of his switch on the iron hook that served as his left hand, "before you undress and kneel against this bench, I must remind you that you owe me a few sols as the price of your punishment."

"What?" I replied. "I'm supposed to pay to be whipped, to have my purse suffer along with my flesh?"

"'Tis the custom, I'm afraid," confessed Dr d'Assas, who appeared very chagrined to have to preside over this execution. "Custom dictates that the patient reimburse the beadle for his labour."

"Well, then, Monsieur Figairasse," I said, affecting a lighthearted tone, "since pay I must, I'll pay. What's your price?"

"There's more than one," said Figairasse, "there are two, depending on the degree of whipping you choose."

"Venerable Dr d'Assas, is this also part of the custom?"

"I'm afraid so," sighed d'Assas, who appeared quite distressed to see me suffer such indignities. I appreciated his concern all the more since I noticed that Fogacer's eyes were unusually bright, but I doubted it was due to any compassion, for I noticed this same expression in the eyes of all of the students who gathered around Merdanson and me, who were shamelessly fighting over front-row seats, so avid were they to observe the spectacle of our punishment.

"All right, then," I said to the beadle, "what are your prices?"

"The prices," said Figairasse, who took his time, spoke well and loved to hear himself speak, "are set according to the degrees of whipping, which are in number, two: the first bloodies you, which is what I'm supposed to do, according to the school tradition."

"Bloodies you?" I asked, surprised that I was the only one involved in this dialogue, since Merdanson didn't say a word, but just sat there looking very sombre.

"You heard me."

"But isn't that cruel?"

"It is," said Figairasse. "And only the students whom I'd call miserly and stingy ever choose the first degree because it costs only five miserable sols. But I don't like it since it's so brutal and lacking in finesse."

"And the second degree?" I asked.

"Ah," said Figairasse, raising his switch towards the heavens, "that requires very great skill—"

"Get on with it, Figairasse," said Dr d'Assas.

"All right, venerable Doctor," said the beadle, "but I must explain why. Considering only the well-being of the patient, the second degree has many advantages. The patient gets off with only a few welts and bruises, which make it painful to sit down for a few days. However, this method is very tiring for me since it demands extreme care in the application of the whip. And so it costs ten sols and not a denier less."

"Samson," I said, "give the beadle ten sols."

"You're a good lad," said Figairasse, as Samson, tears in his eyes, counted out ten sols into the beadle's large palm, "you've acted nobly, paid cash in hand with no bargaining. I'll treat you as well as I can. Your turn, Merdanson."

"Figairasse," said Merdanson emerging from his brown study, "I regret I must disappoint you, but yesterday I accompanied my friends to the brothel in the rue des Étuves and the bitches took everything I had. I've not a sol to my name."

"In that case," said Figairasse, his face darkening by the minute and his eyes full of anger, "tradition dictates that if you've no money the punishment is doubled. I'll have to give you forty lashes instead of twenty and all first degree."

"But couldn't I pay you at the end of the month?" begged Merdanson, whose face was losing colour as he contemplated this frightful menace. "I get my pension then."

"Oh no!" said the beadle. "I'm not a rich man, my friend, I can't afford to reduce your punishment on credit!"

"Samson," I broke in. "Give ten sols to the beadle for Merdanson. He has to be punished in the same way I am. Otherwise the equity of the verdict wouldn't be respected."

"By St Vitus's belly!" gasped Merdanson, looking at me as if he'd never seen me before. "Siorac, you're an honest fellow, novice though you are! I'll pay you back your money."

"No! I'm offering you this gift for the love that should reign between novices and second-years."

"Well said, well said!" cried Dr d'Assas, his eyes growing moist.

All the students broke into applause as if they were at the theatre, though the best comedy was yet to come, as they no doubt knew.

"Undress, my lads, and kneel next to each other to facilitate my task."

We did as he directed and were very ashamed to expose our hidden parts to the curiosity of all.

"Ah, what nice arses you have!" laughed Fogacer as he leapt from the platform and approached us. "My mouth waters at the sight of you!" Although his words elicited belly laughs from the crowd, I found his words ugly and inappropriate, and it hurt me that Fogacer would say such a thing.

"Siorac," whispered Merdanson, as he knelt next to me, "have you ever been whipped?"

"Oh yes! By my father!"

"That's nothing! Listen, take my hand, and when the beadle strikes squeeze it as hard as you can. Grit your teeth as well and flex your muscles. The pain will be less severe."

"Lads, are you ready?" said Figairasse, making his switch whistle over our heads.

"Get on with it," said Dr d'Assas.

"And so I am, venerable Doctor," replied Figairasse, "but I must follow the ceremony. Boys, I'll strike two blows to one and two to the other alternately. Are you ready?"

"Yes! Get it done!" I said.

"Oh, my boy," replied Figairasse, "I'm only beginning, and the time's going to pass very slowly for you before I'm done."

"Begin, I beg you," said d'Assas.

And I received two lashes so strident and burning they took my breath away. But I refused to open my mouth or make any sound.

"Belly of St Vitus!" said Merdanson. "Don't keep quiet! Yell! It helps!"

And when he received his ration, he yelled.

"Ah, that's great!" said Figairasse. "Here's a boy who knows what it's about! I like it when they yell! It soothes me too!"

I received two more blows, which seemed even more painful than the first, but didn't flinch—but when my third turn came, I realized that I wouldn't make it to the end without fainting unless I let out the beast in me, so, seizing the hand offered by Merdanson, who'd never seemed so friendly, I screamed to wake the deaf.

"Well now, our second gentleman is getting into it!" said Figairasse. "I like that better! It's only natural!"

Of course, he was right, and right, too, about the way time stood still. I thought I'd been at the pillory for an hour when we were only at the tenth lash.

"Hold on, Figairasse!" broke in d'Assas. "I think you're losing your touch. These last two lashings seemed to me to be first-degree punishment, not second."

"Ah, no, venerable Doctor, that's not possible!" replied the beadle, quite annoyed to be criticized about his speciality. "I give the patient exactly what he paid for, and when I'm done you'll see blood very near the skin but you won't see a drop spilt. I'm very careful!"

"I hope so, for your sake, Figairasse," said d'Assas with a hard and menacing tone, which very much surprised me since he was normally so benign.

"Venerable Doctor," said Figairasse, "I'm being very careful."

Their dispute (as d'Assas must have hoped) provided a bit of a respite, which I took advantage of to catch my breath, for during the lashings I thought my lungs would give out and venom fill my heart. But when Figairasse started in again, his lashes, despite d'Assas's warning, didn't seem any lighter, quite the contrary.

"Stop, Figairasse!" shouted d'Assas. "How many lashes is that for each boy?"

"Fourteen, venerable Doctor."

"No, it's sixteen."

"Venerable Doctor, I'm sure of my count."

"And I'm certain of mine."

Since Figairasse dared not contradict d'Assas's affirmation, and d'Assas refused to back away from a number he knew to be false, there was a moment of silence.

"So what shall we do?" said the beadle bitterly while making his switch whistle in the air over our backsides.

"Let's wager," said d'Assas.

"Aha!" replied the beadle, suddenly changing his tone of voice and, though my backside was turned towards him, I thought I detected a gleam in his eye. "Let's wager! What shall we wager?"

"Whoever loses, wins. If I'm right, I'll give you a flask of my Frontignan wine."

"Two," countered the beadle.

"All right, two. But it must be in good faith. Search your memory carefully, my friend. You're up to sixteen."

"Venerable Doctor, now that I think about it, there's no doubt. You're absolutely right—and I won: I'm up to sixteen."

"Shake on it!" said d'Assas. "You won! And make sure you lighten your hand for the last four."

He didn't, since the beadle never gave anything for nothing. But suddenly it was all over. Stunned and bruised, I got up and dressed quietly but I did not feel totally undone, and the first faces I saw were Luc, Samson and Fogacer, tears streaming down their cheeks. Yes, Fogacer! And may Satan himself whip me in his infernal kingdom if I ever understand this devil of a man!

"Merdanson," I said, "since we suffered together, let's recover our strength together. I invite you to join us for dinner at the Three Kings. A wounded ass should not go about on an empty stomach!"

"What?" gasped Merdanson. "Did I hear you right? Novice, you're inviting me to eat and drink with you?"

"Friend, you heard right."

"Belly of St Vitus, Siorac, you're the most polished novice I've ever met! It wasn't enough to pay ten sols to get me out of the first degree! You're feeding me! I, who've got no money after the bitches wiped me out yesterday! Siorac, you're a noble fellow! Give me your hand! A novice you may be, but I'm your man! And shit on this shitty beadle! May his shit go back in where it came out and climb right up to his throat so he suffocates in his own excrement and his anus grimaces in agony."

On our way to the inn, Samson shed hot tears as he thought about what we'd endured, but smiled through them to see me whole and not too hobbled by my execution (though my backside was dragging). He kept hugging me, taking my arm, throwing his arm over my neck and kissing my face.

"Aieee!" I cried as I tried to sit down at the Three Kings.

"Aieee!" cried Merdanson as he sat down next to me. "My poor arse! You shitty beadle, may it please God to make you a cuckold as many times as I have welts on my backside."

"Merdanson," said our hostess, "in the meantime, take your hands off *my* arse or I'll give you a slap that will uncurl your red hair. Try this wine instead, it's our best."

"It's not bad. And as bent, broken and messed up as I am, I drink to the very exalted and very farting Monsieur d'Assas for having, by ruse and by Frontignan, got us off two lashes. But my good hostess, to proffer a glass instead of your arse is such a pity! What's life without a little sex?"

"Merdanson," said our hostess, "I like you well enough, but besides the fact that you're as foul-mouthed as any stable boy in Toulouse, your manners are rude and crude. You should take Siorac for a model. He caresses with his eyes and waits until he's invited to move from eye to hand."

"Siorac," agreed Merdanson, "is the most perfect gentleman in all creation. I love him like a brother. Thanks to him I'm able, despite those bitches in the rue des Étuves, to eat my fill and *bibere papaliter.** What's more he's got a beautiful brother, even if he is only an apothecary's apprentice."

At this, the hostess, Merdanson and I all sat in silent contemplation of Samson, for he was indeed so beautiful that just looking at him made you infinitely happy.

"Good hostess," I said, "bring us one of your crispy roast pork dishes that I saw on the spit as I passed the kitchen. And add to that a flagon of your best—no, two, since there are three of us. But, good woman, you're playing with me. As for your 'invitations', I don't see any coming!"

"Patience!" she laughed. "Here's a little down payment." And passing behind me she ran her fingers along my neck. But I didn't move a muscle, for I knew all too well that she belonged to Cossolat. Yet I knew she liked me. So she would give me saucy looks and I would

---

*   "Drink like a Pope."

tease her but that was enough to create an understanding between us that added extra flavour to her succulent roast pork.

But listen to this! No sooner had this delectable roast arrived at our table, been carved and served up, and no sooner had Samson brought his fork to his mouth, than he let it fall onto his doublet. Open mouthed, he turned crimson, then paled and seemed if he were going to pass out: Dame Gertrude du Luc, her blue eyes more beautiful even than I remembered, was standing there looking as though she'd suddenly emerged from beneath the ground, dressed to kill. A veritable vision!

That Samson should have been unable to utter a word was no surprise, but I, who never lack for words, was completely tongue-tied, literally bewitched to see her so beautiful in all her finery. Merdanson, too, fell silent, and this silence might have lasted longer if Dame Gertrude hadn't been the first to speak; she went right to the point: "Good friends," she said, her eyes shining while maintaining an air of formality, "I've just arrived here from Rome where I finished my holy pilgrimage, and finding you here is a rare coincidence. But as happy as I am to see you, I am distressed not to be able to speak further with you: I am on my way to the Saint-Firmin church to thank God for the success of my enterprise."

And, looking Samson directly in the eye in a way that fooled no one (for she knew that he was slow to understand things), she brought her black veil over her hair, adjusted her mask and departed in a majestic sweep of her dress.

9

THE PAIN I SUFFERED at the hands of Figairasse didn't simply make for "some difficulties sitting down" but for difficulties of another kind, which the reader will easily understand, since my arse hurt with every movement I made. And since, every night, Fontanette slipped the bolt of her door and came into my bed, she was every bit as distressed as I was.

"Oh, Pierre," she whispered, her eyes glowing in the darkness, "you never should have taken my virginity. Now I'm so anxious to make the beast with two backs with you, however great a sin it may be, that I could no more do without it than do without my daily bread. I go wandering dreamily about during the day, which is spent only in waiting for night to come, and as soon as I've left your embrace, I start dreaming of it again in my own bed."

"But, Fontanette," I answered, "isn't it sweet to dream thus, and to anticipate such pleasure?"

"It *would* be, Monsieur, if I liked my work. But alas! *She's* watching my every move and especially now that my heart isn't in the work as much as it was before. Dame Rachel is forever quarrelling with me and nagging my master to get rid of me."

"All the more reason, Fontanette," I replied, "to listen to reason: you see what state my backside is in, and that I wince every time I move. Go straight to bed: you'll feel more like working in the morning."

"Oh no, Pierre! Not on your life," she said, her sweet arms round my neck and hugging me close with marvellous vigour. "Let me at least enjoy you a little before I go to bed!"

Whereupon, unable to resist her embraces any longer (for this adorable girl's arsenal was more potent than any brace of pistols), I began sweet-talking her and caressing her, and from caress to caress we slipped inevitably into giving her what she had asked for (and of course what I wanted), despite the grimaces that I made towards the end, when I was again beset by the bruises on my back.

Dear reader, I don't know why, upon rereading this page, I don't rip it to shreds. God knows why I should have written it in such lighthearted and profane terms, I who swore to say no more about my poor Fontanette, since every thought of her and her terrible and pitiful fortune so tears at my heart: a thorn that I could never pull out, even today, without it ripping me apart.

My Samson was in heaven, but at the same time very tormented, for the courses had begun at the Royal College of Medicine and he was required to attend at least some of them, which lasted until five o'clock—at which time he could be seen running madly towards the needle shop, carrying his books, his writing desk and his candle—this last because the lectures began before daybreak. At ten, I would go looking for Samson and, with Miroul on my right, stroll through the deserted streets of Montpellier, swords in hand and pistols in our belts. And it was a good thing we were armed, for one evening—it was a Thursday, if I remember correctly—we found the needle shop under siege by five or six villains, who, having climbed up the eaves, were trying to break open the windows on the second floor, but neither the racket they'd made nor Thomassine's cries for help had brought any neighbours to their windows, so cowardly were they. There was a full moon, and I shot one of them like a pigeon, and Miroul shot two others while the rest fled. At the sound of these detonations, Cossolat, followed by his archers, arrived on the run, swords in hand, furious that anyone in his town had dared attack Thomassine, for whom he had a weakness, austere Huguenot though he was. Of course, he was also sweet on the hostess of the Three Kings, and I don't know if that was the lot, since this sort of man is not easy to satisfy.

Candles were brought into the large room at the needle shop. Thomassine, still shaking with emotion and wearing only her negligee, was a beautiful sight, and more beautiful still, it seemed to me (silly though I might have been), was Dame Gertrude, who, in her confusion and shame, had taken the time to throw on a cloak. Cossolat, seated opposite her, looked her over in a way that made me instantly jealous, if I'd had the right to be so. As for Samson, he was drinking the wine that Azaïs had poured for us, and kept saying, "Whath all thith? Whath all thith?"—very put out that anyone had dared frighten his lady. Certainly he would have been able to repulse the attack all by himself if he'd had a weapon, but, since he'd come straight here from the Royal College, which forbade us to bear arms, he didn't.

"Captain," panted Thomassine, her breasts heaving, "what good are your archers if they can't protect the honest citizens of Montpellier? Without Pierre de Siorac, we'd have all been killed."

"Ah, my good Thomassine," replied Cossolat, "it's a very big city and my archers can't be everywhere at once. What's more, there are as many bad characters here as there are rats in the sewers, and the taverns and brothels are worse than the Augean stables. A river couldn't wash away the vermin that frequent them. I've already told you a hundred times, a woman living alone, who's believed to be rich, draws thieves like a magnet attracts iron. Hire a guard and arm him."

"Who can I find?" moaned Thomassine. "I know a lot of people who've been robbed—and sometimes killed—by their own watchmen."

"Thomassine," I ventured, "if you want my advice you'll hire

Espoumel, when he receives the king's pardon and is released from the jail."

"Sweet Jesus!" cried Azaïs. "A brigand from the Corbières! In our house? With two women! He'd surely rape us!"

Saying that, she looked at Miroul with such effrontery that I thought she was trying to make him jealous or goad him on a bit. But Miroul, who knew the wench too well, remained calm and serene.

"Espoumel," I said, "is done with his days of highway robbery. He's not a bloodthirsty type. Quite the contrary. As long as he's treated well and his pride is not injured—for he's a very proud man—he'll be as faithful as a bulldog."

"I'll think on it," said Thomassine, who, though generous, was nevertheless careful with her money, since she'd known such terrible poverty in the Cévennes and feared falling back into it in her old age when she'd no longer be attractive. And as she fell silent, everyone else did too, but the various exchanges of looks between us spoke volumes! Samson was devouring his lady with his eyes, but she, still feeling ashamed to be there, kept hers lowered, but was clearly aware that she was being looked over by Cossolat. Thomassine, fearing Cossolat's jealousy, would only look at me when he wasn't looking, though he was fully aware of our amours. As for Azaïs, and Miroul, each was trying mightily to pretend not to be looking at the other. Quite a spectacle!

"Siorac," said Cossolat, finally tearing himself away from his fascination with the beautiful Norman, "satisfy my curiosity! What are you doing with all these wooden dolls that Espoumel is carving in his jail for you?"

"Well, Captain!" I replied. "It's a deep dark secret, but I'm going to share it with you since you're my friend. I'm painting some of these *petetas* as English soldiers. By the same magic, I'm turning others into Frenchmen, and Miroul has been building a model of the ramparts of the citadel of Calais out of cardboard. I'm planning on taking this panorama of the battle to little Anne de Joyeuse to show him how Guise, d'Andelot, Sénarpont, my father and a few others recaptured the city from the English after they'd held it for 210 years."

"What a marvellous idea!" cried Cossolat. "Joyeuse will be delighted and even more so his son, who dreams only of battles and heroism. When should I request an audience for you?"

"I'll have finished the project by next Thursday," I smiled, happy to see his zeal, and his willingness to intervene for me in an enterprise from which he himself couldn't fail to gain some credit.

After Cossolat took his leave with his archers—to whom Azaïs had served a round of drinks in the street outside—Dame Gertrude du Luc, with a serious look but a suave tone of voice, asked if she could speak with me alone. Whereupon, seeing my assent, Thomassine (who didn't like this tête-à-tête one bit) nodded to Azaïs, and the latter showed us into a little parlour off the larger room. Samson, although he made no objection, watched our departure with great astonishment. The door scarcely closed behind us, Gertrude threw her arms around me: "Oh, my brother!" she said, giving me a huge hug and showering my face with a thousand little kisses. "I'm so happy to see you and to be able to express privately the extraordinary tenderness I feel for you and thank you for the many beautiful letters you sent when I was in Rome plunged in my devotions."

"Madame," I replied, thrilled that she trusted her privileges as a sister and my own virtue enough to lavish such caresses on me, which, I confess, did not leave me unmoved. "Madame," I said, my voice failing me and saliva filling my mouth, "I was merely the interpreter in these letters of my beloved Samson's great passion for you."

"Of course! I know that!" she answered, dazzling me with her deep-blue eyes and her sweet hands on my face. "But," she added, "the words were yours, so suave and so delectable! Surely, if you found such beautiful ways to express it, you must love me as well!"

"No, Madame, I do not love you," I answered, sensing the danger of such language, and neither daring nor desiring to pull my face away or take my eyes from hers.

"What?" she said with a pout. "Is it possible? Is there some little chambermaid about, whom you've fallen for despite her inferiority of blood and rank?"

I didn't like this tactic at all, and the scales suddenly fell from my eyes. I withdrew my hands from hers, and holding her at arm's length, I said, "Madame, you wished to speak to me, I believe?"

"Ah, yes!" she replied, quickly adopting a businesslike tone. "I told Caudebec that I was lodging with my cousin here, and I think it would be better if we avoided my beloved's comings and goings and asked Maître Sanche if Samson might spend the night here from now on."

"Madame, the thing isn't as simple as you think. Maître Sanche is a very austere gentleman who would not tolerate a certain sin you're all too aware of, even if it were youthful folly. Moreover, my father committed Samson to my care and protection, and I doubt he'd make exceptions to the current arrangement, even for a few days and for an unknown lady."

"But, my brother," she cooed, pulling her hands from mine and throwing them around my neck again, "please consider the danger to which I'm exposed in this house! And the perils that Samson risks walking about at night, not to mention the dangers to which you expose yourself," she added, bringing her face up close to mine and tilting her head slightly as she looked at me, her beautiful red lips opened invitingly, her blue eyes moist with tenderness.

"By the belly of St Anthony!" I thought to myself. "This is a lively widow, pious though she may be! And who leads men around by the nose or by whatever member she can get hold of! It's a lucky thing she's leaving for Normandy soon. Sooner or later she'd make Samson suffer."

"Madame," I said, taking her hands from around my neck, with the pretext of kissing them respectfully (though even these kisses were a little too pleasurable). "I am your servant and will do my best to obey you, but I cannot guarantee that Maître Sanche will look favourably on my request."

"Perhaps, then," said Dame Gertrude, giving in to this possibility and looking at me slyly, "I should ask Cossolat to mount the guard here to protect me?"

"Oh, you she-devil!" I thought. "Even though you had your eyes discreetly lowered, you didn't miss the fact that Cossolat's attentions were getting under my skin."

"Madame," I countered, with some frost in my voice, "if I were you, and Maître Sanche refused, that's what I'd decide."

And, rapidly kissing her hands, I called Miroul and left, thoroughly disappointed, and very much on my guard against this beautiful Circe, having no idea what she intended to do with all of these men whom she wished to enchant, and doubting very much that she had much of an idea herself. "Aha!" I thought. "Now I see her in her true light. Was she never sincere? Not even in her affection for me? Has this coquette always been hidden beneath her prudish exterior? Or is it Rome and the Romans who've returned her to us with such a lusty appetite, not just for one man but for all men?"

I left her feeling very uncomfortable that I was perhaps responsible for Samson's having fallen into such slippery hands. When I got back to the pharmacy, I set about convincing Maître Sanche of the perils that threatened us when we were out walking the streets at night, and I convinced him that Samson should take his lodgings, armed to the teeth, at the needle shop. In this way, Dame Gertrude would have no reason to see Cossolat every day, and I would have no occasion to see her, which was all to the good since, according to my mood, I loved her either too much or too little.

Cossolat didn't forget the mission he'd agreed to undertake for me, and the following Thursday, towards three in the afternoon, Joyeuse sent me his carriage (which made a great noise in the rue de la Barrelerie) to bring me to his mansion with my wooden soldiers, the ramparts of Calais, the citadel and the inlets of La Manche that surrounded it, these last painted in blue on the cardboard and assuredly less icy than they had been in that month of January, when Guise, his brothers, Sénarpont, my father and so many others waded in up to the neck to launch their assault.

I'd thought that I would tell my tale in the great hall of the mansion with only little Anne de Joyeuse for an audience. You may easily imagine my surprise when I discovered that the table and rugs had been removed from the hall and the servants had placed a circle of chairs around the now empty room, on which were seated Anne, his brothers and sisters, the Vicomte de Joyeuse himself, surrounded by his principal officers (Cossolat standing slightly behind him), and, to my considerable astonishment, the beautiful Madame de Joyeuse, who, high and mighty though she was, had deigned to attend this military spectacle, bejewelled like a queen, and behaving a bit like one, surrounded by her ladies-in-waiting, who were dressed almost as elegantly as she was, rustling with silk, strewn with pearls and pulverized with perfumes.

I presented my respects to the vicomte without too much awkwardness, I think, and kissed his wife's hand, heavily adorned with rings, and made no attempt to hide the feelings that her great beauty inspired in me.

At first I felt too shy to speak in front of this magnificent assembly, but once I got over my initial stage fright, I forgot where I was and could think only of how best to narrate this heroic adventure, which had allowed our kingdom to shake off the last English foothold on our soil and which, subsequently, earned for my father the title of baron.

I'd asked the cyclopean Balsa to lend me his wand for the occasion (which he was most reluctant to do, but he ended up consenting to my request since he couldn't figure out how to refuse it). Armed with this long, flexible pointer, I directed Miroul, who was seated on the floor, to move the English and French soldiers, according to the ebb and flow of battle that I was recounting, adopting the same lively and dramatic tone that my father had used when he told us this story at Mespech.

Espoumel had made me some little cannon, which I'd painted bronze, and these, at the direction of my pointer, shot off rounds, which amused Joyeuse and his officers, but totally amazed Anne and his brothers when, thanks to a thread that Miroul had attached to one part of the ramparts, a whole wall of the citadel fell as if struck by cannonballs. In the credulity of their youth, the brothers believed it was really the cannon that had opened the breach in the stone walls of the castle. "Ah, Monsieur de Siorac," cried Anne, clapping and flushing with the excitement of battle, "this is marvellous! Now, have at these cursed English!"

"Here, my lad," I said, handing him the pointer, "do me the honour of commanding the assault!" Whereupon he leapt to his feet, cried, "Have at 'em! Have at 'em! No quarter!" and touched different groups of soldiers, which Miroul then thrust into the hole in the ramparts.

"Hey there! Go easy, my boy!" cried Joyeuse. "Don't rush all your men in at once! You've got to have reserves ready to support the vanguard you've already committed to the fight. The city hasn't been taken yet, only the citadel. It isn't clear yet if you can maintain your position!"

This set Anne to thinking, and he turned to me with a wonderfully naive, sweet and serious demeanour that I couldn't help but admire. It's true that his extraordinary beauty, already so remarkable at such a young age, gave his words great weight.

"Siorac," he said with his sweet, musical voice, "how many men did Guise engage in the assault on the citadel?"

"Five hundred and a good number of gentlemen."

"Including your father, if I remember rightly," added Joyeuse courteously. To which I could only respond with a deep bow, since I was so touched I couldn't find my tongue.

"What about Guise?" asked Anne.

"Guise," I explained, "led the assault, but when the citadel was taken, he waded back across the little channel up to his neck in water to rejoin the main battalion of his troops."

"Oh, if I'd been him," said Anne petulantly, "I would have remained in the citadel so I could be the first one to enter Calais!"

Not knowing how to respond to this, I looked at Joyeuse, who said gravely:

"No, Anne, that was impossible. The 500 French who had taken the citadel were in a very vulnerable position, since the city was entirely occupied by the English garrison, who had cannon. Guise was right to go back to the main body of his troops on terra firma to enable him, if necessary, to pull back from the castle or, if possible, to double the number of troops there."

To which Anne made no other response than to produce one of the charming little pouts that held such sway over his father and that, later, were to have even more effect on Henri III, and would bring him many royal favours: one of which would turn out to be fatal, for if, as a child, he'd paid more attention to the lessons of prudence that his father was always providing, he wouldn't have met his death at the age of twenty-six at the head of Henri's army, which he commanded with such valour and such mad impetuosity.

"Oh," said Anne when I'd finished, "I wish I had some soldiers like these! I'd drill them every day!"

"But they're yours!" I said. "Soldiers, cannon and ramparts. I brought them here to offer them to you!"

"Father!" cried little Anne, his blue eyes blazing in wonder. "Did you hear that?" And without waiting for his answer, and taking advantage of the fact that I was kneeling down to pick up one of the soldiers that had been knocked over by the pointer, Anne threw his arms around my neck and kissed me so many times that I was overwhelmed with tenderness and nearly in tears.

When I stood up, Joyeuse was very gracious with me, and in veiled and fairly vague terms promised to compensate me for the expenses I'd put myself to in order to create my little army. Thereupon he took his leave very graciously and Madame de Joyeuse allowed me to kiss her fingertips, and then they all withdrew. When they'd gone, Cossolat laid his hand on my shoulder and whispered: "By the belly of St Anthony, Siorac, today you've considerably improved your fortunes with Joyeuse, but if I were you, I wouldn't count too much on the compensation he mentioned. He's very careful with his money, both by nature and by necessity."

I put on a brave face when I heard this, but was secretly bitterly disappointed, having wagered on his generosity to provide sums that I'd extracted with great difficulty from Samson to pay for the card-board, the paints, the wood and the sculptor. "Well, that's great men for you!" I mused. "They think everything is owed them. Tomorrow the vicomte will have forgotten his promise and I'll be down twenty-five écus for nothing."

"Don't worry, Captain," I said. "We'll speak no more of it. It's nothing."

"But wait!" said Cossolat suddenly, his eyes lighting up. "There's one of Madame de Joyeuse's ladies-in-waiting heading your way, looking like a trireme under full sail. Maybe this is, if I'm not mistaken, another sort of compensation."

"Monsieur de Siorac," said the lady as she approached, without even appearing to see Cossolat, and bowing gracefully, "Madame de Joyeuse requests the honour of your presence in her apartments."

"Madame," I replied, bowing in return, "I am at Madame de Joyeuse's command." And I followed her through a maze of splendid rooms, my eyes glued to her back, which was a pure delight, for she was a tall brunette, beautifully proportioned, with a graceful step.

But turning round after a moment or two, she said with a half-haughty, half-amused air, "I beg you, Monsieur, walk by my side. I dislike being devoured, especially from behind."

"You forget that I might devour you from the side!"

"No, no!" she laughed. "This way I can keep my eye on you!"

"Madame," I rejoined, "since I have the pleasure of walking by your side, might I have the honour of knowing your name, since you seem to know mine?"

"Monsieur," she said proudly, but with her upper lip tracing a smile, "I am Aglaé de Mérol. My father is the richest man in Provence. As his daughter, my plan is *not* to marry a little brother from Périgord without a penny to his name, even if he is as good-looking as you."

"Madame, I ask you then," I laughed, "which of the two of us first spoke of marriage? You or me? For me the pleasures of looking are enough. I don't need to go further."

Caught off guard and unable to find a suitable reply, Aglaé chose laughter for her answer.

"Yet you dare continue!" she said, observing my eager eyes.

"Madame, it's just that there's more to look at when I'm beside you than behind you!"

"Well, then, walk ahead of me!" she commanded.

"What! Like a condemned man!" But finding our game so pleasant, I did as she commanded and, after a moment or two, I said without turning round, "The problem is I can still see you in my mind's eye. So I'm captive, but only of your beauty."

"What a catch!" replied Aglaé. "A little brother without a penny! A gentleman who intends to be a doctor! Shame on you!"

"Oh, Madame! Don't go despising a doctor! I could work such cures on you!"

She laughed and knocked on the door that stood before us, and, as it opened, she entered, made a deep bow and said, "Madame, I bring you a monster, but at least he'll amuse you!"

"Tell him to come in!" said Madame de Joyeuse, and when I saw her, with all her ladies sitting in a circle around her, their eyes maliciously alight and their little pointed teeth showing through their dangerous little smiles, I felt like one of the early Christians who was being thrown to the lionesses. And yet, I also enjoyed this challenge and felt not a whit inferior to the traps that they might be setting for me.

"Monsieur de Siorac," said Madame de Joyeuse, looking at me quite severely, though I felt not the least abashed in her presence, for the scene struck me as rather comic, "can you explain why it is so important for you to enjoy the good graces of my husband?"

"But, Madame, why does one ever go anywhere except because one hopes to find pleasure?"

At this reply, which was pronounced in a certain tone and accompanied by a certain look, Madame de Joyeuse, forgetting that she was a grande dame, broke out laughing uncontrollably and shamelessly, and her ladies with her. Aglaé, joining in the merriment, cried as if she were proud of me, "Madame, didn't I tell you what a monster he was?"

"And so you are, Monsieur!" said Madame de Joyeuse as she tried to stifle her laughing behind her fan. "A most impertinent fellow! No other gentleman here would have had the audacity to give me the look you did when you kissed my fingers. What's more, you kissed them like a glutton, though the custom is merely to graze them."

"Oh, Madame, if you're not allowed to look or kiss, where's the pleasure in greeting?" At this, all the ladies-in-waiting again burst out laughing uproariously.

"Pleasure, Monsieur? Pleasure?" cried Madame de Joyeuse. "Is that all you think about?"

"What else can I think about, Madame, when I'm at your feet?" And so saying, I threw myself on my knees in front of her.

"Monsieur!" said my hostess, attempting to recover her haughty air, though her attempt seemed altogether forced, since she had to be in her element with a man at her knees. "You must understand that I'm a lady of virtue, though I do love a good laugh, as long as it's innocent. And though I'm courted by every handsome nobleman in Provence, I cause yearning and martyrdom, not happiness."

"Madame," I said, still on my knees but losing none of the effrontery of my looks, "that's exactly how I understand things. But I have discovered in you so many diverse beauties that I cannot but aspire to such martyrdom, if you would consent to it."

"What, Monsieur?" she said with consummate coquetry, while playing with her fan. "Am I so beautiful? I've been told, Monsieur, that my forehead is, perhaps, too high."

"But, Madame, a high forehead is the sign of great wit and intelligence. Hippocrates says so in his aphorisms. And who can focus on your forehead when your eyes are there, large as lakes, deep, golden-brown and full of intriguing shadows?"

At this, the ladies-in-waiting, despite the exchange of some sly smiles, evinced a faint murmur of adulation—sort of an "Amen", but in profane tones.

"Enough about my eyes," said Madame de Joyeuse, "some people say my nose is too long."

"Long, Madame? It is the nose of a noblewoman. But what look could linger on your nose when it could alight on your sweet, fulsome lips, which open to pure little oriental pearls?"

"All right," she conceded with a flutter of her fan, "I'm not unhappy with my mouth, but the nasty people I've mentioned complain that my neck is too fat."

"Fat, Madame? What idiocy! Such people should be tortured for having such lame judgement. May I speak frankly, Madame?"

"If you dare, Monsieur."

"If nature gave you a neck so soft and smooth, it must have been so that a nest of kisses could lodge there."

"Oh, Monsieur!" she said as if scandalized. "That's really too much! A nest of kisses! Did you hear that, Mesdames?"

"Madame," said Aglaé, "he may be a monster, but he's right!"

"Well... all right, we'll accept the nest. But what do you think of my shoulders, Monsieur?"

Dear reader, from the shoulders to the feet—everything except those parts that one neither names nor displays—all had to be reviewed, so hungry was Madame de Joyeuse for compliments. She had clearly reached that age when a woman's beauty begins to fade by the smallest and nearly invisible—but cruel—signs. I suddenly realized that what had begun as pure play had barely hidden the real fears that lurked behind this ridiculous gallantry and that my role was not to make sport but to reassure. And so I played to perfection my role as martyr, persuaded as I was that the martyr wasn't he who threw himself at her feet, but she who, in her fear of ageing, demanded such unbridled praises.

"Madame," Aglaé said when finally we'd arrived at her feet (and it wasn't possible to go any farther), "this monster would make a passably good martyr, at least if he's a true nobleman."

"Good Madame," I replied, rising and pretending to be stung by her question, "my father earned the title of chevalier at Ceresole, and, at Calais, that of baron. I know of no better way in the world to be noble."

"True enough for men," said Madame de Joyeuse gravely, "but, Monsieur, meaning no offence, before I can receive you I must know who your mother is."

"My late mother, Madame, was born Castelnau and Caumont."

"Caumont?" said Madame de Joyeuse. "Are they the Caumonts from Castelnau and Milandes?"

"None other."

"But they're of old and excellent Périgordian stock! Heretics though they may be, the Caumonts are my cousins."

"Your cousins, Madame?" I replied. "Then I have the honour of being your cousin."

Madame de Joyeuse lowered her golden-brown eyes and seemed to be evaluating, on some delicate scales and with infinite meticulousness, the exact degree of our connection, and, having duly weighed it, announced, "Enough parentage, Monsieur, that I may call you 'my little cousin', but not enough that you could call me 'my cousin'."

"Ah, well said, Madame," cried Aglaé. "Very witty indeed! I shall repeat it to everyone!" And all the ladies began to laugh, to applaud and to cackle like pecking hens. But I was not happy, foreseeing what use the nobility of Montpellier would make of such a quip. Marvellously, however, I never had cause for complaint, for once the laughter died down, I was everywhere treated as Madame de Joyeuse's "little cousin"—a title, I later learnt, to which I had no right, but which the good lady granted me in order to be able to include in her company a character as unimportant as a younger brother from Périgord—who was intending to become a doctor!—without lowering herself or offending the rules of etiquette.

"But wait, my little cousin!" continued Madame de Joyeuse, examining me carefully through her lorgnette. "Look how you're done up! Dressed in black from head to toe! Such a little ruffle! And badly worn shoes! You can't appear here dressed like that!"

"Ah, Madame," I moaned, shamed by her reproaches, "you've hit a very sensitive point!"

And so I told her the story of the blue satin doublet I'd requested from my father and how Sauveterre had, in the name of the Brethren, refused categorically to sanction such expense. At which Madame de Joyeuse laughed heartily, her parakeets even more so. Indeed, I thought they'd never stop giggling, chattering, smoothing their plumes and dancing from one foot to the other. "Ah, my little cousin," soothed Madame de Joyeuse, who wasn't entirely lacking in goodwill, "you mustn't be angry, I beg you, with our silliness. But you have to admit that our Huguenots have very strange ways!"

"But, Madame," broke in Aglaé, "didn't your husband promise to compensate our guest for his wooden army? He could use that to buy some new clothes."

"Aglaé," corrected Madame de Joyeuse, "remember this: my husband has two memories. One very good one for what is owed him and another very bad one for his debts."

As one can easily imagine, this quip was immediately applauded loudly by the circle of ladies, though it was not the first time they'd heard it, as Aglaé later explained.

"My little cousin," continued Madame de Joyeuse, when she'd breathed in this incense, "how much money did you spend to create your little army?"

"Oh, Madame," I replied, trying to sound negligent and above such material questions, "in truth, I kept no account of my expenses so I couldn't really say."

"Come now, how much?"

"Fifty écus."

"Very good!" said Madame de Joyeuse, who lacked neither wit nor finesse in matters that did not concern her beauty. "As a gentleman you didn't keep track, but as a good Huguenot, you know to the écu how much you spent."

More laughter. And for my part, knowing what I knew, I adopted my sweetest air and, with the best grace, allowed them to enjoy themselves at my expense, waiting for what would come next. And what came next was overwhelming.

"Aglaé," said Madame de Joyeuse, "when you show my little cousin out, give him 200 écus from my account." And, so saying, she offered me her hand, which, in mute gratitude, I covered with kisses, from her fingers to her wrist and from her wrist to her palm. "My little cousin," she said, frowning through her smile, "come back and see me on Wednesday in decent clothes and, before you devour it, please give me back my hand!"

Thereupon, accompanied by gales of laughter, greatly moved by her generosity, my feet hardly touching the ground, I took my leave of her, with Aglaé de Mérol at my side, looking a bit sad, it seemed to me.

"Monsieur," said Aglaé as soon as we were out of earshot, "you have to admit that you're a monster of ambition, cleverness and deceit."

"Deceit, Madame?" said I, frowning and stopping in my tracks to look her in the eye. "How was I deceitful, Madame?"

"If 'deceitful' stings so much, I withdraw it," she answered hurriedly, alarmed to see me so distressed. "But adroit you are, given all the compliments you lavished on us."

"Was that wrong?" I asked archly. "Am I or am I not Madame de Joyeuse's martyr? Isn't that the role I'm supposed to play?"

"Well then,' she said, placing her hand on my arm, "you're right, I'm sorry. It's just that I love my mistress despite her silly behaviour. And the whole scene, though very funny, causes me much distress. Do you know, Monsieur, there was a time when Madame had so many earnest martyrs surrounding her that we didn't have to go looking for a young, inexperienced lad to pay court to her."

"What, me? Young and inexperienced?" I cried. "I, who fought in the struggles at la Lendrevie and broke up the brigands' band in the Corbières!"

"Easy!" she said. "You don't have to go trumpeting your bravery, we know all about it. But, Monsieur, look at the unvarnished truth: you're a younger brother without a penny and you're a medical student."

"What do you mean, without a penny?" I laughed. "You just gave me 200 écus!" (And, my good reader, you can't imagine how sweet was the sound of those gold coins falling into my purse.)

"But that's nothing!" replied Mademoiselle Mérol, with a sad expression. "My father has a revenue of 100,000 livres a year. Which means that I can't decently marry a man who doesn't have at least half of what my father has. And there are probably not more than four such men in Provence, and they're so ugly and so uninviting that I've refused them all. And so my fortune is sealed. I'll die an old maid."

After that, I began to see her in a different light, astonished that such a beautiful woman should have to submit to such a terrible fate. And I suddenly realized that it was a great pity, when you thought about it, that money governed man's destiny instead of facilitating it.

"Madame," I said, half seriously, half in jest, "if someday I have 50,000 livres, and if I please you, I'll ask for your hand, on condition that you cease to despise the divine art of medicine."

"Divine, Monsieur?" she asked, raising an eyebrow.

"If it's God that gave us life, isn't it something godlike that allows us to hold on to life when it's slipping away?"

"Hold on to it? Can you do that?"

I told her that we could and she said no. We argued about this for a few minutes longer and since every girl enjoys receiving marriage proposals even in jest, Aglaé gradually recovered her lightheartedness and said, "Begone, monster! At least you're not a heartless monster. You will become attached to Madame de Joyeuse and will be a very creditable martyr. And even though you're a younger brother, a doctor and penniless, I feel a great friendship for you already."

This said, she gave me a little kiss on the cheek. And even though it was offered from atop her father's 100,000 pounds, I found it sweet enough to give it back on the little dimple at the corner of her lips, which, by chance, I nibbled a bit. At this she blushed, eyes wide and mouth shut tight, being unaccustomed, I'd wager, to such a caress, whose novelty surprised and, I think, pleased her. Seeing her confusion, and not wishing to wait for her astonishment to become anger, I made a deep bow and departed.

I ran to the Jewish quarter, where there was a little tailor's shop owned by a man named Martinez, who was reputed to make the Vicomte de Joyeuse's doublets. He had olive skin, and was bent double by his profession, but seemed quite robust, with penetrating black eyes, and always looked as though he'd just heard a secret joke.

I explained to him, not without a certain swagger (since my 200 écus gave me great confidence in myself), who I was and whose house I lived in.

My guess is that he already knew, since he was a Sephardic and had his shop near the place des Cévenols, where Maître Sanche had his pharmacy; however, he said not a word, but stood looking at me with his sharp eyes, stroking his beard. He displayed his fabrics, which were very beautiful and which, in the dim light of his shop and in his hands, seemed even more so, but he refused to quote prices for them, and simply said, "The price is not important! We'll settle that later!" Finally, at my repeated insistence, he named a price. It was so high that I pulled away, throwing up my hands, and headed for the door. He grabbed my elbow and began wheedling me, trying to coax me into staying and pleading with me not to take my business elsewhere.

"You'll have my business," I said, "on condition you halve your price."

"Halve it! Fie, Monsieur! A gentleman bargaining with a tailor!"

"My good tailor," I replied, "unlike some gentlemen, whose names I shall not mention since they're so well known, I'll pay you on the nail. It's half your price or nothing. A good healthy half, payable in round gold coins."

"Ah, my lad! You've got your knife to my throat. I'm dying here!"

And his cries brought his family running; his wife, his three sons and his four daughters invaded the small shop, suffocating me with polite greetings and begging me, practically on their knees, not to reduce their father to poverty. I held out, finding as much amusement in this scene as Martinez himself, who seemed like a maestro who, through imperceptible signs and winks, was directing his troupe; and to tell the truth, I had no idea why he would be offering me this comedy; perhaps he was hoping I'd lower my demands. But I wouldn't consider it. I insisted on half of the quoted price and Martinez ultimately accepted my offer, leaving me very satisfied with my business acumen—until the next day, that is, when I learnt from Cossolat that the half I'd held out for was his customary price and that he didn't ask more even from Joyeuse, who, of course, never paid him.

The thing that kept me from abridging the scene of all these lamentations was that Martinez's four daughters were so very beautiful that I couldn't decide which one to look at. So I kept looking from one to the other of these bewitching women, whose gazelle-like eyes shone in the darkness of the shop, and thinking—Aglaé having set me thinking about marriage—that I could not, as a gentleman, marry a tailor's daughter, any more than a Sephardic girl could marry a

313

Christian—and even less a penniless younger brother marry Aglaé. "Oh," I thought, "every way I turn I meet obstacles! If God made the world and made it well, I'd like to know who has so bungled it ever since."

As I mulled over this thought, I walked back to the pharmacy, and it was there that this day, which had started out so auspiciously for my glory and profit, suddenly turned into pain and indelible sadness. Luc was waiting for me in my room, his eyes teary and with a very long face.

"Pierre, my friend," he said in a mournful voice, I have terrible news for you. Dame Rachel has just sacked Fontanette."

"When?" I cried, my throat knotting up.

"Just now."

"Just now?"

"Not an hour ago."

"Ah!" I thought with terrible remorse. "The hour I just spent haggling over my new doublet! I could have seen her if I hadn't done that!"

"Where has she gone?" I moaned faintly.

"That's the problem," said Luc, "nobody knows. No one here knows where she's from, or who her relatives are, except maybe Dame Rachel, who hired her."

"I'll go see Dame Rachel right away," I said clenching my teeth.

"Oh, Pierre," said Luc jumping to his feet, "don't do it! Dame Rachel is furious with you. She's spitting fire and brimstone and demanding that my father kick you out, which he refuses to do."

"She'll spill it," I said, "I'm going to confront her."

Heading downstairs, I went to knock at the door of the lady, who, thinking no doubt it was her husband, bade me enter.

I went in full of resolve. She was sitting at her dressing table putting on her make-up when she saw me in the mirror. She stiffened, turned, sat upright on her tail like a snake (I was astonished that such a beautiful woman could have such a malevolent look and such a tyrannical complexion) and told me to leave at once.

"Madame," I said, "you have sacked Fontanette."

"And you know very well why," she hissed.

"Madame, I'll know why when you have told me."

"And I'll not tell you," she screamed, "since I don't want to dirty my lips, which are pure, by reciting your sins."

"Madame, did she confess?"

"Young man," she spat, her voice breaking under the effect of violence, "I heard that she confessed. I have nothing more to say. If it were up to me, you would not enrage me by your continued presence in this room."

"I thank you, Madame," I answered calmly, "for your very Christian sentiments, but since I find that I am more guilty in this matter than poor Fontanette, I want you to tell me where she has gone and where she lives, so that I may bring her aid and comfort in her distress."

"She has her wages, that's enough."

"Begging your pardon, Madame, but I don't think her wages will get her very far and, from all appearances, she is in great need of support from a friendly hand."

But Dame Rachel remained majestically and stonily silent and inflexible, as though she hadn't heard me, and glared at me with her agate eyes. So I continued, "Surely, Madame, since you hired her, you know where she comes from."

"I knew it," she sneered, a cruelly triumphant light in her eyes, "I did know it," she repeated, "but my memory is such that, the instant I had this pestiferous whore thrown from my house, I erased her from my thoughts and immediately forgot her, her name, her family and the name of her village."

I knew then that I would learn nothing from this flinty vixen, and, drunk with fury as I was, could easily have throttled her to squeeze some little spark of humanity from her body, and from her mouth the name of the village she was hiding. Despite my angry looks, however, she was made of marble and felt nothing, not even fear. Meanwhile, I was trembling from head to toe with the effort of mastering my homicidal rage and I could no longer look her in the eyes, hers being so icy and mine speaking all the hatred and scorn I'd forever feel for her and for the extreme baseness of her actions.

Without a word or a gesture of any kind, I left her standing there. I ran down the stair and, calling to Miroul to saddle Albière, I saddled Accla; as I bridled her, I told Miroul that we were going to look for Fontanette and that the best thing would be to ask the guards at the city gates if they seen a wench of her description; that he should gallop to the la Saulnerie gate, next to the Lattes gate and from there to the la Blanquerie gate while I went to the Pila, Saint-Gély and Peyrou gates.

Sadly, and even more sadly for her, no one had seen Fontanette. It happened, by the worst of luck, to be market day in Montpellier, and that the crowd of labourers and their wives, who had now sold their goods, were now heading en masse towards the city gates to go back to their farms. There was such a crush of people, carts, mules, donkeys and baskets in the streets that Accla could hardly take a step. And who could have picked out of this immense crowd a young girl, dressed like all the others and, tears in her eyes, no doubt, carrying her little bundle? The guards at each gate simply laughed when I asked after her.

"Ah, my lad," said one, "even if I wanted to help, how could I manage to pick out such a needle from a wheat field?"

I waited until the crowds had thinned out and explored for several leagues each of the roads leading out of the city, stopping at each of the nearest villages to describe my poor Fontanette and ask old women enjoying the evening breeze on the benches in front of their farms about her, but I learnt nothing, other than a couple of false leads which were cruelly disappointing.

I came back to our lodgings late that night, exhausted and dusty, and with a throat so tight I could hardly breathe. Miroul had already returned, but had likewise failed in his enquiries, as I could tell just from the sad look in his unmatched eyes. I threw him Accla's bridle and, having no appetite whatsoever, and finding repugnant the idea of sitting down to table with that gorgon, I went up to my room, and without undressing or taking my boots off, fell on my bed where I lay, without a tear or a prayer, too devastated to think. So blinding was the evidence of my loss that I couldn't believe it. I couldn't sleep. And I caught myself listening for the sound of the bolt in Fontanette's door, which she would slide to come into my bed, so round and fresh, her beautiful eyes shining in the darkness with such infinite tenderness.

The next evening, I learnt from my good Thomassine, who seemed quite troubled and angry, that Cossolat had come to see Dame Gertrude du Luc while Samson was attending his lectures at the Royal College, and had stayed for three hours locked in her room. Thomassine wanted me to go and confront this shameless woman and reproach her for her behaviour. But I refused, fearing that this Circe would turn me into a swine in my turn, just by throwing her arms around my neck. Nor did I want to speak to Cossolat about it, for I knew he'd make some joke, since he loved to say that never did a pilgrimage pass through Montpellier without some *roumieuse* deciding that she wanted to forget her saints in his bed. How could I respond to such humour? Laugh with him, or get angry? And where might my anger lead?

Meanwhile, I couldn't help thinking that when my poor Samson happened to hear the news of his mistress's infidelity, he'd be devastated by news that would be cruel for anyone, but so much the more so for one so innocent. Ultimately I became so concerned about him, and so concerned about keeping this news from him, I nearly forgot my anguish about Fontanette.

All that day and the following night I turned over in my mind various strategies but could think of none that would succeed in separating this Circe from Samson, and from Cossolat—and from me, for, to tell the truth, the idea that she took such delight in men was not without its temptations for me, despite the horror I felt at the idea of cheating on my poor brother—and under Thomassine's roof, no less!

Even while listening to Saporta's discussion of Avicenna at the college, this quandary didn't go away, and when Saporta called me up to his podium after his lecture, I thought he was going to take me to task for my inattention. But, after calling my name, he called Merdanson and the surgical apprentice Carajac as well. After having scrutinized us for a moment with his glowering black eyes (for he always seemed invested in convincing us that our present innocence was but the form and substance of our future guilt), he told us that one of the guards at the hospital was offering to the college the body of a beggar who'd just died, and ordered us to go and study this body carefully to see if it was a good subject for dissection.

Off we went, with a certain swagger and the feeling that we were on a very important mission. The guard at the hospital was a balding old man, ugly as sin, with stinking breath and so thin that Merdanson called his case "interesting", and added, for my benefit, "Know what I mean, friend?" The guard said his name was Russec and immediately led us to a small, very dark curtained room that was impregnated with an over-sweet pestilential odour, so foul that we couldn't step over the threshold, preferring Russec's halitosis to the stink of putrefaction. In the centre of the room stood a wooden bed, covered with a straw mat, and on this lay a body shrouded with a dirty sheet.

"So, my scholars!" coughed Russec with a breath so nauseous that I had to cover my nose and mouth with my hand. "I'll warrant you've never seen as handsome a devil as we've got here. He is so vigorous, so well built and so young that he's lacking nothing but the breath of life. He's a marvellous specimen and, what's more, he passed just this morning, so you won't find a fresher cadaver anywhere. And so, my Royal College students, out of my love for medicine, I'm going to offer him to the college for only five sols and not a penny more."

"Five sols," agreed Merdanson, "is worth considering. But we won't buy a pig in a poke; we've got to see it. Please pull the curtain and remove the sheet."

Russec did as Merdanson ordered, and as the light of the sun filled the room, I could see that he was careful to touch the sheet only with his fingertips and stand as far from the bed as he could. Seizing the sheet, he pulled it off. Without taking a step towards the cadaver, we stood staring at it and could hardly believe our eyes: the dead man had a huge bubo from the plague in his armpit and a carbuncle on his right foot.

"Siorac, Carajac!" cried Merdanson, when his fear subsided enough for him to utter a word. "Do you see what I see? By the belly of St Vitus, let's get out of here!"

And the three of us fled madly down the corridor of the hospital, followed by Russec, who was shouting hoarsely, "What is it? Don't you want him? Is there something wrong with him?"

"You bet there's something wrong with him!" shouted Carajac. "And it's a major problem!"

"In that case," cried Russec, "I'll lower my price by a quarter!"

"Not by a quarter or a third!" shouted Merdanson as he burst into the street. Ah, how sweet the fresh air of Montpellier seemed after being in such a pestilential place and with an guard whose breath smelt worse than the cadaver.

"Friends," I proposed, "let's get hold of ourselves. We're near the Three Kings and the hostess is beautiful. Allow me to offer you a glass of wine and some food to build up the red blood in our veins and arteries and thereby strengthen them against contagion."

"That's an excellent and preventive medicine," said Merdanson. "Ambroise Paré recommends it in his treatise on the plague."

"I can subscribe to that!" agreed Carajac (who spoke little but always to the point), "but what's the hostess got to do with it?"

"Beauty," said I, "cures the eye of filthy sights."

Scarcely had I said this when the hostess gave a powerful slap to Merdanson, who, in entering her kitchen and despite her warnings, had given her a pat on her backside.

"Ow!" cried Merdanson. "The wench has a wicked slap! Never mind! Her flesh looks copious and delectable. I'm going to dream about her all night!"

"Shameful creature," said the hostess, "do you want another slap?"

"What? Without getting to touch?" said Merdanson indignantly.

"My friends," I said when she'd withdrawn after serving our food, "I'm worried about this corpse. Do you think we're going to have an epidemic?"

"No, no," said Merdanson, "I heard from Saporta that we see a few cases in the hospital each year but that they never seem to lead to an epidemic. Nevertheless, without this flagon of wine, I'd be mighty sad. In this shithole of a town, everything seems to be in league against medicine. Do you know, my friends, that not a week ago the provost refused to give Saporta the body of a man who was tortured to death, preferring to have his quarters rot from the branches of an olive tree? And today that stinking Russec dares offer us the body of a man with the plague. Goddam it! Medicine is done for if we can't get bodies to dissect. I learn more in one hour from the scalpel of the prosector than in three hours of lectures on Hippocrates. And that foetus Bazin lowered our quota of dissections to four per year! Four, my friends! We should have at least eight! My hostess, since I can't touch your sweet backside, at least leave your beautiful corpse to the college when you die so we can dissect you!"

"Fie, Monsieur!" said our hostess, who was bringing a flagon. "I want to be buried whole in a good Christian burial."

"It's true that we're poor enough," said Carajac. "The college doesn't even have a skeleton. It's scandalous! How can you show the conjunction of bones without a skeleton?"

"I just had a thought," said Merdanson, "which must be a good one, since I pulled it out of this flagon: let's kill Russec. We'd cure him for good of his stinking breath. A gain for him, a gain for everyone. Then, when he's dead, we'll make a skeleton of him. He's pretty thin anyway, his skin's just barely sticking to his bones, so our work's half done already! So from an ugly guard we'll make a handsome skeleton!"

"Friends," I said, conceiving a plan that had nothing to do with what he'd just said, "empty this bottle without me. I see here a gentleman I'd like to have a word with."

When he saw me heading towards him, Caudebec, who had just stuffed half a huge Bigorre sausage into his maw, nearly choked, and, glowering at me, brought his hand to his dagger. But remembering his vain combat of two months ago against a stool, and Cossolat's threats, and seeing me approach with a smile on my face, he greeted me civilly with a nod of his head, but without rising or inviting me to sit with him. His monks lowered their eyes as if they were in the presence of Satan himself.

I was careful not to take offence at this greeting, but, asking a chambermaid to bring me a stool, I sat some distance from Caudebec and said, in a playful voice, "Well, Monsieur! I'm so happy to see you again, all strong and healthy, and your monks as well! And your women look more bewitching than ever." (To which the Norman ladies made a slight bow in my direction, smiled and batted their eyelashes at me.) "They tell me Rome is the most beautiful city in the world. What did you think of it?"

Caudebec groaned at this, but couldn't say more, since his mouth was crammed so full of sausage, and he was busily trying to swallow it like a boa with a rabbit, by a sucking motion of his lips.

"Well!" I continued. "I'm not surprised you like the Eternal City. And what was the purpose of your pilgrimage? Did Heaven grant your prayers? Do you have good news about the health of Madame your wife?"

"No, Monsieur," growled Caudebec, emptying his goblet to water down the sausage. "I received a letter this morning. The ingrate died a month ago, when I'd scarcely arrived in Rome. Ah, Monsieur, I'm furious. What a nasty trick she's played on me. Couldn't she wait at least until I'd made my vows at St Peter's basilica before dying so precipitously?"

"There, there, Monsieur," I said, "try to forgive her. No man living gets to choose the hour of his death. Why, just this morning I saw in the hospital here a poor young rascal in the prime of his youth stretched out dead on a mat with a bubonic sore on his armpit and a carbuncle on his foot."

"What?" cried Caudebec, spitting out his wine. "A bubonic sore! A carbuncle! He had the plague!"

"Well, yes," I answered as innocently as I could, "we have a couple of cases in Montpellier, but don't worry, the city is safe."

"Safe, Monsieur? Safe? Monks!" he cried as he stumbled to his feet. "We're leaving immediately! 'Sblood! I'm not staying another minute in this pestilential town!"

"Monsieur," I said amicably, "since you're leaving, let us part as friends. Give me your hand." And advancing towards him, I held out my right hand. But he leapt backwards, knocking over a stool and shouted:

"Monsieur, don't touch me! You may be infected!"

"Not I," I replied. "Why, I only palpated him a little. Shake hands!" And stepping closer with my right hand extended, and while he retreated from my hand in terror, I pursued him around the table, as he had chased me, dagger in hand, two months previously. But once he'd got on the other side of the table, and seeing the stairs nearby, Caudebec fled, climbing them four at a time and rushing into his room where we heard him double-locking the door.

Whereupon, bowing to the rest of the *roumieux*, who sat mute and paralysed in front of their plates, I went back and sat down at my table with a tranquil air.

"Oh, Pierre," whispered my hostess, "what knavishness is this! You're going to ruin me! All these pretty Norman écus that are fleeing my inn!"

"My friend," I said, lowering my head in mock remorse, "I beg a thousand pardons. My tongue got the better of me. I didn't know what I was saying."

"Now that I don't believe!" she answered. "You never say a word you haven't thought out. I know you too well, and I'll find out why you chased my clientele away."

And she did find out, from Cossolat, who, far from resenting me, when he learnt of the sudden departure of the *roumieux*, laughed until I thought his sides would split.

"Oh, Pierre," he said, "there are two sides to your little trick, so what were you trying to do? Prevent me from giving a pair of horns to your brother? Or prevent yourself from doing it?"

But I knew not how to respond since I was unsure myself. Sometimes it's very difficult to sort out one's feelings, and harder still, one's desires.

*

When this business was done, which had stirred me up quite a lot, I went to look for Maître Sanche, and after politely asking his pardon for all the trouble I'd introduced into his household, I begged him to tell me where I might find Fontanette, for I clearly owed her succour and compensation.

"Alas, my Pierre, I do not know," he sighed. "Dame Rachel knew and doesn't seem to be able to remember. And what choice do I have but to believe her? Oh, my nephew, a woman's will is a boil that no surgeon can ever lance!" He went on to urge me with great feeling to resume taking my meals at his table, since, he said, my absence saddened the whole company. "Except Dame Rachel," I corrected, "who asked you to kick me out."

"I am master of my house," said Maître Sanche, reasserting himself. "I decide who sits at my table. Certainly our rules of morality are stricter in the city than they are in the country, where a younger son's weakness for a chambermaid can have little consequence. And since you were raised in such tolerance, I see no reason to impose our more severe rules."

"Sadly, it is poor Fontanette who must pay the price for both of us."

"Alas, Pierre," said Maître Sanche, suddenly looking very mournful, "I was very fond of the girl. She brightened our lives with her beauty and sweetness. I'm very sad she's gone."

I was very moved by his words, and throwing myself in his arms, I kissed him on both cheeks and promised to return to his table the following Wednesday.

I'd chosen Wednesday, because that was the day Martinez was supposed to deliver my new pale-blue satin doublet, my stockings of the same colour with the red slashes and a small cap with a blue feather—since blue was Madame de Joyeuse's colour, as the tailor had been sure to inform me. I was so thrilled to admire myself in the tailor's full-length mirror and to see how handsome I looked in my new clothes, that I paid the tailor on the spot and even added four écus to the agreed sum.

"Ah, Monsieur de Siorac," Martinez beamed, his olive skin reddening with pleasure, "a gentleman who pays cash on the nail is a rarity indeed! But it's even more rare to be given extra payment. If it weren't for my humble birth, I would embrace you, Monsieur! But I know who can do it for me."

And clapping his hands in a certain way, his four daughters appeared suddenly, and handing each of them one of the four extra écus, he said, "My girls, here's an addition to your purses. Thank Monsieur de Siorac for his generosity and I'll allow you to give him a kiss." Which the four girls did, one after another, in the sweetest manner, leaving me dazzled and almost bewitched by their gazelle-like, smiling eyes.

"Oh, Martinez," I gasped, laughing, "after this you will always be my tailor!"

I stepped out into the rue de la Barrelerie, strutting shamelessly and, since the bells were just striking twelve noon, and there were no passers-by, I had to be my own audience, and so I watched myself on the sly, admiring my nonchalant manner, my mind floating on air. My return to Maître Sanche's table was no abject act of repentance, playing the guilty one clothed in sackcloth, head covered with ashes and rolling in the dust. I managed to time my entrance with that of the master, who, when he saw me, stopped dead in his tracks; Dame Rachel froze at her place, and the others sat mute with astonishment.

"My nephew!" cried Maître Sanche when he'd recovered. "How gallantly you're dressed! What finery! What a splendid doublet! And where might you be going in such elegant clothes?"

"My illustrious master," I replied, "this is not vanity nor ostentation, but simply obligation. I am invited this afternoon to the home of Madame de Joyeuse, since I am, as you know, her little cousin."

"Oh, *que matador! Que matador!*" cried Maître Sanche in his Sephardic jargon. Which was roughly translated as: "How handsome he is!" "My nephew," he continued, "please greet my wife, who has ordered a special dinner to celebrate your return."

Which I did with the best grace in the world, and bowed almost to the ground, but without a trace of a smile, and I have no idea how she received my greeting since, as I bowed, I was careful not to look at her. Shimmering in my blue satin and the object of everyone's eyes, I sat down to this "festive" meal that Maître Sanche had announced, though it scarcely merited this name, but everyone did eat very nearly enough that day. All the while, Fogacer, with one eye on his bowl and the other on my brilliant new doublet, smiled to himself, while Maître Sanche kept repeating, half tenderly, half jokingly, "*Que matador! Que matador!*"

And so the winter passed without much improvement in my relations with Dame Rachel, her agate eyes never seeming to notice me, and, for my part, I made no attempt to repair things with her, since every time I recalled how basely she'd behaved by refusing to tell me where Fontanette had gone, I was again seized with nearly uncontrollable fury. And, to tell the truth, what angered me the most about her behaviour was that she had been able to cover her spite and cruelty under the cloak of religion.

My beloved Samson was so dreamy and so much in his own world that neither Thomassine nor Azaïs ever breathed a word to him of the long conversation that Cossolat had had with his lady in her room at the needle shop. Nor did he ever learn the reasons for the sudden departure of the *roumieux*, and, though he suffered a lot since he was in the bloom of his youth and it was his first love, I consoled myself with the realization that he would have suffered infinitely more had he ever discovered the truth. Upon her return to Normandy, the minx had the gall to write him a very tender letter, to which my brother asked me to respond, but I refused outright and told him he was old enough now to write his own letters. Which he did, but the result was pitifully brief and gauche. She answered nevertheless, and a little trickle of correspondence continued between them for the next four years, though they never saw each other, proof that the lady wasn't without some fondness for him. But this fondness didn't prevent her from leaning elsewhere and dipping her tender leaves into other waters. Alas, what could anyone do? Can you change the nose of a dog that runs in all directions at once? For from censuring such behaviour, I believe that it's no great matter if a woman behaves that way, as long as one doesn't fall in love with her.

I continued to visit Madame de Joyeuse throughout the winter, and things progressed so well between us that ultimately I became the first among her martyrs, though the others, it must be said, had mostly grown weary under the harness, so the lady was pleased to discover in me a freshness, an effrontery, a gaiety—and most of all an imagination capable of inventing new compliments, when the sedative virtues of the old ones had been exhausted. But what drew her to me the most was, in truth, that, grateful for her generosity and goodness, I really loved—and liked—her, and I have to say that she granted me some privileges that a martyr ought not to have received. For example, in the privacy of her cabinet I would massage her back and breasts with ointments, not to mention a variety of kisses we exchanged on the floor next to her bed and a thousand different caresses—but which never passed the threshold beyond which Madame de Joyeuse would have felt she had been unfaithful to her husband.

That threshold, however, seemed to shift, in a way you can easily imagine, and so when I was alone with the lady behind the blue curtains of her four-poster and my kisses and hugs had got her very excited, she allowed herself to say, guiding my hand, "My pretty little cousin, do what I want now." So I good-heartedly gave in to her demands, and she began sighing and moaning and making such violent cries that you would have thought she was giving up the ghost. Certainly I was not so callow that I didn't know what that meant. But I secretly admired the fact that, however much she pursued these pleasures, Madame de Joyeuse was careful never to break faith with her husband. And I've often thought that the little abbot who heard her confession—if, indeed, she confessed all—must have been a very benign or an infinitely tactful priest. For, in truth, the poor lady saw very little of her husband, who was always riding off here and there on his trusty steed, in his travels across France and throughout Provence, in the service of the king, and must have straddled many other mounts that were brought to him at each halting place and which he never got enough of.

Of my intimacies with Madame de Joyeuse, Aglaé couldn't help feeling resentful, and displayed these feelings when we were alone together.

"So, monster," she would say, "what did you do to Madame that made her moan so much?"

"Nothing," I'd answer, "that I wouldn't gladly do to you if you let me."

"Fie then!" she sniffed haughtily. "I'm a virgin! And may the blessed and sacred Virgin keep me in this state until I am married! It seems to me, however," she added after a moment, "the if the Devil were to tempt me enough to make me moan with you, our ages would be much better matched."

I found this something of a betrayal of her mistress, but said nothing. "Aglaé," I replied, "Madame de Joyeuse is such a good person and I love her and I'd be ready to do anything she might ask, even if it meant pulling the moon out of the sky with my teeth. As for her age, it doesn't make any difference between us."

"Well, I see then," she said bitterly and close to tears, "that you're a new kind of martyr: a happy martyr."

And as I looked at her and felt the pain behind the gibe, I tried to pour some balm on this wound.

"With Madame de Joyeuse I am indeed a happy martyr, but with you, Aglaé, I'm an unhappy martyr since, for lack of 50,000 livres, I cannot ask you to marry me." And the word "marry" was like a magic wand. As soon as I'd uttered the word, joy sparkled in Aglaé's eyes.

"Do you really think about it?" she asked, her delectable dimples showing in her smile.

"Yes!" I said. "And I swear it by these dimples!" (Not wanting to swear by any other oath.) And so saying, I gave each of them a little kiss one after the other, but when I went to kiss the left dimple, Aglaé accidentally moved her head in the other direction, and I kissed her lips, a kiss that she was slow to put an end to.

"What impertinence!" she cried, pretending to be ashamed (but also really feeling some shame since she was of a naturally innocent nature). "Monster! Begone!"

On the lawn that filled the courtyard of their mansion, I met the Vicomte de Joyeuse, who, as soon as he caught sight of me, left his officers and came to meet me, embraced me warmly and whispered in my ear, "Ah, Siorac! Or rather my little cousin!" (And here he smiled.) "I'm so grateful to you for entertaining Madame de Joyeuse. You must have a special charm for calming querulous wives. Ever since you've been coming here, there are no more rude words or stinging comments, just smiles and accommodation."

I returned Joyeuse's bow, but hardly knew what to say since my conscience pricked me not a little given his use of the word "charm". And yet it occurred to me that I shouldn't have so many scruples since everyone seemed to be happy. "My, my," I thought as I left their mansion, "very appealing, my blue doublet—by the belly of St

Anthony! I'm in very good standing here!" And saying this—since we are all so blind about what the future holds—I could not possibly have foreseen to what degree, by my own fault, I would need help to get out of a dangerous situation.

Meanwhile, happy with Thomassine, happy in a different way with Madame de Joyeuse, I still thought of my poor Fontanette, even though several months had passed since I'd lost her. And even though I was working very hard at the Royal College—attending lectures, taking notes, organizing them afterwards and, in the evening, rereading the authors that had been commented on that day—and on Wednesdays was very occupied with Madame de Joyeuse, I still managed every Sunday to saddle my Accla and continue my search for Fontanette, village by village, on every road that led out from Montpellier towards the surrounding countryside. But it was all in vain. I couldn't find any trace of the poor girl and, as the months passed, I gave up my search and almost never thought about her any more.

10

I, WHO KNEW the rigours of the Sarlat winters, where snow is not rare in the hills during the coldest months, couldn't help delighting in the moderate climate of Montpellier; the sun shone bright and hot in January almost every day, and the evenings were so mild that we didn't even have to light fires for warmth at night. We would burn scrub oak logs, boxwood branches, old vine-stock, rosemary and heather roots, all of which made beautiful flames, with rich colours, and embalmed the air with their essences. To the curative qualities of these essences I attribute the fact that during my entire stay in Montpellier I never caught a single head cold, though in other locales I'm susceptible to them.

The Montpellierians' high spirits, evident in their daily socializing, regardless of their age or sex, are especially evident during carnival and Mardi Gras, which are originally pagan festivals, despite the fact that tradition links them to the Christian practice of Lent. I have to admit than in my native Sarlat region, we don't have such marvellous exuberance or such a great love of singing, dancing, music and fancy dress. The reader can well imagine that without neglecting my medical studies, at which I laboured daily like a weaver at his loom (in the sense that I was weaving every day the cloth of my future knowledge), I didn't fail to take advantage of these many occasions to join in the joyful processions that wound through the city.

In Montpellier, January is the month when young men give aubades to their sweethearts: for these they hire three musicians (who are otherwise not much in demand that month), two of whom play the oboe or the guitar and the third of whom plays the cymbals, a tambourine or a fife with admirable dexterity. On my return to the pharmacy in the evening, as soon as I saw such a troupe preceded by servants carrying torches, I'd follow them. When they arrived at the home of the girl, the musicians would play their first piece. Then the father would open one of the windows overlooking the street and demand to know the name of the gallant. And if, when the gallant took his mask off and gave his name, the name was agreeable to the father, the window would remain open. If not, the window was closed and the house would remain closed and dark for the rest of the aubade. But there were no insults or ugly words, nor any pots of water, urine or excrement thrown on the performers, as is done, alas, in other regions. Such brutalities are unknown among the Montpellierians, whose customs are as benign and courteous as the climate is mild.

From all this great gaiety at the beginning of the year, one might suppose that every new year brought nothing but happiness, which is certainly not always the case and certainly was not the case for the year 1567, which was beginning, and which would witness, before its end, a renewal of our fratricidal wars, as the Huguenots and the papists began tearing each other apart once again in our unfortunate kingdom.

But the future is like a parchment that's rolled up on itself and can only be deciphered as the days unroll from it, so that, for the time being at least, I felt very lighthearted and could abandon myself with the entire city to the games its friendly inhabitants so enjoyed.

I was very involved in these activities, as you would expect. With eyes and ears wide open, and driven by the insatiable curiosity of

332

my fifteen years, I watched with great interest these games that were unknown in our Périgord.

On Mardi Gras, the most exciting of the day's activities is the hoop dance that takes place on the place de la Canourgue—the most beautiful of the open spaces in Montpellier, where we'd seen the delightful ballet of the sugared almonds on the day we arrived.

Today it wasn't sugared almonds or any other sweets that were being enjoyed but hoops—either white or golden—which were held by a group of young noblewomen, dressed in long white gowns, sparkling with jewellery and wearing masks. Their partners were also dressed in white, and the game, for the men, consisted of jumping through the hoops that the girls held, to the sound of fifes, cymbals and tambourines. If the gallant who wanted to jump through her hoop didn't appeal to the damsel, she would pull it up suddenly, and trip the lad. If she liked him but wanted to test him, she would hold out the hoop only for a moment and then pull it away, so that the suitor would have to dive, head and hands first, through the hoop and somersault onto the paving stones, risking serious injury. If, however, he succeeded in this feat, he would be enthusiastically applauded and the girl, shyly blushing and coyly eyeing her beau, would signify that her hoop was "taken". And even though the purpose and outcome of this dance were obvious to everyone, the admirable thing was that it was accomplished without any coarseness or lewd comments, or ribald laughter, but with an elegance and grace that amazed me.

It was also during the month of January that a series of balls began, which were given at night under torchlight by the nobles or rich merchants of the city. As far as I could tell, however, it was the same group of people who attended all of them, and so, as the "little cousin" of Madame de Joyeuse, I was invited everywhere. Samson was, as well, since he is my brother—and a lad of great beauty—but he declined the honour, declaring that these balls were ridiculous, vain, frivolous and sinful. As soon as his *roumieuse* paramour had departed, my beloved brother had returned to his Huguenot austerity, as to a cloak that he wouldn't have removed except to lie for a few moments in a bed of flowers.

Although I'd never attempted to dance in my life, raised as I was by my Uncle de Sauveterre, I didn't miss any of these balls, and quickly learnt the swing dance, the galliard and the wheel dance, in which I found a double and delicious pleasure: the movements that I made, of course, but also the movements of the girls I danced with that were so graceful and beguiling to watch. For an entire month, until the last day of carnival, when all of the balls end, I never returned to my lodgings until after midnight, my shirt soaked and legs aching with fatigue. But at five the next morning, fresh as the dawn (which hadn't yet arrived), my mind clear and eager for learning, I'd set off for the college, carrying my books, with Miroul at my side with my writing desk and candle. We always wore swords and pistols in our belts since it was still dark out, but when we got to the rue du Bout-du-monde, I took my desk and candle from Miroul and gave him my weapons. I won't claim that I wasn't tired of a morning, or that my thoughts didn't wander somewhere above all the wounds, fevers and sores that our teachers described to us, but I got through the labours of the day well enough. And at nightfall, invited to another ball, I'd start all over again.

On the eve of Mardi Gras, Aglaé's brother, Justin de Mérol, a handsome lad of sixteen who had befriended me, brought me a long white robe, a mask of the same colour, a sack and a wicker basket.

"So what am I supposed to do with all these trappings?" I asked in my surprise.

"Well," said Justin, who had an easy laugh and spoke a very different French from his sister's Parisian dialect, since he'd received very little education, "put on the robe, tie on the mask and attach the sack crosswise in front of you with the two cords."

"And what am I supposed to put in the sack?"

"Ah, that's a secret," he laughed.

"And what's the basket for?"

"It's a secret."

"I'm going to bet," I said, turning it over and over, "that this handle that I see in the centre is to hold it out in front of me like a shield."

"That's a pretty good guess," said Justin. "Pierre, remember that tomorrow, the twelfth of February, is the noblemen's carnival, and we're going to get as crazy as march hares. I'll come find you here at noon, and will explain everything then." And, this said, off he ran, laughing, one of the nicest fellows you'll ever meet, but hardly the brightest—not that it mattered since he'd never have to worry about getting on, his father being worth 100,000 livres.

He was back late the next morning, followed by a valet carrying a large sack.

"Let's go, Pierre! Get your harness on!" he laughed, and his gaiety was so infectious that I couldn't help joining in, intrigued as I was to wear a disguise, and experience what a snake must feel when it loses its skin. So I put on the robe and the mask, hiding my hair under a cap since, being blonde, it would have been too easy to identify me. Justin adjusted my sack crosswise and then announced, "And now for our munitions!"

Hearing this, the valet passed him, one by one, the oranges he'd brought in the sack.

"Oranges?" I gasped. "Am I supposed to throw oranges at people? Isn't that a terrible waste? In Sarlat, if you can find them at all, oranges are very dear."

"But here," said Justin, always laughing, "they're only four deniers for two dozen. Which is to say you can get them for nothing. And look, Pierre, I was careful to choose soft ones so they won't hurt our assailants too much."

"And who am I to assail?"

"Anyone who is harnessed like we are, and wears a red ribbon on his shoulder and not, like us, a blue one. Let's be off, Pierre, it's time, let's not hang about here any longer. Our side agreed to meet in front of Notre-Dame des Tables at noon so we'd have the high ground. My valet will follow us to keep us in ammunition."

"No, no!" I argued. "He's carrying too much weight. He'd slow us down. I'll get Miroul to come with him and carry a second sack with half of our munitions."

It was a glorious battle and we fought like madmen and were watched by great crowds of people of all classes and walks of life, who laughed and applauded and sometimes came up so close behind us to watch the progress of the battle that they'd get hit in the head or the face with the "cannonballs" that were intended for us. Indeed, the people of Montpellier are every bit the inveterate gawkers that Parisians are reputed to be.

The blue and red sides had agreed that once an orange had hit the ground, it shouldn't be picked up and thrown again, the only acceptable munitions being those we had in our sacks, or ones that were caught in flight—an exploit I managed twice, to the great merriment of the crowd. Unfortunately, there were some rogues among the onlookers who, seizing the dirty and burst oranges they found on the ground, began bombarding indiscriminately others in the crowd, sparing no one, not even the more peaceful onlookers. But seeing this, the leaders of both sides got together and suddenly we all presented a united front against these thugs and, advancing on them, we put them to flight under our bombardment, and finished them off by running them down and, in hand-to-hand battle, slapped them silly or kicked their arses so badly that they started yelling "Help! Murder!" as they retreated, a cry taken up by the crowd. This tumult attracted the attention of Cossolat and his archers, who quickly arrived on the scene. When they saw the square before Notre-Dame des Tables strewn with debris—a spectacle that, in truth, offended my Huguenot respect for the fruits of the earth and our duty to be good managers of all that she provides us for our nourishment—he scowled and, given his dark eyes, hair and skin, his visible displeasure had a powerful effect, especially since, as a Huguenot himself, lacking any indulgence for the excesses of the Catholic nobility, the spectacle of this awful waste had clearly exceeded his tolerance. And yet, as a man worried about his future career, and knowing who we were, given our costumes, he didn't want to run the risk of angering the families of Montpellier's finest youth, so, still scowling, he said, half serious, half joking, "My lads, if you weren't who you are, I'd have you enjoy a few days in jail for the commotion you've caused here. So let me just remind you that this game, however traditional it may be, is still forbidden. I'll turn a blind eye to it this time"—though, as I learnt later, he closed his eyes every year—"but on two conditions: first, that you each give a sol to my sergeant so that he can have this mess cleaned up. Second, that you take all the oranges you still have to the hospital and distribute them to the poor there, who will be happy to enjoy them."

We obeyed without any discussion, Cossolat being a man who suffered no answering back. Like everyone else, I gave my sol to the sergeant, very ashamed to have participated in this waste and very glad that my mask allowed me to escape Cossolat's detection. But then I realized he must have known I was there when he saw Miroul among the valets who brought the oranges to the hospital.

Cossolat was withdrawing after having restored order when a fellow hurried by, shouting that there was a beautiful procession in the rue de l'Espazerie, and, like sheep, the crowd set off in that direction, so I followed, along with my peers. And indeed, there was an impressive masquerade there, with costumed players dancing to the sound of tambourines, guitars and fifes. Everyone wore masks, their hair hidden under caps or wigs, some dressed as sailors, brandishing ropes and carrying baskets of fish (which were, thank God, made of painted cardboard), others as pilgrims with indulgences pinned to their backs, stomachs or backsides, still others as labourers, carrying the tools of their trades; finally there came a group of men dressed as women. All were wildly dancing in their gaudy costumes, while singing, jumping up and down and making strange cries; the most delirious of this procession seemed to be the men who were wearing women's dresses, wigs and heels. For these "fellows" were parading like whores in heat, cackling, clucking, wriggling, batting their eyelashes, giving wanton looks and approaching passers-by with lewd gestures and expressions as if they were going to unzip them right there in the street. This made for hilarious laughter among the crowd, and, though I don't like to see such ridiculous characterizations of the fair sex, it might have been funny if the entire group of them hadn't seen our troupe and thrown themselves at us like misery on the poor world, shouting for all to hear that we were the prettiest rascals in all of Montpellier and that they wanted to marry us on the spot. Then, with piercing cries, they began feeling us all over our bodies, without sparing those parts that we reserve for women, trying to pull off our masks and slipping their hands under our robes. The most salacious, craziest and most excessive of these profligates was a tall, thin "woman" wearing a red wig who tried to squeeze me so hard that, to keep "her" hand off my arse, I had to elbow "her" in the stomach as hard as I could, but as the wench came right back at me, I threw a punch at her cheek, which only grazed her, but knocked her mask off. In the brief second or two that it took to readjust the mask, I caught sight of "her" face. I couldn't believe my eyes and just stood there staring: I'd recognized Fogacer.

*

After this discovery I didn't know what to think about it, which is another way of saying that it gave me almost too much to think about. I moved away from the group of masked bawds and their frenetic dancing to the sound of drums, which shook the ground under our feet, and, hearing that there was a group of actors who had made outlandish effigies of famous people and who were about to process around the city preceded by a band, I decided to try to see them. I headed in their direction through the press of the crowds and Miroul somehow caught up with me. We found them in front of the Barbote Tower, where the crowd was even thicker, given the people's appetite for such mordant satire, and I suddenly caught sight of Samson. He recognized me immediately despite my mask, and was so enraged he threw himself into my arms without saying a word. Astonished to see him in such high dudgeon, I pressed him with questions. Finally, recovering his voice, he moaned, "Oh, Pierre. There's more infamy here than I can bear. Merdanson, Carajac, Gast and Rancurel are here too, and are just as furious as I am to see our college so ridiculed and our illustrious master so cruelly disparaged."

"Maître Sanche!" I cried. "What's this all about? What are they doing?"

"Siorac," said Merdanson, his large shoulders breaking a path through the crowd and followed by his lieutenants, Gast and Rancurel, and by Carajac. "Siorac," Merdanson growled, "it's villainy! These shitty shit-heads! May God send the Devil to roast their arses in hell and wrap their guts on his spit! These cowpats, these excreta, these faeces, these turdish turds, these clods of wayward marl! What they've done to Maître Sanche! Siorac, it's villainy! We can't let such an effigy be paraded around the city. It's a dishonour to our college to allow our master to be vilified."

"Especially someone I so love and honour!" said Samson through the fury of his tears.

"Does anyone know who did this?" I asked.

"We don't know," said Carajac, clenching his large fists, "they're wearing masks, but what I do know is that I want to stuff their effigy down their throats!" To which Gast and Rancurel nodded their assent with a resolute air.

"Well, then, let's go feel things out," I suggested.

"What do you mean?" asked Merdanson.

"Find out who they are and how many they are. Stay here, all of you. I'll be right back."

Crying "Give way! Give way there, I say!" I pushed through the crowd, and so great is the authority of one resolute man with a loud voice over a crowd, I was able to move through this Red Sea like Moses, and easily got to the first row of people. It didn't take long to identify the effigy of Maître Sanche among the twenty or so that were displayed there: a big, fat, red-faced fellow with porcine eyes was turning it this way and that to the great amusement of his comrades.

To tell the truth, as grossly made as it was, a little in the manner of a scarecrow on two crossed sticks, it was easy to identify its model: with his head topped by his apothecary's bonnet, his long nose arching down to his long beard, Maître Sanche was easily recognizable by anyone in the city, even if his name hadn't been hung around his neck. But the nastiness of this business wasn't the caricature or the ridicule it conveyed, but the horrific rhymed inscriptions that were pinned to his black robe. One on his buttocks read:

> *We'll stuff right up the arse of any pharm'ist*
> *The pills with which he tries to harm us!*

Another, placed on his virile parts, couldn't help but offend Samson and me:

This old goat, now emasculate,
Likes boys, not she-goats, for his date.

And the third, attached to his stomach, proclaimed:

Pork's a meat Good Christians'll use
But dubious Christians will refuse.

Worse still, as if to make this underhanded accusation even clearer, they'd derisively stuck in various places on his robe bits of fat and pork rind.

I stood agog before such a malicious and stupid piece of cruelty, for Maître Sanche was defamed here in every possible way: in his art, in his private life and in his religious practice—this last insinuation the most odious and perilous of all, for it accused him of heresy and put him at the mercy of the priests.

My blood boiled so hot at this shameful spectacle that it was all I could do to keep from assaulting the fat boor and ripping it out of his hands. But that would have been madness. I would have immediately been overwhelmed by his accomplices, and I had no idea how many of them there were. I'd come to get a sense of the situation, not start a fight. Calming myself down, I put on a friendly face, and approaching the fat churl with a smile (which is all that he could see of my face under my mask) and realizing that my white robe gave me something of an advantage over him, I said with perfect courtesy, "My friend, you've made a marvellous effigy there! It's easily the best of any displayed here! I'm guessing you're a group of medical students who've had enough of Maître Sanche's discipline?"

"Medical students?" said the oaf. "Not on your life. Medicine's nothing but shit, spit and piss. We prefer other food. We're law students."

"Ah, you law students," I said, counterfeiting a sweet hypocrisy, "for me you're the alpha and omega of all knowledge and I hold you in my highest esteem. I'd offer to stand you all a drink after the parade if there weren't so many of you."

"But there are only ten of us here, and if this number doesn't terrify you we'll meet you at the Golden Tavern at five o'clock."

"We'll see you there!" I said, bowing. "At five o'clock sharp!"

When our medical students heard the news that the law students were behind this outrage, they gnashed their teeth and wanted to attack them right away. But we needed to plan our stratagem: wearing our masks we'd greet these oafs in a friendly and lighthearted way and offer to help them carry the effigy. As soon as Samson could get his hands on it, he'd tear it to pieces (with what pious rage you can easily imagine!) while we attacked our adversaries. Everything went exactly according to plan. We had the advantage of surprise. Before the law students could get over their surprise, we had hit them so hard, administering black eyes, split lips, broken teeth, knees to the stomach and kicks to the arse that all ten of them were knocked to the ground like pigs and lay groaning in pain. Samson, as beautiful in his righteous wrath as the Archangel Michael, pulled the effigy apart, deboned its arms, broke its legs, ripped its robe to pieces, stomped the false nose and mouth into the mud and, striking a flint, set fire to the debris. In a minute, the entire effigy, which had cost the lawyers so many hours of venomous labour, was reduced to ashes.

But in the hour of our triumph we fell into great peril, for the crowd, irritated that we'd destroyed such a clever effigy and fearful that we'd go after the others, gathered round us and began to threaten us with such terrible reprisals that we thought they'd pulverize us on the spot. I tried reasoning with them, explaining that we'd only wanted to avenge our master, and that Maître Sanche, far from deserving such treatment, was so illustrious that both Catherine de'

Medici and the king had visited him when they had passed through Montpellier. But they would have none of it. Their anger only seemed to redouble with every word I said, and we were soon surrounded by furious looks, clenched fists and angry shouts. Ah, the good burghers of Montpellier are not very accommodating when they're angry! "At them!" they yelled. "Have at these miscreants! They're trying to ruin our games! Whack and crack 'em! Brothers, let's go! Castrate the rascals!"

We closed ranks and prepared for what promised to be mortal combat, when all of a sudden someone—I found out later that it was Miroul, who quickly and quietly had snuck in among their ranks—shouted, "Watch out! Captain Cossolat's coming!" His shouts were picked up and repeated blindly and in panic by others in the crowd, and suddenly all one could hear from one end of the square to the other was the name of our captain—who was, in fact, still in the rue de l'Espazerie, where he was trying to control the situation there. When he heard, however, that things were turning ugly at the Barbote Tower, he headed our way with his archers, so that, to our immense relief, after the people started shouting "Wolf!" the wolf actually arrived.

As soon as they saw him, the crowd began cheering him and denouncing us with shouts and insults, claiming we'd burnt one of the effigies and brutally assaulted the people who were carrying it.

"What's this?" trumpeted Cossolat, frowning, but managing a quick wink at me to show me that he'd recognized me despite my mask. "What? Destroyed an effigy at carnival time! That's an odious crime! You there!" he said to us. "Not a word out of any of you! I'm taking you to the jail where you'll discover what it feels like to be locked behind bars! Archers, surround them!"

Merdanson opened his mouth to protest, but a quick elbow in the stomach shut his mouth and got him to understand that the jail was a much better alternative than this murderous mob.

When we emerged from the crowd, Cossolat leant over in his saddle and said, half severe, half in jest, "Siorac, I can't believe my eyes! Everywhere there's fighting, there you are!"

"Captain, we had no choice. Did you see this infamous effigy?"

"I saw it," said Cossolat, lowering his voice and looking quite sombre. "I saw it before you destroyed it, and I think it's a very bad omen. Behind these idiotic law students who are simply pawns and don't understand what they're being told to do, there are terrible people who work underground and know how to sabotage things. Pierre, remember this! When they start going after the Sephardics, the Inquisition's not far behind and is polishing its arms to use against the Huguenots. Rumours are flying, which never spread without cause, that Catherine de' Medici is courting the Spanish king, and you know very well what the price will be of any alliance she makes with him. We're going to see a return of our persecutions."

He'd spoken very quietly and didn't say any more until we reached the jail, where we were crowded into a fairly spacious room with a table and some stools. He made us each take an oath not to make jokes about our exploits of the evening, and never say a word about this to anyone.

We were stunned by this admonition, for we hadn't imagined that this business was anything but a dust-up between law students and their medical counterparts. He added: "The people who created this effigy are not going be happy that you destroyed their work, and they have very long memories."

"Captain," asked Merdanson, "when will you release us?"

"At nightfall. One by one, and by a back door. Except for Siorac, for whom I've got other plans."

And indeed, an hour later, a carriage drew up before the door, curtains drawn, and Cossolat said, taking me aside, "Pierre, leave your harness here. Madame de Joyeuse has sent for you. Go put on your blue satin doublet before you visit her. And Pierre," he said, placing his index finger on my sternum, "not a word about this effigy. You weren't there. You saw nothing. On the other hand, regale her as much as you want about the orange battle. In short, amuse her, please her. Give her lots of reasons to remember that you spent the afternoon of carnival day with her."

It's not hard to imagine that I was very much at ease in the luxurious coach, far from the dangers we'd just encountered with the mob. But Cossolat had astonished me. Remembering his final warning, I realized that he had a pair of fine ears listening in on the Joyeuse household, which kept him informed of everything.

"Monster!" cried Madame de Joyeuse as I threw myself on my knees before her and kissed her plump hands. "Monsieur," she continued, "what a tyrant you are in your play! You shock everyone! You knock everything down! You eviscerate your enemies! No quarter! Everyone has to give way!"

"Ho, Madame! So many reproaches for a little tussle!"

"Little? When people are talking about you in nasty little verses pinned to an effigy of Maître Sanche!"

"I saw no effigy," I said quickly. "I was in jail for the battle of the oranges."

"But Justin saw it, and Aglaé can repeat the pasquinade."

"Oh, Madame, I wouldn't dare!" cried Aglaé, putting on her virginal and fierce airs.

"Well then, I will dare! Listen, my friend:

"This old goat, now emasculate,
Likes boys, not she-goats, for his date."

"Madame, that's an infamy! Moreover it's bad poetry and lacks metre!"

345

"Forget the metre!" said Madame de Joyeuse. "Monster, answer straight out. What's going on between this old goat and the boy I see before me?"

"Madame," I replied, suddenly serious, "if it were true, the honour of a certain lady would seal my lips. But the thing is as false as a monk's modesty. The truth is I hate the old goat from his horn to his hoof."

And so I recounted to my benefactress the story of my poor Fontanette.

"Oh my God!" said Madame de Joyeuse, who, though she had a good heart, had no interest in the fate of a chambermaid. "So much ado over a simple girl? The wench has gone back to her village, that's obvious. But, Pierre," she said, suddenly severe, "did you really need this wench as well? Wasn't Thomassine enough to satisfy you?"

"Thomassine, Madame?"

"Oh, don't bother to deny it. Cossolat has told me all. Now, my little cousin, don't go off pouting to the window seat. Come back here. And don't make any claims about Thomassine's honour. Tell me everything. I demand it."

"What, Madame? Everything. In front of your ladies-in-waiting? Some of whom are virgins!"

Madame de Joyeuse seemed delighted by my answer, and, turning to her women, her head to one side and her eyes shining, she said, "Siorac is right. Please withdraw, all of you. There are certain things a girl shouldn't hear before she's married."

To which Aglaé replied through clenched teeth (though I alone could hear her), "Moans, for example, I would guess!" However, all the ladies withdrew, looking very put out, with knowing glances to each other, sly smiles, murmurs and gracious flourishes of their wide gowns.

"Pierre, give me your arm, I beg you, and put me in my bed; I don't know what's come over me but suddenly I'm suffocating. Unhook me, please. What a dear little chambermaid you are, my sweet, every gesture so gentle and every look so caressing" (and indeed, this was a labour I enjoyed more than I can say). "But, Pierre, I don't know whether I can abandon myself to your care undefended, terrible tyrant and brutal killer that you are!"

I didn't answer this, knowing where her thoughts were tending and not wishing either to encourage her or rein her in.

"Oh," she sighed, "unhook this for me as well! Oh my God, I'm almost naked. Pierre, I fear for my modesty. Please close the bed curtains…"

But even with the bed curtains pulled I could still see her well enough, bathing in her blondness in this light-blue light. I paid her a pretty compliment, which made her golden-brown eyes light up. "Oh, Pierre!" she said in a languorous voice. "Your words are honey, your tongue is divine…"

"Well, Madame," I whispered in her ear, "who knows better than you?"

"What effrontery!" she gasped, half laughing, half angry. "You're such a devil to tempt me so. What a pity I'm so faithful to my husband, and such a good Catholic, praying to God every day, confessing every week. If I were Thomassine! Tell me, does she have many lovers?"

"Many."

"Oh!" sighed Madame de Joyeuse. "So many for some, so few for others. Monster, what are you doing?"

"I'm unhooking you some more. Look, you're all red and must be suffocating! You'll feel better this way."

"Monster, you're taking advantage of me! I'm so weak and you're so vigorous and such a tyrant! Oh, my monster," she cooed offering her lips to me. "Aren't you going to storm my last defences? Aren't you tempted to use force with me?"

"Yes, yes, yes, I'm so tempted. And if I offend you, I'll withdraw."

I pretended to pull away, but you can guess how little her scruples held her back and with what strength her weak arms held me to her!

"Oh, Pierre, it's all my fault, I was too tantalizing! I forgive you—you're so young and full of desire. How could you not use force with that body of yours! Are you going to beat me? Are you going to take me by force like any harlot in the street? Oh, you monster! Oh, Pierre, my sweet…"

As I left the Joyeuse mansion and was returning with a warmed heart and light step towards Maître Sanche's lodgings, I saw my tailor, Martinez, in the rue de la Barrelerie, sitting on his doorstep, enjoying the morning air. Seeing me, he rose to greet me, and, seizing my elbow, invited me into his shop to enjoy a goblet of Frontignan. I agreed, since I didn't want to offend him, and was hoping to see his four daughters again. I wasn't disappointed. They were sitting in the shop, sewing, and, seeing me, all four looked up with their gazelle-like eyes, cheeks of apricot and lips as red as any noblewoman's. But then they went back to work with sly, sidelong glances at each other which I found enchanting. Seeing my distraction, Martinez offered to go and fetch the wine, so I remained alone with his daughters. After a moment, giving a great sigh, I said, "If you were all Muslims, I would happily convert and marry all four of you together!"

Of course they all laughed at this, though in a modest way, covering their pretty mouths with their hands, fluttering quietly at this idea of marriage, which always seems to create such a stir in young women. But what does marriage really offer them? An ungrateful and tyrannical husband, the heavy responsibility of the household, a child every year and, sooner or later, death in childbirth.

"So, Monsieur," said Iñez, the eldest, "all four? So you wouldn't have a preference?"

"Of course I would, but I'd only be able to discover it after some time together."

At this, they blushed and giggled a bit, but I suspected the real giggles were reserved for night-time when they were in their beds. But then, hearing their father approaching, they fell silent and went back to their sewing.

"Monsieur de Siorac," said Martinez from the doorway, "may I ask you to join me in my office? We'll be better able to talk there. Monsieur," he said, closing the door and offering me a goblet of Frontignan, "if you would like to have a doublet and leggings of your choice of colours, I'd be happy to make them for you free of charge."

Seeing my great surprise and astonished at his own largesse, he added, "I meant to say, for half of the price we first negotiated, which doesn't really cover the cost of the materials and my work, as you can imagine."

I was sure that, at the price he named, there would be some profit; however, I decided not to protest, but thanked him profusely and asked him to what I owed such kindness.

"Monsieur de Siorac," he said gravely, "everyone in Montpellier knows that when the ugly business of the effigy happened you were in jail for the disturbance with the oranges, and went directly from there to spend the afternoon with Madame de Joyeuse. But there's not a Sephardic in this city who doesn't know to whom we owe the destruction of the odious image that defamed Maître Sanche in his private life and in the practice of his religion, and thereby defamed us all." Then, putting down his glass, his expression changed from gravity to tenderness and he said, "May I give you a hug, noble gentleman that you are?"

"But of course!" I cried. "And as a sign of our friendship!" Whereupon he rubbed his scratchy beard on my cheek, hugged me so hard I thought I'd expire, and gave me such hearty slaps on the back I feared for my shoulder blades.

The minute Maître Sanche saw me when I got back to the pharmacy he, too, embraced me with great warmth, but his throat was so tight all he could do was to utter in a broken voice, "My nephew, oh, my nephew!" And then, very troubled and still in tears, he walked away.

I went up to my room and there was a knock at the door. It was Fogacer. Without hugging or touching me in any way, his face very constrained, he offered me his hand, and sat down on a stool a few feet away and said, "Dame Rachel has asked our illustrious master to send you away."

I sat there, stunned beyond words. When I had recovered sufficiently to speak, I said, "And how did she justify this request?"

"Because of the rhyme about the old goat and the boy. Caesar's wife, she said, should never suffer such calumny."

"By St Anthony's belly! What about Maître Sanche?"

"Sanche lashed out at her with fire and brimstone, and the young she-goat took refuge in her rooms. I doubt her bed will be open to our master for a very long time. That's why he looked so worried."

"But how do you come to know about the rhyme?"

Fogacer looked at me for a moment, raising his black eyebrows.

"I was there. Perhaps, Pierre, you failed to notice that among those infamous effigies that so excited the public's outrage, there was another that caricatured a Présidial judge, whose robe, like Sanche's, bore a little rhyme that attacked his morals for a practice that, no doubt, you can guess."

"And he's a friend of yours?"

"He belongs to a group that I'd dare to call my brotherhood," replied Fogacer with a directness that struck me all the more since he was very pale and ill at ease. "Yet another of those odious effigies," he added, "attacked Abbot Cabassus, accusing him of atheism. So along with the Sephardics and atheists, *we* were in good company." He said this "we" with such a strange inflection of his voice, his face still constrained but with an air of pride as if he defied the entire world.

"Fogacer, were you there when I attacked the effigy of Maître Sanche?"

"Yes, and I recognized you in spite of your mask and, taking advantage of the turmoil, I ripped the incriminating verses from the judge."

"You recognized me despite my mask?" I cried, surprised and angered, looking him in the eye.

"Understand me, Pierre," replied Fogacer with a long face, "when I was behaving so madly on the rue de l'Espazerie, I didn't recognize you, but then, when you knocked off my mask, you saw my face and, for my part, I saw the expression in your eyes, and knew immediately it was you, and I was very grieved and ashamed to have accosted you. And for that," he said, raising his diabolical eyebrow, and in a tone that was not nearly as remorseful as he wanted, said, "I beg you to accept my humblest apology."

"Oh, Fogacer!" I said, leaping to my feet. I went to him and leant over, put my hands on his shoulders and kissed him on both cheeks, a gesture that, to my great surprise, made him blush like a virgin. "Fogacer," I continued, turning away so as not to make him more uncomfortable, and walking back and forth across the room, "you're my friend, we need have no apologies between us. If anyone should apologize it should be me for striking you. Your follies, as you term them make no difference to me. *Medicus sum.** The only difference between us is a difference of complexion or orientation. I'm interested in skirts. You're not. That's all."

"Except that," rejoined Fogacer grimacing a bit, "all the skirts in the world won't put you in danger of being burnt at the stake in public for sodomy."

---

* "I am a doctor."

"And so," I said, pausing and turning to look him in the eye, "you live in constant peril!"

"And all the more so since I'm an atheist," said Fogacer. "But that crime is easier to hide. A little mummery suffices."

Although I didn't much like the word "mummery" applied to the papist rites (since, I believe, Fogacer could also have applied it to our Huguenot rites), I trembled for Fogacer's safety. Though, on second thought, we only have one body to offer our executioner, so that Fogacer couldn't be burnt twice, once for atheism and again for sodomy—but once was already too much. The idea was frightful, knowing the man and valuing so highly his friendship.

"Fogacer," I said, to chase away the vision of the executioner, "Cossolat thinks that there are powerful underground forces behind these effigies."

"*We* think so too," said Fogacer. "As you know, the revolt of the reformed Church in the Low Countries against the Spanish yoke convinced Felipe II to send an army stationed along the French border to knock some sense into these 'beggars' from Flanders, as he calls them. But these 'underground' forces, as you put it, ardently desire that, once Felipe has exterminated those 'beggars', these Spanish allies of our king will come and exterminate all the reformers in France as well. Do you think this is unrelated to the effigies? Not on your life, it isn't. For these same people who consider that no means is too vile or small-minded given the ends they pursue, hope that by taking on all the Sephardics, atheists and sodomites in this city, they're preparing the terrain for the scaffolds on which they'll hang all the Huguenots."

"So I did a good thing by destroying that hateful effigy."

"But you'll do a better thing from here on out by sparing your life, for, however well protected you are by Cossolat, by Joyeuse and by the Sephardics, the people we're talking about are very powerful and very patient."

I would have done well to heed this advice, which was as wise as his escapades and follies were the opposite, but, alas, that was not in my character. But I was also carried away in the enterprise I'm about to relate (and that my father in an angry letter in Latin called "*atrocissimo*") by my great love of medicine—but certainly, also, by the heat of the moment, circumstances and opportunity. If in these memoirs I have, more than once, asked for the reader's indulgence and counted on his goodwill, I need it now more than ever.

Eastertide brought to an end our school year at the Royal College of Medicine, and though Saporta and Bazin stayed on through July and August to give private tutoring for those who could afford it, we were sorry to say goodbye to Dr Feynes and especially to Dr d'Assas, who withdrew to their country estates, the former to pursue his book, in elegant Latin, on smallpox, and the latter to live in indolence and various pleasures, dividing his attentions between his vineyard and his lovely chambermaid, Zara. With the end of our lectures, the work on dissections was finished for the year, contrary to the promises of Dean Bazin, who for reasons of sordid economizing of the college's finances, purchased only three cadavers. The third of these, to our considerable dismay and ultimately angry protests, was a monkey! To be reduced from six, in Rondelet's day, to three (including the monkey) was a scandal, and we complained to Saporta, who malevolently directed us to Bazin, who slammed his door in our faces, being of a nasty and venomous disposition.

"Siorac," Merdanson said one evening as were sitting with Carajac at the Three Kings, "I can't accept this cutback. What was the point of Rondelet's founding the shitty anatomical theatre in Montpellier if we are only going to practise three dissections a year? Three! That foetus Bazin promised four! Three is a joke! How can we improve our knowledge of the human body if all we do is parrot in 1567 what Galen and Hippocrates wrote several centuries before Christ?"

"I think I know a way we could make up this lack," said Carajac, lowering his voice.

The surgical apprentice sitting next to Merdanson looked, despite his broad shoulders, somewhat frail, and was so brown-skinned that he looked like a Turk, which is not so surprising given all the incursions these pagans had made over the last fifty years in Aigues-Mortes, his birthplace, which he bragged about whenever he opened his mouth, which he rarely did. He mostly sat silently by, large as a kitchen cabinet, moving neither head nor hand, his eyelids drooping lazily over his pupils.

"So what's your plan?" asked Merdanson.

"Do you know Cabassus?"

"Isn't he the abbot they made an effigy of at carnival, claiming he's an atheist?" I asked.

"The same. He's abbot of the parish of Saint-Denis in Montpellier, which has a cemetery within its walls from which the papists derive a huge profit, since they charge a lot of money for every inhumation."

Carajac took a deep breath as if he were astonished to have been speaking so much. "I'm thinking we should empty our flagon and go over there and take a look."

"What for?" asked Merdanson.

But since Carajac had used up his provision of words for the day, he made a nod that signified he'd said enough and just sat there silently. His taciturnity was so powerful, however, that without any further questions I called our hostess and paid her. She refused to smile however—she had given me the cold shoulder ever since the business with Caudebec and the plague victim.

Night was falling when we arrived at Cabassus's lodgings, which were situated at some distance from the parish houses. The priests lived together in a sort of community, like monks.

Carajac tapped at the door and identified himself in a hushed voice. The door opened halfway, then the rest of the way, and in the shabby room before us, whose ceiling was so low Carajac's head actually touched it, we could see a very hairy, unnaturally thin little man, whose eyes, in the light of a candle set on the miserable table near him, looked a little crazy, they were so brilliant and so active—and in that respect imitated his arms and legs, which seemed to dance, shake and jump without respite, and without any apparent reason, for Cabassus was merely occupied in cooking his dinner (which smelt like chicken boiled in cabbage) in an old cracked pot over the paltry flame in his hearth.

"My brothers," he said in a falsetto voice, "my brothers—not in God, who doesn't exist—but in our common species: humanity. You are welcome in my humble abode and at my table. Come on over, my brothers, and smell this bird! There's no mystery of the Holy Trinity, but there *is* this chicken! I stole it yesterday from the henhouse of a rich merchant. I've got to live in this poor body, don't I, since I don't believe there's any chance my soul will survive, contrary to the teachings of the Holy Church. The cabbage, on the other hand, is mine, comes right out of my garden, which is next to the cemetery, so it's fat and well nourished. Cabbage and chicken are together going to tease our gullets along with a flagon of good wine, if Carajac kept his promise."

"He's kept it," said Carajac, taking a bottle from under his coat and handing it to our host. Cabassus grabbed hold of it, his whole body shaking and his eyes rolling in their sockets. Then, with extraordinary dexterity, he uncorked it and filled four goblets.

"Let's drink," he proposed, "to the nonexistence of God."

"I'll drink to the existence of God," I answered, "in whom I believe."

"Me too," affirmed Merdanson.

"Me as well," echoed Carajac.

"My brothers," said Cabassus after downing in one gulp the contents of his goblet, "I love you out of love for humanity, but you're plunged into a mortal error. What credence can we give to the confused, contradictory spoken reports of four credulous and popular Hebrews, artisans who, knowing nothing, believed in everything like the poor labourer in our villages who believes in the miracles of his saint? And how does my Church respond to my assertions? With flames at the stake. The brutal weakness of the answer demonstrates all by itself the irrefutable force of inter-rogation. My brothers," he continued, placing his hand on a roll of manuscript pages, "I've written a Latin treatise on the nonexistence of God and on the non-immorality of the soul, which I've entitled *Nego*,* a treatise I expect will illuminate the ignorant minds of our time, if I can find someone willing to publish it. But no one dares. My *Nego* will perish with me."

"Father," asked Carajac, "you also deny the immortality of the soul?"

"Of course I deny it!" replied Cabassus, rolling his eyes. "I've never met a soul that was distinct from the body it lived in. And you, surgeon Carajac, you who have seen many dissections and only want to see more, has any surgeon who's cutting up a cadaver ever discovered a soul under his scalpel?"

"It's impossible," I observed, "the soul is impalpable."

"If it's impalpable," Cabassus shot back, shaking on his stool, and pulling a chicken wing out of his mouth, "then how do you know it's there?"

"Because tradition teaches it," said Merdanson.

"Aha!" said Cabassus. "You Huguenots have rejected, in the name of freedom of thought, a good number of articles of faith that trad-ition taught. But your thinking wasn't free enough. You stopped in

* *I Deny.*

mid journey, as if terrified of your own audacity. By going further, as I did, you would have denied everything!"

At this he plunged the chicken wing back into his mouth and chewed it up, bones and all, with crushing noises that left us all aghast.

As the fire was dying out in the hearth, the little vaulted room seemed as dark as the gates of hell, lit only by the single candle that Cabassus had placed on the back of a cauldron in the middle of the worm-eaten table. I didn't know what to think of Cabassus. No doubt his face, his shaking, his eye-rolling and his other weirdnesses gave him the look of a madman. But when this madman began to reason, despite the fact that everything he said was horrible to contemplate, we all felt less wise and less sure of ourselves than before.

As much as the feeble light of the candle permitted, I looked at Carajac and Merdanson by turns. Neither one seemed to want to argue with Cabassus, the first because of his natural taciturnity, and the second, like me, because he was afraid of losing the argument. Moreover, although we'd begun to understand why we'd come, neither Carajac nor Merdanson had breathed a word about it.

"Nor do I believe in the Last Judgement," continued Cabassus, "or in the resurrection of the dead. For me, I think the dead remain for ever where we've buried them, their flesh eaten by worms, leaving only their skeleton, and the skeleton turning to dust in its turn. Nothing emanates from these 'glorious bodies', as the Church likes to call them. But this language is nothing more than illusion, foolery and fallacy. Dust is nothing but dust. And so I believe that it's perfectly legal for the advancement of our knowledge to open bodies to learn their geography, as you doctors seem to want to do."

"Monsieur," said Merdanson, "what will that cost us?"

"No more than the chicken we just devoured," answered Cabassus with authority. "Not a sol. My brothers in humanity," he continued, rising, "tomorrow afternoon, the parish is opening a grave on the cheap for a whore and an orphan. Which is another way of saying the graves won't be deep. Come back tomorrow night with a couple of long, solid staves, some rope, some flasks, some candles, your scalpels and enough vinegar for disinfectant. I'll provide the shovels. Don't forget, however, that if you're caught, your crime is called 'profanation of a grave' and is punishable by torture or by being shipped out as a galley slave."

"By St Vitus's belly," cried Merdanson, "will your brothers in Christ be armed?"

"They have a crossbow."

"A crossbow!" I cried. "An ancient but very lethal weapon!"

"It'll be pitch dark," said Cabassus, "and the cemetery is never guarded. Rumours have been going round that witches have been celebrating their Sabbath here at night. That's enough to keep most thieves away."

With no further ceremony, and being a man of few words except when denying the existence of God, Cabassus pushed us out of the door, and we headed back through the winding streets of this suburb of Montpellier, having a lot to think about. Before passing through the city gate, which opened only upon request, Carajac stopped short and said in a hushed voice, "Friends, what are we doing? There's terrible danger in this adventure."

"Terrible and very evident," agreed Merdanson, "but I'm in if Siorac is. By the foetus Bazin's excrement, I think I'm as brave as Siorac, but he's better at getting out of a jam."

Both Carajac and Merdanson stood looking at me, and though I could scarcely see their faces in the darkness, I could tell that they were expecting me to make the decision. And to confess the truth, dear reader, I wasn't so sure I wanted to do this. To dig up a dead person, open her up and all of this in profanation of the divine laws; to expose ourselves to a crossbow quarrel, or worse, to dishonour on the public scaffold—there was a lot to think about. Not to mention that cemeteries are places that we loathe, vague borders between heaven and hell, closer to the latter, being overrun by wandering souls, the succubi that pursue them, will-o'-the-wisps, fatal sulphur vapours, mandrakes born of the seed of hanged men, poisons and venoms of the rotting bodies—haunted, if you believe the reputation of the Saint-Denis cemetery, by the witches and their fiends who dance on their graves and consort with the Devil by the light of the moon.

And I have to add that that I didn't relish any kind of complicity with this crazy abbot, with his rolling eyes, his body inhabited by God knows which demon and his demented negation of the existence of God, which seemed to be calling vociferously for the hangman.

"Ah," I began, at first in a hushed voice that got louder and louder as I grew more exalted, "what an arduous challenge Fortune has thrown down to us! My friends, let us meet this challenge! Let's pick up her glove! This is a rare opportunity: we have to seize our advantage! We're always sitting behind doctors and older students during the dissections in the anatomical theatre, so what do we really see? All we do is listen to the royal professor's comments about what the prosector has done. Gestures, but nothing more. Can we actually distinguish any part of the human geography from any other? Do we really know what a vein looks like? A nerve? A ligament? Have we palpated organs? Do we know anything about the volume, weight or consistency of an organ, or the ramifications of these aspects? My friends, if we only dare, tomorrow night we will be able to open up, touch and observe two bodies, one male and one female. This is miraculous! Two bodies and an entire night without a teacher or professor to block our view, the body in our hands, under our eyes, open to our scalpels! In this one night we may advance our medical knowledge more than in an entire year of study!"

Thus roused, Carajac and Merdanson acquiesced and shook on it: I had persuaded them, and by a common and unspoken agreement, I became the leader of the enterprise and began to organize the details.

Oh, dear reader! If anyone had seen us the next night as the darkness fell, all three dressed and masked in black, hair under close-fitting caps, pistols and daggers in our belts, laden with candles and ropes, stakes and blankets, Merdanson carrying an as yet unlit lantern, all three walking at several paces from each other on padded feet, they assuredly would not have thought we were going to do some pious work.

It was a long walk from Montpellier to the Saint-Denis parish. At the town gates, the guard, who must have been well in his cups, scarcely looked at us and waved us by. At Carajac's tap on his door and murmur of his name, Cabassus opened his door and closed it after us, then said in his falsetto voice, his eyes nearly orbiting out of their sockets:

"My brothers, sit down and eat some of this rabbit: it's not so bad. My neighbour's hutch has offered it to us for free. You can't go off on the work you're about to do on an empty stomach! Carajac, I'm going to open your flagon. Eat and drink up, my brothers! This is *not* my flesh, and this good Corbières wine is certainly not my blood. It's all matter, thank God—if I'm allowed to thank a nonexistent being! Matter is but matter. It is; that's all we can say about it. As Maître Heraclitus taught us, the world is one, and no God created it."

Since no one wanted to argue this point, no one answered. The rabbit, although it was savoury enough, upset our stomachs. Our hearts were in our teeth and even the wine had no effect on us. In this shabby room, so low and dark that it seemed already to be a tomb, we ate sparingly of this sad, mortuary meal which the grating and continuous blasphemies of our host did not render more digestible.

"Your Huguenots," Cabassus continued in his shrill and piercing voice that was a veritable torture to our ears, "got rid of the Virgin and wiped the slate clean of the saints! Well done, to be sure. But while they were at it, why didn't they reduce Jesus to his human stature? Jesus was a Hebrew. Like all of his people, he liked to prophesy, and since he was celibate, the habitual compression of his animal tendencies made him eloquent. His disciples convinced him that he could make miracles; he did so, but miracles were abundant in those credulous times! There were everywhere attestations of such wonders! What's more, Jesus said odious things about the high priests and so they had him crucified. If they hadn't, no one today would believe he was divine. So I, Cabassus, as I have written in my *Nego*, find it funny that all it took to make Jesus Christ into a God was four nails and two planks. *Et si faret in terris Heraclitus, tanquam rideret*."*

"Oh, Cabassus," I gasped, my throat knotting up, "please, out of respect for your guests, spare us this atrocious talk. I can hardly swallow your rabbit I'm so upset!"

"Also, would you please explain," said Merdanson, "how a shitty atheist became a priest?"

"Shitty believer," rejoined Cabassus, "you're putting the cart before the horse! I became a priest out of my great taste for learning. But having some instruction, I lost my beautiful faith."

"And it went to the Devil," added Carajac, who seemed to have paled considerably at hearing such thoughts.

But here, Cabassus just shrugged his shoulders, and, rolling his eyes, he raised both hands in the air and cried in a strident voice, "Error! Error! To the Devil? I don't believe in him any more than I believe in God!"

"Neither God nor the Devil!" I cried. "The world would no longer have meaning!"

---

* "And if he was on earth today, Heraclitus would laugh too."

"Oh yes it would—and does!" answered Cabassus. "It is."

But this seemed to me so obscure that I no longer felt like arguing any more, and, rising from my stool, said, "My friends, it's dark out. Let's get our masks on and get going."

Merdanson lit his dark lantern, and Cabassus preceded us through a back door that opened onto his garden, which, as he'd said, abutted the cemetery, and was separated from it by a low hedge of rosemary, which we could easily step over. This was, for us, a very lucky circumstance since the cemetery was otherwise entirely enclosed by the priests' dwellings, or by a very high stone wall that was full of traps set to catch grave-robbers.

"Here's a piece of chalk," whispered Cabassus. "Mark the tombstones each time you make a turn. That way you'll find your way back here when you're done."

"You're not coming along to help us?" I whispered.

"Not on your life! I hate cemeteries, they stink of human vanity. The rich are all strutting about in their marble tombs. When I'm burnt alive, my ashes will be scattered. This is as it should be. Nothing returns to nothingness. Here it is, my brother. Under this mound of earth lies a beautiful courtesan who gave pleasure to many people. And over there, an orphan, only eight years old, who spent his entire life crying. Get to work! I'll wait for you in my lodgings."

"Ah!" breathed Merdanson when Cabassus had disappeared. "Thank God! He's left! This shitty atheist makes my blood boil. May God pardon me for listening to his abominations! By Jesus Christ and His holy wounds, I believe in the Father, the Son and the Holy Spirit! And if it's a sin, as I believe, to open these graves, I humbly beg pardon of my Creator."

"Amen!" I said.

"Amen!" said Carajac. "But you know Cabassus, as completely mad as he is, is not malicious. He gives everything he has to the poor."

"My friends," I said, "enough talk! Let's get to work!"

Merdanson placed the dark lantern on a neighbouring tombstone and each of us, shovel in hand, began to unearth the whore's coffin. Since my hands had gone soft for not having worked in the fields so long, I put on gloves so that I wouldn't hurt my palms on the rough handle of the shovel. We had a thumbnail moon overhead that was frequently covered by clouds, and even though our eyes got used to the darkness, we could see nothing more around us than the white crosses and the tombstones. I would have shivered from the fear and sadness that this sinister place gave me if the effort of shovelling hadn't put me in a sweat. Cabassus had said that since it was a cheap grave the gravedigger wouldn't have gone very deep. But for us, who had to redig it, it seemed like an endless job. We'd been shovelling for about half an hour when Merdanson walked over to me and whispered, "Someone's watching us."

"From where?"

"Behind the yew, in front of you. To the left. I saw a face white as linen." I could feel his hand trembling on my arm. Amazing to say, Merdanson was shaking with fear! I couldn't believe my eyes.

"Friends," I whispered, "keep working. I'm going to take a look."

Leaning back on the tombstone behind me as if I were tired, I put my shovel down and drew my dagger from its sheath, and headed around behind the tomb on padded feet. Then, I bent over and crawled towards the yew tree, my weapon in my hand. I thought my heart was going to jump right out of my chest and my mouth was dry as a bone, unsure whether the spy was man or spirit. Reader, neither the butcher-baron of la Lendrevie, nor the highwaymen of the Corbières, nor Espoumel with his knife, nor Caudebec with his dagger rattled me as much as this white face half hidden among the black branches of the yew tree, the way it appeared to be floating a few feet above the ground.

But when I got right up close to the yew, I could see a very small form leaning against the tree, and, gathering all my strength, I leapt on it and knocked it to the ground without encountering any resistance whatsoever. I remained huddled on top of my prey, panting for breath, and gradually felt reassured since the person I'd subdued was warm (and therefore not a ghost) and, what's more, a girl.

At this moment, the moon reappeared from behind some clouds, and I saw that it was a girl of about eighteen, very pale indeed. But, though she could hardly see me since I was wearing a mask, she nevertheless looked at me with her big black eyes with such adoration that I was astonished.

"Oh, Maître Léonard," she cooed. "Oh, my handsome billy goat! Oh, beloved Monseigneur! Finally! My grandmother told me I'd find you in this cemetery, where I've come every night for a year to give myself to your rut."

"My what? Who are you?"

"You know very well: Ermandine Mangane!" she said. "For having faithfully served your infernal orders, my entire family, except my grandmother and me, were burnt at the stake a year ago."

"So they didn't burn you?"

"If Monseigneur remembers, it was on Monseigneur's orders that I pretended to be deaf, dumb and crazy and thereby escaped."

"So you're the last of the Manganes."

"I won't be the last, Monseigneur, when you've done your work on me and put your fruit in me. The Mangane family will be reborn as ministers of your cult and will go on serving you for ever." And she laughed. "Imagine, Monseigneur, that at first I thought you and your servants were grave-robbers, but when you leapt upon me, I felt your claws beneath those gloves."

"My claws!" I thought. "Oh, the power of the imagination!"

"Child," I said, "tonight, what you ask is impossible! Come back tomorrow at midnight."

"Aha!" she trumpeted. "I *knew* it was you! The prediction said that you would try to get away twice."

"Leave!" I ordered. "I demand it." And getting up, I let go of her. But she held on to me with a degree of strength I wouldn't have imagined possible from such frail arms.

"The prediction's come true!" she exclaimed, holding me close. "You've tried to send me away twice!"

"Wench," I asked, "how did you get in here?"

"Over the wall, with a rope."

"What about the traps?"

"I know them all."

"Wench, if I grant your request, will you leave without turning round one single time so that you don't see my infernal mysteries?"

"I promise to obey, my Great Goat!"

"Wait for me here. I must say a word to my servants."

I left her and, returning to the grave of the whore, I called Merdanson and Carajac over and whispered, "It's the last of the Mangane family. She thinks I'm the Devil, whom she calls the Great Goat, or Maître Léonard, and demands that I impregnate her."

"Go ahead!" said Carajac.

"I'm ashamed to, the wench thinks I'm the Devil!"

"Go ahead!" said Merdanson. "One woman's as good as the next. Witch or no, her sex runs from top to bottom and never from right to left."

"Go ahead!" repeated Carajac. "We don't want this crazy bitch getting in the way here. It would be too dangerous. Screw her and get rid of her."

"But she's a creature of the Devil!" I said, still troubled by the prospect.

"Screw her and pray!" said Merdanson. "Your prayer will steal her fruit from Satan."

I made up my mind, and, going back to the wench, I took her in my arms and, though I found the idea repulsive, wanted to lay her on the grass, and though the moon was but a sliver, could see that she began to glow with a strange brilliance.

"No, no!" said the girl, her eyes shining. "There's a place better than this!" And taking me by the hand, she led me to a sort of mausoleum closed by an iron gate, which did not stop her, for she took a key from her pocket, opened the gate and locked herself in the tiny chapel with me.

"Here! Under this stone," she said, tapping the stone with her foot, a savage fire in her black eyes, "lies the Grand Inquisitor who had the Mangane family burnt at the stake. Sometime later, suffering from an ulcer, he bought some pills from an itinerant charlatan, one of your devils, Monseigneur, and died two months later after agonies much more atrocious than the flames. So it's here on the tomb of our enemy that I want to be impregnated."

I couldn't utter a word, so frozen was I by her words and by the unnatural light of the moon. However, without releasing my hand, the girl stretched out on the tombstone and pulled me down on top of her—again with a degree of strength that astonished me—and I found myself lying beside her while she undressed in the blink of an eye. Her skin was brown and her flesh so round and sweet as to damn you. Alas, I don't use this word lightly, for as busy as I was, not in caressing her but in quietly praying to God (who was already punishing me for profaning the graves of the whore and her orphan), I remained stretched out beside her like a log, without a gesture or a peep, half dead with terror, and attentive only to the moans that seemed to be emanating from under the stone where we lay.

"Ah," said the girl looking at me with her black eyes, whose brilliance in the pale moonlight was almost unbearable, "Monseigneur disdains mortal women, I see, and prefers his games with the succubi in his infernal empire. No matter, sorceress that I am—before becoming Lilith in your kingdom after my death—I am not without my powers over the body of a man, which you've chosen to appear in. Monseigneur, may I use the arts I have learnt on your adored person?"

"Certainly," I said, though my will had no role in my answer, for I continued to pray desperately, for I'd heard the moans from underneath the stone where I lay, which completely froze my bones from my neck to my heels.

But as soon as I had pronounced, in spite of myself, my acquiescence, I felt the girl unhooking my doublet and I was suddenly surrounded by a hot breath of wind. And losing irreparably the words of my prayer and my hearing and any thought of the terrible moans from beneath me, I felt myself floating backwards through the warm air, my body lulled by a thousand little breezes. These pleasures left me so little clear awareness that I'll wager that the girl must have been giving me certain strange and demonic caresses which would have revived the most deficient of men; and even supposing I'd dare try to remember them (which sometimes tempts me) I would never dare describe them without blushing, even these many years later— caresses that no woman born of woman ever gave since. Even then, having become a man again by the magic of her ministrations, and vibrating with desire from head to toe, I did not dare move. Seeing which, the witch straddled me in a frenetic dance and, eyes wild and mouth open, drew from me amidst savage cries the seed she was after. "Oh," I thought, when, with the end of our sensual journey, I regained consciousness, "may God keep this infernal womb from ever bearing fruit!"

When I stood up, the girl threw herself at my feet and began kissing them, then my knees in adoration of her master.

"Wench," I said, "you got what you asked for. Get out of here and don't come back."

"As you wish, Maître Léonard," she replied, her eyes, as she unlocked the gate, brimming with happiness at the thought that she would perpetuate her family. But she complied with my commands, as I verified by following her back through the cemetery. When I rejoined my companions, I discovered they'd made good progress and had entirely uncovered the body of the woman, who was sewn into her shroud.

"My friend," whispered Merdanson, "by St Vitus's belly! Where's the justice in all this? Some fornicate while others do the work."

"Ah, Merdanson," I replied with an involuntary shudder, "it's not funny. I wish I'd been a thousand leagues from here."

"Never would have guessed by the way you were howling!"

"I was howling?"

"Like a demon."

I shivered again at this, since I hadn't heard myself make any noise and was noticing that the moon on my left no longer had the same strange brilliance that had lit the face of the witch when she straddled me.

"My friend," Merdanson continued, while Carajac stood by, his two hands on the handle of this shovel, silent, as usual, and looking very unhappy, "since you like fondling women's parts so much that you're willing to do it with a witch, or succubus or whatever, on a gravestone, get down in that grave and slip this rope under the wench's shoulders, and the other under her legs so we can pull her out of there. It's time for you to do a little work."

And with another curse, he added a joke that was so dirty and unpleasant that I won't repeat it here. Certainly, Merdanson meant no offence; he was just foul-mouthed, not heartless. For my part, I was disappointed to see my companions get so upset about something they'd just urged me to do, but I simply shut my mouth and started to climb down into the grave. My foot slipped, however, and I found myself prostrate on top of the corpse of the poor wench, whose body was all stiff and cold. "Ah!" I thought (and I nearly threw up, beneath Merdanson's jeers). "Anything's better than death!" May Christ pardon me, but I preferred the witch and her hellish heat to this! But I got up, still feeling sick, and, placing my feet on either side of the corpse, slid the ropes under her, as Merdanson had suggested, which wasn't easy, since the woman was tall and heavy, and already stiff with the irrefragable rigidity of death.

It would have taken four strong men pulling on the ropes from both sides to get her out of there. We were but three, and would have been unable to finish the job had not Carajac had the idea of tying one of the ropes to the iron gate of a nearby monument. And so all three, sweating and panting, managed to hoist her out onto the mud. This done, with the aid of the one of the blankets and the two staves we'd brought, Carajac fashioned a kind of stretcher, on which we placed the body.

The exhuming of the child was much easier since it was buried in a very shallow grave, and was so light that Carajac could throw it over his shoulder. Merdanson and I grabbed the handles of the stretcher and we carried the two bodies to Cabassus's lodgings.

Cabassus, seeing the light from our dark lantern, had lit several candles we'd brought, and set them on planks stuck in the fissures between the rough stones of his walls. Five others he placed in a candelabra he'd no doubt pinched from the Virgin in some chapel or other, and that one of us would hold over the table, which he'd not only cleared but actually washed. We lay the body of the whore on this table, and Carajac stood the stiffened body of the orphan against the wall in a corner of the room. I held the candelabra above the dead woman while Merdanson, scalpel in hand, cut the threads of the shroud, which enclosed it from head to foot. But he had the patience to cut it only where it was knotted, so that we could resew it afterwards and return the poor wench to her grave.

"Ah," said Merdanson when we'd removed the shroud, and the white, frozen body lay uncovered before us, "by the belly of St Vitus, what a beautiful big woman she was! Friends, look at her shoulders, her large breasts, her graceful stomach, her wide hips and those long shapely legs that she spread every day to offer her little onion for her clients' pleasure! By the belly of St Vitus, 'tis a pity she's not still alive and warm! I wouldn't use my scalpel to explore her! What a gorgeous young woman! What a waste! She was so healthy, strapping and vigorous! Cabassus, do you know how she rendered her last breath?"

"She died in childbirth yesterday," replied the priest in his falsetto voice. "Bled to death."

"And the baby?"

"Stillborn, thank God." But he added quickly, which he did every time the word God passed his lips: "Who doesn't exist."

"Well, now," said Merdanson, "where shall we start?"

"With her chest," said Carajac. "I'm very eager to explore the heart, the canals that irrigate it and lead away from it."

"No, no!" I argued. "Let's start with the genitalia. The three cadavers that we dissected at the college were males, including the monkey. And since, happily, we have a wench here, let's begin with what makes her a wench."

"Siorac's right," agreed Merdanson, "and as for the heart, before we put her back in the ground, we can remove it and give it to Carajac to work on it at leisure in his lodgings."

Carajac seemed quite happy with this solution.

"Siorac," said Merdanson, "hold the light so I can see properly to cut into her flesh. I'm going to open up the seat of man's pleasure, and from there explore up into the womb and the ovaries."

Merdanson had just received his baccalaureate in medicine with high praise from both Saporta and d'Assas, who had presided over his examination (which was very lucky since Dr Bazin had it in for him, knowing that his student referred to him as "the foetus"). Merdanson's success on his exams was poetic justice, for, other than his indiscretions with the whores on the rue des Étuves, whom he visited regularly, being hurried and coarse in his appetites, and lacking in any patience whatsoever when it came to paying compliments to his women (an art he took to be a waste of time and not always very successful), and other than his gluttonous pleasure in food and drink, which he wolfed down noisily, his great, fierce and unique love was medicine, for the advancement of which he would have given his soul, or at least his life. What's more, he was a good enough Huguenot, but, like me, belonged more to a political party than to a church, and would much rather have missed a service than a medical dissection.

I had just finished my first year and Carajac the same, which meant that we left the scalpel work to our elder, who, having already dissected all the little animals that fell into his hands, was very adroit with this tool. He was also very good at discussing what he saw and I was sorry not to be able to take notes, since my job was to hold the candelabra over his head. Carajac, his sleeves rolled up, stood ready to help with pulling the flesh apart, while Cabassus stood quietly (for once!) on a chair behind Merdanson, absorbed in his admiration of our work—since it was not about God but about the material world— and watching our dissection of the whore with seemingly religious respect.

"I observe," said Merdanson, without any of the coarseness that habitually punctuated his discourse, "that the womb is still very swollen, seeing that the delivery was yesterday. I observe, too, that it was a difficult birth; the vagina displays many deep wounds inflicted by the maladroit and criminal midwife, who was evidently using pincers, and not only killed the child but perforated the womb and peritoneum, causing the bleeding which killed the poor woman. And finally, it's clear that the womb is single, as Vesalius demonstrated, and not double, as Galen claimed."

"So Galen was wrong!" cried Cabassus rubbing his hands with glee, so great was his hatred of the ancients and of all authority.

"But," I laughed, "there are still doctors in our college, Dr Pinarelle, among others, who would rather be wrong with Galen than right with Vesalius."

"That's abominable!" growled Cabassus. "To have eyes and see not!"

But he said no more, since Merdanson was uncovering the Fallopian tubes and an ovary and was explaining their functions. I thought to myself what a delicate marvel a woman's fecundation was, proving, all by herself, the existence of a Creator, who alone in His divine wisdom could have imagined this simple yet extremely subtle mechanism. But I kept these thoughts to myself so as not to set Cabassus off again on his strident negations.

When he'd finished with the genitalia, Merdanson opened her chest to remove the heart, and, as he did this, he said, "Do you realize, Carajac, that Aristotle thought the heart was a hot organ with three cavities?"

"Hah!" opined Cabassus, plunged in the delight of proving that the master his Church so venerated had fallen so low in this mistake.

"I did not know that," said Carajac.

"Aristotle also believed that it was in the heart that blood was formed."

"Ha ha!" sniggered Cabassus.

"Aristotle also believed—listen to this, my friends!—that, as the heart was a hot organ, it tended to overheat and so the lungs functioned as bellows whose job was to send cold air to cool it off."

Here Cabassus broke out in a belly laugh and shook so hard that he very nearly fell off the chair he was perched on.

"As for Galen," Merdanson continued, rolling up his sleeves in order to pull from the thoracic cavity the heart, which he'd separated from its arteries, "as for Galen, he claimed that the cardiacal cavities communicated with each other through pores."

"And he was wrong?" asked Cabassus, who began rubbing his hands together again in his pleasure at seeing so many ancient authorities openly defeated and undone.

"My friends, he was wrong. Vesalius showed in his *De humani corporis fabrica* that the cardiacal cavities have no communication between them. Carajac," he continued, "here's the heart of the poor woman. When she was alive, it beat for more than one man to the rhythm of her little 'onion'." (But he said this out of pity rather than as a crude joke.) "Take good care of it."

Silently and with great gravity, Carajac pulled from his pocket a large handkerchief, and, taking the heart Merdanson handed to him, he wrapped it in the cloth, knotting the corners to form a packet, which somehow reminded me of the little round blocks of butter that the farmers bring to town on market day.

When we'd resewn the wench back into her shroud, for, to be frank, she was beginning to give off a bit of that stale, sweet smell which accompanies the first stage of decomposition, we placed her back on the stretcher. Carajac placed his packet next to the dark lantern, and then picked up the orphan and brought it to the table saying, "He's so light!"

"Orphans don't get too much to eat," observed Merdanson, his scalpel in hand. But scarcely had he opened up the shroud when an unbearable odour invaded our nostrils. And it got much worse, when, advised by Cabassus that the child had died of lung failure, Merdanson opened these up and they immediately produced a stench to turn the hardiest stomach. We doused them in vinegar to combat both the nauseating stink they made and any infection that it may have carried. But in addition to the fact that the vinegar had no effect whatsoever, the lungs were so decomposed that we couldn't see anything or find anything other than small stones—at least, that's what they call these small granulations about the size of a pea and which we couldn't understand, for they're usually found in the urinary tract.

When we'd done dissecting the orphan, we resewed him into his shroud, but before we dealt with him, we decided to bring the wench back to her grave and rebury her. But once the earth was shovelled back over her, Merdanson announced that he'd decided not to reinter the orphan, but to bring him back to his place and bury him in a shed in his garden, and eventually produce a skeleton which he would donate anonymously to the Royal College of Medicine for our teachers to use in their lectures. Moreover, it would be an easy thing to do and require little labour or care, since the poor child had but little flesh on his bones to begin with, having apparently died of consumption.

We were quite surprised by this proposal and objected that it would not only be difficult to do, but very dangerous. How could we carry a cadaver through the streets of Montpellier, especially since Cossolat had doubled the night watch, fearful that, after the Flanders affair, which had everyone riled up, the more excitable papists and reformers might come to blows under the cover of darkness? But we couldn't convince him. As stubborn as a red donkey (whose hair he already bore not only on his head but on other parts of his body) Merdanson refused to give in, and Cabassus, who, like Carajac and me, was initially opposed to the plan, ended up giving in, and it was agreed that he'd find a nice big log that we could bury in place of the child, which we did. And so the three of us, wearing masks, set off with our stakes, our ropes and our lantern, I in the lead, Carajac next, carrying with extreme care the little package of you-know-what, and Merdanson bringing up the rear, carrying on his shoulder the orphan, sewn back into his shroud, itself enveloped in a sheet, a burden whose stench alone was enough to attract the attention of the nightwatchmen.

But we had to get back into Montpellier by a gate that was closed at night. It's true that the guard was an old drunk, but he was possessed of the curiosity of his state, and he wouldn't have failed to ask what was in the sheet. So I asked Merdanson to put his load down a few steps away from the gate, and Carajac his package as well, along with stakes, ropes and all the gear we'd employed in our dissections. Then, with empty hands, but masks still on our faces, we knocked at the gate until the hoary head of the guard appeared at the observation post.

"Guard!" I cried. "Open up!"

"Nay," he replied, "who are you?"

"Honest fellows from Montpellier. We're returning from a village nearby where we were courting some wenches, which dried up our purses and our throats as well. Open up and go get us a flagon of your best wine. We'll pay handsomely and, what's more, we'll drink with you."

That was enough for him. He came down. The gate opened a small way, still held by its chain, and we entered one by one, and he put down his lantern so that he could feel our bodies to be certain we weren't carrying any arms. "How does it happen," he asked, "that you're wearing masks?"

"I'm the son of a nobleman," I replied, "and my friends are the offspring of well-heeled merchants here. We didn't want to be recognized when we were out sowing our wild oats."

"How did your boots get so muddy?" he queried.

"In God's good earth where we were fornicating, for lack of a dwelling."

At which the old drunk burst our laughing, and, seeing him so well disposed towards us, I generously greased his palm and said, "Your wine, old man! Your wine, by the grace of God, or our throats will split from drought!"

"Monsieur," he said, looking over the coins I'd put in his hand, "if you want some Frontignan, it'll be five sols more."

I gave him what he asked, and he hobbled off. Immediately, Merdanson and Carajac, crossing back through the gate, retrieved our various baggages and brought them inside the walls, placing them in a dark corner and at some distance from the postern so that the stench wouldn't attract the guard's attention. After which, all we had to do was clink glasses with the old man and empty his bottle, which we did quite happily, having so parched our throats from our night of such macabre work.

Luckily, Merdanson's lodgings were but a stone's throw from this gate, and when, finally, we'd opened the shed in his garden and stowed the orphan, our tools and ropes, I let out half a sigh. I said "half" by design, for we still had Carajac's bundle in which the whore's heart represented the worst possible proof of what we'd been up to. I tried to convince Carajac that if we saw the night watch coming, he should toss the damnable bundle into a corner or over a wall, but he wouldn't hear of it, fearing irreparable damage to the tender organ from such a fall. I reminded him that his own organ would suffer far more pain if he were arrested and sent to the galleys. But so great was his love of learning that he didn't want to give up at this point. I made no further effort to convince him, but secretly swore to myself that I'd never repeat such a perilous adventure with such stubborn partners.

When I finally took my leave of Carajac, I felt infinitely lighter, now that I had no companion or evidence that would indicate where I was coming from or what I'd been doing, and I believed I had nothing more to fear, except perhaps some nocturnal thievery. So, holding my dagger before me, and walking in the middle of the street as quickly as I could, I felt quite equal to any bad fortune that might befall me.

My walk having warmed me, I removed my mask and gloves and stuffed them in my doublet and so, with one hand on my dagger and the other holding my lantern, I walked along at my ease, proud ~~~~~~~~~ silence, breathing in great lungfuls of the night air, believing myself entirely out of the woods of this perilous business. I should have realized that it's often out of the blue that the worst storms appear.

I'd scarcely turned the corner into the rue de la Barrelerie and was almost home, only a few steps from the pharmacy, when I had the impression of being followed by a shadow, which, however, made no noise on the pavement, but which I could see dancing along behind me in the halo of my lantern. Ah! I should have had the sense to blow out my lantern and run at full speed to my lodgings, but so sure was I of my strength and courage that I turned and rushed at the shadow, turning both light and dagger on it. O Lord! O Holy Christ! My blood nearly froze in my veins, for there before me stood the Mangane girl, whose eyes were throwing sparks, her mouth vomiting more hatred than all hell ever contained. She seized my hand—a contact that paralysed me—and hissed, "Where are your claws, Maître Goat? Where are your black eyes? Where is your tail? Ah, traitor! Ah, you wicked dog! You have vilely abused me! I should have realized the minute you did me that I couldn't feel your claws or your bites or the fire in my belly! Miserable Christian, don't you realize that the Great Léonard fucks his witches seven times before releasing them, panting, clawed, bitten, and their wombs devoured by his flame! His seed is the flame of hell! And yours is inert!"

"Mangane!" I replied in a voice a great deal less self-assured that I wanted, so hellish was the voice that hissed its hatred at me. "There was no deception, no trick. You were mistaken about me, that's all."

"You should have told me, Christian dog!"

"I couldn't. I had to get rid of you—I had a job to do."

"A villain's work!" she screamed, if you can call a scream the terrible hissing sound she made, as if she were a serpent. "I saw everything through Cabassus's window and tomorrow I'll tell all!"

"Hah! Silly witch! If you say a word you'll _____ stake!"

"I aspire with every fibre of my being to burn at the stake, since your sacrilegious embrace has forever robbed me of the arms of my beloved! After I die, a succubus will rise from my ashes and I'll live at his adored feet, submitting to his every desire. But know that for the harm you've committed, I will wreak such revenge on you in this life, tying your member in knots and leaving you forever impotent in the arms of a wench."

"Knot up my member?" I said, sweat running down my cheeks at this terrifying threat. "There's no way, since I'll never marry."

"I can twist the member of anyone I want and at any time I want, in marriage or out of marriage. All I need is a thread in which I make a knot and then throw on the ground, along with a coin. If the coin disappears, then Satan took it and the victim will be forever impotent."

"Mangane!" I cried, weak with terror and my knees trembling beneath me. "I'll give you all my gold if you promise not to!"

"Your gold!" she screamed derisively.

Mad with rage and fear, I gave her a terrible thrust of my dagger, but there was nothing there. She'd disappeared, as if absorbed by the shadows, and I was wondering if I'd even seen her when I heard the sound of a coin on the pavement.

"She's knotted me up!" I cried in a pathetic voice, my throat constricted with fear, and began casting my lantern about trying to see the thread, which I found knotted in a figure of eight, but I did not find the coin, though I was a long time on my knees looking for it. So the infernal powers had granted her wish and consummated her curse. My youth's bloom had faded and I would never recover my ardour for life, or love.

11

I REALIZE THAT in our current century there are many sceptics who, believing neither in God nor the Devil, will find my terror merely amusing, attaching no credence to witchcraft, which, however, is considered by both the Church and many learned men to be excessively maleficent. Certainly, at Mespech we made great fun of the affectations of la Maligou, but la Maligou was not a witch, or considered to be one in Marcuays or the other villages. Otherwise, no one would have laughed at her; they would have trembled with fear at her powers. For sorcerers and witches have the terrifying power to make our herds sick, dry up our wells, make our orchards wither in one night, bewitch people by sticking pins in a doll, compose love philtres or death potions, or knot up the member of a bridegroom.

Nor were we wrong to tremble: these evil doings were not, and are not, rare in the Périgord region nor throughout Provence, where the fear of witches is so widespread that a mere ten out of one hundred bridegrooms will celebrate his marriage publicly in the parish church.

It's a well-known fact, indeed, that at the moment the priest says: "What God hath joined together let not man put asunder," it's enough for a witch to murmur: "But let the Devil do it," and throw over her shoulder a coin and a piece of string tied in a figure of eight, for the man to become permanently impotent and be unable to consummate his marriage. That's why you so often see a young couple sneak off to a church in a neighbouring village to say their vows, hiding the hour, day and place of their wedding from everyone, even their own families (among whom there might be some jealous person) in order to avoid this secret curse, which could weigh on them not just during their lifetimes, but even till Judgement Day, if one of Satan's assistants, inspired by the powers below, decided to wreak his infernal evil on them.

The rest of the night, which was very short, I spent eyes wide open, so terrified about my joyless future that at times, despite the cool night breezes, I found myself sweating from my every pore. But I had to get up in the morning, dog-tired and aching all over, to go hear Saporta's and Bazin's private lectures, and sadly could only listen distractedly with half my attention, the other half busy ruminating on the terrible thoughts you can easily imagine. Not that I feared that the Mangane girl would denounce our secret dissection: who would believe such a wench who, during the trial that condemned her entire family to the flames, passed for a crazy deaf mute? But the knotting of my member and her horrible power over me were not thoughts one could easily dismiss, especially if one derived such pride and such sweet delights from one's virility.

That day dragged on—and was, in fact the longest of the year—but after so many hours of torture by my apprehensions, the lectures were finally done, and I ran straight to see Thomassine and sought refuge in her bosom, which I covered with kisses and caresses; and, in the end, I was so inflamed that I began to believe I'd triumphed over the Mangane girl's curse. But this fire went out all of a sudden, and it was as if a wall had suddenly been erected between her body and mine. I weakened and fell against her bosom, inert and dishonoured. But, however surprised she may have been, in her usual maternal, caring way, Thomassine cradled me gently against her and whispered all the sweet names she'd given me in our love-making. I was so overcome by her tenderness that I broke into sobs and told her about the curse I'd been given that morning (leaving out, of course, any mention of our grave-robbing). Thomassine did not take my story lightly, and with a sombre face told me about the more than ten occasions when, in the Cévennes mountains, some unfortunate who'd been cursed with the knotted string at his wedding, lived the rest of his life without being able to touch his bride—though with other wenches he was entirely potent.

"Oh, Thomassine," I sighed, "I pray to Heaven that this curse will be so selective that it will only target my wife—that I don't have!"

"Since you're not married," replied Thomassine, "then the curse is meant to keep you from enjoying any women at all, and is so much the worse for you, my poor Pierre."

I found no comfort in these words, nor in any of the tales she told me, and I had to interrupt her, since each one drove me further into despair.

"But, Thomassine," I ventured, "is there no remedy? Cannot God undo what the Devil has done? If not, then the Devil is more powerful than God!"

Thomassine had no answer to this since her faith was of the simplest kind. She went to Mass every Sunday at Saint-Firmin, accompanied by Azaïs, who carried her missal, which Thomassine held gravely up to her eyes during the entire Mass without turning a page, for though she could count, she could not read.

"I've never heard tell," she said after a few moments of reflection, during which she raised herself on her elbow and put a cushion under my head, "I've never heard tell of a curse being undone, except in the case of a labourer in my village who confessed the next day to his curate."

"But, Thomassine! You forget that I'm a Huguenot and that I object to confession! What's more, if it were enough to confess to be cured, why would there be so many men undone by the witch's knot?"

"That's true," she sighed. "It's also true that the curate of the labourer I mentioned was something of a sorcerer himself—but a sorcerer for good, not for evil, and was therefore more powerful than the others."

"And is this good sorcerer still in the Cévennes mountains? By the belly of St Anthony, tell me his name and where he lives and I'll saddle Accla and set out immediately to confess to him!"

"He's dead," replied Thomassine.

And along with her words, all hopes died of finding a cure. I left her, infinitely more sombre than before our discussion, and believed I was condemned to the most mournful future, living out in bitterness the torments of chastity—a virtue recommended by our churches, but one I held in absolute horror, feeling that it was against nature, and made a man less than a man, and a woman less than a woman; that it was a detrimental and dangerous diminution of their being, and certainly not an elevation to an ineffably higher state, as it was sometimes claimed to be.

The reader may well ask why my first step after the curse was not to go and consult a reformist minister, despite the absence of confession. Well, of course I thought of it! And if I didn't do it, it's because they are so austere, so unaccommodating and so quick to assume that the victim of such a curse was in some way not entirely innocent. In this, they were not so wrong. Moreover, I have too much respect for my pastors to lie to them or to truncate my story, as I would have done with some papist priest so eager for his money. No, I would have had to tell all, or say nothing. Terrified by this "all"—which would include the profanation of a grave and fornication with a witch—I chose "nothing" and decided to suffer alone and without succour the misfortune that had befallen me.

And so I left the needle shop crestfallen and discomfited, persuaded that, after my terrible impotence with Thomassine, I would fail as well with Madame de Joyeuse. I looked forward with such bitter apprehension to our Wednesday assignation that I couldn't sleep for three nights. I arrived at her door pale, with rings under my eyes and a downcast look, and asked for a private conversation with her. Alarmed by my appearance and my tone of voice, she sent her ladies away, invited me into her boudoir and lay down on her bed, while I sat, silent and ashamed, on a stool beside her, trying to decide how much to reveal in my confession. I was sure that Madame was too clever to accept the abridged version I'd given to Thomassine. She'd immediately want to know the what and wherefore of this great wrath I'd excited in the Mangane girl, and if I told her, wouldn't I then have to tell her the rest of the story?

"Ah, my sweet!" she said after a moment or so in her gentlest tones, looking at me with those golden-brown eyes. "Is it so terrible that you can't even speak of it, even with me? Don't you know that I'm your friend, and that I'll never withhold my friendship or my support no matter what you may have done?"

I was so touched by these words that I began to weep, but still couldn't talk, my throat was in such knots.

"My Pierre," said Madame de Joyeuse, "don't sit there like a log on that stool. Come here, in my arms, like this: rest your head there, and tell me everything—I desire it," she added with an authoritative tone.

This tone convinced me. I obeyed her as I always did, partly because she was fifteen years older than I, partly because she was a grande dame whom I admired, but mostly because I was so infinitely grateful for all her marvellous goodness. And so, snugly nestled into her welcoming body, my cheek on her breast, one arm around her waist, I told her all, without omitting a single detail or disguising anything, confident that she'd pardon me everything. Oh, you papists!

Answer me! Could we ever find a better confessor than the woman who loves us?

This is not to say that Madame de Joyeuse didn't break into my tale with indignant objections and murmurs, such as: "Oh, Pierre! How *could* you?"; "But, my sweet, that's dishonest!"; "Jesus! How horrible!"; "Fie! You're breaking all the laws!"; "O Lord, I've never heard of anything so infamous!"; "What! You did it with a witch? And on a gravestone!" But at each outburst her gestures belied her words, for she caressed my hair with one hand while her other hand was gently squeezing my shoulder, which assured me that I was still her friend.

Finally, I got to the worst part. During my description of what happened in the rue de la Barrelerie, she remained silent and still, not moving a finger. But after a few eloquent sighs, which I concluded were half compassionate on my account and half regretful on hers, she said in a most reassuring tone, "You should know, Pierre, that my husband, who is very worldly-wise, considers such pretensions a huge farce. He thinks the string knotting is neither infernal nor real; that the knot is in the knotter and nowhere else. That it's one's own imagination that produces the impotence. He also says that Michel de Montaigne demonstrated this for him in Bordeaux with many convincing examples and powerful reasons."

I found this somewhat comforting, yet still couldn't persuade myself that I didn't feel some paralysis of the vitality in my body that I didn't believe I could overcome. And feeling thus, I remained nestled up against her, unable to move and as if plunged into abject terror, fearing above all to dishonour myself by failing to finish what I'd started.

"Oh, Pierre!" she said as if she'd heard every one of my inmost thoughts. "You're too young and too brave for this curse, as you call it, to weigh on you more than a week! Good heavens! A string knot! My husband is right. It's just a charlatan's trick! A silly superstition! A trap for the ignorant. Pierre, are you some simple labourer that you should be terrorized by a village sorceress? Are you going to believe the Mangane wench's old wives' tales or Michel de Montaigne's learned reasons?"

"Ah, Madame!" I replied. "I'd dare believe you if I weren't so dog-tired, broken and beaten that I feel like the shadow of my former self."

"That's just the effects of your remorse, my little cousin, for having committed such outrageous and scandalous sins. And your imagination holds such sway over you that this knot business is simply the punishment you think you deserve. In a week, you'll be back to your gallant ways in my arms! I order it!"

"Oh, Madame, must I obey you?"

"You'd better not fail to do so! Are my spells any less powerful than those of that ignorant little girl? Are my potions less effective? Am I any less beautiful?"

"Oh, Madame!" I cried, full of fire. "You're a thousand times more beautiful than that shadowy creature! Your face shines with such brilliance, and your body is divine in all its parts."

She was much moved by this and blushed right down to her breasts, since she was accustomed to hearing such sweet words as a prelude to our love-making. Meanwhile, complaining of the heat, she wriggled about and began unhooking her chemise, and tried very hard to arouse me since I was clearly making no efforts on my own, believing them to be in vain. We remained in this impasse for a few moments, she reddening increasingly from the impulses she was feeling, and I remaining quite still and quiet like a rabbit hidden in a bush. Finally, growing impatient at my immobility, she said with a little laugh to hide her shamelessness, "My sweet, is there any reason why, even if you can't take your own pleasure today, you refuse me mine?"

"Oh, Madame!" I gasped. "I beg you, tell me what to do! There's nothing I wouldn't do for you, I love you so much!"

And so she ordered me to play her chambermaid and to finish undressing her: which I did, not without great sighs of regret that I couldn't enjoy the beauties I could see before me. Then undressed myself. And finally, taking and guiding my hand just as she had the first time she'd initiated me into these intimacies, she said, "My sweet, do that thing I like." I did as she asked, and she began writhing with pleasure, making those moaning sounds that so annoyed Mademoiselle de Mérol. But before finishing her pleasure, she stopped and told me to lie on top of her. Which I did, not without great embarrassment, as you may imagine, because of my inertia, but now she put her hands on my shoulders and gently pushed me downward, showing me with this gesture that she wanted me to put my mouth where my finger had been. And though this caress, that I'd never heard tell of before, seemed at first very strange, or even sinful, I was careful not to disobey Madame, thinking that I owed her this compensation for the insufficiencies fate had inflicted on me. However, once I'd recovered from my surprise, and observing that her moans were becoming more acute, and the writhing more intense, I felt enormous pleasure to be giving such exquisite pleasure to a woman who had been so good to me. This thought increased my appetite for this strange activity, and I applied myself enthusiastically, though not without tenderness, to my caresses, which she must have felt, for she arrived at the height of her pleasure with more panting, moans, cries and tumultuous writhing than I'd ever seen before.

When this tempest subsided into calm, she whispered, still breathless, her arms akimbo, "Oh, my little cousin, if I dared speak this way without blasphemy—which I hope I may do, for I fear God, go to confession and am in church every Sunday—I'd say that was divine and that I'm going to think of it often before I see you healthy and whole again next Wednesday, in the hope that you'll provide me the other pleasure that we share."

She accompanied these words with so many caresses, kisses and great compliments on the way I'd performed (not without adding to her praises a few words of advice on how to do even better the next time) that even though I hadn't been able to possess her, I felt that I was her lover again: this considerably calmed my fears and gave a new spring to my step as I returned to the pharmacy. There, having swallowed my spartan gruel without saying a word to anyone, I ran to my room and threw myself on my bed. Alas! I still couldn't sleep, despite being less anxious about the curse.

During the evening of the following day, a valet wearing Madame de Joyeuse's livery brought me a letter from Madame attached to a small package.

My dear little cousin,

In this packet you will find a sachet of curative herbs that Michel de Montaigne gave to my husband, who was once in a predicament similar to yours. Wear it day and night round your neck, next to the medallion of the Virgin that your mother gave you on her deathbed, even though you don't worship Her, evil Huguenot that you are. This sachet will do wonders. You'll see what I mean next Wednesday, when we shall see each other again.

My little martyred cousin, I offer you my fingertips.

Eléonore de Joyeuse

"Of course, her fingertips!" I laughed to myself. "What an expression! Oh, how elegantly these noblewomen speak—and do—everything, while hiding behind their words." I was nonetheless very touched that she had been so thoughtful as to send me her valet—she who had nothing to do all day. I ran to my room, opened the package and hung the sachet around my neck and never took it off day or night,

388

following the advice of Michel de Montaigne, whom I'd never met but whose wisdom had been highly praised by our late friend Étienne de La Boétie.

On rereading Madame de Joyeuse's letter, however, I noticed a *postscriptum* that I hadn't seen before:

Cossolat will see you at noon tomorrow at the Three Kings.

"Oh, marry!" I moaned to myself. "Did she tell him everything?" For I'd long suspected that there was a secret intelligence between them, though certainly not for the reason you'd imagine, the lady considering herself too elevated for a mere officer of the law, but rather to facilitate various intrigues throughout Provence that she did or undid in the service of her husband. Which reminded me that I'd just done her a disservice by saying that she had nothing to occupy her time all day.

At noon, the hostess of the Three Kings, still full of resentment, made a sour face at me despite my smile, and, pushing me roughly by the shoulder, led me to a little cabinet where Cossolat was sitting down to a roast and flagon, looking quite severe.

"Monsieur," I said, half serious, half in jest, "have you sent for me to throw me into jail?"

"Not yet, Siorac," he replied extremely coldly, "though certain it is that you deserve it."

"He knows everything," I thought, and, my legs shaking with fear, I sat down opposite him. Cossolat continued eating and drinking as if I weren't there, never opening his mouth except to ingest his dinner, which began to irk me no end, being unaccustomed to being treated so badly, especially by him, who was normally so respectful of nobility.

"Monsieur," he said finally, "is there anything left of the 200 écus Madame de Joyeuse gave you?"

"Certainly," I answered, astonished at this indiscretion. "I've spent roughly one quarter of it."

"Then order a roast and a flagon from our hostess, and pay her ten écus."

"Ten écus!" I cried. "For a roast and drink that cost ten sols?"

"Not at all! Ten écus for the money you lost her by scaring off Caudebec and his *roumieux* with your story of the plague."

I'm a good Huguenot and a good enough manager of my money, though not as stingy as Samson or Sauveterre. But I immediately understood that without these ten écus (from which Cossolat would doubtless profit one way or another), I'd never get back into my hostess's good graces, an eventuality I knew I could not risk. So I resigned myself to be squeezed at bit—especially since, for various reasons, I wasn't in a position to be as proud of myself as I'd have liked to be.

"Here are your ten écus," I said, taking them out one by one from my purse and placing them on the table.

Cossolat clapped his hands, and immediately the door to the kitchen opened, and our hostess emerged, her eyes shining at the sight of all my gold. "My girl," said Cossolat, "Siorac, here, would like a bit of roast and some drink and here's his payment. Give him a kiss on the cheek and be his friend."

All honey and smiles, our hostess, having rapidly pocketed my money, obeyed, and never, in all the bloom of my youth, did a kiss cost me so dearly. Cossolat, of course, as he watched her retire with an extra roll of her hips, seemed very happy with the outcome of this business, but his expression changed for the worse.

"Ah! Pierre! Pierre! Pierre! Why didn't you speak to Madame de Joyeuse about your crimes the next day instead of waiting three days! I could have hushed up the whole business, but now I can't. The Présidial got wind of it, had the Mangane girl arrested and tortured her. She gave them Cabassus's name but luckily didn't know your name or those of your friends, but she described you."

At a knock on the door, he fell silent. Preceded by a chambermaid, who brought me a flagon of wine and a knife, our hostess served me my roast, and, as she was leaving, ran her fingers along the back of my neck. "My girl," frowned Cossolat, "you've shown enough gratitude. Enough is enough." She blushed and departed smartly.

"So what's going to happen to Cabassus?"

"What did you say? You're worried about Cabassus and not your own neck? Is your head so light that you're not worried about losing it?"

At this joke, which I did not appreciate, he burst out laughing, being a man of natural coarseness, though he was fiercely devoted to those of his own party. "Cabassus," he answered finally, "is protected by the diocese of Saint-Denis, who prefers to consider him as a madman rather than an atheist. For the last ten years, they've relegated him to that farm for his own protection and stripped him of all his priestly duties. Being a priest, he won't risk much if he can only keep his mouth shut."

"But sadly," I mused, "he's crazy and gabs like a mill wheel."

"In that case," said Cossolat, "he'd better flee and hide."

"He won't do either. Cabassus is very invested in his own unbelief, and only lacks the right occasion to confess *urbi et orbi* this bizarre faith that he has revealed in his treatise, entitled *Nego*."

"What!" cried Cossolat, "He's put all of his crazy ideas in writing? By the belly of St Peter! He's cooked! What can I do now to stop it? If Cabassus is arrested he'll be tortured, and he'll reveal your names and you'll fall as well."

His words gave me such a chill I couldn't eat another bite.

"There, there!" soothed Cossolat, who really wasn't such a mean-spirited fellow. "Eat up! You're not yet kneeling on the scaffold offering your neck to the hangman! You have powerful friends! You know,

Pierre, the worst that can happen is that you'll be obliged to flee the city on the sly, the way your father did in his youth, when he killed that man in a duel."

"Ah, but next to death, I can't imagine a fate worse than exile! I'd never recover. I cannot imagine a life without medicine—it's my great love!"

"I think you love it too much!" rejoined Cossolat.

But how I managed to finish my roast after that, I know not. "Cossolat," I said, "what do *you* think? Is the Mangane girl really a witch? Or are her curses just foolishness and error?"

Cossolat shrugged his shoulders. "The girl is a madwoman raised by crazy people who believed they were witches and who were burnt at the stake based on their own confessions. But whether these confessions were sincere or frightful, stupid boasting I've no way of knowing."

"So what makes you doubt them?" I asked, quite surprised.

"Well, mostly from this girl herself. When she was tortured, she confessed to having fornicated with Beelzebub on the tombstone of the Grand Inquisitor."

"But that was me!" I cried. "And she knows it perfectly well since she then accused me of impersonating Satan himself."

"Well, then, she's lying! It's clear!" said Cossolat. "And if she's lying about that, couldn't she be lying about all the rest? Claiming in her insane pride, at risk of burning at the stake, that she's got a power she doesn't have?"

This set me to thinking, as you might imagine, and doubtless would have calmed my fears about impotence if the threat of an even worse consequence weren't weighing on me. "Ah!" I thought, my throat so constricted I could hardly breathe. "If I had to flee, how would I ever face my father in Mespech?"

"Cossolat," I said, as if he'd been able to hear my thoughts, "what must I do to avoid this terrible extremity?"

"Wait, and keep your ears open."

"What? Aren't yours sufficient?"

And seizing my meaning, Cossolat smiled faintly. "Mine, alas, can't be everywhere. But Fogacer's, now, they'd be more useful than mine."

"Fogacer?" I said, astonished.

"Fogacer," replied Cossolat, "is a friend of the Présidial judge, who was ridiculed in effigy at carnival."

"So this judge might possibly reveal to his friend the contents of his secret instructions."

"Aha! You understand!" said Cossolat. "It's no different with these strange men than it is with us and our wenches. The appetite we have for another can be our Achilles heel. All our weakness can be traced to that. Even I, who consider myself an honest man, just extorted ten écus from you to please our hostess. Though that was a matter of justice," he added as he rose.

I wanted to see Fogacer that very evening, but wasn't able to for two days, as our illustrious master informed me that he was at the country home of a rich merchant who, since Rondelet's death, swore only by my tutor. On the third day, as I was preparing to go to bed, I heard him moving about in his room and went to knock on his door.

He seemed to be happy to see me enter his room with such familiarity, for, since what had happened between us at carnival on the rue de l'Espazerie, he'd put some distance between us, no doubt from shame, which, out of my own shame, I hadn't tried to bridge.

"Ah, Siorac!" he said, raising that satanic eyebrow and hiding his emotions behind his usual humorous tone. "What's that hanging by the medallion of the Virgin? A sachet? What's the meaning of this? Have you become a double-idolater, you, a confirmed Huguenot?"

"Not at all," I replied, "it's just a herbal medicine to counteract a nervous malady that I seem to have, and that occasionally flares up."

"Ah, indeed!" he said sceptically. "You don't look your usual self! But, Pierre, sit down and tell me the what and wherefore of your 'nervous' disorder. If your cheeks weren't so hollow (as you seem to have lost weight) I'd say they were bursting with questions. My son, lance this boil and let the pus out! Who's it about?"

"The Mangane wench."

"Pestilence! Do you run after satanic skirts too? 'Sblood! There are flames and then there are flames and this one could really burn you!"

But I didn't feel like laughing. "I've heard tell," I said gravely, looking him straight in the eye, "that they've put her on trial. And since this trial concerns me to some extent, and thinking perhaps that her testimony might be less of a secret to you than to me, I thought I might ask you to shed some light on what's happening, if you wouldn't mind sharing what you know."

"Aha!" exclaimed Fogacer, and he began silently pacing back and forth (though his room was hardly wide enough to allow it) glancing at me from time to time, but looking very preoccupied and circumspect.

"Pierre," he said finally, "what makes you think I'd know more about these proceedings than you?"

I was ready for this question with an answer that wasn't entirely true, since I didn't want to scare Fogacer by repeating what Cossolat had told me. "On carnival day, you ripped off the nasty poem that was pinned to the effigy of the Présidial judge."

"Ah, so that's it!" he sighed, sitting down, greatly relieved. "What can I say? I don't like people to be defamed. As for the judge," he added nonchalantly, "it's true I know him slightly."

I had to admire this "slightly", but I remained silent.

"Well, what do you want to know?"

"If my name has come up in this business."

"Aha!" said Fogacer. "So that's it! Well, Siorac, so far, you've not been named, but you have been described."

"And was I recognized in this description?"

"Not by the Présidial judge. But I recognized you immediately, for I know you all too well and I know that you're strong, high-handed and impetuous. Of course, I also recognized both Merdanson and Carajac by their large, powerful frames."

"Fogacer," I stammered, my throat tightening into a knot, "did you tell Saporta?"

"I had to. But he declared that he wouldn't throw any of you out of the college unless you were condemned by the Présidial court. And he's in a difficult position, since he recently accepted the gift of a skeleton without knowing where it came from." And at that he began to laugh so hard he got tears in his eyes at the thought that Saporta would be accused of trafficking in cadavers. But since I wasn't able to share the joke, being up to my ears in this whole business, I brought Fogacer back to the subject at hand:

"Fogacer, what do you think about the Mangane wench?"

"It's the trial that produced the witch, not the other way around. If you torture a poor wench to make her confess she fornicated with the Devil, you can be sure she'll say so."

"So you don't think she's in possession of supernatural powers?"

"In my view, no. Not her any more than her entire family, or all of the so-called sorcerers in France and Navarre put together."

"And yet," I ventured as my mouth went dry, "when a witch does the curse of the knot and throws a coin on the ground, the coin disappears. Hasn't the Devil taken it?"

"Oh, my poor, naive friend! That's such a carnival trick. Like peas under moving thimbles! She throws the coin on the ground so you'll hear it and then quickly picks it up. So you can look for it all you want. Why do you think they use a coin, if not to strike terror into you when you can't find it, having heard it fall?"

"But where did you hear this, Fogacer?" I asked, gaping.

"The Présidial judge is in the habit, when he arrests a witch, to put a false witch in jail with her to get her talking."

"So it's all a fraud?"

"Of course!"

"And our judges know this, but burn them at the stake?"

"Because the judges, or at least our judges, consider that such fraud is itself diabolical. In their view, playing at sorcery is every bit as damnable as practising it. For sorcery disrupts the order of the world, adoring Satan and not God."

This provided me much food for thought and I began to believe—as Joyeuse would say—that I had knotted myself. But this was merely a passing thought since I had many more fish to fry and these were more sharks than minnows.

"What about Cabassus?" I asked.

"Ah, Cabassus!" he replied. "Since the Mangane wench named him, the Présidial judge subpoenaed him, but he recused himself, claiming that as a priest, he fell under the jurisdiction of his bishop."

"Well, that's very good!"

"It's very bad! For the Présidial court demanded that the bishop bring Cabassus to trial and since the bishop is not anxious to burn one of his priests, even so bad a one as Cabassus, he's charged his canons to examine the case."

"And if they lock Cabassus in an ecclesiastical jail, will they torture him?"

"I don't know, Siorac," replied Fogacer looking me in the eye, "but if they do, he'll name you, and you'll have to flee."

"Ah," I thought, "if there's still time!" And seeing my discomfiture, Fogacer tried to comfort me, and I left having more confidence in his friendship than I had in my future. When I got back to my room, I slept but fitfully, even if it was for different reasons than the previous nights, for my head seemed very uneasy on my shoulders.

The entire day Tuesday was spent in the greatest distress, terrified and anxious as I was at the idea of dishonouring my father by being beheaded in public for having profaned a grave—and of my two companions, not being noblemen, being hanged high on a scaffold, which is a terrible death, as Espoumel had explained. Oh, reader! What torment and grief I was experiencing in my sixteenth year! Although I'd always believed my life would be a bed of roses, I now felt I was lying in a briar patch, sad and mournful, horrified by my own behaviour, and overwhelmed with misery. As soon as I got back to my room, I began crying and ruminating on my fate, trying to pray to God. I, who was so proud of my body, had made it my idol for all the pleasures it provided me, being uncommonly proud of its vigour, its gallantry and its amorous appetites, and delighted that wenches loved me as much for my body as I loved them for theirs. Oh, Lord! To lose this beautiful and good flesh so quickly and so soon in the bloom of my youth, almost without having had time to live! That was the nearly unbearable and worst suffering I could imagine—even worse than the pain of death itself.

I had to force myself on this Tuesday to go to listen to the private lectures given in the rue du Bout-du-monde by Chancellor Saporta, who loved to look at me from time to time, given the ardour I displayed in listening to him. But that morning, I noticed to my despair that he didn't look my way once, even though I was in the first row and listened to him with my usual fervour. Not once did he condescend to notice my presence. I had the sinister impression from this behaviour that Saporta had already expelled me from the college and from the company of the living. Of course, I understood that he was angry and disappointed that I was going to tarnish the reputation of the school by the trial. But not one single look at me, his own son: this was almost more than I could endure. I stopped listening, laid my pen down on my now useless writing desk, studied the ground in front of me and imagined my burial: rotting, cold and forgotten in the shadows of the tomb, far from the Provençal sun, my head separated from my body to the great shame of my family.

When the lecture was over, I caught sight of Merdanson and Carajac, both pale and crestfallen, their powerful shoulders sagging. I was seized with even greater remorse that I should have dragged them into this calamitous adventure, and I went up to them and proposed that we meet at noon at the Three Kings. From the mournful way they responded, I understood that the gibbet was haunting them every bit as much as I was obsessed with the executioner's block where I'd lay my head.

The hostess at the Three Kings was all smiles and welcomed me warmly, which first comforted me, but then annoyed me a bit since I owed her smiles to the ten écus I'd paid for them. She did, however, agree to allow me the use of her little cabinet, which was normally reserved for people richer than I. As I entered it, Merdanson and Carajac arrived right behind me. I ordered roast meat and three flagons, one for each, hoping to cheer them up—and myself as well—and recover a little bit of our *joie de vivre*. They'd learnt that the Mangane girl had been imprisoned, but didn't know that she'd named Cabassus and that he now risked death, so when I told them this news, they became so terrified that Merdanson started talking about fleeing Montpellier immediately without any more discussion.

We argued bitterly, Carajac for and I against this idea, and I was most unhappy to see them so resentful of my opposition, not that they openly reproached me for dragging them into such a sinkhole with no help in sight, but I could sense that this was on the tips of their tongues and rather wished they could just say it outright.

This is how things were, bitter and growing worse by the minute, given their mounting terror, when there was a knock at the door. It was Cossolat.

When he saw him, Merdanson paled and rose as if to flee, and Carajac, too, looked wildly for some way to escape.

"Monsieur," choked Merdanson, "are you here to arrest me?"

"I don't know, young man, who are you?" replied Cossolat half serious, half in mirth, his eyes shining malevolently. "And you, my friend," he said to Carajac, "what's your name? Given the description the Mangane wench provided, I think I could guess." And, as my two companions just stood there stupidly staring at him, he continued, "I would have guessed it, even if your question, which was really stupid, wasn't enough to incriminate you." This was said with such authority that my two friends sat down again, bristling at being called stupid, yet somehow relieved that Cossolat seemed more jocular than menacing.

"Monsieur de Siorac," said Cossolat, "if I understand correctly, I may speak of your affairs in front of your friends. They have the same interest as you in learning of what's transpired."

"Monsieur," burst in Merdanson without giving me time to respond, "should we flee the town?"

"Why on earth do you keep accusing yourself?" laughed Cossolat. "You're too wet behind the ears to appear before a judge."

"Monsieur," said Carajac with some irritation, "don't make fun of us. You're a Huguenot as we are. Answer us: should we run?"

"Young man," growled Cossolat, raising his voice, "I'll make fun of whomever I please, whenever I please! As a good Huguenot, I don't like people who profane graves. But as for fleeing, it would be pure folly. That's my answer."

A long silence followed. Merdanson and Carajac looked abashed and crestfallen to be so rebuffed.

"Siorac," continued Cossolat, looking very pleased with himself, "what have you learnt from your friend?"

"That Cabassus was hauled before the Présidial judges, but recused himself as a priest, so the judges have asked the bishop to judge the case."

"And that's all?"

"Yes."

"So my visit wasn't in vain," said Cossolat. "Listen to what happened next. The bishop ordered three canons to go to interrogate Cabassus in his hut. He was in bed with a bad cold, which was so severe it made him deaf. They couldn't get anything out of him except a bunch of incoherent sounds, so they decided he was a crazy, senile old wreck. On their way out, however, one of them found his *Nego*. Zounds! According to what I've heard this treatise is incendiary—every one of its hundred pages is like another stick on his pyre and it doesn't take a hundred sticks to burn an atheist."

"Oh," I groaned, "Cabassus is a goner and it's all my fault!"

"All *his* fault" corrected Cossolat. "When you've got such ideas it's pure folly to write them down! The canons have locked him in the ecclesiastical jail."

"Will they torture him?"

"For the moment, they can't because he's a priest. But the canons want to defrock him, and once they do that, and he's a mere layman, they'll hand him back over to the Présidial judges, and they'll torture him." Cossolat looked me in the eye.

"This is where your friend can be infinitely helpful if he can inform you in time."

"To flee?" said Merdanson in a voice stifled by fear.

"Young man," replied Cossolat, "you must realize that if you flee you lose everything: your family, your friends, your city, your studies, your future. Consider it only as a last resort: I hope I've convinced you of this."

"But, Monsieur," said Carajac, "Siorac, here, has powerful friends to protect him. We don't!"

"That's where you're wrong. If Siorac's protection holds, it holds for all three of you. You can't incriminate some but not others, or exculpate one without exculpating all three. Think about this."

This said, he rose and left, in his abrupt and military way, scarcely bowing as he exited, back and neck as stiff as a board.

I spent the rest of the day as best I could, which is to say atrociously, having but one thought, which I turned over and over in my poor head, which I risked losing on the scaffold. By the light of my candle I tried going over my lecture notes in my room after our meagre supper, but they danced before my eyes in total confusion. And what was the good of all this knowledge now, I wondered, that I was trying so hard to memorize? Alas, I couldn't say, feeling as though I were trapped in the hand of Destiny like a fly in the hands of playful children. Convinced of the futility of it all, I threw myself on my bed and, empty of tears to shed, I lay there, prey to an indescribable extremity of despair.

There was a knock at the door, and I raised my head: it was my beloved Samson, whom I'd completely forgotten in my misery, scarcely having more than three words to say to him a day, and hardly a glance for him, whose angelic beauty would have consoled a leper. But here he was, on my threshold, more timid and wild than a virgin, afraid to enter, his copper-coloured locks falling around his ears so gracefully, his azure eyes so pure, his face freckled, framing his perfect mouth.

"Excuthe me, my brother," he said in that delicious lisp he'd had since infancy. "May I come in?"

"You may, Samson,' I replied, raising myself on my elbow, but unable to stand to embrace him. He gave me a troubled glance, noticing my languor, so unlike my usual energetic self, closed the door and came to sit down next to me on the bed. "My brother, are you thuffering from fever? You look tho defeated, pale and thad and you've not thaid a word to me in three dayth. Ith there some hidden reathon that you're thuffering tho?"

"It's nothing, Samson. It will pass." But suddenly thinking that it might easily be on the scaffold that it would pass, I suddenly burst into tears. Samson threw himself down beside me and held me tenderly while I sobbed uncontrollably, and assured me he'd do anything in the world to help if I'd only tell him how, and then himself began crying, mixing his tears with mine.

"Oh, my beloved brother," I sobbed, when I could speak again, "I'm so grateful for the affection you feel for me, and it gives me courage to go on. I cannot tell you for the moment what's so bitterly troubling me but I promise to do so when I figure out how to deal with my predicament. But whether the outcome is a happy or a fatal one, I beg you to go on loving me when you learn of the terrible thing I've done."

"Oh, my brother!" replied Samson, who in his dove-like innocence couldn't imagine any sin greater that this: "You haven't become a papitht have you?"

"No, no!" I laughed through my tears, so touched was I by his simplicity. "I stand firm in my Huguenot beliefs and, God willing, always shall."

"Then you'll be thaved!" said Samson, his face radiant with joy, as if my salvation in the life to come was more important than my fortunes in this one.

May Christ forgive me, but I couldn't take such an elevated view of things, and was less preoccupied by my salvation than my life here below; but I didn't say a word, not wishing to hurt Samson's feelings. I was thoroughly resolved to tell him later about the profanation, but in no wise about the fornication, since for him sins of the flesh were more damnable than any others.

After a thousand assurances that he would always love me and come to my aid, whoever my enemies might be, he left, and the result of his visit and display of his great angelic love for me was that I slept better that night than the dozen nights that had preceded it.

I awoke feeling more lively and vigorous and, as I combed my hair in front of my little mirror, I said to my image, "Well, if my head must fall, let it fall, by the belly of St Anthony! At least I won't die as a coward." And suddenly seeing the whole thing as a comedy I was playing in, I imagined myself climbing the steps of the scaffold surrounded by crowds of onlookers, and stepped across my room with a confident and brash air, my hands behind my back as if tied, and, kneeling before my stool as if it were the executioner's block, I placed my head on it with my neck exposed and told the executioner with great authority: "Strike, villain!"

I was so pleased with this bravado that I replayed the entire scene again and suddenly felt so cured and recovered from the terror that had so eaten away at me that, from that moment on, it was as if I'd removed all its venom by imagining my death, and I altogether ceased trembling or lamenting my fate.

That was on a Wednesday, the day when Madame de Joyeuse was going to "offer her fingertips to me" as she had so prettily expressed it in her letter.

After an excellent repast at the Three Kings, which I washed down with a bottle of Corbières wine (since I'd decided, given how uncertain my future was, to be less careful about my money), I headed towards Madame de Joyeuse's mansion with a lively step, having resolved that morning to consider my impending death as a certainty and therefore cleared my heart of all the rubbish of despair, which was only a sly version of hope.

This change in attitude didn't escape the sparkling eye of Aglaé de Mérol, when she came out to greet me in the antechamber to lead me to Madame de Joyeuse's apartments. In the half-tender, half-ironic tone she had adopted with me, she said, "For a man whose head is hanging by such a thin thread, I have to admit, Siorac, that you look awfully full of yourself!"

"That, Madame, is because I'm so happy to see you!"

"Professor! Keep your inane compliments for others."

"Professor, Madame?" I said, stopping in my tracks and looking her in the eye, "What do you mean by that?"

"Didn't you take on my mistress as a student in your School of Sighs? Well, you must be an excellent teacher, for every Wednesday, I hear her moaning louder than before."

"Madame, if I had the good fortune to be your husband, I'd keep you in school morning, noon and night."

At which she laughed, blushed and undulated from head to toe. "But wouldn't that be too much schooling and too much studying?"

"Not at all! Moaning doesn't require so much work. All you have to do is let yourself go."

She laughed again, those dimples next to her lips showing deliciously.

"Oh, Madame," I said, "your dimples! I'll have to kiss them right away!"

"Why so?" she frowned, affecting disdain. But instead of taking her leave, she turned and seemed to be moving closer.

"Because, Madame, you owe me these dimples since I made you laugh," I said, and, taking her in my arms, I kissed her thrice, once on each dimple, once on her lips.

"Fie, Monsieur," she said in an angry tone, while shuddering with delight, "you're trying to use force to recruit me into your school. Go on by yourself. I'm staying here."

Whereupon she sat down in one of the armchairs, turning away from me, no doubt hoping to hide her confusion from the other ladies-in-waiting. As for me, I made a large bow to the other women but omitted any flourish of compliments since I was in a hurry to be alone with Madame de Joyeuse, after my "heated" exchange with Aglaé.

"Oh, my sweet!" cried Madame de Joyeuse as I pulled the curtains closed on her four-poster. "What's this? What do you want? Jesus, what a man! What? *In medias res?** Am I a chambermaid to be treated this way? Are you a soldier? How tyrannical you are! You're killing me and sacking my castle! Oh, Pierre, this is so crude! Oh, my sweet!"

To be sure, I did not go about things with a light hand in this furious assault, as preoccupied as I was with my virility and my own pleasure, having rediscovered my sword. But given her generous heart and her own intense interest in such activities (whatever her confessor may have thought) she was kind enough not to resent me for my abrupt manners—quite the contrary, in fact, for she laughed with pleasure at the return of calm between us.

"My sweet," she giggled, "Montaigne's sachet has worked miracles! Have you been wearing it every day?"

"I never took it off. But," I added, taking it from around my neck, "I wonder what's in it? It seems woefully thin!"

"Well, let's take a look!" she proposed, and, with a mischievous look, she grabbed a pair of scissors from the bedside table, cut the sachet loose and opened it. It was empty. At the sight of which, she laughed even harder.

"Oh, Madame," I cried, "you knew it!"

"Of course I knew it, since I was the one to sew it!"

"Madame, you've made unfair sport of me!"

"But, my sweet little cousin, I had to! You got knotted up by a trick and had to be untied by another."

"Oh, my joyous lady, what a genius you are!"

"The genius was in the idea, which is Michel de Montaigne's. The execution was mine," she said without a trace of vanity.

---

*   "[You're starting] in the middle?"

At this I threw myself in her arms, thanked her a thousand times and told her I despaired of ever finding a way of adequately demonstrating my gratitude.

"Oh, my Pierre!" she laughed. "Don't despair. You've got a very beautiful way of expressing it!" And as I was lying on top of her, kissing her neck, she placed both of her plump hands on my shoulders and pushed me gradually downwards, letting me know that she wanted the same caresses she'd required of me previously. "Aha!" I thought as I obediently followed her lead. "Aglaé, you were wrong, I think. My mistress is not so much following my schooling as I am following hers." In trying to remember the recommendations she'd given me with as much tact as possible, and following the intensity of her moans, I tried to give her the most exquisite pleasure I could, amazed at our bodies' resources for giving pleasure, during our short stay in this life, to those we cherish.

"My Pierre," she breathed as she emerged from this swell of passion that had swept over her, "tell me where things are in this sad business of yours."

Realizing that she already knew everything through Cossolat, and that she was only asking in order to hide her sources and to learn my own version of these facts, I went through the sequence of events as faithfully as I could, omitting nothing except Fogacer's name, whom I didn't want her to link to the Présidial judge, thinking that Cossolat, as circumspect as he was, would not have named my tutor in his version of the case.

Madame de Joyeuse, who was a very smart and well-informed lady, did not seem offended by this omission, quite the contrary. "Pierre," she agreed, "you're quite right to hide the name of your friend, because he's taking such risks for you. But, listen carefully, the minute you're told that Cabassus gave your name under torture, get yourself here as quickly as possible, whether it's day or night. They'll let you in. I'll give the orders and this house will be an inviolable asylum for you."

"I cannot thank you enough, Madame, for your help. But I'm not alone in this. I have two companions."

"Ah, indeed!" said Madame de Joyeuse frowning. "But they're not noblemen, there's the snag! How can I let them in here?"

Knowing the value she attached to nobility, I couldn't argue with her, and just looked at her without saying a word. After what seemed like an eternity of trying to tell her with my eyes what my lips were forbidden to pronounce, her natural generosity got the better of her feelings about rank, and, finding a compromise which seemed to accommodate the one and the other, she said casually, "Oh, my sweet! Let's not get overwrought about this! Your friends can be guests of my major-domo and can stay with him."

I covered her hands with kisses, then her arms, which were so round and firm and velvety, and lavished praises on them. But then we had to go over her entire body as usual: "Yes, my arms are beautiful, but what about my nose, Pierre? Isn't it too big?"

"But, Madame, not at all! It's a noble nose and can only be judged in the company of your striking face and in the surroundings of your gorgeous blonde curls and in the light of your golden-brown eyes!"

"Yes, my features are pleasant, but what about my neck? What do you think of my neck? Some nasty people—"

"Oh, Madame, don't even mention these vipers! If I knew them, I'd crush them with my heel! Your neck, Madame, is divine, sweet and soft and I never look at it without my lips itching to cover it with a thousand little kisses."

"Well, my sweet," she laughed, "what's stopping you? I couldn't ask for better."

And so, my appetite whetted anew, and happy enough not to exhaust my brain trying to come up with new compliments, I began furiously nibbling at her neck, then her breasts and... But I must desist from the rest of my attentions. Everyone knows that kisses are little animals that like to travel everywhere. And *hic et nunc** the School of Sighs, as Aglaé called it, opened its doors to its two students and, to be honest, I don't know which of the two lectured to the other, so much did our sighs complement each other.

As I left the Joyeuse mansion, someone took my arm from behind. It was Cossolat.

"Zounds, Siorac!" he whispered. "You're snorting and prancing and breathing fire like a stallion in a pasture full of mares! I'm guessing that you've been cured of the curse," he laughed. "But we have to undo some other things as well. Your head is hanging by a thread. The canons have ordered Cabassus to be defrocked tomorrow. The scaffold will be erected in front of the pharmacy, on the Place des Cévenols, virtually under your windows. I'll be there. When the defrocking is over, I'll try to take the ex-abbot to the city jail, where, on orders from the Présidial judge, at about three in the afternoon, they'll begin torturing him." Then, lowering his voice, he added, "Tell Fogacer that he must go to see his friend tomorrow evening and to tell you immediately if Cabassus named you. Every minute will be precious."

The strange thing was, despite the fact that the danger was now so near, armed with my newfound courage I didn't fear it as I had before, and took in this warning calmly, without wincing or blinking. Cossolat was astonished by my impassiveness. At dinner, with Maître Sanche, I was more voluble than usual, and argued heatedly with both my illustrious master and my tutor about the spread of syphilis, my tutor agreeing with the famous doctor of Verona, Girolamo Fracastoro, that the contagion spread from body to body by means of tiny insects, smaller than the eye could see. To which Maître

---

*   "Right then and there."

Sanche replied that since Fracastoro couldn't see them, then they weren't there. It seemed to me as I listened to them that common sense favoured Maître Sanche, but perhaps not a finer logic, for how could it be that in all the maladies that spread from body to body, the contagious agents were never visible to the human eye, even though we knew they were there?

I was awakened the next morning by the hammers of the artisans who were building the platform under my window. On this Thursday morning, neither Dean Bazin nor Chancellor Saporta were giving their private lessons at the Royal College of Medicine, so I remained in my room to go over my notes, and was much more able to concentrate than I would have expected, given how soon we could expect an outcome to this drama.

At exactly eleven, with all the pomp they loved to give their ceremonies, about forty papist priests arrived in a very brilliantly coloured parade of camails and chasubles as if they were processing into a solemn Mass at Notre-Dame des Tables. The vicar general, the canons and curate of Saint-Denis (Cabassus's parish) took their places on the platform, while the smaller fry—abbots, deacons, subdeacons and acolytes—remained standing on the pavement below, but were in the first row, in front of Cossolat and his archers, so that no one would miss the fact that clerical authority trumped lay authority in this matter.

The bishop arrived in an open carriage pulled by four horses, mitre on his head and crozier in hand, loudly acclaimed by the foolish crowd of people who'd rushed to watch this spectacle. The bishop, who appeared to be sick, climbed onto the platform with a majestic slowness, protected from the sun by a purple canopy held by four clerics.

Someone knocked at my door. It was Fogacer, who asked permission to watch the defrocking from my window, since it provided a better view of the proceedings than his. "Ah," he sighed, "there's poor Cabassus, who was imprudent enough to want to correct human failings."

"But where is he?"

"There, way over on the left, flanked by those two fat canons."

I hadn't recognized him at first, since, before bringing him up, they had washed him, shaved him and dressed him in the sacerdotal vestments proper to his rank, notably a gold-embroidered silk chasuble that they were going to defrock him with. And other than the fact that I'd never seen him so clean, or so splendidly dressed, I noticed that he was no longer rolling his eyes, but kept them glued to the ground, and far from chattering, shaking and moving constantly about, he remained quiet and calm with an expression less sad than grave.

"Ah, Fogacer," I said very troubled, "is he going to persist?"

"Of course! He wants to burn and thereby bear witness to his belief in the nonexistence of God. Which is a crazy thing to do, since non-belief, not being belief, but its opposite, doesn't require martyrdom."

The ceremony began with some Latin chants celebrating the glory and power of the divine Lord. Then Monseigneur the bishop, who was very pale and seemed to be suffering from some stomach disorder and intestinal ache, for he kept pressing his hand to his stomach, rose and pronounced a short homily on the same theme. After which he sat down and said to Cabassus in a paternal tone of voice, more sad than severe, "*Fili, credesne in Deum?*"*

"*Domine, non credo in Deum. Nego Deum esse.*"

"*Nominas Deum. Ergo Deus est.*"

"*Deum verbum atque nomen est. In se non est.*"†

At which the bishop sighed, which did not appear to be a ceremonial facade, and I later heard from Monsieur de Joyeuse that, believing,

---

* "My son, do you believe in God?"

† "My Lord, I do not believe in God. I deny that God exists." "You name God, therefore He exists." "God is a word and a name. As a being He does not exist."

as did the curate of Saint-Denis, that Cabassus was crazy, he would never have defrocked him without pressure from the Présidial judges.

"*Fili,*" he continued, "*errare humanum est. Perseverare diabolicum.*"

"*Diabolus non est,*" replied Cabassus.*

The bishop, then turning to a very tall canon sitting on his right, told him in a very tired voice to continue. This canon stood up. He had a very red but handsome face, a more imperious than evangelical look, and a very sonorous voice. And as gentle as the bishop had been with Cabassus, this man was hard and loud. And although his imprecations were useless after Cabassus's public confession, his Latin diatribe lasted a very long half-hour, during which the bishop kept rubbing his stomach and his epigastrium and appeared to be suffering greatly in his body, but even more so in his mind, for he seemed extremely impatient with this eloquence—which he put an end to with a few brief whispered words to the orator. The canon, who appeared to be quite embarrassed by this interruption—this ceremony before a great crowd of people being his moment of glory—next pronounced the official defrocking of Cabassus. Then, turning to the bishop, he asked him if he approved this sentence. The bishop replied in a very soft voice that, yes, he did approve it, and his pain seemed to increase dramatically.

The two canons who were flanking Cabassus, each taking him by the arm, brought him to the centre of the platform, facing the bishop, and proceeded to strip him of his vestments, explaining in Latin the function of each of the different ornaments and the reason it was being removed. The chasuble, which was of purple silk, embroidered with a knotwork of gold, was removed from his neck, a young cleric receiving it with great respect on his two outstretched arms as if it were an idol. This done, they continued to explain in Latin (which was understood by no more than a dozen people other than the priests) the uses and

---

* "My son. To err is human, to persist is diabolical." "The Devil does not exist."

411

symbolism of each ornament, and the canons, each taking a corner of the stole, pulled it over his head and placed it on the chasuble held by the young cleric. And finally, ordering Cabassus to raise his arms, the canons removed his alb, a sort of white chemise decorated at the bottom with embroideries of the same colour. The unfortunate priest stood there in his hose while another cleric brought him some very ugly, threadbare lay garments and helped him put them on.

Next came another cleric carrying a stool. One of the canons ordered Cabassus to sit down and the other held a kind of metal blade with which he scraped Cabassus's tonsure. But his scraping turned out to be purely symbolic, since he was so bald. This done, Cabassus held out his right hand with the index and middle fingers raised, and the canon scraped them as well, explaining in Latin that he was removing the abbot's powers to bless. That was the last act in this long ceremony, which the crowd watched in silence, and which appeared to move several of the priests there to tears. Others however, were frowning in disapproval and looked at poor Cabassus in horror.

The tall canon, who had read the sentence of the tribunal against Cabassus, stood, and, turning to the bishop, asked him what they should do with this man who was now no longer a priest. To this the bishop, his hand painfully gripping his abdomen, and his face distorted in pain, replied in a weak voice, "I order you to deliver him to the secular judges."

The curate of Saint-Denis hid his face in his hands, as though overcome with shame that one of the priests of his parish should have merited such a downfall. But the bishop leant over to Cabassus and, with a look of kindness, said several words in his ear that seemed to calm him. The tall canon made a sign to Cossolat, who, having gathered his archers and set them up in a double row leading to the steps of the platform, climbed to the platform and bowed very civilly to the bishop, who turned away, making scarcely any gesture of response. Of course, I knew why: many priests there considered that Cossolat's Huguenot heresy qualified him every bit as much for the stake as Cabassus's atheism. Cossolat, however, helmeted and wearing his battle armour, appeared to be blissfully unaware of the bishop's snub. Rather, he wore an expression of secret mirth as though he thought this entire papist pomp and ceremony were but another version of carnival.

"Monseigneur," he said, with a respectful coldness, "should I arrest this man?"

The bishop, without even looking at him, nodded briefly, and Cossolat walked up to Cabassus and placed his right hand on the former abbot's shoulder. The defrocked priest, who had managed to remain marvellously serene, composed and firm during the entire ceremony, did not flinch in the least at being delivered over to secular authority, understanding all too well what this would mean for him. Cossolat took his arm, without the least resistance from the abbot, and led him down the stairs, where the crowd, which, up to that point had remained calm, suddenly became enraged and rushed at him, shouting, "Kill him! Kill the atheist!"

Cossolat shouted an order to his archers, who lowered their pikes to a horizontal position and used them as a barrier to repulse these bloodthirsty knaves. Cossolat, sword in hand, grabbed Cabassus by the arm, and they ran through the corridor created by the archers, and climbed into a carriage that had been stationed some twenty paces from the platform. They barely made it into the carriage before some of the spectators (though they probably weren't merely observers, since the whole tumult looked very much as though it had been secretly planned in advance) pushed up against the wheels and tried to tip the carriage over, shouting, "Kill the atheist! Kill the Huguenot! Kill them!" But Cossolat leant over from his seat atop the coach and began administering blows with the flat of his sword (and occasionally with the point, as far as I could tell), and shouted an order to another group of archers who had been stationed in the rue de la Barrelerie, who came charging to the rescue of their comrades and, catching the rascals from behind, pricked their backsides with their pikes and soon put them to flight. Seeing this, Cossolat, shouting at his sergeant to whip on the horses, carried off his prisoner at a gallop, as if the now-precarious life of his prisoner were every bit as precious as his own. But the populace, seeing their prey escaping, continued to shout angrily. The two groups of archers now joined forces, and, led by a lieutenant, charged the crowd with no quarter, since they were so furious that their captain had been insulted and attacked while protecting Cabassus.

When the soldiers finally withdrew, a dozen of these rogues lay bleeding on the cobblestones. They were brought to the pharmacy to be bandaged, and we discovered that they were not from Montpellier, but had been recruited from outlying villages (the countryside being much more stoutly papist than the city). Our local papists had brought these labourers in from their farms and whipped up their religious zeal to provoke the riot. So we could see here the work of the cabal of papists that Cossolat had warned me about, and in no wise the work of the bishop, who seemed very troubled and unhappy to be associated with such damnable excesses.

After having helped Maître Sanche and Fogacer to cleanse the wounds of these wretches—victims of the hate that they'd been taught by their curates—I came back to my room, where Fogacer immediately joined me. "This much is clear," he said, arching his eyebrows, "they've used this poor atheist as an excuse to go after the Huguenots. Don't leave the pharmacy, but have your horse saddled and ready to go. They're going to torture Cabassus with atrocious zeal. The entire Présidial court will be there. And if, as I fear, Cabassus names you, I'll run here to warn you."

I scarcely had time to thank him: he was gone in a flash. I tried to focus on the work at hand, but couldn't, since my ears were ringing with the screams that Cabassus would be making as they tortured him. I threw myself on my bed and, for the first time since I'd got my courage back, I shed hot tears, which did little to soothe me, since it wasn't on my own account that I was crying.

After a few moments, however, I realized I should send Miroul to find Carajac and Merdanson, thinking that we'd be well advised to remain together if we had to get from the pharmacy to the Joyeuse mansion, for the same people who arranged the attack on Cossolat might well, if our names were known, prepare an ambush for us to speed up the work of justice.

Carajac and Merdanson, who had prepared themselves for travel, arrived at my lodgings by different routes, and seemed quite relieved to be in my company in this extremity, especially since asylum had been promised them at the Joyeuse mansion. I told Miroul to saddle his Arabian mare, Albière (since I'd loaned Accla to Fogacer so he could come back as quickly as possible from the secret place he'd agreed to meet his friend once Cabassus's torture was completed). Then I distributed weapons among the three of us, giving each two loaded pistols and a sword.

Four o'clock had just sounded, I think (though my memory is a bit jumbled), when I recognized the sound of Accla's trot outside. I leant out the window and Fogacer, raising his eyes at that moment, nodded gravely.

"Friends," I cried, "we've been named! Let's get out of here!"

We rushed downstairs at breakneck speed. Fogacer handed me Accla's reins, and the three of us were saddled up in the blink of an eye—and not a minute too soon, for as we spurred our horses on, a group of angry men surged towards us from the rue de la Barrelerie, whom I thought I recognized as the same peasants from the morning's riot. Fogacer's friend wasn't the only judge who had leaked the news: Cabassus's torture scarcely ended, our enemies, who know who we were, had moved against us.

"Spurs to horses!" I cried, and our three steeds, leaving sparks on the cobblestones behind them, bounded forward.

12

MADAME DE JOYEUSE was anything but joyous when I was ushered into her presence, and though it was still early in the afternoon, had already slipped into her nightgown and was in bed.

"Oh, Pierre!" she moaned, raising herself on her elbow. "I'm no longer what I was. There was a time when a little supper with a dozen courses, accompanied by two or three flagons of good wine, would leave me feeling fresh as the morning dew the next day. Alas! Those times are no more! What did I eat yesterday? Practically nothing, a few Bigorre sausages, three or four slices of ham, half a carp that was fished that morning, a garlic-roasted capon, an egg cream, a few almond tarts and, finally, some sugared almonds, nougats, fruit compotes, and other sweets that I adore. And very little wine, perhaps two or three glasses of Frontignan. In short, almost nothing! And here I am, Pierre, my liver in revolt, my stomach all angry and, what's worse, my poor dear, my complexion is awful despite all the make-up I applied."

"But, Madame," I soothed, "you have defamed yourself! I don't know what's happening inside, but the outside is as bewitching as ever, and if you weren't so uncomfortable, I'd show you!"

"Oh, please, Pierre, don't kiss me! My breath stinks like a swamp. And don't touch me either. I'm feeling like I'm going to throw up and you can't imagine what that's like!"

"Madame," I said, sitting down on a stool at her bedside, "I'm devastated that you're not well enough to tolerate my particular remedy, which is reputed to be unparalleled when one is built like you."

"Pierre! Pierre! Don't make me laugh either!" she laughed. "My guts are working me over! But tell me," she continued, "is it really true that you think my body is all right?"

"Oh, Madame, you're joking! You're so ravishing in your roundness that I could never forget your beautiful curves cupped so deliciously in the palm of my hand."

"Oh, Pierre, you're such a comfort! You have such a honeyed tongue!"

Hearing this I said nothing in reply, but gave her a very knowing look, which she understood immediately.

"My little cousin," she sighed, "no temptations today, I beg you! I couldn't. Nor would I want to when I'm entirely devoted to my repentance and to God when I'm in such discomfort."

"Madame," I soothed, "the little abbot who confesses you hereby absolves you. Would he be so impertinent as to put you on a diet?"

"We shall see what we shall see!" replied Madame de Joyeuse. "But as soon as this madness comes over me, my conscience goes soft as well. Forgive me!"

"Forgive you, Madame?" I said gravely, kneeling by her bedside. "I who dream only of living at your feet?"

She was very touched by my words, and reached out and ran her fingers through my hair and began caressing my head.

"So," she said, suddenly changing tone and subject, "it seems Cabassus has named you. Here you are, in danger of really losing your head, and I talk of losing mine! I heard there was a great tumult when this fellow was defrocked."

I told her everything I'd seen from my window, and the trap that first Cossolat and then I almost fell victim to when I left the pharmacy.

As she listened to this, she grew quite pale, then frowned and gnashed her teeth, and, when I'd finished my account, she entirely forgot her stomach problems in her wrath, got up out of bed and paced angrily back and forth, biting her fists; suddenly she roared like a lioness defending her cubs, "What! These scoundrels want to assassinate my sweet little man! Do they really think I'm going to let them do this? Do they think I'm going to tolerate this outrage? Zounds! They won't get away with this if I still have any influence on Monsieur de Joyeuse! My little cousin, wait here, and don't move an inch! I'm going to see him and I'll be back soon."

What happened next—the interview between the lieutenant general of Provence and his wife—I learnt only from the account of it given later by Madame de Joyeuse, and which I remember virtually word for word, it was so lively and colourful.

Monsieur de Joyeuse was at dinner when his big knave of a valet announced that Madame de Joyeuse was asking to speak with him.

"Madame!" he said, rising to meet her as she entered. "You don't need to wait to be announced! My door," he added with a smile, "is always open to you, day and night, though I respect your privacy, not wishing to violate the arcane mysteries that surround your beauty."

"My good husband, you are too kind!" she said as he took her hand and led her to an easy chair. "Thank you infinitely for your civility."

"Madame, might I ask you to do me the honour of sharing my repast?"

"Oh, sweet Jesus, Monsieur! Don't talk to me of meat or of eating! I had a little supper last night that seems to have weighed too heavily on my epigastrium."

"I'll wager it wasn't so little," laughed the vicomte. "But, if you'll permit me, I'll continue my dinner while we talk: I'm hungry as a bear, since I just returned from Nîmes, where I fear there's going to be a dust-up between the Huguenots and our Catholics. The bishop,

Bernard d'Elbène was so ill advised as to close the College of Letters since all the professors were of the reformed religion. Alas, when I arrived, the deed was done. I had to support Bernard d'Elbène, whatever the cost. But I fear the worst in Nîmes. From what I hear, on both sides there are anonymous attacks, plots and secret assemblies."

"Well, Monsieur," said Madame de Joyeuse, "I think you're going to have the same predicament here. Has Cossolat told you what happened?"

"I'll meet with him tomorrow."

"And it will be too late!" cried Madame de Joyeuse.

Forthwith, she recounted to her husband the defrocking of Cabassus, the angry mob that followed it, Cabassus's revelations, and the ambush that my friends and I had just barely escaped.

"And where are our three schoolboys now?" asked Monsieur de Joyeuse, frowning at this story, furious that this riot had taken place behind his back when he was in Nîmes.

"Here, within our walls. Two with our major-domo and Monsieur de Siorac in my apartments."

"I'll warrant he's not the most unhappy of the three," smiled the vicomte. "As for me, I'm delighted that your little cousin, who so charms and delights you, should help you pass the time in your solitude, which the duties of my office oblige me to impose all too often on you."

"It is indeed true, Monsieur," Madame de Joyeuse agreed, "that for a woman who is still young and who has managed to conserve at least some of her former beauty, I find myself too often abandoned."

"'Tis but too true, my love," said the vicomte bowing, "and I often reproach myself for this negligence. I don't pay your marvellous beauty the homage it deserves as often as I should, since I'm so constantly riding around the kingdom in the service of the king to preside over his local tribunals."

"But I'm happy to hear that there are some rustic beauties who succeed in offering you at least some comfort."

"Madame," replied the vicomte bowing again, "I'm so delighted that you can offer such generous indulgence to me, who must occasionally dine—you get my gist, I think—on stale bread and in such spare circumstances. But, my heart belongs ever to you, my dear. You have but to command and I will obey."

"But, Monsieur, the king himself is the only one in Provence who may command you."

"Oh, Madame!" lamented the vicomte with a sigh. "Would that you were right! But I have only what Michel de Montaigne has termed 'a very confused authority' in these parts, commanding too few troops to carry much weight on my right and on my left; I must rely more on persuasion than commands. The inhabitants of Montpellier are so rebellious and insubordinate. Do you know what the king of France calls them? 'My little kings of Montpellier!'… Nevertheless, I repeat, your wish is my command."

"My dear husband, I hope that you will agree that we must save our three schoolboys from the Présidial tribunal and from assassination."

"It'll be easier to save them from the first than from the second, our devout papists are so implacable. But, starting tomorrow, I shall employ every means at my disposal on their behalf, Madame, I promise you."

"Oh, Monsieur," said Madame de Joyeuse, "I can't thank you enough! Please let me offer you a token of my gratitude worthy of your immense goodness. I want to make you a gift of the silver dinnerware that I inherited from my father."

"Madame," said the vicomte, leaping to his feet with rather too much vivacity, "that's too much! It's a thousand times too much! I have my own silver service and it's enough for me, a man of simple tastes, and not given to pomp, as you know all too well." (Madame de Joyeuse couldn't keep from laughing outright when she told me this part of their conversation.) "But, Madame, the generosity you've shown with your father's estate is infinite. You are rich. I am not. And if it pleases you to fill my purse on this occasion, I would be infinitely grateful."

"And, Madame, are you going to fill it?" I asked, gaping, as I listened to this account later that evening.

"To the brim! Though it's a bottomless pit!"

"But, Madame," I mused, "from what your husband has told you about Nîmes, if I understood it correctly, and about Montpellier, it would seem that what he fears most of all is an uprising by all the reformists in our provinces. Don't you think that his primary aim is to prevent the fanatics among the papists in our city from murdering three Huguenot schoolboys for fear that our side will take revenge by an uprising that he won't be able to control? And if that's what he's intending to do anyway, why pay him to do it?"

Madame de Joyeuse burst out laughing at my question. "My little cousin," she said, "you're very abrupt in your way of talking, but you're quite right. But I think you'll agree that, for my part, I've acted quite wisely, and since you're so clever, you'll no doubt work out why, if you think about it a bit."

As for what happened the next day at the tribunal between the judges and the lieutenant general of Provence, I had news of it from two different sources. One was Madame de Joyeuse, who'd got it from her husband, the other Fogacer, who'd heard it from his friend. And, all things considered, I prefer the latter version, which I believe to be closer to the truth, since Monsieur de Joyeuse had every reason to want to inflate, in the eyes of his generous wife, the difficulties he encountered in his undertakings there.

The Présidial judges were deliberating my fate and that of my two companions, trying to decide whether they should arrest us based on Cabassus's confession, when the Vicomte de Joyeuse asked to be allowed to meet with them immediately. The judges were quite surprised that the vicomte should condescend to visit them at the court, rather than to summon them to appear in his mansion. However, the most rabid among them understood very well what he was intending to ask them, and were of the opinion that they should decide first and receive him afterwards. But the more moderate group carried the day, judging that they couldn't insult the king's emissary by making him wait and that, in any case, it would be better to hear him before deciding the matter.

The judges all rose and bowed deeply when de Joyeuse was introduced by the beadle, and the vicomte, in turn, greeted them with great civility, and invited them to be seated. After which, he accepted the chair he was offered and began speaking forthwith, without any bitterness, and without raising his voice, speaking in tones that were more laced with chagrin than severity.

"Messieurs, I suppose that you are deliberating the sad case with which a little cousin of my wife's has been most imprudently associated, and although laws are laws and justice applies to all and each alike, I am very unhappy that a relative of mine should be subjected to an outcome that would cast dishonour on me. There is no doubt that a crime has been committed: our three medical students dug up a whore and an orphan, but certainly not for any material gain nor because they intended any sacrilege, but simply because they sought to enlarge their understanding of the geography of the human body, as the great Vesalius himself did when he carried off a hanged man in Louvain. Remember, too, Messieurs, that Chancellor Rondelet was not afraid of dissecting his own son in order to discover the disease that killed him."

"Ah, but that was different," objected one of the judges. "The child hadn't been buried."

"To be sure! To be sure! But consider, I beg you, that by their unhappy decision to dig up two bodies, our schoolboys did not offend any notable family in Montpellier: the orphan had been raised by public charity. As for the wench—a whore living in shame and selling her body—no one knows who were her parents. What's more, after their dissection, the boys reburied the—"

"But without her heart!" remonstrated one of the judges.

"Did she have a heart when she was alive?" asked the vicomte, hoping to sidestep, with this quip, the swamps of a theological discussion about the difficulties for a mutilated corpse of receiving all the benefits at the resurrection of the dead at the Last Judgement. "Now, there's still the matter of the little orphan boy who was turned into a skeleton. This is a capital crime, I grant you. But where is the skeleton now? Do you know? In the Royal College of Medicine! Our schoolboys have made of it an anonymous donation to the chancellor of the college and the chancellor has had the imprudence to accept this gift. It therefore follows that if you arrest my cousin and his two companions, you must also arrest Chancellor Saporta for having trafficked in bodies."

"And why shouldn't we?" asked the most rabid of the judges.

To this reply, which was not without some impertinence, the vicomte reacted with visible annoyance. He didn't answer at first, but when he did, his tone, his face and his behaviour had completely changed. He rose from his seat and, frowning viciously (from feigned or real anger), he said in a most irate voice: "And why not, indeed? And why not also instigate today, as was done yesterday, a riot behind my back? And why not send a bunch of peasants to kill Cossolat, who, Huguenot though he may be, serves me faithfully? Or against my little cousin? Or against his companions? Or against Chancellor Saporta, who's also a Huguenot? Messieurs, it's not enough to judge. You have to know what you want. It's all well and good to throw three heads—including my little cousin's—in the face of the Huguenots of this city. But do you really want them to take up arms and knock down the doors of your Présidial and throw you in the city jail? Do you really want them to seize Montpellier? They have all the arms and talent to do so. And what would I do then but seek refuge with those of you who'd been spared, in the Saint-Pierre fortress to try to hold out against a siege, whose outcome would at best be uncertain?"

The judges, of course, paled at this and, seized by terror, sat there looking at each other, their throats constricted, unable to speak.

"Monsieur de Joyeuse," one of them said finally in a trembling voice, "are you telling us that you don't have the means necessary to defend the loyal subjects of your king?"

"I command a handful of soldiers, some of whom—among the best—are reformists and make no attempt to hide their loyalties."

"But, Monsieur," said one of the more fanatical papists, "we can expect reinforcements. The king and queen mother have just drafted 6,000 Swiss guards."

"Indeed," said the vicomte, his words dripping with irony, "and we won't see a single one of them here. Nor will I see a single écu, for the king needs all his soldiers and all his money if things go badly between the Huguenots and him."

Hearing this, the most fanatical among them began to fear that the hunters would suddenly become the hunted—an infinitely less appealing prospect than the one they'd been nurturing—and, abashed, fell silent. Seeing this, the vicomte walked over to the judges, who had stood up when he had, and looked them each in the eye with great seriousness. Then, with a composed and grave expression, he said: "Messieurs, I have said enough. I invite you now to deliberate, and to do so freely. I bid you good day!"

"Monsieur," said the oldest of the judges, "have I understood you correctly when I declare that, in this trial, we should use great circumspection in a matter which touches the king's interests in Provence?"

"You have understood me perfectly, Monsieur," replied the vicomte with a nod.

"But, Monsieur," continued the judge, "I must now ask you to deign to clarify very precisely what you mean. What does the king's interest require in this case?"

"That public safety and civil order not be troubled in a moment when they hang by a thread."

"And?…"

"Monsieur, since you invite me to do so, I will speak as a soldier. With total candour and honesty. You have Cabassus in your hands. He's an atheist. Burn him. *That should suffice.*" This said, and with a very slight bow, Joyeuse turned on his heels and departed.

"Oh, Fogacer!" I said when he'd finished his account of this encounter. "Tell me! You're leaving out the most important part! What happened in their deliberations?"

"These free deliberations," Fogacer explained, arching his eyebrows, "lasted for half an hour. After which they reread the minutes which related the interrogation of Cabassus under torture and they decided to burn the sections of his confession in which he named the three of you."

"Then I'm safe!" I cried.

"If they don't assassinate you," cautioned Fogacer, "since you're a Huguenot here with enough visibility and courage to cause them to fear some public reprisal if the Huguenots ever take the city. And what better way to punish the vicomte for being a Catholic who's too soft on his enemies than to kill his little cousin?…"

*

Like the summer before it, the summer of 1567 was suffocatingly hot. As before, they sprinkled the streets with water, and stretched reed mats that hung from the first-floor windows of the houses facing each other to give shade to the cobblestones, which otherwise would have been so hot you could have fried an egg on them.

In order to protect myself from my enemies, I obtained special dispensation from Chancellor Saporta to carry a dagger, sword and pistol in the rue du Bout-du-monde and even within the confines of the college. In addition, I never left my lodgings or the college without being accompanied by Miroul and Samson. On Wednesdays, Madame de Joyeuse sent her carriage around to the rue de la Barrelerie, with two huge armed bodyguards positioned on the running boards behind, and an archer with an arquebus next to the coachman in front. She had me return home at night by the same means.

In order not to expose me, Thomassine prohibited me from coming to see her, since the Saint-Firmin quarter was brimming with miserable cadgers who could have been hired to kill me for a couple of sols. Instead, she rented a chair and had herself brought by her guard, Espoumel, and some honest worthy, both armed to the teeth, to my lodgings, where she dared visit me in my room, dressed very elegantly, her features well-hidden behind a black silk veil. She had the temerity to tell the cyclopean Balsa that she was my cousin, and Balsa, very troubled both by her visits and by the falsehood, repeated the latter to Maître Sanche, who, shaking his head, contented himself with quoting a passage from the Koran: "If the mountain won't come to Muhammad, then Muhammad will go to the mountain."

I learnt later from Luc that Dame Rachel, bile dripping from her lips, her eyes flashing venom, unleashed a furious diatribe against her husband, accusing him of tolerating under her very roof the shameless and oft-repeated fornications between a common whore and a grave-robber.

"Fornication, Madame?" replied Maître Sanche, frowning. "Do you listen at Siorac's door, then?"

"Of course not, Concepcion does."

"Concepcion will pack her bags within the hour then," replied the apothecary. "And it was inspired of you to desist, Madame, or else you would have been cooked." Whereupon he turned his back, leaving her boiling and reboiling in the poisons her bitter soul secreted.

Towards the end of August, Cossolat requested my presence at the Three Kings, where I found him in the little cabinet looking very worried as he devoured his roast meat and wine.

"Ah, Pierre," he announced. "Things look very bad. I have it from the vicomte just this morning."

"Very bad? For me? For the reformists?"

"For the kingdom." He emptied his goblet, looked at me very gravely, and continued: "No doubt you remember the alarm we felt when Felipe II drew up a powerful army along our frontier to punish the poor beggars in Flanders—who share our religion. Condé and Coligny asked Catherine de' Medici and the king to gather an army of 6,000 Swiss guards, which was done. But when Felipe's army reached Luxembourg, Catherine de' Medici, no longer fearing for her kingdom, switched camps, as usual, and had 6,000 sacks of wheat delivered to the Spanish king. Pierre, you heard about this infamy, did you not? The king of France supplied food to the troops that were going to massacre our reformed brothers in Flanders! What's worse is that once Felipe had withdrawn, the French king did not dismiss the Swiss guards! Condé requested daily that they be sent home, but to no avail. Do you know what the constable ultimately said to him? 'What's the good of paying these Swiss guards if we don't use them for something?' And use them against whom?" Cossolat continued, banging his fist on the table. "Since the Spanish king was in Flanders!"

There was a knock at the door, and our hostess poked her head in, and asked me if I'd also like some roast meat and wine. "I'd love some," I said, "but this time I won't pay as dearly as last time!"

She and Cossolat both laughed at this, but his laugh was very distracted since he was so up in arms about the situation in the kingdom.

"Do I understand you correctly, Cossolat?" I asked when the hostess had withdrawn. "The Spanish king was fighting the reformists in Flanders, so then when the Swiss guards were no longer a shield against them in Flanders, they became a pistol pointed directly at our reformists in France?"

"You understand me perfectly."

"And so what did Condé do to disarm this pistol?"

"He demanded to be promoted to lieutenant general. If he had obtained this promotion, it wouldn't have been easy to turn the Swiss against the Huguenots, since, in that case, it's Condé who would have commanded them."

"But," I said, quite troubled, "wouldn't it have been over-reaching for a Huguenot, even one who's a royal prince, to solicit a promotion that would have made him second in the kingdom after the king?"

"Assuredly so! How to decide what to do in such a predicament? There's a logic in things. Mistrust is met with mistrust."

"So what did the king do when faced with such great pretension from Condé?"

"He did nothing. The queen mother did everything. She set her other beloved son, her adored sweetheart, the Duc d'Anjou, against Condé. And this baby, still wet behind the ears and who parades around like a woman, spraying perfumes and eating his meats with a little fork—"

"Hah! As for that," I laughed, "Monsieur de Joyeuse does the same thing!"

429

"But that's different. The vicomte is a man. In short, the Duc d'Anjou, in full session of the council, lashed out at Condé, reproaching him for being so insolent as to request a post that belonged to him, as brother of the king. A title he trumpeted with great bravado!"

"What's so astonishing about that?" I asked. "Wouldn't you do the same in his place?"

"But the Duc d'Anjou is such a child!" cried Cossolat. "Excuse me, but he's your age! He's never commanded anything! But the worst was, Pierre, his unspeakable bravado, defiance and threatening manner. He walked right up to Condé, scolded him and defied him like a valet, his hand on the pommel of his sword, at times raising, at times wearing his cap, and saying, among other nasty things, that he'd reduce him to a role as small as the one he wished to have is great."

"Indeed! That's a terrible way to treat a royal prince, and the head of a party as strong as ours! What did Condé do?"

"He listened to this incredible remonstrance, then, bowing, and without saying a word, he left the court immediately, fearing he'd be assassinated."

"Oh, Cossolat! Then it's war! What an incredible shame! A war neither party wants: yet they'll plunge right into it, heads lowered, in the great mistrust they have of each other."

There was another knock at the door, and our hostess entered, bringing my food and drink, and threw us both smiles and saucy looks, which, however, fell quite flat, since both Cossolat and I were sitting there, crestfallen, our hearts passing sore over this great quarrel between subjects of the same king.

"Pierre," said Cossolat when she'd gone, "what will you do if the Huguenots of Montpellier try to take over the city?"

"Ah, Cossolat," I replied, "so that's the reason for our chat! You're trying to sound me out. You've been ordered to sound me out. But you already know the answer. My father never consented to draw his sword against his king during the earlier troubles which so beset France, and on this occasion, I will not draw mine either, except if..."

"Except if?"

"Except if the rabid papists attempt to massacre us as they did at Vassy, five years ago."

"You need have no fear," said Cossolat. "We're stronger than they are here."

"*We*, Captain Cossolat?" I said with a half smile and yet with utter seriousness. "We? In which camp are you? Aren't you one of Monsieur de Joyeuse's officers? So what will you do if he orders you to lead an armed attack against the reformists?"

"Ah, Pierre," he sighed, "that's exactly the point! The answer is, I don't know. I'm loyal and want to serve my king. And yet!..."

I left Cossolat not without some compassion for the great uncertainty I observed in him; he was torn between his faith and his king, not knowing which to choose. And I well remembered my father, when the first civil wars broke out, refusing to join the Huguenot army of Monsieur de Duras (the same one who lay siege to Sarlat) and how tortured he was by his conscience, and how Sauveterre tried to comfort him by saying that, in any situation in which one's loyalties are impossibly divided, "we always end up feeling we were wrong."

On 21st September, as I opened my window to greet the day, I was surprised to see such a dark and menacing sky—since it had been so warm until then; I leant out to see whether the pavement was glistening or not from rain, and caught sight of some men clad in long purple robes building a wood pyre in the middle of the square. I immediately felt my throat tighten and I realized that they were about to burn Cabassus at the stake. This worry was confirmed by Fogacer as he entered my room without knocking, his face deadly pale and sad (for he himself had two reasons, as we know, to fear a similar fate), and silently took up his watch at my side as the executioner and his aides continued their funereal preparations. A few minutes later, Cossolat's archers appeared and took their places around the pile of logs, and in the adjoining streets, in order to control the crowds, now amassing from all sides, as the burning of an atheist was a spectacle not to be missed. Fogacer, noticing that the soldiers were very numerous and dressed for war, concluded that Cossolat feared—not without good reason—a repetition of the riots that had followed the abbot's defrocking.

"Pierre," he advised, "you should close your curtains most of the way, put on a mask and cover your blonde hair, which is so rare in Provence. You do not want to be recognized. I'm going straightaway to advise our illustrious master to close his shop and lock all the doors and windows, for we know that if there's a riot, some of these marauders may begin looting the surrounding shops."

Since my window offered an excellent view of the square, but I myself was thereby visible from below, I followed Fogacer's advice and put on a mask and covered my head. When Samson came into my room, as Fogacer was leaving, he was very surprised by my appearance as well as by the agitation in the square below. His eyes widened in bewilderment and he asked who was to be burnt.

"An atheist," I replied, not wishing to go into any details of the business, having avoided up to that point confessing to my brother what I'd done.

"An atheist?" replied Samson without batting an eyelid. "Well then, they're doing the right thing!"

"My dear brother," I replied in a trembling voice, "this 'they're doing the right thing' makes me very angry. You have such a tender heart and, ordinarily so much pity for others, how can you envision with such a cold lack of humanity the indescribable suffering that this miserable wretch is going to suffer?"

"But he's an atheist!" said Samson. "When the illustrious Michael Servetus denied the Holy Trinity, a denial which was a crime, but certainly a less heinous crime than atheism, our Calvin had him burnt at the stake in Geneva."

"And assuredly that is not one of our Calvin's best achievements."

"What?" cried Samson. "You dare censure Calvin!"

"Calvin is neither a God nor a prophet. Why should he be above censure?"

"But to deny the Holy Trinity is a crime!"

"It's an error, not a crime! Samson, how can we possibly argue for the freedom of conscience for ourselves, which the papists have denied us, if we refuse it to those who have ideas that differ from ours?"

"But an atheist, my brother, an atheist!" cried Samson. "How can we suffer such vermin to exist on the surface of the earth?"

"Well, Samson!" I said, having lost patience with him. "Let's break off this discussion right there. Please return to your room and leave me alone. I don't have the heart to discuss this any further."

Whereupon, visibly wounded by my rebuff, his face crimson and tears already forming on the edges of his eyelids, Samson left me, not without an immediate sense of remorse on my part for my rudeness.

Someone knocked on my door, and Fogacer reappeared, having put on a mask as well, fearing that if he were recognized someone might assume I was with him. At the very instant that he was explaining this, rain began to fall, first in large drops, but then in sheets, accompanied by hail and such a bitter wind that it felt more like winter than the end of summer.

"Oh no!" said Fogacer. "The wood will be wet and will burn slowly. It will take a long time. Cabassus will suffer immensely—unless Vignogoule, at the moment he lights the fire, strangles Cabassus, which I believe he will do," he added after a moment.

"What makes you think so?"

"The post, standing at the centre of the pyre, is pierced with a small hole through which someone has threaded a rope in the form of a noose."

"And who decides that the condemned man should be strangled before the flames reach him?"

"The Présidial judges. But this act of mercy is a secret. And Vignogoule applies it well or badly, according to whether he's well or badly paid by the friends of the condemned. But who, today, would dare befriend an atheist?"

"Me!" I cried. "I'm going right out there to give five écus to Vignogoule so he'll strangle Cabassus properly!" And saying this, I ran to the door like a madman, but before I got there, it opened to reveal Maître Sanche.

"My good nephew," he said with a very severe look, "I couldn't help hearing what you said as I was coming in. This cannot be. The door is closed and every window barred and every exit blocked. Moreover the Présidial has just arrived along with the canons and Cossolat. It would be madness to attempt to bribe the executioner right in front of them."

I ran to the window. He was right: some on horseback, some on mules, the Présidial judges and the canons, who had condemned Cabassus to be defrocked, surrounded the pyre, their faces grave and formal. Some were chatting quietly among themselves and seemed very impatient to get the thing over with. Behind them, forming a kind of rampart to keep the crowds away from the judges and the stake, Cossolat had drawn up a circle of two rows of archers.

The captain was spurring his horse to the right and to the left, his hawk's eyes ceaselessly surveying his surroundings and even the windows of the houses that gave onto the square, which were full of people of both sexes, including some pregnant women and mothers nursing their babies, who were laughing, joking and chattering as if they were going to watch some farce or magic show. The crowd on the square, as best I could judge (for Fogacer, was holding my arms to prevent me from opening the curtains wider) was immense, and I could tell that Cabassus had appeared when a howl went up so loud, strident and savage that it made my blood curdle and I was unable for a moment to make out the words that were shouted with such hatred by thousands of mouths, "Burn, atheist! Burn!"

"Ah," observed Fogacer, as he paled and grabbed my hand, "who said that man is a wolf to his own kind! That's a bad saying: it vilifies the wolf!"

"I can't watch any more," said Maître Sanche, his voice trembling, "I'm going back to my laboratory." And he quickly left us.

Cabassus, flanked by two archers, had neither hands tied nor legs hobbled, but still walked with great difficulty and as though he were staggering, as much because he had not yet recovered from the torture he'd suffered as because someone had tied a huge bundle of hay on his back, which interfered with his steps and was, I suppose, a symbol of the fate that awaited him. The crowd certainly understood its meaning and hurled insults and jokes at him, crying, "Strike the flint, villain, and roast!" But this scene did not suit the canons, perhaps because this burden reminded one, as derisory as it was, of the cross that Christ had had to bear at Golgotha. Eventually, after having argued about it among themselves, the oldest among them, standing up in his stirrups, shouted to Vignogoule to remove the bundle of hay. Which the executioner did, to the great annoyance and displeasure of the crowd, who, not daring to hoot at the clergy, began spitting at him.

At this moment, the rain, which had let up at the arrival of the archers, started in again, not in sheets but in tiny drops that fell like a curtain out of the sky, which was very dark all the way to the horizon with livid openings in the clouds. The soldiers who had escorted

Cabassus having withdrawn, the abbot stood alone at the foot of the pyre, clothed in the ragged old doublet that he had donned when he was defrocked. He no longer rolled his eyes, but was very calm and seemed as resolved as on the day of his degradation.

One of the Présidial judges rode up to Cabassus on his horse, unrolled a scroll that he was holding, and read his sentence in Latin, in French and in Provençal. This done, he asked Cabassus if he had any final words, and Cabassus said in a clear voice:

"I'm dying as a witness to truth."

"This is not a time to argue your case," said the judge, frowning, and turning to Vignogoule he cried in a loud voice: "Villain, do your duty."

At this command, the crowed applauded enthusiastically, stamping their feet with impatience, happy that this spectacle they'd been awaiting in the rain and cold was finally beginning. On the faces I could see in the windows around the square, I perceived only pleasure and relief, as if it were a feast-day bonfire and everyone were going to dance and play around it. You might have said that Cabassus, being an atheist, was a different species entirely from the human, and that it had become as legitimate and pleasant to burn him in the middle of all this wood as it would have been if he'd been one of the insects unlucky enough to have made their nests in those logs.

Vignogoule, hearing the judge, quietly stepped up to Cabassus, and, placing his hands on his shoulders, and in a gesture that seemed more affectionate than brutal, whispered something in his ear, and Cabassus, nodding in assent, sat down on a log, took off his shoes, and next removed his breeches and his doublet, which he then folded with care and laid on a log next to him as if he intended to put them back on after he'd been burnt. This done, standing there on the wet pavement, barefoot and in his shirtsleeves, he waited, his hair matted by the rain, which trickled down his face, without a single muscle moving, other than an occasional shiver. Some of the rogues, seeing this shiver, yelled that he would warm up soon enough. But this joke didn't provoke much laughter since everyone's attention was now fixed on Vignogoule.

The executioner—the same one who would have cut my head off if the Présidial court had condemned me—was a mountain of a man, at least six feet tall, large and fat in all parts of his body, from his rump to his belly and from his belly to his breasts, which fell onto his torso like those of a woman; his face was fleshy as well, his eyes pale and watery, his hair, eyebrows and eyelashes not so much blonde as absent of any colour. Although of prodigious strength, he moved with extreme sloth, his head bobbing, his stomach shaking over his belt, his large backside swaying in his breeches, placing his feet one before the other as quietly as a cat's paw; but this paw was monstrous, like his hands, so big and strong that they could strangle the most robust man in the blink of an eye as easily as if he'd been a pigeon.

In his ordinary behaviour, Vignogoule, it seemed, wouldn't have killed a fly or a mosquito, for from this enormous hulk there issued a very soft voice. His gestures were round and caressing, his expression suave, benign and fawning. But having a heart devoid of any humanity—on the contrary, he had an unimaginable delight in the suffering of others—whenever he got the chance to torture some poor devil, or strangle him, or decapitate, hang or burn him, his eyes, glued to his victim, suddenly glowed with pleasure, his pupils dilated and, opening wide his great maw, his breath would become as hoarse and noisy as if he were mounting a wench.

As much as they loved these spectacles that he provided them, the crowd hated, despised and rejected Vignogoule, doubtless because his cruelty presented a mirror of their own bloodthirstiness and enlarged it. As soon as Cabassus was undressed and in his shirtsleeves, Vignogoule, who towered head and shoulders over his meagre, frail little body, began panting like the bellows in a forge, his huge hands trembling to their fingertips, and his eyes turned up as if in a fit. And even though the populace held its collective breath to watch him, they were unable to bear this odious delight and, bursting out suddenly with hateful imprecations, shouted, "Burn yourself, Vignogoule, burn yourself!"

At this the judge signalled a drum roll, and when silence had returned on the square, he turned to Vignogoule and said with extreme disgust, "Do your duty, villain, and no more delay."

Vignogoule, still panting and rolling his eyes, stepped up to Cabassus and, giving him a gentle push—almost a caress—he showed him the pyre, but said not a word, unable to speak, no doubt, through his laboured breathing. At this, Cabassus started joyfully up the steps that had been fashioned from some of the logs, and sat down at the foot of the stake, his legs folded in front of him—no doubt as he had been instructed by his executioner. In this position, he waited with marvellous patience, his face totally calm, not batting an eyelid, though still shivering occasionally from the cold rain.

Vignogoule, still panting, climbed up in his turn, and, tying Cabassus's hands against his chest, attached his torso to the stake with several turns of the rope, making a knot with each loop, a practice intended, I surmised, to keep the rope in place when the flames began to attack the hemp. Next, he placed the noose that Fogacer had pointed out to me around his neck, and checked to see that the free end could move freely in the hole that had been pierced in the stake. This done, he placed on the logs, at a couple of paces from Cabassus, a copy of the abbot's manuscript on atheism, which the judges had ordered to be burnt with the condemned man. He scrupulously avoided touching the manuscript with his bare hands but held it at arm's length with a pair of long pincers, as though he were afraid being infected by it if he so much as touched it.

Vignogoule accomplished all of this at a snail's pace, his entire body jiggling like jelly with each step, but, in his otherwise calm face, his eyes were rolling, and from his gaping mouth his breath came in loud, hoarse pants, as I have mentioned. As for Cabassus, his expression changed to one of intense sadness when he saw his *Nego* placed on the logs, and he moved his hands desperately in an attempt to reach it. But suddenly he ceased all movement, lowered his eyes and his lips began moving as if in prayer.

This didn't fail to astonish and move the canons, who quickly gathered for a discussion, and the eldest rode up close to the pyre on his horse and asked Cabassus in a loud voice if God had touched his hardened heart and if he'd recovered his faith.

Cabassus shook his head, no.

"And yet, you're praying!" said the canon.

"I'm not praying," replied Cabassus, in a loud and clear voice, "I'm repeating to myself the reasons I have for not believing."

"What reasons can stand up to divine revelation?" cried the canon.

At this Cabassus smiled—I repeat: he *smiled*—and in the silence that fell over the square, he said in a beautifully clear and distinct voice: "My reasons must necessarily prevail since you are forced to burn them!"

The canon, looking very wounded by this assertion, shouted to Vignogoule, "Carry on, villain!" and the executioner struck a flint, lit his torches and gave them to his aides, who set fire to the pyre at the front and on both sides, but not at the back, doubtless to allow the executioner a means to reach the condemned man.

Although the lowest logs burned well enough, having been protected from the rain by the higher ones, the fire seemed unable to rise much and produced much more smoke than flames. These, however, eventually came to lick the *Nego* and suddenly it caught fire, illuminating the visage of poor Cabassus, who turned to face the canons and cried in an extraordinarily loud voice:

"Even though I myself and my *Nego* will be reduced to ashes, our ashes will still cry out to you: 'There is no God!'"

The head judge then made a gesture with the scroll he was holding, and Vignogoule, still panting, climbed up behind Cabassus and, seizing the rope that was threaded through the back of the stake, pulled it towards him, though with a weak gesture, as though regretfully.

"Thank God, he's strangling him!" breathed Fogacer, squeezing my hand, and leaving me quite surprised that he should be invoking the Almighty—which he ordinarily never did.

And, indeed, the noose tightened on Cabassus's neck, his head fell forward on his chest and remained inert, and the crowd, in a single shout, hooted at the executioner, as if they were unhappy that Cabassus should die by the rope and not by the flames. Their spite was of short duration, however, since the flame was now beginning to reach the place where the body was sitting, and suddenly the abbot began writhing convulsively in his bonds, and, raising his head, began to scream in unbearable pain, being attacked by the flames from beneath.

"Oh, Vignogoule!" seethed Fogacer, squeezing my hand so hard I thought it would break. "Oh, you scum! You rogue! You only half strangled him till he passed out, but not more."

Meanwhile, Cabassus screamed to break the hardest of hearts, and all the more so since the pyre, despite being fanned from all sides by the aides with the torches, began to wane, and here and there died out, since the rain was now coming down so heavily.

"Villain!" shouted the head judge, crimson with rage and now standing up in his stirrups. "Get that fire burning or I'll burn *you*!"

Hearing this, Vignogoule ran over to the pharmacy and banged on the door repeatedly, begging to be given oil and turpentine to rekindle the flames. No one answered, so Fogacer left my side to go to see what he could do; as soon as had he gone, I could see, as I leant out, that Maître Sanche had opened the door and was telling the executioner that he'd give him all the oil he had, but that it wouldn't be enough to get the fire going again.

"Executioner!" screamed the head judge. "Get some straw!"

Meanwhile Cabassus was burning slowly, and as the small flames licked at his body, he was convulsed like a madman and emitted unbearably strident and heart-rending cries, yet no one could tell when his suffering would end, since the straw would have to be gathered outside the city and carted in, all of which would take at least an hour. And the victim's screams ultimately so bothered the crowd that the pitiful cries eventually effected a strange revolution in their feelings, and the assembled began to pity his suffering and to grumble about the executioner and even about the judges—and all the more so since suddenly there were blinding flashes of lightning and deafening thunder claps over the city, and it seemed as if God Himself were furious that they were so botching the burning of the very person who denied His existence!

Some crazed fellow (as there seems always to be in large crowds) began prophesying and shouting over and over that Cabassus would soon be struck down by a thunderbolt by the Almighty, and this set off an astonishing flux and reflux of people, some, fearing the lightning, hastening to get as far away from the stake as possible, others hoping to get a first-hand look and surging towards it. Soon, given the clash of these two opposing forces, there were insults, fisticuffs and injuries.

These movements of the multitude began to worry the judges and the canons, who, however, were expected to remain there until the execution was fully completed, no matter how bothered they were by the thick smoke emanating from the pyre, which the wind was blowing their way, and which they couldn't escape since the archers behind them were preventing their departure. Meanwhile, Cossolat, surrounded by a strong platoon of his archers, tried to calm the various scuffles that broke out here and there. Spurring his horse towards them, he cajoled and threatened the crowd as was his wont, but these fractious factions, terrified and maddened by Cabassus's strident screams and by the bolts of lightning that seemed to open up livid holes in the heavens and by the interminable explosions of thunder directly overhead, refused to listen to him but instead hurled savage imprecations in his direction.

I made up my mind in the blink of an eye. I loaded an arquebus and, taking care that its barrel did not stick out from behind the curtains, aimed at Cabassus's heart.

"By all the devils in hell!" screamed Fogacer, as he entered my room, and he rushed over and pushed the barrel aside. "What are you doing, Siorac? Are you crazy? Don't you have enough troubles? Killing a condemned man is murder; it's a capital crime! Are you going to offend the Présidial and risk your head again?"

"Fogacer," I said, "you can see that all of the judges and canons are completely blinded by the smoke, that Cossolat is entirely caught up in managing the crowd, that there are thunder claps every five seconds, that my arquebus won't be heard and that there won't be any trace of my bullet since Cabassus will end up a pile of ashes. Fogacer, am I going to sit by while Cabassus screams in agony for another hour? I had something to do with this execution, as you very well know!"

"You had *nothing* to do with it!" cried Fogacer, still holding my arm lowered. "Cabassus is there because he wrote his *Nego* and because he sought martyrdom at all costs."

"I furnished the occasion for his arrest."

"The occasion but not the cause!" countered my tutor.

"Oh! Ever the logician!" I cried. "Here we are, arguing while he screams! Take your hand from my barrel, Fogacer! I've made up my mind!"

Fogacer looked at me for a moment in silence, then, reading in my eyes that he could not shake my resolve, let go of the weapon. I shouldered it, aimed extremely carefully, held my breath and fired. I stepped back immediately so that no smoke would be visible at the window, then, leaning my arquebus against the wall, ran to the window. Cabassus's head hung on his chest, his body was completely still and his screams had ceased. And, as luck would have it, the thunder ceased, the rain stopped and a great silence fell over the whole square. The crowds of people slowed and then stopped their restless movement, and suddenly everyone was standing in silent amazement, as if nailed to the spot. The canons quickly gathered for another discussion and the eldest, raising himself in his stirrups, turned to the crowd and, in stentorian tones, announced: "The smoke from this impious scoundrel has irritated Heaven and now you see the effect of God's wrath and of His compassion."

The entire crowd erupted in a shout of happy relief at his explanation, which was, indeed, extremely clever, for, without saying that lightning had struck the victim, since no one had seen a flash of lightning, it suggested that God had intervened somehow to punish the atheist and, in His great mercy, to put an end to his interminable agony.

"It is finished!" continued the canon, when the crowd quieted and he could speak again. "Let us pray using the words of the Our Father!"

This done, he began chanting the dominical prayer and everyone took up the response with wonderful fervour and then each one went on his separate way without any further disturbance to the public order.

"Well, Siorac," said Fogacer arching his satanic eyebrows, and speaking with unusual bitterness, "your lips aren't moving. Aren't you going to pray with these foul hypocrites who dare speak of compassion? You're the unique and veritable author of the miracle they're celebrating!"

"Oh, Fogacer," I begged, "please! No joking. This whole thing was an abomination and I'll never forget it as long as I live." I closed the window and sat down on my stool, my head in my hands.

"However that may be," he said, "one thing is certain: after this miracle, no one will ever be able to accuse you of having fired that shot."

But he was mistaken, as he himself informed me the next evening (after he'd seen his friend). The Présidial judges suspected that someone had shot Cabassus from a window, and believed that no one else but me would have had the audacity to do it, or the convenience of a window situated so close to the stake. But after a long debate, they decided that there would be no way to open an inquest on the matter that wouldn't contradict the version of divine intervention that the crowd had been given, or immediately set them against the Vicomte de Joyeuse. But their hatred of me increased in direct proportion to their feelings of impotence in the matter, and Fogacer, repeating their venomous words, advised me to leave the city, at least for a while.

"If you were able to shoot Cabassus from your window," he said, "no doubt some thug could shoot at you from a window as you passed in the street. It wouldn't matter, then, how courageous and well armed you were."

Ten days after Cabassus's execution, they burned the Mangane girl, a punishment I felt very sorry about, despite the fact that the girl had so tortured me with her knot curse. But hadn't I been forced to admit that it was all a farce and false magic like the rest of her affectations? And wasn't Fogacer right when he explained that they didn't burn her because of her satanic powers, but because she was creating panic and fear among the populace by her open adoration of the Devil, who didn't exist? As for the miserable wretch, raised by a bunch of crazy fanatics who dreamt and fantasized that they'd had commerce with the Devil, how could she have failed to believe such stuff when she'd been brought up on these beliefs *ab ovo*? Nourished with thoughts of

God, we believe in Him; fed with visions of the Devil, she believed in him. Was she a witch? I don't believe so. And the proof that she both believed and didn't believe in Satan was that she took me for Beelzebub when it served her desire, and as soon as she'd done with me she regretted her convenient mistake.

I don't know who paid Vignogoule on this second occasion, but I did hear that, unlike his behaviour with Cabassus, he strangled the girl properly as soon as he'd lit the fire, so that, in the fine weather they enjoyed that day, the pyre burned quickly, and rapidly reduced to ashes an inert body. Nevertheless, the crowd, which had so vehemently protested when Cabassus suffered so terribly, protested with equal venom that the Mangane girl hadn't suffered enough.

The same day, at four in the afternoon, a valet came to tell me that a minister of the reformed Church, Abraham de Gasc, wished to see me. Surprised at this request and given that I didn't recognize the valet who delivered it, I feared it was a trap and sent Miroul to ask the pastor if this valet was, in fact, his, and if he had asked for a meeting with me. He replied in the affirmative, and so, trading my blue satin doublet for my everyday black college uniform, which I judged would sit better with this austere minister, I set out, well armed and hugging the walls, to his dwelling. His lodgings were neither poor nor paltry, as Monsieur de Gasc owned a candle shop, selling merchandise he'd brought from Lyons and, it was said, he prospered greatly in this commerce.

Nevertheless, the interior of his house seemed quite spare, and I guessed, seeing it thus, that Gasc preferred keeping his money in his coffers rather than in tapestries on his walls. Monsieur de Gasc was a tall, thin man, with a face so hollow that his skin seemed to be glued to his bones with no flesh intervening, which would have given him the appearance of a skull had his prominent nose and fiery eyes not countered this impression.

"Monsieur," he said, "there are so many rumours circulating in Montpellier on your account that I thought I should ask you what this is all about, given that you profess the reformed religion."

I did not like this introduction one whit and I replied coldly: "Monsieur de Gasc, does my fidelity to the reformed faith require that you hear my confession?"

Since hearing confession was considered by our Huguenots as one of the most shameful and despicable of the papist inventions, I could not have more blatantly confronted the minister than by implying his intention of submitting me to it. And indeed, he turned crimson and remained silent for a long moment.

"Monsieur de Siorac," he said finally, "confession is neither a sacrament nor an obligation for us. Nevertheless, is it not my duty as a minister to enquire about the behaviour of members of our cult?"

"I don't know," I replied, "for no minister has ever asked me any questions."

"Then who enquired about your behaviour in Sarlat?" asked the minister stiffly.

"My father."

"Since your father's not here, why not consider me as your father?"

"But, Monsieur," I said without batting an eyelid, "I already have a father here to whom I am accountable. It's Chancellor Saporta."

"And can you not have the same confidence in me that you have in him?"

This embarrassed me somewhat, and, lowering my eyes, I took some time to think about it. I wanted neither to offend him nor to give in to his demands. "Monsieur," I said finally, "I'd have the same confidence in you as I do in him if your questions were as discreet as his."

"Ha! What kind of a person are you to limit my questions before I've posed them?"

"Monsieur de Gasc, it's better to limit the questions than the answers."

"Are you saying you can't answer sincerely?"

"I'm simply saying that I won't undergo confession against my will."

"Do you feel so guilty?"

"Certainly, Monsieur, I feel very guilty towards my Creator."

"Well! I'm happy to hear that!"

And, indeed, he seemed very relieved of a great weight. I would have been astonished at this if what he said next hadn't immediately revealed his suspicions about me.

"My son," he continued, raising his hands, "you did not lose your faith in your contact with this atheist! You believe in God!"

"But of course I do!" I said, open-mouthed. "And I'm very disappointed you should think so, since I've never missed a single service! Do you think I'm such a hypocrite that I would profess with my lips that which I didn't believe in my heart?"

"My son," said the minister, "please forgive me. I'm infinitely happy that the Devil didn't make you his prey. For, to say the least, my son, your daily habits are hardly edifying. From what I've heard you're something of a skirt-chaser. You were out dancing in the streets at carnival. And you've been seen playing at tric-trac with friends at the Three Kings."

"Ha!" I thought, greatly annoyed to see myself given a dressing-down in this way. "So tric-trac is the sin! Like Clément Marot in Geneva, I'm being censured for playing this innocent game! I'm going to bet that I won't be accused of adultery, since my accomplice is a noblewoman and too well placed to be implicated. Whether you're a papist or a Huguenot, morality seems to stop short, terrified, before the throne of power."

"Monsieur," I said, "your questions are so artfully posed that answers become useless."

"I have one last question to ask you," he replied gravely. "Rumours have been flying among the Présidial judges that, on the twenty-fifth of September, you shot Cabassus in his agony at the stake with an arquebus."

"Monsieur," I said with the iciest tone I could manage, "the Présidial court decided not to pursue this question. Do you want to pursue this inquest on your own?"

"You misunderstand me, Siorac, I'm not interested in the crime, but in the sin. And it is a grave sin to steal from the Lord His just punishment of an atheist."

"Did I hear you correctly?" I gasped. "The person who killed Cabassus committed a sin in putting an end to the earthly suffering of an atheist? Can't we trust God to punish this atheist in the afterlife if He so chooses?"

"Wrong, Siorac! This is a grave error!" cried Monsieur de Gasc, raising his hands heavenward. "The absolute sovereignty of the Lord does not relieve us of our duty, which, in this life, is to pursue and punish impiety."

"So the papists did the right thing to burn Cabassus?"

"We would have burnt him too," replied Gasc gravely.

"And on a slow fire, if the wood didn't burn?"

"Can you believe, young man, that the rain, that day, wasn't an act of God and that whoever tried to shorten the atheist's suffering was acting contrary to divine will?"

"So that's it?" I said. "Cabassus's long and atrocious agony was God's will, and whoever shortened it has committed a sin? For countermanding the will of God? Did I hear you correctly?"

"Assuredly so."

I lowered my eyes, chilled to my very heart by what I'd just heard, which was so contrary to my feelings and my beliefs. Moreover, my instinct didn't fail to alert me to some danger that lurked in all of this, for if Monsieur de Gasc had learnt from the "corridors" of the Présidial court that I'd fired an arquebus shot that I believed to have been merciful but was considered by papists and reformists alike to have been a sin, I knew I should be on my guard. Who knew whether information wasn't flowing in both directions? And whether what I said here wouldn't be repeated in the "corridors" of these judges?

"Well?" said Gasc. "You haven't answered my question. Are you the one who shot Cabassus?"

So, looking him straight in the eye, I said curtly: "No."

To this day, I don't know whether Gasc believed me or not, for without altering his habitual grave expression in the least, he said, "I leave you to your conscience. I hope you can reconcile yourself with your conscience on this matter and your conscience with you."

That was, I'll warrant, an ambiguous conclusion to our discussion, but I took it as a courteous leave-taking. So, maintaining my own marmoreal expression and with eyes respectfully lowered, I bowed deeply (though Monsieur de Gasc neither bowed nor said one word of goodbye) and left. Already the object of intense hatred of the most fanatical papists, I now realized that my own people smelt a rat and considered my faith to be shaken and condemned me for this. And yet I had no doubt that if the former had killed me, the latter would have tried to avenge my death: which was small consolation after the tongue-lashing I'd just endured.

Madame de Joyeuse's carriage was waiting for me in the rue de la Barrelerie, and, taking the time to change back into my blue silk doublet, I thought how ironic it was that it was sent by a "skirt" whom Monsieur de Gasc would never have dared name, no more than he dared mention the grave-robbing in Saint-Denis, perhaps because he knew that the court minutes that incriminated me had been burnt— a sin, moreover, that he considered minor compared to the deadly affront to his God of having shortened the suffering of an atheist by a few minutes in this world when he believed Cabassus's suffering would be eternal in the next.

"Ah," I mused, "what's become of humanity? Where is the God of mercy and love? Haven't we, who claim we are the party of reform, outdone the papists in this domain? Aren't we, like them, still in the shadows of age-old ferocity?"

It seems clear that this arquebus shot had done me a great disservice in all quarters. And great was my distress upon my arrival at the Joyeuse mansion when I did not receive my usual warm welcome, judging by the cold shoulder I got from Aglaé de Mérol, who, as she accompanied me to Madame's chambers, rejected my advances, my compliments and my witticisms, refusing to smile and thereby denying me a glimpse of her dimples, not to mention a kiss, as she left me.

"Ah!" I thought, a pinch at my heart. "What an icy greeting I'm in for with Madame, if her lady-in-waiting is so cold!"

"Monsieur de Siorac," said Madame de Joyeuse as soon as we were alone together, adopting one of her superior airs and refusing me her hand, "you've disgraced yourself in this house, to be frank! The vicomte is very angry with you and said out loud that you no longer deserved his protection, going from folly to folly, committing one crime after another, and this latest one has turned the entire city against you. Scarcely are you out of one quagmire when you throw yourself head-first into another. It's madness! And might I ask you to tell me, Monsieur, what drove you to fire this weapon?"

"Madame," I replied, "my compassion."

Although my heart was passing sore at this greeting, my lady's stiffness had provoked the same attitude in me and I said this last dry-eyed and with a strong sense of pride.

"Monsieur," she snapped, "you've badly misplaced your compassion! An atheist! Are you so fond of blasphemy?"

"Madame," I said, "that is an insult; I believe in God, but for me, Cabassus wasn't just an atheist, he was a man, and I couldn't bear his horrific suffering. If I have sinned, God will judge me."

"Monsieur," said Madame de Joyeuse archly, "does that mean man has no right to judge you? Do you dare remonstrate with me, wet behind the ears as you are?"

"No, Madame," I answered with as firm an expression as I could, but softening my voice. "It would never be my intention to disagree with you. I know the gratitude I owe your gracious kindness, and even though it would cause me great sadness to lose the protection of your husband, especially with all the dangers that beset me, I would be infinitely sorrier to have lost the friendship of one whose beauty and goodness light up my life. But I see, Madame, that I have exhausted your patience and that I am no longer appreciated here, nor is my presence desired. Allow me, then, to take my leave, begging you, before departing, to grant me one last kiss of your precious hand."

Saying this, and feeling very moved, I knelt before her, holding out my right hand. But she did not take it. Which was, of course, embarrassing and, even more, it wounded my heart so deeply that the tears I'd been trying to hold back came rolling down my cheeks. However, raising my eyes to see her beautiful face, I saw her quite undone, pale and without any of the haughtiness she'd displayed when I arrived. She stepped away from me, and fell into one of her armchairs, but kept her eyes lowered and said not a word, which I found quite surprising, since silence was not in her repertoire.

I didn't know what to do next, but since I couldn't stay on my knees for ever in the middle of the room, my right hand extended, I saw no alternative than to do what I'd said I'd do, and, standing, bowed to her and headed towards the door.

"Go ahead, Siorac," she said suddenly, in a bitter and raspy voice, "hurry over to Saint-Firmin and seek consolation from the bawd who

451

lives in public disgrace, whom you've got such pleasure from. Such a beautiful romantic story and so worthy of an atheist and a scoundrel! You were aiming way too high here! You'll be so much better off in the needle shop, having your fun in that dung heap!"

I was deeply wounded by her cruel words and, turning as though I'd been stung by a wasp, I pulled myself up to my full height, looked Madame de Joyeuse in the eye and, in a serious but respectful tone, said, "Madame, I am neither an atheist nor a scoundrel. As for my delights and 'romantic story', I found them here as long as I was welcome. Madame, I am your servant." And bowing deeply I walked proudly to the door, and, without waiting for my usual escort, headed for the antechamber. But blinded by my anger and sorrow, I mistook my way in the maze of corridors and was very heartened to hear the high heels of Aglaé de Mérol behind me.

"Ah, Siorac," she cried, all out of breath, her chest heaving, "where are you rushing off to? That's not the way! Anyway, my mistress requires your presence immediately!"

"So, she hasn't finished tormenting me?"

"Oh, Monsieur!" said Aglaé, putting her hand on my arm. "I know my mistress: she's quick to correct, but she has a good heart. Someone was spreading terrible rumours about you. And ever since that sad arquebus shot, everyone in this city hates you, and even Cossolat refuses to defend you any more!"

"Well then," I replied, "I'll be leaving your beautiful city since I'm no longer appreciated here."

"Are you sure that's so?" she said, raising her eyebrows. "For my part, I find your pride very entertaining, and I think you're the most rascally and most prideful young nobleman in all of Périgord, and I'm perfectly able to tolerate your presence here."

"What! You *tolerate* it? I wouldn't have guessed it from your welcome this morning."

"I was ordered to behave that way," she smiled.

"And this smile now, is it an order too? And your dimples? Is that the net you're throwing over me to drag me back to submit to Madame de Joyeuse's knife?"

"Ah, Monsieur, to bring you back, I'd do much more than that if I had to!" And she leant towards me and kissed my lips. After which, since she was smiling, I applied a few pecks to her dimples, which she managed to endure.

"Madame," I sighed, "I shall follow you. Your mistress must be very good to you if you're devoted to her to this extent."

Meanwhile, this flirtation had considerably calmed me down—as my cunning little devil no doubt had intended, who, though unmarried and a virgin, was familiar with all the little tricks that girls use to bewitch us.

I found Madame de Joyeuse exactly as I had left her, sitting in the armchair, but now with her bodice unhooked, looking very flushed, breathing rapidly, covered with perfumes and, most significantly, in a state of mind I was more familiar with and which reassured me completely.

"Oh, my little cousin," she moaned, "I thought I would die to be so mistreated by you! Are you now sufficiently ashamed and remorseful for behaving like such a ruffian and tyrant towards someone of my rank? That was so unseemly! Have I failed so badly to polish your rude and rustic Périgordian ways that you behave so crassly with me? In your unpardonable arrogance, insolent as a Spanish grandee, you've gone way beyond what I can tolerate! Am I or am I not, Monsieur, the Vicomtesse de Joyeuse?"

"Certainly you are, Madame," I said, putting on a grave face, though smiling happily inside. "How could I doubt it, listening to you?"

"Then, young man, on your knees and humbly beg my forgiveness for the insults you heaped on me!"

I did not kneel, but threw myself at her feet and kissed them.

"Monsieur," she cried, "are you crazy? What are you doing?"

"Madame," I replied without batting an eyelid, "I humbly beg your pardon for having called me a Périgordian knave, unwashed bumpkin, atheist and scoundrel who's wet behind the ears!"

"Oh, Pierre!" she giggled. "No one could resent you for very long. You're so clever and have such wit! All right, I see I'm going to have to give in to you and forgive you! But you must also promise always to be my slave and obey me in everything."

"What, Madame, your slave? When did I ever disobey you?"

But the reader well knows the measure of such repartee and to what sweet nothings and caresses it was leading in our School of Sighs, and what good lessons it would inspire in each of us. But I will not enter into the details of these scholastic activities, having already said much—and perhaps more than I ought to have done—on this subject, despite the licence allowed for such things in this century.

Once our lessons were done and teacher and student had recovered their breath behind the blue curtains, and were enjoying the mirth, laughter and thousand little confidences that they loved to share, suddenly Madame de Joyeuse burst into tears, but wouldn't tell me at first what had provoked such sadness.

"Oh, my sweet!" she said through her tears. "It would have been easier to part in anger, as I tried to do, than this way. But part we must. You must leave Montpellier, at least for the time being. Both my husband and Cossolat are certain that if you stay here you'll be assassinated; you are so hated by the fanatics among the Catholics."

"Me, flee!" I cried. "Run away from these people? And leave you? In the very jaws of death I'd never do such a thing!"

"Oh yes, you will, Pierre!" countered Madame de Joyeuse. "You will when you hear what's being plotted against you and what our spies have learnt."

"I'm listening, Madame. What's happening? A plot against me?"

"No! That's the point! It's your brother who's the target."

"Samson!" I cried, leaping to my feet, terrified. "But he's got nothing to do with any of this! God knows, he's the most innocent being on this earth!"

"Samson is in great danger!"

"But why?"

"Because he's your brother. Because he's not as careful as you. Because he's not so quick to unsheathe his sword as you, or to fire his pistols. And because that would be the worst thing they could do to you, knowing your great love for him."

"But," I cried, beside myself, "what sort of people are these that could strike down an angel from heaven?"

"Fanatics—who are implacable once their anger has been aroused."

"But, Madame," I said, having made my decision in the blink of an eye, "if it will save Samson's life, of course I'll leave, but where shall we go? I can't go back to Mespech without my father's permission."

"Ah! Thank God for that, my sweet! You wouldn't get far! I have a very good friend in Nîmes, Monsieur de Montcalm, who is a royal officer and head judge in the courts there. He was once one of my 'martyrs', and will take good care of you for as long as I want you to stay there, and in Nîmes you'll have nothing to fear, since neither Huguenots nor Catholics there know you. And, although there are some underground agitations going on there—as there are throughout Provence—given the events you're aware of, the city is calm. Nevertheless, my little cousin," she sighed, shedding a few more tears, "I will miss you terribly! You should have thought about me before you fired that awful shot with your arquebus!"

"Madame, Cabassus was suffering so much it was driving everyone crazy who could hear him. Even the crowd who wanted to see him burn couldn't bear his screams."

"But he was an atheist!"

"Oh, Madame! An atheist can suffer as much as anyone else! More, perhaps, since he can expect no consolation in the hereafter."

This idea appeared to be so novel for Madame de Joyeuse that, completely taken aback, she fell silent. Then, hugging me tightly, she gave me permission to leave and I threw myself in her carriage; before returning to my lodgings, I had the coachman take me to the Saint-Firmin church, but, not wanting a coach with the Joyeuse coat of arms to stop in front of the needle shop, I had him drop me on the other side of the church. I crossed the church at the end of the nave, walking as quietly as possible, to reach the side door. Alas! I arrived at the benediction, and though the papists who were there pretended to be deep in their devotions, a few hypocrites with eyes in the backs of their heads caught sight of me, and whispering among themselves, threw me looks that would have killed me if they'd had the power to do so.

I couldn't say goodbye to Thomassine the way I'd hoped. Cossolat was there, seated at her table, a goblet in his hand, and frowned in a most unfriendly way when he saw me.

"Are you leaving?" he said abruptly.

"Tomorrow at dawn, with Samson and Miroul."

"Good," he replied sternly. "Wear a mask and arm yourselves for war, with body armour and a helmet. You'll find three safe-conduct passes and a letter from me to Captain Bouillargues in Nîmes. This captain is one of us, if I can still call you one of us after you insulted Monsieur de Gasc."

"I didn't insult him," I answered stiffly. "I simply refused to have him confess me."

"In any case," said Cossolat, staring into his goblet, "after your last exploit, Monsieur de Gasc has little love for you. And as for myself, I don't care for you much either."

"I'm am very sorry to hear this, Monsieur," I said, bowing, and then turned on my heels and left, wounded deeply by his hard words, since Cossolat had always shown me, despite his military and abrupt manner, a certain friendship.

As I expected, Thomassine caught up with me in the antechamber, and, throwing herself in my arms, hugged me to her breast, and said, "I still love you, Pierre! No matter what you've done, I'll always be your friend."

But I scarcely had time to kiss her back, since Cossolat was calling her angrily. "Aha!" I thought as I walked around behind Saint-Firmin (since I didn't want to walk by the hypocritical stares inside.) "Cossolat is clearly master of the house here, just as he is at the Three Kings, and who knows how many other places! And yet, he is also, no doubt, to hear Monsieur de Gasc tell it, 'one of ours'—proof that they don't mind that the 'Devil has made him his prey' whatever his 'daily habits'. Why, he might even be forgiven a few games of tric-trac since he does so much for so many!"

Turning these bitter thoughts over in my mind, and thoroughly dissatisfied with my fellow men and with the world, I threw myself in the carriage and wondered whether I should also say goodbye to Chancellor Saporta. But of course I knew his sacrosanct rule that I would have to request to see him *in writing*, a request that he would answer a week later with a *written* response. As for going to visit him unannounced—even if he opened his door to me, it would have been like going to look for sticks to hit myself with, to be honest, and I'd already been buffeted enough in one day and was too bruised and bloody to go looking for another thrashing by my teacher.

There was another one—and a very severe one—waiting for me when I got back to the pharmacy. My father had written to answer the letter I'd sent him confessing to everything that had happened: the grave-robbing in the Saint-Denis cemetery, and including even my fornication with the Mangane girl on the tomb of the Grand Inquisitor, an action my father considered, in Latin, "*atrocissimo*". I did not show this letter to Samson any more than I told him about our trip to Nîmes, but, enveloping myself in mystery, frowning and speaking tersely, I told him to pack his bags, and, once done, to help Miroul to tend to the horses, and to be ready to ride the next day at daybreak.

After our evening meal, at which I observed that Dame Rachel displayed a very uncharacteristic but insolent joy, intending, no doubt, to show me how delighted she was that I'd be leaving, I spoke with Maître Sanche alone, and my illustrious master, without raising his voice in the least, without a single word of reproach, embraced me warmly, rubbing his scratchy grey beard against my cheek; then, holding me at arm's length and looking me straight in the eye, he said, "Oh, my good nephew! Go in peace! And come back soon! I am going to miss you here and your brother even more, for he has been a great help to me in my laboratory and adds much to my practice as much by his beauty as by his dove-like amiableness. And by the way, I don't know and don't want to know whether it was you who fired the shot that killed Cabassus, as is the rumour. But if you did fire it, I do not in any way hold it against you. This unhappy Cabassus was suffering and screaming to knot up your intestines, and as we Sephardics know pain only too well, having ourselves suffered in Spain, we cannot lightly bear the sufferings of others. They have called you wicked. I would say, on the contrary, *Nemo proprius ad deum accedit quam qui hominibus salutem dat et beneficium.** Were we going to wait until they brought the hay? You acted from the goodness of your noble and steadfast heart. *Cor nobile, cor immobile.*† By Hippocrates, I couldn't bear another minute of those horrible screams! It seemed as if all the millennial sufferings of the Jews were crying with his

---

* "None is closer to God than he who shows goodness to men and serves them."

† "A noble heart is an unshakable heart."

voice, and in my cowardice I hid my head in my bedcovers! My beautiful nephew, you are young, hotheaded and valiant! You dare to act! Don't pay the least attention to the hate that oppresses you. The word impious is too quickly spoken. Is it piety that counts, or pity? Or to reverse the terms, can there be piety without pity? My nephew, your conscience shines like the leaves of a tree that's bursting with sap! Oh, I pray you! Stay the way you are! It's your greatest strength. *Murus aheneus conscientia sana.** My nephew, I bless you in the name of the Lord Adonai, Amen."

And giving me a huge hug, and combing his beard furiously with his hands, tears brimming in his eyes, he turned away, more bent than ever, one shoulder lower than the other, and muttering under his breath one of those Latin sentences in which he found solace against life's reversals—of which there were plenty, to judge by the constitution of his wife.

Scarcely had I left this excellent gentleman when I ran into Typhème in the corridor leading from the laboratory to our lodgings—which was fairly dark but suddenly seemed illuminated by her Moorish beauty. She stopped and, eyes lowered, said, "You're leaving us, I believe. Our house will seem very empty without you and your brother."

I was completely surprised that she should speak to me, for, in ten months, she hadn't said ten words to me, so shy was she in her virginal reserve. She was promised, as everyone knew, to Dr Saporta, and would enter marriage the way one enters religion—for what convent could be more mournful than the spare lodgings of the chancellor, nor guardian sister more hawk-eyed and ill-tempered than the amazingly withered gorgon that served as his chambermaid? Since I didn't say a word, so amazed was I that she'd spoken to me and that she was alone with me in this dark corridor, she added: "But is it really so? Concepcion told me."

---

* "A healthy conscience is a brass wall."

"Ah!" I said. "So Concepcion is still here! I thought that your illustrious father had sent her away for having listened at my door."

She blushed to the roots of her hair at this and fell silent, having perhaps heard or guessed what Concepcion had been trying to hear. Seeing her confusion, and not wishing to embarrass her further, I continued: "So much the better if Concepcion was pardoned. But, yes, I am leaving with Samson. But only for a time. We will return."

"I'm very happy to hear it," she said, and, taking me by the hand, she squeezed it. And then, blushing even more deeply, eyes lowered, she turned away and, pulling up her skirts to run more quickly, hurried away as if terrified by her own audacity.

"Oh, the poor girl!" I mused. "Having to go live in that tawdry dwelling with that bilious old greybeard! What a jail! What a forsaken dungeon! What a dead end! And yet our very illustrious master is so full of goodness and goodwill. It's incomprehensible that he'd choose such a union for his daughter."

I was going to knock on Luc's door when it opened before me; he fell into my arms, in tears, and couldn't utter a word, but held me tight, so I found myself having to comfort him rather than the other way around.

"Oh," he sobbed finally when he'd recovered his voice, "I can't stand Monsieur de Gasc or the religious bigotry of the elders and deacons! They've thrown fire and flame on you for firing that shot! It's madness! No one can contradict or confront them without peril—especially someone like me, who's a Sephardic, and therefore inevitably suspected of not being sincere in his faith. Oh, Pierre, I'm so weak! Without you, whom I've so relied on, I can't do anything but sit here and tremble like a rabbit in its hole!"

As he was speaking, I heard heavy footsteps on the stairs and there was a knock on the door, and as I cried, "Come in!" Merdanson and

Carajac appeared and quickly filled up the room with their great statures. They'd come, they explained, to say their goodbyes.

"What?" I said open-mouthed. "You knew I was leaving? It's a secret. Who told you?"

"Fogacer."

"Fogacer knows about it? Who told him? Friends, wait here for a moment with Luc. There's a flagon. Uncork it and make yourselves comfortable. I'll be right back."

I went to knock on my tutor's door.

"I was expecting you," said Fogacer, his eyebrows in their familiar arch, and a tone of ironic humour in his voice. "Come in, young and impetuous Siorac! Take a stool. I'm very interested in seeing close up our Christian Iphigenia, for, you should know, there isn't a papist or Huguenot in Montpellier who isn't hungering to put a knife to your throat. And frankly, the Huguenots are particularly eager for your blood, fearing that if they supported you, they'd be suspected of atheism. So, you're leaving, like the goat that Israel sent out into the desert, loaded with all the sins of that clever tribe. But do you know the what and the wherefore of this departure?"

"I'm betting that you know it, Fogacer. Otherwise I wouldn't be here listening to you."

"I do know it," said Fogacer, walking back and forth in his tiny room where his spidery arms and legs seemed even longer than usual, his body thin as a thread and clothed in black from head to toe. "I know," he repeated, stopping and looking at me with his most ironic expression. "Would you like to hear it?"

"Without further delay, I beg you!"

"Well then, listen carefully, Siorac! The Vicomte de Joyeuse, in his Machiavellian diplomacy, approached the papist fanatics—the very ones who were planning to assassinate you."

"He knows them?"

"Like the fingers of his hand."

"Why doesn't he throw them in the city jail?"

"He can't. Nor does he want to. Have you forgotten he's a papist too?"

"So what did he tell these fanatics?"

"He decided to bargain with them: senna for rhubarb. They'll make no attempt on your life, but you'll leave town. At least for a time. The time for the two scandals you created to die down."

"Two? What do you mean, two?"

"The big one and the small one," replied Fogacer.

"The big one's the arquebus shot. What's the little one?"

"Oh, the little one's very little indeed and is hardly worth mentioning. It's exceptionally annoying to the vicomte, who's trying to increase his power and his fortune, that there's a rumour going round that you're not as 'martyred' as you should be by Madame de Joyeuse."

"Ha!" I said. "That's pure calumny!"

"Of course!" agreed Fogacer without batting an eyelid. "But, as you know, Siorac, Caesar's wife must be above suspicion. So the vicomte very adroitly killed two birds with one stone. He protects you and he gets rid of you."

"Two birds with one stone," I thought. "I'll wager that the vicomte has managed his coup so well that his wife is immediately going to fill his purse."

"Well?" said Fogacer. "What do you think of all of these knots being tied so nicely?"

"Ah, Fogacer," I said, after some reflection, which did not sit well with me, "why is man what he is?"

Meanwhile, those who were waiting for me in my room, my medical-college companions, loved me without qualification, reserve or hesitation. And after having emptied the flagon I'd promised them, and another as well, and then a third with Luc, Fogacer, Merdanson

462

and Carajac, Miroul playing his viol (Samson was present but wouldn't touch a drop), I went off to bed, my head throbbing a bit, but my mood much improved. And I still remember that the last thought I had before I fell asleep was that in Nîmes I would finally have some peace and quiet after the incredible series of reversals and troubles I'd suffered ever since the ill-fated grave-robbing in Saint-Denis. By St Anthony's belly! What a blindfold the future had fastened over my eyes! If there were worse things to be endured than what I'd experienced here, I was galloping hell for leather right at them. I was going to put so many leagues under Accla's hooves just to fall from the frying pan into the fire! I was heading straight towards the wolf, and, if not actually into its mouth, I was at least putting myself in the uncomfortable position of trying to hold its ears while avoiding its teeth.

13

READER, YOU CAN easily understand how sad I was to leave Montpellier, a city I loved dearly, and along with it so many people that I'd folded into the secret places of my heart. And yet, at daybreak, as I saddled Accla, masked, helmeted and well plated with armour, I felt excited to be setting out on a new adventure, in the bloom and vigour of my youth, on the great highways of our kingdom, heading for a city I'd never seen and that was famous for its beauty.

Samson, who'd got up very early, was nodding off in his saddle, and managed to stay on Albière by pure force of habit. But Miroul, having to work hard to manage his two Arabians, the one he rode and the one who bore our packs and arms—including the fateful arquebus that was the direct cause of our exile—was nevertheless humming quietly, happy, no doubt, to see me escaping from the very present dangers I was in, given the role my father had assigned him as my guardian angel—at least as far as security was concerned, for his amorous behaviour with Thomassine's Azaïs would not have appeared very angelic to Monsieur de Gasc, if he'd known about it. And why should a brother assume the right, in the name of God, to judge his brother? The devil if I knew!

I was at the head of our little platoon, and focused all my attention on watching the windows under which we passed, ready to fire my two pistols instantly at any gun barrel that a would-be assassin might have the temerity to point at me, but I also had to rein in Accla, whose metal shoes tended to slip on the paving stones, shining with last night's rain. I filled my lungs with the fresh morning air and breathed in the delicious smells of an unknown future, and abandoned myself to the vehement joy that gripped me at the idea that my present troubles were at an end.

We reached the city gate without incident, and there, laden as we were with all our baggage and all three masked, we had to show the guard the three safe-conduct papers Cossolat had provided us.

"My noble gentleman," said the guard, who was as round as a melon and possessed of a benign face, the eyes of a faithful hound and thin lips, "with such spirited horses as you've got, you'll catch up quickly with Captain Cossolat and his platoon of archers. They're escorting Vignogoule and his hideous wife, since his own aides are sick with fever, as they deliver a poor wench to the gibbet to be hanged for killing her newborn baby that was born out of wedlock. A prettier lass I never saw, and it seems to me a great pity that they should destroy what God has created in his own image."

"Ah, but don't they usually hang criminals near the la Saulnerie gate in an olive orchard? I remember that when we first arrived in Montpellier in June of last year, coming from Narbonne, which would be fifteen months ago now, I saw the gibbet among those trees and the dismembered parts of the body of a poor wench they'd hanged there for the same crime."

"Monsieur, they decided to change the venue since the owner of that orchard no longer wanted to rent out his land, claiming the stench of the rotting bodies spoilt his olives. So the city bought an olive orchard whose trees had all gone sterile, two leagues hence on the Nîmes road. That's where you'll see Vignogoule at his dirty work, who'd do better to hang his horrible woman and himself afterwards, so cruel, greedy and odious are they, and so ugly that the mere sight of them makes you want to empty your guts right there. Oh, my young gentleman, how many times have I seen poor girls being brought there because they destroyed the fruit of their wombs? Whereas the fathers of these babies go strolling about town free as the air, and what's worse, proud of themselves for having enjoyed so many of these poor wenches, laughing at the girl's naivety for having believed their promises of marriage!"

"Ah, how right you are, my good man," I agreed. "Man is a scoundrel and justice limps along as best it can."

As for the rest, the guard had been right as well. Our horses were so speedy that we quickly caught up with Cossolat's heavy mounts. The night's rain had more quickly evaporated on the highway than on the stone streets in Montpellier, and the archers' nags raised so much dust that our eyes and throats were blinded and parched by it, so we decided to pass them as quickly as we could. I also wanted to give Cossolat a friendly greeting as we passed, hoping to repair somewhat the feelings he'd expressed at our last meeting at Thomassine's needle shop. Before we spurred on our Arabians, I removed my mask, since the mid-morning sun was so hot and because I no longer needed it now that we had left our enemies behind in Montpellier, stagnating in their hatred within the city's walls.

"Hey, Samson," I called. "Wake up, my brother! You can't go on lazing in your saddle as if you were still in bed. Spur Albière on! These louts have left us their dust to eat! It's our turn to return the favour!"

So I spurred Accla to a gallop, followed by Samson, and, a few paces behind him, Miroul, who was managing his two Arabians so skilfully. Since the cortège that preceded us was taking up the entire width of the road, I slowed down to a trot and hailed the archers in front of us, asking them to let us pass. But they pretended not to hear me, and without turning their heads or reacting at all, they continued as before, despite my cries, and spread out even more across the road, which wasn't very wide at that point, having narrowed between two rocky outcrops. Angry at such insolence, I was contemplating drawing my sword and applying the flat of my blade to the croups of their horses, when Cossolat suddenly appeared, having heard the ruckus. I greeted him coolly, to which he responded much more civilly than I would have expected, perhaps regretting his words of the previous day.

"Monsieur de Siorac," he said, "what do you want?"

"To pass, Monsieur," I replied, "with your permission."

"Archers!" called Cossolat. "Make way for Monsieur de Siorac! He's in a greater hurry than we are!"

At this his soldiers lined up on the right-hand side of the road, and I spurred Accla to a trot, but seeing before me the back of the poor wench they were leading to the gibbet, I slowed to a walk to get a better view of her as we passed, both out of compassion and also because the guard had been so impressed by her beauty. And yet I hesitated to pass, feeling a bit ashamed of my curiosity. While I was trying to make up my mind, I observed that she was riding a mule and was tightly tied to a Moorish saddle, her arms attached behind her with a rope that passed around the stomach of her mount. A hideous fishwife, monstrously fat with a mean and disgusting face, held her mule by the bridle. This ogress was astride a pitiful hack that looked like it got more blows than oats, to judge from its condition. In front of them, I spied, sitting on a raw-boned nag that was nearly crushed by his enormous weight, rode Vignogoule, clothed in the long purple robe that he wore for executions. There was, however, no judge in evidence, but I was not unduly surprised since the Présidial judges doubtless thought it wasn't worth bestirring themselves so early in the morning for hangings of this kind, which were so frequent that they considered them of little consequence.

From the back, the girl looked very comely, though she was clothed in a grey chemise that was torn and dirty and her hair was cut short to allow the noose to choke her neck more easily. Catching up to her, I leant forward to see her better. But the movement I made caught her attention and the poor girl turned her head towards me and let out a terrible cry. Gaping, my blood running cold in my veins, I recognized Fontanette.

"Fontanette," I said, almost suffocating from the knot in my throat, "is it really you I see in this predicament? How did you come to be here, a brave girl like you?"

"Oh, my noble friend," she said. "How can you say that? You who had me kicked out of the pharmacy after falsely accusing me of stealing from you!"

"Me?" I cried. "But who told you that?"

"Dame Rachel."

"The viper lied through her teeth, I swear it on my salvation!"

"Monsieur," broke in Vignogoule, "the condemned girl is going to be hanged, and no one is allowed to speak to her."

I looked at Vignogoule with as much repulsion as if I had seen a hundred toads in a pile. His face was unspeakably vile, as if the venom from his brain had seeped down into his face and corrupted his features: he was cross-eyed; his bent nose was spread wide at its base; his closed lips looked like some awful swollen wound; and his cheeks and chin were greying, hairy and full of pustules—to say nothing of the heap of a body on which this hideous head reposed. I spurred Accla behind the mule that Fontanette was riding and came up on Vignogoule's woman's right hand.

"Good woman," I said, "ten sols for you if you close your ears."

"Monsieur," said the ogress, her little weaselly eyes suddenly aglow, "as soon as the condemned woman is remitted into my husband's hands, she belongs to him: her clothes, her body, her five senses and her breath."

"Good woman," I said, "twenty sols for three minutes."

"Monsieur," croaked la Vignogoule, "even for three minutes I can't sell anything or loan anything that belongs to her: neither her ear nor her breath."

"Good woman, forty sols."

"Monsieur," she replied, "you heard me."

"Wench," I replied, frowning and throwing her a terrible look, "one golden écu in return for what I ask or I'll pass my sword through your guts."

At this threat, which to this day I cannot say whether I would have carried out, so furious was I, la Vignogoule, as tempted though she may have been to raise the bid, didn't dare to confront me or to dispute any further, and without a word held out her hand. I quickly placed an écu in it, which she immediately brought to her bloated lips and bit. This done, she hid it away in her belt and pulled out a rosary from beneath her purple robe, lowered her nose and began to tell her beads, but whether she was praying or only pretending to, only God knows.

I turned Accla and came up next to Fontanette again. "Fontanette," I told her, "I never accused you of having robbed me! Do you believe me now?"

"Alas! I believe you!"

"After you were sent away I searched everywhere for you!"

"Alas! I know! I was in Grabels."

"In Grabels! Fontanette! That's near Montpellier! I went through there ten times, shouting your name!"

"I know. I had told everyone to say they'd never heard of me."

"Oh, Fontanette, you didn't trust me, but you believed Dame Rachel?"

She made no response, but gave me a look that broke my heart, tears streaming down her cheeks.

"And what did you do in Grabels?"

469

"I found employment as a servant on a farm, but the farmer, after promising to marry me, got me pregnant."

"You shouldn't have given in," I said, knowing it was the wrong thing for me, of all people, to say, but doubtless jealousy had something to do with my reaction.

"Oh, Pierre!" she sobbed, and turning her tear-streaked face towards me, she threw me a look of such sad reproach that I was transfixed. "How can you say that? It was you who first mounted me!"

Wholly ashamed, I lowered my eyes, and was unable to say a word, so pricked was I by my conscience. Finally, I said, "Fontanette, you are so good and merciful, how could you kill your baby?"

"Oh, Pierre! I was forced to against my will and conscience. The farmer ordered me to, threatened me, said that if I didn't, he send me away penniless. And how would I have fed my child if I hadn't a crumb to eat myself? Oh, my friend, what a horrible memory I must bear! The minute I was about to give birth, the farmer's mother pushed me into the barn and, on the same straw as the sheep, I delivered the baby without a soul to love or help me. And when the sweetling was there, all I could think of was that it would go to die with me on the roads, so I put my hand over its mouth and when I took it away, it didn't move any more."

And tears again brimmed over her eyes and, amidst great sobs, streamed down her face. She said in a broken voice, "Oh, Pierre, I committed a great sin! So it's truly just that they hang me! And may the Virgin Mary intercede for me with her divine Son! But I'm so afraid of dying by the rope!"

And seeing her trembling with fear so uncontrollably at this sinister thought, with each step of her mule bringing her closer to her Calvary, I asked her more questions to try to distract her.

"So what did you do with the little body?"

"I threw it in the dry well, but la Grenue saw me."

"Who's la Grenue?"

"A neighbour, who can think only of marrying my farmer. La Grenue denounced me to the priest, who sent for me to come to confession. But when he was alone with me, he promised not to tell if he could have me right there. But I didn't want to and was horrified by the idea of sinning with a man of God. So the curate wrote to the judges in Montpellier and a month later they came and arrested me in Grabels and locked me in the city jail."

"Oh, Fontanette!" I thought. "What a chain of terrible people has been soldered together, link by link, to forge your misfortune! Myself, alas! Dame Rachel, the farmer and the very priest of Grabels. May God forgive us the evil we have wrought on you!"

"Pierre," she sobbed, trembling, "I'm terrified. Not of dying, but of being hanged by the neck and suffocating. They told me in the jail that it's a long and frightful torture."

"Monsieur de Siorac," said Cossolat, who'd come up quietly behind us, "it's against the law to talk to the prisoner. Woman," he said to la Vignogoule, "how did it happen that you didn't forbid this?"

"Captain!" protested the ogress, with her most hypocritical look. "I was saying my prayers and didn't hear a thing!"

"Ah, to be sure! I trust your compassion like I'd trust a viper. I know you, wench. A greased palm turns you deaf as a stone. Monsieur de Siorac, a word with you if I might. Let's ride on!"

We galloped ahead, and having put some distance between ourselves and the sinister procession, Cossolat said, "I understand what this wench meant to you. And the Présidial judges better than I. But I want you to know that I did everything I could to put this execution off till tomorrow, to avoid this meeting. But the judges decided otherwise. That's why I brought so many men. Some of the judges are hoping, knowing how impulsive you are, that you'll commit some madness."

"So it's a trap?"

"Assuredly. And I'm the jaws of that trap."

"I won't fall into it. I thank you, Cossolat, for the warning."

"So, no shooting?" said the captain, turning in his saddle to look me straight in the eye.

"No shooting, I promise. But I would like you to grant me the chance to speak privately with the hangman."

"It's not possible," said Cossolat brusquely. "I'm the only one who may speak to Vignogoule."

"Monsieur," I said, gulping, "you may push me to do something you'd have preferred to avoid."

Cossolat fell silent at this prospect and gave me a very severe look, full of resolve. I felt, no doubt, somewhat less resolve than he did, for I couldn't dream of attacking a platoon of archers without a lot of help from Miroul, who already had his hands full with his Arabians, and also from Samson. How could I ask them to risk their lives simply because I was willing to risk mine for this girl?

"Siorac," said Cossolat, "if you promise to forgo any violence whatsoever, I could bring my archers up as a vanguard to do reconnaissance on the road ahead. What you might say to anyone in my absence would assuredly be none of my business."

"Captain," I replied, "I promise."

He spurred his horse and was gone, and I went back alone to the procession.

"Vignogoule," I said, riding up beside him, though not without a good deal of disgust at his odious face and worse odour, "a word with you."

"Monsieur," said the hangman very softly, and looking sideways at me with his watery eyes, which you could barely see through all the fat surrounding them, "you're not s'posed to speak with me."

"A word is all I ask."

"Monsieur, I'm not going to listen to you," he said, turning his head away piously.

"Five écus for you, if you'll agree that, before you put the rope around the girl's neck, you'll put your thumb on her neck and break it. That way she'll die suddenly and you'll string up a dead person on your gibbet."

"'Fraid that's not possible. The judge didn't order that."

"Ten écus."

"Monsieur, if I go against the judge's orders I'll lose my job."

"Who'd know? The captain can't hear us."

"Ah, Monsieur, my *conscience*!"

"Fifteen écus."

"Monsieur, everyone has their weaknesses," said Vignogoule with feigned humility. "For me, it's the pleasure of watching the victim slowly strangle at the end of my rope."

Hearing these odious words, I was nearly beside myself, and cried, "Twenty écus, villain, to comfort your villainous soul."

"Monsieur," said Vignogoule, with a wonderfully false humility, "my soul is not so ugly. What I said comes from the deep love for my profession. Moreover, twenty écus seems pretty paltry when you consider the great friendship you seem to have for the wench."

I thought I was going to be sick at hearing the vile baseness of his sentiments, so I decided that money alone wasn't going to seal the bargain and that I needed a little iron in my arsenal to scare the wretch. "Villain," I suggested, frowning and speaking as rudely as possible, "do you know who I am?"

"Monsieur," said Vignogoule, eyes lowered in a way that was both servile and menacing, "who doesn't know you? And did we not almost get to know each other even better? I'm told you dig up graves to cut people up. I'm even told you shot Cabassus at the stake."

"That wasn't me. But whoever had the front to do that would have no trouble killing a hangman."

"Ah!" rejoined Vignogoule. "You realize that it's a capital crime to kill an executioner."

To which I hissed, "It was a capital crime to kill the condemned man. And whoever dared to do that would have no trouble with the other."

At this, Vignogoule threw me a quick glance through his watery eyes and lowered his heavy lids. I looked at him in turn. His fat face, like a huge block of mud, having both its colour and consistency, made no reaction, but I could see the reins in his enormous hands begin to tremble.

"Villain, did you hear what I said?"

"My noble Monsieur," he said softly, with a loud sigh that swelled his enormous chest, "I would beg you to consider this: if I am to put my thumb where you asked me to, on her throat, the bitch won't suffer any pain. She would die instantly. But that's not an execution, it's a vulgar murder, which is unheard of and despised by my art, and brings dishonour on me."

"So?" I said frowning and placing my hand on my dagger.

He turned this way and that in his saddle, and realizing that the archers were too far away to help, he licked his fat lips and said in a faint voice, "It'll be twenty-five écus and not an écu less."

"It's a bargain!" I said, not wishing to shake or discuss it further with this scoundrel. Then I added, "Twenty-five gold écus on the spot. But, hangman, remember this: if, after this bargain, the victim dies slowly, you will die quickly."

"Monsieur," said Vignogoule, "money down guarantees results."

Coming closer, despite my entire repugnance at the odour of death that emanated from this block of sludge, I counted out his gold, which took some time since he had to bite each coin to test it, just as his horrible woman had done before him. So I was greatly relieved when I left him to return to Fontanette's side.

"My poor Fontanette," I whispered, "I've made a deal with this villain. As soon as he places the noose around your neck, close your eyes. You won't feel a thing and will die instantly."

"Oh, Pierre," she gasped. "Praise be to God and to you too! It's a blessing that I met you to ease my death! And even more so to learn from your lips that you never told Dame Rachel I'd stolen from you!"

"Ah!" I cried, my fists clenched on the reins and gnashing my teeth. "I will crush that evil woman! It's her venom that has done this! Without her, I would have found you in Grabels, and released you from the hands of that awful farmer!"

"Pierre," she sobbed, tears again streaming down her beautiful face, "don't say such things! You're breaking my heart with regret, and I want to have the courage to face what's coming. And Pierre," she said looking at me with those beautiful naive eyes, "do you still love me a little?"

"Fontanette," my throat and eyes stinging, "I love you with great love and friendship and will never forgive myself for having taken your first bloom on that rooftop."

"No, Pierre! Don't say bad things about our moment there under the moon. It was my little moment of paradise. All the bad things came later."

I was so touched by the goodness of these words, which seemed to exonerate me, even though at first she'd seemed to blame me—I'd never know which was the case. And even though Fontanette didn't want to hear any more about the irrevocable chain of events that led her here, I couldn't help coming back to the cause of her unjust fate: "So Dame Rachel didn't tell you she'd learnt from your confessor that you'd consorted with me?"

"No, my love, not a word. The only thing she said was that I'd stolen two handkerchiefs from you."

"And all that time I was looking for you in Grabels! Two or three paces from Accla's hoof beats you were eating your heart out about my supposed injustice! Oh, Fontanette, words, words, words, what a poison they've put in you to separate us!"

"Pierre, let's speak no more of those terrible things. You're here by my side. I can't touch you, for my hands are tied behind my back, but if I could ask you to put your hand on my shoulder I'd be content."

I did what she asked, and scarcely had my fingers touched her when she leant her head over and laid her cheek on them, which had the same effect that a bird's palpitations would, if it lay dying cupped in my hand.

The road inclined sharply upward and our horses and mules slowed to a walk in the heat. At the top of the hill, my blood ran cold all of sudden as I spied, a few toises from us on our right, the gibbet, and beside it, immobile on his horse, Cossolat, who was waiting for us.

"Oh!" said Fontanette. "Here we are! Oh, Pierre, I found you again only to lose you so soon!" And she added in a sad, sweet and piteous voice that broke my heart again, "I'm only eighteen! My life was so short!"

Oh Christ! It was like a brass dome that closed over me! Christ! Can I never forget this moment? This gibbet, the archers, this oafish hangman and my sweet Fontanette, who was going to die right before my eyes! My God, how can I have the strength to tell what happened next? Every word that I write is like a strip of flesh that I'm pulling from my incurable wound thirty years later!

As soon as he saw me, Cossolat came over and tied his horse's reins to mine and I was suddenly separated from Fontanette and surrounded by archers, who kept a careful watch on me, their arquebuses ready and the fuses lit. As for me, my throat was so tight I couldn't speak, as though paralysed by the pain I felt. I saw everything as if through a mist, and yet with extreme attention. I saw Vignogoule get down from his nag, untie the stool he'd strapped on the croup of his mount, and step onto it to arrange a blackened and threadbare rope on the scaffold. This done, he placed the stool directly below the noose and ordered his woman to sit down there, which surprised me, since I couldn't guess what role he'd given her to play. Vignogoule did all of this with a sad expression, head lowered and gestures so slow and limp that you would have thought he was a jellyfish floating between two tides.

Once his woman was seated on the stool, he dragged himself over to Cossolat's horse, his breasts and stomach jiggling at every step, and asked in his high voice if the captain commanded him to continue. At which Cossolat, reddening in anger, stood up in his stirrups and shouted at the top of his voice, "Get on with it, for Christ's sake! Do it and make it fast!" And he added in Provençal, "*Aviat! Aviat!*"

"Captain," whined Vignogoule, "my art disdains doing things in a hurry. Work done slowly is work done well."

"By the seventy devils of hell!" shouted Cossolat. "Get on with it! And don't waste any more of my time or I'll lay my sword on your backside from here back to Montpellier!"

His face an implacable mud pie, Vignogoule, still shaking like gelatin, shuffled over to Fontanette, and, while he untied, with the same disheartening slowness, the cord that attached her to the saddle and the trappings of her mule, his eyes began rolling, and his breathing became louder and more hoarse. I shivered, as if emerging from a trance, and moved my hand towards one of my pistols. But Cossolat, putting his right hand on my arm, said quietly, "Remember your promise, Pierre." And, turning towards the hangman, he again shouted, "*Aviat! Aviat!*"

I fell back into my daze. And Vignogoule, seizing my Fontanette by the waist, lifted her like a feather from her mule and placed her on the ground. Still panting and eyes bulging out of their sockets, he pushed her with the flat of his hand towards the gibbet. She was facing away from me, but when he ordered her to sit down on the lap of his woman, with her neck at the same level as the noose, Fontanette managed to turn enough to look for me in the crowd, and, locking her eyes on mine, never looked away.

As soon as Fontanette had sat down in her lap, the ogress locked her arms around her victim's chest, and squeezed her tight so that she seemed to seep into her monstrous flesh. The hangman, drawing the noose near to him with an infinitely slow gesture, passed it over Fontanette's head and fastened it to her neck. For a terrible moment I was afraid he'd break his promise. But leaning towards her, he squeezed her neck with a single hand, his thumb on her throat. Without making a cry or even a sigh, her head fell inert onto her chest like a strangled pigeon's. Vignogoule ceased his panting. It was over. But I had to stay until he'd hoisted her body to be sure that he hadn't half strangled her, as he'd done with Cabassus.

"All right, Pierre," said Cossolat, touching my arm, "don't hang around here. She's not moving or shaking. Look, no convulsions, or feet dancing in the air. She's dead."

"Dead?" I said, as if disbelieving.

I could say no more, stunned as I was, my eyes fixed on Fontanette's stony white face, her eyes wide open, her neck twisted. Oh God! Was that the sweet wench, so lively, so tender, whom I'd held in my arms under the moon, feeling the swell of her heart's blood beating against mine? Poor lost soul, hanged in the bloom of her youth and destined to be hacked to pieces and to have her parts hung from these sterile olive trees, which would now bear these sad fruits until they rotted away!

"Pierre," Cossolat urged, "don't stay here eating your heart out! Come away! Come! I'll set you on your way again."

And, slapping Accla's croup, he made her leap forward, and we both took off hell for leather, followed by Samson and Miroul. We galloped at least two leagues before we stopped to breathe, and I later understood that Cossolat had forced me to get away from there because he feared that, in the grief-stricken trance I was in, I might kill Vignogoule and his hag before I knew what I was doing.

I was scarcely aware that Cossolat had gone, and hardly noticed where I was going as I rode along, crazy with grief, unable to manage Accla. My head was as benumbed as if I'd been beaten, and I could hardly see anything but the image of the hateful gibbet that I carried with me through hill and dale. I felt as though I were dead to myself, bearing in my frozen heart only the feeling of my immense guilt and infinite sorrow.

At noon, with the sun beating down on us, and we were sweating rivers under our thick armour, Miroul trotted up beside me and dared point out that our horses were exhausted and that we needed to stop. When I finally understood what he wanted, and seeing a small grassy knoll off to our right, I told him in a faint voice that we should make that our stopping place. As I dismounted, I undid my armour plates and threw off my helmet; then, handing Accla's reins to Miroul, I stumbled forward a few steps and dropped, face down, onto the grass, giving way to my fatigue and my grief. Digging my fingers into the ground and burying my face and my mouth in the rich tufts of grass, as warm as a mother's breast, I gave myself over to my tears so convulsively and for so long I thought they'd never end.

Our little troop reached Nîmes on 30th September, as eleven o'clock was chiming over the town, and stopped at a fortified gate, surmounted by a tower, whose parapet was patrolled by about twenty men who seemed dressed so as not to appear to be soldiers, yet who bore a varied assortment of weapons and armour of all kinds, some quite ancient, and including such things as shields, coats of mail and even cuirasses. These fellows seemed very inflamed, and were strutting around pulling on their moustaches with very bullying airs, and as soon as we presented ourselves at the gate, armed for war as we were and wearing helmets, they stared suspiciously at us from their tower, a few going as far as to light the fuses of their arquebuses, as though the three of us had devised a plan to attack the town.

I dismounted and, handing the reins to Samson, I walked up to the gate. "Soldier, please open the gate. We have safe-conduct documents."

"We open to no man," replied the gatekeeper, a twisted little fellow clothed in a suit of armour much too big for him, and holding a halberd that looked way too heavy for him to lift. He added, "Neither in nor out. Them's our orders." This said, he put on a great frown, but finding this expression more for show than for real, I said, in Provençal, in a somewhat lighthearted way,

"Hey, friend, what's the good of a door if you never open it? And where are we going to sleep tonight, if your beautiful city will have none of us, despite our safe-conduct passes?"

"Ah, Monsieur," said the man, softening his manner when he heard my playful tone. "I'm right sorry for you, for you seem an amiable sort of fellow, but there's nothing I can do. Orders are orders."

"Your orders? So you're a soldier?"

"Not a bit of it!" said the little man with a certain swagger. "I have a trade and I'm very good at it. I'm a wool carder. And these others you see up here on the parapet are weavers, bootmakers, cobblers or silk workers, but these last I don't like a bit since they're all stuck up and think they're superior to the rest of us, because they work with silk and not wool."

"But how does it happen that you're all here on a Tuesday guarding the town gate instead of working your trades?"

"What?" replied the carder naively. "You don't know?"

"How could I," I said, "since I'm outside and not inside?"

"It's because today we seized the town from the papists, who are holed up in the chateau."

"Well, this is good news!" I cried. "My brother and I are of the reformed religion. And my valet as well."

"What?" said the carder in surprise. "You're Huguenots? All three? Why didn't you say so? I would have opened the gate for you!"

"Well, open it now!"

"Nay!" said the carder, raising his cap and scratching his head. "Don't know if I ought to now, since I didn't do it before. Orders are orders, even though you're Huguenots. The devil if I know what I should do! What do you think, Monsieur?"

I thought it odd that he should ask me, since I'd already asked it of him and was preparing to persuade him to open up right away, but wagering that after giving my view of it he might hesitate some more, I said, "My friend, my view of it is that you ought to go and ask your boss so he can decide for you."

"By my faith, that's a right good idea!" confessed the carder. "I'll go and ask him right away."

He went off a bit unsteadily in his very large corselet, dragging his halberd behind him, though I was certain he'd never be able to strike anyone with it since he couldn't even lift it. But he hadn't taken three steps before he was back and said, "Monsieur, my name is Jean Vigier."

"Jean Vigier, is it? I like that name very much, as it's the name of a very worthy fellow. They call me Pierre de Siorac."

"Are you a nobleman then, Monsieur, or are you simply pretending to nobility?"

"I'm the younger son of the Baron de Mespech in Périgord."

"Ah, Monsieur! Who would have guessed it to hear you speak so amiably? I see you're not as scornful of artisans as some are."

"Certainly not. A skill is a skill. And the work of a carder is every bit as important as that of a silk worker."

"Monsieur, I like the way you talk! I'll go and fetch my boss." And off he went, dragging his halberd along behind him, and soon returned with a tall, thin, dark-skinned fellow whose countenance was far from being as pleasing as his subaltern's.

"Monsieur," he said, "I'm Jacques de Possaque, house marshal in the cavalry brigade of Captain Bouillargues, and I've just learnt of your request to enter our town. May I ask what business brings you here?"

"The desire to visit your beautiful city," I said, not wishing to reveal that I was intending to reside with Monsieur de Montcalm, who was a royal officer and a papist, and was doubtless not considered by those of our party with much favour at a moment like this. "We are students from Montpellier," I added, "and I have a letter of safe conduct from Captain Cossolat, who's one of ours, addressed to Captain Bouillargues."

As I pulled the letter from my saddlebags, I showed him the address on the letter without handing it to him. But even sealed as it was, this document proved to be an open sesame.

"Monsieur," said Possaque (whose "de" supposedly indicating his noble status struck me as a pretence, as Jean Vigier had put it), "I'll escort you to the Seashell inn where I'll ask you to wait until Captain Bouillargues can see you. However, I doubt that will be before this evening. Except for the chateau—whose garrison is too weak to cause us any alarm—the city is in our hands. And the captain has a few scores to settle with some of the papist fanatics, scores that won't admit of any delay in the settling."

As he said this, Possaque gnashed his teeth and his eyes gleamed in a way that I thought would offer very little comfort to those he had mentioned. "Ah," I thought, "the fanatics aren't just on one side in this mess. Here I am with a reformist cut from the same cloth."

Possaque, having admitted us into the city, invited us to dismount and walk our mounts, which we did. We then followed a platoon of about twenty men, holding a stunning variety of weapons, amongst them Jean Vigier, who'd managed to trade his unwieldy halberd for a short sword. He carried this sword in his hand, having no sheath for it, and seemed so happy to be armed that, as he walked, he would practise great slashes with it in the air. Possaque, worried that he'd wound a comrade with these antics, sent him to the back of the platoon, where he was very happy to find us, and I was just as happy to converse with him, for without him we would never have learnt the particulars of this drama we'd been plunged right into.

As we progressed towards the centre of town, the noise of the tumult seemed to grow louder, not because of any great combat or resistance, for the papists were huddled, terrified, in their homes, but because the streets were full of various brigades, running this way and that, shouting at the top of the lungs, "Close up your shops! All shops closed!"—an order the merchants were careful not to disobey, for they all feared looting. In a trice, Nîmes became a dead city, stalls removed, shutters closed, doors barricaded, and the populace ensconced behind their walls—all except those who ran about, shouting "Kill the papists! Kill! It's a new world!"

"Ha!" I thought. "What kind of a new world is this, that begins with the massacre of people who, when all is said and done, have the same God that we do but worship Him in a different way?"

"What?" I said to Jean Vigier. "Are you planning to kill all the papists here?"

"Oh no!" he replied. "We're not Turks! From what I've heard, none of the women, children or moderate papists will be killed. But as for those who were continually preaching against us and promising that we'd all be burnt at the stake, they'll not piss so high when we've got our hands on them."

483

"Vigier," I said, "do I hear you right? Executions? Without trials and without judges?"

"Oh, as for judges," he replied, "how would we find any? They were all on the other side and against us."

While he was saying this, Possaque called a halt in front of a beautiful house and knocked violently on the door with the handle of his sword. As there was no answer, he ordered his men to break it open, but they were unable to do so since it was a strong oak door, reinforced with iron bands. At this point, an upper window opened, and a well-dressed white-haired woman asked Possaque what he wanted.

"Wench," he shouted, "we want this scoundrel, this rogue, this thief, I mean this first consul of shit, your son, Gui Rochette! We want him to come down here and explain his management of our city!"

"My son," she replied with great dignity, "does not deserve these nasty and filthy words. In any case, he's not here."

"Oh yes, he is, bitch! There's no doubt about it!" yelled Possaque. "Tell him to get himself out here this instant, or I'll set fire to your house!"

"Whether or no you set fire to my house, he's not here, and as Christ is my witness, I repeat and I swear it. Where he is now I have no idea; he left suddenly around noon and without his hat."

Hearing this, our men grumbled and swore a lot with terrible curses that the scoundrel had fled the city. "Quiet!" shouted Possaque. "That's not possible! By noon, we'd closed all the gates!" At this the lady paled visibly; Possaque must have seen her loss of composure and, deciding that she must be telling the truth, ordered his troops to move on.

I foresaw that nothing good could come of this first encounter, nor from the brutal and profane way that Possaque had addressed the old woman, and, turning to Vigier, I whispered, "What did Gui Rochette do to warrant being treated this way?"

"Nothing, Monsieur," said the carder, "except for serving as the first consul and being fiercely opposed to us Huguenots and being the reason that last November they chose four consuls, all four of whom are papists, and not two of theirs and two of ours, as we'd asked for. We protested this election to the lieutenant general, Monsieur de Joyeuse, but that little piece of shit vicomte who eats his meat with a fork (as you've probably heard!) decided against us. Rochette is going to die if we find him, and maybe the three others with him, though it's not so sure about the others since they're less papist than Rochette. He's always sucking up to the bishop, Bernard d'Elbène, kissing his hand and drooling over the stakes they'll erect to burn us all, with the king's blessing! By the belly of St Michael! We're going to wipe out this entire brood!"

"What?" I gasped. "The bishop too?"

"The bishop too! Though he's not such a bad man. But we won't be such Turks as they are. We won't burn them at the stake; that would heat things up too much." (And here he laughed at his little joke.) "No, my lad! A nice thrust of the dagger ought to do the trick and off they go to worship the Virgin Mary in the other world, leaving this one to us!"

Listening to Vigier go on like this, emphasizing his words with great sword thrusts in the air, I began to sense that the intensity of his hatred of the papists and the everlasting persecutions and threats they'd levelled at the reformists was going to lead to some terrible bloodshed before the end of this September day, which had started out so sunny and beautiful.

I was in the midst of these sad thoughts when a troop of Huguenots who were coming from the opposite direction met us and, as we squeezed to the right to let them pass, their leader, a tall redhead, full of spit and vinegar, shouted at the top of his lungs, "Companions! It's a new world! Condé and Coligny have taken the king prisoner at the Château de Monceaux! They've offed the old bitch, Catherine de' Medici! And her two pups, Anjou and Alençon! Comrades! Our brothers have taken Lyons. Soon we'll have Montpellier! Toulouse! Paris!"

I doubted this news the minute I heard it and, indeed, I was right, but it had an extraordinary effect on Samson, whom I quietly urged to be silent, and on the rest of our troop, giving them the false hope that the kingdom was now at their feet and swelling immeasurably their thirst for revenge and the belief they no longer had to answer for their bloody deeds to anyone, not even the king, who was thought to be in their hands. I immediately saw the unfortunate effects of their exaltation when Possaque asked the tall redhead who the two fellows were they had captured.

"Ah! Just small fry that I'm taking to city hall," said the redhead. "Guérinot, a cobbler, and Doladille, a silk worker, both papist fanatics."

"Small fry indeed!" sneered Possaque, shrugging his shoulders.

But Jean Vigier, hearing Doladille's name, turned ashen from anger. And shoving everyone aside, he marched up to the unfortunate silk worker and, taking him by the collar, cried, "Ah, Doladille! Ah, villain! So here you are!" And he struck him with his sword so awkwardly that he opened a deep wound in his left arm. Possaque grabbed Vigier by the arm and berated him soundly, telling him it was not up to him, but up to their leaders, to decide about executions. And after roundly putting him in his place, Possaque sent him to the back of the platoon, where Vigier, observing when we started marching again that I wasn't speaking to him, said innocently, "Hey, what's with you? You don't like me any more?"

"Ah, Vigier! To strike an unarmed man! Fie then! You should be ashamed!"

"But, Monsieur, that's not just any man, that's Doladille!"

"And who's this Doladille?"

"He's a silk worker, as you heard, and is always belittling and despising my work in wool."

"So that's enough reason to kill him?"

"Well, he also cuckolded me with my wife and went about bragging about it!"

"That's a piece of treachery to be sure—"

"Ha, Monsieur! There's worse. Swelled with malice, this Doladille, nasty papist that he is, has gone about saying that since Charles IX outlawed the reformist religion, he's going to kill me with his bare hands and marry my widow, claiming he's got what it takes in his pants to convert her back to the true religion!"

We couldn't argue any further, since Possaque called me to show me the Seashell inn, which he succeeded in getting opened up to us only after many shouts and banging on the doors. The door opened only halfway, however, and the innkeeper, a very pretty, high-breasted woman, with a proud look and an assertive tongue, appeared.

"Who's that?" she asked, fiercely. "I'm closed. I was ordered to do so."

"Well, I'm ordering you to open," snarled Possaque. "Give these gentlemen accommodation and no back talk. They've just arrived from Montpellier and they need a place to stay."

Whereupon, with little show of civility, and Vigier the only one to wave goodbye, the troop continued their hunt for papists, no doubt hoping to bring back to city hall more substantial game than a shoemaker and a silk worker.

Meanwhile, the innkeeper, without a word, her expression as cold as ice, put me in one room and Samson in another, and had her valet help Miroul tend to our horses in the stables.

"My friend," I said, retaining her for a moment by her arm, "what's this! Why do you look so unpleasant? Your eyes are so cold and your mouth pinched so hard. What have I done to displease you so thoroughly?"

"Monsieur," she said, "nothing in your looks, which I could get along with well enough. It's your actions that displease me so."

"My actions? What have I done?"

"Nothing," she replied, her eyes flashing, "except come all the way from Montpellier to join in the massacres here."

"Oh, Madame!" I cried. "This is unjust! I've never killed a soul except in loyal combat. And I'm not about to start in your fair city. I'm in Nîmes to visit a friend who happens to be a papist. But seeing the colour of things here on my arrival, I didn't want to name him. So here I am in your inn, by order of Possaque, and very sorry to be here against your will."

"Monsieur," she softened, "should I believe you?"

"You should, my friend," I replied, putting my hands on her shoulders. "I'm a Huguenot, but not as fanatical and bitter as some that I've seen here."

"Monsieur," she said, growing friendlier, "can I trust you? Can you name the person you were going to stay with?"

"My friend," I answered, "I'll do better: I'll show you the letter that I'm supposed to transmit to him. Here it is," I continued, and, removing my coat of mail, I took from my doublet the letter and held it out to her. "It's not sealed, you may read it."

"Ah, Monsieur," she said, now entirely reassured, "you're acting in such an open and honest way with me that I'm beginning to like you." Then, reddening, she added with evident shame, "I know how to count, Monsieur, but can't read much. May I send for my cook, who reads as well as a bishop? He'll tell me whether I can trust you as much as my feelings are urging me to."

At this she gave me a sweet look and such a warm smile that I could not but consent. And having said a few words privately to her chambermaid, she sat down on a stool, and I sat down in turn, having nothing better to do than wait, and we looked at each other for some time without saying anything, since each of us seemed to be enjoying what we saw, though the time had not yet come to say so.

There was a knock, and at the innkeeper's invitation the cook stepped through the door, a portly fellow with a jolly face, large nose and easy-going manner. My hostess immediately handed him the letter, and asked him politely if he would read it. Hearing this, the cook made me a small bow, but did not remove his white hat, which surprised me a bit. Then, without being invited to do so, he took a seat, with a certain pomp, and read the letter with great seriousness, while the innkeeper listened with a degree of respect that few cooks could expect from their mistresses. When he'd done, the cook rose, made a deep bow, still without removing his chef's hat, handed the letter to the innkeeper, crossed his hands over his stomach and said in a suave voice: "Madame, the letter is from Madame the Vicomtesse de Joyeuse and addressed to Monsieur de Montcalm, our chief magistrate, to whom the vicomtesse recommends this gentleman, who is her little cousin."

"The little cousin of Madame de Joyeuse!" cried the innkeeper, very impressed and looking at me with new respect.

"This gentleman is named Pierre de Siorac," said the cook, raising his hand as if he were not accustomed to being interrupted. "He's the younger son of the Baron de Mespech in Périgord. Monsieur de Siorac and his brother Samson are both students. And as Pierre de Siorac has exhibited some rash behaviour in Montpellier" (and here my hostess looked at me tenderly, never imagining that my indiscretions could be anything other than what she guessed they must be) "the vicomtesse asks Monsieur de Montcalm to host them for a time until things in Montpellier have settled down again. Madame de Joyeuse adds that Pierre de Siorac is, like his father, a Huguenot loyalist, and that in no case would he ever bear arms against his king—"

"Ah, Monsieur!" cried the innkeeper. "That's excellent news! I'm reassured! You now have my entire trust! I will hide nothing from you either!—"

"Madame," the cook broke in, frowning with all the authority his literacy provided him, "you are too quickly investing your trust! Monsieur de Siorac has every appearance of being a true gentleman, but he *is* a Huguenot, no doubt faithful to his sect."

"Of course!" I cried. "But not to the point of assassinating anyone! Nor of taking a city from the king! Comrade," I said, walking up to the cook and taking him by both hands (which were very soft and not at all what one would have expected from his profession), "if I can help anyone here to save his life by preserving him from the excesses that my party may commit, I'll do it!"

And as I said this, with some emotion and fire, I couldn't help thinking that this fellow's toque, which he refused to remove when bowing, may well hide the tonsured head of a priest beneath it, one who might have needed to disguise himself as a cook to escape the hunt that was currently going on in Nîmes for anyone wearing a cassock. "But," I added, "all is not yet lost! They're taking prisoners, but not killing them!"

"Ah, Monsieur de Siorac!" cried the cook, choking back his tears. "You're harbouring false hopes! Don't be fooled. Although the orders are, for the moment, to bring all the captured papists to city hall safe and sound, we've heard that the plan is secretly to execute all of them tonight. And in at least one case, already, their fanatical fury has run ahead of their plans: this morning, a little before noon, the vicar general, Jean Péberan, was surprised in his rooms by the clerk of the magistrate, La Grange, and a score of armed men who cut him down on the spot, stabbing him more than a hundred times with daggers and swords."

"Ah, what villainy!" I gasped. "Now I'm beginning to fear for the safety of Monsieur de Montcalm. Is he considered an enemy of the Huguenots in Nîmes?"

"One of the worst," said the innkeeper. "But rumour has it that he escaped with his wife and daughter before they closed the city gates. And some people claim to have seen the three of them heading west on the Provence road where Montcalm has a well-defended chateau with a moat, towers and machicolations."

"My friend," I said to my hostess, "as soon as you've provided me some victuals, for I'm very hungry, I'll go see what I can find out about Monsieur de Montcalm. Meanwhile, please hide this letter addressed to him in a safe place so that they won't find it on me if I'm searched by the more excitable members of my party."

The innkeeper rose from her stool and very courteously asked the "cook" to prepare my roast meat. This latter, who apparently had no thought of performing this duty, immediately rose as well. But before withdrawing, he stepped over to me, looked at me beseechingly and said in a tone of supplication, "Monsieur, the bishop's palace is next to Monsieur de Montcalm's house, so if you're heading in that direction, I wonder if you could take a look, and keep your ears open as well for any news of our bishop, Bernard d'Elbène, who, so far, has managed to throw his enemies off his tracks."

"Monsieur," I replied, "for the love of Christ, I will do as you ask."

Hearing this, the "cook" gave me a deep bow, his toque still on his head, and returned to his kitchen.

I wanted to eat my meal in my room, alone with Samson. And when we'd finished, speaking with as much urgency as I could muster, I told him that I was going out, but without him, that he should absolutely remain in his room and speak to no one, and that if any Huguenots questioned him he was to say that we were simply here to visit Nîmes and to deliver a letter to Captain Bouillargues, and to leave it at that without saying anything more or giving his opinion on anything that was happening here. I stressed that he was not to get involved in anything that was going on in Nîmes, or say anything that might offend the king or the queen mother or the king's brothers, since I very much doubted the news of their misfortune that had been reported to Possaque. And finally, embracing him tenderly, I told him to remember that our father had always been a Huguenot loyalist and that he'd never consented to take up arms against his king, nor taken part in the siege of Sarlat, believing that it was a rebellion pure and simple, and that he should consider that the executions of priests and of the papist merchants, however fanatical they may have been against our cult, were nothing more than common murders, repugnant to any sense of honour, and bloody infractions of our laws.

I took my dagger and sword, but did not put my armour or helmet on, since the late-September heat was stifling. When the innkeeper let me out by a back door that gave onto an alley, whom did I find waiting for me, armed exactly as I was? "Miroul!" I exclaimed, open-mouthed. "What are you doing here?"

"I'm not leaving you, Monsieur," he said, his chestnut eye twinkling and his blue eye cold as ice.

"But how did you get out here?"

"By that window up there on the second storey."

"Sweet Mother of God!" said the innkeeper. "You'd have to be a fly or a bird to get down from there without breaking your neck!"

"Ha! I've seen him do better than that!" I said, proud of Miroul's nearly unbelievable agility, for, as the reader may remember, he'd once scaled the walls of Mespech and got through all our defences noiselessly to come and steal some ham from our kitchens, poor little rogue that he was back then, dying of hunger.

"Miroul," I said, pretending to be angry, "who told you to follow me?"

"Your father, the Baron de Mespech, everywhere he thought you might be in danger. And it seems like we're in the thick of it here."

"Indeed it does, he's right!" said our hostess. "My noble friend, take care of yourself! And you, Miroul, keep him safe!"

This said, and not without a very sweet look from her beautiful eyes that seemed to send me a sheaf of promises, she closed the door. "Ah!" I mused. "If I get back safely, this house is going to be very welcoming!"

Once in the street we found more platoons of armed men running this way and that, all worked up and tirelessly shouting, "Kill the papists! It's a new world!" and looking us over suspiciously as they went by, since they didn't recognize us. But I managed to look so calm, serious and self-assured that no one dared accost us to ask what we were doing there. And though I had trouble concealing my compassion when I saw, in the midst of these bloodthirsty platoons, monks, priests or papist merchants being led to city hall to be locked in subterranean dungeons, I managed to look the other way and quicken my step and appear as though I were on some urgent mission so that I passed through all the meshes of this enormous net without incident and reached the cathedral, not far from which, according to the innkeeper, were located both the bishop's palace and Monsieur de Montcalm's mansion.

Once there, I felt as though I were out of danger, since, whenever a wave of Huguenots surged onto the cathedral square, they were all focused on their business, some armed, others not, pillaging the churches and sacking them, carrying off crosses, icons, statues and the canons' stalls, hacking these last to pieces, and bearing away any sacred vessels or gold-embroidered vestments. Some had built a great bonfire in the middle of the square, where they were burning the documents and feudal titles belonging to the cathedral, shouting that it was all over—that no one in Nîmes would ever again pay a *sol* in tax to the canons! They were all so drunk with destruction and looting, and displayed such intense focus and unimaginable joy, as if they really believed that out of the cinders of this debris a new world would be born, that Miroul and I could pass through them unnoticed and reach the bishop's palace. But I dared not enter, for the building was full of soldiers who were destroying everything they could, their eyes full of fury and their faces bathed in sweat in the suffocating heat.

Next to the bishop's palace I saw a beautiful mansion, with an exterior stairway in a tower leading to two cantilevered stories, and figured that it must be Montcalm's lodgings. Finding the door wide open, I went in, followed by Miroul, and saw a dozen armed guards, more focused on destruction than pillaging, and whom my arrival seemed seriously to disturb. One of them, whom I recognized as the tall redhead who had announced the supposed death of Catherine de' Medici and the capture of the king by the Huguenots, scowled at me angrily, as though surprised to be caught in such disgraceful looting. Cocksure and disdainful, he headed over to me with a bullying air, brandishing his pistol, and said in the most insulting possible tone, "Hey, you bumpkin, what's your business in here?"

"Monsieur," I replied, standing up to him, "my name is Pierre de Siorac, I'm the younger son of the Baron de Mespech in Périgord, who," I lied, making it up as I went, "holds a bill of credit for 500 livres payable by Monsieur de Montcalm and I'm here to collect it. But perhaps I've come too late? Seeing you all here collecting his goods, I suppose that Monsieur de Montcalm is dead and you're his heirs."

"He's not dead!" yelled one of the looters. "He's fled!"

"Shut your mouth, Vidal!" yelled the redhead. "And as for you, idiot," he said, turning towards me, still snarling and putting on his superior airs, "I don't believe a word of this cock and bull story about credits and barons and such. I already saw your lying face somewhere and I think you're a spy sent by the papists to steal our secrets."

"Monsieur," I said, pulling myself up to my full height, crimson with fury, hands on my hips and speaking very loudly, "if you would please put up your pistol and unsheathe your sword, I'll stuff your dirty accusations back in your throat! I'm of the reformed religion, and better than you, I dare say! For if I'm right about what's going on in here it's more about looting than about faith!"

"Insolent knave," he cried, striding forward and striking me in the chest with his pistol. With his other hand, his eyes suddenly wild, he opened my doublet, which I'd left unbuttoned because of the intense heat, and uncovered the gold medallion to Mary that my mother had given me on her deathbed. Seeing this, his fury redoubled and he screamed: "So you dare pretend you're a Huguenot? And you wear this idolatrous image around your neck! You're a papist, a scoundrel, and, what's worse, a papist spy! And the only thing you'll get from spying on us here is a quick trip to hell!"

But he didn't have time to finish his sentence, since Miroul, with the flat of his palm, had knocked his pistol out of his right hand. Then, with a well-aimed kick, he threw this mountain of a man to the ground, straddled his chest and, whipping his dagger from its sheath, placed its point on the man's throat. It was a marvel to watch this David flatten this Goliath in the twinkling of an eye.

"Monsieur," said Miroul, "should I finish him off for his nasty insults?"

"No, thank you," I replied. I then unsheathed my sword, picked up my assailant's pistol and aimed it at him with one hand while pointing my sword at the group of looters with the other, for they had recovered from their surprise at Miroul's exploit, had pulled themselves together and were now brandishing their weapons with very menacing looks.

"You there!" I shouted, braving their angry stares. "I didn't lie! I'm a Huguenot. It's for love of my dead mother, who was a papist, that I'm wearing this medallion, and not out of idolatry. If any one among you doubts me, take me to your minister and he can test my religious convictions."

My tone, the force of my declaration, my black clothes and my proposal to be examined seemed to give them pause. "Maybe we'd better take him to Monsieur de Chambrun," said the man the redhead had called Vidal. "Otherwise, how're we going to decide?"

"All right," said another, "but who'll take him?"

They looked at each other for a moment in silence, none of them apparently willing to abandon his role in the looting to the others while he escorted me to the minister.

"Monsieur," said Vidal finally, "if your valet will free François Pavée, we'll let you go without any problems.

"Do I have your word?" I replied, and though I gave very little credence to the word of a looter, I realized that I had to accept.

"I give you my word," said Vidal. "Leave, Monsieur!"

"Not before your leader retracts the things he said against me," I shouted, while Miroul continued to hold the point of his dagger at François Pavée's throat.

"I retract what I said," said François Pavée in a faint voice, but hatred was oozing from every pore of his villainous face.

"My friends, that will suffice! Lean your arms against that wall while my valet and I withdraw."

They obeyed, and I discharged Pavée's pistol against the ceiling and then threw it on the floor next to him. Then, making a sign to Miroul and with no regard for my rank, I scooted off like a scared rabbit and crossed the square, Miroul flying along at my side with his usual grace—and it was a good thing we did, for two arquebus shots rang out behind us, but neither hit its target. But as soon as we'd rounded the corner of the nearest street, I stopped and sheathed my sword, convinced that none of those soldiers would follow us, being too busy enriching themselves with their looting.

When I say "soldiers" it's just in a manner of speaking. For this François Pavée, as I learnt later, wasn't a beggar taking advantage of the chaos. He was one of the well-to-do merchants of Nîmes, with a large house, overflowing coffers and property in the countryside, thanks to which he could call himself lord of Servas. But his bigotry, cruelty and avarice had taken over his soul, and he was one of the three Huguenot leaders in Nîmes who, unbeknownst to the other leaders in their community, carried out the sinister massacre that I was to witness.

"Master," said Miroul, "you now have a mortal enemy in this Pavée character. We should leave this city while we still can."

"Yes, but not before seeing Monsieur de Chambrun."

"Why should we go to see him?"

"So he'll know that I'm really a Huguenot and so that he'll tell others. But most of all to try to stop these damnable excesses if we can."

"Ah, my master! You always want to fix everything!" sighed Miroul. But suddenly embarrassed, in his peasant sensitivity, that he'd given the impression of censuring me, he fell silent.

Monsieur de Chambrun, who was as humane and flexible in his thinking as Monsieur de Gasc was imperious and strict, examined me with great care and was happy to recognize that I was not only well versed in all aspects of the reformed religion, but seemed sincere in my feelings and in my observance of its rites. He did, however, reproach me for continuing to wear the medallion of the Virgin around my neck, which certainly gave me the appearance of being an idolater. It was his opinion that I should sacrifice to my faith the word I'd given my dying mother. We argued over this for a good bit without either persuading the other, and finally he "remanded me to my own

497

conscience", a phrase that seemed to be in vogue with our ministers, Gasc having already used it with me. But Monsieur de Chambrun was less bitter about it than his Montpellier counterpart—quite the contrary. On the other hand, when I touched on the present and future excesses of the Nîmes rebellion, and the necessity of trying to rein in these abuses, he threw his hands heavenward and said:

"Monsieur de Siorac! In these times of war, arms will not give way to the cloth! I've reported to the consistory the most violent of our leaders, François Pavée, Captain Bouillargues and Poldo Albenas, but they don't seem to care that these men have taken the law into their own hands. They will respond to my warnings with apparent respect when this is all over. And of course these three will deny everything, accusing others of the executions they themselves have ordered. The only thing the consistory can do is to try to limit the number of executions. And, at best, to put a term on them."

I was stunned by the powerlessness of the Nîmes ministers to limit the cruelty of their captains, and, reflecting on my own fortunes, I realized I was in grave danger, François Pavée now having both the desire and power to kill me with no one to oppose him.

"I agree!" confessed Monsieur de Chambrun. "François Pavée is the worst of them all! And the most arrogant. You've defied him and he's not the man to suffer it. I'll write a note to Captain Bouillargues explaining who you are and the evil suspicions Pavée conceived about you, and ask him to write you a safe-conduct pass so that you may leave Nîmes before Pavée can get his hands on you."

Monsieur de Chambrun did as he had said, and I left him after a thousand compliments and thanks, but precious little reassured. His letter to Captain Bouillargues found its way into my doublet, joining Cossolat's missive to the same captain, who appeared to be impossible to find: these two notes were feeble bulwarks against the armed platoons my enemy commanded.

My alarm wasn't ill-founded: scarcely had we taken a hundred steps after leaving Monsieur de Chambrun's lodgings when we were confronted by a dozen armed men, who pointed their arquebuses at us, fuses lit. Though my heart was pounding like an alarm bell, I stepped boldly up to them, though I was sweating profusely from the sun's heat and from having so many barrels pointed at my chest. But affecting a calm and smiling tone, I yelled, "Comrades! What's this? You're aiming your guns at me? Why so? Do they send people into your town without explaining the what and the why of things? Are you common throat-slashers or seasoned artisans faithful to the reformed religion?"

And even while I was speaking to them with apparent calm, I inwardly trembled lest one of them discharge his arquebus and shorten my sentence for me. But happily they had no thought of such butchery, and were swayed by my words, like most Provençal natives.

"Monsieur!" said one of them, stepping up to me, who turned out to be our old friend, Jean Vigier. "'Tis true you're a friendly fellow despite your birth, and don't despise us workers, but we have orders from François Pavée to kill you within the hour, both you and your valet, as papist spies."

"Ah, Jean Vigier!" I laughed. "I'm neither a spy nor a papist! I'm the son of a Huguenot baron! I'm a Huguenot myself. Want proof? I've got a letter here," I said, pulling the letter from my doublet, "that Monsieur de Chambrun has written to Captain Bouillargues telling him that I'm definitely a member of the reformed Church, whatever François Pavée might claim, and requesting the guards at the gates to allow me to leave the city."

"I can't read," said Jean Vigier, pushing my letter away.

"Comrades," I said, "is there anyone among you who'd like to read this letter?"

But not a one of them knew his letters, and I judged from their faces that there wasn't one of them who didn't resent me for making them admit it. So I changed my tactics hurriedly.

"So," I said, "the important thing isn't the letter! It's that I'm a good Huguenot, and you can see that with your eyes closed! I can sing you the Psalms of David from beginning to end, without skipping a single one. And so can my valet! And I can denounce seventeen papist heresies," I continued, buttoning up my doublet since the chain of my medallion was beginning to burn my skin. "The truth is that François Pavée has sworn to kill me because I caught him looting Montcalm's lodgings, filling up sacks with his personal take while you good fellows were running about the city, sweating in your chain mail. Why didn't François Pavée kill me himself if he really believed I was a spy? The reason is that my father is a powerful Huguenot baron in Périgord, and a great captain who fought at Ceresole and at Calais. And François Pavée was afraid that if he killed me by his own hand, my father would take his revenge on him. So he sent you out to do his dirty work for him, preferring, no doubt, that it should be you lot my father would send to the gibbet!"

This speech did not have the effect on them I'd hoped. I clearly saw that it was as hard to get a new idea to penetrate their skulls as it was to drive an old one out, once it was in there. On the other hand, if my words bounced off their helmets like hail, they didn't seem to think I was such a bad person.

"It's a fact," said one, "that the man doesn't have a bad face."

"And he's pretty young," said another. "And such a handsome fellow it'd be a pity to kill him."

"Nor does he look like a spy," said a little round balding fellow.

"Nay!" said a fourth, who was tall, thin and had a very jaundiced look. "The man doesn't look like a villain. But he's not from Nîmes… What's he doing here?"

"What?" I said. "Does that make everyone who comes to admire your beautiful city a spy?"

"But orders are orders," said Jean Vigier, looking at me with his friendly and naive little eyes. "And by your leave, Monsieur, our orders are to kill you!"

"Jean Vigier," I said, "who's your captain? François Pavée or Captain Bouillargues?"

"The captain."

"And what do you think he'll say when you bring him the letters you'll find on me when you kill me?"

"Ah, now that's a point you've got there!" And raising his helmet he began scratching his head.

"I think," said the tall, thin man, "we ought to dispatch him right here and now and quit all this bargaining. Just remember, he's not from Nîmes. And it's really too hot to stand here arguing with the scoundrel, I'm filling up my armour with sweat. Finish him!"

"Comrade," I said quickly, "you're right about the heat. Let's go and discuss this at the Seashell inn in front of a few good flagons of wine—on me, because I love Nîmes and because I love life!"

Everyone was busy seconding this idea when Jean Vigier broke in, "But wait! We're expressly prohibited from going to the inn today."

"Ah, but not from accompanying me there, since that's where I'm staying," I countered, "and surely you can leave me there if you haven't made up your minds what you're going to do with me!"

"Ah, you've got a point there!" said Jean Vigier.

But still he hesitated.

"Lets go to the inn and have a drink and then we'll kill him," said the tall, thin fellow.

This suggestion won the day, and we all set off, my executioners and I, towards the Seashell inn, they sweating like pigs in their armour, and I in my doublet, the afternoon sun still strong upon our backs.

I suggested we all enter the inn by the back door, so no one would see us. But when we got there we couldn't seem to get anyone to come to open the door, no matter how much noise we made. So I ordered Miroul to scale the wall up to the second floor and to go back through the little window he'd emerged from that morning. Which task he accomplished with an agility that left our dangerous guests gaping with wonder, for he climbed vertically, almost as if he were a fly, and made no sound whatever doing so.

"By my faith," said the thin man, "if I were that rascal, I'd become a thief! I could earn a better living doing that than I do as a cobbler."

Fearing to leave them any time to think, and fearing that they might reconsider our plan, I told them the story of how Miroul had penetrated Mespech's defences by night, by leaping from wall to wall, and I kept them on tenterhooks long enough for the innkeeper to open the door, which she did without the least appearance of fear, but with the aplomb and the self-assurance of a wench who knows how to keep order in her house amidst a group of rowdy men. Moreover, I learnt that Miroul had quickly explained the danger of our situation to her and so she'd known how to win over our mob with her welcoming manner.

"Friends," she said, "you're very welcome in my house as long as you're friends of this Huguenot gentleman, for I've been ordered to give neither crumb nor cup to any papists—though I'm a papist myself."

"It's all right if you are," said Jean Vigier. "We don't touch any women."

"And it's a good thing you don't!" said our hostess. "Otherwise, who'd roast your meat? My friends, put out those fuses on your arquebuses before coming in! And remove your armour and helmets and put 'em in a pile in the corner. I don't want you scratching my table! I'll go and get some nice cool wine and some goblets."

My executioners meekly obeyed all of her commands, as if she'd been the captain of a garrison, and sat down and began drinking. And when, after two or three flagons, the thin man suggested that they decamp and go out and kill me in the back alley, the hostess objected that they couldn't go off without having something to eat, and the chambermaids brought in an entire ham, some Bigorre sausages, a cold roast with mustard, some brook trout and a good deal more wine, which had been cleverly doctored. While my captors were gorging themselves on this feast, I asked Miroul to go and get his viol, and then suggested to each of them that they cite the first verse of the psalm of their choice, and then I sang the entire psalm while Miroul accompanied me. But this was wasted effort, as became quickly evident.

"Well, my friends," I said when I'd finished singing, "what do you think, am I a Huguenot or not?"

"Sure enough," replied Jean Vigier, "that was sweetly sung. But François Pavée warned us that you were very good at pretending to be a Huguenot. And the fact is that you're wearing a medallion to the Virgin Mary around your neck. Do you deny it?"

"No."

"Then you're an idolater."

At this, they all looked at me with as much horror as if they'd caught me kneeling before the golden calf. "Well!" I thought as the sweat dripped down between my shoulder blades. "This time I'm done for. Everything becomes violence and terror the minute you touch religion! Idolatry is fanatical, but so is anti-idolatry. Montluc cut off a man's head for having broken a cross. And these men were going to cut my throat for wearing a medallion."

"My friends," I said, "this medallion was given me by my mother on her deathbed. She was a papist and made me swear to wear it after she died. It's because of my dead mother's idolatry that it's dangling from my neck, *not* because I worship Mary. The truth is that I pray

503

to God the same way you do, without any intercession of Mary or the saints."

"To be sure," sneered Jean Vigier, "you've got a ready tongue! It's quite a story you tell! But is it true? Who shall say?" he added with a burp that would have unstopped a chimney.

"The man's not from Nîmes," mumbled the thin man in his cups. "Listen to me! He's from Montpellier. And as everyone knows, it's no good lying when you've come a long way."

"But I'm not lying!" I cried in desperation. "That I'm a good, loyal and sincere Huguenot is all written down in black and white in the letter Monsieur de Chambrun wrote to Captain Bouillargues! Are you going to cut my throat because you don't know how to read? And why don't you know your letters in the first place? I've heard that all the artisans and labourers who join our religion learn to read right away so they can decipher the Holy Bible."

At this reproach, they all lowered their heads and stared into their goblets, looking quite ashamed, I thought. Then the little round bald-headed man said, in a trembling voice and with tears in his eyes (not just, I think, because of the wine he'd drunk), "Monsieur! We're all recent converts to the true religion and though they told us we'd need to learn to read to be able to decipher the sacred texts, I can't go learning to read when I'm working fifteen hours a day and I've got five mouths to feed with the little I earn. I just don't have the energy, come sundown, to go to work with my head however much I might try. I just can't seem to make any progress."

"I completely understand," I said, "that no one here knows how to read. So, go and fetch Monsieur de Chambrun. He'll tell you what you want to know about my religion."

"By my faith, that's not a bad idea!" said the little round man.

But when he tried to stand, he fell back onto his stool, having lost the use of his legs.

"Ah, bah!" mumbled Jean Vigier, his nose in his goblet. "We've been betrayed. I'm not going to let this go. The man has an idol around his neck." And thereupon he burped.

"Thish wine ishn't sho bad," said the tall, thin man with the yellowing skin. "But I'm not forgedding my order even though I'm not through eading. You shir, jush wait a bit. In a moment we'll kill you."

"What?" said the little round man. "We're not going to fetch Mish-yor de Chambrun?" But when he tried to get up he fell back on his stool.

"Hey!" proclaimed the tall, dark-haired fellow on his left. "Doesn' matter what the minshter thinksh or whether this rascal is papist or Huguenot, lesh jush kill 'im. The Lord up there will decide. Miroul, I'm going to shing a shong about my weaversh' trade becaush I'm a weaver like that little fat fellow over there. Can you accompany me?"

"Depends," said Miroul, "are you going to kill me like my master?"

"Of coursh!"

"With or without an idol?" said Miroul, his brown eye smiling and his blue one cold.

"With or without."

"Then I'm your man. Sing, weaver!"

And, Miroul giving me a quick look, I came over and stood beside him, which is to say, quite near the door, and was reassured to observe that I still had my sword and dagger in my belt, as did Miroul, our executioners never having thought to disarm us, perhaps because there were so many of them and only two of us. And certainly, if it came to a fight, we would have been able to kill more than a few of them. But I had no taste for bloodshed with these fellows, however badly they understood the precepts of religion.

Meanwhile the weaver was singing a song that had nothing to do with weaving and would have made the chambermaids blush if they hadn't been accustomed to hearing such stuff at various banquets.

After the weaver it was the wool carder who had to share his song, then a cobbler, and then a silk worker. In their refrains, in which each one tried to exalt his trade over the others, there was plenty of lewdness. The wool carder's song was about a pretty wench who asked her beau to give her a pretty thread that would make her bobbin fatter.

"Bloody hell!" said the thin man, who, though he was a shoemaker, hadn't wanted to sing a song about his trade. "I think it's downright sinful to sing dirty songs and eat, drink and make merry when we haven't found where this shithead of a bishop is hiding." And at these words the innkeeper looked up with alarm. "Comrades," he continued, banging his fist on the table and rolling his eyes furiously, "we're doing God's work pretty badly here!"

And hearing the words "God's work" I feared the worst, for, whether he's a papist or a Huguenot, a man tends to use them in the service of his worst instincts.

"Friends!" continued the shoemaker, banging on the table. "Let's dispatch this gentleman right now. We've waited long enough!"

"He's right!" agreed Jean Vigier. "He's a traitor. 'Sgot an idol around his neck!"

"So let's do him!" said the shoemaker, drawing his dagger, though he didn't stand up.

"What?" cried the innkeeper, standing over him like a Fury, and no more afraid of his dagger than if he'd had a spoon in his hand. "*What?*" she screamed. "Kill him in here? Shoemaker, is this how a cobbler understands civility? You'll get blood on my floor, and I just washed it!"

"Hadn't thought of that!" mumbled the cobbler, looking vaguely troubled at his dagger as if he were astonished to see it in his hand.

"Cobbler," I said, "your hostess is right. Let's the three of us go outside so we don't ruin her floor."

"Three?" said the cobbler.

"I thought your order was to kill the valet too?" said Miroul gravely. "With or without an idol."

"Well, yes—"

"So, let's be off," I said, hoping this would be a good occasion to finish this business.

"Monsieur!" said the cobbler, struggling with some difficulty to his feet. "It's very nice of you to be so amenable to being killed. I'm not a cruel man so I'll get it over with quickly."

He took several steps towards the door, where he would have fallen flat on his face if we hadn't held him up. Some of his companions made as if to get up and follow, since a man's death is always an enticing spectacle. But our good soldiers' legs were so heavy, their stomachs so anchored to the table and the chambermaids were just now bringing such quantities of delicious wine that they changed their minds. It's no doubt true that these rogues had precious few occasions to eat and drink their fill, working as they did for miserable wages and only getting their fill on holidays.

With Miroul's help, each of us holding an arm, we managed to get the cobbler out into the back courtyard of the place, between the sinkhole and the kitchen, on the threshold of which all the kitchen help had quietly gathered on orders from the cook. At this point the cobbler couldn't take another step and his legs gave way from under him. But since, in falling, he began waving his dagger in the air, Miroul snatched it from him in a trice.

"Monsieur, where's my dagger?" said the cobbler, flexing his fingers and looking wildly at me.

"In your hand."

"Yesh," he garbled, "I shee it but I don feel it."

"That's because your hand is so heavy and the dagger's so light."

"Comrade," he continued, "how come you're not trying to shtop me from killing you?"

"So why is it, now, that you want to kill me?"

"Ah, Monsieur, I'm not happy about it. Indeed I'm thinking maybe you're not a papisht after all."

"So, why do you want me dead?"

"Because you're not from Nîmes. And who can trusht a man who'sh not from Nîmes?"

"How right you are, cobbler. So, do your duty. Strike me right in the heart, now!"

And, seizing his empty fist, I give myself a blow in the chest, and cried, "I'm killed!"

Moving quickly around behind him, I made a sign to Miroul to imitate my death, which he did a marvellous job of, his brown eye gaily glinting. After which I give the cobbler a little push from behind and he fell on his knees, feeling around on the pavement as if he were looking for our bodies, and stammering, "D-did I k-k-kill them?"

I turned to the cook, the one who never removed his toque, and whispered, believing that he'd enjoy taking part in the fun: "Friend, sprinkle some chicken's blood on his face. And on his dagger. And when you've done that, give him a goblet of brandy. That'll help him sleep for about ten hours and dream he killed us. As for you," I said to one of the kitchen boys, "here's two sols. Be a good fellow and saddle and bridle our horses and bring them round to the back door."

I was careful not to return to the dining room, where our valiant soldiers were singing a medley of bawdy songs in a horrible cacophony. Instead I passed by that room after the innkeeper closed the door, and went up to my chamber, where I found Samson biting his nails after hearing from our hostess what was going on at the banquet. I told him the rest as briefly as possible, instructing him and Miroul to arm for war, with helmet and armour.

"Where are we going?" asked Samson. "All the city gates are closed."

"To look for Captain Bouillargues, to give him our safe-conduct letters and ask him to let us leave."

"But aren't we in terrible danger if we go out now when François Pavée is looking for us?"

"Yes, but it's dark out now. Our helmets will partly conceal our faces. And fully armoured as we are—and they are—we're more likely to go unnoticed than if we wore our doublets."

Someone knocked at our door and, opening it part way, I saw that it was our hostess. Not wishing to speak with her in front of Samson, I led her to my room and quickly drew the bolt.

"Oh!" she said. "Have you heard? They haven't taken the bishop. Where's Montcalm?"

"He has fled."

"Thanks be to the Mother of God!" she said. "But," she continued tenderly, "are you leaving this minute, my noble friend? You don't risk anything by staying here. We've taken the idiot cobbler back into the dining room where he announced that he'd killed you both, and then fell asleep like a log. Must you leave right away?"

"My friend," I smiled, "I'm so sorry to have to leave you, but I must find this Bouillargues and get our safe-conduct papers."

"But you have time! It isn't dark enough yet."

"Well then, as we wait, let's talk about you. There's no point in herding sheep if you don't get some wool. Here's five écus to cover that banquet! Will that satisfy you?"

"Ah, my friend," she said, looking at me with a sidelong glance, "no money between us!"

And while she was protesting, the écus found their way into her purse without too much complaint, and as for me, I wasn't sorry to have paid for so much wine to save me from spilling my own blood. But as my fifth écu dropped into her purse, she stood silently looking at me with her eyes like moons, and I, knowing full well what she wanted, and what I desired as well, and being so happy to be alive after having come so close to *not* being so, and so unsure of remaining so after leaving her inn, wanted to enjoy this calm between two storms. However brief this paradise was to be, I wanted to enter it if only for the length of one sigh. Ah, reader, don't frown. If it's a sin to be so worldly, forgive me. Life is so sweet. Was it not marvellous to feel the warmth and vibrancy of this woman's arms when, at that very minute, I could have found myself lying cold and bloody on the cobblestones?

14

I'D HEARD TALK among my executioners around the banquet table of a huge gathering that was to take place at nine o'clock that night in front of the cathedral. I decided to go there with Samson and Miroul, reckoning that if we were ever to find Captain Bouillargues, it would be there, and we could venture out at night with a helmet on, especially in such a large crowd, without being recognized. As soon as we arrived at the cathedral, it was evident, from the babel of local Provençal dialects being spoken here, that hundreds of Huguenots from all the surrounding villages had descended on Nîmes once they'd heard the city had been taken by the reformists. I also saw that far from being despised or treated as suspicious in any way, as my cobbler would have done, these strangers were welcomed by the people of Nîmes.

There was a great feeling of happiness in the crowd, whose members were feeling avenged for the cruel persecutions that had been inflicted on them since the reign of François I. And though many were shouting, "Kill the papists! It's a new world!" I saw no movement whatsoever to spread out into the city, to break into houses and kill the papists without sparing women, girls or babies—as, alas, the papists were to do five years later to our people on that dreadful St Bartholomew's night.

We were there for about an hour, mingling among the populace, before daring to speak to anyone, but finally saw a man with a pleasant face and, according to what we overheard of his conversation, who seemed to know many important people in Nîmes, so I sent Samson over to him, since my brother was as yet entirely unknown in the city, given that he'd never left the inn.

"Greetings, young man!" said the man, staring at Samson as if he'd just met the Archangel Michael descending in glory and beauty from one of the stained-glass windows in the cathedral. And when he'd heard Samson's request, he said, "If you need Captain Bouillargues, you need only follow the platoon of Pierre Cellerier, who's leaving presently for city hall, and there you'll find the captain."

"So is this Pierre Cellerier also a captain?" asked Samson.

"Not at all. He's a jeweller and one of the richest men in Nîmes, but a severe and unbending Huguenot."

I pulled Samson by the elbow, fearing he would talk too much, and we immediately fell in behind the platoon, which was about thirty strong, and marching smartly three abreast. This Miroul, Samson and I imitated, so no one seemed surprised. It was now very dark, and as the platoon was lit by four or five torchbearers at the head of the company, we were able to remain in the shadows.

We arrived at city hall, and instead of the soldiers remaining outside as I would have expected, Pierre Cellerier ordered them to follow him, and, descending several steps, the troop found itself in front of a heavily guarded door, which the guards unlocked for us, giving us access to a large room where the papist prisoners were being held. This room was normally used as an abattoir and butchering shop, to provide meat to sick people during Lent. It was very humid with low ceilings and was unevenly paved, with a central gutter to drain away blood. As for windows there were some small openings with strips of iron across them, which is doubtless why the place had been chosen as a keep for about one hundred prisoners, mostly priests and monks of different orders, but including some merchants and a few artisans, among whom I noticed Doladille, whom Jean Vigier had wounded on the arm.

Since all of these unfortunates had been mildewing in the darkness, as soon as they saw the torchlight and the armed soldiers they backed away, cowering, dazzled and terrified, some blinking like owls in sunlight, others shading their eyes with their hands, but all shrinking as far as possible from us, for they believed we were going to slaughter them on the spot like sheep during Lent. And to tell the truth I feared the same thing, seeing the savage looks Pierre Cellerier and the others were directing at them, their eyes so full of the hatred and bitterness that had been stewed and restewed in the cauldron of persecution.

Pierre Cellerier stepped forward into the space from which the prisoners had retreated, and ordering a torchbearer to give him light, he pulled a list from his doublet and began reading some names. Cellerier was a thickset, broad-shouldered man, though not very tall. His face, lit from the side by the torch, seemed rough-hewn, furrowed by wrinkles and fairly plain. His voice, bearing and expression all suggested a butcher rather than a jeweller, much more at home in this slaughterhouse than with working delicate gems.

He began by calling the name of the first consul, Gui Rochette, whose mother had been so uncivilly questioned by Possaque earlier in the day. Gui Rochette, a handsome, well-dressed man, stepped forward courageously and with dignity, knowing full well the fate that awaited him. And he didn't flinch or say a word when two soldiers rudely seized him by the arms. However, when, after him, Cellerier called, "Robert Grégoire, lawyer," the first consul of Nîmes looked very upset and, turning his head towards the jeweller, whom, till then, he'd affected not to notice, said, "In the name of God, I beg you, Monsieur, not Grégoire. He's done nothing other than to be my brother!"

"It's enough that he's your brother," snarled Cellerier, frowning. But perhaps the cruel absurdity of his words struck him, for he added,

"In any case, the judges have decided it this way." And he repeated, "Robert Grégoire, lawyer!"

And the brother, looking very young and extremely terrified, stepped forward, and was seized by the soldiers, but less roughly, as if they were secretly astonished that he was being delivered up to their knives.

The third man called was a monk, to whom Cellerier gave his title, but in a much more derisive voice than to Grégoire. "Jean Quatrebar, Augustinian prior and ordinary preacher at the cathedral church." He gave a vengeful inflection to the way he pronounced the word "preacher", and as Quatrebar stepped forward, the soldiers hooted at him and I wondered whether in his sermons in the cathedral Quatrebar hadn't more than once damned our Huguenot brothers to the flames of hell—and, what's worse, to the flames of the stake here on earth. He walked towards the soldiers with a bullying and defiant step, his head raised, eyes aflame, and looking down at Cellerier from his height of six feet, he said in a sonorous voice,

"I thank you for offering me a martyr's death!"

The soldiers all groaned at this, but Cellerier merely raised his hand and, disdaining any reply, merely continued down his list: "Nicolas Sausset, Jacobin prior."

This was a little reed of a man, bent over and hoary with age and, either because of his age or because of his present terror, his hands, which were folded over his chest, wouldn't stop trembling. But however inoffensive he seemed, this appearance must have hidden some malice, for our soldiers all hooted at him as much as they had Quatrebar, and were hardly tender with him when they hauled him away.

Cellerier continued: "Étienne Mazoyer, canon of the cathedral church."

This time there were no hoots, but a few sniggers, which suggested that the unfortunate canon must have owed his position more to influence than to his reputation for good works. Moreover, he seemed incredibly old, dreamy and stupid, trembling with senility, and walking laboriously; and, as he advanced, having no idea what he was doing there, he said, "Are they going to free me?"

"In a sense, yes," replied Cellerier.

And however cruel this joke was, it was probably more humane than the truth, and produced but a smattering of laughter among the soldiers, which annoyed the others. However, Mazoyer, his head bobbing and still not understanding, asked again, very hesitatingly, "But where are you taking me, Monsieur?"

"To the bishop's house," replied Cellerier with a smile, which I found greatly offensive. "You'll be better off there than here! Enough talk! Let's go!"

"What about us?" cried a voice from among the remaining papists. "Are you going to call us too the next time? Are we all going to die?"

Cellerier frowned so hard that I thought he wouldn't answer. But after a moment of thought during which he appeared to be trying to decide, honesty won out over cruelty and he said in his rude voice: "I know not. The judges haven't decided yet."

"But you, neighbour?" cried another voice. "What do you think they'll decide?"

Cellerier seemed troubled and blinked, as though he knew this voice and had heard it many times, and, turning away, said over his shoulder, almost as if he were ashamed to make any charitable gesture to the papists, "I believe that you won't all die." Perhaps the cruelty of this sentence wasn't intended, but it merely shifted their fears without eliminating them.

I managed to be the last to leave this room, with Miroul and Samson, so as to remain far from the light of the torches, but there was little risk of being identified, since the soldiers had eyes and ears only for their prisoners, who, with the exception of Nicolas Sausset, displayed great courage, but occasionally as they passed through the streets looked desperately at the houses as if they hoped some last-minute help might come from that direction. Sadly for them, however, the city was dead, and not a single candle shone from the windows; all the shutters were closed and the doors barricaded since the judges had forbidden the papists to stick their noses out of doors that night so that the streets would belong entirely to the Huguenots.

Meanwhile, as we walked along with the prisoners in our midst, Quatrebar, in the sonorous voice that had resonated for years under the cathedral vaults, exhorted the other papists to have courage, repeating every minute or so, with great exaltation: "My brothers! My beloved brothers! I see the heavens opening already to take us up into God's hands!" At which the soldiers began protesting, one of them shouting indignantly, "It's hell that's opening up for you, you idolater!"

"Quiet there!" said Cellerier, turning to his troops. "Silence in the ranks! And you, preacher, preach your last sermon more quietly!"

"Why should I obey you, heretic?" shouted Quatrebar, tossing his head. "You can only kill me once."

"That once will be good enough!" replied Cellerier, his soldiers laughing their approval.

Our destination was the bishop's palace, as Cellerier had joked to Mazoyer, who was so little able to keep up with us that the soldiers were taking turns carrying him. And not the palace itself but the enclosed courtyard in front of it, which was fairly large and well paved and had, in one corner, a large well, surmounted by beautiful ironwork. On the far side stood a bell tower with four windows spaced vertically in its stonework, and on three sides the courtyard was surrounded by a solid wall with a parapet, which was reached by some stairs. On these stairs, on the parapet and in the windows of the bell tower could be seen soldiers holding torches that were flickering, which gave the eerie sense that the paving stones in the courtyard seemed to be shaking. One corner of this courtyard remained in darkness and so I hastened over to it with Samson and Miroul, fearing we might be discovered and questioned before Captain Bouillargues could get there—but we had to wait several hours for him, not daring to move all the while.

Sweat began dripping down my back, and my heart was pounding in my chest as if I myself were facing death. But, unaccustomed to the horror of death as I was, I simply couldn't believe or imagine that this courtyard, which was so beautiful, and lit up as if for a festival, could become the theatre of a horrifying butchery. But, of course, why would they have chosen this high seat of Catholicism except to make it clear to everyone that it would be the tomb of these zealots?

The soldiers—if they could indeed be called soldiers since they were really local artisans and tradesmen commanded by Huguenot merchants—didn't rush headlong into this massacre, perhaps because they weren't accustomed to spilling blood voluntarily, and perhaps, too, because they were waiting to be given the order to do so. Cellerier himself, once the prisoners had arrived at the bishop's palace, was careful to give no order and left immediately with half of his platoon to look for other "outlaws" at the city hall, leaving the other half to decide what they would do with the unfortunates who were gathered there. And I guessed that these soldiers, who had little appetite for this grisly work, would have delayed the execution even longer had not the preacher, Quatrebar, demonstrated such arrogant appetence for martyrdom. Raising himself to his full height and tossing his head, he demanded at the top of his lungs, in his cathedral voice and very insolent manner, permission to pray out loud. Despite their irritation, the soldiers told him he could, on condition that it was the Our Father and nothing else. Hearing this, Quatrebar crossed his arms over his chest and intoned an Ave Maria as if it were a war cry. They shouted and hooted at him to be quiet, but he kept on: so doggedly that they threw themselves on him and stabbed him more than a hundred times, some shouting as they went about their bloody work, "Go to hell, miserable idolater!"

At this, Nicolas Sausset threw himself on his knees and, trembling from head to toe, begged for mercy, crying that he'd never pray to the Virgin again, that he recognized his errors and that he'd convert. But his cowardice seemed to irritate the soldiers every bit as much as Quatrebar's arrogance had, and they massacred him on the spot and stabbed him and covered him with spit even more than they had the preacher.

Poor Mazoyer who, having been left to himself, had had to sit down on the paving stones in the middle of the courtyard, watched these proceedings with horror, and bleated out, "What's this? What's this?"

He was killed, as though in passing, and our troops, with great howls of hatred, threw themselves on the first consul, Gui Rochette. It took them some time to do their business, because he kept parrying their knife thrusts with his elbows, all the while pleading with them to spare his little brother. Of course, his resistance only enraged the soldiers even more, so the minute Rochette was felled, their hatred overflowed onto Robert Grégoire, whose throat was slashed furiously despite the fact that only moments before I'd heard them wondering why he was even here.

Now that they'd warmed to their murderous work and knew that Cellerier was returning with other prisoners, they didn't hesitate to dispatch the rest of their victims. Surprised, in fact, that the others hadn't yet returned, they began stripping the dead of their clothes and their rings and emptying their pockets, complaining that these had already been visited by the soldiers in the escort. As soon as this pillaging began, their mood seemed to change, and it seemed to me that, apart from a few who didn't want to touch anything that had belonged to their victims, the appetite for lucre added to their zeal.

Having stripped the dead of their clothes, I saw one of the soldiers drag the bloody corpse of Nicolas Sausset across the paving stones of the courtyard and I wondered what he intended to do when, after hoisting him onto the curb of the well—which was quite wide—he threw him into it. His example was immediately followed and it was there that the bodies of all of the unfortunates whom they killed that night ended up, as if they'd wanted to pollute for ever the clear water, which bubbled up from beneath, by this despicable use of it. I heard later that the well was virtually filled to the brim by the bodies they threw in it, and that the judges decided the next day to throw enough dirt over them to close it up permanently.

I watched this entire spectacle with feelings I can't begin to describe, my heart frozen with disgust yet my body sweating through all of its pores. What added to the horror we felt was to hear emanating from this well, which was close to the dark corner where we were hiding, the moans emitted weakly by a dying voice, which indicated that some of the victims hadn't been entirely killed and that they continued in the water and ghastly tangle of bodies their interminable agony. Driven by compassion or by the hope of maybe helping one of them—though how could I possibly help since the well was so deep?—I went to lean over the edge, which wasn't very prudent since I was in the full light of the torches, but all I could see was the mass of bodies convulsively moving about in the water, reddened by their blood. Miroul hurried to pull me away from the light, and I returned to our corner and put my arm around Samson, who was quietly crying, his face hidden in his hands. Ah! I should have done the same, so overcome was I by shame and pity. But Miroul, his own face streaming with tears, held my right hand firmly, fearing, no doubt, that I might throw myself like a madman between the assassins and their victims—as indeed I was itching to do.

Gradually, as the night wore on, I noticed that the killing became more mechanical and that the soldiers became more and more hardened to it. Most of the condemned accepted their fate with resignation and prayer at the moment they were struck down. But one of them, named Jean-Pierre, revolted suddenly, and cried that he was only the music master at the cathedral, that he'd never said or done anything against our people, and that he didn't deserve to die! Hearing him, the soldiers laughed uproariously and joked cruelly that he would die because his music was papist. And as Jean-Pierre escaped from their grasp and ran like a madman around the walls, they pursued him shouting, "You run pretty well for a musician!" and when they finally caught him and began stabbing him they said with each blow, "And what do you think of this little note?" And when, in agony, Jean-Pierre screamed, "I'm dead. I can't bear any more!" one of the soldiers laughed and said in Provençal, "You're going all the way to the well!" and, pushing him there, didn't kill him until he'd reached it.

What added to the villainy of the business was that, living in the same city, some even neighbours of each other, murderers and victims often knew each other well, so that, in addition to the zeal and desire for lucre, there were also many old scores being settled here. That became evident in the execution of Doladille, the silk worker whom Jean Vigier had wounded with his sword and who was brought all bloody to the bishop's palace. When he was brought in, there was a torrent of hoots and insults from all sides, since Doladille was, it seemed, a well-known profligate who had, in the words of Vigier, cuckolded more than one of our partisans, parading around town boasting of having something in his pants that could convert all the Huguenot ladies in Nîmes. He was not executed right away, but made to suffer excessively, accompanied by horrible comments and mutilations, before finding his repose in death.

However, after Doladille, there were no more such horrifying outbursts of pleasure, and the executions settled down to a kind of mournful, mechanical routine. Moreover, as day began to dawn, the soldiers slowed down and displayed more repugnance in their sinister work, as if, gorged with so much blood, disgust overcame them—or fatigue, or perhaps a sense of the awful absurdity of these murders.

Just as dawn was breaking, something happened that struck me powerfully, because it restored a little bit of my faith in humankind, whom I'd come to despise so terribly during the night. To witness what I'm about to recount was like a breath of pure air, and convinced me that there are fewer evil men than there are evil thoughts, including this one, which is the worst of all: that nothing is evil which serves the advancement of the true religion. But it's enough for this terrible idea, the cause of all our evils, to subside somewhat for the seeds of goodness to be rediscovered in the hearts of almost all men; like sparks of fire on a flintstone, it takes very little to produce them.

Among the executioners, I'd observed a rascal of about twenty, fairly strong and well built, who, as far as I could tell by the light of the torches, didn't have such a bad face, seemed to kill more out of duty than out of a taste for it, and never insulted his victims, or stripped them, leaving his part of the pillaging to those who enjoyed it. Now it happened that, exhausted from his night's work, this fellow came over and leant against the wall next to us, his bloody sword in his hand, saying with a sigh, "Ah, my mates. We kill and we go on killing! Is this our gospel, then?"

To which, all prudence deserting me, despite the fact that Miroul was squeezing my hand very hard, I couldn't help saying, "Assuredly not."

The rascal turned to get a better look at me, as though surprised by my answer, which, however, he should have expected since it was implied by his question. "So, you didn't kill anyone?" he said finally.

"Not a one," I replied. "We came here for another matter altogether. We're waiting for Captain Bouillargues."

"Ah, my friend, you may count it as a certainty that he's not coming... That fox is too sly to get blood on its paws! And where he is I can tell you—or better yet I can show you as soon as this vile work is done."

I thanked him profusely, and after a few moments, during which he sighed repeatedly, he said, "My name's Anicet, I'm twenty years old and I'm a weaver. And I'd much rather have laboured the night through at my loom than to have killed so many of my fellow men— with the exception of Gui Rochette and Quatrebar, who spew fire and flames against us. But Robert Grégoire was a very quiet sort of papist! Did we have to kill him because he was Rochette's brother?"

"Anicet," I said, "and why even Rochette and Quatrebar? Do we have to kill every papist who calls for our execution?"

"Truly I know not, my friend. Our leaders claim that we have to inherit Nîmes from the papists or the papists will inherit it from us... and that we'll have to kill them before they kill us."

"Ah!" I said. "I don't like this word 'inherit'. It sounds too much like profit and looting."

"My friend," said Anicet, "you're right. You saw here the shameful stripping and picking of pockets that went on. Is that what Calvin preaches?"

As he was speaking, two soldiers, one carrying him by the head, the other by the feet, brought in a lad who couldn't have been more than twenty, and who had a large wound in his left thigh. They threw him down roughly on the paving stones near us, which caused him to groan in pain. But taking no notice, the two soldiers, with terrible curses, began undressing him, having no doubt decided that this was more easily done while he was alive than after they'd dispatched him. Meanwhile, as they were trying to pull off one sleeve of his doublet, the unfortunate boy turned his face towards us, and the torches bathed it in light.

"By the belly of St Anthony!" Anicet cried suddenly in a troubled voice. "I'm not going to tolerate this!" And marching over to them with his sword drawn he yelled, "You there! Stop that! I know this rascal. He's named Pierre Journet. He's a little cleric at the bishop's palace, not even tonsured yet, and he's never done anything against us!"

"No matter," said one of the executioners, "he was found hiding with the bishop in the house of the councillor of Sauvignargues. Robert Aymée wounded him in the leg with a pike and told us to bring him here to be killed with the others."

"What?" cried Anicet. "That idiot Aymée is giving us orders now? No one but the judges or Captain Bouillargues has that right!"

"I don't care if he's got the right or not," said the second soldier. "This rascal is ours 'cause we carried him here. And I'm taking his doublet!"

"I'm taking the rest," said the other.

"By my faith," cried Anicet, pointing his sword at them, "that's pillaging and thievery, and not zeal! Leave the rascal his clothes, mates, and give him back his life or I'll take yours."

At this the two soldiers stood gaping at the lad, then looked at each other silently. Then one, leaning over to the other, whispered something, and the other nodded. Suddenly, they drew their swords, which they'd just sheathed in order to strip Pierre Journet.

"'Sblood!" cried one. "There are two of us! And you're alone! Are you going to try to stop us, friend?"

I tore myself out of Miroul's grasp and, unsheathing my weapon, leapt to Anicet's side in a trice.

"Who's he?" said the soldier.

"The judge of this dispute," I replied. And catching his sword in mine, with a sudden movement of my wrist I flipped it about ten paces away—which wasn't really much of an exploit given the way he was holding it. I then placed the point of my sword on his throat. "And here's my verdict. You're going to carry Pierre Journet to the house where Captain Bouillargues is staying. He'll be the one to decide this case."

"What! Carry him some more?" cried the soldier who had confronted Anicet, mine remaining as mute as a stone.

"Perhaps this will help you decide what to do," I said, seizing the pistol that was hanging from the left side of my belt and aiming it at him.

The man resheathed his sword without further discussion, and prepared to pick up this burden that he now so reviled, since he was no longer sure to get any profit from it. The strangest thing about this controversy was that the other executioners, who had been watching it unfold, simply stood by in silence, as if dazed with fatigue, and seemed almost unable to understand what it was about and unwilling to intervene. One might almost have said that the business no longer concerned them, and that they were now only killing out of some force of habit that had taken hold of them during the night.

We found Captain Bouillargues in his house, armed for war, but, from what I could tell, little inclined to stick his nose out of his burrow, too smart to be seen at the bishop's palace, knowing all too well what was going on there, since it was he and the judges who'd ordered it. He was a big man, heavy and fat, looking like a bear in every aspect but his face, which was definitely more fox than bear, with cunning little eyes and a mobile and ferrety nose, as if designed to sniff out traps before sticking his paw into them. Clearly he was not the kind of thief to raid a chicken coop openly or to participate in looting the house of a papist who'd fled, as François Pavée had done in Montcalm's lodgings! On the other hand, I'd heard from Dame Étienne André herself that she secretly paid 1,000 livres to Bouillargues (in whom everything was false, including his name, which was, in reality, Pierre Suau) to spare the life of her husband, whom he'd had arrested. And long after the "Michelade" was over (which is what this massacre came to be called since it was the day after Michaelmas), I learnt that Bouillargues received ransom money from many people that night and that he operated an open market on the sale of lives of people he had the power to dispatch or save, enriching himself with anonymous monies, and not, like François Pavée and other imprudent fools, with booty whose origins could later be identified.

I wanted to penetrate this lair, where the blood of other people was being trafficked, and left Pierre Journet in the street, groaning but not *in extremis*, in the company of Anicet and the two soldiers, who looked quite crestfallen and were beginning to regret that they were there. Miroul and Samson, whom I didn't want to get mixed up in this business, since I couldn't foresee how things might turn out, had remained behind at the bishop's palace to await my return.

I found Bouillargues surrounded by emissaries, whom he was dispatching every minute or so to various corners of Nîmes, and guarded by four or five secretaries whose palms I had to grease in order to get an audience with him. Even then he received me with crafty reserve, asking who I was and whether I was the kind of fowl that could be plucked, and was clearly ready to up the ante if I was there to try to ransom a friend. I managed to remain calm, without a trace of insolence or brashness, while maintaining the air of someone who's not going to be browbeaten. I told him my name, where I was from and whose son I was, and gave him first the letter from Cossolat that was addressed to him, and, when he'd read that, the letter from Monsieur de Chambrun. The first appeared to impress him more than the second. Seeing that I was under the protection of both Cossolat and Monsieur de Joyeuse (who, even though he was a papist, was someone to be reckoned with), he immediately changed his tone, his countenance and his behaviour, and very politely bade me be seated and asked what had caused my quarrel with François Pavée, looking very distressed upon hearing that Pavée had been usurping his prerogatives by ordering someone to be killed without obtaining his permission. In the heat of his anger, he dictated a letter for Pavée to a secretary, and had it delivered on the spot. This done, he wrote my name, and those of Samson and Miroul, on safe-conduct papers he took from a stack on his table, no doubt prepared in advance to exact money from various papists. When he'd signed them, and I'd placed them with enormous relief in the pocket of my doublet, I told him, without naming him, the story of the little cleric whom Anicet and I had saved from the talons of the vultures at the bishop's palace, and invited him to step out in the street for a moment to adjudicate on the issue. Shrugging his powerful shoulders in a way that showed of what little consequence he considered this matter, and that he only consented to do this as a favour to me, Bouillargues rose and, swaying like a bear, but with a surprising degree of agility, opened the door onto the street. Scarcely had he caught sight of the little cleric, however, when he roared, "Good God, it's you, my little Pierre! Who has done this to you? Who wounded you? Justice will be done! Was it these two?" he added, looking at the two soldiers and seizing his dagger.

"No, no!" I broke in. "It was Robert Aymée."

"Aymée! Well, not very aymée-able at all!" cried Bouillargues. "'Sblood, I'll cut his liver out. Everyone in Nîmes knows that Pierre Journet was raised by my wet nurse and is very dear to me! You rogues, carry Pierre inside and put him gently on my bed. And you," he said, turning to a major-domo who had followed him outside, "send for Domanil, the surgeon; fly like an arrow or I'll have your neck! Monsieur de Siorac," he continued, real tears streaming down his cheeks (seeing which, I could hardly believe my eyes) and giving me an enormous hug, "I'll remember your name if I live to be a hundred."

At this point, he looked over at Anicet and, seeing that he was as poor as Job, wanted to give him an écu, but Anicet refused, saying that he'd merely acted out of compassion. Meanwhile, the two soldiers, now silent, eyes lowered and looking very crestfallen, carried Pierre Journet in and placed him on Bouillargues's bed with as much tender care as they'd previously used cruelty, when, an hour before, they'd thrown him on the paving stones in the courtyard of the bishop's palace. This done, they tried to become as invisible as possible, and left very happily with us, fearing that Bouillargues might still turn the anger on them that, half crying, half roaring, he continued to vent on Robert Aymée. I left Bouillargues after many more expressions of gratitude on his part, and thought how surprising it was that this fox had something resembling a heart after all, even though it seemed to beat only for members of his family, and not for other men, who, by and large, seemed to be rejected outside the community of mankind.

Scarcely had I left his house, however, when, changing my mind, I retraced my steps and found Bouillargues sitting by the bed of the wounded man. I took him aside and whispered, "Captain, I've heard they've arrested Bernard d'Elbène, the bishop of Nîmes. Are they going to kill him too? Haven't we had enough bloodshed?"

Bouillargues lowered his eyes, and said, feigning compassion for the bishop, "For my part, I didn't order him to be dispatched, and I would a thousand times have preferred to hold him hostage and demand a ransom." (This was no doubt true.) "But I don't know what the judges have decided."

"Pardon my curiosity, Captain," I said quietly, "but who are these judges I've heard so much about here?"

"Ah, Monsieur de Siorac, who knows?" replied Bouillargues, squinting at me with the air of a man who knew full well. Whereupon, he gave me a bear hug, thanked me again profusely and, giving me a pat on the back, withdrew.

You can imagine that I wasn't happy to be returning to the courtyard of the bishop's palace, if only to fetch Samson and Miroul, for my imagination was full of the torches, the pavement shining with blood, the screams, the bodies that were despoiled and the well where they threw all those bodies in a tangled mess—horrible scenes that I wished never to have witnessed.

As I walked along, full of these sad thoughts, one of the soldiers who had almost killed Pierre Journet tugged at my sleeve and thanked me for having said that it was Robert Aymée who had wounded the boy. I answered that I didn't want Bouillargues to stab him right then and there, or his friend, but that if they really wanted to express their gratitude, they'd stop the killing and both return to their lodgings. He promised me they would, but excused himself for having to accompany me back to the bishop's palace since they had hidden their loot and didn't want to lose it as they were both tanners and had been out of work for six months and hoped to sell the clothes they'd taken from the papists to buy a bit of bread for their children, who were now thin as cartwheel spokes having had so little to eat for so long. I asked Guillaume (the other soldier was named Louis, but was as quiet as a carp), if there was any money in their loot.

"Alas, no, Monsieur, not a sol. The soldiers who took them to city hall pocketed everything including their rings and jewels, and left us nothing but their clothes."

Hearing this, and touched by what they'd told me about their children, convinced they'd only acted on the orders given them, and moved by the bitter necessity that beset them, I gave each of them an écu, which they accepted, the one silent as ever but face crimson with joy, the other with infinite thanks. As for the latter, Guillaume was as expressive as a puppy, jumping up and down, hugging me and swearing himself at my service should I ever require it. And, seeing that Anicet was feeling a bit out of joint at seeing me being so lavish with our former enemies, I also gave him an écu, which at first he refused, but which he ended up accepting at my insistence, assuring me with some pride that he wasn't out of work and lived by honest means, even if humbly so.

Morning had broken, and the sun was just coming out over the houses, when we reached an intersection that had a well at its centre, called the Well of the Great Table, as I learnt from Guillaume. At the corner, we joined up with a larger platoon, which was guarding a group of three or four papists whom they were taking to the bishop's palace, and these soldiers were very exercised, shouting, "Kill the papists! It's a new world!" which had been the slogan of the previous night.

Anicet suddenly cried, "But that's the bishop, Bernard d'Elbène! And next to him is his major-domo, Maître de Sainte-Sophie!"

As he said this, the large swarthy devil that was commanding the group called a halt, and walked over to the major-domo, a pike in his hand, and cried furiously, "Ah, you scoundrel! You've got fat enough on our money! This will help you lose some of that blubber!" And saying this, with a furious blow, he thrust his pike into the man's stomach, pulled it out and plunged it in again. Seeing this, some of the soldiers set upon the major-domo and began stabbing him, some with daggers, some with swords, so quickly and thoroughly that he hardly had time to moan. He fell, and as he lay in agony on the paving stones, they kept stabbing him.

Some of these, whose bloodlust hadn't yet been satisfied, cried that they should immediately dispatch the bishop! Others protested, saying that they'd received no order to execute him. The bloodthirsty ones, however, couldn't get close enough to the bishop to strike him because others of the soldiers were pressing around him, trying to pull his rings from his fingers.

"Guillaume," I whispered, "who's that tall scoundrel who just killed the major-domo?"

"Robert Aymée."

"What? The one who wounded Pierre Journet?"

"The same!"

Stepping right up to this fellow, I grabbed him by the elbow and said, "Monsieur, I'd like a word with you, if you please. Captain Bouillargues is very distraught and angry with you because when you were at the councillor of Sauvignargues's house you wounded his little 'brother' Pierre Journet. He's so furious about this he's sworn to cut your liver out when he catches up with you."

"What?" gasped Aymée. "The shitty little curate I found this morning with the bishop—"

"Was his protégé."

"But I didn't know that!" cried Aymée, looking very abashed and crestfallen.

"Ah, my friend," I said, searching for the best way to dress up the truth to make it sound as threatening as possible, "the captain thinks that you did know it, and that you did it to spite him! Monsieur Aymée, if I were you I'd go right over to Bouillargues's lodgings to clear this up. He's spitting such fire and brimstone against you it makes a body shudder to hear it."

"I'll go there right away!" said Robert Aymée.

And, calling to his platoon, he said, "Hey there, mates, you don't need me to put the bishop in the palace and drown him in his well!"

And, having launched this ugly pleasantry, by which he tried to hide his terror, he walked off with great strides, without even asking my name, and, as far as I could tell, in a direction diametrically opposite the one that led to Bouillargues's house. I was fairly certain that this Aymée character, as cowardly as he was cruel, was heading home to hide under his bed until Pierre Journet had recovered! Which he did eventually, though he would first spend two months very near death.

Meanwhile, the platoon, without Robert Aymée, continued on to the bishop's palace, and we followed it, Anicet on my right and Guillaume and Louis on my left, and all three intent on letting me know that they felt that it would be a pity to kill the bishop, who, they insisted, was not a bad man, indeed far from it, as he spent the lion's share of his money on charity, lived simply in his palace, ate little and drank less; moreover, they claimed, no one had ever heard him preaching against the Huguenots as Quatrebar and Sausset and certain papist merchants of Nîmes had done, even more zealously than the priests. Their sense was that he was straightforward, good and very welcoming to the artisans and poor of the city. All three felt that the Huguenots could find common ground with him, had it not been for the episcopal court surrounding him, who howled constantly at our heels like a pack of hungry wolves.

Some of the most fanatical of our soldiers had stripped the bishop to his doublet and, to humiliate him, had placed on his head a silly bonnet with lots of ribbon, while others, as we walked along, made cruel jokes about the fate that awaited him. Bernard d'Elbène bore all of this without a murmur, and without any of the defiance that Quatrebar had displayed. He was praying quietly, perhaps not wishing to offend his captors by intoning the Ave Maria; at the same time, without lowering his eyes, he looked at those who were leading him to his Calvary with neither hatred nor resentment, as if he had already pardoned them. His fortitude and his meekness so impressed the most zealous of his captors that they ceased their mockery and threats—all except one man named Simon, of whom I'll say more later. The bishop was of medium height, had a pale complexion, white hair and hands that trembled, but it was clear that this was not from fear but from old age.

As soon as we entered the courtyard of the bishop's palace, Bernard d'Elbène, seeing from the oceans of blood the butchery that had taken place there, threw himself on his knees, and with loud sighs and tears streaming from his eyes began to pray for the salvation of the souls of the martyred. The score of soldiers gathered there, sensing that this great grief was not for himself but for others, immediately began to feel some shame. Moreover, exhausted by the terrible fatigue of their bloody night, they allowed the bishop to pray much longer than they'd permitted anyone else to do. But finally, one among them, growing impatient, approached Bernard d'Elbène and snarled, bloody sword in hand, yet not daring to touch him, "Enough praying! Take off your doublet, Bishop, I don't want to ruin it when I kill you."

At which, the bishop, without batting an eyelid and with perfect composure, removed his doublet and, hesitating for a moment as to whether to lay it on the pavement, not wishing to stain it with the blood that was there, handed it to his executioner, saying gently, "Here, my son. I hope you can make good use of it, though it's a bit threadbare."

The soldier blushed at the idea that the loot was being offered to him by his victim rather than being stolen by him; that this was witnessed by everyone present, which caused some laughter, and that the doublet was threadbare caused him great embarrassment. He stood there with the doublet in one hand and his sword in the other, unable to decide whether or not to strike the man, which seemed greatly to irritate one of the most rabid of his companions, a sort of gnome with a loud mouth, who had spent the entire time during their march lambasting the bishop with ugly lampoons and insults. "Hey, Martin," he called with a hectoring tone, "you idiot! Are you a man or a woman sitting at your loom? Kill him! If you don't have the balls, I still have enough appetite to kill a bishop!"

And, raising his dagger, he would have killed the bishop on the spot, if a young lad who had a good face and a gentle manner hadn't leapt in front of him and pointed his pistol and sword at his chest. "No!" cried this fellow stubbornly. "You're not going to kill him! I'm offering him his life! And no one here's going to take it from him except at the price of his own!"

"What, Coussinal," cried Simon. "What's happened to you? You're defending a papist bishop against your own Huguenot brothers?"

"I don't give a damn whether he's a papist or not," replied Coussinal. "He sheltered my mother, for an entire winter, against famine and cold. And since he saved her life, I'm saving his!"

"Ah, bloody hell! What a pretty story!" cried Simon in the most venomous tone. "I think I'm going to cry! Mates, do you hear this sheep bleating? His mother! 'Sblood! What's this bastard's mother to us? Friends, who was the head of the papists in Nîmes? The bishop! Are we going to kill all the soldiers and then pardon the general? Mates, what's Coussinal up to here if it's not treason? Nothing less than treason! This shitty little Coussinal is just a Huguenot in the pay of the bishop! Friends, have at 'em! Kill them both! Let's off the bishop and this rogue Coussinal with him!"

"We'll see," said Coussinal, who wasn't as eloquent as Simon, but whose eyes were blazing and who, standing in front of the bishop, was leaning into his adversary, his pistol in one hand and his sword in the other.

It seemed to me there were but a dozen or so soldiers who were backing Simon, while the rest seemed to have no more appetite either for killing the bishop or for defending him. Nevertheless, among the former, there was one fellow who had an arquebus, and seeing him strike his flint to light his fuse, I sensed that things were taking a bad turn for Coussinal. Whispering to my companions that they might have to back me up if necessary, I stepped forward, a pistol in each hand, and said to the arquebusier, "Put out your fuse, my friend! Or I'll turn your helmet into a sieve!"

This fellow, who doubtless had acquired some reputation in Nîmes as a marksman, laughed and shouldered his weapon, but in the instant he took aim at me, I fired and, as promised, I put a hole in his helmet, the bullet hitting it with such force that it was ripped from his head, and the poor wretch, thinking he was dead, dropped his weapon and fuse, and seized his head in both hands as if he'd been wounded.

"All right, friend, no need to scowl!" I cried. "You're not hurt. Stamp out your fuse! Your skull isn't as hard as your helmet, and see what I did to the helmet!"

"But who is this man?" cried Simon, crimson with surprise and anger. "Where'd he come from?"

"Simon," I said, "I've just been to see Captain Bouillargues, who told me, I swear this on my salvation, that he had no orders from the judges to kill the bishop and that he doesn't know what they've decided to do with him."

"What?" cried Simon. "Are we going to have to wait all day for their decision? A bishop is a bishop! Robert Aymée ordered us to kill the man! That's enough for me! Come on, mates, there are only two of them! Two traitors bought by the papists! Let's rush them! Kill! Kill the traitors!"

I wheeled around and shouted: "Over here, my lads!" In the blink of an eye, not only Samson and Miroul, but Anicet, Guillaume and Louis were at my side, swords in hand, and surrounding the bishop.

"Monseigneur," I said to Bernard d'Elbène, who throughout the preceding ruckus had remained on his knees in prayer, as peacefully as if he'd been in his chapel, "rise! We're going to get you to a safe place, if we can."

While I was speaking, Simon was screaming loud enough to crack his ribs. And his cries had brought about ten comrades to his side, but none seemed very resolute, nor inclined to precipitate an attack, fearing our firearms. And while Simon was harassing us with his screams and insults, Anicet and Coussinal had quietly consulted with each other on how best to protect the bishop from these fanatics, and the bishop, overhearing them, said that the most secure place would be the house of Jacques de Rochemaure, a lieutenant in the seneschalty, because he had a secret door in his house that communicated with the chateau, where he still had a garrison.

"Let's head that way without delay," I said. "Anicet will walk in front, with Guillaume and Louis, and the rest of us, who have pistols, will serve as rearguard."

"Monsieur," whispered Guillaume in my ear, "would it be all right if I go to fetch my loot before we leave?"

"*Aviat*, Guillaume! *Aviat!*"

He was back in a trice, carrying his loot under one arm and Louis's under the other, which together made a fairly large pile of clothes, though they were bloodstained, I noticed with some disgust. All this time, Simon, the gnome, had been screaming his ear-splitting imprecations, hatred gushing from his eyes and venom from his lips. My father was right when he said, after the fighting in la Lendrevie, which was my first combat, that it's always the most nefarious who incite people to mutiny, for they breathe in blood, exhale war and snort massacres. And ultimately, in the same way that wind starts the wings of a windmill moving, they incite others to murder and mayhem. I resolved to stifle this pestilent wind, and, taking one of Miroul's pistols, since I only had one still loaded, I shouted, loudly enough to cover his voice:

"Simon, I forbid you to follow us! If you violate this order, my first ball will pierce your helmet and the second your skull!"

After that, he yelled some more, but made no effort whatsoever to follow us.

Seeing this, his henchmen didn't move either, being worn out from their night of bloodshed and each one thinking only of getting back to his lodgings to eat a morsel, count his loot and, finally, to sleep. Which is, no doubt, also the reason that the streets we traversed to bring the bishop to Rochemaure's lodgings were strangely deserted, despite the rising sun. The papists remained barricaded behind their walls, and the Huguenots had all gone home, glutted and exhausted from their sad exploits.

Jacques de Rochemaure's door was heavily reinforced by iron bands, but there was a peephole in the upper part (also protected by an iron grid), which opened when we knocked. Monsieur de Rochemaure, seeing us armed, hesitated, and when the bishop saw this, he stepped forward and explained that we had saved him from the hands of his executioners and asked that we be admitted. But Rochemaure refused, fearing a trick and that the bishop was being forced to speak.

He asked us to withdraw to the end of the street, about fifty paces away, and to leave the bishop alone, and on this condition he'd open the door. Bernard d'Elbène took his leave of us in the most touching way, asking each of us our names, thanking each of us and assuring us that he would never fail to remember us in his morning and evening prayers, reminding us that we worshiped the same God, despite the fact that it often did not appear to be true. We left him, and waited at the end of the street until the door had opened and closed behind this holy man, who, as he entered this sanctuary, waved us a fond farewell.

The Michelade massacre came to an end with the failed execution of the bishop, as if the Huguenot judges (who had not ordered it, but wouldn't have been sorry if it had happened) had been surprised that the mutineers had, in this case, mutinied against them.

The judges released, in exchange for huge ransom monies, the rest of the prisoners in the city hall dungeon, who numbered about forty, roughly sixty having perished at the bishop's palace. And, after negotiations on 2nd October with the seneschal, Honoré de Grille, who still held the chateau, they allowed Bernard d'Elbène to leave the city under escort. The bishop withdrew to Tarascon, and there, he willed some lands he owned near Nîmes to the only one of his entourage to have survived, Jean Fardeau. And since he could no longer write, given the extreme weakness of his hands, he dictated a letter to the Vicomte de Joyeuse, in which he recounted in the most glowing terms the role I had played in his rescue. And when this letter was read, reread and published in Montpellier, I was suddenly rehabilitated in that city, and honoured as greatly as I'd previously been execrated, and both for the same reason, as I had done for the bishop nothing other than what I had done for Cabassus.

For my part, I believe that the greatest merit in this entire business was shown by Coussinal, who dared, with such marvellous courage, to confront, all by himself, a score of armed and angry men. I probably wouldn't have acted if Coussinal hadn't provided the example he did, moved as he was by compassion for this old man who demonstrated so much humanity in his last moments.

The three of us left Nîmes without further entanglements, exiting the city by the Carmes gate, and set off on the road named (God knows why) "five lives", which led to Beaucaire.

There we planned to cross the Rhône in order to get to Tarascon, and from Tarascon to reach the Château de Barbentane, where the innkeeper had told us Monsieur de Montcalm, his wife and his daughter had fled when they'd escaped from Nîmes. Since I didn't yet know of the reversal of my fortunes in Montpellier, I thought I should obey Monsieur de Joyeuse's orders to reside with Montcalm, wherever he was, while I waited for permission to return.

My head was full of sad thoughts as we rode along, troubled as I was that it was the Huguenots who had committed the massacre this time, accustomed as we were, ever since Vassy, to be the victims of the papists rather than their executioners. I thought of what Socrates had said on his deathbed: "better to submit to injustice rather than commit it", and decided he must be right, so heavy was my heart after witnessing the murders in the courtyard of the bishop's palace. At the same time, I found myself trying to justify their behaviour by the persecutions they'd endured before. Alas, my defence of them would have been much stronger if I'd been able to foretell what the papists would perpetrate on our people during the St Bartholomew's night massacre—a butchery ordered by the king of France in his Louvre and not by a group of petty tyrants in Nîmes.

I shall not pursue this moral dilemma any further, since I cannot help being a party to the dispute while trying to judge it fairly. And it seems to me as I reread this that I'm making too many excuses for the reformists. In truth there is no excuse: blood does not excuse blood.

During the first day of our trip we made about six leagues. It's true that the road was neither hilly, winding, nor uneasy. By evening, we'd reached Beaucaire, where we spent the night. But according to what we heard at the inn, the more mountainous region ahead, full of hills and dales and woods, had recently been taken over by highway robbers, who killed their victims and stripped them of everything they had. I thus resolved to set out at daybreak, hoping to reach the safety of Barbentane before dark. We made a forced march throughout the day, but I was quite dismayed to discover as we arrived at the chateau that our hosts were not there. Their major-domo, who had been notified by a rider of their flight from Nîmes, had been waiting for them in vain since the previous night, but he'd hesitated to set out to look for them since he was responsible for guarding the chateau, and because the bandits were so close by. His name was Antonio, and this small, dark-haired and twisted fellow seemed very attached to his masters. After having discussed the situation with him, I resolved to set out immediately to look for the Montcalms, leaving only our packhorse in Antonio's care.

It was about two in the afternoon when, after having rested and fed our horses, we set out again, but only at a slow trot, as much to spare our horses as to scour the underbrush on both sides of the road through the la Montagnette woods for any sign of our friends.

We went from one end to the other of these woods without meeting anyone. At the far edge of the forest, there was an abbey that looked more like a fortress, with very thick walls. I galloped up to the gate and rang the bell, until the peephole opened and a monk, looking out at me with cold distrust, told me rudely that the abbey did not take in travellers, but that there was a good inn in Barbentane.

"My brother," I replied, "I don't need shelter. I'm staying at the chateau. I'm looking for Monsieur de Montcalm, who was supposed to have arrived there by now but hasn't appeared."

"What?" cried the monk, now very alarmed. "He's not there? But we saw him last evening, as it was getting dark, with Madame de Montcalm and his daughter! They asked us for some wine and then left immediately. They must have fallen into the hands of the bandits who infest the la Montagnette woods that you just passed through. Monsieur, please wait a moment. I'm going to tell the prior."

The delay was extremely aggravating, and all the more so since the prior, a sharp-eyed man with enormous eyebrows, took me into a little vaulted room with a portcullis, and, attended by two armed monks, asked me endless questions. "By the belly of St Anthony," I thought, "what interrogators these monks and these ministers are!" Furious at all the time we'd wasted, I cut the confession short and showed the prior the letters from Monsieur de Joyeuse and Monsieur de Montcalm. It was an immediate open sesame!

"Ah, Monsieur," said the prior, "now I believe you and I fear the worst. If the Montcalm family has fallen into the hands of those scoundrels, it's going to be no little matter to rescue them. There are at least twelve of these desperadoes. There are only three of you. They know these woods extremely well. You'll be like lost children in there. I'm going to give you Father Anselm and three of our brothers, both to guide you and to fight alongside you. There will be blood. These miscreants always ask for a ransom, but the minute they've got it, they murder the hostages and the messenger."

Once we were on horseback, I took a good look at the monks the prior had sent to help rescue our friends and, to my great relief, I found nothing sanctimonious or canting about them. As far as I could tell, they'd slipped on a coat of mail under their cassocks, and wore large swords at their sides and on their backs round shields with a point in the centre that allowed them to be used as a weapon as well as a defence. But the best thing of all was that they carried crossbows that looked to be as old as the abbey itself, but which were well oiled and greased.

I rode up beside Father Anselm and looked at him out of the corner of my eye, trying to gauge him. He was round, but not soft; indeed his girth announced a good deal of strength, and his black hair was clipped as close as a field after harvest. He had a large nose, a prominent chin, and cheeks tanned dark by the sun: a master monk, more accustomed to the hunt than the reciting of paternosters all day long, and not a grain of hypocrisy in him, it seemed.

"Monsieur," said Father Anselm, turning his large head in my direction and speaking with the jocular air of a peasant, "have you been studying me? Do I meet with your approval?"

"Indeed so!" I said, smiling.

"I'm glad! It's mutual."

"And yet I'm a Huguenot."

"What do I care? Whoever fights with me doesn't require a note of confession. Especially since you're helping us defend our abbey!"

"How so?"

"My son," replied Father Anselm with a humorous look in his brown eyes, "if Monsieur de Montcalm is killed, then these scoundrels will take his chateau, and if the chateau is taken, who will dislodge them? Especially in this time of civil wars when the king's subjects are so concerned with cutting each other's throats. Listen! If the chateau is in their hands, the village of Barbentane will be too. So, from the other side of the woods, they'll storm the abbey, take it and pillage it."

"Nicely reasoned," I laughed, "and even though my aim is to save Montcalm, you won't find me sorry to take this opportunity to be a good Catholic!"

The master monk burst out laughing at this, being of a naturally playful temperament, even when we were on the verge of battle.

"Father Anselm," I said, "you've got a good sword and shield. But wouldn't you like one of our pistols for fighting at a distance?"

"Thank you, no! We've got our crossbows and think they're better than firearms."

I liked this monk, and would have continued our conversation, but he made a sign for me to be quiet. Leaving the trail, he plunged into the underbrush, with me at his heels, and the others at mine. And indeed, listening very carefully, I heard, at some distance, along the path we'd been following, the faint sound of hoof beats. After a moment, with his hand still raised, Father Anselm said, leaving me amazed by his sharp hunter's hearing, "There are three of them and one of the three is Antonio. I recognize his mare's hoof beats."

And it was indeed Antonio, followed by two swarthy valets, armed to the teeth, and who appeared as resolute to fight it out with the bandits as their major-domo, who, thin and bent though he might be, looked like no minor adversary, to judge by the fire in his eyes. For he was furious that the bandits had carried off his master from under his nose, on the very grounds of his chateau, which they'd been infesting for the last month like lice in a tramp's hair, stealing, murdering and openly committing various other crimes. He explained that, just an hour earlier, one of these rogues had shouted up to him, from the other side of their moat, that he was to bring 1,000 écus to a camp at the foot of the Mont de la Mère if he didn't want to see Montcalm's head delivered on a stake at sundown.

"Have you got the ransom, Antonio?" asked Father Anselm.

"I have."

"And you're going to bring it to their camp?"

"I am."

"But that's madness! They'll ambush you! As soon as you appear, they'll kill you, take your money and kill your masters. Dismount, Antonio, and come back with us away from the trail."

He did as ordered, and with our horses tied to the nearby branches, we sat down in a circle on some logs that the foresters had left there.

"We'll have to ambush their ambush," said Father Anselm, and, putting his elbows on his knees, he rested his head in his hands. He remained quietly thinking in this position for some time—so long in fact, that finally I asked:

"So what are we waiting for?"

"My son," he replied without moving a muscle, "when you go hunting, you need to be patient. These rascals must have placed a spy who would have seen Antonio and his valets leaving the chateau. So they'll be waiting for them on the path to the Mont de la Mère. Let them wait a while. Nothing confuses an ambush more than a long wait. We'll surprise them at sundown."

But for us the wait was pretty long as well, though we amused ourselves by watching Miroul throw his knife at a tree, a trick he excelled at, having learnt it from Espoumel. But Miroul got tired and sat down, and no one felt like talking, so we just sat there quietly looking at the ground, each of us reluctant to share his emotions with the others. For there was every reason to think that the battle would be very bitter against these desperate rogues and that more than one of us might be wounded or left dead on the field.

As for me, I prayed to the Lord that if I were to appear before him this day, that He would forgive my sins, especially my sins of the flesh, for I didn't think I was particularly sinful in other ways. And once my prayers were done, I began remembering the wenches I'd known who'd been so sweet to me, but couldn't face thinking about Fontanette since that wound was so fresh.

And so I recalled my most pleasant memories of the sweet maids who, I realized, had been the guarantee of beauty and benevolence in my life, which, deprived of their presence, would have been such an arid path. And though I realized how worldly my musings were compared to the monks', I gleaned a comforting warmth from them, and felt bathed in this warmth as if I were back in Barberine's lap. But alas, that didn't last. For as hard as I tried to avoid the memory of Fontanette, she burst suddenly into my mind and with such force and such anguish that I had to get up from the log and, turning away from my mates, walk into the underbrush with tears rolling down my cheeks.

After a moment, I heard a step behind me, and thought at first it was my beloved Samson, but when I turned around I beheld Father Anselm.

"My son," he said in a grave voice, "you seem very troubled in your conscience. I know, of course, that you and the reformists reject confession, but if, without any of the apparatus—the prayers and absolution that accompany confession—you'd like to tell me, now that we're in the teeth of this great peril, what is so tormenting you, you might feel some comfort having shared it with a friendly ear."

"Oh, Father Anselm," I said, touched as I was by his tone, and speaking in all sincerity, "I am a Huguenot, and not accustomed to confession, or even to confidences. I seem to have no appetite for such things. My Huguenot conscience is like a dark closet in which I've locked up tight my most bitter worries, which sometimes come out to torture me in the most grievous fashion. But I think I've lost the key to let them out and be done with them."

I thought Father Anselm was going to press his advantage, but instead, placing his hand on my shoulder, he said only, "My religion is more open to human failings than yours is. But I'm not trying to vaunt it. I know all too well the abuses that it has allowed to infest its vast body. Monsieur de Siorac, your hand. When we rejoin our companions, let us recite the paternoster since it's the only prayer we have in common."

Which we did, out loud, standing in a circle, in fraternal meditation, as if, Huguenots and papists, we'd forgotten the murders and butcheries that separated us.

Father Anselm ordered us to dismount about a quarter of a league from the encampment at the Mont de la Mère, where the bandits had fixed their rendezvous with Antonio.

"If I'm not mistaken, the ambush should be pretty close by. Miroul," he continued, turning to my valet, "go and see if you can see where they are. You're quick and strong, as I've observed, and you're very handy with a knife. Don't attack the group, my son, but if you come upon a lookout, dispatch him."

It was growing dark when Miroul returned, pale and panting. "I had to kill a sentinel," he said as he regained his breath, "who surprised me, and I feel bad for him, nasty rogue though he was. As for the ambush, they're hiding on the left side of the path that leads to the camp, about 600 paces from us. There are five knaves, lying in a trench with branches on their backs, and I wouldn't have seen them if one of them hadn't stretched from fatigue and shown himself."

"Miroul," I asked, "did you get as far as the encampment?"

"Yes. There are about ten of them, not keeping watch, sitting around in front of an old ruin, where they must have the Montcalms imprisoned."

"So, there are ten of them and that's a lot," said Father Anselm, putting a quarrel in his crossbow. "It's going to be hot. Siorac, let's split up. The monks and I will take care of the ambush, attacking them quietly with our crossbows, which won't alarm the larger group. Meanwhile, go round the encampment, through the woods, and take them from behind. But don't attack until you hear the whistling of our crossbows, and then fire on them with your pistols. You can fight a bear more easily from a distance than up close, as everyone knows!"

Father Anselm was better at strategy than at maths, for there were only four monks and five bandits in the ambush trench, and when four of the latter were pierced by the crossbow quarrels, the fifth leapt out of his hiding place and fled before they could restring their weapons. Running wildly to the encampment, he passed within ten paces of us in the underbrush, and Miroul, seeing him pass, drew his knife to throw it, but unfortunately, before I could stop him, Antonio aimed his arquebus at the wretch, fired and dropped him in his tracks. The shot exploded in the underbrush with such force that it left us aghast.

"Ah, Antonio," I cried, "you've spoilt everything! We've lost the chance to surprise them! Have at them, now! And fast! Speed is our only recourse!"

But, sadly, the alert had been given and the rascals were waiting for us with their arms at the ready. We fired our pistols, but when they were empty, we had to unsheathe our swords and fight hand to hand with ten bloodthirsty rogues, and because we had already engaged them up close, when the monks arrived with their crossbows they couldn't fire without risking hitting us. However, they made marvellous use of their swords and shields, all the time hurling terrible imprecations at their enemies, damning the brigands to hell and damnation. As there were now only three of the enemy left, these attempted to flee, but, sadly for them, they stopped to pick up the crossbows they'd dropped, and the monks were able to shoot two of them. The third got away, but didn't get very far, as I shall relate.

Thinking the day was ours, and the encampment without any defenders, I burst into the house and saw one of the bandits, knife raised, ready to dispatch Monsieur de Montcalm. But I was quicker, and ran his neck through with my sword. But at the same moment, another of the rogues, whom I hadn't seen, delivered a terrible blow with his pike that my armour deflected onto my left shoulder, and this man fell in his turn, Miroul pinning him to the wall with a throw of his knife. As for me, I felt as though I'd been viciously punched in the shoulder and that was the extent of it.

Monsieur de Montcalm was lying with his hands tied to a leg of the table, his face ashen, but quite calm, and Father Anselm, coming in just then, cut his bonds with his cutlass, while Miroul and I tried to untie the women. Strangely enough, Monsieur de Montcalm's first words were for his daughter rather than his wife, whose bonds I was trying to break. "Angelina, are you all right?"

"Yes, my father, I am," said Angelina in a light, sing-song voice that sounded deliciously like music to my ears after the terrible shouts of the bandits and the curses that the monks had hurled at their enemies, not counting mine, which I wasn't even conscious of having shouted in the heat of battle.

"But, Monsieur!" gasped Angelina, whose face was very close to mine as I was untying her. "You're wounded! You're bleeding!"

"It's nothing," I protested, feeling no other pain than the blow I'd received, and quite astonished by the extraordinarily sweet look Angelina was giving me.

"But, Monsieur," she said again as she stood up. "You're wounded! You're bleeding badly!"

But then I looked down at my left arm, and seeing red from the top to the bottom of the sleeve of my doublet, I was suddenly aware of both a terrible pain and debilitating weakness, and, immediately feeling faint, I would have fallen had not Angelina held me up. Then Father Anselm, stretching me out on the table and giving me some spirits from his gourd, dashed some of this alcohol on the wound at my request, which was not pleasant, before he and Samson bandaged me up, the latter seriously limited in his attempt to help by the tears that were blinding him.

I scarcely remember how I was able to get myself onto my horse and return to the Château de Barbentane, so dazed was I. As soon as I was comfortably installed in a bed, Monsieur de Montcalm sent for a doctor, but I sent this ignoramus away since he wanted to bleed me—as if I hadn't lost enough blood already! He also wanted to purge me, as if he believed that to cure my arm he needed to empty my intestines! At this point, we learnt that in Beaucaire there was a surgeon-barber who'd studied under Ambroise Paré, and I asked Monsieur de Montcalm to send for him. And this barber did very well, indeed, contenting himself with cleaning my wound with brandy, rebandaging it and giving me some opium to ease the pain.

The battle had cost us three of our people: Antonio, one of the monks and the valet who was watching our horses and did so badly at it that one of the escaping bandits surprised him and fled on one of the monks' steeds—a wonderfully bad choice, since Miroul leapt on his Arabian, caught up with him in less than an hour and dropped him with a pistol shot. As for the wounded in our troop, there were many. With the exception of Miroul and my beloved Samson, almost all had some injury, although the others were less serious than mine.

Monsieur de Montcalm came to visit me every morning in my room and thanked me profusely for having saved him, his wife and his daughter—these last, moreover, not just from death but also from dishonour. He was a tall man with very bushy eyebrows and an imposing face but a good heart, although he was somewhat narrow-minded and held too closely to his Catholicism, which I realized from a few words that escaped him and that convinced me that he would have liked me better if I'd shared his religious views. These were, no doubt, the reason he was held in such umbrage by the Huguenots of Nîmes, who would have killed him, I fear, if he hadn't fled in time.

Monsieur de Montcalm was very devoted to his daughter, who was his only remaining child, but whom he often quarrelled with, since both had very quick tempers. And each of them would become as obstinate as rams in their arguments, locking horns and refusing to give ground. These quarrels were, I imagine, their way of expressing the great love they had for each other, and which they would have been quite embarrassed to express in any other way. As for Madame de Montcalm, who, verbally at least, shared her husband's views, she seemed very kind, but carried in her heart a sad longing for the happiness she'd never really enjoyed as a girl, and was very dedicated to sharing her daughter's delights, basking in her happiness while taking some umbrage at it. All of which seemed to make her very mercurial, sometimes approving her daughter's behaviour, at other times thwarting the same tendencies.

Monsieur de Montcalm came to visit me at ten every morning, Madame de Montcalm at noon and Angelina during the afternoon: which made my mornings seem very long, so much so that I tried to shorten them by sleeping a lot. However, as my strength gradually returned, my sleep gave way to daydreams that grew in intensity the more I looked forward to seeing Angelina each afternoon.

Angelina enchanted me by the marvellous tenderness in her eyes, which was clearly not feigned, as it might have been in other girls, but seemed wholly natural to her and reflected her deeply angelic character, for she looked on everything and everyone with the same grace and benign compassion. She felt genuine sadness at others' pain or loss, including the death of a mouse or a sparrow, and greeted everyone she met with the same instinctive goodwill, even the most bitter and nasty of characters who were ill-disposed towards her, and, rather than return their spite, pitied them and pardoned the injury the instant she received it. As for the eyes through which this generous soul was revealed, they were large, languid, widely spaced and of a deep, black, oriental colour, as if there were some Saracen or Sephardic ancestry in the Montcalm family. Her nose was on the strong side, but without disturbing the harmony of her fair features, and her curly tresses framed her face with a Venetian tint of red.

My room was large and well lit by two leaded windows facing south, and was situated at the end of a long corridor, which allowed me to hear the approach of my visitors, and I amused myself by recognizing the footsteps of each of them, and sometimes mistook one person's steps for those of another, but never Angelina's. For Angelina, being one of those tallish women who are by nature slow and phlegmatic (except when she was angry), walked, despite her long legs, with such astonishing languidness that she would take but one step in the time I might take three.

Monsieur de Montcalm got in quite a state of anxiety at Barbentane when he learnt how François Pavée had looted his lodgings in Nîmes. He wrote to the parliament in Aix, complaining bitterly about this damage, and they responded in their wisdom that everything would be restored to order after these damnable excesses, when the king's authority had been re-established in that city. But this was not to be, for we were heading towards civil war, and the two sides appeared to be at equal strength for the moment. And so Monsieur de Montcalm, uneasy, stumbling along, too idle and muddle-headed, tried to manage his estate at Barbentane, where, it seemed to me, he was much less successful than the Brethren at Mespech, lacking their Huguenot virtues of economy.

He liked me well enough despite my religion and admired the fact that, in the bloom of my youth, I'd already had so many adventures, and, to distract him, he'd get me to tell him about them. When Angelina heard about this, she was very dismayed, since, given that her mother slept so late, she had to supervise the chambermaids during the time of her father's visits with me. In her dealings with her servants she displayed infinite kindness, but they always obeyed her every command out of love and respect for her.

"Ah, Monsieur de Siorac!" she said, sitting on the stool next to my bed one afternoon, "I'm so disappointed that my household duties prevent me from hearing the stories you tell my father every morning!" Saying this without the slightest coquetry, or consciousness of the sweetness of her look, she looked at me with her deep, black eyes, which were so tender that you had only to glimpse them to feel you'd never get enough of their radiance.

"Oh, Madame," I replied, "I'm at your service and would be only too happy to repeat these stories, if it would amuse you, during your afternoon visits."

"Oh, would you?" she said with such vivacity and joy that I could suddenly envision the little girl in her I'd never known.

"Of course!"

"And it wouldn't tire you out too much?"

"Not at all!"

"Ah, Monsieur de Siorac, you're too kind!"

She said no more, being somewhat unskilled in speech, and displaying in our conversations that same languid distraction she had when she walked. And yet, when she trusted me completely, which would not take long, she talked much more freely.

Since my stories required more time than the brief visits Angelina was accustomed to, we had to ask Monsieur de Montcalm's permission to extend her afternoons with me. He granted it, took it away, gave it back again, demanded to be present, got tired of listening to stories he'd already heard, left, returned and, ultimately, left us alone for as long as we wished.

For Monsieur de Montcalm, I wove very serious, ceremonial stories; when necessary, very repentant and moral tales that were careful to appeal to his papism. But for Angelina, as soon as her father had thrown in the towel, I told much livelier stories though *ad usum delphinae*—well within what a young woman should hear—in which my lovers became mere friends; the conversations were of an innocence of which she who listened to them was a model. By now I was able to get up and move around, though I could as yet not move my left arm to gesticulate appropriately, and mimed my adventures, marching here and there in the room as if it were a stage, changing tone and voice to imitate my characters. Angeline drank all of this in with both eyes and ears and, living the adventures I was recounting, suffered or rejoiced, imitating my expressions, living my life and paling terribly when the story of the gravedigging and mercy killing of Cabassus put me in such danger of being burnt at the stake.

"Oh, Pierre!" she exclaimed. "What troubles! What incredible dangers! How I tremble for you!" And her eyes would fill with such tender compassion that I would be too overcome by their maternal concern to find my words.

She remained agitated even when we were apart at night and in the morning, and every afternoon she'd ask me an embarrassment of questions, which would have been indiscreet if she who asked them hadn't been so naive.

"But, Pierre," she said, "why did you visit Madame de Joyeuse so often? What interest could you possibly have had in an such an old woman well over the age of thirty?"

"She taught me many things," I said without batting an eyelid. Which was, of course, true, but not in the sense I allowed her to believe.

Samson might have taken umbrage at my constant commerce with Angelina had Monsieur de Montcalm not taken a liking to him and invited him to go hunting every day after our midday meal. Not that Samson had much taste for the murder of feathered and furry beings that men practise in these parts, but he would not have wanted to offend his host by turning up his nose at this amusement. Moreover, he was dying of boredom in Barbentane, being so far from Maître Sanche and from the apothecary studies that he'd become so passionate about, which surprised me, since I couldn't understand how anyone could maintain such a love for such inert things. Certainly, if it were me, I would not have failed to respond to the flirtations of the chambermaids of the chateau, some of whom were quite pretty, and seemed available enough and were visibly enamoured of his bewitching beauty. But they might as well have been flirting with pretty images in a book! The poor wenches were all but transparent: Samson didn't notice them. Nor did he notice Angelina, which annoyed her at first, since she was accustomed to receiving attention from the men around her.

"Pierre," she said one day, "where does Samson come by this immense disdain of the beautiful sex? I might as well be a witch's broom given how coldly he looks at me. Is he one of those unfortunates who doesn't love women?"

"Not at all. He loves one. The rest don't interest him."

"Is she so beautiful?" asked Angelina, looking at me for the first time with a hint of coquetry.

"She is, but not as beautiful as some women I could name."

Hearing this, Angelina lowered her pretty eyes, and rising to go (my story for the day having come to an end) she wished me a good evening, and with her usual languor left my room, though I certainly couldn't fault the slow pace with which she did so, since it afforded me more time to watch her depart.

My brother wasn't entirely without anything to do: he was trying to write to Dame Gertrude du Luc, and, sweating blood and water, managed to tie a few sentences together, bringing them to me each morning for my corrections, very annoyed that I'd categorically refused to write his letters for him. But, without telling him why, I'd been obstinate in my refusal ever since she'd left, being disgusted by her betrayal of my brother with Cossolat—and all the more so since, in order to resist her advances, I'd had to armour my virtue: not an easy thing for me.

There were opportunities enough to test my virtue at Barbentane, where the chambermaids, rejected by my brother, would happily have taken revenge on me! But although my strength was returning, along with my great thirst for life, I resisted their advances as best I could. For I must confess that, in the silence of my nights and in my daydreams, I'd given my love entirely to Angelina, being persuaded that I'd never find in this vast world, however far and wide I searched, a woman who would unite such beauty and such heart. I didn't breathe a word of this to her, however, since I had no way of knowing whether her feelings matched mine, which were so strong I couldn't think about leaving her without suffering frightfully. But as little assured as I was of ever earning her love, I didn't want to do anything to risk losing it. Certainly, if it depended only on me, I could have, as Madame de Joyeuse was wont to say, "enjoyed a crust of bread on the other side of a thicket". But I doubt Angelina would have accepted such behaviour. Although she was two years older than I, she seemed too naive to distinguish between love and the tyranny of desire, not being, as I was, accustomed to give in to the latter.

I received two letters from Madame de Joyeuse. One, twenty days after I was wounded, urging me to return to Montpellier, since the report sent by the bishop of Nîmes to the vicomte had swayed public opinion in my favour.

The other, a fortnight later, sang an entirely different song:

My Little Cousin,

Oh, our poor king! Our poor kingdom! What a terrible thing is this misfortune we've just experienced! I think I'll die of heartbreak or lose the little beauty I have left! Those nasty Huguenots (who are your allies, my sweet little cousin), have taken Montpellier by force, and the vicomte, with a handful of men, took refuge in the Saint-Pierre fortress, taking his wife and children and his silverware. But as these fanatics were preparing to lay siege to the fortress, the vicomte fled by a secret door. Once outside, he made a bargain with the rebels to let us leave—me, his children and his silverware. This arrangement was brokered by our good Cossolat, who's got a foot in both camps, being a Huguenot but loyal to his king, so this enterprise was successful—at least for me and my children. For the rebels kept the silver and, after we had escaped, very devoutly pillaged the fortress, taking everything, even the small forks. My cousin, is this what your Calvin teaches?

The vicomte is furious at this loss, and at Pézenas where we've taken refuge, he's nursing his anger at these scoundrels. So, in order to calm him down and bend him to my own designs, I offered him my complete gold-plated serving dishes.

All in vain! At the first word I uttered about having you join us here, he threw up his hands and shouted, "Madame, rumours are flying already! You want more? Montpellier was one thing. He was studying medicine there. But what possible pretext could there be for bringing him to Pézenas? Especially since he's a Huguenot! Are you looking to have me ridiculed?"

My sweet cousin, you can well imagine that I threw fire and flames on such odious suspicions. And you can also well imagine with what annoyance I rejected his innuendos about the innocence of our relationship. But, alas! my little cousin, my efforts and goodwill on your behalf were without any effect on the vicomte, who's closed up like an oyster on this matter. Oh, my sweet cousin, you, at least, obey me, and when I think about it (and I think about it often) you're the only one in the world to whom I can say, "My sweet, do that thing I like," and be assured that you'll obey. And you can be sure that not to be able to say it makes me very sad indeed!

My little cousin, as you read this, have pity on me! To live in Pézenas without my ladies-in-waiting and in such cramped quarters! Without all my things! Without my little martyr! Ah, it's too terrible! My beauty is fading, I won't survive such a misfortune!

My little cousin, I offer my fingertips to your lips...

Eléonore de Joyeuse

As tenderly as I felt about Madame de Joyeuse, and as unhypocritical as was my nature, how could I answer this letter, except hypocritically? My pen took pity on Madame de Joyeuse because she wished it so. And while awaiting my answer, she lamented the fate that kept me so far from her indestructible beauty. But one can easily imagine that I was not loath to remain at Barbentane, since things had taken such a pleasant turn here.

Alas, however, these days spent in secret delight—since nothing had been said on either side—these days were numbered. My father, to whom I'd made a faithful report of what had happened in Nîmes and what was now going on in Montpellier, wrote to me that he didn't want me to return to that city because of the terrible excesses the Huguenots were committing there, killing priests and demolishing entire churches. But he didn't want us to attempt by ourselves to return to Mespech either, given that the three of us would be too few to travel in such perilous times, and so he proposed to come to fetch us in Barbentane with the best of Mespech's fighters. But the fact that my father would have to come through the Auvergne mountains to reach us—a long and difficult journey—gave me some unexpected extra time to enjoy my present circumstances.

With Angelina listening with both eyes and ears to the recitation of my exploits, I was in no hurry to conclude my odyssey, not least since our conversations always began with her prattling on sweetly about her morning activities and my news about Samson, Miroul, my father and Uncle de Sauveterre. But after an hour of trading the journals of our respective chateaux, she begged me to continue my history from the point where I'd left off the previous afternoon.

But I reached a point in my narrative where I suddenly felt exceedingly sad and couldn't say a word. I was telling her about leaving Montpellier to head to Nîmes, and how I left the city at daybreak and found myself at the foot of the gibbet. Angelina saw my confusion and asked what was the matter, so I told her that what I had to tell about that day was so infinitely sad and painful that I was unsure whether to exclude it from my account or to include it.

"Oh," she said, "you must choose the latter! If one of your characters has earned your compassion, she needs it now in her distress!"

This sentiment seemed so touching and so finely tuned to the goodness of her soul that I decided to tell her the lamentable ending of my poor Fontanette, hiding from her the relationship we had enjoyed for such a short time.

Angelia was sitting in a high-backed chair between the two leaded windows, caressing the black cat named Belzebuth, who was sitting purring in her lap. This name was an insult to such a suave and nonchalant tom, who loved his mistress and followed her about like a lapdog.

It's easy to remember this moment, which, even after so many years, is still painted with such lively colours in my mind. The afternoon sun flowing in through the open windows—that October was so mild—lit with a kind of dusty aura her Venetian red hair that fell about her face in such wavy curls. She was not wearing a high collar since Belzebuth had scratched her when playing with it, but an open collar displaying a cross on a golden chain. Her dress, of pale-green silk with dark-green ribbons, moved me all by itself, since green had been my mother's favourite colour. There was something in Angela's wide-eyed expression that I loved very much. Her coal-black irises glowed with a soft, quiet light, so tender and friendly that I've never seen the like, even in a doe, and I felt an almost irresistible urge to leap into her lap like a child, but also the desire to protect her.

I began my story in my usual way, standing and moving this way and that around the room, miming each voice, reliving my memories, but as soon as Fontanette entered this one, riding on her mule, she reappeared with such incredible force, her hands tied behind her back, that a terrible charm began to work on me. I believed I could see her as if she were still alive, and imitated her tiny, pitiful voice, feeling the tears flowing down her cheeks, and how the evil of men had brought her to the gibbet. Christ! It was all right in front of me again! I touched her shoulder with my hand. She rested her cheek on my hand. I would never have thought that words could contain a magic powerful enough to resuscitate a memory to the point of making it tangible, and of twisting my heart to the point of breaking it, of tying such a terrible knot in my throat, altering and squeezing my voice, that I could scarcely whisper my hoarse and stuttering account.

I couldn't finish. I broke into sobs. My eyes blinded by my tears, I approached Angelina, whose hair was shining in a halo of sun. Belzebuth, seized by some kind of fright, leapt from Angelina's lap when he saw me, and she made no effort to stop him, looking only at me, her eyes shining with compassion. In my distress I dared to do something I never would have had the courage to venture otherwise. I threw myself at Angelina's feet and cried, my head in my hands, tormented by the desire to put it in her lap to be comforted, but not daring to go that far, so great was my respect for her innocence. She didn't move a muscle for a very long time, though I could feel her trembling in every part of her body, but since my tears just kept flowing and my emotional tumult did not abate, she finally put her right hand on my head and very lightly began caressing my hair, as a mother might do to her child. And since I didn't know whether to attribute this gesture to pity or to some stronger feeling, astonished by my very uncertainty and, thus, distracted from my grief, I found myself feeling more peaceful and fell silent, continuing to hold my hands up to my face, fearing that if I removed them, she would feel ashamed and withdraw her hand from my head.

Finally the desire to see her won out. I withdrew my hands. She withdrew hers from my hair and suddenly said: "Pierre, did you love this poor wench?"

"It was friendship. Until this very moment, I've never loved anyone."

Hearing this, she held me in her gaze for a very long time, yet remained silent as if she expected me to continue. Which I did, encouraged by her silence, and I began speaking in words that surprised me since they appeared before I'd thought of them. "Angelina," I said, "I am the younger son of a baron and I must make my fortune. Would you consent to wait for me?"

Saying this, I rose from my knees and took a step back, to show her that I didn't presume on the liberty I'd taken. She seemed to be stunned by my words. But as she lowered her eyes, I couldn't tell how she had taken my proposal, since, with her eyes closed, her face no longer mirrored her thoughts.

Finally, she rose with her usual nonchalance and, bowing her head, said without either looking at me or saying my name, "I wish you a good evening."

My heart was breaking. I thought I'd lost everything as she walked towards the door with what seemed like infinite slowness, but as she reached it, her right hand on the doorknob, she turned slightly and looked over her shoulder at me with great seriousness and said, not without some force and resolve:

"Monsieur, I will wait for you."

That Angelina had confided in her mother and reported our conversation was very quickly made clear to me as I was sitting on a stone bench under an open window in the courtyard of the chateau later that evening. I heard footsteps in the room and recognized the voice of Monsieur de Montcalm and his wife, but since I couldn't hear what they were saying, I didn't move, and when I could, it was too late; they would have seen me as I stood up, and would have thought I was dishonest—especially given the subject of their conversation, which I couldn't help overhearing, since they were speaking with such great animation and in such lively dispute.

"Madame, I've already told you how I feel. Pierre is too young."

"Monsieur, my husband," replied Madame de Montcalm, "the difference in their ages is very small. Moreover, Pierre is a man and already very mature. Angelina is a child."

"Perhaps. But I have other plans for her."

"Sadly, she won't agree."

"She'll agree."

"No. You know her. She's more stubborn than a goat."

"All right, then. The convent will bring her around."

"Convent, Monsieur?" gasped Madame de Montcalm and then laughed out loud.

"You're laughing, Madame. Why make light of this?"

"Monsieur, would you have the heart to lock Angelina in jail?"

"And why not? Isn't that where many fathers put their daughters when they're insubordinate and rebellious?"

"Those fathers aren't you. You've always been crazy about your daughter."

"Madame," said Monsieur de Montcalm after a moment of thought. "I'm not so weak. I *will* be obeyed."

"Who's talking about disobedience? You have to admit Pierre is a very likeable young man."

"Yes, but he's got no fortune."

"He'll make one."

"If he's not killed first. He's high-handed and madly courageous."

"Ah, Monsieur! Would you reproach these qualities? Without his 'mad courage' neither you, nor I, nor your daughter would be here arguing about this!"

"Madame!" growled Monsieur de Montcalm, with great irritation. "Are you going to split my ears with this rescue every single day of my life?"

"No, Monsieur. I will henceforth rely on your gratitude."

"Now you're making light of things again."

"Not at all!"

"Madame, merely because Pierre helped save our lives, must I give him my chateau, my wife, my daughter, my house in Nîmes and my position as royal officer?"

"Monsieur, he asks only for your daughter."

"He won't have her! He's a heretic!"

"Ah, Monsieur, what a big word! You're not in Nîmes. Pierre is a loyalist Huguenot and hardly a zealot."

"Zealot or not, he's a reformist."

"As is everyone else in your family in Montpellier. To my knowledge, you're the only Montcalm who has remained in the faith of your fathers."

"I glory in that distinction!"

"My husband, you might have remained Catholic with a bit more moderation. We might not have been made outlaws in our own town and had our house pillaged."

"What are you saying, Madame?" cried Monsieur de Montcalm angrily. "Do you dare censure me? Are you in league with my enemies?"

There ensued a long silence, during which, I gather, she was using some of her charms, which she knew to have an effect on her husband, and then she said very sweetly, "My dear husband, I'm very sorry to have displeased you. If I have offended you, I shall withdraw immediately. I shall dine in my room."

"Stay, my friend!" countered Monsieur de Montcalm in more temperate tones. "It would distress me no end if you left me. You know I love everything about you, even our quarrels."

"Ah, Monsieur, you are too good to me! I'm a silly old fool to bother you so! It's true that Pierre is too young for Angelina. But what will happen if he changes his mind when he's made his fortune?"

"Oh, I'm not the least worried about that! I completely trust his word. He's a gentleman."

"Well, as for that, his nobility is a lot less ancient than yours. It was more than 300 years ago that your ancestor Dieudonné de Gozon killed the dragon of Rhodes!"

"Assuredly so! But why should we despise new nobility when it, too, was won in combat as the Baron de Mespech's was? And we mustn't forget that Pierre's mother is a Castelnau and Caumont, one of the oldest families in Périgord. And the baron is reputed to be quite rich, though a bit miserly in the Huguenot way."

"Yes, but Pierre's his younger son."

"True, and yet he abounds in talent that will assure his success in the world."

"What you say is true, my friend, but the difference in our religions is of no little consequence in this business."

"Oh, Madame, there's the problem! But Pierre is not the least zealous, and we can hope for his conversion!"

"I wouldn't hold my breath if I were you. He'd be too afraid to displease his father, who seems to be his god."

At this, they left the room, to my immense relief, leaving me on my bench, prey to a variety of feelings, in which hope and despair were mingled, since I was neither fully accepted nor fully rejected. However, I would have been happier if Madame de Montcalm hadn't seemed so mercurial. So much so indeed that, no matter how hard I tried, I simply couldn't understand how she could, almost in the same breath, support her daughter's inclinations and harm them, refuting her arguments only moments after making them and undoing the web she had just so carefully woven for us.

Meanwhile, nothing seemed to have changed in our daily routines, and I was able to see Angelina as much as I desired, though I never ventured a kiss or even a touch of her hand for fear of displeasing her, and without having her mother any more present than before, being a woman as lively and agitated as her daughter was languorous, and unable to stay more than half an hour in the same place without needing to go somewhere else. As for Monsieur de Montcalm, he put on a brave face about things, and one afternoon I even heard him say to Samson, whom he was very taken with, that he was very sorry that my father was coming to fetch us: he would have been happy to keep us the whole winter with him.

But alas, that was not to be. I was living on borrowed time, and, as sweet as the days were, they were flowing by too quickly, whereas those of my convalescence had seemed too long. My father arrived in mid November, accompanied by our Siorac cousins, by Cabusse and by Jonas, our stonecutter, all armed to the teeth, their great hulks terrible to behold and their skin tanned nut-brown.

Oh, reader! What a mad embrace it was! As soon as my father dismounted, I was in his arms, and how he hugged me to him, his blue eyes shining with joy! My gentle Samson wisely awaited his turn, which was just as emotional, for if my father admired me more, he loved Samson every bit as much, bastard though he was. Our Siorac cousins clutched us to them next. They could now be distinguished one from the other since Michel had a scar on his left cheek that he'd got in the fighting at la Lendrevie. I gave each of them a hug, of course, but Cabusse was anxious for his turn as well, looking very proud and wearing a prominent moustache.

"Ah, Cabusse!" I cried, rediscovering my words, which the sight of my father had momentarily taken from me. "What are you doing here without Coulondre?"

"He had to stay behind in his mill, there's no lack of work!"

"And your Cathau?"

"She's expecting!" said Cabusse in a very heroic tone, his strong hands pulling at his moustache. He was so faithful to the image I'd always had of him, I gave him a huge embrace.

"May I, Monsieur?" asked the Herculean Jonas, who, not being a veteran of the Brethren, didn't have the same familiarity with us as the others.

"Oh, Jonas! You have to ask? How is Sarrazine?"

"She's expecting," blushed Jonas, looking down.

"You seem unhappy…"

"Oh, Monsieur, there are so many wenches who die in childbirth, my heart fails at the thought."

"Then don't think about it!" said my father, who nevertheless thought about how my mother had died that way, and suddenly looked sad.

Meanwhile, Monsieur de Montcalm, alerted by his valet, was coming across the lawn of the chateau to greet the new arrivals, his hands extended.

"Ah, Monsieur!" he said, "I'm so honoured to have as my guest the hero of Ceresole and Calais!"

"Monsieur de Montcalm," said my father in his jocular way, always a little self-effacing, "the only heroism seems to have been to survive… The rest is the luck of war. Besides, I only had to deal with men, whereas your ancestor, Dieudonné de Gozon, had to kill a dragon all by himself!"

"I'm not sure I'm very worthy of him," replied Monsieur de Montcalm, delighted that my father, far away in Périgord, knew about his illustrious lineage. "But, as you know, I've abandoned the practice of arms for the position of royal official."

"*Cedant arma togae*,"* said my father, tasting a bit of his Latin the way one might taste the new wine in a good year.

"But in your case," said Monsieur de Montcalm, looking very pleased with himself, "*cedant arma aratro*."† Whereupon both smiled, for each had rendered homage, one to the other's bravery, one to

---

* "Arms bow before the toga."

† "Arms bow before the plough."

the other's ancestry, and had exhibited his prowess in Latin, which each was rather proud of, and I was quite sure that they were going to become good friends, since both were great hunters and, what's more, adept at chasing skirts—and still managed to outrun more than a few, since neither seemed to be ageing much in this respect.

"You have a beautiful chateau here," added my father, continuing the compliment. "And, I see, with excellent ramparts."

"But I would have lost it without your sons," said Monsieur de Montcalm, "who are as handsome as they are courageous."

This moved my father so much that not only did he blush, but he was unable to speak, and so made no answer, but contented himself with a bow to his host. Seeing this, Monsieur de Montcalm, whose great chagrin was to have lost two sons, understood how deep my father's love was for us, and, trembling suddenly at the idea that he should ever lose us, put his hand on my father's arm and said, "Madame de Montcalm and my daughter are very anxious to meet you."

"It will be an enormous pleasure!" said my father. "But here I am, all booted and armed for war, and covered by the dust of our journey. I hope you will allow me to clean myself up a bit before daring to appear before such elegant ladies."

Monsieur de Montcalm, Samson and I waited together for the Baron de Mespech in the great hall of the chateau, while, up in his room, he dressed for the occasion. And I hope that I will not be considered too frivolous if I confess that I hoped my father would not reappear dressed in black, since the Huguenots, disdaining ostentation, preferred this colour, as everyone knows. But I hadn't counted on the finesse of my father, who, before leaving Sarlat, had allowed himself a few expenses in order to appear to his advantage and to that of his sons, which purchases, I'll wager, did not exactly fit Uncle de Sauveterre's economical standards. In any case, when he appeared, I was very happy to see him wearing a light-green satin doublet—green, as I have mentioned, being my late mother's favourite colour—and decked out in an elegant knurled ruff instead of the little Huguenot ruff that Madame de Joyeuse considered so paltry. Monsieur de Montcalm was very satisfied with his guest's appearance, as were to an even greater extent Madame de Montcalm and her daughter, who entered the hall at the same time he did, dressed in all their finery and their beautiful jewellery. Angelina was all smiles, and Madame de Montcalm quite civil, but somewhat reticent, secretly curious about my father, who, from her perspective, had but recently emerged from the estate of the commons. My father, sensing this nuance, deployed all of his charm and immediately enveloped his hostess with his full arsenal of graces and conquered her in a trice.

Oh, I so admired my father and wanted to be him! And so I followed with much appreciation his assault, the way his eyes twinkled, ever slightly jocular and smiling, yet proud, knowing when to be silent, when to speak, his back so straight and his movements so lively. He behaved so well in this first encounter with them, that his hosts, who had been deprived of their house in the city, and who'd had quite enough of country living, were so delighted with him that they would have kept him for a month! But, while lavishing a thousand compliments on Monsieur and Madame de Montcalm with his Périgordian ease, the Baron de Mespech would agree only to spend "a short week". And short it seemed, indeed! For as happy as I was to see my father again, I was immeasurably sad to take my leave of Angelina, and found myself in the same position as Gargantua, who, when his son Pantagruel was born, and his wife had died in childbirth, didn't know whether he should weep at the death of his wife or laugh for joy at the birth of his son.

On the eve of the day we were to depart, Angelina, walking with me around the parapet of Barbentane, stopped and, fixing her marvellous eyes on me, took from her middle finger a little ring adorned with a blue gem.

"My Pierre," she said gravely, "this is a ring that I inherited. If it fits on your little finger, I would like to give it to you."

I tried it on and it fit perfectly. Angelina seemed delighted, seeing this as a good omen, and added, "Don't wear it until you've left Barbentane. But always wear it and no other."

"I give you my oath," I said, joyfully, understanding that with this gift she was engaging her faith and mine. "But, alas, I have nothing to offer you in return, since the only jewel I wear is my mother's medallion to Mary, which she gave me on her deathbed and which I've never removed."

"And it's a good thing you haven't," said Angelina.

Her beautiful lips arched in a smile, she said, "I have a favour to ask of you. Let's go into this turret and I'll tell it you."

This turret was a little, round, walled extension of the tower of the chateau and was decorated with a series of loopholes.

"I brought you in here so no one would see us, for I want to cut a lock of your hair. May I, Pierre?"

I agreed and she pulled from her brocaded purse a small pair of silver scissors, and told me to lower my head. But I didn't have to lower it very far, since, when she stood on tiptoe, she was as tall as I was. And when she had made her little harvest of my hair—a very little one—and tucked it away in her purse with the scissors, I said, smiling, my smile being the only way I could hide my emotion: "You didn't make a very large harvest, so I won't lose all of my strength."

And since she opened her eyes wide at this and didn't seem to want to leave the turret, but remain there longer with me, I told her the story of Samson and Delilah, which she had never heard, being a papist.

"Alas," she said, saddening suddenly, "we're not of the same religion. It may be a great obstacle, I fear, to our projects."

"I, too, fear this," I said, embarrassed to tell her how I had learnt this. She fell silent then, not wanting to say any more, but opened her lips slightly and seemed to be breathing more rapidly. The turret was so small that we were forced to stand quite close to one another, as the defenders of the castle would have, had they been firing through the loopholes at their assailants. And, though neither Angelina nor I, as we stood in this turret, had any assailants to repulse, we were, in a sense, besieged by opposing forces in our young lives.

"My nurse often told me," said Angelina, "that if a wench gives a ring to a man to wear on his little finger, he'll want her whole arm."

"It seems to me," I said, as I felt my heart beating furiously, and my voice nearly strangled, "that it depends on the man. And it isn't true if he respects you."

"Is this true, Pierre?" Then, after hesitating a moment, she added, "And if I give you a kiss, would you demand another?"

"Angelina," I replied with great seriousness, "I want only what you want, nothing more."

And so she put both her hands on my shoulders and, keeping her arms half extended, and without touching me in any part of my body, she placed a kiss on my lips. And certainly this was a very small, very short and very light kiss, in comparison to all of the ones I'd received up until then. And isn't it a marvel that it had such an effect on me that, to this day, I can still remember it as well as if I were still standing there with Angelina, in that turret on a balmy autumn afternoon, her hands on my shoulders?

"My Pierre," she said, "this is our last meeting, and I wouldn't want you to look at me, when you're leaving tomorrow, in front of all the people gathered there, as you've often done, with looks that are too expressive."

"Ah!" I said. "So what should I do? Turn away?"

"No, no! I want us to look each other in the eyes one last time."

But no matter how careful I was, in our adieux, to obey Angelina, my father didn't fail to notice my feelings, or perhaps he had already discerned them. For as we were passing through the Barbentane woods, he noticed how more dreamy and sad I looked the farther we got from the Montcalms' chateau, and ordered me to gallop ahead of the others for a moment to scout out the road.

And so I obeyed him. But after a few minutes, I heard hoof beats behind me, and saw my father approach and pull even with me.

"My son," he said in his usual jocular way, his blue eyes searching mine, "I see you have a beautiful ring on your finger, which I didn't see yesterday. Have you plighted your troth to some lady?"

"Yes, father, with your permission."

"Ha!" said Jean de Siorac, half jokingly. "My permission! It seems to me you're asking for it a bit after the fact!"

"Monsieur," I confessed, "I beg you to excuse me. You weren't there. The event was pressing."

"I understand, of course. But you're still young. You're a younger brother. You've got no money."

"We'll wait till I've made my fortune."

"And do you think Monsieur and Madame de Montcalm will agree?"

"As to that, I don't know," I said, not wishing to confess the great doubts that beset me.

At this, his countenance, though always expressing some amusement (but perhaps that was a mask to cover the awkwardness he felt at this conversation), became more serious, as if he were gauging and weighing the matter in his scales.

"Well," he said, "as far as I can tell, they seem to respect your father in this family, and Samson, and you. And they are very grateful to you, which is rare. And though papist, they don't express their emotions too freely. They are clearly not vainglorious. They have heart. In a word, they are good people and have good connections throughout

569

Provence, and are rich enough, though their lands are not managed well, and their only fault seems to be that they're a bit too proud of their lineage. But after all, that's a small sin. Who knows what your grandchildren will say about Calais? To hear them, I managed to take the city single-handedly!"

Here he stopped, and throwing his head back began to laugh uproariously. Oh, how I loved him then! Both for his way of laughing at himself and for what he had said of the Montcalm family, which gave me some hope.

"As for your chances," he continued, turning serious again, "they seem to me, to tell you frankly, to vary a good deal. As far as I could tell, the girl is entirely devoted to you. The mother is half for you, the father half against."

"And what about you, father?"

"*Distinguo* between the person and the religion. As for the person, you couldn't do better. She is very beautiful, my Pierre. But as important as this commodity is in a woman, it's nothing compared to heart, and Angelina has an excellent heart, as I have observed every day I've been here. It's a pity she's a papist."

"Father!" I blurted out, suddenly afraid. "Didn't you marry a papist?"

"Yes, of course," said Jean de Siorac, growing sombre. "And it was my life's cross to bear."

And after saying this, he fell silent, and I as well. And yet, after a moment, my heart was beating so hard, and, fearing that my father might line himself up with the "noes", as, no doubt, Uncle de Sauveterre would, I said with little self-assurance, "Father, if mother came back to life, wouldn't you be very happy?"

"Oh, yes of course! Of course!" said Jean de Siorac, his voice catching in his throat.

And, seizing me by the left hand, he leant over, looked me in the eyes and said, "Have no fear, my son! I'm not such a zealot. And even if I were, out of love for your dead mother, I would put no obstacles in your way. The ones you already have are sufficiently big already! I don't need to add any of my own."

I thanked him as best I could, being scarcely able to say a word I was so overcome with gratitude.

"Let's gallop on, father!" I cried, trying to hide the tumult that was inside me.

And I sat up straight in my saddle, my chest raised and my nostrils open wide.

"Gallop on!" shouted Jean de Siorac, smiling, because he so well understood what I was feeling.

And off we went, side by side, my father, still so young and vigorous, loving me more than his barony, and I, full of the great love that I felt for him. The earth flew by under our horses' hooves. And, my head full of thoughts of Angelina, it seemed to me as I leant over my steed, that I was riding not my valiant mare, but the years of the beautiful future that awaited me.

Next in the *Fortunes of France* series

HERETIC DAWN

Pushkin Press

Pushkin Press was founded in 1997, and publishes novels, essays, memoirs, children's books—everything from timeless classics to the urgent and contemporary.

Our books represent exciting, high-quality writing from around the world: we publish some of the twentieth century's most widely acclaimed, brilliant authors such as Stefan Zweig, Marcel Aymé, Antal Szerb, Paul Morand and Yasushi Inoue, as well as compelling and award-winning contemporary writers, including Andrés Neuman, Edith Pearlman and Ryu Murakami.

Pushkin Press publishes the world's best stories, to be read and read again. Here are just some of the titles from our long and varied list. For more amazing stories, visit www.pushkinpress.com.

===

THE SPECTRE OF ALEXANDER WOLF
GAITO GAZDANOV

'A mesmerising work of literature' Antony Beevor

BINOCULAR VISION
EDITH PEARLMAN

'A genius of the short story' Mark Lawson, *Guardian*

TRAVELLER OF THE CENTURY
ANDRÉS NEUMAN

'A beautiful, accomplished novel: as ambitious as it is generous, as moving as it is smart' Juan Gabriel Vásquez, *Guardian*

BEWARE OF PITY
STEFAN ZWEIG

'Zweig's fictional masterpiece' *Guardian*